D1525582

LEO
TOLSTOY

COLLECTED
SHORTER
FICTION
(in two volumes)

Written over a period of more than half a
century, these stories reflect every aspect of
Tolstoy's art and personality. They cover
his experiences as a soldier in the Caucasus,
his married life, his passionate interest in
the peasantry, his cult of truth and simplicity, and, above all, his growing preoccupa-
tion with religion. Ranging in scope from
novellas like *The Kreutzer Sonata* and *Hadji
Murad* to folk-tales only a few pages long,
they provide a marvelous opportunity to
become closely acquainted with Russia's
great novelist. Aylmer and Louise Maude's
classic translations are supplemented by
new translations by Nigel J. Cooper of six
stories, including two that have never before
appeared in English.

EVERYMAN'S LIBRARY

EVERYMAN,
I WILL GO WITH THEE,
AND BE THY GUIDE,
IN THY MOST NEED
TO GO BY THY SIDE

LEO TOLSTOY

Collected Shorter Fiction

Translated from the Russian by Louise and Aylmer Maude
and Nigel J. Cooper
with an Introduction by John Bayley

VOLUME 1

EVERYMAN'S LIBRARY

Alfred A. Knopf New York Toronto

243

THIS IS A BORZOI BOOK

PUBLISHED BY ALFRED A. KNOPF

First included in Everyman's Library, 2001
Introduction, Bibliography and Chronology Copyright © 2001
by Everyman Publishers plc
Translations in the Appendix Copyright © 2001 by Nigel J. Cooper
Typography by Peter B. Willberg
Second printing

www.randomhouse.com/everymans

ISBN 0-375-41172-0

Library of Congress Cataloging-in-Publication Data
Tolstoy, Leo, graf, 1828–1910.
[Short stories. English. Selections]
The collected shorter fiction / Leo Tolstoy; translated by Aylmer
Maude and Nigel J. Cooper; with an introduction by John Bayley.
p.   cm.
ISBN 0-375-41172-0 (alk. paper)—ISBN 0-375-41287-5 (alk. paper)
1. Tolstoy, Leo, graf, 1828-1910—Translations into English.
I. Maude, Aylmer, 1858–1938. II. Cooper, Nigel J. III. Title.
PG3366.A13 M3 2001   00-053487
891.73'3—dc21   CIP

Book Design by Barbara de Wilde and Carol Devine Carson

Printed and bound in Germany
by GGP Media, Pössneck

CONTENTS OF VOLUME 1

CONTENTS OF VOLUME 2

INTRODUCTION

Tolstoy was not a particularly precocious young man, although from an early age he had vague ideas about becoming a writer. But he detested the artificiality and the hypocrisy which, as he felt, were an integral part of the way writers went about making things up. His ideal was an absolute simplicity and a straightforwardness which would describe people just as they were, and events exactly as they happened. Soon after he had written *Childhood, Boyhood and Youth* he came to dislike everything in it except the original childhood section. The later parts, he said, were 'an awkward mixture of fact and fiction', and it was the fictional element that repelled him.

Some time even before *Childhood* he had begun an experimental piece which he called 'A History of Yesterday'. It is indeed just that; and as nothing much happened to Tolstoy on that particular yesterday it cannot be said to hold the reader's attention very closely: indeed it is almost a refutation in itself of its author's view that if the writing is simple enough it is bound to be of interest to all. The story is of interest none the less, because of its startling affinity with fictional experiments, like those of Virginia Woolf, in our own century, although Tolstoy's manner is too precise and too beady-eyed to give the impressionist effect so important to a sketch of hers like 'The Mark on the Wall'.

Tolstoy greatly admired the first part of Dickens' *David Copperfield*, which was appearing in the Russian periodical *Sovremennik* while he was meditating his own book. At least one touch in Dickens – David's curiosity about his own grief after his mother's death, and his pride in it before his schoolfellows – may have suggested to Tolstoy his own kind of unremitting analysis of the same state of mind. But at times *Childhood* can remind us of the flatness of the 'History of Yesterday', although it has become an inspired kind of flatness.

At first I felt sorry for her, I wondered whether I ought not to try and console her, and how to do it: but finally I became vexed that she should place me in such an awkward situation.

xi

'Oh God, how absurd it is to keep on crying! I loved your mother so, we were such friends ... we ... and ...'

She found her handkerchief, covered her face with it and continued to cry. My position was again an awkward one, and continued to be so for a good while. I felt vexed and yet sorry for her. Her tears seemed sincere, but I felt that she was not crying so much about my mother as because she herself was not happy now, and things had been much better in those days.

The bereaved boy is sorry for this old friend of his mother's as he has been sorry for himself, but Tolstoy goes on adding to the list of other considerations that come into question. The writing, though so simple, is wonderfully accurate, as *Childhood* itself is wonderful, but Tolstoy is still a very young writer who has not yet the strange power, which will take hold of him in the composition, on its epic scale, of *War and Peace*, of seeming both to comfort and to inspire the reader, even while he is insisting on a multitude of extraneous and sometimes tedious details. We see the remarkable shrewdness and truth of the narrator's perception; but the scene also brings, as it has done in real life, a dull feeling of discouragement and discomfort. It is precisely because the thing is so like life that our interest droops and our curiosity seems futile, even impertinent. Tolstoy has not the knack in his stories, as Chekhov has, of raising what is random and hapless and inconsolable to the level of art. In order to understand people with love, and to present them so that they are understood in the same way by us, he needs a story on the scale of *War and Peace*, or *Anna Karenina*.

And yet Tolstoy's stories, varied as they are, have their own brand of unique fascination. Some are long and on the scale of *nouvelles*, like *The Cossacks*, *The Death of Ivan Ilych* and *Hadji Murad*. Some are very short, like 'The Wood-Felling', from Tolstoy's own army experiences, or his brief parables like 'God Sees the Truth, but Waits'. All are distinguished by the same sense of a subject worked away on, made to reveal the utmost of itself that it can. And yet one could say that Tolstoy had a light touch. Turgenev, who admired his youthful tales, none the less displeased their author by telling him 'My dear Leo, you really shouldn't spend quite so long telling us the exact way the hero puts his hand in his pocket.' An exaggeration, but a telling one. The stories do spend a disproportionate time going into such details. And yet so compulsive is Tolstoy's method, and so penetrating and powerful the mind and observation at work, that he manages not to forfeit the reader's attention for a second.

Irtenyev, the 'hero' of *Childhood, Boyhood and Youth*, has a good deal in common with Olenin, the young officer who is the centre of consciousness in *The Cossacks*. That is to say of course that both have a good deal in common with the author himself, though by no means everything. Tolstoy kept just as beady an eye on his own failings and vanities as he did on those of other people; and at the same time he could present, as he does in the character of Ivan Ilych, a man who is like all men, whose suffering and fate are inseparable from the smallness of his outlook and the necessary triviality of his life. But by the time he wrote *The Death of Ivan Ilych* the preacher in Tolstoy had got the upper hand. The life of Ivan Ilych is remorselessly chronicled: Tolstoy seems determined that it should appear as 'unexamined', in Socrates' sense, as he can make it, and his death correspondingly without dignity or redemption. But Tolstoy cheats in the manner in which he finally presents that death itself. It is a black bag into which Ivan Ilych is being thrust, but at the bottom of that black hole there is a light. Characteristically Tolstoy produces an odd metaphor for what he sees as the process, drawn from every-day life:

What had happened to him was like the sensation one sometimes experiences in a railway carriage when one thinks one is going backwards while one is really going forwards and suddenly becomes aware of the real direction.

Well, maybe. Tolstoy, the expert on physical being, 'the seer of the flesh' as the critic Merezhkovsky called him, has no hesitation in projecting his knowledge into the last moments of a dying man. Undeniably the effect is strangely impressive: everyone who has read the story remembers that black bag and the moment of light that follows. And – who knows? – perhaps Tolstoy is not cheating here after all.

LEO TOLSTOY

The Russian historian Prince Mirsky used to say that up to the time he wrote *War and Peace* Tolstoy saw life as an enchanted ballroom: afterwards it seemed to him like Ivan Ilych's black bag. Certainly the experiences he underwent, and afterwards wrote about in *A Confession*, changed not only his outlook but his manner of writing. But this too it is possible to exaggerate, at least where the stories are concerned. *Hadji Murad* is one of his last, his finest and in a sense one of his most epically tranquil tales: one would not guess that the man who wrote it had become a religious crank and a fervent disbeliever in literary art. The way in which Tolstoy describes Hadji Murad's death in action is in sharp contrast to the way he concludes the story of Ivan Ilych: but at the same time he claims the right of a 'seer of the flesh' to know how the flesh dies.

Surrounded by his enemies and wounded by pistol-shots and sabre-cuts, Hadji Murad is on the very verge of physical extinction:

> He did not move but still he felt.
> When Hadji Aga, who was the first to reach him, struck him on the head with a large dagger, it seemed to Hadji Murad that someone was striking him with a hammer and he could not understand who was doing it or why. That was his last consciousness of any connexion with his body. He felt nothing more and his enemies kicked and hacked at what had no longer anything in common with him.

Survival after death? Tolstoy probably never believed in it: his consciousness as a writer was too absorbed in his own being, and in the awareness of the body. But of course he was intensely curious about it, and often gives the impression that he cannot really believe death can possibly take place or at least that he himself can die, although he is careful not to make any such claim on behalf of Ivan Ilych.

As he dies Hadji Murad recalls the moment in babyhood when his mother washed him and shaved his head; a memory of Tolstoy's own, of which in the story he makes an austere but touching use. He virtually claimed to remember the moment of being born in the same spirit in which he claims knowledge of the body in its last moments. It is touching too that in his last moments he kept repeating 'I do not understand what it is I have to do.' It was as if he could not believe that his will and being and power of action were about to be taken away from him, and that he had to do nothing now but cease to exist.

Certainly death has a surprisingly prominent part in the stories, almost acting as if it were itself a narrative device. One of the most powerful, *Master and Man*, was written in 1895, years after the spiritual crisis which had caused him to renounce art, and to reject the great novels he had written twenty years earlier. I feel it to be the most impressive story that Tolstoy ever wrote, and for that reason worth choosing for a detailed commentary. Part of the interest lies in its exemplification of his own theory of art, developed in this later period. His dogmatic essay *What is Art?* is perverse in many ways, even absurd; but the main point it makes, that all good art has to be simple, in order to appeal to the simplest people, is brilliantly exemplified in *Master and Man* and justified by its total success as a story.

And the story it tells is indeed very simple. Brekhunov, a merchant proud of his ability to drive a hard bargain, sets out by sleigh on a business trip with his servant Nikita. A snow storm blows up, and the pair take refuge with a well-off peasant family. The writing is as vivid here as it ever was in Tolstoy's younger days, and amusing too. The son of the house who is sent to guide them keeps shouting lines from Pushkin's poem 'Winter Evening', which he has learnt in school. On that snowy evening poetry and reality unexpectedly coincide, and the comedy of this (Tolstoy's humour, though uncertain and cautious, is always to be reckoned with) is deadpan. His view of poetry, even Pushkin's, was never high, but 'Winter Evening' is both a wonderful and a simple poem, and the boy's pleasure in it shows that it meets Tolstoy's requirements as set out in *What is Art?* Tolstoy is setting out to write a story as simple and as effective as Pushkin's poem. One that is not 'a lie'. 'But why did I write a lie?' the narrator in *Childhood* asks himself when he has had to write a birthday poem for his grandmother; and in *War and Peace* the essential falsity of the relations between Boris and Julie is exemplified by the album verses they write to each other.

Pushkin's snow-storm verses pass the test because their young guide who keeps reciting lines about 'snowy circles wheeling wild' finds they 'described what was happening outside so aptly that it cheered him up'. Having set the travellers on the high road he bids them farewell and goes off home. But soon they lose their way again in the blizzard; and now poetry contrasts with the terrifying starkness of Tolstoy's prose as he calmly describes what happens. When Nikita decides it is futile to travel through the night, Brekhunov leaves him and goes on alone. He has in fact gone blindly round in a circle, but seeing a dark patch ahead he thinks he has come to a village:

But the dark patch was not stationary, it kept moving; and it was not a village but some tall stalks of wormwood sticking up through the snow on the boundary between two fields, and desperately tossing about under the pressure of the wind which beat it all to one side and whistled through it.

The reader feels the terror of the lost moment almost as vividly as Brekhunov did. No wonder Tolstoy commented scornfully to a friend that a story by the young Andreyev, a fashionable writer in the 1890s, always seemed to be saying hopefully to its reader 'Are you frightened? – Are you frightened *now*?' when the reader was merely bored by the author's attempts to make him so. Tolstoy's accumulation of telling detail really does make the reader feel frightened. So does the unobtrusive way in which he gives us portraits, as the tale goes on, of the master who has so much to live for and the servant who has nothing, and so accepts their increasingly desperate situation with stoic fatalism.

The travellers are reunited. Nikita, poorly clad, is soon nearly dead from exposure, and Brekhunov seems to come to a decision. 'Suddenly, with the same resolution with which he used to strike hands when making a good purchase', he sets about organizing what shelter he can for both of them. Then putting the servant in the sledge he lies down on him in his heavy fur coat. He is surprised by the pleasure he feels in looking after another human being. He sheds tears, and longs to share his joy with someone else, so he tells Nikita, who only answers drowsily from below that he is getting nice and warm. But Brekhunov is being far from selfless. 'Nikita kept him warm from below and his fur coat from above', a calculation that he made just as he used to strike a bargain.

When they are found next day the merchant is dead, but Nikita is just alive and recovers. 'When he realized that he was still in this world he was sorry rather than glad, especially when he found that the toes on both his feet were frozen.'

Tolstoy's early story *The Snow Storm* is almost equally vivid, but it lacks the quiet accumulation of telling detail which is so effective in *Master and Man*. The moral of the story works without strain, because the personality of Brekhunov is fully established, and he remains true to it throughout. Mirsky remarks that 'his is a horrifying death', but this is surely wrong. One feels on the other hand that Ivan Ilych is not, so to speak, allowed to die in his own way, but is thrust into the black bag by Tolstoy, as into his final moment of tranquillity and brightness. One can quote Tolstoy's own rather portentous words against him: 'When characters do what in their nature they are unable to do it is a terrible thing.'

Brekhunov's end is moving, and also, in a curious way, both happy and comic. It makes us want to laugh and cry, an objectionable formula when used in a blurb, or in praise of Russian 'soulfulness', but here neither more nor less than the truth. One is left feeling that Tolstoy's humour here is something he is not in the least concerned with, and that probably he would despise the notion. None the less humour comes out from under his hand involuntarily when his narrative is at its best. There is the same sort of involuntary humour in the detail of the narrator's visit to the monastery in *Youth*.

It may be Tolstoy's lavish and always graphic use of detail, together of course with its romance and exotic setting, which for many readers has made *The Cossacks* the most popular of all his works. Conrad and Hemingway greatly admired it, and the latter virtually copied from it. And yet Tolstoy himself was never satisfied with the story, and said hard things about it in the heyday of his artistry, when he was writing *War and Peace*. It is true the joints of the narrative creak a little. The young Olenin's departure from Moscow and his arrival in the mountains of the Caucasus are wonderfully done; but the Cossacks themselves seem to occupy a kind of pastoral space into which Olenin blunders, like an eighteenth-century French hero among a tribe of Noble Savages. When the Chechen braves, the *abreks*, cross the river Terek, what do they come for? Obviously to ambush and attack the Russians. But the Cossack village appears to take few if any precautions against them, and the one who swims over by night seems to do it chiefly in order that Tolstoy should make a fine set-piece description out of his killing.

After Tolstoy joined the army and was posted as a young lieutenant to the Caucasus, he became seriously interested in military life and made his own kind of study of it. One of his sketches from that period, *The Wood-Felling*, is a little master-piece, revealing Tolstoy's close observation of officers and simple soldiers, and his sympathy with the latter. The story is slight – merely an account of how his artillery unit is required to cut down a band of forest so that the Chechens who lurk there, with whom they are in perpetual guerrilla conflict, can be kept under fire. The soldiers come to life even more vividly in this tale than they do in the *Sevastopol Sketches* which Tolstoy wrote a little later whilst on active service during the Crimean war. He had a mania just then for lists, definitions, and ways of analysing human beings, their conduct and character, and *The Wood-Felling* contains an amusing specimen of this, dividing soldiers into three types: the submissive, the reckless and the domineering – the last being classed under two sub-types, 'the sternly domineering' and 'the diplomatically domineering'.

Shortly after he left the army Tolstoy wrote *Two Hussars*, a striking tale which shows his continuing interest in such types, and also the growing conservatism of his outlook, a conservatism which will permeate in a more disguised form the philosophy of *War and Peace*. The older officer in the story has many faults – recklessness, bravado, and the love of gambling which Tolstoy himself indulged at one stage of his army career. But he is open and honest and would not cheat or lie. His conduct contrasts with that of the young Hussar of the next generation, a cold-hearted correct creature, who maintains appearances but has few if any scruples.

After leaving the army Tolstoy settled on the family estate at Yasnaya Polyana and began to think about marriage and a family. He became interested in various girls, and with his usual wish to get everything settled in his own mind he began to plan a sort of experimental *nouvelle*, setting out what he conceived a marriage in its early stages should be like. The result was *Family Happiness*, a work which contains much admirable writing and its author's usual shrewd observation, but which possesses a certain awkwardness arising from what was for him the hypothetical nature of the relationship. Tolstoy had to know such things intimately before he could really settle down to writing about them. In spite of the idyll which *Family Happiness* hopefully suggests, and which was implemented in the marriages of Mary and Nicholas and Natasha and Pierre in *War and Peace*, it also contains the themes of uneasiness and guilt, themes that will become obsessive in the long stories Tolstoy wrote after his spiritual crisis in middle age.

The strangest and most morbid of these is *The Kreutzer Sonata*. It is full of the more tormented side of Tolstoy's own personality, which he exaggerates immensely to create the pathological figure of Pozdnyshev. The relation between author and character is thus exceptionally unbalanced: as if Shakespeare had let us know that he hated sex, but not as much as Hamlet does, or Timon. The playwright was silent on the issue but Tolstoy was not, and he cannot detach himself and his own views from those of the character he has created. No writer explores the marriageness of marriage so directly and so exhaustively as Tolstoy, and *The Kreutzer Sonata* gives us another view of the question, which in part at least was coming to be Tolstoy's own. In *Family Happiness* he envisaged marriage; in *War and Peace* he described it; and in *The Kreutzer Sonata* he denounces it.

Like many more ordinary stories it has a strong element of daydream, and also of nightmare.

I think of running away from her, hiding myself, going to America. I get as far as dreaming of how I shall get rid of her, how splendid that will be, and how I shall unite with another, an admirable woman – quite different ...

The intended power of the tale is to compel us to own up – who doesn't sometimes have similar daydreams? – but the accusing finger fails to disconcert us as much as it wants to. The melodrama of the murder is sensational rather than moving, but the conclusion of the story surely moves us very much. Its narrator says goodbye to Pozdnyshev in the railway carriage where the tale has been told.

'Good-bye,' I said, holding out my hand. He gave me his and smiled slightly but so piteously that I felt ready to weep.

'Yes, forgive me . . .' he said, repeating the same words with which he had concluded his story.

'Forgive' is almost the same word in Russian as 'goodbye'. Since his wife's death has deprived him of forgiveness, Pozdnyshev can only ask it of strangers.

Guilt is also the theme of another story, *The Devil*, which Tolstoy wrote just before *The Kreutzer Sonata*. It too concerns marriage, and the sexual guilt which the author himself had come to be obsessed by in his own life. But the longest, most detached and most successful working out of the theme is the story told in *Resurrection*, meditated for some time by Tolstoy and completed in 1899. He made use of a character to whom we were first introduced in *Youth*. Nekhlyudov there is essentially a comic character, beautifully perceived and described; the sort of person who takes himself more seriously than his friends do, and who often does the opposite of what he really wants because it gives him a feeling of self-satisfaction. In this way he takes up as a friend a poor student whom he does not like and with whom he has nothing in common. This philanthropic act makes him feel happy, but the student who is the hapless object of his philanthropy soon becomes very uncomfortable under the burden of supporting his patron's self-esteem.

As a result of his actions in that story, and their consequences, Nekhlyudov in *Resurrection* becomes very much more of a serious character. But his essential temperament remains the same; and the way Tolstoy now presents it adds considerably to the interest of a story which might otherwise be too much like an enlarged version of Tolstoy's parable tales. The young Nekhlyudov in *Youth* has the unconscious and slightly comic innocence of a clever young man: in *Resurrection* he has the innocence of a determined and conscientious convert; yet never loses the reader's sympathy and even affection. But his motives, none the less, are not able to stand up to Tolstoy's always remorseless and as if automatic powers of analysis. Maslova too, the girl he originally seduced and who has ended up in prison, is quite able to see in Nekhlyudov's obstinate attachment to her not so much true remorse and repentance as the desire to display these qualities, to her but above all to himself. As she puts it to him once with brutal simplicity: 'You want to use me now spiritually as you once did physically.'

Maslova too is very much a real personality in her own right. The fact that she had ended up as a convict on the way to Siberia is, in the circumstances, both wholly convincing and deeply pitiable as well. Tolstoy does not dismiss human justice wholesale, but he shows what may happen if it goes wrong, and how inertia and ineptitude reinforce official rigidity at each step of Maslova's trial. If only they had done this, and had not forgotten to ask that ... Is the system, corrupting and deforming those who attempt to supervise its working, always unjust, or has an exceptional miscarriage of justice occurred here? This is a point of some importance, but Tolstoy ignores it. He has to, because he believes all governmental procedures to be inherently wrong and bad. The information about such procedures which he acquired for the occasion, and which he deploys in such detail, emphasizes this underlying anomaly. He did a great deal of research. He found out about senatorial protocol, and what clauses in the penal code dealt with the various offences and with degrees of guilt. The Tolstoy archives in Moscow contain long lists of such queries.

In the end, though, the strength of *Resurrection*, as in the case of the other longer stories, is in the power and pictorial animation of its individual scenes – Maslova's trial, the Siberian prison, the prison fortress of Peter and Paul at St Petersburg, the convicts' march across Moscow. It is on such pages that the author's magnificence as narrator and storyteller is at its height. They leave one wondering, too, at the vitality and above all at the variety of these stories by the man whom Turgenev called 'Great writer of our Russian land'. They can be read again and again: there is always something new and fascinating to find in them.

John Bayley

SELECT BIBLIOGRAPHY

BIOGRAPHY

MAUDE, AYLMER: *The Life of Tolstoy*, 2 volumes, Oxford University Press, 1930 (revised version of the 1908–10 edition). Besides translating Tolstoy's writings, Maude was Tolstoy's friend and follower, and has insights not available to later biographers. This *Life* remains a classic.

SIMMONS, ERNEST J.: *Leo Tolstoy*, 2 volumes, Vintage Books, Boston, 1945–46 (Vintage paperback edition 1960), Routledge, London, 1973. A detailed and scholarly account by a distinguished American critic.

TROYAT, HENRI: *Tolstoy* (first published in French, 1965), Doubleday, New York, 1967, W. H. Allen, London, 1968, Penguin Books, Harmondsworth, 1970. A detailed and popular biography (denounced by Nabokov as 'a vile *biographie romancée*'). Highly readable if somewhat bland, and thin on the implications of Tolstoy's ideas. Comprehensive in its references to the shorter fiction.

CRANKSHAW, EDWARD: *Tolstoy – The Making of a Novelist*, Weidenfeld & Nicolson, London, 1974. Less detailed and more idiosyncratic than the titles above, but a knowledgeable and well-illustrated study concentrating largely on Tolstoy's personal and spiritual development before 1880.

WILSON, A. N.: *Tolstoy*, Hamish Hamilton, London, 1988, Penguin Books, Harmondsworth, 1989. A stimulating, consciously unreverential treatment which is very readable, and good on the ideas as well as the literary writings. Refers to most of the more important short fiction.

AUTOBIOGRAPHICAL SOURCES

CHRISTIAN, R. F. (editor and translator): *Tolstoy's Letters*, 2 volumes, Athlone Press, London and Scribner's, New York, 1978.

CHRISTIAN, R. F. (editor and translator): *Tolstoy's Diaries*, 2 volumes, Athlone Press, London and Scribner's, New York, 1985.

These two comprehensive collections, clearly presented and well annotated, provide invaluable tools for the reader who wants to explore the connections between Tolstoy's life and his fictions.

LITERARY CRITICISM

BAYLEY, JOHN: *Tolstoy and the Novel*, Chatto & Windus, London, 1966 (paperback edition 1968). The main focus is on *War and Peace*, but there are many references to the shorter writings.

CAIN, T. G. S.: *Tolstoy* (*Novelists and their World* series), Paul Elek, London, 1977. A survey of Tolstoy's work which foregrounds his ethical and spiritual struggles. Includes discussions of *Family Happiness*, the post-conversion writings and *Hadji Murad*.

CHRISTIAN, R. F.: *Tolstoy, a Critical Introduction*, Cambridge University Press, 1969. A methodical and detailed survey of Tolstoy's writings. Includes a discussion of Tolstoy's earliest writings and a chapter on the later stories.

EIKHENBAUM, B. M.: *The Young Tolstoy*, tr. G. Kerne, Ardis, Ann Arbor, Michigan, 1972. A translation of the great Soviet critic's 1922 study which has much to say about narrative technique.

GIFFORD, HENRY (editor): *Leo Tolstoy – A Critical Anthology*, Penguin Books, 1971. An interesting anthology of reactions to Tolstoy's writing, from contemporaries and later readers.

GREENWOOD, E. B.: *Tolstoy – The Comprehensive Vision*, Dent, London, 1975, paperback edition Methuen, London, 1980. A densely written survey covering the full range of Tolstoy's fiction with an emphasis on psychology and ideas. Devotes more space than most critics to the shorter fiction of the early, middle and late periods.

JONES, MALCOLM (editor): *New Essays on Tolstoy*, Cambridge University Press, 1978. A symposium of contributions by ten writers which includes an essay on *Hadji Murad* by A. D. P. Briggs and a bibliography of Tolstoy studies in Great Britain.

KNOWLES, A. V. (editor): *Tolstoy – The Critical Heritage*, Routledge, London and Boston, 1978. A rich collection of criticism and comment on his works from Tolstoy's own lifetime.

MATLAW, RALPH E.: *Tolstoy – A Collection of Critical Essays*, Prentice-Hall, Englewood Cliffs, New Jersey, 1967. A representative collection of a dozen essays drawn from a wide range of writers. Half the pieces are thematic but Wasiolek's thoughts on *Ivan Ilych* are included, as well as Shestov's essay on Tolstoy's late works which focuses on *Diary of a Madman* and discusses *After the Ball* and *Master and Man*.

ORWIN, DONNA TUSSING: *Tolstoy's Art and Thought, 1847–1880*, Princeton University Press, 1993. A detailed examination of the main philosophical and intellectual influences on Tolstoy during his major creative period.

STEINER, GEORGE: *Tolstoy or Dostoevsky – An Essay in Contrast*, Faber, London, 1960. A remarkably full introduction to Tolstoy's world view and art, considering that he shares the focus of the book with Dostoevsky. Many references to the shorter fiction.

WASIOLEK, EDWARD: *Tolstoy's Major Fiction*, University of Chicago Press, Chicago and London, 1978. A concise overview of Tolstoy's fiction which gives the shorter works unusual prominence: Wasiolek includes useful sections on *Three Deaths*, *Polikushka* and *Family Happiness*, as well as chapters devoted to *The Death of Ivan Ilych* and *Master and Man*.

C H R O N O L O G Y

———

DATE	AUTHOR'S LIFE	LITERARY CONTEXT
1828	Lev Nikolayevich Tolstoy born 28 August at Yasnaya Polyana, his father's estate 130 miles south of Moscow.	
1830	Death of his mother.	Stendhal: *Scarlet and Black*. Pushkin: *Boris Godunov*.
1832		
1833		Pushkin: *Eugene Onegin*.
1835		Balzac: *Old Goriot*.
1836	The family moves to Moscow.	Gogol: *The Government Inspector*.
1837	Death of his father.	Pushkin dies after a duel. Dickens: *Oliver Twist* (to 1838).
1838	Death of his grandmother.	
1840		Lermontov: *A Hero of Our Time*.
1841	On the death of their guardian (an aunt), the Tolstoy children move to Kazan to live with another aunt.	Lermontov killed in a duel.
1842	Loses his virginity. Starts to read Rousseau.	Gogol: *Dead Souls Part 1*, *The Overcoat*.
1843		Dickens: *Martin Chuzzlewit* (to 1844).
1844	Enters Kazan University.	Thackeray: *Barry Lyndon*.
1846		Dostoevsky: *Poor Folk*, *The Double*.
1847	Inherits Yasnaya Polyana and leaves Kazan University without graduating. Suffering from a venereal disease. Returns to Yasnaya Polyana and attempts to institute a programme of social reform directed at the peasants.	Herzen: *Who is to Blame?* Goncharov: *An Ordinary Story*. Belinsky: *Letter to Gogol*. Charlotte Brontë: *Jane Eyre*. Emily Brontë: *Wuthering Heights*. Thackeray: *Vanity Fair* (to 1848). Herzen: *From the Other Shore* (to 1851). Turgenev: *A Sportsman's Notebook* (to 1852).
1848	Goes to Moscow.	

France: July Revolution.
Rebellion in Poland (to 1831).
Great Britain: First Reform Act.
Great Britain: Factory Act.

Great Britain: Accession of Queen Victoria.
First Russian railway line constructed.

Ban on sale of individual peasants.

Tsar Nicholas I visits England.

Herzen leaves Russia.

Revolution in France: Second Republic declared.
First Californian Gold Rush.

LEO TOLSTOY

CHRONOLOGY

LEO TOLSTOY

DATE	AUTHOR'S LIFE	LITERARY CONTEXT
1860	Second (and last) visit to western Europe. Death of his brother Nikolai, in France. Visits Rome.	Turgenev: *On the Eve, First Love.* Eliot: *The Mill on the Floss.* Dickens: *Great Expectations* (to 1861). Chekhov born.
1861	Visits Paris, London, Brussels. Back in Russia, quarrels with Turgenev. Serves as Arbiter of the Peace. Resumes school work at Yasnaya Polyana.	Dostoevsky: *The House of the Dead.* Herzen: *My Past and Thoughts* (to 1867).
1862	Starts publication of educational magazine. Gives up being Arbiter of the Peace. Police raid on his house. Marries Sofya Andreyevna Behrs, daughter of a court physician. Closes the school.	Turgenev: *Fathers and Children.* Hugo: *Les Misérables.* Flaubert: *Salammbô.*
1863	Publishes *The Cossacks, Polikushka.* Sergei born (first of thirteen children).	Death of Thackeray. Chernyshevsky: *What is to be Done?*
1864		Dostoevsky: *Notes from Underground.* Nekrasov: *Who can Live Happy in Russia?* (to 1876). Dickens: *Our Mutual Friend* (to 1865).
1865–6	Publishes *1805* (volumes 1 and 2 of *War and Peace*).	Leskov: *Lady Macbeth of Mtsensk.*
1866	Unsuccessful defence of soldier court-martialled for striking an officer.	Dostoevsky: *Crime and Punishment.*
1867	*War and Peace* volume 3 published.	Turgenev: *Smoke.*
1868	*War and Peace* volume 4 published.	Dostoevsky; *The Idiot.* Gorky born.
1869	*War and Peace* volumes 5 and 6 published. Experiences acute fear of death in a hotel room at Arzamas.	Goncharov: *The Precipice.*
1870	Begins a novel about Peter the Great. Starts learning Ancient Greek.	Death of Dickens, Herzen. Kuprin born.
1871		Dostoevsky: *Demons* (to 1872).
1872	Reopens Yasnaya Polyana school. Poor health. Reading philosophers, notably Schopenhauer. Writes *A Prisoner in the Caucasus, God sees the Truth but Waits.*	Leskov: *Cathedral Folk.*

CHRONOLOGY

DATE	AUTHOR'S LIFE	LITERARY CONTEXT
1873	Begins writing *Anna Karenina*.	Leskov: *The Enchanted Wanderer*.
1875	Publishes *New Primer, Russian Reader*. Increasingly preoccupied with religious problems, troubled by war with Turkey.	Saltykov-Shchedrin: *The Golovlyovs* (to 1880).
1875–7	*Anna Karenina* appears in instalments.	
1876	Begins to practise Orthodoxy.	James: *Roderick Hudson*. Twain: *Tom Sawyer*.
1877		Turgenev: *Virgin Soil*. Garshin: *Four Days*.
1878	*Anna Karenina* published in book form. Reconciliation with Turgenev. Moral crisis leads him into theological studies. Abandons practice of Orthodoxy.	Hardy: *The Return of the Native*.
1879	Begins writing *A Confession*.	Dostoevsky: *The Brothers Karamazov* (to 1880).
1880	Begins *Critique of Dogmatic Theology, Translation and Harmony of the Gospels*. 4th edition of *Collected Works* appears (11 vols).	Death of Flaubert. Blok, Bely born.
1881	Writes to the Tsar asking for a pardon for the assassins of Alexander II. Visits monastery of Optina Pustyn.	Death of Dostoevsky. James: *The Portrait of a Lady*.
1882	Finishes *A Confession* (banned in Russia). Studies Hebrew. Moves his family to Moscow.	
1883	Writes *What I Believe*. Hands over control of property to his wife. Chertkov arrives as a visitor, stays as a disciple.	Death of Turgenev. Korolenko: *Makar's Dream*. Garshin: *The Scarlet Flower*.
1884	*What I Believe* banned. Publishes fragments from *The Decembrists* (unfinished novel). Writes *Memoirs of a Madman*.	Huysmans: *Against Nature*. Zamyatin born.
1885	Renounces hunting, meat, tobacco and alcohol. Publishes 'popular' tales including *What Men Live By, Where Love is, God is, Ivan the Fool, Two Old Men*.	Zola: *Germinal*.

C H R O N O L O G Y

Russian Populist movement begins.
Russia invades Chinese Turkestan.
Universal Exhibition in Vienna.

Land and Liberty movement formed in Russia.

Russia declares war on Turkey.

Russo-Turkish War ends. Congress of Berlin.
Afghan War.
Trial of Vera Zasulich.

People's Will party formed in Russia.
Governor of Kharkov assassinated.
Osip Vissarionovich Djugashvili (Stalin) born.

Alexander II assassinated. Accession of Alexander III.
Jewish residence in Russia severely restricted.

Great Britain: Married Women's Property Act.
University riots. Censorship laws strengthened.

Plekhanov and others form Marxist study groups.

LEO TOLSTOY

DATE	AUTHOR'S LIFE	LITERARY CONTEXT
1886	*The Death of Ivan Ilych, How Much Land Does a Man Need?, The Godson* published. Tolstoy's play *The Power of Darkness* offends the Tsar and is forbidden. Finishes *What Then Must We Do?* Denounced as heretic by Archbishop of Kherson.	Chekhov: first volume of stories. James: *The Bostonians, The Princess Casamassima.*
1887		
1888	Publishes *Strider* (written 1861). *The Power of Darkness* performed in Paris.	Chekhov: *The Steppe.* Death of Garshin.
1889	Begins writing *Resurrection.* Publication of *Collected Works* (12 vols). Unauthorized copies of *The Kreutzer Sonata* in circulation.	Akhmatova born.
1890	Tsar gives permission for publication of an edited version of *The Kreutzer Sonata.* Writes *The Devil.*	Pasternak born. Wilde: *The Picture of Dorian Gray.*
1891	Renounces copyright on his works post-1881, divides property among family. Writes *Why do Men Stupefy Themselves?*	Ehrenburg, Bulgakov born.
1891–2	Engaged in famine relief work.	
1892	*The Fruits of Enlightenment* produced in Moscow.	Chekhov: *Ward No. 6.* Merezhkovsky: *Symbols.* Gorky publishes his first story. Mandelstam, Tsvetayeva born.
1893	Publishes *The Kingdom of God is within you.*	Death of Maupassant.
1894	Publishes *Christianity and Patriotism, Reason and Religion, Religion and Morality, How to Read the Gospels, Walk in the Light.*	Babel born.
1895	Publishes *Master and Man.* Intervenes to defend the Dukhobors against persecution.	
1896		Chekhov: *The Seagull.* Merezhkovsky: *Christ and Anti-Christ* (to 1905).
1897	Chertkov arrested and exiled.	
1898	Finishes *Father Sergius.* Publishes a censored version of *What is Art?*	Zola: *J'Accuse.* Blok: *Ante Lucem* (to 1900).

CHRONOLOGY

Five students (including Lenin's brother) hanged for an attempt on the Tsar's life.

Second International founded.

Beginning of Trans-Siberian Railway construction.
Famine in southern Russia.

Witte becomes Finance Minister.

Famine in some Russian regions.
Massacres in Armenia.
Great Britain: Independent Labour Party founded.
Death of Tsar Alexander III. Accession of Tsar Nicholas II.
Great Britain: Greenwich bomb outrage.

Socialist Revolutionary Party founded in Russia.

Pobedonostsev urges the Tsar to imprison Tolstoy.

Spanish–American War. Curies discover radium.
Russian Social Democrat Party founded.

DATE	AUTHOR'S LIFE	LITERARY CONTEXT
1899	Publishes *Resurrection* (begun 1889). Son Sergei accompanies Dukhobors to Canada.	Leonov, Olesha, Nabokov born. Gorky: *Foma Gordeyev*. Chekhov: *The Lady with the Dog*.
1900		Freud: *The Interpretation of Dreams*. Chekhov: *In the Ravine*.
1901	Excommunicated by the Holy Synod of the Russian Orthodox Church. Writes *Reply to the Synod's Edict*. Convalescing in Crimea, meets Gorky, Chekhov.	Chekhov: *Three Sisters*. Fadeyev born.
1902	Writes to the Tsar about the evils of autocracy and private land ownership. Finishes *What is Religion?*	Gorky: *The Lower Depths*. Death of Zola.
1903	Protests against anti-Jewish pogroms in Kishinyov and contributes three short stories for a benefit anthology published in Warsaw. Writes *After the Ball*.	Kuprin: *The Duel*.
1903–6	Writes *Reminiscences*.	
1904	Death of brother Sergei. Finishes *Hadji Murad*. Writes a pamphlet against the war with Japan, *Bethink Yourselves!*, published in England. Writes *The Forged Coupon, Divine and Human*.	Chekhov: *The Cherry Orchard*. Death of Chekhov. Blok: *Verses about the Beautiful Lady*. Bely: *Gold in Azure*.
1905	Writes *Alyosha Gorshok, Fëdor Kuzmich. The One Thing Needful* seized by police.	Rilke: *The Book of Hours*. Sholokhov, Panova born. Sologub: *The Petty Demon* (to 1907).
1906	Writes *What For?* Wife seriously ill.	
1907	Police raid Yasnaya Polyana and seize books.	Gorky: *Mother*. Blok: *The Snow Mask*. Bryusov: *The Fiery Angel*.
1908	Writes *I Cannot Be Silent*, a protest against the hanging of the 1905 revolutionaries. Tolstoy's secretary Gusyev arrested and exiled. Chertkov returns from exile to live nearby.	Andreyev: *The Seven who were Hanged*.

HISTORICAL EVENTS

Student riots: temporary closure of universities.
Boer War begins.

Russia occupies Manchuria.
Social Democrat Party brings out newspaper *The Spark*.

Great Britain: Death of Queen Victoria; accession of Edward VII.

Wave of political assassinations in Russia.
Boer War ends.

Lenin's faction (Bolsheviks) prevails at Social Democrat Party congress in London.
Massacre of Jews in Kishinyov.

Lenin launches newspaper *Forward*.
Russo-Japanese War (to 1905); Russian fleet destroyed in Tsushima Straits.

First Russian Revolution: Bloody Sunday, general strike, Tsar's October Manifesto. Witte becomes First Minister.

Meeting of the first Duma (elected parliament).

Austria annexes Bosnia-Herzegovina.

LEO TOLSTOY

DATE	AUTHOR'S LIFE	LITERARY CONTEXT
1908 *cont.*	Growing quarrels with his wife and Chertkov about mss. and copyright ownership.	
1909	Draws up will relinquishing copyright on his published works since 1881 and his unpublished works from before 1881. Chertkov expelled, goes to Moscow.	Bely: *The Silver Dove, Ashes, The Urn.* Wells: *Tono-Bungay.*
1910	More quarrels with wife (now seriously unbalanced) about wills and copyright. Tolstoy leaves home and sets out to visit the monastery at Optina Pustyn. Taken ill on a train, he dies at the station of Astapovo on 7 November, aged 82. His body is buried without religious rites on the edge of the forest near Yasnaya Polyana.	Kuprin: *The Pit.* Bunin: *The Village.* Forster: *Howards End.* Rilke: *Sketches of Malte Laurids Brigge.*

CHRONOLOGY

THE RAID
A VOLUNTEER'S STORY

The portions of this story enclosed in square brackets
are those the Censor suppressed; they were
published in English for the first time in
Aylmer Maude's translation (1935).

Chapter I

[WAR always interested me: not war in the sense of man-
œuvres devised by great generals – my imagination refused to
follow such immense movements, I did not understand them –
but the reality of war, the actual killing. I was more interested
to know in what way and under the influence of what feeling
one soldier kills another than to know how the armies were
arranged at Austerlitz and Borodinó.

I had long passed the time when, pacing the room alone and
waving my arms, I imagined myself a hero instantaneously
slaughtering an immense number of men and receiving a
generalship as well as imperishable glory for so doing. The
question now occupying me was different: under the influence
of what feeling does a man, with no apparent advantage to
himself, decide to subject himself to danger and, what is more
surprising still, to kill his fellow men? I always wished to think
that this is done under the influence of anger, but we cannot
suppose that all those who fight are angry all the time, and
I had to postulate feelings of self-preservation and duty.

What is courage – that quality respected in all ages and
among all nations? Why is this good quality – contrary to all
others – sometimes met with in vicious men? Can it be that to
endure danger calmly is merely a physical capacity and
that people respect it in the same way that they do a man's
tall stature or robust frame? Can a horse be called brave,
which fearing the whip throws itself down a steep place
where it will be smashed to pieces; or a child who fearing to
be punished runs into a forest where it will lose itself; or a
woman who for fear of shame kills her baby and has to endure
penal prosecution; or a man who from vanity resolves to kill a

fellow creature and exposes himself to the danger of being killed?

In every danger there is a choice. Does it not depend on whether the choice is prompted by a noble feeling or a base one whether it should be called courage or cowardice? These were the questions and the doubts that occupied my mind and to decide which I intended to avail myself of the first opportunity to go into action.

In the summer of 184– I was living in the Caucasus at the small fortified post of N—.]

On the twelfth of July Captain Khlópov entered the low door of my earth-hut. He was wearing epaulettes and carrying a sword, which I had never before seen him do since I had reached the Caucasus.

'I come straight from the colonel's,' he said in answer to my questioning look. 'To-morrow our battalion is to march.'

'Where to?' I asked.

'To M. The forces are to assemble there.'

'And from there I suppose they will go into action?'

'I expect so.'

'In what direction? What do you think?'

'What is there to think about? I am telling you what I know. A Tartar galloped here last night and brought orders from the general for the battalion to march with two days' rations of rusks. But where to, why, and for how long, we do not ask, my friend. We are told to go – and that's enough.'

'But if you are to take only two days' rations of rusks it proves that the troops won't be out longer than that.'

'It proves nothing at all!'

'How is that?' I asked with surprise.

'Because it is so. We went to Dargo and took one week's rations of rusks, but we stayed there nearly a month.'

'Can I go with you?' I asked after a pause.

'You could, no doubt, but my advice is, don't. Why run risks?'

'Oh, but you must allow me not to take your advice. I have been here a whole month solely on the chance of seeing an action, and you wish me to miss it!'

'Well, you must please yourself. But really you had better stay behind. You could wait for us here and might go hunting – and we would go our way, and it would be splendid,' he said with such conviction that for a moment it really seemed to me too that it would be 'splendid'. However, I told him decidedly that nothing would induce me to stay behind.

'But what is there for you to see?' the captain went on, still trying to dissuade me. 'Do you want to know what battles are like? Read Mikháylovski Danílevski's *Description of War*. It's a fine book, it gives a detailed account of everything. It gives the position of every corps and describes how battles are fought.'

'All that does not interest me,' I replied.

'What is it then? Do you simply wish to see how people are killed? – In 1832 we had a fellow here, also a civilian, a Spaniard I think he was. He took part with us in two campaigns, wearing some kind of blue mantle. Well, they did for the fine fellow. You won't astonish anyone here, friend!'

Humiliating though it was that the captain so misjudged my motives, I did not try to disabuse him.

'Was he brave?' I asked.

'Heaven only knows: he always used to ride in front, and where there was firing there he always was.'

'Then he must have been brave,' said I.

'No. Pushing oneself in where one is not needed does not prove one to be brave.'

'Then what do you call brave?'

'Brave? . . . Brave?' repeated the captain with the air of one to whom such a question presents itself for the first time. 'He who does what he ought to do is brave,' he said after thinking awhile.

I remembered that Plato defines courage as 'The knowledge of what should and what should not be feared', and despite the looseness and vagueness of the captain's definition I thought that the fundamental ideas of the two were not so different as they might appear, and that the captain's definition was even more correct than that of the Greek philosopher. For if the captain had been able to express himself like Plato he would no doubt have said that, 'He is brave who fears only what should be feared and not what should not be feared'.

I wished to explain my idea to the captain.

'Yes,' said I, 'it seems to me that in every danger there is a choice, and a choice made under the influence of a sense of duty is courage, but a choice made under the influence of a base motive is cowardice. Therefore a man who risks his life from vanity, curiosity, or greed, cannot be called brave; while on the other hand he who avoids a danger from honest consideration for his family, or simply from conviction, cannot be called a coward.'

The captain looked at me with a curious expression while I was speaking.

'Well, that I cannot prove to you,' he said, filling his pipe, 'but we have a cadet here who is fond of philosophizing. You should have a talk with him. He also writes verses.'

I had known of the captain before I left Russia, but I had only made his acquaintance in the Caucasus. His mother, Mary Ivánovna Khlópova, a small and poor landowner, lives within two miles of my estate. Before I left for the Caucasus I had called on her. The old lady was very glad to hear that I should see her 'Páshenka', by which pet name she called the grey-haired elderly captain, and that I, 'a living letter', could tell him all about her and take him a small parcel from her. Having treated me to excellent pie and smoked goose, Mary Ivánovna went into her bedroom and returned with a black bag to which a black silk ribbon was attached.

'Here, this is the icon of our Mother Mediatress of the Burning Bush,' said she, crossing herself and kissing the icon of the Virgin and placing it in my hands. 'Please let him have it. You see, when he went to the Caucasus I had a Mass said for him and promised, if he remained alive and safe, to order this icon of the Mother of God for him. And now for eighteen years the Mediatress and the Holy Saints have had mercy on him, he has not been wounded once, and yet in what battles has he not taken part? . . . What Michael who went with him told me was enough, believe me, to make one's hair stand on end. You see, what I know about him is only from others. He, my pet, never writes me about his campaigns for fear of frightening me.'

(After I reached the Caucasus I learnt, and then not from the captain himself, that he had been severely wounded four times and of course never wrote to his mother either about his wounds or his campaigns.)

'So let him now wear this holy image,' she continued. 'I give it him with my blessing. May the Most Holy Mediatress guard him. Especially when going into battle let him wear it. Tell him so, dear friend. Say "Your mother wishes it."'

I promised to carry out her instructions carefully.

'I know you will grow fond of my Páshenka,' continued the old lady. 'He is such a splendid fellow. Will you believe it, he never lets a year pass without sending me some money, and he also helps my daughter Ánnushka a good deal, and all out of his pay! I thank God for having given me such a child,' she continued with tears in her eyes.

'Does he often write to you?' I asked.

'Seldom, my dear: perhaps once a year. Only when he sends the money, not otherwise. He says, "If I don't write to you, mother, that means I am alive and well. Should anything befall me, which God forbid, they'll tell you without me."'

When I handed his mother's present to the captain (it was in my own quarters) he asked for a bit of paper, carefully wrapped it up, and then put it away. I told him many things about his mother's life. He remained silent, and when I had finished speaking he went to a corner of the room and busied himself for what seemed a long time, filling his pipe.

'Yes, she's a splendid old woman!' he said from there in a rather muffled voice. 'Will God ever let me see her again?'

These simple words expressed much love and sadness.

'Why do you serve here?' I asked.

'One has to serve,' he answered with conviction.

['You should transfer to Russia. You would then be nearer to her.'

'To Russia? To Russia?' repeated the captain, dubiously swaying his head and smiling mournfully. 'Here I am still of some use, but there I should be the least of the officers. And besides, the double pay we get here also means something to a poor man.'

'Can it be, Pável Ivánovich, that living as you do the ordinary pay would not suffice?'

'And does the double pay suffice?' interjected the captain. 'Look at our officers! Have any of them a brass farthing? They all go on tick at the sutler's, and are all up to their ears in debt. You say "living as I do"...Do you really think that living as I do I have anything over out of my salary? Not a farthing! You don't yet know what prices are like here; everything is three times dearer...']

The captain lived economically, did not play cards, rarely went carousing, and smoked the cheapest tobacco (which for some reason he called home-grown tobacco). I had liked him before – he had one of those simple, calm, Russian faces which are easy and pleasant to look straight in the eyes – and after this talk I felt a sincere regard for him.

Chapter II

NEXT morning at four o'clock the captain came for me. He wore an old threadbare coat without epaulettes, wide Caucasian trousers, a white sheepskin cap the wool of which had grown yellow and limp, and had a shabby Asiatic sword strapped round his shoulder. The small white horse he rode ambled along with short strides, hanging its head down and swinging its thin tail. Although the worthy captain's figure was not very martial or even good-looking, it expressed such equanimity towards everything around him that it involuntarily inspired respect.

I did not keep him waiting a single moment, but mounted my horse at once, and we rode together through the gates of the fort.

The battalion was some five hundred yards ahead of us and looked like a dense, oscillating, black mass. It was only possible to guess that it was an infantry battalion by the bayonets which looked like needles standing close together, and by the sound of the soldiers' songs which occasionally reached us, the beating of a drum, and the delightful voice of the Sixth Company's second tenor, which had often charmed me at the fort. The road lay along the middle of a deep and broad ravine by the side of a stream which had overflowed its banks. Flocks of wild pigeons whirled above it, now alighting on the rocky banks, now turning in the air in rapid circles and vanishing out of sight. The sun was not yet visible, but the crest of the right side of the ravine was just beginning to be lit up. The grey and whitish rock, the yellowish-green moss, the dew-covered bushes of Christ's Thorn, dogberry, and dwarf elm, appeared extraordinarily distinct and salient in the golden morning light, but the other side and the valley, wrapped in thick mist which floated in uneven layers, were damp and gloomy and presented an indefinite mingling of colours: pale purple, almost black, dark green, and white. Right in front of us, strikingly distinct against the dark-blue horizon, rose the bright, dead-white masses of the snowy mountains, with their shadows and out-lines fantastic and yet exquisite in every detail. Crickets, grass-hoppers, and thousands of other insects, awoke in the tall grasses and filled the air with their clear and ceaseless sounds: it was as if innumerable tiny bells were ringing inside our very ears. The air was full of the scent of water, grass, and mist: the scent of a lovely early summer morning. The captain struck a light and lit his pipe, and the smell of his cheap tobacco and of the tinder seemed to me extraordinarily pleasant.

To overtake the infantry more quickly we left the road. The captain appeared more thoughtful than usual, did not take his Daghestan pipe from his mouth, and at every step touched with his heels his horse, which swaying from side to side left a scarcely perceptible green track in the tall wet grass. From under its very feet, with the cry and the whirr of wings which involuntarily sends a thrill through every sportsman, a pheasant rose, and flew slowly upwards. The captain did not take the least notice of it.

We had nearly overtaken the battalion when we heard the thud of a horse galloping behind us, and that same moment a good-looking youth in an officer's uniform and white sheep-skin cap galloped past us. He smiled in passing, nodded to the captain, and flourished his whip. I only had time to notice that he sat his horse and held his reins with peculiar grace, that he had beautiful black eyes, a fine nose, and only the first indications of a moustache. What specially pleased me about him was that he could not repress a smile when he noticed our admiration. This smile alone showed him to be very young.

'Where is he galloping to?' muttered the captain with a dissatisfied air, without taking the pipe from his mouth.

'Who is he?' I replied.

'Ensign Alánin, a subaltern in my company. He came from the Cadet Corps only a month ago.'

'I suppose he is going into action for the first time,' I said.

'That's why he is so delighted,' answered the captain, thoughtfully shaking his head. 'Youth!'

'But how could he help being pleased? I can fancy how interesting it must be for a young officer.'

The captain remained silent for a minute or two.

'That is just why I say "youth",' he added in a deep voice. 'What is there to be pleased at without ever having seen the thing? When one has seen it many times one is not so pleased. There are now, let us say, twenty of us officers here: one or other is sure to be killed or wounded, that is quite certain. To-day it may be I, to-morrow he, the next day a third. So what is there to be pleased about?'

Chapter III

As soon as the bright sun appeared above the hill and lit up the valley along which we were marching, the wavy clouds of mist cleared and it grew hot. The soldiers, with muskets and sacks on their shoulders, marched slowly along the dusty road. Now and then Ukrainian words and laughter could be heard in their ranks. Several old soldiers in white blouses (most of them non-commissioned officers) walked together by the roadside, smoking their pipes and conversing gravely. Heavily laden wagons drawn by three horses moved steadily along, raising thick clouds of dust that hung motionless in the air. The officers rode in front: some of them caracoled – whipping their horses, making them take three or four leaps and then, pulling their heads round, stopping abruptly. Others were occupied with the singers, who in spite of the heat and sultriness sang song after song.

With the mounted Tartars, about two hundred yards ahead of the infantry, rode a tall handsome lieutenant in Asiatic costume on a large white horse. He was known in the regiment as a desperate dare-devil who would spit the truth out at anybody. He wore a black tunic trimmed with gold braid, leggings to match, soft closely fitting gold-braided oriental shoes, a yellow coat and a tall sheepskin cap pushed back from his forehead. Fastened to the silver strap that lay across his chest and back, he carried a powder-flask, and a pistol behind him. Another pistol and a silver-mounted dagger hung from his girdle, and above these a sword in a red leather sheath, and a musket in a black cover, were slung over his shoulder. By his clothing, by the way he sat his horse, by his general bearing, in fact by his every movement, one could see that he tried to resemble a Tartar. He even spoke to the Tartars with whom he was riding in a language I did not know, and from the bewildered and amused looks with which they glanced at one another I surmised that they did not understand him either. He was one of our young officers, dare-devil braves who shape their lives on the model of Lérmontov's and Marlínsky's heroes. These officers see the Caucasus only through the prism of such books as *A Hero of our Time*, and *Mullah-Nur*,[1] and are guided in their actions not by their own inclinations but by the examples of their models.

The lieutenant, for instance, may perhaps have liked the company of well-bred women and men of rank: generals, colonels, and aides-de-camp (it is even my conviction that he liked such society very much, for he was exceedingly ambitious), but he considered it his imperative duty to turn his roughest side to all important men, though he was strictly moderate in his rudeness to them; and when any lady came to the fort he considered it his duty to walk before her window with his bosom friends, in a red shirt and with slippers on his

1 Novels by the above-mentioned authors.

bare feet, and shout and swear at the top of his voice. But all this he did not so much with the intention of offending her as to let her see what beautiful white feet he had, and how easy it would be to fall in love with him should he desire it. Or he would often go with two or three friendly Tartars to the hills at night to lie in ambush by the roadside to watch for passing hostile Tartars and kill them: and though his heart told him more than once that there was nothing valiant in this, he considered himself bound to cause suffering to people with whom he affected to be disillusioned and whom he chose to hate and despise. He always carried two things: a large icon hanging round his neck, and a dagger which he wore over his shirt even when in bed. He sincerely believed that he had enemies. To persuade himself that he must avenge himself on someone and wash away some insult with blood was his greatest enjoyment. He was convinced that hatred, vengeance, and contempt for the human race were the noblest and most poetic of emotions. But his mistress (a Circassian of course) whom I happened to meet subsequently, used to say that he was the kindest and mildest of men, and that every evening he wrote down his dismal thoughts in his diary, as well as his accounts on ruled paper, and prayed to God on his knees. And how much he suffered merely to appear in his own eyes what he wished to be! For his comrades and the soldiers could never see him as he wished to appear. Once on one of his nocturnal expeditions on the road with his bosom friends he happened to wound a hostile Chechen with a bullet in the leg, and took him prisoner. After that the Chechen lived for seven weeks with the lieutenant, who attended to him and nursed him as he would have nursed his dearest friend, and when the Chechen recovered he gave him presents and set him free. After that, during one of our expeditions when the lieutenant was retreating with the soldiers of the cordon and firing to keep back the foe, he heard someone among the enemy call him by name, and the man he had wounded rode forward and made signs to the lieutenant to do the same. The lieutenant rode up to his friend and pressed his hand. The hillsmen stood some way back and did not fire, but scarcely had the lieutenant turned his horse to return before several men shot at him and a bullet grazed the small of his back. Another time, at night, when a fire had broken out in the fort and two companies of soldiers were putting it out, I myself saw how the tall figure of a man mounted on a black horse and lit up by the red glow of the fire suddenly appeared among the crowd and, pushing through, rode up to the very flames. When quite close the lieutenant jumped from his horse and rushed into the house, one side of which was burning. Five minutes later he came out with singed hair and scorched elbow, carrying in his bosom two pigeons he had rescued from the flames.

His name was Rosenkranz, yet he often spoke of his descent, deducing it somehow from the Varángians (the first rulers of Russia), and clearly demonstrated that he and his ancestors were pure Russians.

Chapter IV

THE sun had done half its journey, and cast its hot rays through the glowing air onto the dry earth. The dark blue sky was perfectly clear, and only the base of the snowy mountains began to clothe itself in lilac-tinged white clouds. The motionless air seemed full of transparent dust, the heat was becoming unbearable.

Half-way on their march the troops reached a small stream and halted. The soldiers stacked their muskets and rushed to the stream; the commander of the battalion sat down in the shade on a drum, his full face assuming the correct expression denoting the greatness of his rank. He, together with some other officers, prepared to have a snack. The captain lay down on the grass under his company's wagon. The brave Lieutenant Rosenkranz and some other young officers disposed themselves on their outspread cloaks and got ready for a drinking-bout, as could be gathered from the bottles and flasks arranged round them, as well as from the peculiar animation of the singers who, standing before them in a semicircle, sang a Caucasian dance-song with a whistling obbligato interjected:

Shamyl, he began to riot
In the days gone by,
Try-ry-rataty,
In the days gone by!

Among these officers was the young ensign who had overtaken us in the morning. He was very amusing: his eyes shone,
he spoke rather thickly, and he wished to kiss and declare his
love to everyone. Poor boy! He did not know that he might
appear funny in such a situation, that the frankness and tenderness with which he assailed everyone predisposed them not to
the affection he so longed for, but to ridicule; nor did he know
that when, quite heated, he at last threw himself down on the
cloak and rested on his elbow with his thick black hair thrown
back, he looked uncommonly charming.

[In a word, everyone was cheerful, except perhaps one
officer who, sitting under his company's cart, had lost the
horse he was riding to another officer at cards and had agreed
to hand it over when they reached head-quarters. He was
vainly trying to induce the other to play again, offering to
stake a casket which everyone could confirm he had bought
for thirty rubles from a Jew, but which – merely because he
was in difficulties – he was now willing to stake for fifteen. His
opponent looked casually into the distance and persistently
remained silent, till at last he remarked that he was terribly
anxious to have a doze.

I confess that from the time I started from the fort and
decided to take part in this action, gloomy reflections involuntarily rose in my mind, and so – since one has a tendency
to judge of others by oneself] I listened with curiosity to the
conversation of the soldiers and officers and attentively
watched the expression of their faces, but could find absolutely
no trace of the anxiety I myself experienced: jokes, laughter
and anecdotes, gambling and drunkenness, expressed the general carelessness and indifference to the impending danger [as if
all these people had long ago finished their affairs in this world.
What was this – firmness, habituation to danger, or carelessness
and indifference to life? Or was it all these things together as

well as others I did not know, forming a complex but powerful moral motive of human nature termed *esprit de corps* – a subtle code embracing within itself a general expression of all the virtues and vices of men banded together in any permanent condition, a code each new member involuntarily submits to unmurmuringly and which does not change with the individuals, since whoever they may be the sum total of human tendencies everywhere and always remains the same?]

Chapter V

TOWARDS seven that evening, dusty and tired, we entered the wide fortified gate of Fort M. The sun was already setting and threw its rosy slanting rays on the picturesque little batteries, on the gardens with their tall poplars which surrounded the fortress, on the yellow gleaming cultivated fields, and on the white clouds that crowding round the snowy peaks had, as if trying to imitate them, formed a range not less fantastic and beautiful. On the horizon the new moon appeared delicate as a little cloud. In the Tartar village, from the roof of a hut, a Tartar was calling the faithful to prayer, and our singers raised their voices with renewed energy and vigour.

After a rest and after tidying myself up a bit, I went to an adjutant of my acquaintance to ask him to let the general know of my intention. On my way from the suburb where I had put up I noticed in Fort M. something I did not at all expect: a pretty little brougham overtook me, in which I caught sight of a fashionable bonnet and from which I overheard some French words. The sounds of some 'Lizzie' or 'Kátenka' polka, played on a bad ramshackle piano, reached me through the windows of the commander's house. In a little grocery and wine shop which I passed, some clerks with cigarettes in their fingers sat drinking wine, and I heard one of them say to another, 'No, excuse me, as to politics, Mary Gregórevna is first of our ladies.' A Jew in a worn-out coat, with a bent back and sickly countenance, was dragging along a wheezy barrel-organ and the whole suburb resounded to the tones of the finale of 'Lucia'. Two women in rustling dresses with silk kerchiefs on their heads and carrying bright-coloured parasols passed by along the planks that did duty for a pavement. Two girls, one in a pink, the other in a blue dress, stood bareheaded beside the earth-embankments of a low-roofed house, and shrieked with high-pitched, forced laughter, evidently to attract the attention of passing officers. Officers, dressed in new uniforms with glittering epaulettes and white gloves, flaunted along the street and on the boulevard.

I found my acquaintance on the ground floor of the general's house. I had scarcely had time to explain my wish to him and to get his reply that it could easily be fulfilled, when the pretty little brougham I had noticed outside rattled past the window we were sitting at. A tall, well-built man in an infantry major's uniform and epaulettes got out and entered the house.

'Oh, please excuse me,' said the adjutant, rising, 'I must go and announce them to the general.'

'Who is it?' I asked.

'The countess,' he replied, and buttoning his uniform he rushed upstairs.

A few minutes later a very handsome man in a frock coat without epaulettes and with a white cross in his buttonhole went out into the porch. He was not tall but remarkably good-looking. He was followed by the major, an adjutant, and a couple of other officers. The general's gait, voice, and all his movements, showed him to be a man well aware of his own value.

'*Bonsoir, madame la comtesse*,'[1] he said, offering his hand through the carriage window.

A small hand in a kid glove pressed his, and a pretty smiling face in a yellow bonnet appeared at the carriage window.

Of the conversation which lasted several minutes I only overheard the general say laughingly as I passed by:

'*Vous savez que j'ai fait vœu de combattre les infidèles; prenez donc garde de la devenir.*'[2]

1 'Good evening, Countess.'
2 'You know I have sworn to fight the infidels (the unfaithful), so beware of becoming one.'

A laugh replied from inside the carriage.

'*Adieu donc, cher général!*'[1]

'*Non, au revoir,*' said the general, ascending the steps of the porch. '*N'oubliez pas, que je m'invite pour la soirée de demain.*'[2]

The carriage rattled off [and the general went into the sitting-room with the major. Passing by the open window of the adjutant's room, he noticed my un-uniformed figure and turned his kind attention to me. Having heard my request he announced his complete agreement with it and passed on into his room.]

'There again,' I thought as I walked home, 'is a man who possesses all that Russians strive after: rank, riches, distinction; and this man, the day before an engagement the outcome of which is known only to God, jokes with a pretty woman and promises to have tea with her next day, just as if they had met at a ball!'

[I remembered a reflection I had heard a Tartar utter, to the effect that only a pauper can be brave. '*Become rich, become a coward,*' said he, not at all to offend his comrade but as a common and unquestionable rule. But the general could lose, together with his life, much more than anyone else I had had an opportunity of observing and, contrary to the Tartar's rule, no one had shown such a pleasant, graceful indifference and confidence as he. My conceptions of courage became completely confused.]

At that same adjutant's I met a young man who surprised me even more. He was a young lieutenant of the K. regiment who was noted for his almost feminine meekness and timidity and who had come to the adjutant to pour out his vexation and resentment against those who, he said, had intrigued against him to keep him from taking part in the impending action. He said it was mean to behave in that way, that it was unfriendly, that he would not forget it, and so forth. Intently as I watched the expression of his face and listened to the sound of his voice,

1 'Good-bye then, dear general.'
2 'No, *au revoir*. Don't forget that I am inviting myself for to-morrow's soirée.'

I could not help feeling convinced that he was not pretending but was genuinely filled with indignation and grief at not being allowed to go and shoot Circassians and expose himself to their fire. He was grieving like a little child who has been unjustly birched . . . I could make nothing at all of it.

Chapter VI

THE troops were to start at ten in the evening. At half-past eight I mounted and rode to the general's, but thinking that he and his adjutant were busy I tied my horse to the fence and sat down on an earth-bank intending to catch the general when he came out.

The heat and glare of the sun were now replaced by the coolness of night and the soft light of the young moon, which had formed a pale glimmering semi-circle around itself on the deep blue of the starry sky and was already setting. Lights appeared in the windows of the houses and shone through cracks in the shutters of the earth-huts. The stately poplars, beyond the white moonlit earth-huts with their rush-thatched roofs, looked darker and taller than ever against the horizon.

The long shadows of the houses, the trees, and the fences, stretched out daintily on the dusty road. . . . From the river came the ringing voices of frogs;[1] along the street came the sound of hurried steps and voices talking, or the gallop of a horse, and from the suburb the tones of a barrel-organ playing now 'The winds are blowing', now some 'Aurora Waltz'.

I will not say in what meditations I was absorbed: first, because I should be ashamed to confess the gloomy waves of thought that insistently flooded my soul while around me I noticed nothing but gaiety and joy, and secondly, because it would not suit my story. I was so absorbed in thought that I did not even notice the bell strike eleven and the general with his suite ride past me.

---

1 Frogs in the Caucasus make a noise quite different from the croaking of frogs elsewhere. L. T.

[Hastily mounting my horse I set out to overtake the detachment.]

The rear-guard was still within the gates of the fort. I had great difficulty in making my way across the bridge among the guns, ammunition wagons, carts of different companies, and officers noisily giving orders. Once outside the gates I trotted past the troops who, stretching out over nearly three-quarters of a mile, were silently moving on amid the darkness, and I overtook the general. As I rode past the guns drawn out in single file, and the officers who rode between them, I was hurt as by a discord in the quiet and solemn harmony by the German accents of a voice shouting, 'A linstock, you devil!' and the voice of a soldier hurriedly exclaiming, 'Shévchenko, the lieutenant wants a light!'

The greater part of the sky was now overcast by long strips of dark grey clouds; it was only here and there that a few stars twinkled dimly among them. The moon had already sunk behind the near horizon of the black hills visible to the right and threw a faint trembling light on their peaks, in sharp contrast to the impenetrable darkness enveloping their base. The air was so warm and still that it seemed as if not a single blade of grass, not a single cloudlet, was moving. It was so dark that even objects close at hand could not be distinguished. By the sides of the road I seemed to see now rocks, now animals, now some strange kind of men, and I discovered that they were merely bushes only when I heard them rustle, or felt the dew with which they were sprinkled.

Before me I saw a dense heaving wall followed by some dark moving spots; this was the cavalry vanguard and the general with his suite. Another similar dark mass, only lower, moved beside us; this was the infantry.

The silence that reigned over the whole division was so great that all the mingling sounds of night with their mysterious charm were distinctly audible: the far-off mournful howling of jackals, now like agonized weeping, now like chuckling; the monotonous resounding song of crickets, frogs, and quails; a sort of rumbling I could not at all account for but which seemed to draw nearer; and all those scarcely audible motions of Nature which can neither be understood nor defined, mingled into one beautiful harmony which we call the stillness of night. This stillness was interrupted by, or rather combined with, the dull thud of hoofs and the rustling of the tall grass caused by the slowly advancing detachment.

Only very occasionally could the clang of a heavy gun, the sound of bayonets touching one another, hushed voices, or the snorting of a horse, be heard. [By the scent of the wet juicy grass which sank under our horses' feet, by the light steam rising from the ground and by the horizons seen on two sides of us, it was evident that we were moving across a wide, luxuriant meadow.] Nature seemed to breathe with pacifying beauty and power.

Can it be that there is not room for all men on this beautiful earth under those immeasurable starry heavens? Can it be possible that in the midst of this entrancing Nature feelings of hatred, vengeance, or the desire to exterminate their fellows, can endure in the souls of men? All that is unkind in the hearts of men should, one would think, vanish at contact with Nature – that most direct expression of beauty and goodness.

[War! What an incomprehensible phenomenon! When one's reason asks: 'Is it just, is it necessary?' an inner voice always replies 'No'. Only the persistence of this unnatural occurrence makes it seem natural, and a feeling of self-preservation makes it seem just.

Who will doubt that in the war of the Russians against the mountain-tribes, justice – resulting from a feeling of self-preservation – is on our side? Were it not for this war, what would secure the neighbouring rich and cultured Russian territories from robbery, murder, and raids by wild and warlike tribes? But consider two private persons. On whose side is the feeling of self-preservation and consequently of justice? Is it on the side of this ragamuffin – some Djemi or other – who hearing of the approach of the Russians snatches down his old gun from the wall, puts three or four charges (which he will only reluctantly discharge) in his pouch and runs to meet the giaours, and on seeing that the Russians still advance, approaching the fields he has sown which they will tread down and his hut which they will burn, and the ravine where his mother, his wife, and his children have hidden themselves, shaking with fear – seeing that he will be deprived of all that constitutes his happiness – in impotent anger and with a cry of despair tears off his tattered jacket, flings down his gun, and drawing his sheepskin cap over his eyes sings his death-song and flings himself headlong onto the Russian bayonets with only a dagger in his hand? Is justice on his side or on that of this officer on the general's staff who is singing French chansonettes so well just as he rides past us? He has a family in Russia, relations, friends, serfs, and obligations towards them, but has no reason or desire to be at enmity with the hillsmen, and has come to the Caucasus just by chance and to show his courage. Or is it on the side of my acquaintance the adjutant, who only wishes to obtain a captaincy and a comfortable position as soon as possible and for that reason has become the hillsmen's enemy? Or is it on the side of this young German who, with a strong German accent, is demanding a linstock from the artillerymen? What devil has brought him from his fatherland and set him down in this distant region? Why should this Saxon, Kaspar Lavréntich, mix himself up in our blood-thirsty conflict with these turbulent neighbours?]

Chapter VII

W E had been riding for more than two hours. I was beginning to shiver and feel drowsy. Through the gloom I still seemed to see the same indefinite forms; a little way in front the same black wall and the moving spots. Close in front of me I could see the crupper of a white horse which swung its tail and threw its hind legs wide apart, the back of a white Circassian coat on which could be discerned a musket in a black case, and the glimmering butt of a pistol in an embroidered holster; the glow of a cigarette lit up a fair moustache, a beaver collar and a hand in a chamois glove. Every now and then I leant over my horse's neck, shutting my eyes and forgetting myself for a few minutes, then startled by the familiar tramping and rustling I glanced round, and felt as if I were standing still and the black wall in front was moving towards me, or that it had stopped and I should in a moment ride into it. At one such moment the rumbling which increased and seemed to approach, and the cause of which I could not guess, struck me forcibly: it was the sound of water. We were entering a deep gorge and approaching a mountain-stream that was over-flowing its banks.[1] The rumbling increased, the damp grass became thicker and taller and the bushes closer, while the horizon gradually narrowed. Now and then bright lights appeared here and there against the dark background of the hills, and vanished instantly.

'Tell me, please, what are those lights?' I asked in a whisper of a Tartar riding beside me.

'Don't you know?' he replied.

'No.'

'The hillsmen have tied straw to poles and are waving it about alight.'

'Why are they doing that?'

'So that everyone should know that the Russians have come. Oh, oh! What a bustle is going on now in the *aouls*! Everybody's dragging his belongings into the ravine,' he said laughing.

'Why, do they already know in the mountains that a detach-ment is on its way?' I asked him.

'How can they help knowing? They always know. Our people are like that.'

'Then Shamyl[2] too is preparing for action?' I asked.

'No,' he answered, shaking his head, 'Shamyl won't go into action; Shamyl will send his *naibs*,[3] and he himself will look on through a telescope from above.'

'Does he live far away?'

'Not far. Some eight miles to the left.'

'How do you know?' I asked. 'Have you been there?'

1 In the Caucasus rivers are apt to overflow in July. L. T.
2 Shamyl was the leader (in 1834–59) of the Caucasian hill-tribes in their resistance to Russia.
3 A *naib* was a man to whom Shamyl had entrusted some administrative office. L. T.

'I have. Our people have all been.'

'Have you seen Shamyl?'

'Such as we don't see Shamyl! There are a hundred, three hundred, a thousand *murids*[1] all round him, and Shamyl is in the centre,' he said, with an expression of servile admiration.

Looking up, it was possible to discern that the sky, now cleared, was beginning to grow lighter in the east and the pleiades to sink towards the horizon, but the ravine through which we were marching was still damp and gloomy.

Suddenly a little way in front of us several lights flashed through the darkness; at the same moment some bullets flew whizzing past amid the surrounding silence [and sharp abrupt firing could be heard and loud cries, as piercing as cries of despair but expressing instead of fear such a passion of brutal audacity and rage that one could not but shudder at hearing it.] It was the enemy's advanced picket. The Tartars who composed it whooped, fired at random, and then ran in different directions.

All became silent again. The general called up an interpreter. A Tartar in a white Circassian coat rode up to him and, gesticulating and whispering, talked with him for some time.

'Colonel Khasánov! Order the cordon to take open order,' commanded the general with a quiet but distinct drawl.

The detachment advanced to the river, the black hills and gorges were left behind, the dawn appeared. The vault of the heavens, in which a few pale stars were still dimly visible, seemed higher; the sunrise glow beyond shone brightly in the east, a fresh penetrating breeze blew from the west and the white mists rose like steam above the rushing stream.

Chapter VIII

OUR guide pointed out a ford and the cavalry vanguard, followed by the general, began crossing the stream. The

---

1 The word *murid* has several meanings, but here it denotes something between an adjutant and a bodyguard.

water which reached to the horses' chests rushed with tremend-ous force between the white boulders which here and there appeared on a level with its surface, and formed foaming and gurgling ripples round the horses' legs. The horses, surprised by the noise of the water, lifted their heads and pricked their ears, but stepped evenly and carefully against the current on the uneven bottom of the stream. Their riders lifted their feet and their weapons. The infantry, literally in nothing but their shirts, linked arm in arm by twenties and holding above the water their muskets to which their bundles of clothing were fastened, made great efforts (as the strained expression of their faces showed) to resist the force of the current. The mounted artillerymen with loud shouts drove their horses into the water at a trot. The guns and green ammunition wagons, over which the water occasionally splashed, rang against the stony bottom, but the sturdy little horses, churning the water, pulled at the traces in unison and with dripping manes and tails clambered out on the opposite bank.

As soon as the crossing was accomplished the general's face suddenly assumed a meditative and serious look and he turned his horse and, followed by the cavalry, rode at a trot down a broad glade which opened out before us in the midst of the forest. A cordon of mounted Cossacks was scattered along the skirts of the forest.

In the woods we noticed a man on foot dressed in a Cir-cassian coat and wearing a tall cap – then a second and a third. One of the officers said: 'Those are Tartars.' Then a puff of smoke appeared from behind a tree, a shot, and another.... Our rapid fire drowns the enemy's. Only now and then a bullet, with a slow sound like the buzzing of a bee's wings, passes by and proves that the firing is not all ours. Now the infantry at a run and the guns at a trot pass into the cordon. You can hear the boom of the guns, the metallic sounds of flying grape-shot, the hissing of rockets, and the crackle of musketry. Over the wide glade on all sides you can see cavalry, infantry, and artillery. Puffs of smoke mingle with the dew-covered verdure and the mist. Colonel Khasánov, approaching the general at full gallop, suddenly reins in his horse.

'Your Excellency, shall we order the cavalry to charge?' he says, raising his hand to his cap. 'The enemy's colours[1] are in sight,' and he points with his whip to some mounted Tartars in front of whom ride two men on white horses with bits of blue and red stuff fastened to poles in their hands.

'Go, and God be with you, Iván Mikháylovich!' says the general.

The colonel turns his horse sharply round, draws his sword, and shouts 'Hurrah!'

'Hurrah! Hurrah! Hurrah!' comes from the ranks, and the cavalry gallop after him. . . .

Everyone looks on with interest: there is a colour, another, a third and a fourth. . . .

The enemy, not waiting for the attack, hides in the wood and thence opens a small-arms fire. Bullets come flying more and more frequently.

'*Quel charmant coup d'œil!*'[2] says the general, rising slightly, English fashion, in his saddle on his slim-legged black horse.

'*Charmant!*' answers the major, rolling his r's, and striking his horse he rides up to the general: '*C'est un vrai plaisir que la guerre dans un aussi beau pays,*'[3] he says.

'*Et surtout en bonne compagnie,*'[4] replies the general with a pleasant smile.

The major bows.

At that moment a hostile cannon-ball flies past with a disagreeable whiz, and strikes something. We hear behind us the moan of a wounded man.

This moaning strikes me so strangely that the warlike scene instantly loses all its charm for me. But no one except myself seems to notice it: the major laughs with apparently greater gusto, another officer repeats with perfect calm the first words of a sentence he had just been saying, the general looks the

---

1 The colours among the hillsmen correspond to those of our troops, except that every *dzhigit* or 'brave' among them may make his own colours and carry them. L. T.
2 'What a charming view.'
3 'Charming . . . War in such beautiful country is a real pleasure.'
4 'Especially in good company.'

other way and with the quietest smile says something in French.

'Shall we reply to their fire?' asks the commander of the artillery, galloping up.

'Yes, frighten them a bit!' carelessly replies the general, lighting a cigar.

The battery takes up its position and the firing begins. The earth groans under the shots, the discharges flash out incessantly, and smoke, through which it is scarcely possible to distinguish the artillerymen moving round their guns, veils your sight.

The *aoul* has been bombarded. Colonel Khasánov rides up again, and at the general's command gallops towards the *aoul*. The war-cry is again heard and the cavalry disappears in the cloud of dust it has raised.

The spectacle was truly magnificent. The one thing that spoilt the general impression for me – who took no part in the affair and was unaccustomed to it – was that this movement and the animation and the shouting appeared unnecessary. The comparison involuntarily suggested itself to me of a man swinging his arms vigorously to cut the air with an axe.

Chapter IX

OUR troops had taken possession of the village and not a single soul of the enemy remained in it when the general and his suite, to which I had attached myself, rode up to it.

The long clean huts, with their flat earthen roofs and shapely chimneys, stood on irregular stony mounds between which flowed a small stream. On one side were green gardens with enormous pear and small plum trees brightly lit up by the sun, on the other strange upright shadows, the perpendicular stones of the cemetery, and long poles with balls and many-coloured flags fastened to their ends. (These marked the graves of *dzhigits*.)

The troops were drawn up outside the gates.

['Well, how about it, Colonel?' said the general. 'Let them loot. I see they are terribly anxious to,' he added with a smile, pointing at the Cossacks.

You cannot imagine how striking was the contrast between the carelessness with which the general uttered these words, and their import and the military surroundings.]

A moment later, dragoons, Cossacks, and infantry spread with evident delight through the crooked lanes and in an instant the empty village was animated again. Here a roof crashes, an axe rings against the hard wood of a door that is being forced open, here a stack of hay, a fence, a hut, is set on fire and a pillar of thick smoke rises up in the clear air. Here is a Cossack dragging along a sack of flour and a carpet, there a soldier, with a delighted look on his face, brings a tin basin and some rag out of a hut, another is trying with outstretched arms to catch two hens that struggle and cackle beside a fence, a third has somewhere discovered an enormous pot of milk and after drinking some of it throws the rest on the ground with a loud laugh.

The battalion with which I had come from Fort N. was also in the *aoul*. The captain sat on the roof of a hut and sent thin whiffs of cheap tobacco smoke through his short pipe with such an expression of indifference on his face that on seeing him I forgot that I was in a hostile *aoul* and felt quite at home.

'Ah, you are here too?' he said when he noticed me.

The tall figure of Lieutenant Rosenkranz flitted here and there in the village. He gave orders unceasingly and appeared exceedingly engrossed in his task. I saw him with a triumphant air emerge from a hut followed by two soldiers leading an old Tartar. The old man, whose only clothing consisted of a mottled tunic all in rags and patchwork trousers, was so frail that his arms, tightly bound behind his bent back, seemed scarcely to hold onto his shoulders, and he could scarcely drag his bare crooked legs along. His face and even part of his shaven head were deeply furrowed. His wry toothless mouth kept moving beneath his close-cut moustache and beard, as if he were chewing something; but a gleam still sparkled in his red lashless eyes which clearly expressed an old man's indifference to life.

Rosenkranz asked him, through an interpreter, why he had not gone away with the others.

'Where should I go?' he answered, looking quietly away.

'Where the others have gone,' someone remarked.

'The *dzhigits* have gone to fight the Russians, but I am an old man.'

'Are you not afraid of the Russians?'

'What will the Russians do to me? I am old,' he repeated, again glancing carelessly round the circle that had formed about him.

Later, as I was returning, I saw that old man bareheaded, with his arms tied, being jolted along behind the saddle of a Cossack, and he was looking round with the same expression of indifference on his face. He was needed for the exchange of prisoners.

I climbed onto the roof and sat down beside the captain.

[A bugler who had vodka and provisions was sent for. The captain's calmness and equanimity involuntarily produced an effect on me. We ate roasted pheasant and chatted, without at all reflecting that the owners of that hut had not merely no desire to see us there but could hardly have imagined our existence.]

'There don't seem to have been many of the enemy,' I said, wishing to know his opinion of the action that had taken place.

'The enemy?' he repeated with surprise. 'The enemy was not there at all! Do you call those the enemy? . . . Wait till the evening when we go back, and you will see how they will speed us on our way: what a lot of them will pour out from there,' he said, pointing to a thicket we had passed in the morning.

'What is that?' I asked anxiously, interrupting the captain and pointing to a group of Don Cossacks who had collected round something not far from us.

A sound of something like a child's cry came from there, and the words:

'Stop . . . don't hack it . . . you'll be seen . . . Have you a knife, Evstignéich . . . Lend me a knife. . . .'

'They are up to something, the scoundrels . . .' replied the captain calmly.

But at that moment the young ensign, his comely face flushed and frightened, came suddenly running from behind a corner and rushed towards the Cossacks waving his arms.

'Don't touch it! Don't kill it!' he cried in a childish voice.

Seeing the officer, the Cossacks stepped apart and released a little white kid. The young ensign was quite abashed, muttered something, and stopped before us with a confused face. Seeing the captain and me on the roof he blushed still more and ran leaping towards us.

'I thought they were killing a child,' he said with a bashful smile.

Chapter X

THE general went ahead with the cavalry. The battalion with which I had come from Fort N. remained in the rear-guard. Captain Khlópov's and Lieutenant Rosenkranz's battalions retired together.

The captain's prediction was fully justified. No sooner had we entered the narrow thicket he had mentioned, than on both sides of us we caught glimpses of hillsmen mounted and on foot, and so near were they that I could distinctly see how some of them ran stooping, rifle in hand, from one tree to another.

The captain took off his cap and piously crossed himself, some of the older soldiers did the same. From the wood were heard war-cries and the words '*Iay giaour*', '*Urus! iay!*' Sharp short rifle-shots, following one another fast, whizzed on both sides of us. Our men answered silently with a running fire, and only now and then remarks like the following were made in the ranks: 'See where *he*[1] fires from! It's all right for him inside the wood. We ought to use cannon,' and so forth.

Our ordnance was brought out, and after some grape-shot had been fired the enemy seemed to grow weaker, but a moment later and at every step taken by our troops, the enemy's fire again grew hotter and the shouting louder.

---

1 *He* is a collective noun by which the soldiers indicate the enemy. L. T.

We had hardly gone seven hundred yards from the village before enemy cannon-balls began whistling over our heads. I saw a soldier killed by one. . . . But why should I describe the details of that terrible picture which I would myself give much to be able to forget!

Lieutenant Rosenkranz kept firing, and incessantly shouted in a hoarse voice at the soldiers and galloped from one end of the cordon to the other. He was rather pale and this suited his martial countenance very well.

The good-looking young ensign was in raptures: his beautiful dark eyes shone with daring, his lips were slightly smiling, and he kept riding up to the captain and begging permission to charge.

'We will repel them,' he said persuasively, 'we certainly will.'

'It's not necessary,' replied the captain abruptly. 'We must retreat.'

The captain's company held the skirts of the wood, the men lying down and replying to the enemy's fire. The captain in his shabby coat and shabby cap sat silent on his white horse, with loose reins, bent knees, his feet in the stirrups, and did not stir from his place. (The soldiers knew and did their work so well that there was no need to give them any orders.) Only at rare intervals he raised his voice to shout at those who exposed their heads. There was nothing at all martial about the captain's appearance, but there was something so sincere and simple in it that I was unusually struck by it. 'It is he who is really brave,' I involuntarily said to myself.

He was just the same as I had always seen him: the same calm movements, the same guileless expression on his plain but frank face, only his eyes, which were brighter than usual, showed the concentration of one quietly engaged on his duties. 'As I had always seen him' is easily said, but how many different shades have I noticed in the behaviour of others; one wishing to appear quieter, another sterner, a third merrier, than usual, but the captain's face showed that he did not even see why he should appear anything but what he was.

The Frenchman at Waterloo who said, '*La garde meurt, mais ne se rend pas,*'[1] and other, particularly French, heroes who uttered memorable sayings were brave, and really uttered remarkable words, but between their courage and the captain's there was this difference, that even if a great saying had in any circumstance stirred in the soul of my hero, I am convinced that he would not have uttered it: first because by uttering a great saying he would have feared to spoil a great deed, and secondly because when a man feels within himself the capacity to perform a great deed no talk of any kind is needed. That, I think, is a peculiar and a lofty characteristic of Russian courage, and that being so, how can a Russian heart help aching when our young Russian warriors utter trivial French phrases intended to imitate antiquated French chivalry?

Suddenly from the side where our young ensign stood with his platoon we heard a not very hearty or loud 'Hurrah!' Looking round to where the shout came from, I saw some thirty soldiers with sacks on their shoulders and muskets in their hands managing with very great difficulty to run across a ploughed field. They kept stumbling, but nevertheless ran on and shouted. In front of them, sword in hand, galloped the young ensign.

They all disappeared into the wood. . . .

After a few minutes of whooping and clatter a frightened horse ran out of the wood, and soldiers appeared bringing back the dead and wounded. Among the latter was the young ensign. Two soldiers supported him under his arms. He was as pale as a sheet, and his pretty head, on which only a shadow remained of the warlike enthusiasm that had animated him a few minutes before, was dreadfully sunk between his shoulders and drooped on his chest. There was a small spot of blood on the white shirt beneath his unbuttoned coat.

'Ah, what a pity!' I said, involuntarily turning away from this sad spectacle.

'Of course it's a pity,' said an old soldier, who stood leaning on his musket beside me with a gloomy expression on his face.

1 'The Guard dies, but does not surrender.'

'He's not afraid of anything. How can one do such things?' he added, looking intently at the wounded lad. 'He was still foolish and now he has paid for it!'

'And you?' I asked. 'Are you afraid?'

'What do you expect?'

Chapter XI

FOUR soldiers were carrying the ensign on a stretcher and behind them an ambulance soldier was leading a thin, broken-winded horse with two green boxes on its back containing surgical appliances. They waited for the doctor. Some officers rode up to the stretcher and tried to cheer and comfort the wounded lad.

'Well, friend Alánin, it will be some time before you will dance again with castanets,' said Lieutenant Rosenkranz, riding up to the stretcher with a smile.

He probably supposed that these words would raise the young ensign's spirits, but as far as one could judge by the latter's coldly sad look the words had not the desired effect.

The captain rode up too. He looked intently at the wounded man and his usually calm and cold face expressed sincere sympathy. 'Well, my dear Anatól Ivánich,' he said, in a voice of tender sympathy such as I never expected from him, 'evidently it was God's will.'

The wounded lad looked round and his pale face lit up with a sad smile. 'Yes, I disobeyed you.'

'Say rather, it was God's will,' repeated the captain.

The doctor when he arrived, [as far as could be judged by the shakiness of his legs and the redness of his eyes, was in no fit condition to bandage the patient: however, he] took from his assistant bandages, a probe, and another instrument, rolled up his sleeves and stepped up to the ensign with an encouraging smile.

'So it seems they have made a hole in a sound spot for you too,' he said in a carelessly playful tone. 'Let me see.'

The ensign obeyed, but the look he gave the merry doctor expressed astonishment and reproof which the inebriated practitioner did not notice. He touched the wound so awk-wardly, quite unnecessarily pressing on it with his unsteady fingers, that the wounded ensign, driven beyond the limits of endurance, pushed away his hand with a deep groan.

'Let me alone!' he said in a scarcely audible voice. 'I shall die anyway.'

[Then, addressing the captain, he said with difficulty: 'Please, Captain . . . yesterday I lost . . . twenty rubles to Drónov. . . . When my things are sold . . . let him be paid.']

With those words he fell back, and five minutes later when I passed the group that had formed around him, and asked a soldier, 'How is the ensign?' the answer was, 'Passing away.'

Chapter XII

I T was late in the day when the detachment, formed into a broad column and singing, approached the Fort.

[The general rode in front and by his merry countenance one could see that the raid had been successful. In fact, with little loss, we had that day been in Mukay *aoul* – where from immemorial times no Russian foot had trod.

The Saxon, Kaspar Lavréntich, narrated to another officer that he had himself seen how three Chechens had aimed straight at his breast. In the mind of Ensign Rosenkranz a complete story of the day's action had formulated itself. Captain Khlópov walked with thoughtful face in front of his company, leading his little white horse by its bridle.]

The sun had hidden behind the snowy mountain range and threw its last rosy beams on a long thin cloud stretching motionless across the clear horizon. The snow peaks began to disappear in purple mist and only their top outline was visible, wonderfully distinct in the crimson sunset glow. The delicate moon, which had risen long since, began to grow pale against the deep azure. The green of the grass and trees was turning black and becoming covered with dew. The dark masses of troops moved with measured sounds over the luxur-iant meadows. Tambourines, drums, and merry songs were heard from various sides. The voice of the second tenor of the Sixth Company rang out with full force and the sounds of his clear chest-notes, full of feeling and power, floated through the clear evening air.

THE WOOD-FELLING

A CADET'S STORY

Chapter I

In the middle of the winter of 185– a division of one battery
was on service with the detachment operating in that part of
the Térek Territory[1] called the Great Chéchnya. On the
evening of February 14, knowing that the platoon which I in
the absence of any officer was commanding, was to join a
column told off to fell wood next day, and having given and
received the necessary orders, I retired to my tent earlier than
usual. As I had not contracted the bad habit of warming my
tent with hot charcoal, I lay down without undressing on my
bed, which was supported on stakes driven into the ground,
drew my fur cap over my eyes, tucked myself up in my sheepskin cloak, and fell into that peculiar, heavy, and deep sleep
which comes at times of anxiety and when one is awaiting
danger. The expectation of the next day's affair had this effect
on me.

At three next morning, while it was still quite dark, the
warm sheepskin was pulled off me and my eyes, heavy with
sleep, were unpleasantly struck by the red light of a candle.

'Get up, please,' said a voice. I shut my eyes, unconsciously
pulled the sheepskin back over myself, and again fell asleep.
'Get up, please,' said Dmítry once more, remorselessly shaking
me by the shoulder: 'the infantry are starting.' The reality
suddenly flashed on my mind, I sat up and jumped to my
feet. After hurriedly drinking a glass of tea and washing myself
with icy water I crept out of the tent and went to the 'park'
(the place where the cannon were). It was dark, misty, and

1 The Térek Territory lies to the north-east of the Caucasian Mountains.
The Great and Little Chéchnya are districts in the southern part of it.

37

cold. The dim red light of the night-fires, which gleaming here and there in the camp showed up the figures of the sleepy soldiers who lay near them, seemed only to make the darkness more intense.

Near by, quiet regular snoring could be heard, and from farther off, sounds of movements, voices, and the clatter of the muskets of the infantry preparing to start. There was a smell of smoke, manure, torches, and mist; the morning air caused cold shivers to run down one's back, and one's teeth chattered involuntarily.

It was only by the snorting and occasional stamping of the horses harnessed to them that we could tell where the limbers and ammunition wagons stood in the impenetrable darkness; and only the fiery dots of the linstocks showed where the guns were. 'God be with us!' With these words came the clanging sound of the first gun moving, then the noise of the ammunition wagon – and the platoon started. We all took off our caps and crossed ourselves. Having occupied the interval between the infantry companies, the platoon stopped and waited a quarter of an hour for the whole column to collect and for the commander to appear.

'One of our men is missing, Nicholas Petróvich.' With these words a black figure approached me, whom I only knew by the voice to be the gun-sergeant of the platoon, Maksímov.

'Who is it?'

'Velenchúk is missing. He was there all the time they were harnessing – I saw him myself – but now he's gone.'

As the column could not be expected to start at once, we decided to send Corporal Antónov to look for Velenchúk. Directly after that, several horsemen trotted past us in the dark. They were the commander and his suite; and immediately the head of the column moved and started and so at last did we also, but Antónov and Velenchúk were still absent. We had, however, hardly gone a hundred yards before they both over-took us.

'Where was he?' I asked Antónov.

'Asleep in the "park".'

'Why, has he had a drop too much?'

'Oh, no.'

'Then how is it he fell asleep?'

'I can't make out.'

For about three hours we moved slowly on in silence and darkness over some unploughed fields bare of snow and over low bushes that crackled under the wheels of the gun-carriages. At last, after we had crossed a shallow but extremely rapid stream, we were stopped, and we heard the abrupt reports of *vintóvkas*[1] in the direction of the vanguard.

These sounds as usual had a most exhilarating effect on everyone. The detachment seemed to wake up: sounds of talking, movement, and laughter were heard in the ranks. Here a soldier wrestled with a comrade, there another hopped from foot to foot. Here was one chewing hard-tack, or to while away the time shouldering and grounding arms. Meanwhile the mist began to grow distinctly whiter in the east, the damp became more intense, and the surrounding objects gradually emerged from the gloom. I could already discern the green gun-carriages and ammunition wagons, the brass of the guns covered with moisture by the mist, the familiar figures of my soldiers, every minute detail of which I had involuntarily studied, the bay horses, and the lines of infantry with their bright bayonets, their bags, their ramrods, and the kettles they carried on their backs.

We were soon again moved forward a few hundred yards where there was no road, and then we were shown our position. To the right one could see the steep bank of a winding stream and the high wooden posts of a Tartar cemetery; to the left and in front a black strip was visible through the mist. The platoon unlimbered. The Eighth Company, which covered us, piled their muskets, and a battalion with axes and muskets went to the forest.

---

1 The *vintóvka* was a long Asiatic rifle used by the Circassians (Cherkéses). When firing, they rested the barrel on a support formed by two thin spiked sticks tied at the top by a strap.

Before five minutes were over fires were crackling and smoking in all directions. The soldiers dispersed, blew the fires and stirred them with hands and feet, dragged logs and branches, while the forest resounded with the unceasing noise of hundreds of axes and the crashing of falling trees.

The artillery, with a certain rivalry of the infantry, heaped their pile high, and though it was already burning so that one could hardly come within two paces of it and thick black smoke was rising through the frozen branches, which the soldiers pressed down into the fire (and from which drops fell sizzling into the flames), and though the charcoal was glowing beneath and the grass was scorched all around, the soldiers were not satisfied, but kept throwing great logs on to the pile, feeding it with dry grass beneath and heaping it higher and higher.

When I came up to the fire to smoke a cigarette, Velenchúk, always officious, but to-day feeling guilty and bustling about more than anyone, in a fit of zeal snatched a piece of charcoal from the fire with his bare hand and, after tossing it from hand to hand a couple of times, dropped it on the ground.

'Light a twig and hold it up,' said a soldier.

'No, better get a linstock, lad,' said another.

When I had at length lit my cigarette without the aid of Velenchúk, who was again trying to take a piece of charcoal in his hand, he rubbed his burnt fingers on the skirts of his sheepskin coat and then, probably for want of something else to do, lifted a large piece of plane-tree wood and swung it into the fire. When at last he felt free to rest a bit, he came close up to the fire, threw open his cloak which he wore like a mantle fastened by one button, spread out his legs, held out his big, black hands, and drawing his mouth a bit to one side, screwed up his eyes.

'Ah, I've gone and forgot my pipe. Here's a go, lads!' said he after a short silence, not addressing anyone in particular.

Chapter II

IN Russia there are three predominant types of soldier under which the men of all our forces – whether line, guards, infantry, cavalry, artillery, army of the Caucasus, or what not – may be classified.

These principal types, including many sub-divisions and combinations, are:

1. The submissive;
2. The domineering;
3. The reckless.

The submissive are divided into (*a*) the calmly submissive and (*b*) the bustlingly submissive.

The domineering are divided into (*a*) the sternly domineering and (*b*) the diplomatically domineering.

The reckless are divided into (*a*) the amusingly reckless and (*b*) the viciously reckless.

The type most often met with – a type more lovable and attractive than the others and generally accompanied by the best Christian virtues, – meekness, piety, patience, and devotion to the will of God, – is the submissive type in general. The distinctive feature of the calmly submissive is his invincible resignation to and contempt for all the reverses of fate which may befall him; the distinctive features of the submissive drunkard are a mild, poetic disposition and sensibility; the distinctive feature of the bustlingly submissive is limited mental capacity combined with purposeless industry and zeal.

The domineering type in general is found chiefly among the higher grade of soldiers: the corporals, sergeants, sergeant-majors and so on. The first sub-division, the sternly domineering, is a noble, energetic, pre-eminently military type and does not exclude high poetic impulses (Corporal Antónov, with whom I wish to acquaint the reader, belonged to this type). The second sub-division, formed by the diplomatically domineering, has for some time past been increasing largely. A man of this type is always eloquent and literate,[1] wears pink shirts, won't eat out of the common pot, sometimes smokes tobacco of Mousátov's brand, and thinks himself much superior to the

---

1 A distinction very frequently met with in Russian is between *literate* and *illiterate* people; i.e. between those who can and those who cannot read and write.

common soldier, but is rarely himself as good a soldier as the domineering of the first sub-division.

The reckless type, like the domineering type, is good in its first sub-division, the amusingly reckless, whose characteristic traits are irresistible mirth, great capacity of all kinds, and a highly gifted and daring nature. As with the domineering class, the second sub-division is bad; the viciously reckless are terribly bad, but to the honour of the Russian army it must be said that this type is very rare, and when found it is excluded from companionship by the public opinion of the soldiers themselves. Unbelief and a kind of boldness in vice are the chief traits characteristic of this class.

Velenchúk belonged to the bustlingly submissive. He was an Ukrainian by birth, had already served for fifteen years, and although not a showy or smart soldier he was simple-minded, kindly, extremely though often inopportunely zealous, and also exceedingly honest. I say exceedingly honest, because an incident had occurred the year before which made this characteristic quality of his very evident. It must be remembered that almost every soldier knows a trade. The most usual trades are tailoring and boot-making. Velenchúk taught himself the former, and judging from the fact that even Michael Doroféich, the sergeant-major, ordered clothes from him, he must have attained some proficiency at his craft. Last year, in camp, Velenchúk undertook to make a fine cloth coat for Michael Doroféich; but that very night after he had cut out the coat and measured out the trimmings and put them all under his pillow in the tent, a misfortune befell him: the cloth that had cost *seven rubles*, disappeared during the night! Velenchúk, with tears in his eyes, trembling white lips and suppressed sobs, informed the sergeant-major of the occurrence. Michael Doroféich was enraged. In the first moment of irritation he threatened the tailor; but afterwards, being a man with means and kindly, he just waved his hand and did not demand from Velenchúk payment of the value of the cloth. In spite of all the fuss made by the fussy Velenchúk, in spite of all the tears he shed when telling of his mishap, the thief was not found. A strong suspicion fell on the viciously reckless soldier Chernóv, who slept in the same tent; but there were no positive proofs. The diplomatically domineering Michael Doroféich, being a man with means and having some little business transactions with the master-at-arms and the caterer of the mess (the aristocracy of the battery), very soon forgot all about the loss of his mufti coat. Not so Velenchúk. He did not forget his misfortune. The soldiers said they feared at the time that he might commit suicide or run away into the mountains, so great was the effect of his mishap upon him. He neither ate nor drank and could not even work, but was continually crying. When three days had passed he appeared, quite pale, before Michael Doroféich, took with trembling fingers a gold coin from under his cuff and gave it him. 'Heaven's my witness, Michael Doroféich, that it's all I have, and even that I borrowed from Zhdánov,' said he, sobbing again; 'and the other two rubles I swear I will also return as soon as I have earned them. He' (whom 'he' meant Velenchúk did not himself know) 'has made me appear like a rascal before you. He – with his loathsome, viper soul – he takes the last morsel from his brother soldier, after I have served for fifteen years. . . .' To the honour of Michael Doroféich be it said, he did not take the remaining two rubles, though Velenchúk brought them to him two months later.

Chapter III

BESIDES Velenchúk, five other soldiers of my platoon sat warming themselves by our fire.

In the best place, on a butt with his back to the wind, sat Maksímov, the gun-sergeant of the platoon, smoking a pipe. The habit of commanding and the consciousness of his dignity were betrayed by the pose, the look, and by every movement of this man, not to mention his nankeen-covered sheepskin coat and the butt he was sitting on, which latter is an emblem of power at a halting-place.

When I came up he turned his head towards me without removing his eyes from the fire, and his look, following the direction his head had taken, only fell on me some time later.

Maksímov was not a serf but a peasant-yeoman; he had some money, had qualified to take a class in the school-brigade, and had stuffed his head with erudition. He was awfully rich and awfully learned, so the soldiers said. I remember how once when we were practising plunging fire with a quadrant, he explained to the soldiers gathered round, that a spirit level *is nothing but as it occurs that atmospheric mercury has its motion*. In reality, Maksímov was far from being stupid, and understood his work thoroughly; but he had the unfortunate peculiarity of sometimes purposely speaking so that there was no possibility of understanding him and so that, I am convinced, he did not understand his own words. He was particularly fond of the words 'as it occurs' and 'continues', so that when I heard him say 'as it occurs' or 'continues', I knew beforehand that I should understand nothing of what followed. The soldiers on the other hand, as far as I could judge, liked to hear his 'as it occurs' and suspected it of being fraught with deep meaning, though they did not understand a word of it any more than I did. This they attributed entirely to their own stupidity, and respected Theodor Maksímov all the more. In a word, Maksimov was one of the diplomatically domineering.

The soldier next to him, who had bared his sinewy red legs and was putting on his boots again by the fire, was Antónov, – that same Corporal Antónov who in 1837, remaining with only two others in charge of an exposed gun, persisted in firing back at a powerful enemy and, with two bullets in his leg, continued to serve his gun and to reload it.

The soldiers used to say that he would have been made a gun-sergeant long ago but for his character. And his character really was very peculiar. No one could have been calmer, gentler, or more accurate than he was when sober; but when he had a fit of drinking he became quite another man; he would not submit to authority, fought, brawled, and became a perfectly good-for-nothing soldier. Only the week before this, during the Carnival, he had had a drinking-bout, and in spite of all threats, persuasions, and being tied to a cannon, he went on drinking and brawling up to the first day of Lent. During the whole of Lent, though the division had been ordered not to fast, he fed on dried bread, and during the first week would not even drink the regulation cup of vodka. But one had to see his sturdy thick-set figure, as of wrought iron, on its stumpy bandy legs, and his shiny moustached visage when in a tipsy mood he took the *balaláyka* in his sinewy hands and looking carelessly round played *Lady*, or walked down the street with his cloak thrown loosely over his shoulders, his medals dangling, his hands in the pockets of his blue nankeen trousers, and a look on his countenance of soldierly pride and of contempt for all that was not of the artillery – one had to see all this in order to understand how impossible it was for him at such a moment to abstain from fighting an orderly, a Cossack, an infantryman, a peasant (in fact, anyone not of the artillery) who was rude to him or happened merely to be in his way. He fought and rioted not so much for his own pleasure as to maintain the spirit of soldiership in general, of which he felt himself to be the representative.

The third soldier, who sat on his heels smoking a clay pipe, was the artillery driver Chíkin. He had an ear-ring in one of his ears, bristling little moustaches, and the physiognomy of a bird. 'Dear old Chíkin,' as the soldiers called him, was a wit. During the bitterest frost, or up to his knees in mud, or after going two days without food, on the march, on parade, or at drill, the 'dear fellow' was always and everywhere making faces, twisting his legs about, or cracking jokes that convulsed the whole platoon with laughter. At every halting-place, and in the camp, there was always a circle of young soldiers collected round Chíkin, who played *Fílka*[1] with them, told them stories about the cunning soldier and the English *milord*, personated a Tartar or a German, or simply made remarks of his own at which everyone roared with laughter. It is true that his reputation as a wit was so well established in the battery that it was sufficient for him to open his mouth and wink in order to produce a general guffaw, but really there was much in him that was truly humorous and surprising. He saw something special, something that never entered anybody else's head, in

1 A soldier's card game. L. T.

everything, and above all, this capacity for seeing the funny side of things was proof against any and every trial.

The fourth soldier was an insignificant-looking boy recruited the year before and this was his first campaign. He stood surrounded by the smoke and so near the flames that his threadbare cloak seemed in danger of catching fire, yet judging by the way he extended the skirts of his cloak and bent out his calves, and by his quiet self-satisfied pose, he was feeling highly contented.

The fifth and last of the soldiers was Daddy Zhdánov. He sat a little way off, cutting a stick. Zhdánov had been serving in the battery longer than anyone else, had known all the others as recruits, and they were all in the habit of calling him 'daddy'. It was said of him that he never drank, smoked, or played cards (not even 'noses'), and never used bad language. He spent all his spare time boot-making, went to church on holidays where that was possible, or else put a farthing taper before his icon and opened the book of psalms, the only book he could read. He seldom kept company with the other soldiers. To those who were his seniors in rank though his juniors in years he was coldly respectful; with his equals he had few opportunities of mixing, not being a drinker. He liked the recruits and the youngest soldiers best: he always took them under his protection, admonished them, and often helped them. Everyone in the battery considered him a capitalist because he had some twenty-five rubles, out of which he was always ready to lend something to a soldier in real need.

The same Maksímov who was now gun-sergeant told me that ten years ago, when he first came as a recruit and drank all he had with the old soldiers who were in the habit of drinking, Zhdánov, noticing his unfortunate position, called him up, severely reprimanded him for his conduct and even beat him, delivered a lecture on how one should live in the army, and sent him away after giving him a shirt (which Maksímov lacked) and half-a-ruble in money. 'He made a man of me,' Maksímov always used to say with respect and gratitude. He also helped Velenchúk (whom he had taken under his protection since he was a recruit) at the time of his misfortune.

When the coat was stolen he helped him as he had helped many and many another during the twenty-five years of his service.

One could not hope to find a man in the service who knew his work more thoroughly or was a better or more conscientious soldier than he; but he was too meek and insignificant-looking to be made a gun-sergeant, though he had been bombardier for fifteen years. Zhdánov's one enjoyment and passion was song. He had a few favourite songs, always collected a circle of singers from among the younger soldiers, and though he could not sing himself he would stand by them, his hands in the pockets of his cloak, his eyes closed, showing sympathy by the movements of his head and jaw. I don't know why, but that regular movement of the jaws below the ears, which I never noticed in anyone else, seemed to me extremely expressive. His snow-white head, his blackened moustaches, and his sunburnt, wrinkled face, gave him at first sight a stern and harsh expression; but on looking closer into his large round eyes, especially when they smiled (he never laughed with his lips), you were suddenly struck by something remarkable in their unusually mild, almost childlike look.

Chapter IV

'I'll be blowed! I've gone and forgot my pipe. Here's a go, lads!' repeated Velenchúk.

'You should smoke *cikars*, old fellow!' began Chíkin, drawing his mouth to one side and winking. 'There, now, I always smoke *cikars* when I'm at home – them's sweeter.'

Of course everybody burst out laughing.

'Forgot your pipe, indeed!' interrupted Maksímov without heeding the general mirth, and beating the tobacco out of his pipe into the palm of his left hand with the proud air of a superior; 'where did you vanish to – eh, Velenchúk?'

Velenchúk, half turning round to him, was about to raise his hand to his cap, but dropped it again.

'Seems to me you hadn't your sleep out after yesterday – falling asleep when you are once up! It's not thanks the likes of you get for such goings on.'

'May I die, Theodor Maksímov, if a drop has passed my lips; I don't myself know what happened to me,' answered Velenchúk. 'Much cause I had for revelling,' he muttered.

'Just so; but we have to answer to the authorities because of the likes of you, and you continue – it's quite scandalous!' the eloquent Maksímov concluded in a calmer tone.

'It's quite wonderful, lads,' Velenchúk went on after a moment's silence, scratching his head and addressing no one in particular; 'really quite wonderful, lads! Here have I been serving for the last sixteen years and such a thing never happened to me. When we were ordered to appear for muster I was all right, but at the "park", there *it* suddenly clutches hold of me, and clutches and clutches, and down it throws me, down on the ground and no more ado – and I did not myself know how I fell asleep, lads! That must have been the trances,' he concluded.

'True enough, I hardly managed to wake you,' said Antónov as he pulled on his boot. 'I had to push and push just as if you'd been a log!'

'Fancy now,' said Velenchúk, 'if I'd been drunk now! . . .'

'That's just like a woman we had at home,' began Chíkin; 'she hardly got off the stove for two years. Once they began waking her – they thought she was asleep – and she was already dead. She used to be taken sleepy that way. That's what it is, old fellow!'

'Now then, Chíkin, won't you tell us how you set the tone during your leave of absence?' said Maksímov, looking at me with a smile as if to say: 'Would you, too, like to hear the stupid fellow?'

'What tone, Theodor Maksímov?' said Chíkin, giving me a rapid side-glance. 'In course I told them what sort of a *Cawcusses* we'd got here.'

'Well, yes, how did you do it? There! don't give yourself airs; tell us how you *administrated* it to them.'

'How should I administrate it? In course they asked me how we live,' Chíkin began rapidly with the air of a man recounting something he had repeated several times before. ' "We live well, old fellow," says I. "Provisions in plenty we get: morning and night a cup of *chokelad* for every *soldier lad*, and at noon barley broth before us is set, such as gentle-folks get, and instead of vodka we get a pint of Modera wine from Devirier, such as costs forty-four – with the bottle ten more!"'

'Fine Modera,' Velenchúk shouted louder than anyone, rolling with laughter: 'that's Modera of the right sort!'

'Well, and what did you tell them about the Asiaites?' Maksímov went on to ask when the general mirth had subsided a little.

Chíkin stooped over the fire, poked out a bit of charcoal with a stick, put it to his pipe, and long continued puffing at his shag as though not noticing the silent curiosity awakened in his hearers. When he had at last drawn enough smoke he threw the bit of charcoal away, pushed his cap yet farther back, and, stretching himself, continued with a slight smile –

'Well, so they asked, "What's that Cherkés fellow or Turk as you've got down in your Cawcusses", they say, "as fights?" and so I says, "Them's not all of one sort; there's different Cherkéses, old fellow. There's the Wagabones, them as lives in the stony mountains and eat stones instead of bread. They're big," says I, "as big as a good-sized beam, they've one eye in the forehead and wear burning red caps," just such as yours, old fellow,' he added, turning to the young recruit, who really wore an absurd cap with a red crown.

At this unexpected sally the recruit suddenly collapsed, slapped his knees, and burst out laughing and coughing so that he hardly managed to utter in a stifled voice, 'Them Wagabones is the right sort!'

'"Then", says I, "there's also the Mopingers,"' continued Chíkin, making his cap slip onto his forehead with a movement of his head: '"These others are little twins, so big . . . all in pairs," says I, "they run about hand in hand at such a rate," says I, "that you couldn't catch 'em on a horse!" – "Then how's it, lad," they say, "how's them Mopingers, be they born hand in hand?"' He said this in a hoarse bass, pretending to imitate a peasant. '"Yes," says I, "he's naturally like that. Tear their hands apart and they'll bleed just like a Chinaman: take a Chinaman's cap off and it'll bleed." – "And tell us, lad, how do they fight?" – "That's how," says I, "they catch you and rip your belly up and wind your bowels round your arm, and wind and wind. They go on winding and you go on laughing till your breath all goes."'

'Well, and did they believe you, Chíkin?' said Maksímov with a slight smile, while all the rest were dying with laughter.

'Such queer people, Theodor Maksímych, they believe everything. On my word they do. But when I told them about Mount Kazbék and said that the snow didn't melt on it all the summer, they mocked at me! "What are you bragging for, lad," they says; "a big mountain and the snow on it don't melt? Why, lad, when the thaw sets in here every tiny bit of a hillock thaws first while the snow still lies in the hollows." There now!' Chíkin concluded with a wink.

Chapter V

THE bright disk of the sun shining through the milky-white mist had already risen to a considerable height. The purple-grey horizon gradually widened, but though it had receded considerably it was still as sharply outlined by a deceptive white wall of mist.

Beyond the felled wood a good-sized plain now opened in front of us. The black or milky-white or purple smoke of the fires expanded and fantastic shapes of white mist-clouds floated above the plain. An occasional group of mounted Tartars appeared far in the distance before us and at rare intervals the reports of our rifles[1] and of their *vintóvkas* and cannon were to be heard.

This, as Captain Khlópov said, was 'not yet business, but only play'.

The commander of the 9th Company of Chasseurs, that formed our support, came up to our guns, pointed to three Tartars[2] on horseback skirting the forest some 1,400 yards from

1 Most of the Russian army at that time were armed with smooth-bore muskets, but a few had wide-calibred muzzle-loading rifles (*stútzers*), which were difficult to handle and slow to load. *Vintóvkas* were also rifles.
2 Russians in the Caucasus used the word 'Tartar' loosely for any of the native Mohammedan tribes (Circassians, Kabardáns, &c.).

us, and with the fondness for artillery fire common among infantry officers in general, asked me to let off a ball or bomb at them.

'Do you see?' he said with a kind and persuasive smile as he stretched his hand from behind my shoulder, 'in front of those big trees there . . . one on a white horse and in a black Circassian cloak and two others behind. Do you see? Could you not, please?'

'And there are three more riding at the outskirt of the forest,' said Antónov, who had astonishingly sharp eyesight, coming up to us, and hiding behind his back the pipe he had been smoking. 'There, the one in front has taken his gun out of its case. They can be seen distinctly, y'r honour!'

'Look there! he's fired, lads. D'ye see the white smoke?' said Velenchúk, who was one of a group of soldiers standing a little behind us.

'At our line surely, the blackguard!' remarked another.

'See what a lot of 'em come streaming out of the forest. Must be looking round . . . want to place a gun,' said a third.

'Supposing now a bomb was sent right into that lot, wouldn't they spit!'

'And what d'ye think, old fellow – that it would just reach 'em?' said Chíkin.

'Twelve hundred or twelve hundred and fifty yards: not more than that,' said Maksímov calmly and as if speaking to himself, though it was evident he was just as anxious to fire as the rest: 'if we were to give an elevation of forty-five lines to our "unicorn"[1] we could hit the very point, that is to say, perfectly.'

'D'ye know, if you were now to aim at that group you would be sure to hit somebody. There now, they are all together – please be quick and give the order to fire,' the company commander continued to entreat me.

'Are we to point the gun?' suddenly asked Antónov in an abrupt bass with a look as if of gloomy anger.

---

1 The 'unicorn' was a type of gun, narrowing towards the muzzle, used in the Russian artillery at that time.

I must admit that I also felt a strong wish to fire, so I ordered the second gun to be trained.

I had hardly given the order before the shell was charged and rammed in and Antónov, leaning against the cheek of the gun-carriage and holding two of his thick fingers to the base-ring, was directing the movement of the tail of the gun. 'Right, left – a bit to the left, a wee bit – more – more – right!' he said, stepping from the gun with a look of pride.

The infantry officer, I, and Maksímov, one after the other, approached, put our heads to the sights, and expressed our various opinions.

'By Heavens, it will shoot over,' remarked Velenchúk, clicking his tongue, though he was only looking over Antónov's shoulder and therefore had no grounds for this supposition. 'By Hea – vens it will shoot over; it will hit that there tree, my lads!'

I gave the order: 'Two.'

The men stepped away from the gun. Antónov ran aside to watch the flight of the shot. The touch-hole flashed and the brass rang. At the same moment we were enveloped in a cloud of powder-smoke and, emerging from the overpowering boom of the discharge, the humming, metallic sound of the flying shot receded with the swiftness of lightning and died away in the distance amid general silence.

A little beyond the group of horsemen a white cloudlet appeared; the Tartars galloped away in all directions and the report of the explosion reached us. 'That was very fine!' 'Ah, how they galloped!' 'The devils don't like that!' came the words of approval and ridicule from the ranks of the artillery and infantry.

'If we had had the gun pointed only a touch lower we should just have caught him. I said it would hit the tree and sure enough it did go to the right,' remarked Velenchúk.

Chapter VI

LEAVING the soldiers to discuss how the Tartars galloped off when they saw the shell, why they had been riding there, and whether there were many of them in the forest, I went and sat down with the company commander under a tree a few steps off to wait while the cutlets he had invited me to share were being warmed up. The company commander, Bólkhov, was one of the officers nicknamed 'bonjourists' in the regiment. He was a man of some means, had formerly served in the Guards, and spoke French. But in spite of all this his comrades liked him. He was clever enough, and had tact enough, to wear a coat of Petersburg make, to eat a good dinner, and to speak French, without too much offending his fellow officers. After talking about the weather, the military operations, our mutual acquaintances among the officers, and having assured ourselves of the satisfactory state of each other's ideas by questions and answers and the views expressed, we involuntarily passed to more intimate conversation. And when people belonging to the same circle meet in the Caucasus a very evident, even if unspoken, question arises: 'Why are you here?' and it was to this silent question of mine that, as it seemed to me, my companion wished to reply.

'When will this expedition end?' he said lazily. 'It is so dull.'

'I don't think it dull,' said I. 'It's much worse on the staff.'

'Oh, it's ten thousand times worse on the staff,' he said irascibly. 'No, I mean when will the whole thing end?'

'What is it you want to end?' I asked.

'Everything, – the whole affair!... Are the cutlets ready, Nikoláyev?'

'Then why did you come to serve here if you so dislike the Caucasus?' I said.

'Do you know why?' he answered with resolute frankness. 'In obedience to tradition! You know there exists in Russia a most curious tradition about the Caucasus, making it out to be a "promised land" for all unfortunates.'

'Yes, that is almost true,' said I. 'Most of us —'

'But the best of it is,' he said, interrupting me, 'that all of us who came to the Caucasus in obedience to the tradition made a terrible mistake in our calculations and I can't for the life of me see why one should, in consequence of an unfortunate love affair or of financial troubles, choose to go and serve in the

Caucasus rather than in Kazán or Kalúga. Why in Russia they imagine the Caucasus to be something majestic: eternal virgin ice, rushing torrents, daggers, mantles, fair Circassians, and an atmosphere of terror and romance; but in reality there is nothing amusing in it. If they only realized that we never get to the virgin ice, that it would not be at all amusing if we did, and that the Caucasus is divided into governments – Stavrópol, Tiflís, and so on.'

'Yes,' said I, laughing, 'we look very differently at the Caucasus when we are in Russia and when we are here. It is like what you may have experienced when reading verses in a language you are not familiar with; you imagine them to be much better than they are.'

'I really don't know; but I dislike this Caucasus awfully,' he said interrupting me.

'Well, no; I still like the Caucasus only in a different way.'

'Perhaps it is all right,' he continued irritably; 'all I know is that I'm not all right in the Caucasus.'

'Why is that?' I asked, to say something.

'Well, first because it has deceived me. All that I, in obedience to tradition, came to the Caucasus to be cured of has followed me here, only with the difference that there it was all on a big scale and now it is on a little dirty one where at each step I find millions of petty anxieties, shabbinesses, and insults; and next because I feel that I am sinking, morally, lower and lower every day; but chiefly, because I do not feel fit for the service here. I can't stand running risks. The fact of the matter is simply that I am not brave.'

He stopped and looked at me, not joking.

Though this unasked-for confession surprised me very much, I did not contradict him as he evidently wished me to do, but waited for his own refutation of his words, which always follows in such cases.

'Do you know, in coming on this expedition I am taking part in an action for the first time,' he continued, 'and you can't think what was going on in me yesterday. When the sergeant-major brought the order that my company was to join the column, I turned as white as a sheet and could not speak for excitement. And if you only knew what a night I had! If it were true that one's hair turns white from fear, mine ought to be perfectly white to-day, because I don't think anyone condemned to death ever suffered more in a night than I did; and even now, though I feel a bit easier than in the night, this is what goes on inside!' he added, turning his fist about before his chest. 'And what is funny is that while a most fearful tragedy is being enacted, here one sits eating cutlets and onions and making believe that it is great fun. – Have we any wine, Nikoláyev?' he added, yawning.

'That's *him*, my lads!' came the excited voice of one of the soldiers, and all eyes turned towards the border of the distant forest.

In the distance a puff of bluish smoke expanded and rose, blown about by the wind. When I had understood that this was a shot fired at us by the enemy, all before my eyes at the moment assumed a sort of new and majestic character. The piles of arms, the smoke of the fires, the blue sky, the green gun-carriages, Nikoláyev's sunburnt, moustached face – all seemed telling me that the ball that had already emerged from the smoke and was at that moment flying through space might be directed straight at my breast.

'Where did you get the wine?' I asked Bólkhov lazily, while deep in my soul two voices spoke with equal clearness. One said, 'Lord receive my soul in peace,' the other, 'I hope I shall not stoop, but smile, while the ball is passing,' and at that moment something terribly unpleasant whistled past our heads and a cannon ball crashed down a couple of paces from us.

'There now, had I been a Napoleon or a Frederick I should certainly have paid you a compliment,' Bólkhov remarked, turning towards me quite calmly.

'You have done so as it is,' I answered, with difficulty hiding the excitement produced in me by the danger just passed.

'Well, what if I have? – no one will write it down.'

'Yes, I will.'

'Well, if you do put it down, it will only be "for critikism", as Míschenkov says,' he added with a smile.

'Ugh! the damned thing!' just then remarked Antónov behind us, as he spat over his shoulder with vexation, 'just missed my legs!'

All my attempts to seem calm, and all our cunning phrases, suddenly seemed to me insufferably silly after that simple exclamation.

Chapter VII

THE enemy had really placed two guns where we had seen the Tartars riding, and they fired a shot every twenty or thirty minutes at our men who were felling the wood. My platoon was ordered forward to the plain to answer the enemy's fire. A puff of smoke appeared on the outskirts of the forest, then followed a report and a whistle, and a ball fell in front or behind us. The enemy's shots fell fortunately for us and we sustained no losses.

The artillerymen behaved splendidly as they always do; loaded quickly, pointed carefully at the spots where the puffs of smoke were, and quietly joked with one another.

The infantry supports lay near in silent inaction awaiting their turn. The wood-fellers went on with their work, the axes rang faster and more unintermittently through the forest; but when the whistle of a shot became audible all were suddenly silent and, in the midst of the deathly stillness, voices not quite calm exclaimed, 'Scatter, lads!' and all eyes followed the ball ricocheting over wood piles and strewn branches.

The mist had now risen quite high and, turning into clouds, gradually disappeared into the dark-blue depths of the sky; the unveiled sun shone brightly, throwing sparkling reflections from the steel bayonets, the brass of the guns, the thawing earth, and the glittering hoar-frost. In the air one felt the freshness of the morning frost together with the warmth of the spring sunshine; thousands of different hues and tints mingled in the dry leaves of the forest, and the shining, beaten track plainly showed the traces left by wheels and the marks of rough-shod horses' feet.

The movement became greater and more noticeable between the two forces. On all sides the blue smoke of the guns appeared more and more frequently. Dragoons rode forward, the streamers of their lances flying; from the infantry companies one heard songs, and the carts laden with firewood formed into a train in our rear. The general rode up to our platoon and ordered us to prepare to retire. The enemy settled in the bushes on our left flank and their snipers began to molest us seriously. A bullet came humming from the woods to the left and struck a gun-carriage, then came another, and a third. . . . The infantry supports that had been lying near us rose noisily, took up their muskets and formed into line.

The small-arm firing increased and bullets flew more and more frequently. The retreat commenced and consequently the serious part of the action, as is usual in the Caucasus.

Everything showed that the artillerymen liked the bullets as little as the infantry had liked the cannon-balls. Antónov frowned, Chíkin imitated the bullets and joked about them, but it was easy to see he did not like them. 'It's in a mighty hurry,' he said of one of them; another he called 'little bee'; a third, which seemed to fly slowly past overhead with a kind of piteous wail, he called an 'orphan', which caused general laughter.

The recruit who, unaccustomed to such scenes, bent his head to one side and stretched his neck every time a bullet passed, also made the soldiers laugh. 'What, is that a friend of yours you're bowing to?' they said to him. Velenchúk also, usually quite indifferent to danger, was now excited: he was evidently vexed that we did not fire case-shot in the direction whence the bullets came. He repeated several times in a discontented tone, 'Why is *he* allowed to go for us and gets nothing in return? If we turned a gun that way and gave them a taste of case-shot they'd hold their noise, no fear!'

It was true that it was time to do this, so I ordered them to fire a last bomb and then to load with case-shot.

'Case-shot!' Antónov called out briskly as he went through the thick of the smoke to sponge out the gun as soon as it was discharged.

At that moment I heard just behind me the rapid whiz of a bullet suddenly stopped by something, with a dull thud. My heart ceased beating. 'Someone of the men has been hit,' I thought, while a sad presentiment made me afraid to turn round. And really that sound was followed by the heavy fall of a body, and the heart-rending 'Oh-o-oh' of someone who had been wounded. 'I'm hit, lads!' a voice I knew exclaimed with an effort. It was Velenchúk. He was lying on his back between the limbers and a cannon. The cartridge-bag he had been carrying was thrown to one side. His forehead was covered with blood, and a thick red stream was running down over his right eye and nose. He was wounded in the stomach but hardly bled at all there; his forehead he had hurt against a log in falling.

All this I made out much later; the first moment I could only see an indistinct mass and, as it seemed to me, a tremendous quantity of blood.

Not one of the soldiers who were loading said a word, only the young recruit muttered something that sounded like 'Dear me! he's bleeding', and Antónov, frowning, gave an angry grunt; but it was clear that the thought of death passed through the soul of each. All set to work very actively and the gun was loaded in a moment, but the ammunition-bearer bringing the case-shot went two or three steps round the spot where Velenchúk still lay groaning.

Chapter VIII

EVERYONE who has been in action undoubtedly knows that strange and though illogical yet powerful feeling of aversion for the spot where someone has been killed or wounded. It was evident that for a moment my men gave way to this feeling when Velenchúk had to be taken to the cart that came up to fetch him. Zhdánov came up angrily to the wounded man and, taking him under the arms, lifted him without heeding his loud screams. 'Now then, what are you standing there for? take hold!' he shouted, and about ten assistants, some of them superfluous, immediately surrounded

Velenchúk. But hardly had they moved him when he began screaming and struggling terribly.

'What are you screaming like a hare for?' said Antónov roughly, holding his leg; 'mind, or we'll just leave you.'

And the wounded man really became quiet and only now and then uttered, 'Oh, it's my death! Oh, oh, oh, lads!'

When he was laid in the cart he even stopped moaning and I heard him speak to his comrades in low clear tones, probably saying farewell to them.

No one likes to look at a wounded man during an action and, instinctively hurrying to end this scene, I ordered him to be taken quickly to the ambulance, and returned to the guns. But after a few minutes I was told that Velenchúk was asking for me, and I went up to the cart.

The wounded man lay at the bottom of the cart holding on to the sides with both hands. His broad healthy face had completely changed during those few moments; he seemed to have grown thinner and years older, his lips were thin and pale and pressed together with an evident strain. The hasty and dull expression of his glance was replaced by a kind of bright clear radiance, and on the bloody forehead and nose already lay the impress of death. Though the least movement caused him excruciating pain, he nevertheless asked to have a small *chérez*[1] with money taken from his left leg.

The sight of his bare, white, healthy leg, when his jack-boot had been taken off and the purse untied, produced in me a terribly sad feeling.

'Here are three rubles and a half,' he said, as I took the purse: 'you'll take care of them.'

The cart was starting, but he stopped it.

'I was making a cloak for Lieutenant Sulimóvsky. He gave me two rubles. I bought buttons for one and a half, and half a ruble is in my bag with the buttons. Please let him have it.'

'All right! all right!' said I. 'Get well again, old fellow.'

---

1 The *chérez* is a purse in the form of a garter, usually worn by soldiers below the knee. L. T.

He did not answer; the cart started and he again began to groan and cry out in a terrible, heart-rending voice. It was as if, having done with the business of this life, he did not think it necessary to restrain himself and considered it permissible to allow himself this relief.

Chapter IX

'WHERE are you off to? Come back! Where are you going?' I shouted to the recruit, who with his reserve linstock under his arm and a stick of some sort in his hand was, in the coolest manner, following the cart that bore the wounded man.

But the recruit only looked at me lazily, muttered something or other, and continued on his way, so that I had to send a soldier to bring him back. He took off his red cap and looked at me with a stupid smile.

'Where were you going?' I asked.

'To the camp.'

'Why?'

'Why? . . . Velenchúk is wounded,' he said, again smiling.

'What's that to you? You must stay here.'

He looked at me with surprise, then turned quietly round, put on his cap, and went back to his place.

The affair in general was successful. The Cossacks, as we heard, had made a fine charge and brought back three dead Tartars;[1] the infantry had provided itself with firewood and had only half-a-dozen men wounded; the artillery had lost only Velenchúk and two horses. For that, two miles of forest had been cut down and the place so cleared as to be unrecognizable. Instead of the thick outskirts of the forest you saw before you a large plain covered with smoking fires and cavalry and infantry marching back to camp.

---

1 The 'Tartars', being Mohammedans, made a point of not letting the bodies of their slain fall into the hands of the 'unbelievers', but removed them and buried them as heroes. The capture of three bodies therefore indicates the vigour of the attack and the demoralization of the enemy.

Though the enemy continued to pursue us with artillery and small-arms fire up to the cemetery by the little river we had crossed in the morning, the retirement was successfully accomplished. I was already beginning to dream of the cabbage-soup and mutton-ribs with buckwheat that were awaiting me in camp, when a message came from the General ordering a redoubt to be constructed by the river, and the 3rd battalion of the K— Regiment and the platoon of the 4th Battery to remain there till next day.

The carts with the wood and the wounded, the Cossacks, the artillery, the infantry with muskets and faggots on their shoulders, all passed us with noise and songs. Every face expressed animation and pleasure caused by the escape from danger and the hope of rest. Only we and the 3rd battalion had to postpone those pleasant feelings till to-morrow.

Chapter X

WHILE we of the artillery were busy with the guns – parking the limbers and the ammunition wagons and arranging the picket-ropes – the infantry had already piled their muskets, made up camp-fires, built little huts of branches and maize straw, and begun boiling their buckwheat.

The twilight had set in. Bluish white clouds crept over the sky. The mist, turning into fine dank drizzle, wetted the earth and the soldiers' cloaks; the horizon narrowed and all the surroundings assumed a gloomier hue. The damp I felt through my boots and on my neck, the ceaseless movement and talk in which I took no part, the sticky mud on which my feet kept slipping, and my empty stomach, all combined to put me into the dreariest, most unpleasant frame of mind after the physical and moral weariness of the day. I could not get Velenchúk out of my head. The whole simple story of his soldier-life depicted itself persistently in my imagination.

His last moments were as clear and calm as his whole life had been. He had lived too honestly and been too artless for his simple faith in a future heavenly life to be shaken at the decisive moment.

'Your honour!' said Nikoláyev, coming up to me, 'the captain asks you to come and have tea with him.'

Having scrambled through, as best I could, between the piles of arms and the camp-fires, I followed Nikoláyev to where Bólkhov was, thinking with pleasure of a tumbler of hot tea and a cheerful conversation which would disperse my gloomy thoughts.

'Have you found him?' I heard Bólkhov's voice say from inside a maize-hut in which a light was burning.

'I've brought him, y'r honour,' answered Nikoláyev's bass voice.

Inside the hut Bólkhov was sitting on a dry mantle, with unbuttoned coat and no cap. A samovar stood boiling by his side and on a drum were light refreshments. A bayonet holding a candle was stuck into the ground.

'What do you think of it?' he asked, looking proudly round his cosy establishment. It really was so nice inside the hut that at tea I quite forgot the damp, the darkness, and Velenchúk's wound. We talked of Moscow and of things that had not the least relation to the war or to the Caucasus.

After a moment of silence such as sometimes occurs in the most animated conversation, Bólkhov looked at me with a smile.

'I think our conversation this morning struck you as being very strange,' he said.

'No, why do you think so? It only seemed to me that you were too frank; there are things which we all know, but which should never be mentioned.'

'Why not? If there were the least possibility of changing this life for the lowest and poorest without danger and without service, I should not hesitate a moment.'

'Then why don't you return to Russia?' I asked.

'Why?' he repeated. 'Oh, I have thought about that long ago. I can't return to Russia now until I have the Anna and Vladímir orders: an Anna round my neck and the rank of major, as I planned when I came here.'

'Why? – if, as you say, you feel unfit for the service here.'

'But what if I feel still more unfit to go back to Russia to the same position that I left? That is also one of the traditions in

Russia, confirmed by Pássek, Sleptsóv and others, that one need only go to the Caucasus to be laden with rewards. Everyone expects and demands it of us; and I have been here for two years, have been on two expeditions, and have got nothing. But still I have so much ambition that I won't leave on any account until I am a major with a Vladímir and Anna round my neck. I have become so concerned about it that it upsets me when Gnilokíshkin gets a reward and I don't. And then how am I to show myself in Russia, to the village elder, to the merchant Kotëlnikov to whom I sell my corn, to my Moscow aunt, and to all those good people, if after two years spent in the Caucasus I return without any reward? It is true I don't at all wish to know all those people, and they no doubt care very little about me either; but man is so made that, though I don't want to know them, yet on account of them I'm wasting the best years of my life, all my life's happiness, and am ruining my future.'

Chapter XI

JUST then we heard the voice of the commander of the battalion outside, addressing Bólkhov.

'Who is with you, Nicholas Fëdorovich?'

Bólkhov gave him my name, and then three officers scrambled into the hut – Major Kirsánov; the adjutant of his battalion; and Captain Trosénko.

Kirsánov was not tall but stout, he had black moustaches, rosy cheeks, and oily little eyes. These eyes were his most remarkable feature. When he laughed nothing remained of them but two tiny moist stars, and these little stars together with his wide-stretched lips and outstretched neck often gave him an extraordinarily senseless look. In the regiment Kirsánov behaved himself and bore himself better than anyone else; his subordinates did not complain of him and his superiors respected him – though the general opinion was that he was very limited. He knew the service, was exact and zealous, always had ready money, kept a carriage and a man-cook, and knew how to make an admirable pretence of being proud.

'What were you talking about, Nicholas Fëdorovich?'

'Why, about the attractions of the service here.'

But just then Kirsánov noticed me, a cadet, and to impress me with his importance he paid no attention to Bólkhov's reply, but looked at the drum and said –

'Are you tired, Nicholas Fëdorovich?'

'No, you see we —' Bólkhov began.

But again the dignity of the commander of the battalion seemed to make it necessary to interrupt, and to ask another question.

'That was a famous affair to-day, was it not?'

The adjutant of the battalion was a young ensign recently promoted from being a cadet, a modest, quiet lad with a bashful and kindly-pleasant face. I had met him at Bólkhov's before. The lad would often come there, bow, sit down in a corner, and remain silent for hours making cigarettes and smoking them; then he would rise, bow, and go away. He was the type of a poor Russian nobleman's son who had chosen the military career as the only one possible to him with his education, and who esteemed his position as an officer above everything else in the world – a simple-minded and lovable type notwithstanding the comical appurtenances inseparable from it: the tobacco-pouch, dressing-gown, guitar, and little moustache-brush we are accustomed to associate with it. It was told of him in the regiment that he bragged about being just but strict with his orderly, and that he used to say, 'I punish seldom, but when I am compelled to do it it's no joke,' but that when his tipsy orderly robbed him outrageously and even began to insult him, he, the master, took him to the guard-house and ordered everything to be prepared for a flogging, but was so upset at the sight of the preparations that he could only say, 'There now, you see, I could —' and becoming quite disconcerted, ran home in great confusion and was henceforth afraid to look his man Chernóv in the eyes. His comrades gave the simple-minded boy no rest but teased him continually about this episode, and more than once I heard how he defended himself, and blushing to the tips of his ears assured them that it was not true, but just the contrary.

The third visitor, Captain Trosénko, was a thoroughgoing old Caucasian – that is, a man for whom the company he commanded had become his family; the fortress where the staff was, his home; and the soldiers' singing his only pleasure in life. He was a man for whom everything unconnected with the Caucasus was contemptible and scarcely worthy of being considered probable, and everything connected with the Caucasus was divided into two halves: ours and not ours. The first he loved, the second he hated with all the power of his soul; but above all he was a man of steeled, calm courage, wonderfully kind in his behaviour to his comrades and subordinates and desperately frank and even rude to aides-de-camp and 'bonjourists', for whom for some reason he had a great dislike. On entering the hut he nearly caved the roof in with his head, then suddenly sank down and sat on the ground.

'Well?' he said, and then suddenly remarking me whom he did not know, he stopped and gazed at me with a dull, fixed look.

'Well, and what have you been conversing about?' asked the major, taking out his watch and looking at it, though I am perfectly certain he had no need to.

'Why, I've been asked my reasons for serving here —'

'Of course, Nicholas Fëdorovich wishes to distinguish himself here, and then to return home,' said the major.

'Well, and you, Abram Ilých,' said Bólkhov, addressing Kirsánov, 'tell me why you are serving in the Caucasus.'

'I serve because in the first place, as you know, it is everyone's duty to serve.... What?' he then added, though no one had spoken. 'I had a letter from Russia yesterday, Nicholas Fëdorovich,' he continued, evidently wishing to change the subject; 'they write that ... they ask such strange questions.'

'What questions?' asked Bólkhov.

The major began laughing.

'Very queer questions.... They ask, can jealousy exist where there is no love.... What?' he asked, turning round and glancing at us all.

'Dear me!' said Bólkhov, with a smile.

'Yes, you know, it is nice in Russia,' continued the major, just as if his sentences flowed naturally from one another. 'When I was in Tambóv in '52 they received me everywhere as if I had been some emperor's aide-de-camp. Will you believe it that at a ball at the governor's, when I came in, you know . . . well, they received me very well. The general's wife herself, you know, talked to me and asked me about the Caucasus, and everybody was . . . so that I hardly knew. . . . They examined my gold sabre as if it were some curiosity; they asked for what I had received the sabre, for what the Anna, for what the Vladímir . . . so I just told them. . . . What? That's what the Caucasus is good for, Nicholas Fëdorovich!' he continued without waiting for any reply: – 'There they think very well of us Caucasians. You know a young man that's a staff-officer and has an Anna and a Vladímir . . . that counts for a good deal in Russia. . . . What?'

'And you, no doubt, piled it on a bit, Abram Ilých?' said Bólkhov.

'He – he!' laughed the major stupidly. 'You know one has to do that. And didn't I feed well those two months!'

'And tell me, is it nice there in Russia?' said Trosénko, inquiring about Russia as though it were China or Japan.

'Yes, and the champagne we drank those two months, it was awful!'

'Eh, nonsense! You'll have drunk nothing but lemonade. There now, I'd have burst to let them see how Caucasians drink. I'd have given them something to talk about. I'd have shown them how one drinks; eh, Bólkhov?' said Trosénko.

'But you, Daddy, have been more than ten years in the Caucasus,' said Bólkhov, 'and you remember what Ermólov[1] said? . . . And Abram Ilých has been only six.'

---

1 General A. P. Ermólov (1772–1861), who was renowned for his firmness and justness as a ruler in the Caucasus, and who subdued Chéchnya and Daghestán, used to say that after ten years in the Caucasus an officer 'either takes to drink or marries a loose woman'.

'Ten indeed!...nearly sixteen....Well, Bólkhov, let us have some sage-vodka. It's damp, b-r-r-r!...Eh?' said Trosénko, smiling, 'Will you have a drink, Major?'

But the major had been displeased by the old captain's first remarks to him, and plainly drew back and sought refuge in his own grandeur. He hummed something, and again looked at his watch.

'For my part I shall never go there!' Trosénko continued without heeding the major's frowns. 'I have lost the habit of speaking and walking in the Russian way. They'd ask, "What curious creature is this coming here? Asia, that's what it is." Am I right, Nicholas Fëdorovich? Besides, what have I to go to Russia for? What does it matter? I shall be shot here some day. They'll ask, "Where's Trosénko?" "Shot!" What will you do with the 8th Company then, eh?' he added, always addressing the major.

'Send the officer on duty!' shouted the major, without answering the captain, though I again felt sure there was no need for him to give any orders.

'And you, young man, are glad, I suppose, to be drawing double pay?'[1] said the major, turning to the adjutant of the battalion after some moments of silence.

'Yes, sir, very glad of course.'

'I think our pay now very high, Nicholas Fëdorovich,' continued the major; 'a young man can live very decently and even permit himself some small luxuries.'

'No, really, Abram Ilých,' said the adjutant bashfully. 'Though it's double it's barely enough. You see one must have a horse.'

'What are you telling me, young man? I have been an ensign myself and know. Believe me, one can live very well with care. But there! count it up,' added he, bending the little finger of his left hand.

---

1 An officer's allowance in Russia proper was very small, but when on service in Poland, the Caucasus, Siberia, &c., they received a higher rate of pay.

'We always draw our salaries in advance; isn't that account enough for you?' said Trosénko, emptying a glass of vodka.

'Well, yes, but what do you expect. . . . What?'

Just then a white head with a flat nose thrust itself into the opening of the hut and a sharp voice said with a German accent –

'Are you there, Abram Ilých? The officer on duty is looking for you.'

'Come in, Kraft!' said Bólkhov.

A long figure in the uniform of the general staff crept in at the door and began shaking hands all round with peculiar fervour.

'Ah, dear Captain, are you here too?' said he, turning to Trosénko.

In spite of the darkness the new visitor made his way to the captain and to the latter's extreme surprise and dismay as it seemed to me, kissed him on the lips.

'This is a German trying to be hail fellow well met,' thought I.

Chapter XII

My surmise was at once confirmed. Captain Kraft asked for vodka, calling it a 'warmer', croaked horribly, and throwing back his head emptied the glass.

'Well, gentlemen, we have scoured the plains of Chéchnya to-day, have we not?' he began, but seeing the officer on duty, stopped at once to allow the major to give his orders.

'Have you been round the lines?'

'Yes, sir.'

'Have the ambuscades been placed?'

'Yes, sir.'

'Then give the company commanders orders to be as cautious as possible.'

'Yes, sir.'

The major screwed up his eyes in profound contemplation.

'Yes, and tell the men they may now boil their buckwheat.'

'They are already boiling it, sir.'

'All right! you may go, sir.'

'Well, we were just reckoning up how much an officer needs,' continued the major, turning to us with a condescending smile. 'Let us count. You want a uniform and a pair of trousers, don't you?'

'Certainly.'

'That, let us say, is 50 rubles for two years; therefore 25 rubles a year for clothes. Then for food, 40 kopeks a day – is that right?'

'Oh yes, that is even too much.'

'Well, never mind, I'll leave it so. Then for a horse and repair of harness and saddle – 30 rubles. And that is all. So it's 25, and 120, and 30 – that's 175 rubles. So you have for luxuries – tea, sugar, tobacco – a matter of 20 rubles left. So you see . . . Isn't it so, Nicholas Fëdorovich?'

'No, but excuse me, Abram Ilých,' said the adjutant timidly, 'nothing remains for tea and sugar. You allow one suit in two years; but it's hardly possible to keep oneself in trousers with all this marching. And boots? I wear out a pair almost every month. Then underclothing – shirts, towels, leg-bands,[1] – it all has to be bought. When one comes to reckon it all up nothing remains over. That's really so, Abram Ilých.'

'Ah, it's splendid to wear leg-bands,' Kraft suddenly remarked after a moment's silence, uttering the word 'leg-bands' in specially tender tones. 'It's so simple, you know; quite Russian!'

'I'll tell you something,' Trosénko remarked. 'Reckon what way you like and you'll find we might as well put our teeth away on a shelf, and yet here we are all alive, drinking tea, smoking tobacco, and drinking vodka. When you've served as long as I have,' he went on, turning to the ensign, 'you'll have also learned how to live. Why, gentlemen, do you know how he treats the orderlies?'

And Trosénko, dying with laughter, told us the whole story about the ensign and his orderly, though we had all heard it hundreds of times.

---

1 It is customary, especially among the peasants and soldiers, to wrap long strips of linen round the feet and legs instead of wearing stockings.

'Why do you look so like a rose, old chap?' continued he, addressing the ensign, who blushed, perspired, and smiled, so that it was pitiful to see him. 'Never mind, old chap! I was just like you once and now look what a fine fellow I am. You let a young fellow straight from Russia in here – haven't we seen them? – and he gets spasms or rheumatism or something; and here am I settled here, and it's my house and my bed and all, d'you see?'

And thereupon he drank another glass of vodka and looking fixedly at Kraft, said, 'Eh?'

'That is what I respect! Here's a genuine old Caucasian! Permit me to shake hands.'

And Kraft, pushing us all aside, forced his way to Trosénko and catching hold of his hand shook it with peculiar emotion.

'Yes,' continued Kraft, 'we may say we have gone through every kind of experience here. In '45 you were present, Captain, were you not? – you remember the night between the 12th and 13th, when we spent the night knee-deep in mud and next day captured the barricades they had made of felled trees. I was attached to the commander-in-chief at the time and we took fifteen barricades that one day, – you remember, Captain?'

Trosénko nodded affirmatively, stuck out his nether lip and screwed up his eyes.

'You see . . .' began Kraft with great animation, making unsuitable gestures with his hands and addressing the major.

But the major, who had in all probability heard the story more than once, suddenly looked at the speaker with such dim, dull eyes that Kraft turned away from him and addressed me and Bólkhov, looking alternately at one and the other. But he did not give a single glance at Trosénko during the whole of his narration.

'Well then, you see, when we went out in the morning the commander-in-chief said to me, "Kraft, take those barricades!" Well, you know, a soldier's duty is not to reason – it's hand to cap, and "Yes, your Excellency!" and off. Only as we drew near the first barricade I turned and said to the soldiers, "Now then, lads, don't funk it but look sharp. If anyone hangs back I'll cut him down myself!" With Russian soldiers, you know, one has to speak straight out. Suddenly a bomb . . . I look, one soldier down, another, a third . . . then bullets came whizzing . . . vzin! . . . vzin! . . . vzin! . . . "On!" I cry, "On, follow me!" Just as we got there I look and see a . . . a . . . you know . . . what do you call it?' and the narrator flourished his arms, trying to find the word he wanted.

'A scarp?' suggested Bólkhov.

'No . . . Ach! what is the word? Good heavens, what is it? . . . A scarp!' he said quickly. 'So, "fix bayonets! Hurrah! ta-ra, ta-ta-ta!" not a sign of the enemy! Everybody was surprised, you know. Well, that's all right; we go on to the second barricade. Ah, that was a totally different matter. Our mettle was now up, you know. Just as we reached it I look and see the second barricade, and we could not advance. There was a what's-its-name . . . now what do you call it? Ach, what is it? . . . '

'Another scarp, perhaps,' I suggested.

'Not at all,' he said crossly: 'not a scarp but – oh dear, what do you call it?' and he made an awkward gesture with his hands. 'Oh, good heavens, what is it?' He seemed so distressed that one involuntarily wished to help him.

'A river, perhaps,' said Bólkhov.

'No, only a scarp! Hardly had we got down, when, will you believe it, such a hell of fire . . . '

At this moment someone outside the tent asked for me. It was Maksímov. And as after having heard the different histories of these two barricades there were still thirteen left, I was glad to seize the excuse to return to my platoon. Trosénko came out with me.

'It's all lies,' he said to me when we were a few steps from the hut; 'he never was near those barricades at all,' and Trosénko laughed so heartily that I, too, enjoyed the joke.

Chapter XIII

I T was already dark and only the watch-fires dimly lit up the camp when, after the horses were groomed, I rejoined my men. A large stump lay smouldering on the charcoal. Only three men sat round it: Antónov, who was turning a little pot of *ryábco*[1] on the fire; Zhdánov, who was dreamily poking the embers with a stick, and Chíkin, with his pipe, which never would draw well. The rest had already lain down to sleep – some under the ammunition wagons, some on the hay, some by the camp-fires. By the dim light of the charcoal I could distinguish familiar backs, legs, and heads, and among the latter that of the young recruit who, drawn close to the fire, seemed to be already sleeping. Antónov made room for me. I sat down by him and lit a cigarette. The smell of mist and the smoke of damp wood filled the air and made one's eyes smart and, as before, a dank drizzle kept falling from the dismal sky.

One could hear the regular sound of snoring near by, the crackling of branches in the fire, a few words now and then, and the clattering of muskets among the infantry. The camp watch-fires glowed all around, lighting up within narrow circles the dark shadows of the soldiers near them. Where the light fell by the nearest fires I could distinguish the figures of naked soldiers waving their shirts close over the fire. There were still many who had not lain down, but moved and spoke, collected on a space of some eighty square yards; but the gloomy dull night gave a peculiar mysterious character to all this movement as if each one felt the dark silence and feared to break its calm monotony.

When I began to speak I felt that my voice sounded strange, and I discerned the same frame of mind reflected in the faces of all the soldiers sitting near me. I thought that before I joined them they had been talking about their wounded comrade, but it had not been so at all. Chíkin had been telling them about receiving supplies at Tiflís and about the scamps there.

I have noticed always and everywhere, but especially in the Caucasus, the peculiar tact with which our soldiers avoid mentioning anything that might have a bad effect on a comrade's spirits. A Russian soldier's spirit does not rest on easily inflammable enthusiasm which cools quickly like the courage of Southern nations; it is as difficult to inflame him as it is to depress him. He does not need scenes, speeches, war-cries,

1 *Ryábco*, soldier's food, made of soaked hard-tack and dripping. L. T.

songs, and drums; on the contrary he needs quiet, order, and an absence of any affectation. In a Russian, a real Russian, soldier you will never find any bragging, swagger, or desire to befog or excite himself in time of danger; on the contrary, modesty, simplicity, and a capacity for seeing in peril something quite else than the danger, are the distinctive features of his character. I have seen a soldier wounded in the leg, who in the first instant thought only of the hole in his new sheepskin cloak; and an artillery outrider who, creeping from beneath a horse that was killed under him, began unbuckling the girths to save the saddle. Who does not remember the incident at the siege of Gergebel when the fuse of a loaded bomb caught fire in the laboratory and an artillery sergeant ordered two soldiers to take the bomb and run to throw it into the ditch, and how the soldiers did not run to the nearest spot by the colonel's tent, which stood over the ditch, but took it farther on so as not to wake the gentlemen asleep in the tent and were consequently both blown to pieces? I remember also how, in the expedition of 1852, something led a young soldier while in action to say he thought the platoon would never escape, and how the whole platoon angrily attacked him for such evil words which they did not like even to repeat. And now, when the thought of Velenchúk must have been in the mind of each one and when we might expect Tartars to steal up at any moment and fire a volley at us, everyone listened to Chíkin's sprightly stories and no one referred either to the day's action, or to the present danger, or to the wounded man; as if it had all happened goodness knows how long ago or had never happened at all. But it seemed to me that their faces were rather sterner than usual, that they did not listen to Chíkin so very attentively, and that even Chíkin himself felt he was not being listened to, but talked for the sake of talking.

Maksímov joined us at the fire and sat down beside me. Chíkin made room for him, stopped speaking, and started sucking at his pipe once more.

'The infantry have been sending to the camp for vodka,' said Maksímov after a considerable silence; 'they have just returned.' He spat into the fire. 'The sergeant says they saw our man.'

'Is he alive?' asked Antónov, turning the pot.

'No, he's dead.'

The young recruit suddenly raised his head in the little red cap, looked intently for a minute over the fire at Maksímov and at me, then quickly let his head sink again and wrapped himself in his cloak.

'There now, it wasn't for naught that death had laid its hand on him when I had to wake him in the "park" this morning,' said Antónov.

'Nonsense!' said Zhdánov, turning the smouldering log, and all were silent.

Then, amid the general silence, came the report of a gun from the camp behind us. Our drummers beat an answering tattoo. When the last vibration ceased Zhdánov rose first, taking off his cap. We all followed his example.

Through the deep silence of the night rose a harmonious choir of manly voices:

'Our Father which art in heaven, hallowed be Thy name. Thy kingdom come. Thy will be done as in heaven so on earth. Give us day by day our daily bread. And forgive us our debts as we forgive our debtors. And lead us not into temptation; but deliver us from the evil one.'

'We had a man in '45 who was wounded in the same place,' said Antónov when we had put on our caps and again sat down by the fire. 'We carried him about with us on a gun for two days – do you remember Shévchenko, Zhdánov? – and then we just left him there under a tree.'

At this moment an infantryman with tremendous whiskers and moustaches came up to our fire, carrying a musket and pouch.

'Give me a light for my pipe, comrades,' said he.

'All right, smoke away: there's fire enough,' remarked Chíkin.

'I suppose it's about Dargo[1] you are telling, comrade,' said the infantry soldier to Antónov.

1 Dargo, in the Térek Territory, was the head-quarters of Shamyl until 1845.

'Yes, about Dargo in '45,' Antónov replied.

The infantryman shook his head, screwed up his eyes, and sat down on his heels near us.

'Yes, all sorts of things happened there,' he remarked.

'Why did you leave him behind?' I asked Antónov.

'He was suffering a lot with his stomach. As long as we halted it was all right, but as soon as we moved on he screamed aloud and asked for God's sake to be left behind – but we felt it a pity. But when *he* began to give it us hot, killed three of our men from the guns and an officer besides and we somehow got separated from our battery. . . . It was such a go! We thought we shouldn't get our guns away. It was muddy and no mistake!'

'The mud was worst under the Indéysky[1] Mountain,' remarked one of the soldiers.

'Yes, it was there he got more worse! So we considered it with Anóshenka – he was an old artillery sergeant. "Now really he can't live and he's asking for God's sake to be left behind; let us leave him here." So we decided. There was a tree, such a branchy one, growing there. Well, we took some soaked hard-tack Zhdánov had, and put it near him, leant him against the tree, put a clean shirt on him, and said good-bye, – all as it should be – and left him.'

'And was he a good soldier?'

'Yes, he was all right as a soldier,' remarked Zhdánov.

'And what became of him God only knows,' continued Antónov; 'many of the likes of us perished there.'

'What, at Dargo?' said the infantryman as he rose, scraping out his pipe and again half-closing his eyes and shaking his head; 'all sorts of things happened there.'

And he left us.

'And have we many still in the battery who were at Dargo?' I asked.

'Many? Why, there's Zhdánov, myself, Patsán who is now on furlough, and there may be six others, not more.'

---

1 The soldier miscalls the Andíysky chain of mountains 'Indéysky', apparently connecting them with India.

'And why's our Patsán holiday-making all this time?' said Chíkin, stretching out his legs and lying down with his head on a log. 'I reckon he's been away getting on for a year.'

'And you, have you had your year at home?' I asked Zhdánov.

'No, I didn't go,' he answered unwillingly.

'You see, it's all right to go,' said Antónov, 'if they're well off at home or if you are yourself fit to work; then it's tempting to go and they're glad to see you.'

'But where's the use of going when one's one of two brothers?' continued Zhdánov. 'It's all they can do to get their bread; how should they feed a soldier like me? I'm no help to them after twenty-five years' service. And who knows whether they're alive still?'

'Haven't you ever written?' I asked.

'Yes, indeed! I wrote two letters, but never had an answer. Either they're dead, or simply won't write because they're living in poverty themselves; so where's the good?'

'And is it long since you wrote?'

'I wrote last when we returned from Dargo... Won't you sing us "The Birch-Tree"?' he said, turning to Antónov, who sat leaning his elbows on his knees and humming a song.

Antónov began to sing 'The Birch-Tree'.

'This is the song Daddy Zhdánov likes most best of all,' said Chíkin to me in a whisper, pulling at my cloak. 'Sometimes he right down weeps when Philip Antónych sings it.'

Zhdánov at first sat quite motionless with eyes fixed on the glimmering embers, and his face, lit up by the reddish light, seemed very gloomy; then his jaws below his ears began to move faster and faster, and at last he rose, and spreading out his cloak, lay down in the shadow behind the fire. Either it was his tossing and groaning as he settled down to sleep, or it may have been the effect of Velenchúk's death and of the dull weather, but it really seemed to me that he was crying.

The bottom of the charred log, bursting every now and then into flames, lit up Antónov's figure with his grey moustaches, red face, and the medals on the cloak that he had thrown over his shoulders, or it lit up someone's boots, head, or back. The same gloomy drizzle fell from above, the air was still full of moisture and smoke, all around were the same bright spots of fires, now dying down, and amid the general stillness came the mournful sound of Antónov's song; and when that stopped for an instant the faint nocturnal sounds of the camp – snoring, clanking of sentries' muskets, voices speaking in low tones – took part.

'Second watch! Makatyúk and Zhdánov!' cried Maksímov.

Antónov stopped singing. Zhdánov rose, sighed, stepped across the log, and went slowly towards the guns.

SEVASTOPOL

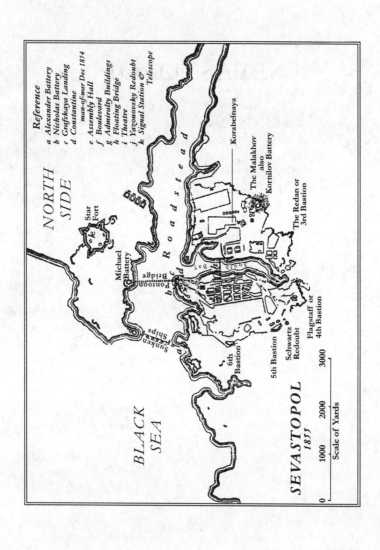

Reference

a Alexander Battery
b Nicholas Battery
c Grafskaya Landing
d Constantine
     man-of-war Dec 1814
e Assembly Hall
f Boulevard
g Admiralty Buildings
h Floating Bridge
i Theatre
j Yazonovsky Redoubt
k Signal Station &
     Telescope

NORTH
SIDE

Star
Fort

Michael
Battery

Pontoon Bridge

Roadstead

Korabelnaya

The Malakhov
also
Kornilov Battery

The Redan or
3rd Bastion

SOUTH BAY

Sunken
Ships

6th
Bastion

5th Bastion

Schwartz
Redoubt

Flagstaff or
4th Bastion

BLACK
SEA

SEVASTOPOL
1855

Scale of Yards

0   1000   2000   3000

SEVASTOPOL IN DECEMBER 1854

THE early dawn is just beginning to colour the horizon above the Sapún Hill. The dark blue surface of the sea has already thrown off the gloom of night and is only awaiting the first ray of the sun to begin sparkling merrily. A current of cold misty air blows from the bay; there is no snow on the hard black ground, but the sharp morning frost crunches under your feet and makes your face tingle. The distant, incessant murmur of the sea, occasionally interrupted by the reverberating boom of cannon from Sevastopol, alone infringes the stillness of the morning. All is quiet on the ships. It strikes eight bells.

On the north side the activity of day is beginning gradually to replace the quiet of night: here some soldiers with clanking muskets pass to relieve the guard, there a doctor is already hurrying to the hospital, and there a soldier, having crept out of his dug-out, washes his weather-beaten face with icy water and then turning to the reddening horizon says his prayers, rapidly crossing himself: a creaking Tartar cart drawn by camels crawls past on its way to the cemetery to bury the blood-stained dead with which it is loaded almost to the top. As you approach the harbour you are struck by the peculiar smell of coal-smoke, manure, dampness, and meat. Thousands of different objects are lying in heaps by the harbour: firewood, meat, gabions, sacks of flour, iron, and so on. Soldiers of various regiments, some carrying bags and muskets and others empty-handed, are crowded together here, smoking, quarrelling, and hauling heavy loads onto the steamer which lies close to the wharf, its funnel smoking. Private boats crowded with all sorts of people – soldiers, sailors, merchants, and women – keep arriving at the landing stage or leaving it.

'To the Gráfskaya, your Honour? Please to get in!' two or three old salts offer you their services, getting out of their boats.

You choose the one nearest to you, step across the half-decayed carcass of a bay horse that lies in the mud close to the boat, and pass on towards the rudder. You push off from the landing stage, and around you is the sea, now glittering in the morning sunshine. In front of you the old sailor in his camel-hair coat, and a flaxen-haired boy, silently and steadily ply the oars. You gaze at the enormous striped ships scattered far and wide over the bay, at the ships' boats that move about over the sparkling azure like small black dots, at the opposite bank where the handsome light-coloured buildings of the town are lit up by the rosy rays of the morning sun, at the foaming white line by the breakwater and around the sunken vessels, the black tops of whose masts here and there stand mournfully out of the water, at the enemy's fleet looming on the crystal horizon of the sea, and at the foaming and bubbling wash of the oars. You listen to the steady sound of voices that reaches you across the water, and to the majestic sound of firing from Sevastopol which as it seems to you is growing more intense.

It is impossible for some feeling of heroism and pride not to penetrate your soul at the thought that you, too, are in Sevastopol, and for the blood not to run faster in your veins.

'Straight past the *Kistentin*,[1] your Honour!' the old sailor tells you, turning round to verify the direction towards the right in which you are steering.

'And she's still got all her guns!'[2] says the flaxen-headed boy, examining the ship in passing.

'Well, of course. She's a new one. Kornílov lived on her,' remarks the old seaman, also looking up at the ship.

'Look where it's burst!' the boy says after a long silence, watching a small white cloud of dispersing smoke that has suddenly appeared high above the South Bay accompanied by the sharp sound of a bursting bomb.

1 The vessel, the *Constantine*.
2 The guns were removed from most of the ships for use on the fortifications.

'That's *him* firing from the new battery to-day,' adds the old seaman, calmly spitting on his hand. 'Now then, pull away Míshka! Let's get ahead of that long-boat.' And your skiff travels faster over the broad swell of the Roadstead, gets ahead of the heavy long-boat laden with sacks and unsteadily and clumsily rowed by soldiers, and making its way among all sorts of boats moored there, is made fast to the Gráfsky landing.

Crowds of grey-clad soldiers, sailors in black, and gaily-dressed women, throng noisily about the quay. Here are women selling buns, Russian peasants with samovars[1] are shouting, 'Hot sbíten!',[2] and here too on the very first steps lie rusty cannon-balls, bombs, grape-shot, and cannon of various sizes. A little farther on is a large open space where some enormous beams are lying, together with gun carriages and sleeping soldiers. Horses, carts, cannon, green ammunition wagons, and stacked muskets, are standing there. Soldiers, sailors, officers, women, children, and tradespeople, are moving about, carts loaded with hay, sacks, and casks, are passing, and now and then a Cossack, a mounted officer, or a general in a vehicle. To the right is a street closed by a barricade on which some small guns are mounted in embrasures and beside which sits a sailor smoking a pipe. To the left is a handsome building with Roman figures engraved on its frontage and before which soldiers are standing with blood-stained stretchers. Everywhere you will see the unpleasant indications of a war camp. Your first impressions will certainly be most disagreeable: the strange mixture of camp-life and town-life – of a fine town and a dirty bivouac – is not only ugly but looks like horrible disorder: it will even seem to you that everyone is scared, in a commotion, and at a loss what to do. But look more closely at the faces of these people moving about around you and you will get a very different impression. Take for instance this convoy soldier muttering something to himself as he goes to water those three bay horses, and doing it all so

1 The samovár, or 'self-boiler', is an urn in which water can be boiled and kept hot without any other fire having to be lit.
2 A hot drink made with treacle and lemon, or honey and spice.

quietly that he evidently will not get lost in this motley crowd which does not even exist as far as he is concerned, but will do his job be it what it may – watering horses or hauling guns – as calmly, self-confidently, and unconcernedly as if it were all happening in Túla or Saránsk. You will read the same thing on the face of this officer passing by in immaculate white gloves, on the face of the sailor who sits smoking on the barricade, on the faces of the soldiers waiting in the portico of what used to be the Assembly Hall, and on the face of that girl who, afraid of getting her pink dress muddy, is jumping from stone to stone as she crosses the street.

Yes, disenchantment certainly awaits you on entering Sevastopol for the first time. You will look in vain in any of these faces for signs of disquiet, perplexity, or even of enthusiasm, determination, or readiness for death – there is nothing of the kind. What you see are ordinary people quietly occupied with ordinary activities, so that perhaps you may reproach yourself for having felt undue enthusiasm and may doubt the justice of the ideas you had formed of the heroism of the defenders of Sevastopol, based on the tales and descriptions and sights and sounds seen and heard from the North Side. But before yielding to such doubts go to the bastions and see the defenders of Sevastopol at the very place of the defence, or better still go straight into that building opposite which was once the Sevastopol Assembly Rooms and in the portico of which stand soldiers with stretchers. There you will see the defenders of Sevastopol and will see terrible and lamentable, solemn and amusing, but astounding and soul-elevating sights.

You enter the large Assembly Hall. As soon as you open the door you are struck by the sight and smell of forty or fifty amputation and most seriously wounded cases, some in cots but most of them on the floor. Do not trust the feeling that checks you at the threshold, it is a wrong feeling. Go on, do not be ashamed of seeming to have come to *look* at the sufferers, do not hesitate to go up and speak to them. Sufferers like to see a sympathetic human face, like to speak of their sufferings, and to hear words of love and sympathy. You pass between the rows of beds and look for a face less stern and full of suffering, which you feel you can approach and speak to.

'Where are you wounded?' you inquire hesitatingly and timidly of an emaciated old soldier who is sitting up in his cot and following you with a kindly look as if inviting you to approach him. I say 'inquire timidly' because, besides strong sympathy, sufferings seem to inspire a dread of offending, as well as a great respect for him who endures them.

'In the leg,' the soldier replies, and at the same moment you yourself notice from the fold of his blanket that one leg is missing from above the knee. 'Now, God be thanked,' he adds, 'I am ready to leave the hospital.'

'Is it long since you were wounded?'

'Well, it's over five weeks now, your Honour.'

'And are you still in pain?'

'No, I'm not in any pain now; only when it's bad weather I seem to feel a pain in the calf, else it's all right.'

'And how did it happen that you were wounded?'

'It was on the Fifth Bastion, your Honour, at the first *bondbarment*. I trained the gun and was stepping across to the next embrasure, when *he* hits me in the leg, just as if I had stumbled into a hole. I look – and the leg is gone.'

'Do you mean to say you felt no pain the first moment?'

'Nothing much, only as if something hot had shoved against my leg.'

'And afterwards?'

'And nothing much afterwards except when they began to draw the skin together, then it did seem to smart. The chief thing, your Honour, is *not to think*; if you don't think it's nothing much. It's most because of a man thinking.'

At this moment a woman in a grey striped dress and with a black kerchief tied round her head comes up to you and enters into your conversation with the sailor. She begins telling you about him, about his sufferings, the desperate condition he was in for four weeks, and of how when he was wounded he stopped his stretcher-bearers that he might see a volley fired from our battery; and how the Grand Duke spoke to him and gave him twenty-five rubles, and how he had told them he wanted to go back to the bastion to teach the young ones, if he could not himself work any longer. As she says all this in a breath, the woman keeps looking now at you and now at the sailor, who having turned away is picking lint on his pillow as if not listening, and her eyes shine with a peculiar rapture.

'She's my missus, your Honour!' he remarks with a look that seems to say: 'You must excuse her. It's a woman's way to talk nonsense.'

You begin now to understand the defenders of Sevastopol, and for some reason begin to feel ashamed of yourself in the presence of this man. You want to say too much, in order to express your sympathy and admiration, but you can't find the right words and are dissatisfied with those that occur to you, and so you silently bow your head before this taciturn and unconscious grandeur and firmness of spirit — which is ashamed to have its worth revealed.

'Well, may God help you to get well soon,' you say to him, and turn to another patient who is lying on the floor apparently awaiting death in unspeakable torment.

He is a fair-haired man with a puffy pale face. He is lying on his back with his left arm thrown back in a position that indicates cruel suffering. His hoarse breathing comes with difficulty through his parched, open mouth; his leaden blue eyes are rolled upwards, and what remains of his bandaged right arm is thrust out from under his tumbled blanket. The oppressive smell of mortified flesh assails you yet more strongly, and the feverish inner heat in all the sufferer's limbs seems to penetrate you also.

'Is he unconscious?' you ask the woman who follows you and looks at you kindly as at someone akin to her.

'No, he can still hear, but not at all well,' and she adds in a whisper: 'I gave him some tea to drink to-day — what if he is a stranger, one must have pity — but he hardly drank any of it.'

'How do you feel?' you ask him.

The wounded man turns his eyes at the sound of your voice, but neither sees nor understands you.

'My heart's on fire,' he mumbles.

A little farther on you see an old soldier who is changing his shirt. His face and body are a kind of reddish brown and as gaunt as a skeleton. Nothing is left of one of his arms. It has been amputated at the shoulder. He sits up firmly, he is convalescent; but his dull, heavy look, his terrible emaciation and the wrinkles on his face, show that the best part of this man's life has been consumed by his sufferings.

In a cot on the opposite side you see a woman's pale, delicate face, full of suffering, a hectic flush suffusing her cheek.

'That's the wife of one of our sailors: she was hit in the leg by a bomb on the 5th,'[1] your guide will tell you. 'She was taking her husband's dinner to him at the bastion.'

'Amputated?'

'Yes, cut off above the knee.'

Now, if your nerves are strong, go in at the door to the left; it is there they bandage and operate. There you will see doctors with pale, gloomy faces, and arms red with blood up to the elbows, busy at a bed on which a wounded man lies under chloroform. His eyes are open and he utters, as if in delirium, incoherent but sometimes simple and pathetic words. The doctors are engaged on the horrible but beneficent work of amputation. You will see the sharp curved knife enter the healthy white flesh; you will see the wounded man come back to life with terrible, heart-rending screams and curses. You will see the doctor's assistant toss the amputated arm into a corner and in the same room you will see another wounded man on a stretcher watching the operation, and writhing and groaning not so much from physical pain as from the mental torture of anticipation. You will see ghastly sights that will rend your soul; you will see war not with its orderly beautiful and brilliant ranks, its music and beating drums, its waving banners, its generals on prancing horses, but war in its real aspect of blood, suffering, and death. . . .

---

1 The first bombardment of Sevastopol was on the 5th of October 1854, old style, that is, the 17th of October, new style.

On coming out of this house of pain you will be sure to experience a sense of relief, you will draw deeper breaths of the fresh air, and rejoice in the consciousness of your own health. Yet the contemplation of those sufferings will have made you realize your own insignificance, and you will go calmly and unhesitatingly to the bastions.

'What matters the death and suffering of so insignificant a worm as I, compared to so many deaths, so much suffering?' But the sight of the clear sky, the brilliant sun, the beautiful town, the open church, and the soldiers moving in all directions, will soon bring your spirit back to its normal state of frivolity, its petty cares and absorption in the present. You may meet the funeral procession of an officer as it leaves the church, the pink coffin accompanied by waving banners and music, and the sound of firing from the bastions may reach your ears. But these things will not bring back your former thoughts. The funeral will seem a very beautiful military pageant, the sounds very beautiful warlike sounds; and neither to these sights nor these sounds will you attach the clear and personal sense of suffering and death that came to you in the hospital.

Passing the church and the barricade you enter that part of the town where everyday life is most active. On both sides of the street hang the signboards[1] of shops and restaurants. Tradesmen, women with bonnets or kerchiefs on their heads, dandified officers – everything speaks of the firmness, self-confidence, and security of the inhabitants.

If you care to hear the conversation of army and navy officers, enter the restaurant on the right. There you are sure to hear them talk about last night, about Fanny, about the affair of the 24th,[2] about how dear and badly served the cutlets are, and how such and such of their comrades have been killed.

1 Among a population largely illiterate, the signboards were usually pictorial. The bakers showed loaves and rolls, the bootmakers boots and shoes, and so on.
2 The 24th October o.s. = 5th November n.s., the date of the Battle of Inkerman.

'Things were confoundedly bad at our place to-day!' a fair beardless little naval officer with a green knitted scarf round his neck says in a bass voice.

'Where was that?' asks another.

'Oh, in the Fourth Bastion,' answers the young officer, and at the words 'Fourth Bastion' you will certainly look more attentively and even with a certain respect at this fair-complex-ioned officer. The excessive freedom of his manner, his ges-ticulations, and his loud voice and laugh, which had appeared to you impudent before, now seem to indicate that peculiarly combative frame of mind noticeable in some young men after they have been in danger, but all the same you expect him to say how bad the bombs and bullets made things in the Fourth Bastion. Not at all! It was the mud that made things so bad. 'One can scarcely get to the battery,' he continues, pointing to his boots, which are muddy even above the calves. 'And I have lost my best gunner,' says another, 'hit right in the forehead.' 'Who's that? Mitúkhin?' 'No . . . but am I ever to have my veal, you rascal?' he adds, addressing the waiter. 'Not Mitúkhin but Abrámov – such a fine fellow. He was out in six sallies.'

At another corner of the table sit two infantry officers with plates of cutlets and peas before them and a bottle of sour Crimean wine called 'Bordeaux'. One of them, a young man with a red collar and two little stars on his cloak, is talking to the other, who has a black collar and no stars, about the Alma affair. The former has already been drinking and the pauses he makes, the indecision in his face – expressive of his doubt of being believed – and especially the fact that his own part in the account he is giving is too important and the thing is too terrible, show that he is diverging considerably from the strict truth. But you do not care much for stories of this kind, which will long be current all over Russia; you want to get quickly to the bastions, especially to that Fourth Bastion about which you have been told so many and such different tales. When anyone says: 'I am going to the Fourth Bastion' he always betrays a slight agitation or too marked an indifference; if anyone wishes to chaff you, he says: 'You should be sent to the Fourth

Bastion.' When you meet someone carried on a stretcher and ask, 'Where from?' the answer usually is, 'From the Fourth Bastion'. Two quite different opinions are current concerning this terrible bastion:[1] that of those who have never been there and who are convinced it is a certain grave for anyone who goes, and that of those who, like the fair-complexioned midshipman, live there and who when speaking of the Fourth Bastion will tell you whether it is dry or muddy, whether it is cold or warm in the dug-outs, and so forth.

During the half-hour you have spent in the restaurant the weather has changed. The mist that spread over the sea has gathered into dull grey moist clouds which hide the sun, and a kind of dismal sleet showers down and wets the roofs, the pavements, and the soldiers' overcoats.

Passing another barricade you go through some doors to the right and up a broad street. Beyond this barricade the houses on both sides of the street are unoccupied: there are no signboards, the doors are boarded up, the windows smashed, here a corner of the wall is knocked down and there a roof is broken in. The buildings look like old veterans who have borne much sorrow and privation; they even seem to gaze proudly and somewhat contemptuously at you. On the road you stumble over cannon-balls that lie about, and into holes made in the stony ground by bombs and full of water. You meet and overtake detachments of soldiers, Cossacks, officers, and occasionally a woman or a child; only it will not be a woman wearing a bonnet, but a sailor's wife wearing an old cloak and soldiers' boots. After you have descended a little slope farther down the same street you will no longer see any houses, but only ruined walls amid strange heaps of bricks, boards, clay, and beams, and before you, up a steep hill, you see a black untidy space cut up by ditches. This space you are approaching is the Fourth Bastion. . . . Here you will meet still fewer people and no women at all, the soldiers walk briskly by, there are traces of blood on the road, and you are sure to meet four soldiers carrying a stretcher and on the stretcher probably a

[1] Called by the English the 'Flagstaff Bastion'.

pale yellow face and a blood-stained overcoat. If you ask, 'Where is he wounded?' the bearers without looking at you will answer crossly, 'in the leg' or 'in the arm' if the man is not severely wounded, or will remain sternly silent if no head is raised on the stretcher and the man is either dead or seriously wounded.

The whiz of cannon-ball or bomb nearby impresses you unpleasantly as you ascend the hill, and the meaning of the sounds is very different from what it seemed to be when they reached you in the town. Some peaceful and joyous memory will suddenly flash through your mind; self-consciousness begins to supersede the activity of your observation: you are less attentive to all that is around you and a disagreeable feeling of indecision suddenly seizes you. But silencing this despicable little voice that has suddenly made itself heard within you at the sight of danger – especially after seeing a soldier run past you laughing, waving his arms, and slipping downhill through the yellow mud – you involuntarily expand your chest, raise your head higher, and clamber up the slippery clay hill. You have climbed only a little way before bullets begin to whiz past you to the right and left, and you will perhaps consider whether you had not better walk inside the trench which runs parallel to the road; but the trench is full of such yellow liquid stinking mud, more than knee deep, that you are sure to choose the road, especially as *everybody* does so. After walking a couple of hundred yards you come to a muddy place much cut up, surrounded by gabions, cellars, platforms, and dug-outs, and on which large cast-iron cannon are mounted and cannon-balls lie piled in orderly heaps. It all seems placed without any plan, aim, connexion, or order. Here a group of sailors are sitting in the battery; here in the middle of the open space, half sunk in mud, lies a shattered cannon; and there a foot-soldier is crossing the battery, drawing his feet with difficulty out of the sticky mud. Everywhere, on all sides and all about, you see fragments of bombs, unexploded bombs, cannon-balls, and various traces of an encampment, all sunk in the liquid, sticky mud. You think you hear the thud of a cannon-ball not far off and you seem to hear the different sounds of bullets all around,

some humming like bees, some whistling, and some rapidly
flying past with a shrill screech like the string of some instrument. You hear the dreadful boom of a shot that sends a shock
all through you and seems most terrible.

'So this is the Fourth Bastion! This is that terrible, truly
dreadful spot!' So you think, experiencing a slight feeling of
pride and a strong feeling of suppressed fear. But you are
mistaken, this is not the Fourth Bastion yet. This is only
Yazónovsky Redoubt – comparatively a very safe and not at
all dreadful place. To get to the Fourth Bastion you must turn
to the right along that narrow trench where a foot-soldier has
just passed, stooping down. In this trench you may again meet
men with stretchers and perhaps a sailor or a soldier with a
spade. You will see the mouths of mines, dug-outs into which
only two men can crawl, and there you will see the Cossacks of
the Black Sea battalions changing their boots, eating, smoking
their pipes, and in short living. And again you will see the same
stinking mud, the traces of camp life and cast-iron refuse of
every shape and form. When you have gone some three
hundred steps more you will come out at another battery – a
flat space with many holes, surrounded with gabions filled
with earth, and cannons on platforms, and the whole walled
in with earthworks. Here you will perhaps see four or five
soldiers playing cards under shelter of the breastworks, and a
naval officer, noticing that you are a stranger and inquisitive,
will be pleased to show you his 'household' and everything
that can interest you. This officer sits on a cannon rolling a
yellow cigarette so composedly, walks from one embrasure to
another so quietly, talks to you so calmly and with such an
absence of affectation, that in spite of the bullets whizzing
around you oftener than before you yourself grow cooler,
question him carefully and listen to his stories. He will tell
you (but only if you ask) about the bombardment on the 5th of
October; will tell you that only one gun of his battery
remained usable and only eight gunners of the crew were
left, and that nevertheless he fired all his guns next morning,
the 6th. He will tell you how a bomb dropped into one of the
dug-outs and knocked over eleven sailors; from an embrasure

he will show you the enemy's batteries and trenches which are here not more than seventy-five to eighty-five yards distant. I am afraid though, that when you lean out of the embrasure to have a look at the enemy the whiz of the flying bullets will hinder you from seeing anything, but if you do see anything you will be much surprised to find that this whitish stone wall – which is so near you and from which puffs of white smoke keep bursting – is the enemy: *he*, as the soldiers and sailors say.

It is even very likely that the naval officer from vanity, or merely for a little recreation, will wish to show you some firing. 'Call the gunner and crew to the cannon!' and fourteen sailors – their hob-nailed boots clattering on the platform, one putting his pipe in his pocket, another still chewing a rusk – will quickly and cheerfully man the gun and begin loading. Look well into these faces and note the bearing and carriage of these men. In every wrinkle of that tanned face with its high cheek-bones, in every muscle, in the breadth of those shoulders, the thickness of those legs in their enormous boots, in every movement, quiet, firm, and deliberate, can be seen the chief characteristic of the strength of the Russian – his simplicity and obstinacy.

Suddenly the most fearful roar strikes not only your ears but your whole being and makes you shudder all over. It is followed by the whistle of the departing ball, and a thick cloud of powder-smoke envelops you, the platform, and the black moving figures of the sailors. You will hear various comments made by the sailors concerning this shot of ours and you will notice their animation, the evidences of a feeling you had not perhaps expected: the feeling of animosity and thirst for vengeance which lies hidden in each man's soul. You will hear joyful exclamations: 'It's gone right into the embrasure! It's killed two, I think. . . . There, they're carrying them off!' 'And now *he's* riled and will send one this way,' someone remarks; and really, soon after, you will see before you a flash and some smoke; the sentinel standing on the breastwork will call out 'Ca-n-non!', and then a ball will whiz past you and bury itself in the earth, throwing out a circle of stones and mud. The commander of the battery will be irritated by this shot and will give orders to fire another and another cannon, the enemy will reply in like manner, and you will experience interesting sensations and see interesting sights. The sentinel will again call 'Cannon!' and you will have the same sound and shock, and the mud will be splashed around as before. Or he will call out 'Mortar!' and you will hear the regular and rather pleasant whistle – which it is difficult to connect with the thought of anything dreadful – of a bomb; you will hear this whistle coming nearer and faster towards you, then you will see a black ball, feel the shock as it strikes the ground, and will hear the ringing explosion. The bomb will fly apart into whizzing and shrieking fragments, stones will rattle in the air, and you will be bespattered with mud.

At these sounds you will experience a strange feeling of mingled pleasure and fear. At the moment you know the shot is flying towards you, you are sure to imagine that it will kill you, but a feeling of pride will support you and no one will know of the knife that cuts at your heart. But when the shot has flown past without hitting you, you revive and are seized, though only for a moment, by an inexpressibly joyful emotion, so that you feel a peculiar delight in the danger – in this game of life and death – and wish the bombs and balls to fall nearer and nearer to you.

But again the sentinel in his loud gruff voice shouts 'Mortar!', again a whistle, a fall, an explosion; and mingled with this last you are startled by a man's groans. You approach the wounded sailor just as the stretchers are brought. Covered with blood and dirt he presents a strange, scarcely human, appearance. Part of his breast has been torn away. For the first few moments only terror and the kind of feigned, premature, look of suffering, common to men in this state, appear on his mud-besprinkled face, but when the stretcher is brought and he himself lies down on it on his healthy side you notice that his expression changes. His eyes shine more brightly, his teeth are clenched, he raises his head higher with difficulty, and when the stretcher is lifted he stops the bearers for a moment and turning to his comrades says with an effort, in a trembling voice, 'Forgive me, brothers!'[1] He wishes to say more, something pathetic, but only repeats, 'Forgive me, brothers!' At this moment a sailor approaches him, places the cap on the head the wounded man holds up towards him, and then placidly swinging his arms returns quietly to his cannon.

'That's the way with seven or eight every day,' the naval officer remarks to you, answering the look of horror on your face, and he yawns as he rolls another yellow cigarette.

So now you have seen the defenders of Sevastopol where they are defending it, and somehow you return with a tranquil heightened spirit, paying no heed to the balls and bombs whose whistle accompanies you all the way to the ruined theatre. The principal thought you have brought away with you is a joyous conviction of the strength of the Russian people; and this conviction you have gained not by looking at all those traverses, breastworks, cunningly interlaced trenches, mines, cannon, one after another, of which you could make nothing; but from the eyes, words, and actions – in short from seeing what is called the 'spirit' – of the defenders of Sevastopol. What they do is all done so simply, with so little effort, that you feel convinced that they could do a hundred times as much. . . . You understand that the feeling which actuates them is not that petty ambition or forgetfulness which you yourself experienced, but something more powerful, which has made them able to live so quietly under the flying balls, exposed to a hundred chances of death besides the one all men are subject to – and this amid conditions of constant toil, lack of sleep, and dirt. Men could not accept such terrible conditions of life for the sake of a cross, or promotion, or because of a threat: there must be some other and higher motive power.

It is only now that the tales of the early days of the siege of Sevastopol are no longer beautiful historical legends for you,

[1] 'Forgive me' and 'farewell' are almost interchangeable expressions in Russian. 'Good-bye' (*prostcháyte*) etymologically means 'forgive'. The form (*prostíte*) here used, however, means primarily 'forgive me'.

but have become realities: the tales of the time when it was not fortified, when there was no army to defend it, when it seemed a physical impossibility to retain it and yet there was not the slightest idea of abandoning it to the enemy – of the time when Kornílov, that hero worthy of ancient Greece, making his round of the troops, said, 'Lads, we will die, but will not surrender Sevastopol!' and our Russians, incapable of phrase-making, replied, 'We will die! Hurrah!' You will clearly recognize in the men you have just seen those heroes who gladly prepared for death and whose spirits did not flag during those dismal days, but rose.

The evening is closing in. Just before setting, the sun emerges from behind the grey clouds that covered the sky and suddenly lights up with its bright red glow the purple clouds, the greenish sea with the ships and boats rocking on its broad even swell, the white buildings of the town, and the people moving in the streets. The sound of some old valse played by a military band on the boulevard is carried across the water and mingles strangely with the sound of firing on the bastions.

SEVASTOPOL IN MAY 1855

I

Six months have passed since the first cannon-ball went whistling from the bastions of Sevastopol and threw up the earth of the enemy's entrenchments. Since then bullets, balls, and bombs by the thousand have flown continually from the bastions to the entrenchments and from the entrenchments to the bastions, and above them the angel of death has hovered unceasingly.

Thousands of human ambitions have had time to be mortified, thousands to be gratified and extend, thousands to be lulled to rest in the arms of death. What numbers of pink coffins and linen palls! And still the same sounds from the bastions fill the air; the French still look from their camp with involuntary trepidation and fear at the yellowy earth of the bastions of Sevastopol and count the embrasures from which the iron cannon frown fiercely; as before, through the fixed telescope on the elevation of the signal-station the pilot still watches the bright-coloured figures of the French, their batteries, their tents, their columns on the green hill, and the puffs of smoke that rise from the entrenchments; and as before, crowds of different men, with a still greater variety of desires, stream with the same ardour from many parts of the world to this fatal spot. But the question the diplomatists did not settle still remains unsettled by powder and blood.

II

A regimental band was playing on the boulevard near the pavilion in the besieged town of Sevastopol, and crowds of women and military men strolled along the paths making

97

holiday. The bright spring sun had risen in the morning above the English entrenchments, had reached the bastions, then the town and the Nicholas Barracks, shining with equal joy on all, and was now sinking down to the distant blue sea which, rocking with an even motion, glittered with silvery light.

A tall infantry officer with a slight stoop, drawing on a presentable though not very white glove, passed out of the gate of one of the small sailors' houses built on the left side of the Morskáya Street and gazing thoughtfully at the ground ascended the hill towards the boulevard. The expression of his plain face did not reveal much intellectual power, but rather good-nature, common sense, honesty, and an inclination to respectability. He was badly built, and seemed rather shy and awkward in his movements. His cap was nearly new, a gold watch-chain showed from under his thin cloak of a rather peculiar lilac shade, and he wore trousers with foot-straps, and clean, shiny calf-skin boots. He might have been a German (but that his features indicated his purely Russian origin), an adjutant, or a regimental quartermaster (but in that case he would have worn spurs), or an officer transferred from the cavalry or the Guards for the duration of the war. He was in fact an officer who had exchanged from the cavalry, and as he ascended the hill towards the boulevard he was thinking of a letter he had received from a former comrade now retired from the army, a landed proprietor in the government of T—, and of his great friend, the pale, blue-eyed Natásha, that comrade's wife. He recalled a part of the letter where his comrade wrote:

'When we receive the *Invalide*,[1] Púpka' (so the retired Uhlan called his wife) 'rushes headlong into the hall, seizes the paper, and runs with it to a seat in the arbour or the drawing-room – in which, you remember, we spent such jolly winter evenings when your regiment was stationed in our town – and reads of *your* heroic deeds with an ardour you

1 The Army and Navy Gazette.

cannot imagine. She often speaks of you. "There now," she says, "Mikháylov is a *darling*. I am ready to cover him with kisses when I see him. He [is fighting on the bastions and] is certain to receive a St George's Cross, and they'll write about him in the papers," &c., &c., so that I am beginning to be quite jealous of you.'

In another place he wrote: 'The papers reach us awfully late, and though there are plenty of rumours one cannot believe them all. For instance, those musical young ladies you know of, were saying yesterday that Napoleon has been captured by our Cossacks and sent to St Petersburg, but you can imagine how much of this I believe. One fresh arrival from Petersburg tells us for certain (he is a capital fellow, sent by the Minister on special business – and now there is no one in the town you can't think what a *resource* he is to us), that we have taken Eupatoria [so that the French are cut off from Balaclava], and that we lost two hundred in the affair and the French as many as fifteen thousand. My wife was in such raptures that she *caroused* all night and said that a presentiment assured her that you distinguished yourself in that affair.'

In spite of the words and expressions I have purposely italicized, and the whole tone of the letter, Lieutenant-Captain Mikháylov thought with an inexpressibly melancholy pleasure about his pale-faced provincial friend and how he used to sit with her of an evening in the arbour, talking *sentiment*. He thought of his kind comrade the Uhlan: how the latter used to get angry and lose when they played cards in the study for kopek points and how his wife used to laugh at him. He recalled the friendship these people had for him (perhaps he thought there was something more on the side of the pale-faced friend): these people and their surroundings flitted through his memory in a wonderfully sweet, joyously rosy light and, smiling at the recollection, he put his hand to the pocket where this *dear* letter lay.

From these recollections Lieutenant-Captain Mikháylov involuntarily passed to dreams and hopes. 'How surprised and pleased Natásha will be,' he thought as he passed along a narrow side-street, 'when she reads in the *Invalide* of my being the first to climb on the cannon, and receiving the St George! I ought to be made full captain on that former recommendation. Then I may easily become a major this year by seniority, because so many of our fellows have been killed and no doubt many more will be killed this campaign. Then there'll be more fighting and I, as a well-known man, shall be entrusted with a regiment...then a lieutenant-colonel, the order of St Anna...a colonel'...and he was already a general, honouring with a visit Natásha, the widow of his comrade (who would be dead by that time according to his day-dream) – when the sounds of the music on the boulevard reached his ears more distinctly, a crowd of people appeared before his eyes, and he realized that he was on the boulevard and a lieutenant-captain of infantry as before.

III

HE went first to the pavilion, beside which stood the band with soldiers of the same regiment acting as music-stands and holding open the music books, while around them clerks, cadets, nursemaids, and children formed a circle, looking on rather than listening. Most of the people who were standing, sitting, and sauntering round the pavilion were naval officers, adjutants, and white-gloved army officers. Along the broad avenue of the boulevard walked officers of all sorts and women of all sorts – a few of the latter in hats, but the greater part with kerchiefs on their heads, and some with neither kerchiefs nor hats – but it was remarkable that there was not a single old woman amongst them – all were young. Lower down, in the scented alleys shaded by the white acacias, isolated groups sat or strolled.

No one was particularly glad to meet Lieutenant-Captain Mikháylov on the boulevard, except perhaps Captain Obzhógov of his regiment and Captain Súslikov who pressed his hand warmly, but the first of these wore camel-hair trousers, no gloves, and a shabby overcoat, and his face was red and perspiring, and the second shouted so loud and was so free and easy that one felt ashamed to be seen walking with him,

especially by those white-gloved officers – to one of whom, an
adjutant, Mikháylov bowed, and he might have bowed to
another, a Staff officer whom he had twice met at the house
of a mutual acquaintance. Besides, what was the fun of walking
with Obzhógov and Súslikov when as it was he met them and
shook hands with them six times a day? Was this what he had
come to hear *the music* for?

He would have liked to accost the adjutant whom he had
bowed to and to talk with those gentlemen, not at all that he
wanted Captains Obzhógov and Súslikov and Lieutenant
Pashtétski and others to see him talking to them, but simply
because they were pleasant people who knew all the news and
might have told him something.

But why is Lieutenant-Captain Mikháylov afraid and
unable to muster courage to approach them? 'Supposing they
don't return my greeting,' he thinks, 'or merely bow and go
on talking among themselves as if I were not there, or simply
walk away and leave me standing among the aristocrats?' The
word aristocrats (in the sense of the highest and most select
circle of any class) has lately gained great popularity in Russia,
where one would think it ought not to exist. It has made its
way to every part of the country, and into every grade of
society which can be reached by vanity – and to what conditions of time and circumstance does this pitiful propensity not
penetrate? You find it among merchants, officials, clerks,
officers – in Sarátov, Mamadíshi, Vínnitza, in fact wherever
men are to be found. And since there are many men, and
consequently much vanity, in the besieged town of Sevastopol, aristocrats are to be found here too, though death hangs
over everyone, be he aristocrat or not.

To Captain Obzhógov, Lieutenant-Captain Mikháylov was
an aristocrat, and to Lieutenant-Captain Mikháylov, Adjutant
Kalúgin was an aristocrat, because he was an adjutant and
intimate with another adjutant. To Adjutant Kalúgin, Count
Nórdov was an aristocrat, because he was an aide-de-camp to
the Emperor.

Vanity! vanity! vanity! everywhere, even on the brink of the
grave and among men ready to die for a noble cause. Vanity! It

seems to be the characteristic feature and special malady of our time. How is it that among our predecessors no mention was made of this passion, as of small-pox and cholera? How is it that in our time there are only three kinds of people: those who, considering vanity an inevitably existing fact and therefore justifiable, freely submit to it; those who regard it as a sad but unavoidable condition; and those who act unconsciously and slavishly under its influence? Why did the Homers and Shakespeares speak of love, glory, and suffering, while the literature of to-day is an endless story of snobbery and vanity?

Twice the lieutenant-captain passed irresolutely by the group of his aristocrats, but drawing near them for the third time he made an effort and walked up to them. The group consisted of four officers: Adjutant Kalúgin, Mikháylov's acquaintance, Adjutant Prince Gáltsin who was rather an aristocrat even for Kalúgin himself, Lieutenant-Colonel Neférdov, one of the so-called 'two hundred and twenty-two' society men, who being on the retired list re-entered the army for this war, and Cavalry-Captain Praskúkhin, also of the 'two hundred and twenty-two'. Luckily for Mikháylov, Kalúgin was in splendid spirits (the general had just spoken to him in a very confidential manner, and Prince Gáltsin who had arrived from Petersburg was staying with him), so he did not think it beneath his dignity to shake hands with Mikháylov, which was more than Praskúkhin did though he had often met Mikháylov on the bastion, had more than once drunk his wine and vodka, and even owed him twelve and a half rubles lost at cards. Not being yet well acquainted with Prince Gáltsin he did not like to appear to be acquainted with a mere lieutenant-captain of infantry. So he only bowed slightly.

'Well, Captain,' said Kalúgin, 'when will you be visiting the bastion again? Do you remember our meeting at the Schwartz Redoubt? Things were hot, weren't they, eh?'

'Yes, very,' said Mikháylov, and he recalled how when making his way along the trench to the bastion he had met Kalúgin walking bravely along, his sabre clanking smartly.

'My turn's to-morrow by rights, but we have an officer ill', continued Mikháylov, 'so —'

He wanted to say that it was not his turn but as the Commander of the 8th Company was ill and only the ensign was left in the company, he felt it his duty to go in place of Lieutenant Nepshisétski and would therefore be at the bastion that evening. But Kalúgin did not hear him out.

'I feel sure that something is going to happen in a day or two,' he said to Prince Gáltsin.

'How about to-day? Will nothing happen to-day?' Mikháylov asked shyly, looking first at Kalúgin and then at Gáltsin.

No one replied. Prince Gáltsin only puckered up his face in a curious way and looking over Mikháylov's cap said after a short silence:

'Fine girl that, with the red kerchief. You know her, don't you, Captain?'

'She lives near my lodgings, she's a sailor's daughter,' answered the lieutenant-captain.

'Come, let's have a good look at her.'

And Prince Gáltsin gave one of his arms to Kalúgin and the other to the lieutenant-captain, being sure he would confer great pleasure on the latter by so doing, which was really quite true.

The lieutenant-captain was superstitious and considered it a great sin to amuse himself with women before going into action; but on this occasion he pretended to be a *roué*, which Prince Gáltsin and Kalúgin evidently did not believe and which greatly surprised the girl with the red kerchief, who had more than once noticed how the lieutenant-captain blushed when he passed her window. Praskúkhin walked behind them, and kept touching Prince Gáltsin's arm and making various remarks in French, but as four people could not walk abreast on the path he was obliged to go alone until, on the second round, he took the arm of a well-known brave naval officer, Servyágin, who came up and spoke to him, being also anxious to join the aristocrats. And the well-known hero gladly passed his honest muscular hand under the elbow of Praskúkhin, whom everybody, including Servyágin himself, knew to be no better than he should be. When, wishing to explain his acquaintance with this sailor, Praskúkhin whispered to Prince Gáltsin that this was the well-known hero, Prince Gáltsin – who had been in the Fourth Bastion the day before and seen a shell burst at some twenty yards' distance – considering himself not less courageous than the newcomer, and believing that many reputations are obtained by luck, paid not the slightest attention to Servyágin.

Lieutenant-Captain Mikháylov found it so pleasant to walk in this company that he forgot the nice letter from T— and his gloomy forebodings at the thought of having to go to the bastion. He remained with them till they began talking exclusively among themselves, avoiding his eyes to show that he might go, and at last walked away from him. But all the same the lieutenant-captain was contented, and when he passed Cadet Baron Pesth – who was particularly conceited and self-satisfied since the previous night, when for the first time in his life he had been in the bomb-proof of the Fifth Bastion and had consequently become a hero in his own estimation – he was not at all hurt by the suspiciously haughty expression with which the cadet saluted him.

IV

BUT the lieutenant-captain had hardly crossed the threshold of his lodgings before very different thoughts entered his head. He saw his little room with its uneven earth floor, its crooked windows, the broken panes mended with paper, his old bed-stead with two Túla pistols and a rug (showing a lady on horseback) nailed to the wall beside it,[1] as well as the dirty bed of the cadet who lived with him, with its cotton quilt. He saw his man Nikíta, with his rough greasy hair, rise from the floor scratching himself, he saw his old cloak, his common boots, a little bundle tied in a handkerchief ready for him to take to the bastion, from which peeped a bit of cheese and the neck of a porter bottle containing vodka – and he suddenly

1 A common way in Russia of protecting a bed from the damp or cold of a wall, is to nail a rug or carpet to the wall by the side of the bed.

remembered that he had to go with his company to spend the whole night at the lodgements.

'I shall certainly be killed to-night,' thought he, 'I feel I shall. And there was really no need for me to go – I offered to do it of my own accord. And it always happens that the one who offers himself gets killed. And what is the matter with that confounded Nepshisétski? He may not be ill at all, and they'll go and kill me because of him – they're sure to. Still, if they don't kill me I shall certainly be recommended for promotion. I saw how pleased the regimental commander was when I said: "Allow me to go if Lieutenant Nepshisétski is ill." If I'm not made a major then I'll get the Order of Vladímir for certain. Why, I am going to the bastion for the thirteenth time. Oh dear, the thirteenth! Unlucky number! I am certain to be killed. I feel I shall . . . but somebody had to go: the company can't go with only an ensign. Supposing something were to happen. . . . Why, the honour of the regiment, the honour of the army is at stake. It is my *duty* to go. Yes, my sacred duty. . . . But I have a presentiment.'

The lieutenant-captain forgot that it was not the first time he had felt this presentiment: that in a greater or lesser degree he had it whenever he was going to the bastion, and he did not know that before going into action everyone has such forebodings more or less strongly. Having calmed himself by appealing to his sense of duty – which was highly developed and very strong – the lieutenant-captain sat down at the table and began writing a farewell letter to his father. Ten minutes later, having finished his letter, he rose from the table his eyes wet with tears, and repeating mentally all the prayers he knew he began to dress. His rather tipsy and rude servant lazily handed him his new cloak – the old one which the lieutenant-captain usually wore at the bastion not being mended.

'Why isn't my cloak mended? You do nothing but sleep,' said Mikháylov angrily.

'Sleep indeed!' grumbled Nikíta, 'I do nothing but run about like a dog the whole day, and when I get fagged I mayn't even go to sleep!'

'I see you are drunk again.'

'It's not at your expense if I am, so you needn't complain.'

'Hold your tongue, you dolt!' shouted the lieutenant-captain, ready to strike the man.

Already upset, he now quite lost patience and felt hurt by the rudeness of Nikíta, who had lived with him for the last twelve years and whom he was fond of and even spoilt.

'Dolt? Dolt?' repeated the servant. 'And why do you, sir, abuse me and call me a dolt? You know in times like these it isn't right to abuse people.'

Recalling where he was about to go Mikháylov felt ashamed.

'But you know, Nikíta, you would try anyone's patience!' he said mildly. 'That letter to my father on the table you may leave where it is. Don't touch it,' he added reddening.

'Yes, sir,' said Nikíta, becoming sentimental under the influence of the vodka he had drunk, as he said, at his own expense, and blinking with an evident inclination to weep.

But at the porch, when the lieutenant-captain said, 'Good-bye, Nikíta,' Nikíta burst into forced sobs and rushed to kiss his master's hand, saying, 'Good-bye, sir,' in a broken voice. A sailor's widow who was also standing in the porch could not, as a woman, help joining in this tender scene, and began wiping her eyes on her dirty sleeve, saying something about people who, though they were gentlefolk, took such sufferings upon themselves while she, poor woman, was left a widow. And she told the tipsy Nikíta for the hundredth time about her sorrows; how her husband had been killed in the first *bondbarment*, and how her hut had been shattered (the one she lived in now was not her own) and so on. After his master was gone Nikíta lit his pipe, asked the landlady's little girl to get some vodka, very soon left off crying, and even had a quarrel with the old woman about a pail he said she had smashed for him.

'But perhaps I shall only be wounded,' reasoned the lieutenant-captain as he drew near the bastion with his company when twilight had already begun to fall. 'But where, and how? Here or here?' he said to himself, mentally passing his chest, his stomach, and his thighs in review. 'Supposing it's here' (he thought of his thighs) 'and goes right round. . . . Or goes here with a piece of a bomb, then it will be all up.'

The lieutenant-captain passed along the trenches and reached the lodgements safely. In perfect darkness he and an officer of Engineers set the men to their work, after which he sat down in a pit under the breastwork. There was little firing; only now and again there was a lightning flash on our side or *his*, and the brilliant fuse of a bomb formed a fiery arc on the dark, star-speckled sky. But all the bombs fell far beyond or far to the right of the lodgement where the lieutenant-captain sat in his pit. He drank some vodka, ate some cheese, smoked a cigarette, said his prayers, and felt inclined to sleep for a while.

V

PRINCE GÁLTSIN, Lieutenant-Colonel Nefërdov, and Praskúkhin – whom no one had invited and to whom no one spoke, but who still stuck to them – went to Kalúgin's to tea.

'But you did not finish telling me about Váska Méndel,' said Kalúgin, when he had taken off his cloak and sat in a soft easy chair by the window unbuttoning the collar of his clean starched shirt. 'How did he get married?'

'It was a joke, my boy! . . . *Je vous dis, il y avait un temps, on ne parlait que de ça à Pétersbourg*,'[1] said Prince Gáltsin, laughing as he jumped up from the piano-stool and sat down near Kalúgin on the window-sill,[2] 'a capital joke. I know all about it.'

And he told, amusingly, cleverly, and with animation, a love story which, as it has no interest for us, we will omit.

It was noticeable that not only Prince Gáltsin but each of these gentlemen who established themselves, one on the window-sill, another with his legs in the air, and a third by the piano, seemed quite different people now from what they had been on the boulevard. There was none of the absurd arrogance and haughtiness they had shown towards the infantry officers; here among themselves they were natural, and Kalúgin and Prince Gáltsin in particular showed themselves very

1 'I tell you, at one time it was the only thing talked of in Petersburg.'
2 The thick walls of Russian houses allow ample space to sit or lounge at the windows.

pleasant, merry, and good-natured young fellows. Their conversation was about their Petersburg fellow officers and acquaintances.

'What of Máslovski?'

'Which one – the Leib-Uhlan, or the Horse Guard?'

'I know them both. The one in the Horse Guards I knew when he was a boy just out of school. But the eldest – is he a captain yet?'

'Oh yes, long ago.'

'Is he still fussing about with his gipsy?'

'No, he has dropped her. . . .' And so on in the same strain.

Later on Prince Gáltsin went to the piano and gave an excellent rendering of a gipsy song. Praskúkhin, chiming in unasked, put in a second and did it so well that he was invited to continue, and this delighted him.

A servant brought tea, cream, and cracknels on a silver tray.

'Serve the prince,' said Kalúgin.

'Isn't it strange to think that we're in a besieged town,' said Gáltsin, taking his tea to the window, 'and here's a *pianerforty*, tea with cream, and a house such as I should really be glad to have in Petersburg?'

'Well, if we hadn't even that much,' said the old and ever-dissatisfied lieutenant-colonel, 'the constant uncertainty we are living in – seeing people killed day after day and no end to it – would be intolerable. And to have dirt and discomfort added to it —.'

'But our infantry officers live at the bastions with their men in the bomb-proofs and eat the soldiers' soup', said Kalúgin, 'what of them?'

'What of them? Well, though it's true they don't change their shirts for ten days at a time, they are heroes all the same – wonderful fellows.'

Just then an infantry officer entered the room.

'I . . . I have orders . . . may I see the gen . . . his Excellency? I have come with a message from General N.,' he said with a timid bow.

Kalúgin rose and without returning the officer's greeting asked with an offensive, affected, official smile if he would not have the goodness to wait; and without asking him to sit down or taking any further notice of him he turned to Gáltsin and began talking French, so that the poor officer left alone in the middle of the room did not in the least know what to do with himself.

'It is a matter of the utmost urgency, sir,' he said after a short silence.

'Ah! Well then, please come with me,' said Kalúgin, putting on his cloak and accompanying the officer to the door.

* * *

'*Eh bien, messieurs, je crois que cela chauffera cette nuit*,'[1] said Kalúgin when he returned from the general's.

'Ah! What is it – a sortie?' asked the others.

'That I don't know. You will see for yourselves,' replied Kalúgin with a mysterious smile.

'And my commander is at the bastion, so I suppose I must go too,' said Praskúkhin, buckling on his sabre.

No one replied, it was his business to know whether he had to go or not.

Praskúkhin and Nefërdov left to go to their appointed posts.

'Good-bye gentlemen. *Au revoir!* We'll meet again before the night is over,' shouted Kalúgin from the window as Praskúkhin and Nefërdov, stooping on their Cossack saddles, trotted past. The tramp of their Cossack horses soon died away in the dark street.

'*Non, dites-moi, est-ce qu'il y aura véritablement quelque chose cette nuit?*'[2] said Gáltsin as he lounged in the window-sill beside Kalúgin and watched the bombs that rose above the bastions.

'I can tell *you*, you see . . . you have been to the bastions?' (Gáltsin nodded, though he had only been once to the Fourth Bastion). 'You remember just in front of our lunette there is a trench,' – and Kalúgin, with the air of one who without being a specialist considers his military judgement very sound, began,

1 'Well, gentlemen, I think there will be warm work to-night.'
2 'No, tell me, will there really be anything to-night?'

in a rather confused way and misusing the technical terms, to explain the position of the enemy, and of our own works, and the plan of the intended action.

'But I say, they're banging away at the lodgements! Oho! I wonder if that's ours or *his*? . . . Now it's burst,' said they as they lounged on the window-sill looking at the fiery trails of the bombs crossing one another in the air, at flashes that for a moment lit up the dark sky, at puffs of white smoke, and listened to the more and more rapid reports of the firing.

'*Quel charmant coup d'œil! a?*[1] said Kalúgin, drawing his guest's attention to the really beautiful sight. 'Do you know, you sometimes can't distinguish a bomb from a star.'

'Yes, I thought that was a star just now and then saw it fall . . . there! it's burst. And that big star – what do you call it? – looks just like a bomb.'

'Do you know I am so used to these bombs that I am sure when I'm back in Russia I shall fancy I see bombs every starlight night – one gets so used to them.'

'But hadn't I better go with this sortie?' said Prince Gáltsin after a moment's pause.

'Humbug, my dear fellow! Don't think of such a thing. Besides, I won't let you,' answered Kalúgin. 'You will have plenty of opportunities later on.'

'Really? You think I need not go, eh?'

At that moment, from the direction in which these gentlemen were looking, amid the boom of the cannon came the terrible rattle of musketry, and thousands of little fires flaming up in quick succession flashed all along the line.

'There! Now it's the real thing!' said Kalúgin. 'I can't keep cool when I hear the noise of muskets. It seems to seize one's very soul, you know. There's an *hurrah*!' he added, listening intently to the distant and prolonged roar of hundreds of voices – 'Ah – ah – ah' – which came from the bastions.

'Whose *hurrah* was it? Theirs or ours?'

'I don't know, but it's hand-to-hand fighting now, for the firing has ceased.'

1 'What a charming sight, eh?'

At that moment an officer followed by a Cossack galloped under the window and alighted from his horse at the porch.

'Where are you from?'

'From the bastion. I want the general.'

'Come along. Well, what's happened?'

'The lodgements have been attacked – and occupied. The French brought up tremendous reserves – attacked us – we had only two battalions,' said the officer, panting. He was the same officer who had been there that evening, but though he was now out of breath he walked to the door with full self-possession.

'Well, have we retired?' asked Kalúgin.

'No,' angrily replied the officer, 'another battalion came up in time – we drove them back, but the colonel is killed and many officers. I have orders to ask for reinforcements.'

And saying this he went with Kalúgin to the general's, where we shall not follow him.

Five minutes later Kalúgin was already on his Cossack horse (again in the semi-Cossack manner which I have noticed that all adjutants, for some reason, seem to consider the proper thing), and rode off at a trot towards the bastion to deliver some orders and await the final result of the affair. Prince Gáltsin, under the influence of that oppressive excitement usually produced in a spectator by proximity to an action in which he is not engaged, went out, and began aimlessly pacing up and down the street.

VI

SOLDIERS passed carrying the wounded on stretchers or supporting them under their arms. It was quite dark in the streets, lights could be seen here and there, but only in the hospital windows or where some officers were sitting up. From the bastions still came the thunder of cannon and the rattle of muskets,[1] and flashes kept on lighting up the dark sky

1 Rifles, except some clumsy *stutzers*, had not been introduced into the Russian army, but were used by the besiegers, who had a still greater advantage in artillery. It is characteristic of Tolstoy that, occupied with

as before. From time to time the tramp of hoofs could be heard as an orderly galloped past, or the groans of a wounded man, the steps and voices of stretcher-bearers, or the words of some frightened women who had come out onto their porches to watch the cannonade.

Among the spectators were our friend Nikíta, the old sailor's widow with whom he had again made friends, and her ten-year-old daughter.

'O Lord God! Holy Mary, Mother of God!' said the old woman, sighing as she looked at the bombs that kept flying across from side to side like balls of fire; 'What horrors! What horrors! Ah, ah! Oh, oh! Even at the first *bondbarment* it wasn't like that. Look now where the cursed thing has burst just over our house in the suburb.'

'No, that's further, they keep tumbling into Aunt Irene's garden,' said the girl.

'And where, where, is master now?' drawled Nikíta, who was not quite sober yet. 'Oh! You don't know how I love that master of mine! I love him so that if he were killed in a sinful way, which God forbid, then would you believe it, granny, after that I myself don't know what I wouldn't do to myself! I don't! . . . My master is that sort, there's only one word for it. Would I change him for such as them there, playing cards? What are they? Ugh! There's only one word for it!' concluded Nikíta, pointing to the lighted window of his master's room to which, in the absence of the lieutenant-captain, Cadet Zhvad-chévski had invited Sub-Lieutenants Ugróvich and Nepshi-sétski – the latter suffering from face-ache – and where he was having a spree in honour of a medal he had received.

'Look at the stars! Look how they're rolling!' the little girl broke the silence that followed Nikíta's words as she stood gazing at the sky. 'There's another rolled down. What is it a sign of, mother?'

'They'll smash up our hut altogether,' said the old woman with a sigh, leaving her daughter unanswered.

---

men rather than mechanics, he does not in these sketches dwell on this disparity of equipment.

'As we went there to-day with uncle, mother,' the little girl continued in a sing-song tone, becoming loquacious, 'there was such a b – i – g cannon-ball inside the room close to the cupboard. Must have smashed in through the passage and right into the room! Such a big one – you couldn't lift it.'

'Those who had husbands and money all moved away,' said the old woman, 'and there's the hut, all that was left me, and that's been smashed. Just look at *him* blazing away! The fiend! . . . O Lord! O Lord!'

'And just as we were going out, comes a bomb fly-ing, and goes and bur-sts and co-o-vers us with dust. A bit of it nearly hit me and uncle.'

VII

PRINCE GÁLTSIN met more and more wounded carried on stretchers or walking supported by others who were talking loudly.

'Up they sprang, friends,' said the bass voice of a tall soldier with two guns slung from his shoulder, 'up they sprang, shouting "Allah! Allah!"[1] and just climbing one over another. You kill one and another's there, you couldn't do anything; no end of 'em —'

But at this point in the story Gáltsin interrupted him.

'You are from the bastion?'

'Yes, your Honour.'

'Well, what happened? Tell me.'

'What happened? Well, your Honour, such a force of 'em poured down on us over the rampart, it was all up. They quite overpowered us, your Honour!'

'Overpowered? . . . But you repulsed them?'

'How could we repulse them when *his* whole force came on, killed all our men, and no re'forcements were given us?'

The soldier was mistaken, the trench had remained ours; but it is a curious fact which anyone may notice, that a soldier

---

1 Our soldiers fighting the Turks have become so accustomed to this cry of the enemy that they now always say that the French also shout 'Allah!' L. T.

wounded in action always thinks the affair lost and imagines it to have been a very bloody fight.

'How is that? I was told they had been repulsed,' said Gáltsin irritably. 'Perhaps they were driven back after you left? Is it long since you came away?'

'I am straight from there, your Honour,' answered the soldier, 'it is hardly possible. They must have kept the trench, *he* quite overpowered us.'

'And aren't you ashamed to have lost the trench? It's terrible!' said Gáltsin, provoked by such indifference.

'Why, if the strength is on their side . . .' muttered the soldier.

'Ah, your Honour,' began a soldier from a stretcher which had just come up to them, 'how could we help giving it up when *he* had killed almost all our men? If we'd had the strength we wouldn't have given it up, not on any account. But as it was, what could we do? I stuck one, and then something hits me. Oh, oh-h! Steady, lads, steady! Oh, oh!' groaned the wounded man.

'Really, there seem to be too many men returning,' said Gáltsin, again stopping the tall soldier with the two guns. 'Why are you retiring? You there, stop!'

The soldier stopped and took off his cap with his left hand.

'Where are you going, and why?' shouted Gáltsin severely, 'you scoun—'

But having come close up to the soldier, Gáltsin noticed that no hand was visible beneath the soldier's right cuff and that the sleeve was soaked in blood to the elbow.

'I am wounded, your Honour.'

'Wounded? How?'

'Here. Must have been with a bullet,' said the man, pointing to his arm, 'but I don't know what struck my head here,' and bending his head he showed the matted hair at the back stuck together with blood.

'And whose is this other gun?'

'It's a French rifle I took, your Honour. But I wouldn't have come away if it weren't to lead this fellow – he may fall,' he added, pointing to a soldier who was walking a little in front leaning on his gun and painfully dragging his left leg.

Prince Gáltsin suddenly felt horribly ashamed of his unjust suspicions. He felt himself blushing, turned away, and went to the hospital without either questioning or watching the wounded men any more.

Having with difficulty pushed his way through the porch among the wounded who had come on foot and the bearers who were carrying in the wounded and bringing out the dead, Gáltsin entered the first room, gave a look round, and involuntarily turned back and ran out into the street: it was too terrible.

VIII

THE large, lofty, dark hall, lit up only by the four or five candles with which the doctors examined the wounded, was quite full. Yet the bearers kept bringing in more wounded – laying them side by side on the floor which was already so packed that the unfortunate patients were jostled together, staining one another with their blood – and going to fetch more wounded. The pools of blood visible in the unoccupied spaces, the feverish breathing of several hundred men, and the perspiration of the bearers with the stretchers, filled the air with a peculiar, heavy, thick, fetid mist, in which the candles burnt dimly in different parts of the hall. All sorts of groans, sighs, death-rattles, now and then interrupted by shrill screams, filled the whole room. Sisters with quiet faces, expressing no empty feminine tearful pity, but active practical sympathy, stepped here and there across the wounded with medicines, water, bandages, and lint, flitting among the blood-stained coats and shirts. The doctors, kneeling with rolled-up sleeves beside the wounded, by the light of the candles their assistants held, examined, felt, and probed their wounds, heedless of the terrible groans and entreaties of the sufferers. One doctor sat at a table near the door and at the moment Gáltsin came in was already entering No. 532.

'Iván Bogáev, Private, Company Three, S— Regiment, *fractura femuris complicata!*' shouted another doctor from the end of the room, examining a shattered leg. 'Turn him over.'

'Oh, oh, fathers! Oh, you're our fathers!' screamed the soldier, beseeching them not to touch him.

'*Perforatio capitis!*'

'Simon Nefërdov, Lieutenant-Colonel of the N— Infantry Regiment. Have a little patience, Colonel, or it is quite impossible: I shall give it up!' said a third doctor, poking about with some kind of hook in the unfortunate colonel's skull.

'Oh, don't! Oh, for God's sake be quick! Be quick! Ah —!'

'*Perforatio pectoris* . . . Sebastian Seredá, Private . . . what regiment? But you need not write that: *moritur*. Carry him away,' said the doctor, leaving the soldier, whose eyes turned up and in whose throat the death-rattle already sounded.

About forty soldier stretcher-bearers stood at the door waiting to carry the bandaged to the wards and the dead to the chapel. They looked on at the scene before them in silence, only broken now and then by a heavy sigh.

IX

ON his way to the bastion Kalúgin met many wounded, but knowing by experience that in action such sights have a bad effect on one's spirits, he did not stop to question them but tried on the contrary not to notice them. At the foot of the hill he met an orderly-officer galloping fast from the bastion.

'Zóbkin! Zóbkin! Wait a bit!'

'Well, what is it?'

'Where are you from?'

'The lodgements.'

'How are things there – hot?'

'Oh, awful!'

And the orderly galloped on.

In fact, though there was now but little small-arms firing, the cannonade had recommenced with fresh heat and persistence.

'Ah, that's bad!' thought Kalúgin with an unpleasant sensation, and he too had a presentiment – a very usual thought, the thought of death. But Kalúgin was ambitious and blessed with nerves of oak – in a word, he was what is called brave. He did not yield to the first feeling but began to nerve himself. He recalled how an adjutant, Napoleon's he thought, having delivered an order, galloped with bleeding head full speed to Napoleon. '*Vous êtes blessé?*'[1] said Napoleon. '*Je vous demande pardon, sire, je suis mort,*'[2] and the adjutant fell from his horse, dead.

That seemed to him very fine, and he pictured himself for a moment in the role of that adjutant. Then he whipped his horse, assuming a still more dashing Cossack seat, looked back at the Cossack who, standing up in his stirrups, was trotting behind, and rode quite gallantly up to the spot where he had to dismount. Here he found four soldiers sitting on some stones smoking their pipes.

'What are you doing there?' he shouted at them.

'Been carrying off a wounded man and sat down to rest a bit, your Honour,' said one of them, hiding his pipe behind his back and taking off his cap.

'Resting, indeed! . . . To your places, march!'

And he went up the hill with them through the trench, meeting wounded men at every step.

After ascending the hill he turned to the left, and a few steps farther on found himself quite alone. A splinter of a bomb whizzed near him and fell into the trench. Another bomb rose in front of him and seemed flying straight at him. He suddenly felt frightened, ran a few steps at full speed, and lay down flat. When the bomb burst a considerable distance off he felt exceedingly vexed with himself and rose, looking round to see if anyone had noticed his downfall, but no one was near.

But when fear has once entered the soul it does not easily yield to any other feeling. He, who always boasted that he never even stooped, now hurried along the trench almost on all fours. He stumbled, and thought, 'Oh, it's awful! They'll kill me for certain!' His breath came with difficulty, and perspiration broke out over his whole body.

1 'You are wounded?'
2 'Excuse me, sire, I am dead.'

He was surprised at himself but no longer strove to master his feelings.

Suddenly he heard footsteps in front. Quickly straightening himself he raised his head, and boldly clanking his sabre went on more deliberately. He felt himself quite a different man. When he met an officer of the Engineers and a sailor, and the officer shouted to him to lie down, pointing to a bright spot which growing brighter and brighter approached more and more swiftly and came crashing down close to the trench, he only bent a little, involuntarily influenced by the frightened cry, and went on.

'That's a brave one,' said the sailor, looking quite calmly at the bomb and with experienced eye deciding at once that the splinters could not fly into the trench, 'he won't even lie down.'

It was only a few steps across open ground to the bomb-proof shelter of the commander of the bastion, when Kalúgin's mind again became clouded and the same stupid terror seized him: his heart beat more violently, the blood rushed to his head, and he had to make an effort to force himself to run to the bomb-proof.

'Why are you so out of breath?' said the general, when Kalúgin had reported his instructions.

'I walked very fast, your Excellency!'

'Won't you have a glass of wine?'

Kalúgin drank a glass of wine and lit a cigarette. The action was over, only a fierce cannonade still continued from both sides. In the bomb-proof sat General N—, the commander of the bastion, and some six other officers among whom was Praskúkhin. They were discussing various details of the action. Sitting in this comfortable room with blue wall-paper, a sofa, a bed, a table with papers on it, a wall-clock with a lamp burning before it, and an icon[1] – looking at these signs of habitation, at

1 The Russian icons are paintings in Byzantine style of God, the Holy Virgin, Christ, or some saint, martyr, or angel. They are usually on wood and often covered over, except the face and hands, with an embossed gilt cover.

the beams more than two feet thick that formed the ceiling, and listening to the shots that sounded faint here in the shelter, Kalúgin could not understand how he had twice allowed himself to be overcome by such unpardonable weakness. He was angry with himself and wished for danger in order to test his nerve once more.

'Ah! I'm glad you are here, Captain,' said he to a naval officer with big moustaches who wore a staff-officer's coat with a St George's Cross and had just entered the shelter and asked the general to give him some men to repair two embrasures of his battery which had become blocked. When the general had finished speaking to the captain, Kalúgin said: 'The commander-in-chief told me to ask if your guns can fire case-shot into the trenches.'

'Only one of them can,' said the captain sullenly.

'All the same, let us go and see.'

The captain frowned and gave an angry grunt.

'I have been standing there all night and have come in to get a bit of rest – couldn't you go alone?' he added. 'My assistant, Lieutenant Kartz, is there and can show you everything.'

The captain had already been more than six months in command of this, one of the most dangerous batteries. From the time the siege began, even before the bomb-proof shelters were constructed, he had lived continuously on the bastion and had a great reputation for courage among the sailors. That is why his refusal struck and surprised Kalúgin. 'So much for reputation,' thought he.

'Well then, I will go alone if I may,' he said in a slightly sarcastic tone to the captain, who however paid no attention to his words.

Kalúgin did not realize that whereas he had spent some fifty hours all in all at different times on the bastions, the captain had lived there for six months. Kalúgin was still actuated by vanity, the wish to shine, the hope of rewards, of gaining a reputation, and the charm of running risks. But the captain had already lived through all that: at first he had felt vain, had shown off his courage, had been foolhardy, had hoped for rewards and reputation and had even gained them, but now all these incentives had lost their power over him and he saw things differently. He fulfilled his duty exactly, but quite understanding how much the chances of life were against him after six months at the bastion, he no longer ran risks without serious need, and so the young lieutenant who had joined the battery a week ago and was now showing it to Kalúgin, with whom he vied in uselessly leaning out of the embrasures and climbing out on the banquette, seemed ten times braver than the captain.

Returning to the shelter after examining the battery, Kalúgin in the dark came upon the general, who accompanied by his staff-officers was going to the watch-tower.

'Captain Praskúkhin,' he heard the general say, 'please go to the right lodgement and tell the second battalion of the M— Regiment which is at work there to cease their work, leave the place, and noiselessly rejoin their regiment which is stationed in reserve at the foot of the hill. Do you understand? Lead them yourself to the regiment.'

'Yes, sir.'

And Praskúkhin started at full speed towards the lodgements.

The firing was now becoming less frequent.

X

'Is this the second battalion of the M— Regiment?' asked Praskúkhin, having run to his destination and coming across some soldiers carrying earth in sacks.

'It is, your Honour.'

'Where is the commander?'

Mikháylov, thinking that the commander of the company was being asked for, got out of his pit and taking Praskúkhin for a commanding officer saluted and approached him.

'The general's orders are . . . that you . . . should go . . . quickly . . . and above all quietly . . . back – no, not back, but to the reserves,' said Praskúkhin, looking askance in the direction of the enemy's fire.

Having recognized Praskúkhin and made out what was wanted, Mikháylov dropped his hand and passed on the order. The battalion became alert, the men took up their muskets, put on their cloaks, and set out.

No one without experiencing it can imagine the delight a man feels when, after three hours' bombardment, he leaves so dangerous a spot as the lodgements. During those three hours Mikháylov, who more than once and not without reason had thought his end at hand, had had time to accustom himself to the conviction that he would certainly be killed and that he no longer belonged to this world. But in spite of that he had great difficulty in keeping his legs from running away with him when, leading the company with Praskúkhin at his side, he left the lodgement.

'*Au revoir!*' said a major with whom Mikháylov had eaten bread and cheese sitting in the pit under the breastwork and who was remaining at the bastion in command of another battalion. 'I wish you a lucky journey.'

'And I wish you a lucky defence. It seems to be getting quieter now.'

But scarcely had he uttered these words before the enemy, probably observing the movement in the lodgement, began to fire more and more frequently. Our guns replied and a heavy firing recommenced.

The stars were high in the sky but shone feebly. The night was pitch dark, only the flashes of the guns and the bursting bombs made things around suddenly visible. The soldiers walked quickly and silently, involuntarily outpacing one another; only their measured footfall on the dry road was heard besides the incessant roll of the guns, the ringing of bayonets when they touched one another, a sigh, or the prayer of some poor soldier lad: 'Lord, O Lord! What does it mean?' Now and again the moaning of a man who was hit could be heard, and the cry, 'Stretchers!' (In the company Mikháylov commanded artillery fire alone carried off twenty-six men that night.) A flash on the dark and distant horizon, the cry, 'Can-n-on!' from the sentinel on the bastion, and a ball flew buzzing above the company and plunged into the earth, making the stones fly.

'What the devil are they so slow for?' thought Praskúkhin, continually looking back as he marched beside Mikháylov. 'I'd really better run on. I've delivered the order. . . . But no, they might afterwards say I'm a coward. What must be will be. I'll keep beside him.'

'Now why is he walking with me?' thought Mikháylov on his part. 'I have noticed over and over again that he always brings ill luck. Here it comes, I believe, straight for us.'

After they had gone a few hundred paces they met Kalúgin, who was walking briskly towards the lodgements clanking his sabre. He had been ordered by the general to find out how the works were progressing there. But when he met Mikháylov he thought that instead of going there himself under such a terrible fire – which he was not ordered to do – he might just as well find out all about it from an officer who had been there. And having heard from Mikháylov full details of the work and walked a little way with him, Kalúgin turned off into a trench leading to the bomb-proof shelter.

'Well, what news?' asked an officer who was eating his supper there all alone.

'Nothing much. It seems that the affair is over.'

'Over? How so? On the contrary, the general has just gone again to the watch-tower and another regiment has arrived. Yes, there it is. Listen! The muskets again! Don't you go – why should you?' added the officer, noticing that Kalúgin made a movement.

'I certainly ought to be there,' thought Kalúgin, 'but I have already exposed myself a great deal to-day: the firing is awful!'

'Yes, I think I'd better wait here for him,' he said.

And really about twenty minutes later the general and the officers who were with him returned. Among them was Cadet Baron Pesth but not Praskúkhin. The lodgements had been retaken and occupied by us.

After receiving a full account of the affair Kalúgin, accompanied by Pesth, left the bomb-proof shelter.

XI

'There's blood on your coat! You don't mean to say you were in the hand-to-hand fight?' asked Kalúgin.

'Oh, it was awful! Just fancy —'

And Pesth began to relate how he had led his company, how the company-commander had been killed, how he himself had stabbed a Frenchman, and how if it had not been for him we should have lost the day.

This tale was founded on fact: the company-commander had been killed and Pesth had bayoneted a Frenchman, but in recounting the details the cadet invented and bragged.

He bragged unintentionally, because during the whole of the affair he had been as it were in a fog and so bewildered that all he remembered of what had happened seemed to have happened somewhere, at some time, and to somebody. And very naturally he tried to recall the details in a light advantageous to himself. What really occurred was this:

The battalion the cadet had been ordered to join for the sortie stood under fire for two hours close to some low wall. Then the battalion-commander in front said something, the company-commanders became active, the battalion advanced from behind the breastwork, and after going about a hundred paces stopped to form into company columns. Pesth was told to take his place on the right flank of the second company.

Quite unable to realize where he was and why he was there, the cadet took his place, and involuntarily holding his breath while cold shivers ran down his back he gazed into the dark distance expecting something dreadful. He was however not so much frightened (for there was no firing) as disturbed and agitated at being in the field beyond the fortifications.

Again the battalion-commander in front said something. Again the officers spoke in whispers passing on the order, and the black wall, formed by the first company, suddenly sank out of sight. The order was to lie down. The second

company also lay down and in lying down Pesth hurt his hand
on a sharp prickle. Only the commander of the second company remained standing. His short figure brandishing a sword
moved in front of the company and he spoke incessantly.

'Mind lads! Show them what you're made of! Don't fire,
but give it them with the bayonet – the dogs! – when I cry
"Hurrah!" Altogether, mind, that's the thing! We'll let them
see who we are. We won't disgrace ourselves, eh lads? For our
father the Tsar!'

'What's your company-commander's name?' asked Pesth of
a cadet lying near him. 'How brave he is!'

'Yes he always is, in action,' answered the cadet. 'His name
is Lisinkóvski.'

Just then a flame suddenly flashed up right in front of the
company, who were deafened by a resounding crash. High up
in the air stones and splinters clattered. (Some fifty seconds
later a stone fell from above and severed a soldier's leg.) It was a
bomb fired from an elevated stand, and the fact that it reached
the company showed that the French had noticed the column.

'You're sending bombs, are you? Wait a bit till we get at
you, then you'll taste a three-edged Russian bayonet, damn
you!' said the company-commander so loud that the battalion-
commander had to order him to hold his tongue and not make
so much noise.

After that the first company got up, then the second. They
were ordered to fix bayonets and the battalion advanced. Pesth
was in such a fright that he could not in the least make out how
long it lasted, where he went, or who was who. He went on as
if he were drunk. But suddenly a million fires flashed from all
sides, and something whistled and clattered. He shouted and
ran somewhere, because everyone shouted and ran. Then he
stumbled and fell over something. It was the company-commander, who had been wounded at the head of his company,
and who taking the cadet for a Frenchman had seized him by
the leg. Then when Pesth had freed his leg and got up, someone else ran against him from behind in the dark and nearly
knocked him down again. 'Run him through!' someone else
shouted. 'Why are you stopping?' Then someone seized a

bayonet and stuck it into something soft. '*Ah Dieu!*' came a dreadful, piercing voice and Pesth only then understood that he had bayoneted a Frenchman. A cold sweat covered his whole body, he trembled as in a fever and threw down his musket. But this lasted only a moment; the thought immediately entered his head that he was a hero. He again seized his musket, and shouting 'Hurrah!' ran with the crowd away from the dead Frenchman. Having run twenty paces he came to a trench. Some of our men were there with the battalion-commander.

'And I have killed one!' said Pesth to the commander.

'You're a fine fellow, Baron!'

XII

'Do you know Praskúkhin is killed?' said Pesth, while accompanying Kalúgin on his way home.

'Impossible!'

'It is true. I saw him myself.'

'Well, good-bye . . . I must be off.'

'This is capital!' thought Kalúgin, as he came to his lodgings. 'It's the first time I have had such luck when on duty. It's first-rate. I am alive and well, and shall certainly get an excellent recommendation and am sure of a gold sabre. And I really have deserved it.'

After reporting what was necessary to the general he went to his room, where Prince Gáltsin, long since returned, sat awaiting him, reading a book he had found on Kalúgin's table.

It was with extraordinary pleasure that Kalúgin found himself safe at home again, and having put on his night-shirt and got into bed he gave Gáltsin all the details of the affair, telling them very naturally from a point of view where those details showed what a capable and brave officer he, Kalúgin, was (which it seems to me it was hardly necessary to allude to, since everybody knew it and had no right or reason to question it, except perhaps the deceased Captain Praskúkhin who, though he had considered it an honour to walk arm in arm with Kalúgin, had privately told a friend only yesterday that though Kalúgin was a first-rate fellow, yet, 'between you and me, he was awfully disinclined to go to the bastions').

Praskúkhin, who had been walking beside Mikháylov after Kalúgin had slipped away from him, had scarcely begun to revive a little on approaching a safer place, than he suddenly saw a bright light flash up behind him and heard the sentinel shout 'Mortar!' and a soldier walking behind him say: 'That's coming straight for the bastion!'

Mikháylov looked round. The bright spot seemed to have stopped at its zenith, in the position which makes it absolutely impossible to define its direction. But that only lasted a moment: the bomb, coming faster and faster, nearer and nearer, so that the sparks of its fuse were already visible and its fatal whistle audible, descended towards the centre of the battalion.

'Lie down!' shouted someone.

Mikháylov and Praskúkhin lay flat on the ground. Praskúkhin, closing his eyes, only heard the bomb crash down on the hard earth close by. A second passed which seemed an hour: the bomb had not exploded. Praskúkhin was afraid. Perhaps he had played the coward for nothing. Perhaps the bomb had fallen far away and it only seemed to him that its fuse was fizzing close by. He opened his eyes and was pleased to see Mikháylov lying immovable at his feet. But at that moment he caught sight of the glowing fuse of the bomb which was spinning on the ground not a yard off. Terror, cold terror excluding every other thought and feeling, seized his whole being. He covered his face with his hands.

Another second passed – a second during which a whole world of feelings, thoughts, hopes, and memories flashed before his imagination.

'Whom will it hit – Mikháylov or me? Or both of us? And if it's me, where? In the head? Then I'm done for. But if it's the leg, they'll cut it off (I'll certainly ask for chloroform) and I may survive. But perhaps only Mikháylov will be hit. Then I will tell how we were going side by side and how he was killed and I was splashed with his blood. No, it's nearer to me . . . it will be I.'

Then he remembered the twelve rubles he owed Mikháylov, remembered also a debt in Petersburg that should have
been paid long ago, and the gipsy song he had sung that
evening. The woman he loved rose in his imagination wearing
a cap with lilac ribbons. He remembered a man who had
insulted him five years ago and whom he had not yet paid
out. And yet, inseparable from all these and thousands of other
recollections, the present thought, the expectation of death,
did not leave him for an instant. 'Perhaps it won't explode,'
and with desperate decision he resolved to open his eyes. But
at that instant a red flame pierced through the still closed lids
and something struck him in the middle of his chest with a
terrible crash. He jumped up and began to run, but stumbling
over the sabre that got between his legs he fell on his side.

'Thank God, I'm only bruised!' was his first thought, and he
was about to touch his chest with his hand, but his arms
seemed tied to his sides and he felt as if a vice were squeezing
his head. Soldiers flitted past him and he counted them unconsciously: 'One, two, three soldiers! And there's an officer with
his cloak tucked up,' he thought. Then lightning flashed
before his eyes and he wondered whether the shot was fired
from a mortar or a cannon. 'A cannon, probably. And there's
another shot and here are more soldiers – five, six, seven
soldiers.... They all pass by!' He was suddenly seized with
fear that they would crush him. He wished to shout that he
was hurt, but his mouth was so dry that his tongue clove to the
roof of his mouth and a terrible thirst tormented him. He felt a
wetness about his chest and this sensation of being wet made
him think of water, and he longed to drink even this that made
him feel wet. 'I suppose I hit myself in falling and made myself
bleed,' thought he, and giving way more and more to fear lest
the soldiers who kept flitting past might trample on him, he
gathered all his strength and tried to shout, 'Take me with
you!' but instead of that he uttered such a terrible groan that
the sound frightened him. Then some other red fires began
dancing before his eyes and it seemed to him that the soldiers
put stones on him. The fires danced less and less but the stones
they put on him pressed more and more heavily. He made an

effort to push off the stones, stretched himself, and saw and heard and felt nothing more. He had been killed on the spot by a bomb-splinter in the middle of his chest.

XIII

WHEN Mikháylov dropped to the ground on seeing the bomb he too, like Praskúkhin, lived through an infinitude of thoughts and feelings in the two seconds that elapsed before the bomb burst. He prayed mentally and repeated, 'Thy will be done.' And at the same time he thought, 'Why did I enter the army? And why did I join the infantry to take part in this campaign? Wouldn't it have been better to have remained with the Uhlan regiment at T— and spent my time with my friend Natásha? And now here I am ...' and he began to count, 'One, two, three, four,' deciding that if the bomb burst at an even number he would live but if at an odd number he would be killed. 'It is all over, I'm killed!' he thought when the bomb burst (he did not remember whether at an odd or even number) and he felt a blow and a cruel pain in his head. 'Lord, forgive me my trespasses!' he muttered, folding his hands. He rose, but fell on his back senseless.

When he came to, his first sensations were that of blood trickling down his nose, and the pain in his head which had become much less violent. 'That's the soul passing,' he thought. 'How will it be *there*? Lord, receive my soul in peace! ... Only it's strange,' thought he, 'that while dying I should hear the steps of the soldiers and the sounds of the firing so distinctly.'

'Bring stretchers! Eh, the captain has been hit!' shouted a voice above his head, which he recognized as the voice of the drummer Ignátyev.

Someone took him by the shoulders. With an effort he opened his eyes and saw above him the sky, some groups of stars, and two bombs racing one another as they flew over him. He saw Ignátyev, soldiers with stretchers and guns, the embankment, the trenches, and suddenly realized that he was not yet in the other world.

He had been slightly wounded in the head by a stone. His first feeling was one almost of regret: he had prepared himself so well and so calmly to go *there* that the return to reality, with its bombs, stretchers, and blood, seemed unpleasant. The second feeling was unconscious joy at being alive, and the third a wish to get away from the bastion as quickly as possible. The drummer tied a handkerchief round his commander's head and taking his arm led him towards the ambulance station.

'But why and where am I going?' thought the lieutenant-captain when he had collected his senses. 'My duty is to remain with the company and not leave it behind – especially,' whispered a voice, 'as it will soon be out of range of the guns.'

'Don't trouble about me, my lad,' said he, drawing his hand away from the attentive drummer. 'I won't go to the ambulance station: I'll stay with the company.'

And he turned back.

'It would be better to have it properly bandaged, your Honour,' said Ignátyev. 'It's only in the heat of the moment that it seems nothing. Mind it doesn't get worse. . . . And just see what warm work it is here. . . . Really, your Honour —'

Mikháylov stood for a moment undecided, and would probably have followed Ignátyev's advice had he not reflected how many severely wounded there must be at the ambulance station. 'Perhaps the doctors will smile at my scratch,' thought the lieutenant-captain, and in spite of the drummer's arguments he returned to his company.

'And where is the orderly officer Praskúkhin, who was with me?' he asked when he met the ensign who was leading the company.

'I don't know. Killed, I think,' replied the ensign unwillingly.

'Killed? Or only wounded? How is it you don't know? Wasn't he going with us? And why didn't you bring him away?'

'How could we, under such a fire?'

'But how could you do such a thing, Michael Iványch?' said Mikháylov angrily. 'How could you leave him supposing he is alive? Even if he's dead his body ought to have been brought away.'

'Alive indeed, when I tell you I went up and saw him myself!' said the ensign. 'Excuse me.... It's hard enough to collect our own. There, those villains are at it again!' he added. 'They're sending up cannon-balls now.'

Mikháylov sat down and lifted his hands to his head, which ached terribly when he moved.

'No, it is absolutely necessary to go back and fetch him,' he said. 'He may still be alive. It is our *duty*, Michael Iványch.'

Michael Iványch did not answer.

'O Lord! Just because he didn't bring him in at the time, soldiers will have to be sent back alone now...and yet can I possibly send them under this terrible fire? They may be killed for nothing,' thought Mikháylov.

'Lads! Someone will have to go back to fetch the officer who was wounded out there in the ditch,' said he, not very loudly or peremptorily, for he felt how unpleasant it would be for the soldiers to execute this order. And he was right. Since he had not named anyone in particular no one came forward to obey the order.

'And after all he may be dead already. It isn't worth exposing men uselessly to such danger. It's all my fault, I ought to have seen to it. I'll go back myself and find out whether he is alive. It is my *duty*,' said Mikháylov to himself.

'Michael Iványch, you lead the company, I'll catch you up,' said he, and holding up his cloak with one hand while with the other he kept touching a small icon of St Metrophanes that hung round his neck and in which he had great faith, he ran quickly along the trench.

Having convinced himself that Praskúkhin was dead he dragged himself back panting, holding the bandage that had slipped on his head, which was beginning to ache very badly. When he overtook the battalion it was already at the foot of the hill and almost beyond the range of the shots. I say 'almost', for a stray bomb reached even here now and then.

'To-morrow I had better go and be entered at the ambulance station,' thought the lieutenant-captain, while a medical assistant, who had turned up, was bandaging his head.

XIV

HUNDREDS of bodies, which a couple of hours before had been men full of various lofty or trivial hopes and wishes, were lying with fresh bloodstains on their stiffened limbs in the dewy, flowery valley which separated the bastions from the trenches and on the smooth floor of the mortuary chapel in Sevastopol. Hundreds of men with curses or prayers on their parched lips, crawled, writhed, and groaned, some among the dead in the flowery valley, some on stretchers, or beds, or on the blood-stained floor of the ambulance station. Yet the dawn broke behind the Sapún hill, the twinkling stars grew pale and the white mists spread from the dark roaring sea just as on other days, and the rosy morning glow lit up the east, long streaks of red clouds spread along the pale-blue horizon, and just as in the old days the sun rose in power and glory, promising joy, love, and happiness to all the awakening world.

XV

NEXT evening the Chasseurs' band was again playing on the boulevard, and officers, cadets, soldiers, and young women, again promenaded round the pavilion and along the side-walks under the acacias with their sweet-scented white blossoms.

Kalúgin was walking arm in arm with Prince Gáltsin and a colonel near the pavilion and talking of last night's affair. The main theme of their conversation, as usual in such cases, was not the affair itself, but the part each of the speakers had taken in it. Their faces and the tone of their voices were serious, almost sorrowful, as if the losses of the night had touched and saddened them all. But to tell the truth, as none of them had lost anyone very dear to him, this sorrowful expression was only an official one they considered it their duty to exhibit.

Kalúgin and the colonel in fact, though they were first-rate fellows, were ready to see such an affair every day if they could gain a gold sword and be made major-general each time. It is all very well to call some conqueror a monster because he destroys millions to gratify his ambition, but go and ask any

Ensign Petrúshev or Sub-Lieutenant Antónov on their conscience, and you will find that every one of us is a little
Napoleon, a petty monster ready to start a battle and kill a
hundred men merely to get an extra medal or one-third
additional pay.

'No, I beg your pardon,' said the colonel. 'It began first on
the left side. I was there myself.'

'Well, perhaps,' said Kalúgin. 'I spent more time on the
right. I went there twice: first to look for the general, and then
just to see the lodgements. It was hot there, I can tell you!'

'Kalúgin ought to know,' said Gáltsin. 'By the way, V—
told *me* to-day that you are a trump —'

'But the losses, the losses are terrible!' said the colonel. 'In
my regiment we had four hundred casualties. It is astonishing
that I'm still alive.'

Just then the figure of Mikháylov, with his head bandaged,
appeared at the end of the boulevard walking towards these
gentlemen.

'What, are you wounded, Captain?' said Kalúgin.

'Yes, slightly, with a stone,' answered Mikháylov.

'*Est-ce que le pavillon est baissé déjà?*'[1] asked Prince Gáltsin,
glancing at the lieutenant-captain's cap and not addressing
anyone in particular.

'*Non, pas encore,*'[2] answered Mikháylov, wishing to show
that he understood and spoke French.

'Do you mean to say the truce still continues?' said Gáltsin,
politely addressing him in Russian and thereby (so it seemed to
the lieutenant-captain) suggesting: 'It must no doubt be difficult for you to have to speak French, so hadn't we better
simply...' and with that the adjutants went away. The
lieutenant-captain again felt exceedingly lonely, just as he
had done the day before. After bowing to various people –
some of whom he did not wish and some of whom he did not
venture to join – he sat down near the Kazárski monument
and smoked a cigarette.

1 'Is the flag (of truce) lowered already?'
2 'No, not yet.'

Baron Pesth also turned up on the boulevard. He mentioned that he had been at the parley and had spoken to the French officers. According to his account one of them had said to him: '*S'il n'avait pas fait clair encore pendant une demi-heure, les ambuscades auraient été reprises,*'[1] and he replied, '*Monsieur, je ne dis pas non, pour ne pas vous donner un démenti,*'[2] and he told how pat it had come out, and so on.

But though he had been at the parley he had not really managed to say anything in particular, though he much wished to speak with the French ('for it's awfully jolly to speak to those fellows'). He had paced up and down the line for a long time asking the Frenchmen near him: '*De quel régiment êtes-vous?*'[3] and had got his answer and nothing more. When he went too far beyond the line, the French sentry, not suspecting that 'that soldier' knew French, abused him in the third person singular: '*Il vient regarder nos travaux, ce sacré —*'[4] in consequence of which Cadet Baron Pesth, finding nothing more to interest him at the parley, rode home, and on his way back composed the French phrases he now repeated.

On the boulevard was Captain Zóbov talking very loud, and Captain Obzhógov, the artillery captain who never curried favour with anyone, was there too, in a dishevelled condition, and also the cadet who was always fortunate in his love affairs, and all the same people as yesterday, with the same motives as always. Only Praskúkhin, Neférdov, and a few more were missing, and hardly anyone now remembered or thought of them, though there had not yet been time for their bodies to be washed, laid out, and put into the ground.

XVI

WHITE flags are hung out on our bastions and on the French trenches, and in the flowery valley between them lie heaps of

1 'Had it remained dark for another half-hour, the ambuscades would have been recaptured.'
2 'Sir, I will not say no, lest I give you the lie.'
3 'What regiment do you belong to?'
4 'He's come to look at our works, the confounded —'

mangled corpses without boots, some clad in blue and others in grey, which workmen are removing and piling onto carts. The air is filled with the smell of decaying flesh. Crowds of people have poured out from Sevastopol and from the French camp to see the sight, and with eager and friendly curiosity draw near to one another.

Listen to what these people are saying.

Here, in a circle of Russians and Frenchmen who have collected round him, a young officer, who speaks French badly but sufficiently to be understood, is examining a guardsman's pouch.

'*Eh sussy, poor quah se waso lié?*'[1]

'*Parce que c'est une giberne d'un régiment de la garde, monsieur, qui porte l'aigle impérial.*'[2]

'*Eh voo de la guard?*'[3]

'*Pardon, monsieur, du 6-ème de ligne.*'[4]

'*Eh sussy oo ashtay?*'[5] pointing to a cigarette-holder of yellow wood, in which the Frenchman is smoking a cigarette.

'*A Balaclava, monsieur. C'est tout simple en bois de palme.*'[6]

'*Joli,*'[7] says the officer, guided in his remarks not so much by what he wants to say as by the French words he happens to know.

'*Si vous voulez bien garder cela comme souvenir de cette rencontre, vous m'obligerez.*'[8]

And the polite Frenchman puts out his cigarette and presents the holder to the officer with a slight bow. The officer gives him his, and all present, both French and Russian, smile and seem pleased.

---

1 'And what is this tied bird for?'
2 'Because this is a cartridge pouch of a guard regiment, monsieur, and bears the Imperial eagle.'
3 'And do you belong to the Guards?'
4 'No, monsieur, to the 6th regiment of the line.'
5 'And where did you buy this?'
6 'At Balaclava, monsieur. It's only made of palm wood.'
7 'Pretty.'
8 'If you will be so good as to keep it as a souvenir of this meeting you will do me a favour.'

Here is a bold infantryman in a pink shirt with his cloak thrown over his shoulders, accompanied by other soldiers standing near him with their hands folded behind their backs and with merry inquisitive faces. He has approached a Frenchman and asked for a light for his pipe. The Frenchman draws at and stirs up the tobacco in his own short pipe and shakes a light into that of the Russian.

'*Tabac boon?*' says the soldier in the pink shirt, and the spectators smile. '*Oui, bon tabac, tabac turc,*' says the Frenchman. '*Chez vous autres tabac – Russe? Bon?*'[1]

'*Roos boon,*' says the soldier in the pink shirt while the onlookers shake with laughter. '*Fransay* not *boon. Bongjour, mossier!*', and having let off his whole stock of French at once, he slaps the Frenchman on the stomach and laughs. The French also laugh.

'*Ils ne sont pas jolis ces b— de Russes,*'[2] says a Zouave among the French.

'*De quoi est-ce qu'ils rient donc?*'[3] says another with an Italian accent, a dark man, coming up to our men.

'Coat *boon,*' says the cheeky soldier, examining the embroidery of the Zouave's coat, and everybody laughs again.

'*Ne sors pas de ta ligne, à vos places, sacré nom!*'[4] cries a French corporal, and the soldiers separate with evident reluctance.

And here, in the midst of a group of French officers, one of our young cavalry officers is gushing. They are talking about some Count Sazónov, '*que j'ai beaucoup connu, monsieur,*' says a French officer with only one epaulette – '*c'est un de ces vrais comtes russes, comme nous les aimons.*'[5]

'*Il y a un Sazónoff, que j'ai connu,*' says the cavalry officer, '*mais il n'est pas comte, à moins que je sache, un petit brun de votre âge à peu près.*'[6]

1 'Yes, good tobacco, Turkish tobacco... You others have Russian tobacco. Is it good?'
2 'They are not handsome, these d— Russians.'
3 'What are they laughing about?'
4 'Don't leave your ranks. To your places, damn it!'
5 'Whom I knew very intimately, monsieur. He is one of those real Russian counts of whom we are so fond.'
6 'I am acquainted with a Sazónov, but he is not a count, as far as I know – a small dark man, of about your age.'

'*C'est ça, monsieur, c'est lui. Oh! que je voudrais le voir, ce cher comte. Si vous le voyez, je vous prie bien de lui faire mes compliments – Capitaine Latour,*'[1] he said, bowing.

'*N'est-ce pas terrible la triste besogne que nous faisons? Ça chauffait cette nuit, n'est-ce pas?*'[2] said the cavalry officer, wishing to maintain the conversation and pointing to the corpses.

'*Oh, monsieur, c'est affreux! Mais quels gaillards vos soldats, quels gaillards! C'est un plaisir que de se battre avec des gaillards comme eux.*'[3]

'*Il faut avouer que les vôtres ne se mouchent pas du pied non plus,*'[4] said the cavalry officer, bowing and imagining himself very agreeable.

But enough.

Let us rather look at this ten-year-old boy in an old cap (probably his father's), with shoes on his stockingless feet and nankeen trousers held up by one brace. At the very beginning of the truce he came over the entrenchments, and has been walking about the valley ever since, looking with dull curiosity at the French and at the corpses that lie on the ground and gathering the blue flowers with which the valley is strewn. Returning home with a large bunch of flowers he holds his nose to escape the smell that is borne towards him by the wind, and stopping near a heap of corpses gazes for a long time at a terrible headless body that lies nearest to him. After standing there some time he draws nearer and touches with his foot the stiff outstretched arm of the corpse. The arm trembles a little. He touches it again more boldly; it moves and falls back to its old position. The boy gives a sudden scream, hides his face in his flowers, and runs towards the fortifications as fast as his legs can carry him.

---

1 'Just so, monsieur, that is he. Oh, how I should like to meet the dear count. If you should see him, please be so kind as to give him my compliments – Captain Latour.'
2 'Isn't it terrible, this sad duty we are engaged in? It was warm work last night, wasn't it?'
3 'Ah, monsieur, it is terrible! But what fine fellows your men are, what fine fellows! It is a pleasure to fight with such fellows!'
4 'It must be admitted that yours are no fools either.' (Literally, 'don't wipe their noses with their feet'.)

Yes, there are white flags on the bastions and the trenches but the flowery valley is covered with dead bodies. The glorious sun is sinking towards the blue sea, and the undulating blue sea glitters in the golden light. Thousands of people crowd together, look at, speak to, and smile at one another. And these people – Christians professing the one great law of love and self-sacrifice – on seeing what they have done do not at once fall repentant on their knees before Him who has given them life and laid in the soul of each a fear of death and a love of the good and the beautiful, and do not embrace like brothers with tears of joy and gladness.

The white flags are lowered, the engines of death and suffering are sounding again, innocent blood is flowing and the air is filled with moans and curses.

There, I have said what I wished to say this time. But I am seized by an oppressive doubt. Perhaps I ought to have left it unsaid. What I have said perhaps belongs to that class of evil truths that lie unconsciously hidden in the soul of each man and should not be uttered lest they become harmful, as the dregs in a bottle must not be disturbed for fear of spoiling the wine. . . .

Where in this tale is the evil that should be avoided, and where the good that should be imitated? Who is the villain and who the hero of the story? All are good and all are bad.

Not Kalúgin, with his brilliant courage – *bravoure de gentilhomme* – and the vanity that influences all his actions, not Praskúkhin, the empty harmless fellow (though he fell in battle for faith, throne, and fatherland), not Mikháylov with his shyness, nor Pesth, a child without firm principles or convictions, can be either the villain or the hero of the tale.

The hero of my tale – whom I love with all the power of my soul, whom I have tried to portray in all his beauty, who has been, is, and will be beautiful – is Truth.

SEVASTOPOL IN AUGUST 1855

I

TOWARDS the end of August, through the hot thick dust of the rocky and hilly highway between Duvánka[1] and Bakhchi-saráy, an officer's vehicle was slowly toiling towards Sevastopol (that peculiar kind of vehicle you never meet anywhere else – something between a Jewish *britzka*, a Russian cart, and a basket).

In the front of the trap, pulling at the reins, squatted an orderly in a nankeen coat and wearing a cap, now quite limp, that had once belonged to an officer: behind, on bundles and bales covered with a soldier's overcoat, sat an infantry officer in a summer cloak. The officer, as far as one could judge while he was sitting, was not tall but very broad and massive, not across the shoulders so much as from back to chest. His neck and the back of his head were much developed and very solid. He had no waist, and yet his body did not appear to be stout in that part: on the contrary he was rather lean, especially in the face, which was burnt to an unwholesome yellow. He would have been good-looking had it not been for a certain puffiness and the broad soft wrinkles, not due to age, that blurred the out-lines of his features, making them seem larger and giving the face a general look of coarseness and lack of freshness. His small eyes were hazel, with a daring and even insolent expression: he had very thick but not wide moustaches the ends of which were bitten off, and his chin and especially his jaws were covered with an exceedingly strong, thick, black stubble of two days' growth.

1 The last posting-station north of Sevastopol. L. T.

This officer had been wounded in the head by a bomb splinter on 10 May[1] and still wore a bandage, but having felt well again for the past week, he had left the hospital at Simferópol and was now on his way to rejoin his regiment stationed somewhere in the direction of the firing – but whether in Sevastopol itself, on the North Side, or at Inkerman, no one had yet been able to tell him for certain. The sound of frequent firing, especially at times when no hills intercepted it and the wind carried it this way, was already very distinct and seemed quite near. Now an explosion shook the air and made one start involuntarily, now less violent sounds followed one another in quick succession like the roll of drums, broken now and then by a startling boom, and now again all these sounds mingled into a kind of rolling crash, like peals of thunder when a storm is raging in all its fury and rain has just begun to fall in torrents. Everyone was remarking (and one could moreover hear for oneself) that a terrific bombardment was going on. The officer kept telling his orderly to drive faster; he seemed in a hurry to get to his destination. They met a train of Russian peasant-carts that had taken provisions to Sevastopol and were now returning laden with sick and wounded soldiers in grey uniforms, sailors in black cloaks, volunteers with red fezes on their heads, and bearded militiamen. The officer's trap had to stand still in the thick motionless cloud of dust raised by this train of carts and, frowning and blinking at the dust that filled his eyes, he sat looking at the faces of the sick and wounded as they drove past.

'There's a soldier of our company – that one who is so weak!' said the orderly, turning to his master and pointing to a cart laden with wounded men which had just come up to them.

A bearded Russian in a felt hat sat sideways in the front of the cart plaiting the lash of a whip, the handle of which he held to his side with his elbow. Behind him in the cart five or six soldiers were being jolted along, some lying and some sitting in

---

1 There were a series of desperate night conflicts on the 9 to 11 May o.s. (21 to 23 May n.s.).

different positions. One with a bandaged arm and his cloak thrown loosely over his very dirty shirt, though he looked pale and thin, sat upright in the middle of the cart and raised his hand as if to salute the officer, but probably remembering that he was wounded, pretended that he only meant to scratch his head. Beside him on the bottom of the cart lay a man of whom all that was visible was his two hands holding on to the sides of the cart and his lifted knees swaying to and fro like rags. A third, whose face was swollen and who had a soldier's cap stuck on the top of his bandaged head, sat on the side of the cart with his legs hanging down over the wheel, and, resting his elbows on his knees, seemed to be dozing. The officer addressed him: 'Dolzhnikóv!' he cried.

'Here!' answered the soldier, opening his eyes and taking off his cap and speaking in such a deep and abrupt bass that it sounded as if twenty soldiers had shouted all together.

'When were you wounded, lad?'

The soldier's leaden eyes with their swollen lids brightened. He had evidently recognized his officer.

'Good-day, your Honour!' said he in the same abrupt bass.

'Where is your regiment stationed now?'

'In Sevastopol. We were going to move on Wednesday, your Honour!'

'Where to?'

'Don't know, your Honour – to the North Side, maybe. . . . Now they're firing right across, your Honour!' he added in a long-drawn tone, replacing his cap. 'Mostly bombs – they reach us right across the bay. *He's* giving it us awful hot now . . .'

What the soldier said further could not be heard, but the expression of his face and his pose showed that his words, spoken with the bitterness of one suffering, were not reassuring.

The officer in the trap, Lieutenant Kozeltsóv, was not an ordinary type of man. He was not one of those who live and act this way or that because others live and act so: he did what he chose, and others followed his example and felt sure it was right. He was by nature endowed with many minor gifts: he sang well, played the guitar, talked to the point, and wrote very easily (especially official papers – a knack for writing which he had acquired when he was adjutant of his battalion), but his most remarkable characteristic was his ambitious energy, which though chiefly founded on those same minor talents was in itself a marked and striking feature. He had ambition of a kind most frequently found among men and especially in military circles, and this had become so much a part of his life that he could imagine no other course than to lead or to perish. Ambition was at the root of his innermost impulses and even in his private thoughts he liked to put himself first when he compared himself with others.

'It's likely I should pay attention to the chatter of a private!' he muttered, with a feeling of heaviness and apathy at heart and a certain dimness of thought left by the sight of the convoy of wounded men and the words of the soldier, enforced as they were by the sounds of the cannonade.

'Funny fellow, that soldier! Now then, Nikoláev, get on!... Are you asleep?' he added rather fretfully as he arranged the skirt of his cloak.

Nikoláev jerked the reins, clicked his tongue, and the trap rolled on at a trot.

'We'll only stop just to feed the horse, and then go on at once, to-night,' said the officer.

II

WHEN he was entering what was left of a street of ruined stone Tartar houses in Duvánka, Lieutenant Kozeltsóv was stopped by a convoy of bombs and cannon-balls on its way to Sevastopol, that blocked the road.

Two infantrymen sat on the stones of a ruined wall amid a cloud of dust, eating a water-melon and some bread.

'Going far, comrade?' asked one of them, with his mouth full of bread, as another soldier with a little bag on his back stopped beside them.

'Going to join our regiment,' answered the soldier, looking past the water-melon and readjusting his bag. 'We've been nearly three weeks in the province looking for hay for our company, and now we've all been recalled, but we don't know where the regiment is. Some say it crossed to the Korábelnaya last week. Perhaps you have heard, friends?'

'In the town, mate. It's quartered in the town,' muttered the other, an old convoy soldier who was digging a clasp-knife into an unripe, whitish water-melon. 'We only left there this afternoon. [It's so awful there, mate, you'd better not go, but fall down here somewhere among the hay and lie there for a day or two!]'

'What do you mean, friend?'

'Why, can't you hear? They're firing from all sides today, there's not a place left whole. As for the likes of us as has been killed – there's no counting 'em!' And making an expressive gesture with his hand, the speaker set his cap straight.

The soldier who had stopped shook his head thoughtfully and clicked his tongue, then he took a pipe out of the leg of his boot, and not filling it but merely loosening the scorched tobacco in it, he lit a bit of tinder at the pipe of one of the others. Then he raised his cap and said:

'One can't get away from God, friends! Good-bye.' And straightening his bag with a jerk he went his way.

'It would be far better to wait!' the man who was digging into the water-melon said with conviction.

'It can't be helped!' muttered the newcomer, as he squeezed between the wheels of the crowded carts. ['It seems I too must buy a water-melon for my supper. Just think what people are saying!']

III

THE post-station was full of people when Kozeltsóv drove up. The first one he met in the porch was a very thin young man, the superintendent, bickering with two officers who were following him.

'It's not only three days you'll have to wait but maybe ten.... Even generals have to wait, my good sir!' said the superintendent, evidently wishing to hurt the travellers' feelings. 'I can't hitch myself to a cart for you, can I?'

'Then don't give horses to anyone, if you have none! Why did you give them to that lackey with the baggage?' shouted the elder of the officers, who had a tumbler of tea in his hand.

'Just consider a moment, Mr Superintendent,' said the other, a very young officer, hesitatingly. 'We are not going for our own pleasure. You see, we are evidently wanted there, since we have been summoned. I shall really have to report it to the general. It will never do, you know.... It seems you don't respect an officer's position.'

But the elder man interrupted him crossly. 'You always spoil everything! You only hinder me ... a man has to know how to speak to these people. There you see, he has lost all respect.... Horses, I say, this very minute!'

'Willingly, my dear sir, but where am I to get them from?'

The superintendent was silent for a few minutes. Then he suddenly flared up and waving his arms began:

'I know it all very well, my dear sir, and fully understand it, but what am I to do? You give me but' (a ray of hope showed itself on the faces of the officers) ... 'let me but hold out to the end of the month, and I'll stay here no longer. I'd rather go to the Malákhov Hill than remain here, I swear I would! Let them do what they please. There's not a single sound vehicle left in the whole place, and it's the third day the horses haven't had a wisp of hay.' And the superintendent disappeared through the gate.

Kozeltsóv entered the room together with the officers.

'Well,' said the elder calmly to the younger, though the moment before he had seemed quite beside himself, 'we've been three months on the road already and can wait a bit longer. No matter, we'll get there soon enough!'

The dirty, smoky room was so full of officers and trunks that Kozeltsóv had some difficulty in finding a seat on the window-sill. While observing the faces and listening to the conversation of the others he began rolling himself a cigarette. To the right of the door sat the principal group round a crooked, greasy table on which stood two samovars with verdigris showing on them here and there, and with sugar spread on various bits of paper. A young officer who had not yet grown a moustache, in a new, quilted Caucasian coat which had certainly been made out of a woman's dressing-gown, was filling a teapot, and there were four other equally young officers in different parts of the room. One of them lay asleep on the sofa with a fur coat of some kind rolled up under his head; another was standing at the table cutting up some roast mutton for a one-armed officer who sat there. Two officers, one in an adjutant's cloak, the other in infantry uniform made of fine cloth and with a satchel across his shoulders, were sitting by the stove, and from the way they looked at the others and the manner in which the one with the satchel smoked his cigar, it was plain that they were not officers of the line and were glad they were not. Their manner did not show contempt so much as a certain calm self-satisfaction founded partly on money and partly on intimacy with generals – a consciousness of superiority extending even to a desire to conceal it. Then there was a thick-lipped young doctor and an artillery officer who looked like a German – these were sitting on the sofa almost on the feet of the sleeping officer, counting money. There were also several orderlies, some dozing, others near the door busy with bundles and portmanteaux. Among all these people Kozeltsóv did not recognize a single acquaintance, but he listened with interest to their conversation. He liked the young officers who, as he at once concluded from their appearance, had come straight from the Cadet College; they reminded him of the fact that his brother, who was coming straight from the College too, ought to reach one of the batteries in Sevastopol in a few days' time. But he did not like the officer with the satchel, whose face he had seen somewhere before – everything about him seemed insolent and repellent. 'We'll put him down if he ventures to say anything!' he thought, and he even moved from the window to the stove and sat down there. Belonging to a line regiment and being a good officer, he had a general dislike for those 'on the Staff', and such he at once recognized these officers to be.

IV

'I SAY, isn't it an awful nuisance that being so near we can't get there?' said one of the young officers. 'There may be an action to-day and we shan't be in it.'

The high-pitched voice and the fresh rosy spots which appeared on his face betrayed the charming youthful bashfulness of one in constant fear of not saying the right thing.

The officer who had lost an arm looked at him with a smile.

'You'll get there soon enough, believe me,' he said.

The young officer looked respectfully at the crippled man, whose emaciated face suddenly lit up with a smile, and then silently turned his attention to making his tea. And really the face, the attitude, and especially the empty sleeve of the officer expressed a kind of calm indifference that seemed to say in reply to every word and action: 'Yes, all that is admirable, but I know it all, and can do it all if only I wish to.'

'Well, and how shall we decide it?' the young officer began again, turning to his comrade in the Caucasian coat. 'Shall we stay the night here or go on with our own horse?'

His comrade decided to stay.

'Just fancy, Captain,' continued the one who was making the tea, addressing the one-armed officer and handing him a knife he had dropped, 'we are told that horses were awfully dear in Sevastopol, so we two bought one together in Simferópol.'

'I expect they made you pay a stiff price.'

'I really don't know, Captain. We paid ninety rubles for it with the trap. Is that very much?' he said, turning to the company in general, including Kozeltsóv, who was looking at him.

'It's not much if it's a young horse,' said Kozeltsóv.

'You think not?... And we were told it was too much. Only it limps a bit, but that will pass. We were told it's strong.'

'What Cadet College were you at?' asked Kozeltsóv, who wished to get news of his brother.

'We are now from the Nobles' Regiment. There are six of us and we are all going to Sevastopol – by our own desire,' said the talkative young officer. 'Only we don't know where our battery is. Some say it is Sevastopol, but those fellows there say it's in Odessa.'

'Couldn't you have found out in Simferópol?' asked Kozeltsóv.

'They didn't know.... Only think, one of our comrades went to the Chancellery there and got nothing but rudeness.

Just think how unpleasant! Would you like a ready-made cigarette?' he said to the one-armed officer who was trying to get out his cigar-case.

He attended to this officer's wants with a kind of servile enthusiasm.

'And are you from Sevastopol too?' he continued. 'How wonderful it is! How all of us in Petersburg used to think about you all and all our heroes!' he said, addressing Kozeltsóv with respect and kindly affection.

'Well then, you may find that you have to go back?' asked the lieutenant.

'That's just what we are afraid of. Just fancy, when we had bought the horse and got all we needed – a coffee-pot with a spirit-lamp and other necessary little things – we had no money left at all,' he said in a low tone, glancing at his comrade, 'so that if we have to return we don't at all know how we are to manage.'

'Didn't you receive your travelling allowance, then?' asked Kozeltsóv.

'No,' answered the young officer in a whisper, 'they promised to give it us here.'

'Have you the certificate?'

'I know that a certificate is the principal thing, but when I was in Moscow, a senator – he's my uncle and I was at his house – told me they would give it to me here, or else he would have given it me himself. But will they give me one in Sevastopol?'

'Certainly they will.'

'Yes, I think so too,' said the lad in a tone which showed that, having asked the same question at some thirty other post-stations and having everywhere received different answers, he did not now quite believe anyone.

V

['How can they help giving it?' suddenly remarked the officer who had quarrelled with the station-master on the porch and had now approached the speakers, addressing himself partly to the staff-officers who were sitting near by, as to listeners more worthy of attention. 'Why, I myself wanted to join the active army just as these gentlemen do. I even gave up a splendid post and asked to be sent right into Sevastopol. And they gave me nothing but a hundred and thirty-six rubles for post-horses from Petersburg and I have already spent more than a hundred and fifty rubles of my own money. Only think of it! It's only eight hundred versts and this is the third month we have been on the way. I have been travelling with these gentlemen here for two months. A good thing I had money of my own, but suppose I hadn't had any?'

'The third month? Is it possible?' someone asked.

'Yes, and what can one do?' the speaker continued. 'You see if I had not wanted to go I would not have volunteered and left a good post, so I haven't been stopping at places on the road because I was afraid. . . . It was just impossible. For instance I lived a fortnight in Perekóp, and the station-master wouldn't even speak to me. . . . "Go when you like; here are a whole pile of requisition forms for couriers alone." . . . It must be my fate. . . . You see I want – but it's just my fate. It's not because there's a bombardment going on, but it evidently makes no difference whether one hurries or not – and yet how I should like. . . .'

The officer was at such pains to explain his delays and seemed so keen to vindicate himself that it involuntarily occurred to one that he was afraid. This was still more evident when he began to ask where his regiment was, and whether it was dangerous there. He even grew pale and his voice faltered when the one-armed officer, who belonged to the same regiment, told him that during those last two days they had lost seventeen officers.

In fact this officer was just then a thorough coward, though six months previously he had been very different. A change had come over him which many others experienced both before and after him. He had had an excellent and quiet post in one of our provincial towns in which there is a Cadet College, but reading in the papers and in private letters of the heroic deeds performed at Sevastopol by his former comrades, he was suddenly inspired by ambition and still more by patriotic heroism.

He sacrificed much to this feeling: his well-established position, his little home with its comfortable furniture painstakingly acquired by five years' effort, his acquaintances, and his hopes of making a good marriage. He threw all this up, and in February already had volunteered for active service, dreaming of deathless honours and of a general's epaulettes. Two months after he had sent in his application he received an official inquiry whether he would require assistance from the government. He replied in the negative, and continued to wait patiently for an appointment, though his patriotic ardour had had time to cool considerably during those eight weeks. After another two months he received an inquiry as to whether he belonged to a Freemasons' Lodge,[1] and other similar questions, and having replied in the negative, he at last, in the fifth month, received his appointment. But all that time his friends, and still more that subconscious feeling which always awakens at any change in one's position, had had time to convince him that he was committing an act of extreme folly by entering the active army. And when he found himself alone, with a dry throat and his face covered with dust, at the first post-station – where he met a courier from Sevastopol who told him of the horrors of the war, and where he had to spend twelve hours waiting for relay horses – he quite repented of his thoughtlessness, reflecting with vague horror on what awaited him, and without realizing it continued on his way as to a sacrifice. This feeling constantly increased during his three months' travelling from station to station, at which he always had to wait and where he met officers returning from Sevastopol with dreadful stories, and at last this poor officer – from being a hero prepared for desperate deeds, as in the provincial town he had imagined himself to be – arrived in Djánka

1 A number of Freemasons were involved in the Decembrist mutiny in 1825, when Nicholas I ascended the throne. He was consequently very suspicious of that organization, which at the time of the Crimean War was prohibited in Russia. The inquiry made would therefore be offensive to a loyal and patriotic volunteer.

a wretched coward, and having a month ago come across some young fellows from the Cadet College, he tried to travel as slowly as possible, considering these days to be his last on earth, and at every station put up his bed, unpacked his canteen, played preference, looked through the station complaint-book for amusement, and felt glad when horses were not to be had.

Had he gone at once from home to the bastions he would really have been a hero, but now he would have to go through much moral suffering before he could become such a calm, patient man, facing toil and danger, as Russian officers generally are. But it would by this time have been difficult to reawaken enthusiasm in him.]

VI

'WHO ordered soup?' demanded the landlady, a rather dirty, fat woman of about forty, as she came into the room with a tureen of cabbage-soup.

The conversation immediately stopped, and everyone in the room fixed his eyes on the landlady. One officer even winked to another with a glance at her.

'Oh, Kozeltsóv ordered it,' said the young officer. 'We must wake him up. . . . Get up for dinner!' he said, going up to the sofa and shaking the sleeper's shoulder. A lad of about seventeen, with merry black eyes and very rosy cheeks, jumped up energetically and stepped into the middle of the room rubbing his eyes.

'Oh, I beg your pardon,' he said to the doctor, whom he had knocked against in rising.

Lieutenant Kozeltsóv at once recognized his brother and went up to him.

'Don't you know me?' he asked with a smile.

'Ah-h-h!' cried the younger Kozeltsóv. 'This is wonderful!' And he began kissing his brother.

They kissed three times, but hesitated before the third kiss, as if the thought, 'Why has it to be just three times?' had struck them both.

'Well, I *am* glad!' said the elder, looking into his brother's face. 'Come out into the porch and let's have a chat.'

'Yes, come along. I don't want any soup. You eat it, Féderson,' he said to his comrade.

'But you wanted something to eat.'

'I don't want anything now.'

Out on the porch the younger one kept asking his brother: 'Well, and how are you? Tell me how things are!' and saying how glad he was to see him, but he did not tell him anything about himself.

When five minutes had passed and they had paused for a moment, the elder brother asked why the younger had not entered the Guards as everyone had expected him to do.

['Oh, yes!' the younger replied, blushing at the very recollection, 'that upsets me terribly. I never expected such a thing could happen. Just imagine, at the very end of the term three of us went to have a smoke – you remember that little room by the hall-porter's lodge? It must have been there in your time – but just imagine, that beast of a hall-porter saw us and ran to tell the officer on duty (though we had tipped that porter several times) and the officer crept up on tiptoe. As soon as we noticed him the others threw away their cigarettes and bolted out by the side door – you know – but I hadn't the chance. The officer was very nasty to me, and of course I answered him back. Well, he told the Inspector, and there was a row. Because of that, you see, they didn't give me full marks for conduct, though for everything else my marks were excellent, except for mechanics, for which I got twelve. And so they wouldn't let me enter the Guards. They promised to transfer me later . . . but I no longer wanted it, and applied to be sent to the front.'

'Dear me!'

'Really, I tell you seriously, I was so disgusted with everything that] I wanted to get to Sevastopol as quickly as possible. And you see, if things turn out well here one can get on quicker than in the Guards. There it takes ten years to become a colonel, but here in two years Todleben from a lieutenant-colonel has become a general. And if one gets killed – well, it can't be helped.'

'So that's the sort of stuff you are made of!' said his brother, with a smile.

'But the chief thing, you know,' said the younger brother, smiling and blushing as if he were going to say something very shameful – 'the chief thing was that I felt rather ashamed to be living in Petersburg while here men are dying for the Fatherland. And besides, I wanted to be with you,' he added, still more shyly.

The other did not look at him. 'What a funny fellow you are!' he said, taking out his cigarette-case. 'Only the pity is that we shan't be together.'

'I say, tell me quite frankly: is it very dreadful at the bastions?' asked the younger suddenly.

'It seems dreadful at first but one gets used to it. You'll see for yourself.'

'Yes . . . and another thing: Do you think they will take Sevastopol? I don't think they will. I'm certain they won't.'

'Heaven only knows.'

'It's so provoking. . . . Just think what a misfortune! Do you know, we've had a whole bundle of things stolen on the way and my shako was inside so that I am in a terrible position. Whatever shall I appear in? [You know we have new shakos now, and in general there are many changes, all improvements. I can tell you all about it. I have been everywhere in Moscow.]'

The younger Kozeltsóv, Vladímir, was very like his brother Michael, but it was the likeness of an opening rosebud to a withered dog-rose. He had the same fair hair as his brother, but it was thick and curled about his temples, and a little tuft of it grew down the delicate white nape of his neck – a sign of luck according to the nurses. The delicate white skin of his face did not always show colour, but the full young blood rushing to it betrayed his every emotion. His eyes were like his brother's, but more open and brighter, and seemed especially so because a slight moisture often made them glisten. Soft, fair down was beginning to appear on his cheeks and above the red lips, on which a shy smile often played disclosing his white and glistening teeth. Straight, broad-shouldered, the uniform over his red Russian shirt unbuttoned – as he stood there before his brother, cigarette in hand, leaning against the banisters of the porch, his face and attitude expressing naïve joy, he was such a charming, handsome boy that one could not help wishing to look at him. He was very pleased to see his brother, and looked at him with respect and pride, imagining him to be a hero; but in some respects, namely, in what in society is considered good form (being able to speak good French, knowing how to behave in the presence of people of high position, dancing, and so on) he was rather ashamed of his brother, looked down on him, and even hoped if possible to educate him. All his views were still those he had acquired in Petersburg, particularly in the house of a lady who liked good-looking lads and had got him to spend his holidays at her house; and at a senator's house in Moscow, where he had once danced at a grand ball.

VII

HAVING talked almost their fill, and reached that stage which often comes when two people find that though they are fond of one another they have little in common, the brothers remained silent for some time.

'Well then, collect your things and let us be off!' said the elder.

The younger suddenly blushed and became confused.

'Do we go straight to Sevastopol?' he asked after a moment's silence.

'Well of course. You haven't got much luggage, I suppose. We'll get it all in.'

'All right! Let's start at once,' said the younger with a sigh, and went towards the room.

But he stopped in the passage without opening the door, hung his head sorrowfully and began thinking.

'Now, at once, straight to Sevastopol . . . into that hell . . . terrible! Ah well, never mind. It had to be sooner or later. And now at least I'll have my brother with me. . . .'

In fact, only now, at the thought that after getting into the trap there would be nothing more to detain him and that he would not alight again before reaching Sevastopol, did he clearly realize the danger he had been seeking, and he grew confused and frightened at the mere thought of the nearness of that danger. Having mastered himself as well as he could, he went into the room; but a quarter of an hour passed and he did not return to his brother, so the latter at last opened the door to call him. The younger Kozeltsóv, in the attitude of a guilty schoolboy, was talking to an officer. When his brother opened the door he seemed quite disconcerted.

'Yes, yes, I'm just coming!' he cried, waving his hand to prevent his brother coming in. 'Please wait for me there.'

A few minutes later he came out and went up to his brother with a sigh. 'Just fancy,' he said, 'it turns out that I can't go with you, after all!'

'What? What nonsense!'

'I'll tell you the whole truth, Mísha . . . none of us have any money left and we are all in debt to that lieutenant-captain whom you saw in there. It's such a shame!'

The elder brother frowned, and remained silent for some time.

'Do you owe much?' he asked at last, looking at his brother from under his brows.

'Much? No, not very much, but I feel terribly ashamed. He paid for me at three post-stations, and the sugar was always his, so that I don't. . . . Yes, and we played preference . . . and I lost a little to him.'

'That's bad, Volódya! Now what would you have done if you hadn't met me?' the elder remarked sternly without looking at him.

'Well, you see, I thought I'd pay when I got my travelling allowance in Sevastopol. I could do that, couldn't I? . . . So I'd better drive on with him to-morrow.'

The elder brother drew out his purse and with slightly trembling fingers produced two ten-ruble notes and one of three rubles.

'There's the money I have,' he said. 'How much do you owe?'

Kozeltsóv did not speak quite truly when he made it appear as if this were all the money he had. He had four gold coins sewn into his cuff in case of special need, but he had resolved not to touch them.

As it turned out the younger Kozeltsóv owed only eight rubles, including the sugar and the preference, his brother gave them to him, merely remarking that it would never do to go playing preference when one had no money.

'How high did you play?'

The younger did not reply. The question seemed to suggest a doubt of his honour.

Vexed with himself, ashamed of having done anything that could give rise to such suspicions, and hurt at such offensive words from the brother he so loved, his impressionable nature suffered so keenly that he did not answer. Feeling that he could not suppress the sobs that were gathering in his throat he took the money without looking at it and returned to his comrades.

VIII

NIKOLÁEV, who had fortified himself in Duvánka with two cups of vodka[1] sold by a soldier he had met on the bridge, kept pulling at the reins, and the trap bumped along the stony road that leads by the Belbék[2] to Sevastopol. The two brothers, their legs touching as they jolted along, sat in obstinate silence though they never ceased to think about each other.

'Why did he say that?' thought the younger. 'Couldn't he have left it unsaid? Just as if he thought me a thief! And I believe he's still angry, so that we have gone apart for good. And yet how fine it would have been for us to be together in Sevastopol! Two brothers, friends with one another, fighting the enemy side by side: one, the elder, not highly educated but a brave warrior, and the other young but ... also a fine fellow. . . . In a week's time I would have proved to everybody that I am not so very young! I shall leave off blushing and my

1 Vodka is a spirit distilled from rye. It is the commonest form of strong drink in Russia.
2 The Belbék is a river.

face will look manly; my moustaches, too, will have grown by that time – not very big but quite sufficiently,' and he pulled at the short down that showed at the corners of his mouth. 'Perhaps when we get there to-day we may go straight into action, he and I together. And I'm certain he is very brave and steadfast – a man who says little, but does more than others. I wonder whether he is pushing me to the very edge of the trap on purpose? I expect he knows I am uncomfortable but pretends he doesn't notice me.' Pressing close to the edge of the trap for fear of his brother's noticing his discomfort, he continued his meditations: 'Well then, we shall get there to-day, and then perhaps straight to the bastion – I with the guns and my brother with his company, both together. Suddenly the French will fall upon us. I shall fire and fire. I shall kill quite a lot of them, but they will still keep coming straight at me. I can no longer fire and of course there is no escape for me, but suddenly my brother rushes to the front with his sword drawn and I seize a musket, and we run on with the soldiers. The French attack my brother: I run forward, kill one Frenchman, then another, and save my brother. I am wounded in the arm, I seize the gun in the other hand and still run on. Then my brother falls at my side, shot dead by a bullet. I stop for a moment, bend sadly over him, draw myself up and cry: "Follow me, we will avenge him! I loved my brother more than anything on earth," I shall say. "I have lost him. Let us avenge him, let us annihilate the foe or let us all die here!" They will all rush after me shouting. Then all the French army, with Pélissier himself, will advance. We shall slaughter them, but at last I shall be wounded a second and a third time and shall fall down dying. Then they will all rush to me and Gorchakóv himself will come and ask if I want anything. I shall say that I want nothing – only to be laid near my brother: that I wish to die beside him. They will carry me and lay me down by the blood-stained corpse of my brother. I shall raise myself, and say only, "Yes, you did not know how to value two men who really loved the Fatherland: now they have both fallen. May God forgive you!" . . . and then I'll die.'

Who knows how much of these dreams will come true?

'I say, have you ever been in a hand-to-hand fight?' he suddenly asked, having quite forgotten that he was not going to speak to his brother.

'No, never,' answered the elder. 'We lost two thousand men from the regiment, but it was all at the trenches, and I was wounded while doing my work there. War is not carried on at all in the way you imagine, Volódya.'

The pet name Volódya touched the younger brother. He longed to put matters right with the elder, who had no idea that he had given offence.

'You are not angry with me, Mísha?' he asked after a minute's pause.

'Angry? What for?'

'Oh, nothing...only because of what happened...it's nothing.'

'Not at all,' answered the other, turning towards him and slapping him on the knee.

'Then forgive me if I have pained you, Mísha!' And the younger brother turned away to hide the tears that suddenly filled his eyes.

IX

'CAN this be Sevastopol already?' asked the younger brother when they reached the top of the hill.

Spread out before them they saw the Roadstead with the masts of the ships, the sea with the enemy's fleet in the distance, the white shore-batteries, the barracks, the aqueducts, the docks, the buildings of the town, and the white and purple clouds of smoke that, rising continually from the yellow hills surrounding the town, floated in the blue sky lit up by the rosy rays of the sun, which was reflected brilliantly in the sea towards whose dark horizon it was already sinking.

Volódya looked without the slightest trepidation at the dreadful place that had so long been in his mind. He even gazed with concentrated attention at this really splendid and unique sight, feeling aesthetic pleasure and a heroic sense of satisfaction at the thought that in another half-hour he would be there, and he continued gazing until they came to the commissariat of his brother's regiment, on the North Side, where they had to ascertain the exact location of the regiment and of the battery.

The officer in charge of the commissariat lived near the so-called 'new town' (a number of wooden sheds constructed by the sailors' families) in a tent connected with a good-sized shed constructed of green oak branches that had not yet had time to dry completely.

The brothers found the officer seated at a dirty table on which stood a tumbler of cold tea, a tray with a vodka bottle, and bits of dry caviare and bread. He was wearing a dirty yellowish shirt, and, with the aid of a big abacus, was counting an enormous pile of bank-notes. But before speaking of the personality of this officer and of his conversation, we must examine the interior of the shed more attentively and see something of his occupations and way of living. His newly built shed was as big, as strongly wattled, and as conveniently arranged with tables and seats made of turf, as though it were built for a general or the commander of a regiment. To keep the dry leaves from falling in, the top and sides were lined with three carpets, which though hideous were new and must have cost money. On the iron bedstead, beside which a most striking carpet was fastened to the wall (the pattern of which represented a lady on horseback), lay a bright red plush coverlet, a torn and dirty leather pillow, and an overcoat lined with racoon fur. On the table was a looking-glass in a silver frame, an exceedingly dirty silver-backed hair-brush, a broken horn comb full of greasy hair, a silver candlestick, a bottle of liqueur with an enormous red and gold label, a gold watch with a portrait of Peter I, two gold rings, a box of some kind of capsules, a crust of bread, and a scattered pack of old cards. Bottles, full and empty, were stowed away under the bed. This officer was in charge of the regimental commissariat and the forage for the horses. With him lived his great friend, the commissioner employed on contracts. When the brothers entered, the latter was asleep in the tent while the commissariat officer was making up the regimental accounts for the month.

He had a very handsome and military appearance: tall, with large moustaches and a portly figure. What was unpleasant about him was merely that his white face was so puffy as almost to hide his small grey eyes (as if he were filled with porter), and his extreme lack of cleanliness, from his thin greasy hair to his big bare feet thrust into ermine-lined slippers of some kind.

'What a heap of money!' said the elder Kozeltsóv on entering the shed, as he fixed his eyes eagerly on the pile of bank-notes. 'If only you'd lend me half, Vasíli Mikháylovich!'

The commissariat officer shrank back when he saw his visitor, as if caught stealing, and gathering up the money bowed without rising.

'Oh, if it were mine! But it's Government money, my dear fellow. . . . And who is that with you?' he asked, placing the money in a cash-box that stood near him and looking at Volódya.

'It's my brother, straight from the training college. We've come to learn from you where our regiment is stationed.'

'Take a seat, gentlemen. Won't you have something to drink? A glass of porter perhaps?' he said, and without taking any further notice of his visitors he rose and went out into the tent.

'I don't mind if I do, Vasíli Mikháylovich.'

Volódya was struck by the grandeur of the commissariat officer, his off-hand manner, and the respect with which his brother addressed him.

'I expect this is one of their best officers, whom they all respect – probably simple-minded but hospitable and brave,' he thought as he sat down modestly and shyly on the sofa.

'Then where is our regiment stationed?' shouted the elder brother across to the tent.

'What?'

The question was repeated.

'Seifert was here this morning. He says the regiment has gone over to the Fifth Bastion.'

'Is that certain?'

'If I say so of course it's certain. Still, the devil only knows if he told the truth! It wouldn't take much to make him tell a lie either. Well, will you have some porter?' said the commissariat officer, still speaking from the tent.

'Well, yes, I think I will,' said Kozeltsóv.

'And you, Osip Ignátevich, will you have some?' continued the voice from the tent, apparently addressing the sleeping contractor. 'Wake up, it's past four!'

'Why do you bother me? I'm not asleep,' answered a thin voice lazily, pronouncing the *ls* and *rs* with a pleasant lisp.

'Well, get up, it's dull without you,' and the commissariat officer came out to his visitors.

'A bottle of Simferópol porter!' he cried.

The orderly entered the shed with an expression of pride as it seemed to Volódya, and in getting the porter from under the seat he even jostled Volódya.

['Yes, sir,' said the commissariat officer, filling the glasses. 'We have a new commander of the regiment now. Money is needed to get all that is required.'

'Well, this one is quite a special type of the new generation,' remarked Kozeltsóv, politely raising his glass.

'Yes, of a new generation! He'll be just as close-fisted as the battalion-commander was. How he used to shout when he was in command! But now he sings a different tune.'

'Can't be helped, old fellow. It just is so.'

The younger brother understood nothing of what was being said, but vaguely felt that his brother was not expressing what he thought, and spoke in that way only because he was drinking the commissariat officer's porter.]

The bottle of porter was already emptied and the conversation had continued for some time in the same strain, when the flap of the tent opened and out stepped a rather short, fresh-looking man in a blue satin dressing-gown with tassels and a cap with a red band and a cockade. He came in twisting his little black moustaches, looking somewhere in the direction of one of the carpets, and answered the greetings of the officers with a scarcely perceptible movement of the shoulders.

'I think I'll have a glass too,' he said, sitting down to the table.

'Have you come from Petersburg, young man?' he remarked, addressing Volódya in a friendly manner.

'Yes, sir, and I'm going to Sevastopol.'

'At your own request?'

'Yes, sir.'

'Now why do you do it, gentlemen? I don't understand it,' remarked the commissioner. 'I'd be ready to walk to Petersburg on foot, I think, if they'd let me go. My God, I'm sick of this damned life!'

'What have you to complain of?' asked the elder Kozeltsóv – 'As if you weren't well enough off here!'

The contractor gave him a look and turned away.

'The danger, privations, lack of everything,' he continued, addressing Volódya. 'Whatever induces you to do it? I don't at all understand you, gentlemen. If you got any profit out of it – but no! Now would it be pleasant, at your age, to be crippled for life?'

'Some want to make a profit and others serve for honour,' said the elder Kozeltsóv crossly, again intervening in the conversation.

'Where does the honour come in if you've nothing to eat?' said the contractor, laughing disdainfully and addressing the commissariat officer, who also laughed. 'Wind up and let's have the tune from *Lucia*,' he added, pointing to a musical box. 'I like it.'

'What sort of a fellow is that Vasíli Mikháylovich?' asked Volódya when he and his brother had left the shed and were driving to Sevastopol in the dusk of the evening.

'So-so, but terribly stingy! [You know he gets at least three hundred rubles a month, but lives like a pig, as you saw.] But that contractor I can't bear to look at. I'll give him a thrashing some day! [Why, that rascal carried off some twelve thousand rubles from Turkey. . . .'

And Kozeltsóv began to enlarge on the subject of usury, rather (to tell the truth) with the bitterness of one who condemns it not because it is an evil, but because he is vexed that there are people who take advantage of it.]

X

I t was almost night when they reached Sevastopol. Driving towards the large bridge across the Roadstead Volódya was not exactly dispirited, but his heart was heavy. All he saw and heard was so different from his past, still recent, experience: the large, light examination hall with its parquet floor, the jolly, friendly voices and laughter of his comrades, the new uniform, the beloved Tsar he had been accustomed to see for the past seven years, and who at parting from them with tears in his eyes had called them his children – all he saw now was so little like his beautiful, radiant, high-souled dreams.

'Well, here we are,' said the elder brother when they reached the Michael Battery and dismounted from their trap. 'If they let us cross the bridge we will go at once to the Nicholas Barracks. You can stay there till the morning, and I'll go to the regiment and find out where your battery is and come for you to-morrow.'

'Oh, why? Let's go together,' said Volódya. 'I'll go to the bastion with you. It doesn't matter. One must get used to it sooner or later. If you go, so can I.'

'Better not.'

'Yes, please! I shall at least find out how. . . .'

'My advice is don't go . . . however —'

The sky was clear and dark. The stars, the flash of the guns and the continual flare of the bombs already showed up brightly in the darkness, and the large white building of the battery and the entry to the bridge[1] loomed out. The air was shaken every second by a quick succession of artillery shots and explosions which became ever louder and more distinct. Through this roar, and as if answering it, came the dull murmur of the Roadstead. A slight breeze blew in from the sea and the air smelt moist. The brothers reached the bridge. A recruit,

---

1 This pontoon bridge was erected during the summer of 1855. At first it was feared that the water was too rough in the Roadstead for a secure bridge to be built, but it served its purpose, and later on even stood the strain put upon it by the retreat of the Russian army to the North Side.

awkwardly striking his gun against his hand, called out, 'Who goes there?'

'Soldier!'

'No one's allowed to pass!'

'How is that? We must.'

'Ask the officer.'

The officer, who was sitting on an anchor dozing, rose and ordered that they should be allowed to pass.

'You may go there, but not back.'

'Where are you driving, all of a heap?' he shouted to the regimental wagons which, laden high with gabions, were crowding the entrance.

As the brothers were descending to the first pontoon, they came upon some soldiers going the other way and talking loudly.

'If he's had his outfit money his account is squared – that's so.'

'Ah, lads,' said another, 'when one gets to the North Side one sees light again. It's a different air altogether.'

'Is it though?' said the first. 'Why, only the other day a damned ball flew over and tore two soldiers' legs off for them, even there. . . .'

Waiting for the trap the brothers after crossing the first pontoon stopped on the second, which was washed here and there by the waves. The wind which seemed gentle on land was strong and gusty here; the bridge swayed and the waves broke noisily against beams, anchors, and ropes, and washed over the boards. To the right, divided from the light blue-grey starry horizon by a smooth, endless black line, was the sea, dark, misty, and with a hostile sullen roar. Far off in the distance gleamed the lights of the enemy's fleet. To the left loomed the black hulk of one of our ships, against whose sides the waves beat audibly. A steamer too was visible moving quickly and noisily from the North Side. The flash of a bomb exploding near the steamer lit up for a moment the gabions piled high on its deck, two men standing on the paddle-box, and the white foam and splash of the greenish waves cut by the vessel. On the edge of the bridge, his feet dangling in the water, a man in his shirt sat chopping something on the pontoon. In front, above Sevastopol, similar flashes were seen, and the terrible sounds became louder and louder. A wave flowing in from the sea washed over the right side of the bridge and wetted Volódya's boots, and two soldiers passed by him splashing their feet through the water. Suddenly something came crashing down which lit up the bridge ahead of them, a cart driving over it, and a horseman, and fragments of a bomb fell whistling and splashing into the water.

'Ah, Michael Semënich!'[1] said the rider, stopping his horse in front of the elder Kozeltsóv. 'Have you recovered?'

'As you see. And where is fate taking you?'

'To the North Side for cartridges. You see I'm taking the place of the regimental adjutant to-day. . . . We're expecting an attack from hour to hour.'

'And where is Mártsov?'

'His leg was torn off yesterday while he was sleeping in his room in town. . . . Did you know him?'

'Is it true that the regiment is at the Fifth Bastion now?'

'Yes, we have replaced the M— regiment. You'd better call at the Ambulance, you'll find some of our fellows there – they'll show you the way.'

'And my lodgings in the Morskáya Street, are they safe?'

'Safe, my dear fellow! They've long since been shattered by bombs. You won't know Sevastopol again. Not a woman left, not a restaurant, no music! The last brothel left yesterday. It's melancholy enough now. Good-bye!'

And the officer trotted away.

Terrible fear suddenly overcame Volódya. He felt as if a ball or a bomb-splinter would come the next moment and hit him

1 In addressing anyone in Russian, it is usual to employ the Christian name and patronymic: i.e. to the Christian name (in this case Michael) the father's Christian name is joined (in this case Semën) with the termination *vich* (*o-vich* or *e-vich*) which means 'son of'. The termination is often shortened to *ich*, and colloquially to *ych*. Surnames are less used than in English, for the patronymic is suitable for all circumstances of life – both for speaking to and of anyone – except that people on very intimate terms use only the Christian name, or a pet name.

straight on the head. The damp darkness, all these sounds, especially the murmur of the splashing water – all seemed to tell him to go no farther, that no good awaited him here, that he would never again set foot on this side of the bay, that he should turn back at once and run somewhere as far as possible from this dreadful place of death. 'But perhaps it is too late, it is already decided now,' thought he shuddering, partly at that thought and partly because the water had soaked through his boots and was making his feet wet.

He sighed deeply and moved a few steps away from his brother.

'O Lord! Shall I really be killed – just I? Lord, have mercy on me!' he whispered, and made the sign of the cross.

'Well, Volódya, come on!' said the elder brother when the trap had driven on to the bridge. 'Did you see the bomb?'

On the bridge they met carts loaded with wounded men, with gabions, and one with furniture driven by a woman. No one stopped them at the farther side.

Keeping instinctively under the wall of the Nicholas Battery and listening to the bombs that here were bursting overhead, and to the howling of the falling fragments, the brothers came silently to that part of the battery where the icon hangs. Here they heard that the Fifth Light Artillery, to which Volódya was appointed, was stationed at the Korábelnaya[1] and they decided that Volódya, in spite of the danger, should spend the night with his elder brother at the Fifth Bastion and go from there to his battery next morning. After turning into a corridor and stepping across the legs of the soldiers who lay sleeping all along the wall of the battery they at last reached the Ambulance Station.

XI

ON entering the first room, full of beds on which lay wounded men and permeated by a horribly disgusting hospital smell, they met two Sisters of Mercy just going out.

1 The Korábelnaya was a suburb of Sevastopol lying to the east of the South Bay and to the south of the Roadstead. Like the 'North Side' it was connected with Sevastopol by a floating bridge.

One, a woman of fifty, with black eyes and a stern expression, was carrying bandages and lint and giving orders to a young lad, a medical assistant, who was following her. The other, a very pretty girl of about twenty whose pale, delicate, fair face looked from under her white cap with a peculiarly sweet helplessness, was walking by the side of the older woman with her hands in her apron pockets, and seemed afraid of being left behind.

Kozeltsóv asked them if they knew where Mártsov was, whose leg had been torn off the day before.

'He is of the P— regiment, I think?' asked the elder. 'Is he a relation of yours?'

'No, just a comrade.'

'Take them to him,' she said to the young sister in French. 'It is this way,' and she herself went up to one of the patients, followed by the assistant.

'Come along, what are you looking at?' said Kozeltsóv to Volódya, who stood with raised eyebrows and a look of suffering on his face, unable to tear his eyes from the wounded. 'Come now!'

Volódya followed his brother but still kept looking back and repeating unconsciously, 'O, my God! My God!'

'I suppose he has not been here long?' the sister remarked to Kozeltsóv, indicating Volódya, who followed them along the corridor with exclamations and sighs.

'He has only just come.'

The pretty sister looked at Volódya and suddenly began to cry.

'My God! My God! When will it all end?' she said in a despairing voice.

They entered the officers' ward. Mártsov was lying on his back, his sinewy arms bare to the elbow thrown back behind his head, and on his yellow face the expression of one who has clenched his teeth to prevent himself from screaming with pain. His sound leg with a stocking on showed from under the blanket and one could see the toes moving spasmodically.

'Well, how are you?' asked the sister, raising his slightly bald head with her slender delicate fingers (on one of which Volódya noticed a gold ring) and arranging his pillow.

'In pain of course!' he answered angrily. 'That'll do – the pillow's all right!' and the toes in the stocking moved still faster. 'How d'you do? What's your name?' ... 'Excuse me,' he added, when Kozeltsóv had told him. 'Ah yes, I beg your pardon. One forgets everything here. Why, we lived together,' he remarked without any sign of pleasure, and looked inquiringly at Volódya.

'This is my brother, arrived to-day from Petersburg.'

'H'm! And I have got my discharge!' said the wounded man, frowning. 'Oh, how it hurts! If only it would be over quicker!'

He drew up his leg and, moving his toes still more rapidly, covered his face with his hands.

'He must be left alone,' said the sister in a whisper while tears filled her eyes. 'He is very ill.'

While still on the North Side the brothers had agreed to go to the Fifth Bastion together, but as they passed out of the Nicholas Battery it was as if they had agreed not to run unnecessary risks and for each to go his own way.

'But how will you find it, Volódya?' said the elder. 'Look here! Nikoláev shall take you to the Korábelnaya and I'll go on alone and come to you to-morrow.'

Nothing more was said at this last parting between the brothers.

XII

THE thunder of the cannonade continued with unabated violence. Ekaterína Street, down which Volódya walked followed by the silent Nikoláev, was quiet and deserted. All he could distinguish in the dark was the broad street with its large white houses, many of them in ruins, and the stone pavement along which he was walking. Now and then he met soldiers and officers. As he was passing by the left side of the Admiralty Building, a bright light inside showed him the acacias planted along the side-walk of the streets with green stakes to support them and sickly, dusty leaves. He distinctly heard his own footsteps and those of Nikoláev, who followed him breathing heavily. He was not thinking of anything: the pretty Sister of

Mercy, Mártsov's foot with the toes moving in the stocking, the darkness, the bombs, and different images of death, floated dimly before his imagination. His whole young impressionable soul was weighed down and crushed by a sense of loneliness and of the general indifference shown to his fate in these dangerous surroundings. 'I shall be killed, I shall suffer, endure torments, and no one will shed a tear!' And all this instead of the heroic life abounding in energy and sympathy of which he had had such glorious dreams. The bombs whistled and burst nearer and nearer. Nikoláev sighed more and more often, but did not speak. As they were crossing the bridge that led to the Korábelnaya he saw a whistling something fall and disappear into the water near by, lighting the purple waves to a flaming red for a second and then come splashing up again.

'Just look! Not quenched!' said Nikoláev in a hoarse voice.

'No,' answered Volódya in an involuntarily high-pitched plaintive tone which surprised him.

They met wounded men carried on stretchers and more carts loaded with gabions. In the Korábelnaya they met a regiment, and men on horseback rode past. One of these was an officer followed by a Cossack. He was riding at a trot, but seeing Volódya he reined up his horse, looked in his face, turned away, and rode on, touching his horse with the whip.

'Alone, alone! No one cares whether I live or not,' thought the lad, and felt inclined to cry in real earnest.

Having gone up the hill past a high white wall he came into a street of small shattered houses, continually lit up by the bombs. A dishevelled, tipsy woman, coming out of a gate with a sailor, knocked up against Volódya.

'Because if he'sh an on'ble man,' she muttered – 'pardon y'r exshensh offisher!'

The poor lad's heart ached more and more. On the dark horizon the lightnings flashed oftener and oftener and the bombs whistled and exploded more and more frequently around them. Nikoláev sighed and suddenly began to speak in what seemed to Volódya a lifeless tone.

'There now, and we were in such a hurry to leave home! "We must go! We must go!" Fine place to hurry to! [Wise gentlemen when they are the least bit wounded lie up quietly in 'orspital. It's so nice, what better can you want?]'

'Well, but if my brother had recovered his health,' answered Volódya, hoping by conversation to disperse the dreadful feeling that had seized him.

'Health indeed! Where's his health, when he's quite ill? Even them as is really well had best lie in 'orspital these times. Not much pleasure to be got. All you get is a leg or an arm carried off. It's done before you know where you are! It's horrible enough even here in the town, but what's it like at the *baksions*! You say all the prayers you know when you're going there. See how the beastly thing twangs past you!' he added, listening to the buzzing of a flying fragment.

'Now,' he continued, 'I'm to show y'r Honour the way. Our business is o' course to obey orders: what's ordered has to be done. But the trap's been left with some private or other, and the bundle's untied.... "Go, go!" but if something's lost, why Nikoláev answers for it!'

A few more steps brought them to a square. Nikoláev did not speak but kept sighing. Then he said suddenly:

'There, y'r Honour, there's where your *antillary's* stationed. Ask the sentinel, he'll show you.'

A few steps farther on Volódya no longer heard Nikoláev sighing behind him. He suddenly felt himself utterly and finally deserted. This sense of loneliness, face to face as it seemed to him with death, pressed like a heavy, cold stone on his heart. He stopped in the middle of the square, glanced round to see if anyone was looking, seized his head and thought with horror:

'O Lord, am I really a vile, miserable coward...when it's for my Fatherland, for the Tsar for whom I used to long to die? Yes! I am a miserable, wretched being!' And Volódya, filled with despair and disappointed at himself, asked the sentinel the way to the house of the commander of the battery and went where he was directed.

XIII

THE commander of the battery lived in a small two-storeyed house with an entrance from the yard, which the sentinel pointed out. The faint light of a candle shone through a window patched up with paper. An orderly, who sat on the steps smoking his pipe, went in to inform the commander of the battery of Volódya's arrival and then showed him into the room. In the room, under a broken mirror between two windows, was a table littered with official papers; there were also several chairs and an iron bedstead with clean bedding, with a small rug beside it.

Just beside the door stood a handsome sergeant-major with large moustaches, wearing side-arms, and with a cross and a Hungarian medal[1] on his uniform. A staff-officer, a short man of about forty in a thin old cloak and with a swollen cheek tied round with a bandage, was pacing up and down the room.

'I have the honour to report myself, Ensign Kozeltsóv, secundus, ordered to join the Fifth Light Artillery,' said Volódya on entering the room, repeating the sentence he had been taught.

The commander answered his greeting dryly and without shaking hands asked him to take a seat.

Volódya sat down shyly on a chair by the writing table, and began playing with a pair of scissors his hand happened to fall on. The commander, with his hands at his back and with drooping head, continued to pace the room in silence as if trying to remember something, only now and then glancing at the hand that was playing with the scissors.

The commander of the battery was rather stout, with a large bald patch on his head, thick moustaches hanging straight down over his mouth, and pleasant hazel eyes. His hands were plump, well-shaped, and clean, his small feet were much turned out and he trod with firmness in a way that indicated that he was not a diffident man.

---

1 That is, a medal granted for service in the suppression of the Hungarian rising in 1849, when Nicholas I helped Austria to suppress the insurgent Hungarians.

'Yes,' he said, stopping opposite the sergeant-major, 'the ammunition horses must have an extra peck beginning from to-morrow. They are getting very thin. Don't you think so?'

'Well, we can manage an extra peck, your Honour! Oats are a bit cheaper now,' answered the sergeant-major, standing at attention but moving his fingers, which evidently liked to aid his conversation by gestures. 'Then our forage-master, Frantchúk, sent me a note from the convoy yesterday that we must be sure, your Excellency, to buy axles there. They say they can be got cheap. Will you give the order?'

'Well, let him buy them – he has the money,' said the commander, and again began to pace the room. 'And where are your things?' he suddenly asked, stopping short in front of Volódya.

Poor Volódya was so oppressed by the thought that he was a coward, that he saw contempt for himself as a miserable craven in every look and every word. He felt as if the commander of the battery had already discerned his secret, and was chaffing him. He was abashed, and replied that his things were at the Gráfskaya and that his brother had promised to send them on next day.

The commander did not stop to hear him out, but turning to the sergeant-major asked, 'Where could we put the ensign up?'

'The ensign, sir?' said the sergeant-major, making Volódya still more confused by casting a rapid glance at him which seemed to ask: 'What sort of an ensign is he?'

'Why, downstairs, your Excellency. We can put his Honour up in the lieutenant-captain's room,' he continued after a moment's thought. 'The lieutenant-captain is at the *baksion* at present, so there's his bed empty.'

'Well then, if you don't mind for the present,' said the commander. 'I should think you are tired, and we'll make better arrangements to-morrow.'

Volódya rose and bowed.

'Would you like a glass of tea?' said the commander of the battery when Volódya had nearly reached the door. 'The samovar can be lit.'

Volódya bowed and went out. The colonel's orderly showed him downstairs into a bare, dirty room, where all sorts of rubbish was lying about and a man in a pink shirt and covered with a thick coat lay asleep on a bed without sheets or blankets. Volódya took him for a soldier.

'Peter Nikoláevich!' said the orderly, shaking the sleeper by the shoulder. 'The ensign will sleep here. . . . This is our cadet,' he added, turning to Volódya.

'Oh, please don't let me disturb you!' said Volódya, but the cadet, a tall, solid young man with a handsome but very stupid face, rose from the bed, threw the cloak over his shoulders, and evidently not yet quite awake, left the room saying: 'Never mind, I'll lie down in the yard.'

XIV

LEFT alone with his thoughts Volódya's first feeling was one of fear at the disordered and cheerless state of his own soul. He longed to fall asleep, to forget all that surrounded him and especially himself. Putting out the candle, he took off his cloak and lay down on the bed, drawing the cloak over his head to shut out the darkness, of which he had been afraid from childhood. But suddenly the thought occurred to him that now, immediately, a bomb would crash through the roof and kill him, and he began listening. Just above his head he heard the steps of the commander of the battery.

'If it does come,' he thought, 'it will first kill those upstairs and then me — anyway not me alone.' This thought comforted him a little and he was about to fall asleep.

'But supposing that suddenly, to-night, Sevastopol is taken and the French break in here? What shall I defend myself with?' He rose and paced up and down the room. The fear of real danger drove away the fanciful fear of the darkness. A saddle and a samovar were the only hard things in the room.

'What a wretch I am — a coward, a despicable coward!' he thought again, and once more the oppressive feeling of contempt and even disgust for himself came over him. He lay down again and tried not to think. Then, under the influence of the

unceasing noise which made the panes rattle in the one window
of the room, the impressions of the day rose in his imagination,
reminding him of danger. Now he seemed to see wounds and
blood, then bombs and splinters flying into the room, then the
pretty Sister of Mercy bandaging his wounds and crying over
him as he lay dying, then his mother seeing him off in the little
country town and praying fervently with tears in her eyes before
the wonder-working icon – and again sleep seemed impossible.
But suddenly the thought of God Almighty, who can do anything and hears every prayer, came clearly into his mind. He
knelt down, crossed himself, and folded his hands as he had been
taught to do when a child. This attitude suddenly brought back
to him an old, long-forgotten sense of comfort.

'If I must die, if I must cease to exist, then do it, Lord,' he
thought, 'do it quickly, but if courage is needed and firmness,
which I lack, grant them to me! Deliver me from the shame
and disgrace which are more than I can bear, and teach me
what I must do to fulfil Thy Will.'

The frightened, cramped, childish soul suddenly matured,
brightened, and became aware of new, bright, and broad
horizons. He thought and felt many things during the short
time this state continued, but soon fell into a sweet untroubled
slumber, amid the continued booming of the cannonade and
rattle of the window-panes.

O Lord Almighty! Thou alone hast heard and knowest the
simple yet burning and desperate prayers of ignorance, of confused repentance, prayers for bodily health and for spiritual
enlightenment, that have risen to Thee from this dreadful place
of death: from the general who, an instant after his mind has been
absorbed by the Order of St George upon his neck, feels with
trepidation the nearness of Thy presence – to the private soldier
prostrate on the bare floor of the Nicholas Battery, who prays for
the future reward he dimly expects for all his sufferings.

XV

THE elder Kozeltsóv happening to meet a soldier of his regiment in the street went with him straight to the Fifth Bastion.

'Keep to the wall, your Honour!' said the soldier.

'Why?'

'It's dangerous, your Honour. There it is, flying over us!' said the soldier, listening to the sound of a ball that whistled past and fell on the hard ground on the other side of the road.

[Without heeding the soldier's words Kozeltsóv went boldly down the middle of the road.]

Here were still the same streets, the same or even more frequent firing, the same sounds, the same groans from the wounded one met on the way, and the same batteries, breastworks, and trenches, as when he was in Sevastopol in the spring; but somehow it all seemed more melancholy now and yet more vigorous. There were more holes in the houses, there were no lights in any of the windows except those of Kústchin's house (a hospital), not a woman was to be seen, and the place no longer bore its former customary character and air of unconcern, but seemed burdened with heavy suspense and weariness.

But here is the last trench and the voice of a soldier of the P— regiment who has recognized his former company-commander, and there stands the third battalion, pressing against the wall in the darkness, now and then lit up for an instant by the firing, and sounds are heard, subdued talking and the clatter of muskets.

'Where is the commander of the regiment?' asked Kozeltsóv.

'In the naval officers' casemate, your Honour,' answers an obliging soldier. 'Let me show you the way.'

Passing from trench to trench, the soldier led the way to a cutting in the trench. A sailor sat there smoking a pipe. Behind him was a door through a chink in which a light shone.

'Can I go in?'

'I'll announce you at once,' and the sailor went in at the door. Two voices were heard talking inside.

'If Prussia remains neutral,' said one voice, 'Austria will too. . . .'

'What does Austria matter?' said the other, 'when the Slavonic lands. . . . Well, ask him in.'

Kozeltsóv had never been in this casemate and was struck by its elegance. It had a parquet floor and a screen in front of the door, two beds stood against the walls, and in a corner of the room there was a large icon – the Mother of God with an embossed gilt cover – with a pink lamp alight before it. A naval officer, fully dressed, was lying asleep on one of the beds. On the other, before a table on which stood two uncorked bottles of wine, sat the speakers – the new regimental commander and his adjutant. Though Kozeltsóv was far from being a coward and was not at all guilty of any offence either against the government or the regimental commander, still he felt abashed in the presence of his former comrade the colonel, so proudly did that colonel rise and give him his attention.

[And the adjutant who was sitting there also made Kozeltsóv feel abashed by his pose and look, that seemed to say: 'I am only a friend of your regimental commander's. You have not come to present yourself to me, and I can't and don't wish to demand any deference from you.']

'How strange!' thought Kolzeltsóv as he looked at his commander, 'It's only seven weeks since he took the command, and yet all his surroundings – his dress, manner, and looks – already indicate the power a regimental commander has: [a power based not so much on his age, seniority, or military worth, as on his wealth as a regimental commander.] It isn't long since this same Batríshchev used to hobnob with us, wore one and the same dark cotton print shirt a whole week, ate rissoles and curd dumplings every day, never asking anyone to share them – but look at him now! [A fine linen shirt showing from under his wide-sleeved cloth coat, a ten-ruble cigar in his hand, a six-ruble bottle of claret on the table – all bought at incredible prices through the quartermaster at Simferópol – and] in his eyes that look of the cold pride of a wealthy aristocrat, which says: though as a regimental commander of the new school I am your comrade [don't forget that your pay is sixty rubles once in four months, while tens of thousands pass through my hands, and] believe me I know very well that you'd give half your life to be in my place!'

'You have been under treatment a long time,' said the colonel, with a cold look at Kozeltsóv.

'I have been ill, Colonel. The wound is not thoroughly closed even now.'

'Then it's a pity you've come,' said the colonel, looking suspiciously at the officer's solid figure. 'But still, you are capable of taking duty?'

'Certainly sir, I am.'

'I am very glad to hear it. Then you'll take over from Ensign Záytsev the Ninth Company that you had before. You will receive your orders at once.'

'Yes, sir.'

'Be so good as to send the regimental adjutant to me when you go.' The commander finished with a slight bow, thereby intimating that the audience was at an end.

On leaving the casemate Kozeltsóv muttered something to himself several times, and shrugged his shoulders as if he were hurt, or uncomfortable, or provoked – and provoked not with the colonel (he had no ground to be so) but with himself, and he felt dissatisfied with everything around him.

[Discipline and the subordination that goes with it, like every legalized relationship, is pleasant only when it rests on a mutual consciousness of its necessity, and of a superiority in experience, military worth, or simply on a moral superiority recognized by the inferior. But if the discipline is founded on arbitrary or pecuniary considerations, as is often the case among us, it always turns into pretentiousness on the one side and into suppressed envy and irritation on the other, and instead of a useful influence uniting the mass into one whole it produces a quite opposite effect. A man who does not feel that he can inspire respect by his own worth, instinctively fears intimacy with his subordinates and tries by ostentation to keep criticism at a distance. The subordinates, seeing only this external side which is offensive to themselves, suppose (often unjustly) that there is nothing good behind it.]

XVI

BEFORE going to join his fellow officers Kozeltsóv went to greet the men of his company and to see where it was stationed.

The breastworks of gabions, the plan of the trenches, the cannon he passed, and even the fragments and bombs he stumbled over on the way, all lit up incessantly by the flashes of the firing, were quite familiar to him. All this had vividly impressed itself on his memory three months before, when he had spent two consecutive weeks at this bastion. Though there was much that was dreadful in the recollection, a certain charm of old times was mingled with it and he recognized all the familiar places and objects with pleasure, as if the fortnight spent there had been an agreeable one. His company was stationed against the wall of defence on the side towards the Sixth Bastion.

Kozeltsóv entered a long bomb-proof, quite open on the entrance side, where he was told he would find the Ninth Company. There was literally no room to set one's foot in the whole shelter: it was crowded with soldiers from the very entrance. At one side burned a crooked tallow candle which a soldier, lying on the ground, held over the book another was reading from, spelling out the words. Through the smoky atmosphere of the place, in the dim light near the candle, heads were visible, raised eagerly to listen to the reader. The book was a primer, and on entering the bomb-proof Kozeltsóv heard the following:

'Pra-yer af-ter les-sons. We Thank Thee, O Cre-a-tor. . . .'

'Snuff the candle!' said a voice. 'It's a fine book.'

'God . . . is' . . . continued the reader.

When Kozeltsóv asked for the sergeant-major the reader stopped and the soldiers began moving, coughing and blowing their noses, as is usual after a restrained silence. The sergeant-major, buttoning his uniform, rose not far from the reader's group, and stepping over and onto the legs of those who could not get out of his way for lack of room, came up to the officer.

'Good evening, friend! Is this the whole of our company?'

'We wish your Honour health. Welcome back, your Honour!' answered the sergeant-major with a cheerful and friendly look at Kozeltsóv. 'How is your health getting on, your Honour? Thank God you're better! We have missed you.'

It was easy to see that Kozeltsóv was liked by his company.

Far back in the bomb-proof voices were heard saying: 'Our old company-commander has come back!' 'Him that was wounded.' 'Kozeltsóv.' 'Michael Semënich,' and so on. Some men even moved nearer to him, and the drummer greeted him.

'How do you do, Obantchúk?' said Kozeltsóv. 'Still whole? Good evening, lads!' he added, raising his voice.

The answer, 'Wish your Honour health!' resounded through the casemate.

'How are you getting on, lads?'

'Badly, your Honour. The French are getting the better of us. They give it us hot from behind their 'trenchments, but don't come out into the open.'

'Perhaps it will be my luck to see them coming out into the open, lads,' said Kozeltsóv. 'It won't be the first time . . . you and I will give them a thrashing.'

'We'll do our best, your Honour,' several voices replied.

'Yes, he's really brave!' said a voice.

'Awfully brave!' said the drummer to another soldier, not loud but so as to be heard, and as if justifying the commander's words to himself and proving that there was nothing boastful or unlikely in what he had said.

From the soldiers, Kozeltsóv went to join his fellow officers in the Defence Barracks.

XVII

IN the large caserne there was a crowd of naval, artillery, and infantry officers. Some slept, others talked, sitting on a chest of some kind and on the carriage of a garrison gun, but the largest and noisiest group sat on two Cossack cloaks spread out on the floor beyond the arch, and were drinking porter and playing cards.

'Ah, Kozeltsóv! Kozeltsóv! . . . So you've come! That's good. . . . You're a brick. . . . How's your wound?' It was evident that he was liked here also, and that his return gave pleasure.

When he had shaken hands with those he knew, Kozeltsóv joined the noisy group of officers playing cards. With some of them he was acquainted. A thin, dark, handsome man, with a long thin nose and large moustaches which joined his whiskers, was keeping the bank and dealt the cards with thin white fingers on one of which he wore a large seal-ring with a crest. He dealt straight ahead and carelessly, being evidently excited about something, and only trying to appear at ease. On his right lay a grey-haired major leaning on his elbows who with affected coolness kept staking half-rubles and paying at once. On his left squatted an officer with a red perspiring face, smiling unnaturally and joking. When his cards lost he kept fumbling with one hand in his empty trouser pocket. He was playing high, but evidently no longer for ready money, and it was this that upset the handsome dark man. A bald, thin, pale officer with a huge nose and mouth paced the room with a large bundle of paper money in his hand and continually staked *va-banque* for ready money and won. Kozeltsóv drank a glass of vodka and sat down with the players.

'Stake something, Michael Semënich!' said the banker. 'You must have brought back heaps of money.'

'Where should I get money? On the contrary, what I had I've spent in the town.'

'Never! ... You've surely cleared someone out in Simferópol!'

'I've really very little,' said Koseltsóv, but evidently not wishing to be believed he unbuttoned his uniform and took up an old pack of cards.

'Well, suppose I have a try! Who knows what the devil may do for one? Even a mosquito, you know, wins his battles sometimes. But I must have a drink to keep up my courage.'

And having drunk another glass of vodka and some porter he soon lost his last three rubles.

A hundred and fifty rubles were noted down against the perspiring little officer.

'No, I've no luck,' he said, carelessly preparing another card.

'I'll trouble you to hand up the money,' said the banker, ceasing to deal the cards for a moment and looking at him.

'Allow me to send it to-morrow,' replied the other, rising and fumbling with renewed vigour in his empty pocket.

The banker cleared his throat loudly, and angrily throwing the cards right and left finished the deal.

'But this won't do. I give up the bank. This won't do, Zakhár Ivánich,' he repeated. 'We were playing for cash, not on credit.'

'What? Don't you trust me? It's really too ridiculous!'

'Who am I to receive from?' muttered the major, who was quite drunk by this time and had won some eight rubles. 'I have paid up more than twenty rubles and when I win I get nothing.'

'What am I to pay with,' said the banker, 'when there's no money on the board?'

'That's not my business,' shouted the major, rising. 'I'm playing with you, *with honest people*, and not with him.'

The perspiring officer suddenly flared up:

'I shall pay to-morrow, I tell you. How dare you insult me?'

'I shall say what I please! *Honest people don't behave like that.* So there!' shouted the major.

'That's enough, Fëdor Fëdorich!' said everybody, trying to pacify him.

But let us hasten to drop the curtain on this scene. To-morrow or to-day, perhaps, each of these men will cheerfully and proudly go to face death, and die steadfastly and calmly; but the only relief in these inhuman conditions, horrible even to the coldest imagination and from which there is no hope of escape, is to forget and to suppress consciousness. Deep in each soul is a noble spark capable of making its possessor a hero, but it wearies of burning brightly – till a fateful moment comes when it will flash into flame and illumine great deeds.

XVIII

THE bombardment continued with equal vigour the next day. At about eleven o'clock Volódya Kozeltsóv was sitting among the officers of his battery whom he was already beginning to get used to. He was examining the new faces, observing, asking questions, and talking. The modest conversation, with some pretension to knowledge, of these artillery officers inspired him with respect and pleased him, and on the other hand, Volódya's bashful and innocent good looks inclined the officers in his favour. The senior of the battery, a captain, a short man with reddish hair standing up in a tuft above his forehead and brushed smooth on his temples, brought up in the old artillery traditions, a ladies' man with pretensions to scientific knowledge, questioned Volódya about what he knew of artillery and new inventions, joked in a friendly manner about his youth and his pretty face, and in general treated him like a son – and this pleased Volódya very much. Sub-lieutenant Dyádenko, a young officer who spoke with an Ukrainian accent and who wore a torn cloak and had dishevelled hair – though he talked loudly, snatched every opportunity to begin a hot dispute, and was abrupt in his movements – nevertheless seemed attractive to Volódya, for he could not help seeing that a very kind heart and much that was good lay beneath this rough exterior. Dyádenko kept offering to be of use to Volódya, and demonstrating to him that none of the guns in Sevastopol were placed according to rule.

The only one Volódya did not like was Lieutenant Tchernovítski with his arched eyebrows, though he was the most polite of them all, and wore a coat which was clean enough and neatly patched if not very new, and though he displayed a gold chain over his satin waistcoat. He kept asking what the Emperor and the Minister of War were doing, and told him with unnatural rapture of feats of valour performed in Sevastopol, regretted [the ill-advised arrangements that were being made, and] that there were so few real patriots, and in general displayed much knowledge, intelligence, and noble feeling; but for some reason it all seemed unnatural and unpleasant. Volódya noticed in particular that the other officers hardly spoke to Tchernovítski. Cadet Vlang, whom Volódya had disturbed the night before, was also there. He did not speak, but sitting modestly in a corner laughed when there was anything funny, helped to recall anything that was forgotten, handed the vodka bottle, and made cigarettes for all the officers. Whether it was the modest, courteous manner of Volódya, who treated him as an officer and did not order him about as if he were a boy, or whether Volódya's attractive appearance charmed Vlánga (as the soldiers called him, giving a feminine form to his name), at any rate he did not take his large kindly eyes from the new officer, foresaw and anticipated his wants, and was all the time in a state of enamoured ecstasy which of course the officers noticed and made fun of.

Before dinner the lieutenant-captain was relieved from the bastion and joined them. Lieutenant-Captain Kraut was a fair-haired, handsome, vivacious officer with big sandy moustaches and whiskers. He spoke Russian excellently, but too accurately and elegantly for a Russian. In the service and in his life he was just the same as in his speech: he served admirably, was a first-rate comrade, most reliable in money matters, but as a man he seemed to lack something just because everything about him was so satisfactory. Like all Russo-Germans, in strange contra-distinction to the idealist German-Germans, he was *praktisch* in the extreme.

'Here he comes – our hero!' said the captain, as Kraut entered the room swinging his arms and jingling his spurs. 'What will you take, Friedrich Christiánich, tea or vodka?'

'I have already ordered some tea,' answered Kraut, 'but meanwhile I do not mind taking a drop of vodka as a refresh-ment for my soul. . . . Very pleased to make your acquaintance. I hope you will favour me with your company and your friendship,' he added, turning to Volódya, who rose and bowed to him. 'Lieutenant-Captain Kraut. . . . The master-gunner at our bastion told me yesterday that you had arrived.'

'I am very grateful to you for your bed: I slept on it.'

'But were you comfortable? One of the legs is broken; no one has time to mend it in this state of siege, it has to be propped up.'

'Well, what luck have you had on duty?' asked Dyádenko.

'Oh, all right; only Skvortsóv was hit, and yesterday we had to mend a gun-carriage – the cheek was blown to shivers.'

He rose and began to walk up and down. It was evident that he was under the influence of that pleasant feeling men experience who have just left a post of danger.

'Well, Dmítri Gavrílich,' he said, shaking the captain by his knee, 'how are you getting on? What of your recommendation? Is it still silent?'

'There's no news as yet.'

'And there won't be any,' began Dyádenko. 'I told you so before.'

'Why won't there be?'

'Because the report was not written properly.'

'Ah, you wrangler! You wrangler!' said Kraut, smiling merrily. 'A real obstinate Ukrainian! There now, just to spite you you'll get a lieutenancy.'

'No I shan't!'

'Vlang, get me my pipe and fill it,' said Kraut, turning to the cadet, who rose at once and readily ran for the pipe.

Kraut brightened them all up: he talked of the bombardment, asked what had been going on in his absence, and spoke to everybody.

XIX

'WELL, have you established yourself satisfactorily among us?' Kraut asked Volódya. 'Excuse me, what is your name and patronymic? You know that's our custom in the artillery.... Have you a horse?'

'No,' said Volódya, 'I don't know what I'm to do. I was telling the captain ... I have no horse nor any money until I get my forage-money and travelling expenses paid. I thought meanwhile of asking the commander of the battery to let me have a horse, but I'm afraid he'll refuse.'

'Apollón Sergéich ...?' and Kraut made a sound with his lips expressive of strong doubt, and looking at the captain added, 'Hardly!'

'Well, if he does refuse there'll be no harm done,' said the captain. 'To tell you the truth, a horse is not much wanted here. Still, it's worth trying. I will ask him to-day.'

'How little you know him,' Dyádenko put in: 'he might refuse anything else, but not that.... Will you bet?'

'Oh, we know you can't help contradicting!'

'I contradict because I know. He's close in other matters, but he'll give a horse because he gains nothing by refusing.'

'Gains nothing when oats are eight rubles?' said Kraut. 'The gain is not having to keep an extra horse.'

'You ask for Skvoréts, Vladímir Semënich,' said Vlang, returning with Kraut's pipe. 'He's a capital horse.'

'Off which you fell into a ditch in Soróki, eh, Vlánga?' remarked the lieutenant-captain.

'What does it matter if oats are eight rubles, when in his estimates they figure at ten and a half?[1] That's where the gain comes in,' said Dyádenko, continuing to argue.

'Well naturally you can't expect him to keep nothing. When you're commander of a battery I daresay you won't let a man have a horse to ride into town.'

'When I'm commander of a battery my horses will get four measures each and I shan't make an income, no fear!'

'We shall see if we live...' said the lieutenant-captain. 'You'll act in just the same way – and so will he,' pointing to Volódya.

'Why do you think that he too would wish to make a profit?' said Tchernovítski to Kraut. 'He may have private means, then why should he want to make a profit?'

'Oh no, I ... excuse me, Captain,' said Volódya, blushing up to his ears, 'but I should think such a thing dishonourable.'

'Dear me! What a severe fellow he is!' said Kraut.

'No, I only mean that I think that if the money is not mine I ought not to take it.'

'But I'll tell you something, young man,' began the lieutenant-captain in a more serious tone. 'Do you know that if you are commanding a battery you have to conduct things

---

1 Referring to the custom of charging the government more than the actual price of supplies, and thereby making an income which was supposed to go for the benefit of the regiment, but part of which frequently remained unaccounted for.

properly, and that's enough. The commander of a battery doesn't interfere with the soldiers' supplies: that's always been the custom in the artillery. If you are a bad manager you will have no surplus. But you have to spend over and above what's in the estimates: for shoeing – that's one' (he bent down one finger), 'and for medicine – that's two' (and he bent down another finger), 'for office expenses – that's three: then for off-horses one has to pay up to five hundred rubles my dear fellow – that's four: you have to supply the soldiers with new collars, spend a good bit on charcoal for the samovars, and keep open table for the officers. If you are in command of a battery you must live decently: you must have a carriage and a fur coat, and one thing and another. . . . It's quite plain!'

'And above all,' interrupted the captain, who had been silent all the time, 'look here, Vladímir Semënich – imagine a man like myself say, serving for twenty years with a pay of first two hundred, then three hundred rubles a year. Can one refuse him a crust of bread in his old age, after all his service?'

'Ah, what's the good of talking,' began the lieutenant-captain again. 'Don't be in a hurry to judge, but live and serve.'

Volódya felt horribly confused and ashamed of what he had so thoughtlessly said. He muttered something, and then listened in silence while Dyádenko began very irritably to dispute and to argue the contrary of what had been said. The dispute was interrupted by the colonel's orderly who came to call them to dinner.

'Ask Apollón Sergéich to give us some wine to-day,' said Tchernovítski to the captain, buttoning his uniform. 'Why is he so stingy? If we get killed, it will all be wasted.'

'Ask him yourself.'

'Oh no, you're the senior officer. We must observe order in everything.'

XX

IN the room where Volódya had presented himself to the colonel the evening before, the table had been moved away from the wall and covered with a dirty table-cloth. To-day the

commander of the battery shook hands with him and asked
him for the Petersburg news, and about his journey.

'Well, gentlemen, who takes vodka? Please help yourselves.
. . . Ensigns don't take any,' he added with a smile.

Altogether he did not seem at all as stern as the night before; on
the contrary he seemed a kind and hospitable host and an elder
comrade among fellow officers. But in spite of it all, the officers
from the old captain down to Ensign Dyádenko showed him
great respect, if only by the way they addressed him, politely
looking him straight in the eyes, and by the timid way they came
up one by one to the side-table to drink their glass of vodka.

The dinner consisted of Polish cutlets with mustard, dumplings with butter that was not very fresh, and a large tureen of
cabbage-soup in which floated pieces of fat beef with an
enormous quantity of pepper and bay-leaves. There were no
napkins, the spoons were of tin or wood, there were only two
tumblers, and there was only water on the table, in a bottle
with a broken neck; but the meal was not dull and the conversation never flagged. At first they talked about the battle of
Inkerman, in which the battery had taken part, and each gave
his own impressions of it and reasons for our reverse, but all
were silent as soon as the commander spoke. Then the conversation naturally passed to the insufficient calibre of our
field-guns, and to the subject of the new lighter guns, which
gave Volódya an opportunity to show his knowledge of
artillery. But the conversation never touched on the present
terrible condition of Sevastopol: it was as if each man had
thought so much on this subject that he did not wish to
speak of it. Nor to Volódya's great surprise and regret was
there any mention at all of the duties of the service he would
have to perform. It was as if he had come to Sevastopol solely
to discuss lighter guns and to dine with the commander of the
battery. During dinner a bomb fell near the house they were
in. The floor and walls shook as if from an earthquake, and the
windows were darkened by the powder smoke.

'You didn't see that sort of thing in Petersburg, I fancy, but
here we get many such surprises,' said the commander of the
battery. 'Vlang, go and see where it burst.'

Vlang went out to see, and reported that it had fallen in the square, and no more was said about the bomb.

Just before dinner ended, a little old man, the battery clerk, came into the room with three sealed envelopes and handed them to the commander: 'This one is very important: a Cossack has just brought it from the Chief of the Artillery.'

The officers all watched with eager impatience as the commander with practised fingers broke the seal and drew out the *very important* paper. 'What can it be?' each one asked himself. It might be an order to retire from Sevastopol to recuperate, or the whole battery might be ordered to the bastions.

'Again!' said the commander, angrily throwing the paper on the table.

'What is it, Apollón Sergéich?' asked the senior officer.

'They order an officer and men to some mortar-battery or other. . . . As it is I have only four officers, and not enough men for the gun detachments,' grumbled the commander of the battery, 'and here they are taking more away. . . . However, gentlemen, someone will have to go,' he said after a short silence, 'the order is, to be at the outposts at seven. Send the sergeant-major to me. Well, who will go? Decide, gentlemen.'

'There's your man – he's not been anywhere yet,' said Tchernovítski, pointing to Volódya.

The commander of the battery did not answer.

'Yes, I should like to go,' said Volódya, feeling a cold sweat break out on his back and neck.

'No, why should he?' interrupted the captain. 'Of course no one would refuse, but one need not offer oneself either: if Apollón Sergéich leaves it to us, let us cast lots as we did last time.'

All agreed. Kraut cut up some paper, rolled up the pieces, and threw them into a cap. The captain joked and on this occasion even ventured to ask the colonel for some wine – to keep up their courage, as he said. Dyádenko sat looking grim, something made Volódya smile. Tchernovítski declared he was sure to draw it. Kraut was perfectly calm. Volódya was allowed to draw first. He took a roll of paper a bit longer than the others but then decided to change it, and taking a thinner and shorter one unrolled it and read, 'Go.'

'It's I,' he said with a sigh.

'Well, God be with you! You'll get your baptism of fire at once,' said the commander, looking at the ensign's perturbed face with a kindly smile. 'But make haste and get ready, and to make it more cheerful for you, Vlang shall go with you as gun-sergeant.'

XXI

VLANG was extremely pleased with his appointment, ran off quickly to get ready, and when dressed came to help Volódya, trying to persuade him to take with him a bed, a fur coat, some back numbers of *Fatherland Records*, the coffee-pot with the spirit-lamp, and other unnecessary things. The captain advised Volódya to read up in the Handbook (Bezák's *Artillery Officer's Handbook*) about firing mortars, and especially to copy out the tables in it. Volódya set to work at once and noticed to his surprise and joy that his fear of the danger and even greater fear that he was a coward, though it still troubled him a little, was far from what it had been the night before. This was partly the effect of daylight and activity, but was chiefly due to the fact that fear, like every strong feeling, cannot long continue with the same intensity. In short he had already had time to live through the worst of it. At about seven o'clock, just as the sun began to disappear behind the Nicholas Barracks, the sergeant-major came and announced that the men were ready and waiting.

'I have given Vlánga the list, your Honour will please receive it from him,' said he.

About twenty artillerymen, with side-arms only, stood behind the corner of the house. Volódya and the cadet walked up to them. 'Shall I make them a little speech or simply say "Good-day lads," or say nothing at all?' he thought. 'But why not say "Good-day lads", it is even right that I should,' and he cried boldly with his ringing voice, 'Good-day lads!' The soldiers answered gaily. The fresh young voice sounded pleasantly in the ears of each. Volódya went briskly in front of the soldiers, and though his heart beat as fast as if he had run full-speed for miles his step was light and his face cheerful. As they approached the Malákhov Redoubt and mounted the hill he noticed that Vlang, who kept close to him all the time and had seemed so brave before leaving the house, was continually dodging and stooping, as if all the bombs and cannon-balls, which whistled past very frequently here, were flying straight at him. Some of the soldiers did the same, and in general most of the faces expressed uneasiness if not exactly alarm. These circumstances emboldened Volódya and completely comforted him.

'So here am I too on the Malákhov mound, which I fancied a thousand times more terrible. And I get along without bowing to the balls, and am even much less frightened than the others. So I am no coward,' he thought with pleasure, and even with a certain self-complacent rapture.

This feeling however was quickly shaken by a sight he came upon in the twilight at the Kornílov Battery while looking for the commander of the bastion. Four sailors stood by the breastwork holding by its arms and legs the blood-stained corpse of a man without boots or coat and swinging it before heaving it over. (On the second day of this bombardment it was found impossible in some parts to clear away the corpses from the bastions, and they were therefore thrown out into the ditch so as not to be in the way at the batteries.) Volódya felt stunned for a moment when he saw the body bump on the top of the breastwork and then roll down into the ditch, but luckily for him the commander of the bastion met him just then and gave him his orders and a guide to show him the way to the battery and to the bomb-proof assigned to his men. We will not speak of all the dangers and disenchantments our hero lived through that evening: how – instead of the firing he was used to on the Vólkov field amid conditions of perfect exactitude and order which he had expected to meet with here also – he found two damaged mortars, one with its muzzle battered in by a ball, the other standing on the splinters of its shattered platform; how he could not get workmen before the morning to mend the platform; how not a single charge was of the weight specified in the Handbook; how two of the men under him were wounded, and how he was twenty times within a hair's-breadth of death. Fortunately a gigantic gunner, a sea-

man who had served with the mortars since the commencement of the siege, had been appointed to assist Volódya, and
convinced him of the possibility of using the mortars. By the
light of a lantern this gunner showed him all over the battery as
he might have shown him over his own kitchen-garden, and
undertook to have everything right by the morning. The
bomb-proof to which his guide led him was an oblong hole
dug in the rocky ground, twenty-five cubic yards in size and
covered with oak beams two and a half feet thick. He and all
his soldiers installed themselves in it.

As soon as he discovered the little door, not three feet high,
Vlang rushed in headlong before anyone else, and at the risk of
breaking his limbs against the stone bottom squeezed into the
farthest corner and remained there. Volódya, when all the
soldiers had settled on the ground along the walls and some
had lit their pipes, made up his own bed in a corner, lit a
candle, and after lighting a cigarette, lay down.

The reports of continuous firing could be heard overhead
but not very distinctly, except from one cannon which stood
quite close and shook the bomb-proof with its thunder. In the
bomb-proof all was quiet, except when one or other of the
soldiers, still rather shy in the presence of the new officer,
spoke, asking a neighbour to move a little or to give him a
light for his pipe, when a rat scratched somewhere among the
stones, or when Vlang, who had not yet recovered and was still
looking wildly around him, heaved a deep sigh.

Volódya, on his bed in this quiet corner crammed with
people and lighted by a solitary candle, experienced a sensation
of cosiness such as he had felt as a child when, playing hide-
and-seek, he used to creep into a cupboard or under his
mother's skirt and sit listening in breathless silence, afraid of
the dark yet conscious of enjoyment. It felt rather uncanny, yet
his spirits were high.

XXII

AFTER ten minutes or so the soldiers grew bolder and began
to talk. The more important ones – two non-commissioned

officers: an old grey-haired one with every possible medal and
cross except the St George, and a young one, a Cantonist,[1] who
was smoking cigarettes he had rolled himself – settled nearest to
the light and to the officer's bed. The drummer had as usual
assumed the duty of waiting upon the officer. The bombardiers
and those who had medals came next, and farther off, in the
shadow nearer the entrance, sat the humbler folk. It was these
last who started a conversation, caused by the noise a man made
who came tumbling hurriedly into the bomb-proof.

'Hullo, old fellow! Why don't you stay outside? Don't the
lasses play merrily enough out there?' said a voice.

'They're playing such tunes as we never hear in our village,'
laughingly replied the man who had just run in.

'Ah, Vásin don't like bombs – that he don't!' said someone
in the aristocratic corner.

'If it was necessary, that would be a different matter,' replied
Vásin slowly, and when he spoke all the others were silent. 'On
the 24th we were at least firing, but why grumble at me now?
The authorities won't thank the likes of us for getting killed
uselessly.'

At these words everyone laughed.

'There's Mélnikov – he's out there now, I fancy,' said
someone.

'Go and send Mélnikov in here,' said the old sergeant, 'or
else he really will get killed uselessly.'

'Who is Mélnikov?' asked Volódya.

'Oh, he's a poor silly soldier of ours, your Honour. He's just
afraid of nothing, and he's walking about outside now. You
should have a look at him, he's just like a bear.'

'He knows a charm,' came Vásin's long-drawn accents from
the other corner.

Mélnikov entered the bomb-proof. He was stout (an
extremely rare thing among soldiers), red-haired and red-
faced, with an enormous bulging forehead and prominent
pale-blue eyes.

1 The Cantonists, under serfdom, which still prevailed at the time of the
Crimean War, were the sons of soldiers, condemned by law and heredity to
be soldiers also.

'Aren't you afraid of the bombs?' asked Volódya.

'What's there to be afraid of in them bombs?' answered Mélnikov, wriggling and scratching himself. 'They won't kill me with a bomb, I know.'

'So you'd like to live here?'

''Course I should. It's jolly here,' he said and burst out laughing.

'Oh, then they should take you for a sortie! Shall I speak to the general about it?' said Volódya, though he did not know a single general in the place.

'Like, indeed! 'Course I should!' And Mélnikov hid behind the others.

'Let's have a game of "noses" lads! Who has the cards?' his voice was heard to say hurriedly.

And soon the game had started in the far corner: laughter could be heard, and noses being smacked and trumps declared. The drummer having heated the samovar for him, Volódya drank some tea, treated the non-commissioned officers to some, and, wishing to gain popularity, joked and talked with them and felt very pleased at the respect paid him. The soldiers, seeing that the gentleman gave himself no airs, became talkative too. One of them explained that the siege of Sevastopol would not last much longer, because a reliable fellow in the fleet had told him that Constantine, the Tsar's brother, was coming with the 'merican fleet to help us, and also that there would soon be an agreement not to fire for a fortnight, but to have a rest, and that if anyone did fire, he'd have to pay a fine of seventy-five kopeks for each shot. Vásin, who was a small man with whiskers and large kind eyes, as Volódya had already noticed, related, first amid general silence and then amid roars of laughter, how he had gone home on leave and at first everyone was glad to see him, but then his father had begun sending him to work while the forester-lieutenant sent a horse and trap to fetch his wife! All this amused Volódya very much. He not only felt no fear or annoyance because of the overcrowding and bad air in the bomb-proof, but on the contrary felt exceedingly bright and contented.

Many of the soldiers were already snoring. Vlang had also stretched himself out on the floor, and the old sergeant having spread his cloak on the ground was crossing himself and muttering prayers before going to sleep, when Volódya felt moved to go out of the bomb-proof and see what was happening outside.

'Draw in your legs!' the soldiers called to one another as soon as he rose, and the legs were drawn in to make room for him.

Vlang, who had seemed to be asleep, suddenly raised his head and seized Volódya by the skirts of his cloak.

'Don't go! Don't go – how can you?' he began in a tearfully persuasive voice. 'You don't know what it's like. Cannon-balls are falling all the time out there. It's better in here.'

But in spite of Vlang's entreaties Volódya made his way out of the bomb-proof and sat down on the threshold, where Mélnikov was already sitting making his feet comfortable.

The air was pure and fresh, especially after that of the bomb-proof, and the night was clear and calm. Mingling with the booming of the cannon could be heard the rumbling of the wheels of carts bringing gabions, and voices of men at work in the powder-vault. High overhead stretched the starry sky, across which the fiery trails of the bombs ran incessantly. On the left was another bomb-proof, through the three-foot opening of which the legs and backs of the sailors who lived there could be seen and their voices heard. In front was the roof of the powder-vault, past which flitted the figures of stooping men, while on the top of it, under the bullets and bombs that kept flying past, was a tall figure in a black cloak with its hands in its pockets, treading down the earth the others carried up in sacks. Many a bomb flew past and exploded very near the vault. The soldiers who were carrying the earth stooped and stepped aside, but the black figure continued calmly to stamp the earth down with its feet and remained on the spot in the same position.

'Who is that black fellow there?' said Volódya to Mélnikov.

'Can't say. I'll go and see.'

'No, don't. There's no need.'

But Mélnikov rose without heeding him, approached the black figure, and for a long time stood beside it just as indifferent and immovable.

'That's the powder-master, your Honour!' he said when he returned. 'The vault has been knocked in by a bomb, so the infantry are carrying earth there.'

Now and then a bomb seemed to fly straight at the door of the bomb-proof. Then Volódya pressed behind the corner, but soon crept out again looking up to see if another was coming that way. Though Vlang from inside the bomb-proof again and again entreated him to come in, Volódya sat at the threshold for about three hours, finding a kind of pleasure in tempting fate and watching the flying bombs. By the end of the evening he knew how many guns were firing, from which positions, and where their shots fell.

XXIII

The next morning, 27 August, Volódya, fresh and vigorous after ten hours' sleep, stepped across the threshold of the bomb-proof. Vlang too came out, but at the first sound of a bullet rushed wildly back to the entrance, pushing his way through the crowd with his head amid the general laughter of the soldiers, most of whom had also come out into the fresh air.

Vlang, the old sergeant, and a few others only came out into the trench at rare intervals, but the rest could not be kept inside: they all crept out of the stuffy bomb-proof into the fresh morning air and in spite of the firing, which continued as violently as on the day before, settled themselves – some by the threshold of the bomb-proof and some under the breastwork. Mélnikov had been strolling about from battery to battery since early dawn, looking calmly upwards.

Near the threshold sat two old soldiers and one young curly-haired one, a Jew transferred to the battery from an infantry regiment. This latter had picked up one of the bullets that were lying about, and after flattening it out on a stone with the fragment of a bomb, was now carving out a cross like the Order of St George. The others sat talking and watching his work. The cross was really turning out very well.

'I say,' said one of them, 'if we stay here much longer we shall all have served our time and get discharged when there's peace.'

'You're right. Why I had only four years left to serve, and I've been five months already in Sevastopol.'

'That won't be reckoned specially towards our discharge, it seems,' said another.

At that moment a cannon-ball flew over the heads of the speakers and fell a couple of feet from Mélnikov, who was coming towards them through the trench.

'That one nearly killed Mélnikov,' said one of them.

'It won't kill me,' said Mélnikov.

'Then I present you with this cross for your courage,' said the young soldier, giving him the cross he had made.

'... No, my lad, a month's service here counts as a year for everything – that was said in the proclamation,' continued one of the soldiers.

'You may say what you like, but when we have peace we're sure to have an Imperial review at Warsaw, and then if we don't all get our discharge we shall be put on the permanent reserve.'

Just then a shrieking, glancing rifle-bullet flew just over the speakers' heads and struck a stone.

'Look out, or you'll be getting your discharge in full before to-night,' said one of the soldiers.

They all laughed.

And not only before night, but before two hours had passed, two of them had got their discharge in full and five more were wounded, but the rest went on joking just the same.

By the morning the two mortars had really been put into such a condition that they could be fired, and at ten o'clock Volódya called out his company and marched with it to the battery, in accordance with the order he had received from the commander of the bastion.

Not a trace of the fear noticeable the day before remained among the men as soon as they were actively engaged. Only Vlang could not master himself, but hid and ducked in the same old way, and Vásin lost some of his composure, fidgeted, and kept dodging. Volódya was in ecstasies, the thought of danger never entered his head. Joy at fulfilling his duty, at finding that not only was he no coward but that he was even quite brave, the sense of commanding and being in the presence of twenty men who were he knew watching him with curiosity, made him quite valiant. He was even vain of his courage and showed off before the soldiers, climbing out onto the banquette and unfastening his cloak on purpose to be more conspicuous. The commander of the bastion making the round of his 'household' as he expressed it, accustomed as he had grown during the last eight months to courage of all kinds, could not help admiring this handsome lad, with his coat unbuttoned showing a red shirt fitting close to his delicate white neck, who with flushed face and shining eyes clapped his hands, gave the order, 'One – two!' in ringing tones, and ran gaily onto the breastwork to see where his bombs were falling. At half-past eleven the firing slackened on both sides, and at twelve o'clock precisely the storming of the Malákhov Redoubt, and of the Second, Third (the Redan), and Fifth Bastions, began.

XXIV

On the North Side of the Roadstead, towards midday, two sailors were standing on the telegraph hill between Inkerman and the Northern entrenchment: one of them, an officer, was looking at Sevastopol through the telescope fixed there. Another officer with a Cossack had just ridden up to the signal-post.

The sun shone brightly high above the Roadstead, and with its warm bright light played on the stationary vessels, the flapping sails, and the rowing boats. A light wind scarcely swayed the withering leaves of the oak-scrub near the telegraph post, filled the sails of the boats, and ruffled the waves.

Sevastopol, still the same, with its unfinished church, its column, its quay, its boulevard showing green on the hill, and the elegant building of its library; with its little azure creeks bristling with masts, the picturesque arches of its aqueducts, and with clouds of blue powder-smoke now and then lit up by red flashes from the guns – this same beautiful, festive, proud Sevastopol, surrounded on one side by yellow smoking hills and on the other by the bright blue sea playing in the sunlight – could still be seen on the opposite side of the Roadstead. Above the rim of the sea, along which spread a streak of black smoke from a steamer, drifted long white clouds that portended rain. Along the whole line of entrenchments, especially on the hills to the left, compressed puffs of thick white smoke continually appeared several at a time, accompanied by flashes that sometimes gleamed like lightning even in the noontide light; and these puffs grew larger and assumed various shapes, rising and seeming darker against the sky.

They started now here now there from the hills, from the enemy's batteries, from the town, and high up in the sky. The noise of the reports never ceased, and mingling with one another they shook the air.

Towards noon the cloudlets of smoke showed less and less often and the air was less shaken by the booming.

'There now, the Second Bastion doesn't reply at all!' said the mounted hussar officer. 'It's absolutely knocked to bits. It's terrible!'

'Yes, and the Malákhov hardly fires one shot for three of theirs,' replied the man who was looking through the telescope. 'It makes me mad that ours are silent. They are firing straight into the Kornílov Battery and it doesn't reply at all.'

'But look here, I told you they always stop bombarding at noon. And it's the same to-day. We'd better go to lunch . . . they'll be waiting for us as it is. . . . There's nothing to look at now.'

'Wait a bit! Don't bother me!' said the man in possession of the telescope, looking eagerly at Sevastopol.

'What is it? What?'

'A movement in the trenches – dense columns advancing.'

'Yes, one can see it with the naked eye,' said the sailor. 'They are advancing in columns. We must give the alarm.'

'Look! Look! They have left the trenches.'

And one could really see with the naked eye what seemed like dark spots coming down the hill, across the ravine from the French batteries towards our bastions. In front of these spots, dark streaks could already be seen near our lines. From our bastions white cloudlets of firing burst out at different points as if crossing one another. The wind brought a sound of small-arms firing, like rain pelting against window-panes. The dark streaks were moving nearer and nearer right amid the smoke. The sounds of firing grew louder and louder and merged into a prolonged rumbling peal. The smoke, rising more and more often, spread rapidly along the lines and at last merged into one light-purple cloud curling and uncurling, amid which here and there flashes just flickered and dark dots appeared: all the separate sounds blended into one thundering crash.

'An assault!' said the officer, growing pale and letting the sailor have the telescope.

Cossacks galloped down the road, officers on horseback passed by, and the commander-in-chief in a carriage accompanied by his suite. On every face there was an expression of painful agitation and expectancy.

'They can't have taken it!' cried the mounted officer.

'By God, a standard! Look! Look!' said the officer, panting and moving away from the telescope – 'A French standard on the Malákhov!'

'Impossible!'

XXV

T H E elder Kozeltsóv, who had found time that night to win back his money and to lose it all again, including the gold pieces sewn in his cuff, was lying towards morning in a heavy, unhealthy, and deep sleep in the Defence Barracks of the Fifth Bastion, when a desperate cry arose, repeated by many voices –

'The alarm!'

'Why are you sleeping, Michael Semënich? We are attacked!' shouted someone.

'It must be a hoax,' he said, opening his eyes incredulously.

Then he saw an officer running from one corner of the barracks to the other without any apparent reason and with such a pale face that he realized it all. The thought that they might take him for a coward who did not wish to be with his company at a critical moment upset him terribly, and he rushed full speed to join it. The artillery firing had ceased, but the clatter of musketry was at its height. The bullets did not whistle as single ones do but came in swarms like a flock of autumn birds flying overhead.

The whole place where his battalion had been stationed the day before was hidden in smoke, and enemy shouts and exclamations could be heard. As he went he met crowds of wounded and unwounded soldiers. Having run another thirty paces he saw his own company pressed to the wall.

'The Schwartz Redoubt is taken!' said a young officer, whose teeth were chattering. 'All is lost!'

'Nonsense!' said Kozeltsóv angrily, and [wishing to rouse himself by a gesture] he drew his blunt little iron sword and cried:

'Forward, lads! Hurrah!'

His voice sounded loud and clear and roused Kozeltsóv himself. He ran forward along the traverse, and about fifty soldiers ran shouting after him. From the traverse he ran out into the open ground. The bullets fell just like hailstones. Two hit him, but where, and what they had done – bruised him or wounded him – he had no time to determine. Before him through the smoke he could already see blue coats and red trousers, and hear shouts that were not Russian. One French-man stood on the breastwork waving his cap and shouting something. Kozeltsóv felt sure he would be killed, and this increased his courage. He ran on and on. Several soldiers outran him, others appeared from somewhere else and also ran. The blue uniforms were always at the same distance from him, running back to their trenches, but there were dead and wounded on the ground under his feet. When he had run to the outer ditch, everything became blurred in Kozeltsóv's eyes and he felt a pain in his chest.

Half an hour later he was lying on a stretcher near the Nicholas Barracks and knew that he was wounded, but felt hardly any pain. He only wished for something cool to drink, and to lie more comfortably.

A plump little doctor with large black whiskers came up to him and unbuttoned his cloak. Kozeltsóv looked over his chin to see the doctor's face and what he was doing to his wound, but he still felt no pain. The doctor covered the wound with the shirt, wiped his fingers on the skirt of his cloak and silently, without looking at the wounded man, passed on to another patient. Kozeltsóv unconsciously watched what was going on around him and, remembering what had happened at the Fifth Bastion with exceedingly joyful self-satisfaction, felt that he had performed his duty well – that for the first time in the whole of his service he had acted as well as it was possible to act, and that he had nothing to reproach himself with. The doctor, bandaging another man, pointed to Kozeltsóv and said something to a priest with a large red beard, who stood near by with a cross.

'Am I dying?' asked Kozeltsóv when the priest approached him.

The priest did not reply, but said a prayer and held a cross to the wounded man's lips.

Death did not frighten Kozeltsóv. He took the cross with his weak hands, pressed it to his lips, and began to weep.

'Were the French driven back?' he asked the priest firmly.

'The victory is ours at all points,' answered the latter to console the wounded man, concealing from him the fact that a French standard was already waving from the Malákhov Redoubt.

'Thank God!' exclaimed the dying man, not feeling the tears that ran down his cheeks, [and experiencing inexpressible delight at the consciousness of having performed a heroic deed.]

The thought of his brother flashed through his brain. 'God grant him as good a fate!' thought he.

XXVI

But a different fate awaited Volódya. He was listening to a tale Vásin was telling when he heard the cry 'The French are coming!' The blood suddenly rushed to his heart and he felt his cheeks grow cold and pale. He remained immovable for a moment, but glancing round saw the soldiers fastening their uniforms and crawling out one after the other fairly coolly. One of them – Mélnikov probably – even joked, saying, 'Take them some bread and salt.'[1]

Volódya, and Vlang who followed him like a shadow, climbed out of the bomb-proof and ran to the battery. There was no artillery firing at all from either side. The coolness of the soldiers did less to rouse Volódya than the pitiful cowardice of the cadet. 'Can I possibly be like him?' he thought, and ran gaily to the breastwork where his mortars stood. He could plainly see the French running straight towards him across the open ground, and crowds of them moving in the nearer trenches, their bayonets glittering in the sunshine. One short, broad-shouldered fellow in a Zouave uniform was running in front, sword in hand, jumping across the pits.

'Fire case-shot!' cried Volódya, running back from the banquette, but the soldiers had already arranged matters without him and the metallic ring of the discharged case-shot whistled over his head first from one mortar and then from the other. 'One – two!' ordered Volódya, running the distance between the two mortars and quite forgetting the danger. From one side and near at hand was heard the clatter of the musketry of our supports, and excited cries.

Suddenly a wild cry of despair arose on the left. 'They're behind us! Behind us!' repeated several voices. Volódya looked round. About twenty Frenchmen appeared behind him. One of them, a handsome man with a black beard, was in front of the rest, but having run up to within ten paces of the battery he stopped, fired point-blank at Volódya, and then again started running towards him. For a moment Volódya stood petrified,

1 It is a Russian custom to offer bread and salt to new arrivals.

unable to believe his eyes. When he recovered and glanced round he saw French uniforms on the breastwork before him; two Frenchmen were even spiking a cannon some ten paces from him. No one was near but Mélnikov, who had fallen at his side killed by a bullet, and Vlang, who had seized a linstock and was rushing forward with a furious look on his face, rolling his eyes and shouting.

'Follow me, Vladímir Semënich!... Follow me!' he cried in a desperate voice, brandishing his linstock at the Frenchmen who had appeared from behind. The furious figure of the cadet perplexed them. Vlang hit the front one on the head, the others involuntarily hesitated, and he ran to the trench where our infantry lay firing at the French, continually look-ing back and shouting desperately, 'Come with me, Vladímir Semënich! Why are you stopping? Run!' Having jumped in, he climbed out again to see what his adored ensign was doing. Something in a cloak lay prostrate where Volódya had stood, and that whole place was occupied by Frenchmen firing at our men.

XXVII

VLANG found his battery at the second line of defence. Of the twenty soldiers belonging to the mortar battery only eight were left.

Towards nine in the evening Vlang crossed over with the battery to the North Side on a steamer crowded with soldiers, cannon, horses, and wounded men. There was no firing any-where. The stars shone as brightly in the sky as they had done the night before, but the sea was rocked by a strong wind. On the First and Second Bastions flames kept bursting up along the ground, explosions rent the air and lit up strange dark objects and the stones flying in the air around them. Something was burning near the docks and the red glare was reflected on the water. The bridge thronged with people was illuminated by a fire at the Nicholas Battery. A large flame seemed to stand above the water on the distant little headland of the Alexander Battery, lighting up from below the clouds of smoke that hung above it, and quiet, bold lights gleamed over the sea, as they had done yesterday, from the distant enemy fleet, and the fresh wind raised waves in the Roadstead. By the glaring light of the conflagration one could see the masts of our sinking ships as they slowly descended deeper and deeper into the water. There was no talking on board, only words of command given by the captain, the snorting and stamping of the horses on the vessel, and the moaning of the wounded, could be heard above the steam and the regular swish of the parting waters. Vlang, who had had nothing to eat all day, took a piece of bread from his pocket and began munching it, but suddenly remembering Volódya he began to sob so loud that the soldiers near him heard it.

'Look! He's eating bread and yet he's sobbing, is our Vlánga!' said Vásin.

'That's queer!' said another.

'Look! Our barrack's been set on fire too,' he continued with a sigh. 'What a lot of the likes of us perished there; and now the Frenchmen have got it for nothing.'

'At all events we have got off alive, thank God!' said Vásin.

'All the same, it's a shame.'

'Where's the shame? D'you think they'll get a chance of amusing themselves there? See if ours don't retake it. No matter how many of the likes of us are lost; if the Emperor gives the word, as sure as there's a God we'll take it back. You don't suppose we'll leave it like that? No fear! There, take the bare walls. . . . The 'trenchments are all blown up. . . . Yes, I daresay. . . . *He's* stuck his flag on the mound, but he's not shoved himself into the town. . . . You wait a bit! The real reckoning will come yet – only wait a bit!' he concluded, admonishing the French.

'Of course it will!' said another with conviction.

Along the whole line of the Sevastopol bastions – which for so many months had been seething with such extraordinary life and energy, for so many months had seen heroes relieved by death as they fell one after another, and for so many months had aroused the fear, the hatred, and at last the admiration of the enemy – no one was now to be seen: all was dead, ghastly, terrible. But it was not silent: destruction was still going on. Everywhere on the ground, blasted and strewn around by fresh explosions, lay shattered gun-carriages crushing the corpses of foes and Russians alike, cast-iron cannons thrown with terrific force into holes and half-buried in the earth and silenced for ever, bombs, cannon-balls and more dead bodies; then holes and splintered beams of what had been bomb-proofs, and again silent corpses in grey or blue uniforms. All this still shuddered again and again, and was lit up by the lurid flames of the explosions that continued to shake the air.

The enemy saw that something incomprehensible was happening in awe-inspiring Sevastopol. The explosions and the deathly stillness on the bastions made them shudder, but under the influence of the strong and firm resistance of that day they did not yet dare to believe that their unflinching foe had disappeared, and they awaited the end of the gloomy night silently, motionless and anxious.

The Sevastopol army, surging and spreading like the sea on a rough dark night, its whole mass anxiously palpitating, slowly swayed through the thick darkness by the bridge over the Roadstead and onto the North Side, away from the place where it was leaving so many brave comrades, from the place saturated with its blood, the place it had held for eleven months against a far stronger foe, but which it was now ordered to abandon without a struggle.

The first effect this command had on every Russian was one of oppressive bewilderment. The next feeling was a fear of pursuit. The men felt helpless as soon as they had left the places where they were accustomed to fight, and crowded anxiously together in the darkness at the entrance to the bridge which was rocked by the strong wind. With bayonets clashing, regiments, vehicles, and militia crowded together and pressed forward to the bay. While mounted officers pushed through with orders, the inhabitants wept, orderlies carrying forbidden luggage entreated, and artillery with rattling wheels hurried to get away. Notwithstanding the diversion resulting from their various and bustling occupations, the instinct of self-preservation and the desire to get away as quickly as possible from this dreadful place of death was present in the soul of each. It was present in the mortally wounded soldier who lay among the five hundred other wounded men on the pavement of the Pávlov Quay praying to God for death; in the militia-man pushing with all his might among the dense crowd to make way for a general who was riding past; in the general who conducted the crossing, firmly restraining the impetuosity of the soldiers; in the sailor who, having got among a moving battalion, was squeezed by the swaying crowd till he could scarcely breathe; in the wounded officer whom four soldiers had been carrying on a stretcher, but stopped by the throng had put down on the ground near the Nicholas Battery; in the artilleryman who having served with the same gun for sixteen years was now, in obedience to an officer's order quite incomprehensible to him, with the help of his comrades pushing that gun down the steep bank into the Roadstead, and in the sailors of the fleet who, having just scuttled their ships, were briskly rowing away from them in the long-boats. On reaching the North Side and leaving the bridge almost every man took off his cap and crossed himself. But behind this feeling of self-preservation there was another, a deeper feeling, sad and gnawing, akin to remorse, shame, and anger. Almost every soldier looking back at the abandoned town from the North Side, sighed with inexpressible bitterness in his heart and made a menacing gesture towards the enemy.

A BILLIARD-MARKER'S
NOTES

IT was going on for three when it happened. The gentlemen playing were 'the big guest' (as our people called him), the prince (who always goes about with him), the gentleman with whiskers, the little hussar, Oliver (the one who has been an actor), and the *pan*.[1] There were a good many people.

The big guest was playing with the prince. I just go round the table with the rest in my hand, counting 'ten and forty-eight, twelve and forty-eight'. Everybody knows what it is to be a billiard-marker. You haven't had a bite all day, nor slept for two nights, but you must keep calling the score and taking the balls out. I go on counting and look round – there's a new gentleman coming in at the door. He looks and looks and then sits down on the sofa. All right.

'Who may that be? – Of what class, I mean?' think I to myself. He was well dressed – oh, very smartly – all his clothes looked as if they had just come out of a bandbox: fine cloth checked trousers, short fashionable coat, a plush waistcoat, and a gold chain with all sorts of little things hanging from it.

Handsomely dressed, but still handsomer himself: slim, tall, hair brushed to the front, latest fashion, and with a red and white complexion – in a word, a fine fellow.

Of course, in our business we see all sorts of people: the grandest that ever were and much trash also, so that though you are a marker you fit in with people, if you are artful enough I mean.

I looked at the gentleman and noticed that he was sitting quietly and did not know anybody, and his clothes were as

1 *Pan* in Polish and Ukrainian means 'squire' or 'gentleman'.

new as could be. So I think to myself: 'He is either a foreigner – an Englishman – or some count who has turned up. He bears himself well although he is young.' Oliver was sitting beside him and even moved to make room for him.

The game was finished – the big guest had lost and shouted at me:

'You always blunder! You keep looking at something else instead of counting properly.'

He swore, threw down the cue, and went out. What can you make of it? He'll play a fifty-ruble game with the prince of an evening, but now when he loses a bottle of Burgundy he's quite beside himself. He's that kind of character! Sometimes he plays with the prince till two in the morning. They don't put their stakes in the pockets,[1] and I know they haven't either of them got any money, but they just swagger.

'Shall we play double or quits for twenty-five?'

'All right.'

But if you just dare to yawn or don't put a ball right – after all, one is not made of stone – then they just jump down your throat:

'We are not playing for chips, but for money!'

That one plagues me more than all the rest...

Well – so the prince says to the new gentleman, when the big one has gone:

'Would you care to have a game with me?'

'With pleasure!' he says.

As long as he was sitting down he looked quite a sport, and seemed to have plenty of confidence, but when he got up and came to the table he was – not exactly timid – no, he was not timid, but one could see he was upset. Whether he was uncomfortable in his new clothes, or frightened because everybody was looking at him, anyhow his confidence was gone. He walked somehow sideways, his pocket catching the table pockets. When chalking the cue he dropped the chalk,

---

1 The players put the money they staked in the pockets of the billiard-table, and the player who pocketed a ball took the money when he took the ball out.

and when he did get a ball into a pocket he kept looking round and blushing. Not like the prince – he was used to it – he would chalk the cue and his hand, turn up his sleeve, and just smash the balls into the pockets, small as he was.

They played two or three games – I don't quite remember – and the prince put down the cue and said:

'Allow me to ask your name . . .'

'Nekhlyúdov,' he says.

'Didn't your father command a corps?'

'Yes,' he says.

Then they began talking quickly in French, and I didn't understand. Probably talking about their relations.

'*Au revoir*,' says the prince, 'I'm very glad to have made your acquaintance.'

He washed his hands and went out to get something to eat, but the other remained beside the table with his cue, shoving the balls about.

Of course everyone knows in our business that the ruder one is with a newcomer the better, so I began collecting the balls. He blushed and said:

'Can I go on playing?'

'Of course,' I says, 'that's what the billiard-table is for – to be played on.'

But I didn't look at him and put away the cues.

'Will you play with me?'

'Of course, sir,' say I.

I placed the balls.

'Is it to be a crawl?'

'What do you mean by a crawl?'

So I say: 'You pay half a ruble, and I crawl under the table if I lose.'

Of course never having seen such a thing it seemed funny to him and he laughed.

'Let's!' he says.

'All right. How much will you allow me?' I ask.

'Why, do you play worse than I?'

'Of course,' I say. 'I can see there are few players to match you.'

We began to play. He really thought himself a master at it. He banged the balls about dreadfully, and the *pan* sat there and kept saying:

'What a ball! What a stroke!'

What indeed! He could make strokes, but there was no calculation about it. Well, I lost the first game as is the usual thing, and began crawling under the table and groaning. Here Oliver and the *pan* jumped up and knocked with their cues.

'Splendid! Go on!' they said. 'Go on!'

Go on indeed! The *pan* especially... for half a ruble he would himself have been glad not only to crawl under the table but under the Blue Bridge. And then he shouted:

'Splendid!' he says. 'But you haven't swept up all the dust yet.'

I am Petrúshka the marker. Everybody knows me. It used to be Tyúrik the marker, but now it is Petrúshka.

But of course I did not show my game. I lost another one.

'I can't play level with you, sir,' I says.

He laughed. Then after I had won three games – and when he had a score of forty-nine and I nothing, I put my cue on the table and said: 'Will you make it double or quits, sir?'

'Quits, what do you mean?' he says.

'Either you'll owe me three rubles, or nothing,' I say.

'What?' he says. 'Am I playing you for money? You fool!'

He even blushed.

Very well. He lost the game.

'Enough!' he says.

He got out his pocket-book, quite a new one bought at the *Magasin Anglais*, and opened it. I see that he wants to show off. It was chock full of notes, all hundred-ruble ones.

'No,' he says, 'there's no change there,' and he took three rubles out of his purse.

'There you are,' he says, 'two for the games, and the rest for you to have a drink.'

'Thank you very much,' I say. I saw he was a nice gentleman. One can do a little crawling for such as him. The pity was that he didn't want to play for money – 'or else,' think I, 'I'd manage to get maybe twenty or even forty rubles off him.'

When the *pan* saw the young gentleman's money he says: 'Would you care to play a game with me? You play so splendidly!' he says, fawning on him like a fox.

'No,' he says, 'excuse me, please, I haven't time,' and he went away.

I don't know who that *pan* was. Someone nicknamed him 'the *pan*' and the name stuck to him. He'd sit all day long in the billiard-room looking on. He had been beaten and sworn at, and no one would play with him. He would bring his pipe and sit by himself and smoke. But he could play a careful game . . . the beast!

Well, Nekhlyúdov came a second and a third time and began coming often. He'd come in the morning and in the evening. Billiards, pool, snooker, he learnt them all. He grew bolder, got to know everybody, and began to play a decent game. Naturally, being a young man of good family and with money, everybody respected him. Only once he had a row with the big guest.

It was all about a trifle.

They played pool – the prince, the big guest, Nekhlyúdov, Oliver, and someone else. Nekhlyúdov stands by the stove talking to someone, it was the big one's turn to play. His ball happened to come just opposite the stove: there was not much room there, and he likes to play with a big swing.

Well, whether he didn't see Nekhlyúdov or did it on purpose, he took a big swing at the ball and hit Nekhlyúdov hard in the chest with the butt of his cue. The poor fellow even groaned a little. And what next? He didn't even say 'beg pardon' – the rude fellow – but went on without looking at him, and even muttered: 'Why do they shove themselves forward? It has made me lose a ball.' As if there was not plenty of room!

The other goes up to him, very pale, and says quite politely as if nothing had happened: 'You should apologize first, sir. You pushed me.'

'It's not the time for me to apologize. I ought to have won,' he says, 'and now that fellow will score off my ball.'

The other says again: 'You must apologize.'

'Be off!' he says. 'Pestering like this!' and keeps looking at his ball.

Nekhlyúdov came still nearer and took hold of his arm.

'You're a boor, sir,' he says.

For all that he's slim and young and rosy as a girl, yet his eyes glittered as fierce as if he were ready to eat him. The big guest is a strong man, and tall. Much bigger than Nekhlyúdov.

'What?' he says. 'Do you call me a boor?'

And he shouts, and lifts his arm to strike him, but the others there jumped up, seized their arms, and dragged them apart.

They talk and talk – and Nekhlyúdov says:

'Let him give me satisfaction! He has insulted me,' he says – meaning that he wanted him to fight a duel. Of course they were gentlefolk – they have such customs . . . nothing can be done with them . . . in a word, they're gentlefolk!

'I won't give him any kind of satisfaction. He's only a boy – that's all he is. I'll pull his ears for him.'

'If you don't want to fight,' he says, 'you are not an honourable man.' And he himself was almost weeping.

'And you're just an urchin – it's impossible for you to insult me!'

Well, they got them apart and took them into separate rooms, as is usually done. Nekhlyúdov was friendly with the prince.

'For God's sake go and persuade him to accept a duel,' he says. 'He was drunk, but he may have come to his senses by this time. The affair must not end like this.'

The prince went. The big one says:

'I have fought duels and I have fought in war, but I won't fight a mere lad – I don't want to: that's all about it.'

Well, they talked and talked and finally left off; only the big guest left off coming to our place.

As far as sensitiveness went Nekhlyúdov was like a cockerel, very ambitious, but in other matters he had no sense at all. I remember once the prince says to him: 'Whom have you with you here?'

'Nobody,' he says.

'How's that – nobody?'

'Why should there be anybody?'

'What do you mean by "Why should there be anybody?"'

'I've lived by myself up to now,' he says, 'so why is it impossible?'

'Lived by yourself? You don't mean it!'

And the prince roars with laughter, and the whiskered gentleman too. They did make fun of him!

'So you've never...?' they say.

'Never!'

They died with laughter. Of course I understood at once why they laughed at him so. I watched to see what would come of it.

'Come along now,' says the prince. 'At once!'

'No, not on any account,' he says.

'Come, that's enough, it's too ridiculous,' he says. 'Have a drink to buck you up, and come along.'

I brought them a bottle of champagne. They drank it, and took the youngster along.

They returned after midnight and sat down to supper. There were a lot of them – all the very best: Atánov, Prince Rázin, Count Shustákh, and Mírtsov. They all congratulate Nekhlyúdov and laugh. They called me in, and I see they are all rather gay.

'Congratulate the gentleman!' they say.

'On what?' I ask.

Whatever did he call it?... On his *initiation* or *instigation* – I don't quite remember.

'I have the honour to congratulate you,' I say.

And he sits there, quite red, and only smiles. How they laughed!

Well, they come afterwards into the billiard-room all very merry, but Nekhlyúdov was unlike himself: his eyes were bleared, his lips twitching, and he kept hiccoughing and couldn't say a word properly. Of course, it being the first time, he was feeling bowled over. He went up to the table, put his elbows on it, and said:

'To you it seems funny, but I am sad. Why did I do it? I shall not forgive myself, or you, prince, for it all my life!'

And he bursts into tears and weeps. Of course he had drunk too much and didn't know himself what he was saying. The prince went up to him smiling.

'That's enough!' he says. 'It's a mere trifle! . . . Come home, Anatole.'

'I won't go anywhere. Why did I do it?' And he sobs. He wouldn't go away from the billiard-table, and that was all there was to it. What it is when a fellow is young and not used to it . . . And he spoilt the table there and then. Next day he paid eighty rubles for having cut the cloth.

So he often used to come to us. Once he came in with the prince and the whiskered gentleman who always went about with the prince. He was an official, or a retired officer – Heaven only knows – but the gentlemen all called him 'Fedót'. He had high cheek-bones and was very ugly, but dressed well and came in a carriage. Why the gentlemen liked him so, God only knows. It's 'Fedót, Fedót,' and you see them treating him to food and drink, paying for him. But he was a desperate fellow! If he lost he did not pay, but if he won – that was different! The big guest has abused him and beaten him before my eyes, and challenged him to a duel. . . . But he always went about arm-in-arm with the prince. 'You'd be lost without me!' he says. 'I'm Fedót and the others are not.' Such a wag.

Well, so they come in, and say:

'Let's play pool, the three of us.'

'All right,' they say.

They began playing for three-ruble stakes. Nekhlyúdov and the prince jabber together. 'You should just see,' he says, 'what a foot she has!'

'Never mind her foot – it's her hair that's so beautiful.'

Of course they didn't attend to the game but only talked together. But Fedót knows his business and plays trickily while they miss or run in. And he wins six rubles of each of them. Heaven only knows what accounts he had with the prince – they never paid one another any money; but Nekhlyúdov got out two three-ruble notes and held them out to him.

'No,' he says, 'I won't take the money from you. Let's play an ordinary game – double or quits, I mean either twice as much or nothing.'

I placed the balls for them. Fedót took odds and they began the game. Nekhlyúdov made strokes just to show off, and when he had a chance to pocket a ball and run out, he says: 'No, I don't want it – it's too easy,' but Fedót doesn't neglect his business and keeps on scoring. Of course he didn't show what he could do, but won the game as if by chance.

'Let's play double or quits again,' he says.

'All right.'

He won again.

'We began with a trifle,' he says. 'I don't want to take so much from you. Double or quits again, yes?'

'Yes.'

Say what one will one's sorry to lose fifty rubles, and Nekhlyúdov himself says: 'Let's have double or quits again.' So it went on and on, more and more. At last he'd lost two hundred and eighty rubles. Fedót knows all the tricks: he would lose a single stake and win a double; and the prince sits there and sees that things are getting serious.

'*Assez*,' he says, '*assez!*'

Not a bit of it! They keep increasing the stakes.

At last Nekhlyúdov owed him over five hundred rubles. Fedót puts down his cue and says:

'Haven't we had enough? I am tired,' he says.

But really he was ready to play till sunrise if there was money in it – all his craftiness of course. The other was still more anxious to go on. 'Let's play, let's play!' he says.

'No, really I'm tired . . . Come upstairs. You can take your revenge there.'

At our place gentlemen played cards upstairs. They'd start with preference and then go on to a gambling game.

Well, from that day on Fedót netted Nekhlyúdov so that he began coming to us every day. They'd have a game or two, and then it was 'Upstairs, upstairs!'

What they did there Heaven only knows, but Nekhlyúdov became a different man, and everything was flourishing with Fedót.

Formerly Nekhlyúdov had been smart, clean, his hair well brushed; but now he was only like his real self in the morning; after having been upstairs he would come down dishevelled, with fluff on his coat and his hands dirty.

One day he comes down with the prince like that, pale, his lips trembling, and disputing about something.

'I won't permit *him*,' he says, 'to tell me I am . . .' – however did he put it? . . . 'unwell-mannered' or something like that – 'and that *he* won't win against me. I have paid *him*,' he says, 'ten thousand rubles so *he* ought to be more careful before others.'

'Come now,' says the prince, 'is it worth being angry with Fedót?'

'No,' he says, 'I won't put up with it.'

'Stop!' he says. 'How can you lower yourself so far as to have an affair with Fedót?'

'But outsiders were present.'

'What if there were outsiders! If you like, I'll make him beg your pardon at once.'

'No,' says he.

And they jabbered something in French that I did not understand. Well, what do you think? That same evening they had supper with Fedót and the friendship continued.

Well, he'd sometimes come along.

'How is it?' he'd say. 'Do I play well?'

Of course it's our business to please everyone. 'Very well,' I say. But lord! – he just knocks the balls about without any kind of judgement. And ever since he got thick with Fedót he always played for money. Before that he did not like playing for any kind of stakes, not even for a lunch or champagne. Sometimes the prince would say:

'Let's play for a bottle of champagne.'

'No,' he'd say, 'I'd rather just order one. Hullo there! Bring a bottle of champagne!'

But now he began to play only for money. He'd walk up and down all day at our place either playing billiards with someone or going upstairs. So I thinks to myself: 'Why should others get it all, and not me?'

'Why haven't you played with me for such a long time, sir?' I says.

And we started playing.

When I had won some five rubles off him: 'Shall we play double or quits, sir?' I says.

He doesn't answer – doesn't say 'Fool!' as he did before. So we play double or quits again and again. I won some eighty rubles off him. Well, what d'you think? He played with me every day. Only he'd wait till no one else was there, because of course he was ashamed to play with a marker. One day he happened to get a bit excited when he already owed me some sixty rubles.

'Shall we play for the whole amount?' he says.

'All right,' I say.

I won.

'One hundred and twenty to one hundred and twenty?'

'All right.'

I won again.

'Two hundred and forty to two hundred and forty?'

'Isn't that too much?' I says.

He doesn't answer. We play. I win again.

'Four hundred and eighty to four hundred and eighty?'

I say: 'Why should I take advantage of you, sir? Play for a hundred rubles or leave it as it is.'

How he did shout! And how quiet he used to be!

'I'll knock you to bits!' he says. 'Either you play or you don't!'

Well, I see there is no help for it.

'Let it be three hundred and eighty,' I says.

Of course I meant to lose.

I allowed him forty points. His score was fifty-two and mine thirty-six. He potted the yellow and scored eighteen,[1] but left my ball standing well.

---

1 In the game of 'five balls' to pot the yellow ball in the middle pocket scores twelve, and to run in off it counts six, so that the two together at one stroke scores eighteen.

I struck the ball hard to make it rebound. No good, it cannoned and ran in and won the game again.

'Listen, Peter,' he says – he did not call me 'Petrúshka' – 'I can't pay you the whole now, but in two months' time I could pay you three thousand, if necessary.'

And he flushed quite red and his voice even trembled.

'Very good, sir,' I says, and put down the cue. He paced up and down a bit and the perspiration just ran down his face.

'Peter,' he says, 'let's play for the whole amount!'

He was nearly crying.

I say:

'What, play again, sir?'

'Do please!'

And he hands me the cue himself. I took the cue and flung the balls on the table so that they fell onto the floor – of course I had to show off – and I say: 'All right, sir!'

He was in such a hurry that he himself picked a ball up. I thought to myself: 'I shan't get the seven hundred anyway, so I might as well lose.' So I purposely played badly. And what do you think?

'Why,' he says, 'do you play badly on purpose?'

And his hands tremble, and when a ball rolls towards a pocket he spreads out his fingers, his mouth goes awry, and he stretches his head and his hands towards the pocket. So that I say:

'That won't help, sir!'

Well, when he had won that game, I says:

'You'll owe me a hundred and eighty rubles and a hundred and fifty games – and I'll go and have supper.'

I put down my cue and went away.

I sit down at a little table by the door and look to see what he'll do. What d'you think? He walks up and down – thinking I expect that nobody sees him – and pulls so at his hair! Then he walks about again muttering to himself, and suddenly gives another pull!

After that we didn't see him for eight days or so. Then he came in once into the dining-room, looking as gloomy as anything, but didn't go into the billiard-room.

The prince noticed him.

'Come, let's have a game!' he said.

'No,' he says, 'I won't play any more.'

'Oh, nonsense! Come along!'

'No,' he says, 'I won't. It would do you no good for me to come and it would do me harm.'

So he didn't come for another ten days. Then in the holidays he looked in one day in a dress suit – evidently he had been paying calls – and remained for the rest of the day playing all the time: next day he came again, and the day after, and then things went on in the old way. I wanted to play with him again.

'No, I won't play with you,' he says, 'but come to me in a month's time for the hundred and eighty rubles I owe you and you shall have them.'

All right. A month later I went to him.

'On my word,' he says, 'I haven't got it, but come back on Thursday.'

I went on the Thursday. He had such an excellent little flat.

'Is the master at home?' I says.

'Not up yet,' they tell me.

'All right. I'll wait.'

His valet was a serf of his own – an old, grey-haired fellow, simple and not up to any tricks. So we had a talk together.

'What are we living here for?' he says. 'My master is running quite to waste, and we get no honour nor profit in this Petersburg of yours. When we came from the country we thought we'd be as it used to be when the old master – the Kingdom of Heaven be his! – was alive; visiting princes, counts, and generals. We thought we'd get some queenly countess with a dowry, and live like a nobleman; but it turns out that we do nothing but run from one restaurant to another – quite bad! Princess Rtíshcheva, you know, is an aunt of ours, and Prince Borotýnzev is our godfather. What d'you think? He's only been to see them once, at Christmas, and hasn't shown his nose there since. Even their servants laugh at me: "Seems your master doesn't take after his papa!" they say. I once said to him:

' "Why don't you go to see your auntie, sir? She is sad at not having seen you so long."

' "It's dull there, Demyánych!" he says.

'Just look at that! The only pleasure he's found is at the restaurants. If only he were in public service somewhere – but no, he is only interested in cards and the like, and such doings never lead to any good . . . Eh, eh, we're ruining ourselves – ruining ourselves for nothing! We inherited from our deceased mistress – the Kingdom of Heaven be hers! – a very rich estate: more than a thousand serfs and more than three hundred thousand rubles' worth of forest land. He's mortgaged it all now, sold the forest, ruined the peasants, and nothing comes of it. In the master's absence a steward is more than a master, as is well known. What does the steward care? He skins the peasants completely, and there's an end of it. All he wants is to stuff his own pockets, though they all die of hunger. The other day two peasants came here to complain from the whole commune.

' "He's ruined the serfs completely," they said.

'Well, he read the complaints, gave the peasants ten rubles each and said: "I shall come myself soon. As soon as I receive money I'll settle up and leave town."

'But "settle up" indeed, when we keep making debts! Why, we have lived here the winter and have got through some eighty thousand rubles, and now there's not a ruble left in the house! And it's all because of his charitableness. Oh, what a simple gentleman he is – there are no words for it. It's because of that he is perishing, perishing just for nothing!'

And the old man almost wept.

Nekhlyúdov woke up about eleven and called me in.

'They haven't sent me the money, but it is not my fault,' he says. 'Shut the door.'

I shut it.

'Here,' he says, 'take this watch or this diamond pin and pawn it. They'll give you more than a hundred and eighty rubles for it, and when I get the money I will buy them out,' he says.

'All right, sir,' I say. 'If you have no money it can't be helped: let me have the watch – I'll pawn it for you.'

I could see myself that the watch was worth three hundred rubles.

Well, I pawned it for a hundred rubles and brought him the ticket.

'You'll owe me eighty rubles, and you can redeem the watch yourself,' I says.

Those eighty rubles are still owing me to this day!

So he kept coming to us every day again. I don't know what arrangements there were between them but he and the prince always went about together, or they went upstairs with Fedót to play cards. And they had some queer accounts among the three of them! One gave to another, the other to the third, but you could not at all make out who was owing whom.

And he came to us in this way almost every day for two years. Only he had lost his old manner: he became bold, and it got to such a pitch that at times he'd borrow a ruble from me to pay his cab fare; yet he still played with the prince for a hundred rubles a game.

He grew thin, sallow, and gloomy. He'd come in, order a glass of absinthe at once, have a snack, and wash it down with port wine, and then he would seem a bit brighter.

He came one day during Carnival, and began playing with some hussar.

'Do you want to have something on the game?' says the hussar.

'Certainly,' he says. 'How much?'

'Shall it be a bottle of burgundy?'

'All right.'

Well, the hussar won, and they sat down to dinner. They sat down, and Nekhlyúdov says at once:

'Simon, a bottle of Clos Vougeot – and mind it's properly warmed.'

Simon went out and brought some food, but no bottle.

'Well, and the wine?'

Simon ran out and brought the joint.

'Bring the wine,' says Nekhlyúdov.

Simon says nothing.

'Have you gone mad? We're finishing dinner and there's no wine. Who drinks it with the dessert?'

Simon ran out.

'The proprietor would like to see you,' he says.

Nekhlyúdov went quite red and jumped up from the table –

'What does he want?' he says.

The proprietor was standing at the door.

'I can't give you any more credit unless you pay me what you owe.'

'But I told you I'd pay at the beginning of next month!'

'As you please, but I can't go on giving credit and not receiving anything. As it is I lose tens of thousands by bad debts.'

'Oh, come, *mon cher,*' he says, 'surely you can trust me! Send up the bottle, and I will try to pay you as soon as possible.'

And he ran back.

'What did they call you away for?' asked the hussar.

'Just to ask me about something.'

'A little warm wine now would be just the thing,' says the hussar.

'Well, Simon, how about it?'

Poor Simon ran out again. Again there was no wine or anything. It was a bad lookout. Nekhlyúdov got up from the table and came to me.

'For God's sake, Petrúshka,' he says, 'let me have six rubles.'

He looked beside himself.

'I haven't got it, sir, on my word! As it is you're owing me a lot.'

'I'll give you forty rubles in a week's time for the six!'

'If I had it,' I says, 'I wouldn't dare refuse you, but really I haven't got it.'

And what do you think? He rushed out, clenching his teeth, and ran up and down the corridor like a madman, banging himself on the forehead.

'Oh, my God!' he says. 'What does it mean?'

He didn't even go back to the dining-room, but jumped into a carriage and drove off.

How they laughed! The hussar says:

'Where's the gentleman who was dining with me?'

'Gone,' they say.

'What do you mean – gone? What message did he leave?'

'He didn't leave any message,' they tell him. 'He just got in and drove away.'

'A fine goose!' he says.

'Well,' I think to myself, 'now he won't come for a long time, after such a disgrace.' But next day towards evening he came again, just the same. He went to the billiard-room with a box of some kind he had brought with him. He took off his overcoat.

'Let's play!' he says, looking from under his brows very cross.

We played a game.

'That's enough,' he says. 'Go and get me a pen and paper. I have to write a letter.'

Thinking nothing and guessing nothing, I brought the paper and put it on the table in the little room.

'It's all ready, sir,' I says.

Well, so he sat down at the table and wrote and wrote something; then he jumped up frowning.

'Go and see if my carriage has come!'

It happened on the Friday in Carnival Week, so none of our gentlemen were there: they had all gone to balls.

I was just going to find out about the carriage, but was hardly out of the door when he cried: 'Petrúshka! Petrúshka!' as if frightened of something.

I came back, and there he stood as white as a sheet, looking at me.

'You were pleased to call me, sir?' I says.

He was silent.

'What is it you want, sir?'

He was still silent.

'Oh, yes! Let's have another game,' he says.

Well, he won the game.

'Have I learnt to play well?' he says.

'Yes,' says I.

'That's it,' he says. 'Now go and find out about my carriage.'

And he paces up and down the room.

Without thinking anything, I went out onto the porch and saw that there was no carriage there at all, and went back.

As I go back it sounds as if someone had given a knock with a cue.

I go into the billiard-room – there's a strange smell.

I look: and there he lies on the floor covered with blood, with a pistol thrown down beside him. I was so frightened that I could not say a word.

He jerked his leg again and again and stretched himself. Then his throat rattled, and he stretched out like this.

And why such a sinful thing happened to him – I mean, why he ruined his soul – God alone knows: he left nothing but this paper behind, but I can't understand it at all.

Really, what things gentlemen do! . . . Gentlefolk – that's it – gentlefolk!

'God gave me everything man can desire: wealth, a name, intelligence, and noble aspirations. I wanted to enjoy myself and trampled in the mire all that was good in me.

'I am not dishonoured, not unfortunate, have committed no crime; but I have done worse – I have killed my feelings, my reason, my youth.

'I am enmeshed in a dirty net from which I cannot free myself and to which I cannot get used. I continually fall and fall, feel myself falling, and cannot stop.

'It would be easier if I were dishonoured, unfortunate, or a criminal. Then there would be some consolation of gloomy greatness in my despair. If I were dishonoured I could raise myself above the perception of honour held in our society and could despise it.

'If I were unfortunate I could complain. If I had committed a crime I might redeem it by repentance or by suffering punishment: but I am merely base, nasty – I know it and cannot raise myself.

'And what has ruined me? Had I some strong passion which could be my excuse? No.

'Sevens, aces, champagne, the yellow in the middle pocket, grey or rainbow-coloured currency notes, cigarettes, women who could be bought – those are my recollections!

'One terrible moment when I forgot myself, a humiliation I shall never wipe out, has made me recollect myself. I was horrified when I saw what an immeasurable gulf separates me from what I wished to be and might have been. In my imagination the dreams and thoughts of my youth reappeared.

'Where are those bright thoughts of life, of eternity, of God, which filled my soul so clearly and powerfully? Where is that force of love – not confined to any person – that filled my soul with such joyful warmth? Where is my hope of development, my sympathy with all that is excellent, my love of my relations, neighbours, work, and fame? Where is my sense of duty?

'I was insulted – and challenged the man to a duel and thought I had fully satisfied the demands of honour. I needed money to satisfy my vices and vanity, and I ruined a thousand families entrusted to me by God and did it without shame – I who so well understood those sacred obligations. A dishonourable man told me that I had no conscience and that I wished to steal – and I remained friends with him because he was a dishonourable man and told me that he had not meant to offend me. I was told that it was ridiculous to be chaste and I abandoned without regret the flower of my soul – my innocence – to a purchasable woman.

'And how good and happy I might have been had I trodden the path which on entering life my fresh mind and my child-like, genuine feeling indicated to me! More than once I tried to escape from the rut in which my life was moving and get back to that bright path. I told myself: I will use all the will I have – but I could not. When I remained alone I felt awkward and afraid of myself. When I was with others I no longer heard the inner voice at all, and sank lower and lower.

'At last I reached the terrible conviction that I could not rise, and left off thinking of doing so and tried to forget myself; but hopeless remorse tormented me still more. Then the idea – terrible to others but comforting to me – of suicide first occurred to me. But in that respect also I was mean and base. Only yesterday's stupid affair with the hussar gave me sufficient resolution to carry out my intention. Nothing honourable remained in me – only vanity, and out of vanity I am doing the one good action of my life. I formerly thought that the proximity of death would uplift my soul. I was mistaken. In a quarter of an hour I shall be no more, yet my views have not changed at all. I still see, still hear, still think, in the same way. There is the same strange inconsistency, inconsequence, vacillation, and levity in my thoughts – so contrary to the unity and clarity that man is – God knows why – able to conceive of. Thoughts of what will be beyond the tomb and of what will be said tomorrow about my death at Aunt Rtíshcheva's present themselves to me with equal force.'

THE SNOW STORM
A SHORT STORY

I

HAVING drunk tea towards seven o'clock in the evening, I left a station, the name of which I have forgotten, though I know it was somewhere in the district of the Don Cossack Army near Novocherkássk. It was already dark when, having wrapped myself in my fur coat, I took my seat under the apron beside Alëshka in the sledge. Near the post-station it seemed mild and calm. Though no snow was falling, not a star was visible overhead and the sky looked extremely low and black, in contrast to the clean snowy plain spread out before us.

We had hardly passed the dark shapes of the windmills, one of which clumsily turned its large sails, and left the settlement behind us, when I noticed that the road had become heavier and deeper in snow, that the wind blew more fiercely on the left, tossing the horses' tails and manes sideways, and that it kept carrying away the snow stirred up by the hoofs and sledge-runners. The sound of the bell began to die down, and through some opening in my sleeve a stream of cold air forced its way behind my back, and I recalled the station-master's advice, not to start for fear of going astray all night and being frozen on the road.

'Shan't we be losing our way?' I said to the driver, and not receiving an answer I put my question more definitely: 'I say, driver, do you think we shall reach the next station without losing our way?'

'God only knows,' he answered without turning his head. 'Just see how the snow drifts along the ground! Nothing of the road to be seen. O Lord!'

'Yes, but you'd better tell me whether you expect to get me to the next station or not?' I insisted. 'Shall we get there?'

'We ought to manage it,' said the driver, and went on to add something the wind prevented my hearing.

I did not feel inclined to turn back, but the idea of straying about all night in the frost and snow storm on the perfectly bare steppe which made up that part of the Don Army district was also far from pleasant. Moreover, though I could not see my driver very well in the dark, I did not much like the look of him and he did not inspire me with confidence. He sat exactly in the middle of his seat with his legs in, instead of to one side; he was too big, he spoke lazily, his cap, not like those usually worn by drivers, was too big and flopped from side to side; besides, he did not urge the horses on properly, but held the reins in both hands, like a footman who had taken the coachman's place on the box. But my chief reason for not believing in him was because he had a kerchief tied over his ears. In a word he did not please me, and that solemn stooping back of his looming in front of me seemed to bode no good.

'In my opinion we'd better turn back,' remarked Alëshka. 'There's no sense in getting lost!'

'O Lord! Just look how the snow is driving, nothing of the road to be seen, and it's closing my eyes right up . . . O Lord!' muttered the driver.

We had not been going a quarter of an hour before the driver handed the reins to Alëshka, clumsily liberated his legs, and making the snow crunch with his big boots went to look for the track.

'What is it? Where are you going? Are we off the road?' I asked. But the driver did not answer and, turning his face away from the wind which was beating into his eyes, walked away from the sledge.

'Well, is there a road?' I asked when he returned.

'No, there's nothing,' he answered with sudden impatience and irritation, as if I were to blame that he had strayed off the track, and having slowly thrust his big legs again into the front of the sledge he began arranging the reins with his frozen gloves.

'What are we to do?' I asked when we had started again.

'What are we to do? We'll drive where God sends us.'

And though we were quite evidently not following a road, we went on at the same slow trot, now through dry snow five inches deep, and now over brittle crusts of frozen snow.

Though it was cold, the snow on my fur collar melted very quickly; the drift along the ground grew worse and worse, and a few dry flakes began to fall from above.

It was plain that we were going heaven knows where, for having driven for another quarter of an hour we had not seen a single verst-post.

'Well, what do you think?' I asked the driver again. 'Shall we get to the station?'

'What station? We shall get back, if we give the horses their head they will take us there, but hardly to the next station – we might just perish.'

'Well then, let us go back,' I said. 'And really . . .'

'Then I am to turn back?' said the driver.

'Yes, yes, turn back!'

The driver gave the horses the reins. They began to run faster, and though I did not notice that we were turning, I felt the wind blowing from a different quarter, and we soon saw the windmills appearing through the snow. The driver cheered up and began to talk.

'The other day the return sledges from the other station spent the whole night in a snow storm among haystacks and did not get in till the morning. Lucky that they got among those stacks, else they'd have all been frozen, it was so cold. As it is one of them had his feet frozen, and was at death's door for three weeks with them.'

'But it's not cold now, and it seems calmer,' I said. 'We might perhaps go on?'

'It's warm enough, that's true, but the snow is drifting. Now that we have it at our back it seems easier, but the snow is driving strongly. I might go if it were on courier-duty or something of the kind, but not of my own free will. It's no joke if a passenger gets frozen. How am I to answer for your honour afterwards?'

II

JUST then we heard behind us the bells of several tróykas[1] which were rapidly overtaking us.

'It's the courier's bell,' said my driver. 'There's no other like it in the district.'

And in fact the bell of the front tróyka, the sound of which was already clearly borne to us by the wind, was exceedingly fine: clear, sonorous, deep, and slightly quivering. As I learnt afterwards it had been chosen by men who made a hobby of tróyka bells. There were three bells – a large one in the middle with what is called a *crimson* tone, and two small ones tuned to a third and a fifth. The ringing of that third and of the quivering fifth echoing in the air was extraordinarily effective and strangely beautiful in that silent and deserted steppe.

'The post is going,' said my driver, when the first of the three tróykas overtook us. 'How is the road? Is it usable?' he called out to the driver of the last sledge, but the man only shouted at his horses and did not reply.

The sound of the bells was quickly lost in the wind as soon as the post sledges had passed us.

I suppose my driver felt ashamed.

'Well, let us try it again, sir!' he said to me. 'Others have made their way through and their tracks will be fresh.'

I agreed, and we turned again, facing the wind and struggling forward through the deep snow. I kept my eyes on the side of the road so as not to lose the track left by the tróykas. For some two versts the track was plainly visible, then only a slight unevenness where the runners had gone, and soon I was quite unable to tell whether it was a track or only a layer of driven snow. My eyes were dimmed by looking at the snow monotonously receding under the runners, and I began to look ahead. We saw the third verst-post, but were quite unable to find a fourth. As before we drove against the wind, and with the wind, and to the right and to the left, and at last we came to such a pass that the driver said we must have turned off to the

---

1 A tróyka is a three-horse sledge, or, more correctly, a team of three horses.

right, I said we had gone to the left, and Alëshka was sure we had turned right back. Again we stopped several times and the driver disengaged his big feet and climbed out to look for the road, but all in vain. I too once went to see whether something I caught a glimpse of was not the road, but hardly had I taken some six steps with difficulty against the wind before I became convinced that similar layers of snow lay everywhere, and that I had seen the road only in my imagination. When I could no longer see the sledge I cried out: 'Driver! Alëshka!' but I felt how the wind caught my voice straight from my mouth and bore it instantly to a distance. I went to where the sledge had been – but it was not there; I went to the right, it was not there either. I am ashamed to remember in what a loud, piercing, and even rather despairing voice I again shouted 'Driver!' and there he was within two steps of me. His black figure, with the little whip and enormous cap pushed to one side, suddenly loomed up before me. He led me to the sledge.

'Thank the Lord, it's still warm,' he said, 'if the frost seized us it would be terrible . . . O Lord!'

'Give the horses their head: let them take us back,' I said, having seated myself in the sledge. 'They will take us back, driver, eh?'

'They ought to.'

He let go of the reins, struck the harness-pad of the middle horse with the whip, and we again moved on somewhere. We had travelled on for about half an hour when suddenly ahead of us we recognized the connoisseur's bell and the other two, but this time they were coming towards us. There were the same three tróykas, which having delivered the mail were now returning to the station with relay horses attached. The courier's tróyka with its big horses and musical bells ran quickly in front, with one driver on the driver's seat shouting vigorously. Two drivers were sitting in the middle of each of the empty sledges that followed, and one could hear their loud and merry voices. One of them was smoking a pipe, and the spark that flared up in the wind showed part of his face.

Looking at them I felt ashamed that I had been afraid to go on, and my driver probably shared the same feeling, for we both said at once: 'Let us follow them!'

III

M y driver, before the third tróyka had passed, began turning so clumsily that his shafts hit the horses attached behind it. They all three shied, broke their strap, and galloped aside.

'You cross-eyed devil! Can't you see when you're turning into someone, you devil?' one of the drivers seated in the last sledge – a short old man, as far as I could judge by his voice and figure – began to curse in hoarse, quivering tones, and quickly jumping out of the sledge he ran after the horses, still continuing his coarse and harsh abuse of my driver.

But the horses did not stop. The driver followed them, and in a moment both he and they were lost in the white mist of driving snow.

'Vasí-i-li! Bring along the dun horse! I can't catch them without,' came his voice.

One of the other drivers, a very tall man, got out of his sledge, silently unfastened his three horses, climbed on one of them by its breeching, and disappeared at a clumsy gallop in the direction of the first driver.

We and the other two tróykas started after the courier's tróyka, which with its bell ringing went along at full trot though there was no road.

'Catch them! Not likely!' said my driver of the one who had run after the horses. 'If a horse won't come to other horses, that shows it's bewitched and will take you somewhere you'll never return from.'

From the time he began following the others my driver seemed more cheerful and talkative, a fact of which I naturally took advantage, as I did not yet feel sleepy. I began asking where he came from, and why, and who he was, and it turned out that like myself he was from Túla province, a serf from Kirpíchnoe village, that they were short of land there and had had bad harvests since the cholera year. He was one of two brothers in the family, the third having gone as a soldier; that they had not enough grain to last till Christmas, and had to live on outside earnings. His youngest brother was head of the house, being married, while he himself was a widower. An *artél*[1] of drivers came from their village to these parts every year. Though he had not driven before, he had taken the job to help his brother, and lived, thank God, quite well, earning a hundred and twenty assignation rubles a year, of which he sent a hundred home to the family; and that life would be quite good 'if only the couriers were not such beasts, and the people hereabouts not so abusive'.

'Now why did that driver scold me so? O Lord! Did I set his horses loose on purpose? Do I mean harm to anybody? And why did he go galloping after them? They'd have come back of themselves, and now he'll only tire out the horses and get lost himself,' said the God-fearing peasant.

'And what is that black thing there?' I asked, noticing several dark objects in front of us.

'Why, a train of carts. That's pleasant driving!' he went on, when we had come abreast of the huge mat-covered wagons on wheels, following one another. 'Look, you can't see a single soul – they're all asleep. Wise horses know of themselves ... you can't make them miss the way anyhow ... We've driven that way on contract work ourselves,' he added, 'so we know.'

It really was strange to see those huge wagons covered with snow from their matted tops to their very wheels, and moving along all alone. Only in the front corner of the wagon did the matting, covered two inches thick with snow, lift a bit and a cap appear for a moment from under it as our bells tinkled past. The large piebald horse, stretching its neck and straining its back, went evenly along the completely snow-hidden road, monotonously shaking its shaggy head under the whitened harness-bow, and pricking one snow-covered ear when we overtook it.

---

1 An *artél* was a voluntary association of workers, which had a manager, contracted as a unit, and divided its earnings among its members.

When we had gone on for another half-hour the driver again turned to me.

'What d'you think, sir, are we going right?'

'I don't know,' I answered.

'At first the wind came that way, and now we are going right under the wind. No, we are not going where we ought, we are going astray again,' he said quite calmly.

One saw that, though he was inclined to be a coward, yet 'death itself is pleasant in company' as the saying is, and he had become quite tranquil now that there were several of us and he no longer had to lead and be responsible. He made remarks on the blunders of the driver in front with the greatest coolness, as if it were none of his business. And in fact I noticed that we sometimes saw the front tróyka on the left and sometimes on the right; it even seemed to me that we were going round in a very small circle. However, that might be an optical illusion, like the impression that the leading tróyka was sometimes going uphill, and then along a slope, or downhill, whereas I knew that the steppe was perfectly level.

After we had gone on again for some time, I saw a long way off, on the very horizon as it seemed to me, a long, dark, moving stripe; and a moment later it became clear that it was the same train of wagons we had passed before. The snow was still covering their creaking wheels, some of which did not even turn any longer, the men were still asleep as before under the matting, and the piebald horse in front blew out its nostrils as before, sniffed at the road, and pricked its ears.

'There, we've turned and turned and come back to the same wagons!' exclaimed my driver in a dissatisfied voice. 'The courier's horses are good ones, that's why he's driving them so recklessly, but ours will stop altogether if we go on like this all night.'

He cleared his throat.

'Let us turn back, sir, before we get into trouble!'

'No! Why? We shall get somewhere.'

'Where shall we get to? We shall spend the night in the steppe. How it is blowing! . . . O Lord!'

Though I was surprised that the driver of the front tróyka, having evidently lost the road and the direction, went on at a fast trot without looking for the road, and cheerfully shouting, I did not want to lag behind them.

'Follow them!' I said.

My driver obeyed, whipping up his horses more reluctantly than before, and did not turn to talk to me any more.

IV

THE storm grew more and more violent, and the snow fell dry and fine. I thought it was beginning to freeze: my cheeks and nose felt colder than before, and streams of cold air made their way more frequently under my fur coat, so that I had to wrap it closer around me. Sometimes the sledge bumped on the bare ice-glazed ground from which the wind had swept the snow. As I had already travelled more than five hundred versts without stopping anywhere for the night, I involuntarily kept closing my eyes and dozing off, although I was much interested to know how our wandering would end. Once when I opened my eyes I was struck for a moment by what seemed to me a bright light falling on the white plain; the horizon had widened considerably, the lowering black sky had suddenly vanished, and on all sides slanting white streaks of falling snow could be seen. The outlines of the front tróykas were more distinct, and as I looked up it seemed for a minute as though the clouds had dispersed, and that only the falling snow veiled the sky. While I was dozing the moon had risen and was casting its cold bright light through the tenuous clouds and the falling snow. The only things I saw clearly were my sledge, the horses, my driver, and the three tróykas in front of us: the courier's sledge in which a driver still sat, as before, driving at a fast trot; the second, in which two drivers having laid down the reins and made a shelter for themselves out of a coat sat smoking their pipes all the time, as could be seen by the sparks that flew from them; and the third in which no one was visible, as probably the driver was lying asleep in the body of the sledge. The driver of the first tróyka, however, at the time

I awoke, occasionally stopped his horses and sought for the
road. As soon as we stopped the howling of the wind sounded
louder and the vast quantity of snow borne through the air
became more apparent. In the snow-shrouded moonlight
I could see the driver's short figure probing the snow in
front of him with the handle of his whip, moving backwards
and forwards in the white dimness, again returning to his
sledge and jumping sideways onto his seat, and again amid
the monotonous whistling of the wind I heard his dexterous,
resonant cries urging on the horses, and the ringing of the
bells. Whenever the driver of the front tróyka got out to search
for some sign of a road or haystacks, there came from the
second tróyka the bold, self-confident voice of one of the
drivers shouting to him:

'Hey, Ignáshka, you've borne quite to the left! Bear to the
right, facing the wind!' Or: 'What are you twisting about for,
quite uselessly? Follow the snow, see how the drifts lie, and
we'll come out just right.' Or: 'Take to the right, to the right,
mate! See, there's something black – it must be a post.' Or:
'What are you straying about for? Unhitch the piebald and let
him run in front, he'll lead you right out onto the road. That
would be better.'

But the man who was giving this advice not only did not
unhitch one of his own side-horses or get out to look for the
road, but did not show his nose from under his sheltering coat,
and when Ignáshka, the leader, shouted in reply to one of his
counsels that he should take on the lead himself if he knew
which way to go, the advice-giver replied that if he were
driving the courier's tróyka he would take the lead and take
us right onto the road. 'But our horses won't take the lead in a
snow storm!' he shouted – 'they're not that kind of horses!'

'Then don't bother me!' Ignáshka replied, whistling cheerfully to his horses.

The other driver in the second sledge did not speak to
Ignáshka at all, and in general took no part in the matter,
though he was not asleep, as I concluded from his pipe being
always alight, and because, whenever we stopped, I heard the
even and continuous sound of his voice. He was telling a folk

tale. Only once, when Ignáshka stopped for the sixth or seventh time, he apparently grew vexed at being interrupted during the pleasure of his drive, and shouted to him:

'Hullo, why have you stopped again? Just look, he wants to find the road! He's been told there's a snow storm! The surveyor himself couldn't find the road now. You should drive on as long as the horses will go, and then maybe we shan't freeze to death ... Go on, do!'

'I daresay! Didn't a postillion freeze to death last year?' my driver remarked.

The driver of the third sledge did not wake up all the time. Once when we had stopped the advice-giver shouted:

'Philip! Hullo, Philip!' and receiving no reply remarked: 'Hasn't he frozen, perhaps? ... Go and have a look, Ignáshka.'

Ignáshka, who found time for everything, walked up to the sledge and began to shake the sleeping man.

'Just see what half a bottle of vodka has done! Talk about freezing!' he said, shaking him.

The sleeper grunted something and cursed.

'He's alive, all right,' said Ignáshka, and ran forward again. We drove on, and so fast that the little off-side sorrel of my tróyka, which my driver continually touched with the whip near his tail, now and then broke into an awkward little gallop.

V

IT was I think already near midnight when the little old man and Vasíli, who had gone after the runaway horses, rode up to us. They had managed to catch the horses and to find and overtake us; but how they had managed to do this in the thick blinding snow storm amid the bare steppe will always remain a mystery to me. The old man, swinging his elbows and legs, was riding the shaft-horse at a trot (the two side-horses were attached to its collar: one dare not let horses loose in a snow storm). When he came abreast of us he again began to scold my driver.

'Look at the cross-eyed devil, really ...'

'Eh, Uncle Mítrich!' the folk-tale teller in the second sledge called out: 'Are you alive? Get in here with us.'

But the old man did not reply and continued his abuse. When he thought he had said enough he rode up to the second sledge.

'Have you caught them all?' someone in it asked.

'What do you think?'

His small figure threw itself forward on the back of the trotting horse, then jumped down on the snow, and without stopping he ran after the sledge and tumbled in, his legs sticking out over its side. The tall Vasíli silently took his old place in the front sledge beside Ignáshka, and the two began to look for the road together.

'How the old man nags . . . Lord God!' muttered my driver.

For a long time after that we drove on without stopping over the white waste, in the cold, pellucid, and quivering light of the snow storm. I would open my eyes and the same clumsy snow-covered cap and back would be jolting before me: the same low shaft-bow, under which, between the taut leather reins and always at the same distance from me, the head of our shaft-horse kept bobbing with its black mane blown to one side by the wind. Looking across its back I could see the same little piebald off-horse on the right, with its tail tied up short, and the swingletree which sometimes knocked against the front of the sledge. I would look down − there was the same scurrying snow through which our runners were cutting, and which the wind resolutely bore away to one side. In front, always at the same distance away, glided the first tróyka, while to right and left everything glimmered white and dim. Vainly did my eye look for any new object: neither post, nor haystack, nor fence was to be seen. Everywhere all was white and fluctuating: now the horizon seemed immeasurably distant, now it closed in on all sides to within two paces of me; suddenly a high white wall would seem to rise up on the right and run beside the sledge, then it would suddenly vanish and rise again in front, only to glide on farther and farther away and again disappear. When I looked up it would seem lighter for a moment, as if I might see the stars through the haze, but the stars would run away higher and higher from my sight and only the snow would be visible, falling past my eyes onto my face and the collar of my fur cloak. The sky everywhere remained equally light, equally white, monotonous, colourless, and constantly shifting. The wind seemed to be changing: now it blew in my face and the snow plastered my eyes, now it blew from one side and annoyingly tossed the fur-collar of my cloak against my head and mockingly flapped my face with it; now it howled through some opening. I heard the soft incessant crunching of the hoofs and the runners on the snow, and the clang of the bells dying down when we drove through deep drifts. Only now and then, when we drove against the snow and glided over bare frozen ground, did Ignáshka's energetic whistling and the sonorous sound of the bell with its accompanying bare fifth reach me, and give sudden relief to the dismal character of the desert; and then again the bells would sound mono-tonous, playing always with insufferable precision the same tune, which I involuntarily imagined I was hearing. One of my feet began to feel the frost, and when I turned to wrap myself up better, the snow that had settled on my collar and cap shifted down my neck and made me shiver, but on the whole I still felt warm in my fur cloak, and drowsiness over-came me.

VI

RECOLLECTIONS and pictures of the distant past superseded one another with increasing rapidity in my imagination.

'That advice-giver who is always calling out from the second sledge – what sort of fellow can he be?' I thought. 'Probably red-haired, thick-set, and with short legs, like Theo-dore Filípych, our old butler.' And I saw the staircase of our big house and five domestic serfs with heavy steps bringing a piano from the wing on slings made of towels, and Theodore Filípych with the sleeves of his nankeen coat turned up, hold-ing one of the pedals, running forward, lifting a latch, pulling here at the slings, pushing there, crawling between people's legs, getting into everybody's way, and shouting incessantly in an anxious voice:

'Lean it against yourselves, you there in front, you in front! That's the way – the tail end up, up, up! Turn into the door! That's the way.'

'Just let us do it, Theodore Filípych! We can manage it alone,' timidly remarks the gardener, pressed against the banisters quite red with straining, and with great effort holding up one corner of the grand piano.

But Theodore Filípych will not be quiet.

'What does it mean?' I reflect. 'Does he think he is useful or necessary for the work in hand, or is he simply glad God has given him this self-confident persuasive eloquence, and enjoys dispensing it? That must be it.' And then somehow I see the lake, and tired domestic serfs up to their knees in the water dragging a fishing-net, and again Theodore Filípych with a watering-pot, shouting at everybody as he runs up and down on the bank, now and then approaching the brink to empty out some turbid water and to take up fresh, while holding back the golden carp with his hand. But now it is a July noon. I am going somewhere over the freshly-mown grass in the garden, under the burning, vertical rays of the sun; I am still very young, and I feel a lack of something and a desire to fill that lack. I go to my favourite place by the lake, between the briar-rose bed and the birch avenue, and lie down to sleep. I remember the feeling with which, lying down, I looked across between the prickly red stems of the rose trees at the dark, dry, crumbly earth, and at the bright blue mirror of the lake. It is a feeling of naïve self-satisfaction and melancholy. Everything around me is beautiful, and that beauty affects me so powerfully that it seems to me that I myself am good, and the one thing that vexes me is that nobody is there to admire me. It is hot. I try to sleep so as to console myself, but the flies, the unendurable flies, give me no peace here either: they gather round me and, with a kind of dull persistence, hard as cherry-stones, jump from my forehead onto my hands. A bee buzzes not far from me in the blazing sunlight; yellow-winged butterflies fly from one blade of grass to another as if exhausted by the heat. I look up: it hurts my eyes – the sun glitters too brightly through the light foliage of the curly birch tree whose branches sway softly high above me, and it seems hotter than ever. I cover my face with my handkerchief: it feels stifling, and the flies seem to stick to my hands which begin to perspire. In the very centre of the wild rose bush sparrows begin to bustle about. One of them hops to the ground about two feet from me, energetically pretends to peck at the ground a couple of times, flies back into the bush, rustling the twigs, and chirping merrily flies away. Another also hops down, jerks his little tail, looks about him, chirps, and flies off quick as an arrow after the first one. From the lake comes a sound of beetles[1] beating the wet linen, and the sound re-echoes and is borne down along the lake. Sounds of laughter and the voices and splashing of bathers are heard. A gust of wind rustles the crowns of the birch trees, still far from me, now it comes nearer and I hear it stir the grass, and now the leaves of the wild roses begin to flutter, pressed against their stems, and at last a fresh stream of air reaches me, lifting a corner of my handkerchief and tickling my moist face. Through the gap where the corner of the kerchief was lifted a fly comes in and flutters with fright close to my moist mouth. A dry twig presses against my back. No, I can't lie still: I had better go and have a bathe. But just then, close to the rose bush, I hear hurried steps and a woman's frightened voice:

'O God! How could such a thing happen! And none of the men are here!'

'What is it? What is it?' running out into the sunshine I ask a woman serf who hurries past me groaning. She only looks round, waves her arms, and runs on. But here comes seventy-year-old Matrëna hurrying to the lake, holding down with one hand the kerchief which is slipping off her head, and hopping and dragging one of her feet in its worsted stocking. Two little girls come running up hand in hand, and a ten-year-old boy,

---

1 The women take their clothes to rinse in lakes or streams, where they beat them with wooden beetles.

wearing his father's coat and clutching the homespun skirt of one of the girls, keeps close behind them.

'What has happened?' I ask them.

'A peasant is drowning.'

'Where?'

'In the lake.'

'Who is he? One of ours?'

'No, a stranger.'

Iván the coachman, dragging his heavy boots through the newly-mown grass, and the fat clerk Jacob, all out of breath, run to the pond and I after them.

I remember the feeling which said to me: 'There you are, plunge in and pull out the peasant and save him, and everyone will admire you,' which was exactly what I wanted.

'Where is he? Where?' I ask the throng of domestic serfs gathered on the bank.

'Out there, in the very deepest part near the other bank, almost at the boathouse,' says the washerwoman, hanging the wet linen on her wooden yoke. 'I look, and see him dive; he just comes up and is gone, then comes up again and calls out: "I'm drowning, help!" and goes down again, and nothing but bubbles come up. Then I see that the man is drowning, so I give a yell: "Folk! A peasant's drowning!"'

And lifting the yoke to her shoulder the laundress waddles sideways along the path away from the lake.

'Oh gracious, what a business!' says Jacob Ivánov, the office clerk, in a despairing tone. 'What a bother there'll be with the rural court. We'll never get through with it!'

A peasant carrying a scythe pushes his way through the throng of women, children, and old men who have gathered on the farther shore, and hanging his scythe on the branch of a willow slowly begins to take off his boots.

'Where? Where did he go down?' I keep asking, wishing to rush there and do something extraordinary.

But they point to the smooth surface of the lake which is occasionally rippled by the passing breeze. I do not understand how he came to drown; the water is just as smooth, lovely, and calm above him, shining golden in the midday sun, and it seems that I can do nothing and can astonish no one, especially as I am a very poor swimmer and the peasant is already pulling his shirt over his head and ready to plunge in. Everybody looks at him hopefully and with bated breath, but after going in up to his shoulders he slowly turns back and puts his shirt on again – he cannot swim.

People still come running and the thing grows and grows; the women cling to one another, but nobody does anything to help. Those who have just come give advice, and sigh, and their faces express fear and despair; but of those who have been there awhile, some, tired with standing, sit down on the grass, while some go away. Old Matrëna asks her daughter whether she shut the oven door, and the boy who is wearing his father's coat diligently throws small stones into the water.

But now Theodore Filípych's dog Tresórka, barking and looking back in perplexity, comes running down the hill, and then Theodore himself, running downhill and shouting, appears from behind the briar-rose bushes:

'What are you standing there for?' he cries, taking off his coat as he runs, 'A man drowning, and they stand there! . . . Get me a rope!'

Everybody looks at Theodore Filípych with hope and fear as, leaning his hand on the shoulder of an obliging domestic serf, he prises off his right boot with the toe of the left.

'Over there, where the people are, a little to the right of the willow, Theodore Filípych, just there!' someone says to him.

'I know,' he replies, and knitting his brows, in response, no doubt, to the signs of shame among the crowd of women, he pulls off his shirt, removes the cross from his neck and hands it to the gardener's boy who stands obsequiously before him, and then, stepping energetically over the cut grass, approaches the lake.

Tresórka, perplexed by the quickness of his master's movements, has stopped near the crowd and with a smack of his lips eats a few blades of grass near the bank, then looks at his master intently and with a joyful yelp suddenly plunges with him into the water. For a moment nothing can be seen but foam and spray, which even reaches to us; but now Theodore Filípych,

gracefully swinging his arms and rhythmically raising and lowering his back, swims briskly with long strokes to the opposite
shore. Tresórka, having swallowed some water, returns
hurriedly, shakes himself near the throng, and rubs his back
on the grass. Just as Theodore Filípych reaches the opposite
shore two coachmen come running up to the willow with a
fishing-net wrapped round a pole. Theodore Filípych for
some unknown reason lifts his arms, dives down once and
then a second and a third time, on each occasion squirting a jet
of water from his mouth, and gracefully tosses back his hair
without answering the questions that are hurled at him from all
sides. At last he comes out onto the bank, and as far as I can see
only gives instructions as to spreading out the net. The net is
drawn in, but there is nothing in it except ooze with a few
small carp entangled in it. While the net is being lowered again
I go round to that side.

The only sounds to be heard are Theodore Filípych's voice
giving orders, the plashing of the wet rope on the water, and
sighs of terror. The wet rope attached to the right side of the
net, more and more covered by grass, comes farther and farther
out of the water.

'Now then, pull together, harder, all together!' shouts
Theodore Filípych.

The floats appear dripping with water.

'There is something coming, mates. It pulls heavy!' someone calls out.

Now the net – in which two or three little carp are struggling – is dragged to the bank, wetting and pressing down the
grass. And in the extended wings of the net, through a thin
swaying layer of turbid water, something white comes in sight.
Amid dead silence an impressive, though not loud, gasp of
horror passes through the crowd.

'Pull harder, onto the land!' comes Theodore Filípych's
resolute voice, and the drowned body is dragged out to the
willow over the stubble of burdock and thistle.

And now I see my good old aunt in her silk dress, with her
face ready to burst into tears. I see her lilac sunshade with its
fringe, which seems somehow incongruous in this scene of

death, so terrible in its simplicity. I recall the disappointment her face expressed because arnica could be of no use, and I also recall the painful feeling of annoyance I experienced when, with the naïve egotism of love, she said: 'Come away my dear. Oh, how dreadful it is! And you always go bathing and swimming by yourself.'

I remember how bright and hot the sun was as it baked the powdery earth underfoot; how it sparkled and mirrored in the lake; how the plump carp plashed near the banks and shoals of little fish rippled the water in the middle; how a hawk hovering high in the air circled over the ducklings, which quacking and splashing had come swimming out through the reeds into the middle of the lake; how curling white thunder-clouds gathered on the horizon; how the mud drawn out onto the bank by the net gradually receded; and how as I crossed the dike I again heard the blows of the beetles re-echoing over the lake.

But that beetle sounds as if two beetles were beating together in thirds, and that sound torments and worries me, the more so because I know that this beetle is a bell, and that Theodore Filípych will not make it stop. Then that beetle, like an instrument of torture, presses my foot which is freezing, and I fall asleep.

I am awakened, as it seems to me, by our galloping very fast and by two voices calling out quite close to me:

'I say, Ignát! Eh, Ignát!' my driver is saying. 'You take my passenger. You have to go on anyhow, but what's the use of my goading my horses uselessly? You take him!'

Ignát's voice quite close to me replies:

'Where's the pleasure of making myself responsible for the passenger? . . . Will you stand me a bottle?'

'Oh, come, a bottle . . . say half a bottle.'

'Half a bottle, indeed!' shouts another voice. 'Wear out the horses for half a bottle!'

I open my eyes. Before them still flickers the same intolerable swaying snow, the same drivers and horses, but now we are abreast of another sledge. My driver has overtaken Ignát, and we drive side by side for some time. Though the voice from the other sledge advises him not to accept less than a bottle, Ignát suddenly reins in his tróyka.

'Well, shift over. So be it! It's your luck. You'll stand half a bottle when we return to-morrow. Is there much luggage?'

My driver jumps out into the snow with unusual alacrity for him, bows to me, and begs me to change over into Ignát's sledge. I am quite willing to, but evidently the God-fearing peasant is so pleased that he has to pour out his gratitude and delight to someone. He bows and thanks me, Alëshka, and Ignát.

'There now, the Lord be praised! What was it like...O Lord! We have been driving half the night and don't know where we are going. He'll get you there, dear sir, but my horses are quite worn out.'

And he shifts my things with increased zeal.

While my things were being transferred I went with the wind, which almost lifted me off my feet, to the second sledge. That sledge, especially outside the coat which had been arranged over the two men's heads to shelter them from the wind, was more than six inches deep in snow, but behind the coat it was quiet and comfortable. The old man still lay with his legs sticking out, and the story-teller was still going on with his tale:

'Well, when the general comes to Mary in prison, in the King's name, you know, Mary at once says to him: "General, I don't need you and can't love you, and so, you see, you are not my lover, but my lover is the prince himself..."'

'And just then...' he went on, but seeing me he stopped for a moment and began filling his pipe.

'Well, sir, have you come to listen to the tale?' asked the other whom I called the advice-giver.

'Yes, you're well off here, quite jolly,' I said.

'Why not? It whiles away the time, anyhow it keeps one from thinking.'

'And do you know where we are now?'

This question did not seem to please the drivers.

'Who can make out where we are? Maybe we've driven into the Kulmýk country,' answered the advice-giver.

'Then what are we going to do?' I asked.

'What can we do? We'll go on, and maybe we'll get some-where,' he said in a dissatisfied tone.

'But suppose we don't get anywhere, and the horses stick in the snow – what then?'

'What then? Why, nothing.'

'But we might freeze.'

'Of course we might, because one can't even see any hay-stacks: we have got right among the Kulmýks. The chief thing is to watch the snow.'

'And you seem afraid of getting frozen, sir,' remarked the old man in a shaky voice.

Though he seemed to be chaffing me, it was evident that he was chilled to his very bones.

'Yes, it is getting very cold,' I said.

'Eh, sir, you should do as I do, take a run now and then, that will warm you up.'

'Yes, the chief thing is to have a run behind the sledge,' said the advice-giver.

VII

'We're ready, your honour!' shouted Alëshka from the front sledge.

The storm was so violent that, though I bent almost double and clutched the skirts of my cloak with both hands, I was hardly able to walk the few steps that separated me from the sledge, over the drifting snow which the wind swept from under my feet. My former driver was already kneeling in the middle of his empty sledge, but when he saw me going he took off his big cap (whereupon the wind lifted his hair furiously) and asked for a tip. Evidently he did not expect me to give him one, for my refusal did not grieve him in the least. He thanked me anyway, put his cap on again, and said: 'God keep you, sir...' and jerking his reins and clicking his tongue, turned away from us. Then Ignát swayed his whole back and shouted to the horses, and the sound of the snow crunching under their hoofs, the cries, and the bells, replaced the howling of the wind which had been peculiarly noticeable while we stood still.

For a quarter of an hour after my transfer I kept awake and amused myself watching my new driver and his horses. Ignát sat like a mettlesome fellow, continually rising in his seat, flourishing over the horses the arm from which his whip was hung, shouting, beating one foot against the other, and bending forward to adjust the breeching of the shaft-horse, which kept slipping to the right. He was not tall, but seemed to be well built. Over his sheepskin he wore a large, loose cloak without a girdle, the collar of which was turned down so that his neck was bare. He wore not felt but leather boots, and a small cap which he kept taking off and putting straight. His ears were only protected by his hair. In all his movements one was aware not only of energy, but even more, as it seemed to me, of a desire to arouse that energy in himself. And the farther we went the more often he straightened himself out, rose in his seat, beat his feet together, and addressed himself to Alëshka and me. It seemed to me that he was afraid of losing courage. And there was good reason for it: though the horses were good the road grew heavier and heavier at every step, and it was plain that they were running less willingly: it was already necessary to touch them up with the whip, and the shaft-horse, a good, big, shaggy animal, stumbled more than once, though immediately, as if frightened, it jerked forward again and tossed its shaggy head almost as high as the bell hanging from the bow above it. The right off-horse, which I could not help watching, with a long leather tassel to its breeching which shook and jerked on its off side, noticeably let its traces slacken and required the whip, but from habit as a good and even mettlesome horse seemed vexed at its own weakness, and angrily lowered and tossed its head at the reins. It was terrible to realize that the snow storm and the frost were increasing, the horses growing weaker, the road becoming worse, and that we did not at all know where we were, or where we were going – or whether we should reach a station or even a shelter of any sort; it seemed strange and ridiculous to hear the bells ringing so easily and cheerfully, and Ignát shouting as lustily and pleasantly as if we were out for a drive along a village street on a frosty noon during a Twelfth Night holiday – and it was stranger still that we were always driving and driving fast somewhere from where we were. Ignát began to sing some song in a horrid falsetto, but so loud and with such intervals, during which he whistled, that it seemed ridiculous to be afraid while one heard him.

'Hey there, what are you splitting your throat for, Ignát?' came the advice-giver's voice. 'Stop a minute!'

'What?'

'Sto-o-op!'

Ignát stopped. Again all became silent, and the wind howled and whined, and the whirling snow fell still more thickly into the sledge. The advice-giver came up to us.

'Well, what now?'

'What now? Where are we going?'

'Who can tell?'

'Are your feet freezing, that you knock them together so?'

'Quite numb!'

'You should go over there: look, where there's something glimmering. It must be a Kulmýk camp. It would warm your feet too.'

'All right. Hold the reins . . . here you are.'

And Ignát ran in the direction indicated.

'You always have to go about a bit and look, then you find the way, or else what's the good of driving about like a fool?' the advice-giver said to me. 'See how the horses are steaming.'

All the time Ignát was gone – and that lasted so long that I even began to fear he might have lost his way – the advice-giver kept telling me in a self-confident and calm tone how one should behave in a snow storm, that it was best to unharness a horse and let it go, and, as God is holy, it would be sure to lead one out, and how it is sometimes possible to find the way by the stars, and that had he been driving in front we should long ago have reached the station.

'Well, is there anything?' he asked Ignát when the latter came back, stepping with difficulty knee-deep through the snow.

'There is, there is a camp of some sort,' replied Ignát, gasping for breath, 'but I can't tell what it is. We must have strayed right into the Prológov estate. We must bear off to the left.'

'What's he jabbering about? It's our camp that's behind the Cossack village,' rejoined the advice-giver.

'I tell you it's not!'

'Well, I've had a look too, and I know: that's what it is, and if it isn't, then it's Tamýshevsk. Anyhow we must bear to the right, and then we'll come right out to the big bridge at the eighth verst.'

'I tell you it's nothing of the sort. Haven't I looked?' said Ignát with annoyance.

'Eh, mate, and you call yourself a driver!'

'Yes, a driver! . . . Go and look for yourself.'

'Why should I go? I know without going.'

Ignát had evidently grown angry: he jumped into the sledge without replying and drove on.

'How numb my legs have got! I can't warm them up,' said he to Alëshka, knocking his feet together oftener and oftener, and scooping up and emptying out the snow that had got into his boot-legs.

I felt dreadfully sleepy.

VIII

'CAN it be that I am freezing to death?' I thought, half asleep. 'They say it always begins with drowsiness. It would be better to drown than to freeze – let them drag me out with a net; but it does not matter much whether I freeze or drown if only that stick, or whatever it is, would not prod me in the back and I could forget myself!'

I did so for a few seconds.

'But how will all this end?' I suddenly asked myself, opening my eyes for a moment and peering into the white expanse before me. 'How will it all end? If we don't find any haystacks and the horses stop, as they seem likely to do soon, we shall all freeze to death.' I confess that, though I was a little afraid, the desire that something extraordinary, something rather tragic, should happen to us, was stronger in me than that fear. It seemed to me that it would not be bad if towards morning the horses brought us of their own accord, half-frozen, to some far-off unknown village, or if some of us were even to perish of the cold. Fancies of this kind presented themselves to me with extraordinary clearness and rapidity. The horses stop, the snow drifts higher and higher, and now nothing is seen of the horses but their ears and the bows above their heads, but suddenly Ignát appears above us with his tróyka, and drives past. We entreat him, we shout that he should take us, but the wind carries our voices away – we have no voices left. Ignát grins, shouts to his horses, whistles, and disappears into some deep, snow-covered ravine. The little old man jumps astride a horse, flourishes his elbows and tries to gallop away, but cannot stir from the spot; my former driver with the big cap rushes at him, drags him to the ground and tramples him into the snow. 'You're a wizard!' he shouts. 'You're a scold! We shall all be lost together!' But the old man breaks through the heap of snow with his head; and now he is not so much an old man as a hare, and leaps away from us. All the dogs bound after him. The advice-giver, who is Theodore Filípych, tells us all to sit round in a circle, that if the snow covers us it will be all right – we shall be warm that way. And really we are warm and cosy, only I want a drink. I fetch out my lunch-basket, and treat everybody to rum and sugar, and enjoy a drink myself. The story-teller spins a tale about the rainbow, and now there is a ceiling of snow and a rainbow above us. 'Now let us each make himself a room in the snow and let us go to sleep!' I say. The snow is soft and warm, like fur. I make myself a room and want to enter it, but Theodore Filípych, who has seen the money in my lunch-basket, says: 'Stop! Give me your money – you have to die anyway!' And he grabs me by the leg. I hand over the money and only ask him to let me go; but they won't believe it is all the money I have, and want to kill me. I seize the old man's hand and begin to kiss it with inexpressible pleasure: his hand is tender and sweet. At first he snatches it from me, but afterwards lets me have it, and even caresses me with his other hand. Then Theodore Filípych comes near and threatens me. I run away into my room: it is, however, no longer a room but a long white corridor, and someone is holding my legs. I wrench myself free. My clothes and part of my skin remain in the hands of the man who was holding me, but I only feel cold and ashamed – all the more ashamed because my aunt with her parasol and homoeopathic medicine-chest under her arm is coming towards me arm-in-arm with the drowned man. They are laughing and do not understand the signs I make to them. I throw myself into the sledge, my feet trail behind me in the snow, but the old man rushes after me flapping his elbows. He is already near, but I hear two church bells ringing in front of me, and know that I shall be saved when I get to them. The church bells sound nearer and nearer; but the little old man has caught up with me and falls with his stomach on my face, so that I can scarcely hear the bells. I again grasp his hand and begin to kiss it, but the little old man is no longer the little old man, he is the man who was drowned . . . and he shouts: 'Ignát, stop! There are the Akhmétkins' stacks, I think! Go and have a look at them!' This is too terrible. No, I had better wake up . . .

I open my eyes. The wind has thrown the flap of Alëshka's cloak over my face, my knee is uncovered, we are going over the bare frozen road, and the bells with their quivering third can be distinctly heard.

I look to see the haystacks, but now that my eyes are open I see no stacks, but a house with a balcony and the crenellated wall of a fortress. I am not interested enough to scrutinize this house and fortress: I am chiefly anxious to see the white corridor along which I ran, to hear the sound of the church bells, and to kiss the little old man's hand. I close my eyes again and fall asleep.

IX

I SLEPT soundly, but heard the ringing of the bells all the time. They appeared to me in my dream now in the guise of a dog that barked and attacked me, now of an organ in which I was one of the pipes, and now of some French verses I was composing. Sometimes those bells seemed to be an instrument of torture which kept squeezing my right heel. I felt that so strongly that I woke up and opened my eyes, rubbing my foot. It was getting frost-bitten. The night was still light, misty, and white. The same motion was still shaking me and the sledge; the same Ignát sat sideways, knocking his feet together; the same off-horse with outstretched neck ran at a trot over the deep snow without lifting its feet much, while the tassel on the breeching bobbed and flapped against its belly. The head of the shaft-horse with its flying mane stooped and rose rhythmically as it alternately drew the reins tight and loosened them. But all this was covered with snow even more than before. The snow whirled about in front, at the side it covered the horses' legs knee-deep, and the runners of the sledge, while it fell from above on our collars and caps. The wind blew now from the right, now from the left, playing with Ignát's collar, the skirt of his cloak, the mane of the side-horse, and howling between the shafts and above the bow over the shaft-horse's head.

It was growing terribly cold, and hardly had I put my head out of my coat-collar before the frosty, crisp, whirling snow covered my eyelashes, got into my nose and mouth, and penetrated behind my neck. When I looked round, everything was white, light and snowy, there was nothing to be seen but the dull light and the snow. I became seriously frightened. Alëshka was asleep at my feet at the bottom of the sledge, his whole back covered by a thick layer of snow. Ignát did not lose courage: he kept pulling at the reins, shouting, and clapping his feet together. The bell went on ringing just as wonderfully. The horses snorted a little, but ran more slowly and stumbled more and more often. Ignát again leaped up, waved his mitten, and again began singing in his strained falsetto. Before finishing the song he stopped the tróyka, threw down the reins on the front of the sledge, and got out. The wind howled furiously; the snow poured on the skirts of our cloaks as out of a scoop. I turned round: the third tróyka was not to be seen (it had lagged behind somewhere). Near the second sledge, in the snowy mist, I saw the little old man jumping from foot to foot.

Ignát went some three steps from the sledge, and sitting down in the snow undid his girdle and pulled off his boots.

'What are you doing?' I asked.

'I must change, or my feet will be quite frozen,' he replied, and went on with what he was doing.

It was too cold to keep my neck out of my collar to watch what he was doing. I sat up straight, looking at the off-horse, which with one leg wearily stretched out, painfully whisked its tail that was tied in a knot and covered with snow. The thump Ignát gave the sledge as he jumped onto his seat roused me.

'Where are we now?' I asked. 'Shall we get anywhere – say by daybreak?'

'Don't worry, we'll get you there,' he replied. 'Now that I have changed, my feet are much warmer.'

And he drove on, the bell began to ring, the sledge swayed again, and the wind whistled under the runners. We again started to swim over the limitless sea of snow.

X

I FELL soundly asleep. When Alëshka woke me up by pushing me with his foot, and I opened my eyes, it was already morning. It seemed even colder than in the night. No more snow was falling from above, but a stiff dry wind continued to sweep the powdery snow across the plain, and especially under the hoofs of the horses and the runners of the sledge. In the east, to our right, the sky was heavy and of a dark bluish colour, but bright orange oblique streaks were growing more and more defined in it. Overhead, through flying white clouds as yet scarcely tinged, gleamed the pale blue of the sky; on the left, bright, light clouds were drifting. Everywhere, as far as eye could see, deep snow lay over the plain in sharply defined layers. Here and there could be seen greyish mounds, over which fine, crisp, powdery snow swept steadily. No track either of sledge, man, or beast could be seen. The outlines and colour of the driver's back and of the horses were clearly and sharply visible even on the white background. The rim of

Ignát's dark-blue cap, his collar, his hair, and even his boots were white. The sledge was completely covered with snow. The right side and forelock of the grey shaft-horse were thick with snow, the legs of the off-horse on my side were covered with it up to the knee, and its curly sweating flank was covered and frozen to a rough surface. The tassel still bobbed up and down in tune to any rhythm you liked to imagine, and the off-horse itself kept running in the same way, only the sunken, heaving belly and drooping ears showing how exhausted she was. The one novel object that attracted my attention was a verst-post from which the snow was falling to the ground, and near which to the right the snow was swept into a mound by the wind, which still kept raging and throwing the crisp snow from side to side. I was very much surprised that we had travelled all night, twelve hours, with the same horses, without knowing where, and had arrived after all. Our bell seemed to tinkle yet more cheerfully. Ignát kept wrapping his cloak around him and shouting; the horses behind us snorted, and the bells of the little old man's and the advice-giver's tróyka tinkled, but the driver who had been asleep had certainly strayed from us in the steppe. After going another half-mile we came across the fresh, only partly obliterated, traces of a three-horsed sledge, and here and there pink spots of blood, probably from a horse that had overreached itself.

'That's Philip. Fancy his being ahead of us!' said Ignát.

But here by the roadside a lonely little house with a signboard was seen in the midst of the snow, which covered it almost to the top of the windows and to the roof. Near the inn stood a tróyka of grey horses, their coats curly with sweat, their legs outstretched and their heads drooping wearily. At the door there was a shovel and the snow had been cleared away, but the howling wind continued to sweep and whirl snow off the roof.

At the sound of our bells, a tall, ruddy-faced, red-haired peasant came out with a glass of vodka in his hand, and shouted something. Ignát turned to me and asked permission to stop. Then for the first time I fairly saw his face.

XI

His face was not swarthy and lean with a straight nose, as I had expected judging by his hair and figure. It was a round, jolly, very snub-nosed face, with a large mouth and bright light-blue eyes. His cheeks and neck were red, as if rubbed with a flannel; his eyebrows, his long eyelashes, and the down that smoothly covered the bottom of his face, were plastered with snow and were quite white. We were only half a mile from our station and we stopped.

'Only be quick about it!' I said.

'Just one moment,' replied Ignát, springing down and walking over to Philip.

'Let's have it, brother,' he said, taking the mitten from his right hand and throwing it down with his whip on the snow, and tossing back his head he emptied at a gulp the glass that was handed to him.

The innkeeper, probably a discharged Cossack, came out with a half-bottle in his hand.

'Who shall I serve?' said he.

Tall Vasíli, a thin, brown-haired peasant, with a goatee beard, and the advice-giver, a stout, light-haired man with a thick beard framing his red face, came forward and also drank a glass each. The little old man too went over to the drinkers, but was not served, and he went back to his horses, which were fastened behind the sledge, and began stroking one of them on the back and croup.

The little old man's appearance was just what I had imagined it to be: small, thin, with a wrinkled livid face, a scanty beard, sharp little nose, and worn yellow teeth. He had a new driver's cap on, but his coat was shabby, worn, smeared with tar, torn on one shoulder, had holes in the skirt, and did not cover his knees and the homespun trousers which were tucked into his huge felt boots. He himself was bent double, puckered up, his face and knees trembled, and he tramped about near the sledge evidently trying to get warm.

'Come, Mítrich, you should have a glass; you'd get fine and warm,' said the advice-giver.

Mítrich's face twitched. He adjusted the harness of one of his horses, straightened the bow above its head, and came over to me.

'Well, sir,' he said, taking the cap off his grey head and bending low, 'we have been wandering about together all night, looking for the road: won't you give me enough for a small glass? Really sir, your honour! I haven't anything to get warm on,' he added with an ingratiating smile.

I gave him a quarter-ruble.[1] The innkeeper brought out a small glass of vodka and handed it to the old man. He took off his mitten, together with the whip that hung on it, and put out his small, dark, rough, and rather livid hand towards the glass; but his thumb refused to obey him, as though it did not belong to him. He was unable to hold the glass and dropped it on the snow, spilling the vodka.

All the drivers burst out laughing.

'See how frozen Mítrich is, he can't even hold the vodka.'

But Mítrich was greatly grieved at having spilt the vodka.

However, they filled another glass for him and poured it into his mouth. He became cheerful in a moment, ran into the inn, lit his pipe, showed his worn yellow teeth, and began to swear at every word he spoke. Having drained the last glass, the drivers returned to their tróykas and we started again.

The snow kept growing whiter and brighter so that it hurt one's eyes to look at it. The orange-tinted reddish streaks rose higher and higher, and growing brighter and brighter spread upwards over the sky; even the red disk of the sun became visible on the horizon through the blue-grey clouds; the sky grew more brilliant and of a deeper blue. On the road near the settlement the sledge tracks were clear, distinct, and yellowish, and here and there we were jolted by cradle-holes in the road; one could feel a pleasant lightness and freshness in the tense, frosty air.

My tróyka went very fast. The head of the shaft-horse, and its neck with its mane fluttering around the bow, swayed swiftly from side to side almost in one place under the special

1 At that time about sixpence.

bell, the tongue of which no longer struck the sides but scraped against them. The good off-horses tugged together at the frozen and twisted traces, and sprang energetically, while the tassel bobbed from right under the horse's belly to the breeching. Now and then an off-horse would stumble from the beaten track into the snowdrift, throwing up the snow into one's eyes as it briskly got out again. Ignát shouted in his merry tenor; the dry frosty snow squeaked under the runners; behind us two little bells were ringing resonantly and festively, and I could hear the tipsy shouting of the drivers. I looked back. The grey shaggy off-horses, with their necks outstretched and breathing evenly, their bits awry, were leaping over the snow. Philip, flourishing his whip, was adjusting his cap; the little old man, with his legs hanging out, lay in the middle of the sledge as before.

Two minutes later my sledge scraped over the boards before the clean-swept entrance of the station house, and Ignát turned to me his snow-covered merry face, smelling of frost.

'We've got you here after all, sir!' he said.

TWO HUSSARS

A STORY

'Jomini and Jomini –
Not half a word of vodka.' – D. DAVÝDOV.[1]

---

1 From *The Song of an old Hussar*, in which the great days of the past are contrasted with the trivial present. D. V. Davýdov is referred to in *War and Peace*.

EARLY in the nineteenth century, when there were as yet no railways or macadamized roads, no gaslight, no stearine candles, no low couches with sprung cushions, no unvarnished furniture, no disillusioned youths with eye-glasses, no liberalizing women philosophers, nor any charming *dames aux camélias* of whom there are so many in our times, in those naïve days, when leaving Moscow for Petersburg in a coach or carriage provided with a kitchenful of home-made provisions one travelled for eight days along a soft, dusty, or muddy road and believed in chopped cutlets, sledge-bells, and plain rolls; when in the long autumn evenings the tallow candles, around which family groups of twenty or thirty people gathered, had to be snuffed; when ball-rooms were illuminated by candelabra with wax or spermaceti candles, when furniture was arranged symmetrically, when our fathers were still young and proved it not only by the absence of wrinkles and grey hair but by fighting duels for the sake of a woman and rushing from the opposite corner of a room to pick up a bit of a handkerchief purposely or accidentally dropped; when our mothers wore short-waisted dresses and enormous sleeves and decided family affairs by drawing lots, when the charming *dames aux camélias* hid from the light of day – in those naïve days of Masonic lodges,[1]

_____

1 Freemasonry in Russia was a secret association, the original purpose of which was the moral perfecting of people on the basis of equality and universal brotherhood. Commencing as a mystical-religious movement in the eighteenth century, it became political during the reign of Alexander I, and was suppressed in 1822.

Martinists,[1] and Tugendbunds,[2] the days of Milorádoviches[3] and Davýdovs[4] and Púshkins – a meeting of landed proprietors was held in the Government town of K—, and the nobility elections[5] were being concluded.

I

'WELL, never mind, the saloon will do,' said a young officer in a fur cloak and hussar's cap, who had just got out of a post-sledge and was entering the best hotel in the town of K—.

'The assembly, your Excellency, is enormous,' said the boots, who had already managed to learn from the orderly that the hussar's name was Count Túrbin, and therefore addressed him as 'your Excellency'.

'The proprietress of Afrémovo with her daughters has said she is leaving this evening, so No. 11 will be at your disposal as soon as they go,' continued the boots, stepping softly before the count along the passage and continually looking round.

In the general saloon at a little table under the dingy full-length portrait of the Emperor Alexander the First, several men, probably belonging to the local nobility, sat drinking champagne, while at another side of the room sat some travellers – tradesmen in blue, fur-lined cloaks.

Entering the room and calling in Blücher, a gigantic grey mastiff he had brought with him, the count threw off his cloak,

1 The Martinists were a society of Russian Freemasons founded in 1780 and named after the French theosophist, Louis Claude Saint-Martin.
2 The Tugenbund (League of Virtue) was a German association founded in 1808 with the acknowledged purpose of cultivating patriotism, reorganizing the army, and encouraging education, and with the secret aim of throwing off the French yoke. Dissolved on Napoleon's demand in 1809, it continued to exist secretly, and exerted great influence in 1812. It was suspected of having revolutionary tendencies, and was in very bad odour with the Russian government at the time of the Holy Alliance.
3 M. H. Milorádovich (1770–1825) distinguished himself in the Napoleonic war, became Governor-General of Petersburg, and was killed when suppressing the 'Decembrist' mutiny in 1825. He appears in *War and Peace*.
4 D. V. Davýdov (1784–1839), a popular poet, and leader of a guerrilla force in the war of 1812. A. S. Púshkin (1799–1837), the greatest of Russian poets, was his contemporary.
5 The *nobility* included not merely those who had titles, but all who in England would be called the gentry.

the collar of which was still covered with hoar-frost, called for vodka, sat down at the table in his blue satin Cossack jacket, and entered into conversation with the gentlemen there.

The handsome open countenance of the newcomer immediately predisposed them in his favour and they offered him a glass of champagne. The count first drank a glass of vodka and then ordered another bottle of champagne to treat his new acquaintances. The sledge-driver came in to ask for a tip.

'Sáshka!' shouted the count. 'Give him something!'

The driver went out with Sáshka but came back again with the money in his hand.

'Look here, y'r 'xcelence, haven't I done my very best for y'r honour? Didn't you promise me half a ruble, and he's only given me a quarter!'

'Give him a ruble, Sáshka.'

Sáshka cast down his eyes and looked at the driver's feet.

'He's had enough!' he said, in a bass voice. 'And besides, I have no more money.'

The count drew from his pocket-book the two five-ruble notes which were all it contained, and gave one of them to the driver, who kissed his hand and went off.

'I've run it pretty close!' said the count. 'These are my last five rubles.'

'Real hussar fashion, Count,' said one of the nobles who from his moustache, voice, and a certain energetic freedom about his legs, was evidently a retired cavalryman. 'Are you staying here some time, Count?'

'I must get some money. I shouldn't have stayed here at all but for that. And there are no rooms to be had, devil take them, in this accursed pub.'

'Permit me, Count,' said the cavalryman. 'Will you not join me? My room is No. 7 . . . . If you do not mind, just for the night. And then you'll stay a couple of days with us? It happens that the *Maréchal de la Noblesse* is giving a ball to-night. You would make him very happy by going.'

'Yes, Count, do stay,' said another, a handsome young man. 'You have surely no reason to hurry away! You know this only comes once in three years – the elections, I mean. You should at least have a look at our young ladies, Count!'

'Sáshka, get my clean linen ready. I am going to the bath,'[1] said the count, rising, 'and from there perhaps I may look in at the Marshal's.'

Then, having called the waiter and whispered something to him to which the latter replied with a smile, 'That can all be arranged,' he went out.[2]

'So I'll order my trunk to be taken to your room, old fellow,' shouted the count from the passage.

'Please do, I shall be most happy,' replied the cavalryman, running to the door. 'No. 7 – don't forget.'

When the count's footsteps could no longer be heard the cavalryman returned to his place and sitting close to one of the group – a Government official – and looking him straight in the face with smiling eyes, said:

'It is the very man, you know!'

'No!'

'I tell you it is! It is the very same duellist hussar – the famous Túrbin. He knew me – I bet you anything he knew me. Why, he and I went on the spree for three weeks without a break when I was at Lebedyáni[3] for remounts. There was one thing he and I did together. . . . He's a fine fellow, eh?'

'A splendid fellow. And so pleasant in his manner! Doesn't show a grain of – what d'you call it?' answered the handsome young man. 'How quickly we became intimate. . . . He's not more than twenty-five, is he?'

'Oh no, that's what he looks but he is more than that. One has to get to know him, you know. Who abducted Migúnova? He. It was he who killed Sáblin. It was he who dropped Matněv out of the window by his legs. It was he who won three hundred thousand rubles from Prince Néstorov. He is a regular dare-devil, you know: a gambler, a duellist, a seducer, but a jewel of an hussar – a real jewel. The rumours that are

1 For a Russian bath, as for a Turkish bath, one goes to a public establishment and subjects oneself to heat that produces profuse perspiration.
2 It was not unusual at the bath to associate with a woman.
3 A town in the Tambóv province noted for its horse fair.

afloat about us are nothing to the reality – if anyone knew what a true hussar is! Ah yes, those were times!'

And the cavalryman told his interlocutor of such a spree with the count in Lebedyáni as not only never had, but never even could have, taken place.

It could not have done so, first because he had never seen the count till that day and had left the army two years before the count entered it; and secondly because the cavalryman had never really served in the cavalry at all, but had for four years been the humblest of cadets in the Belévski regiment, and retired as soon as ever he became ensign. But ten years ago he had inherited some money and had really been in Lebedyáni where he squandered seven hundred rubles with some officers who were there buying remounts. He had even gone so far as to have an uhlan uniform made with orange facings, meaning to enter an uhlan regiment. This desire to enter the cavalry, and the three weeks spent with the remount officers at Lebedyáni, remained the brightest and happiest memories of his life, so he transformed the desire first into a reality and then into a reminiscence and came to believe firmly in his past as a cavalry officer – all of which did not prevent his being, as to gentleness and honesty, a most worthy man.

'Yes, those who have never served in the cavalry will never understand us fellows.'

He sat astride a chair and thrusting out his lower jaw began to speak in a bass voice. 'You ride at the head of your squadron, not a horse but the devil incarnate prancing about under you, and you just sit in devil-may-care style. The squadron commander rides up to review: "Lieutenant," he says. "We can't get on without you – please lead the squadron to parade." "All right," you say, and there you are: you turn round, shout to your moustached fellows. . . . Ah, devil take it, those were times!'

The count returned from the bath-house very red and with wet hair, and went straight to No. 7, where the cavalryman was already sitting in his dressing-gown smoking a pipe and considering with pleasure, and not without some apprehension, the happiness that had befallen him of sharing a room with the celebrated Túrbin. 'Now suppose,' he thought, 'that he suddenly takes me, strips me naked, drives me to the town gates and sets me in the snow, or ... tars me, or simply. . . . But no,' he consoled himself, 'he wouldn't do that to a comrade.'

'Sáshka, feed Blücher!' shouted the count.

Sáshka, who had taken a tumbler of vodka to refresh himself after the journey and was decidedly tipsy, came in.

'What, already! You've been drinking, you rascal! . . . Feed Blücher!'

'He won't starve anyway: see how sleek he is!' answered Sáshka, stroking the dog.

'Silence! Be off and feed him!'

'You want the dog to be fed, but when a man drinks a glass you reproach him.'

'Hey! I'll thrash you!' shouted the count in a voice that made the window-panes rattle and even frightened the cavalryman a bit.

'You should ask if Sáshka has had a bite to-day! Yes, beat me if you think more of a dog than of a man,' muttered Sáshka.

But here he received such a terrible blow in the face from the count's fist that he fell, knocked his head against the partition, and clutching his nose fled from the room and fell on a settee in the passage.

'He's knocked my teeth out,' grunted Sáshka, wiping his bleeding nose with one hand while with the other he scratched the back of Blücher, who was licking himself. 'He's knocked my teeth out, Blüchy, but still he's my count and I'd go through fire for him – I would! Because he – is my count. Do you understand, Blüchy? Want your dinner, eh?'

After lying still for a while he rose, fed the dog, and then, almost sobered, went in to wait on his count and to offer him some tea.

'I shall really feel hurt,' the cavalryman was saying meekly, as he stood before the count who was lying on the other's bed with his legs up against the partition. 'You see I also am an old army man and, if I may say so, a comrade. Why should you borrow from anyone else when I shall be delighted to lend you a couple of hundred rubles? I haven't got them just now – only a hundred rubles – but I'll get the rest to-day. You would really hurt my feelings, Count.'

'Thank you, old man,' said the count, instantly discerning what kind of relations had to be established between them, and slapping the cavalryman on the shoulder: 'Thanks! Well then, we'll go to the ball if it must be so. But what are we to do now? Tell me what you have in your town. What pretty girls? What men fit for a spree? What gaming?'

The cavalryman explained that there would be an abundance of pretty creatures at the ball, that Kólkov, who had been re-elected Captain of Police, was the best hand at a spree, only he lacked the true hussar go – otherwise he was a good sort of a chap: that the Ilyúshin gipsy chorus had been singing in the town since the elections began, Stëshka leading, and that everybody meant to go to hear them after leaving the Marshal's that evening.

'And there's a devilish lot of card-playing too,' he went on. 'Lúkhnov plays. He has money and is staying here to break his journey, and Ilyín, an uhlan cornet who has room No. 8, has lost a lot. They have already begun in his room. They play every evening. And what a fine fellow that Ilyín is! I tell you, Count, he's not mean – he'll let his last shirt go.'

'Well then, let us go to his room. Let's see what sort of people they are,' said the count.

'Yes do – pray do. They'll be devilish glad.'

II

THE uhlan cornet, Ilyín, had not long been awake. The evening before he had sat down to cards at eight o'clock and had lost pretty steadily for fifteen hours on end – till eleven in the morning. He had lost a considerable sum, but did not know exactly how much, because he had about three thousand rubles of his own, and fifteen thousand of Crown money which had long since got mixed up with his own, and he feared to count lest his fears that some of the Crown money was already gone should be confirmed. It was nearly noon when he fell asleep and he had slept that heavy dreamless sleep which only very young men sleep after a heavy loss. Waking at six o'clock (just when Count Túrbin arrived at the hotel), and seeing the floor all around strewn with cards and bits of chalk, and the chalk-marked tables in the middle of the room, he recalled with horror last night's play, and the last card – a knave on which he lost five hundred rubles; but not yet quite convinced of the reality of all this, he drew his money from under the pillow and began to count it. He recognized some notes which had passed from hand to hand several times with 'corners' and 'transports', and he recalled the whole course of the game. He had none of his own three thousand rubles left, and some two thousand five hundred of the Government money was also gone.

Ilyín had been playing for four nights running.

He had come from Moscow where the Crown money had been entrusted to him, and at K— had been detained by the superintendent of the post-house on the pretext that there were no horses, but really because the superintendent had an agreement with the hotel-keeper to detain all travellers for a day. The uhlan, a bright young lad who had just received three thousand rubles from his parents in Moscow for his equipment on entering his regiment, was glad to spend a few days in the town of K— during the elections, and hoped to enjoy himself thoroughly. He knew one of the landed gentry there who had a family, and he was thinking of looking them up and flirting with the daughters, when the cavalryman turned up to make his acquaintance. Without any evil intention the cavalryman introduced him that same evening, in the general saloon or common room of the hotel, to his acquaintances, Lúkhnov and other gamblers. And ever since then the uhlan had been playing cards, not asking at the post-station for horses, much less going to visit his acquaintance the landed proprietor, and not even leaving his room for four days on end.

Having dressed and drunk tea he went to the window. He felt that he would like to go for a stroll to get rid of the recollections that haunted him, and he put on his cloak and went out into the street. The sun was already hidden behind the white houses with their red roofs and it was getting dusk. It was warm for winter. Large wet snowflakes were falling slowly into the muddy street. Suddenly at the thought that he had slept all through the day now ending, a feeling of intolerable sadness overcame him.

'This day, now past, can never be recovered,' he thought.

'I have ruined my youth!' he suddenly said to himself, not because he really thought he had ruined his youth – he did not even think about it – but because the phrase happened to occur to him.

'And what am I to do now?' thought he. 'Borrow from someone and go away?' A lady passed him along the pavement. 'There's a stupid woman,' thought he for some reason. 'There's no one to borrow from . . . I have ruined my youth!' He came to the bazaar. A tradesman in a fox-fur cloak stood at the door of his shop touting for customers. 'If I had not withdrawn that eight I should have recovered my losses.' An old beggar-woman followed him whimpering. 'There's no one to borrow from.' A man drove past in a bearskin cloak; a policeman was standing at his post. 'What unusual thing could I do? Fire at them? No, it's dull . . . I have ruined my youth! . . . Ah, those are fine horse-collars and trappings hanging there! Ah, if only I could drive in a tróyka: Gee-up, beauties! . . . I'll go back. Lúkhnov will come soon, and we'll play.'

He returned to the hotel and again counted his money. No, he had made no mistake the first time: there were still two thousand five hundred rubles of Crown money missing. 'I'll stake twenty-five rubles, then make a "corner" . . . seven-fold it, fifteen-fold, thirty, sixty . . . three thousand rubles. Then I'll buy the horse-collars and be off. He won't let me, the rascal! I have ruined my youth!'

That is what was going on in the uhlan's head when Lúkhnov actually entered the room.

'Have you been up long, Michael Vasílich?' asked Lúkhnov slowly removing the gold spectacles from his skinny nose and carefully wiping them with a red silk handkerchief.

'No, I've only just got up – I slept uncommonly well.'

'Some hussar or other has arrived. He has put up with Zavalshévski – had you heard?'

'No, I hadn't. But how is it no one else is here yet?'

'They must have gone to Pryákhin's. They'll be here directly.'

And sure enough a little later there came into the room a garrison officer who always accompanied Lúkhnov; a Greek merchant with an enormous brown hooked nose and sunken black eyes; and a fat puffy landowner, the proprietor of a distillery, who played whole nights, always staking 'simples' of half a ruble each. Everybody wished to begin playing as soon as possible, but the principal gamesters, especially Lúkhnov who was telling about a robbery in Moscow in an exceedingly calm manner, did not refer to the subject.

'Just fancy,' he said, 'a city like Moscow, the historic capital, a metropolis, and men dressed up as devils go about there with crooks, frighten stupid people and rob the passers-by − and that's the end of it! What are the police about? That's the question.'

The uhlan listened attentively to the story about the robbers, but when a pause came he rose and quietly ordered cards to be brought. The fat landowner was the first to speak out.

'Well, gentlemen, why lose precious time? If we mean business let's begin.'

'Yes, you walked off with a pile of half-rubles last night so you like it,' said the Greek.

'I think we might start,' said the garrison officer.

Ilyín looked at Lúkhnov. Lúkhnov looking him in the eye quietly continued his story about robbers dressed up like devils with claws.

'Will you keep the bank?' asked the uhlan.

'Isn't it too early?'

'Belóv!' shouted the uhlan, blushing for some unknown reason, 'bring me some dinner − I haven't had anything to eat yet, gentlemen − and a bottle of champagne and some cards.'

At this moment the count and Zavalshévski entered the room. It turned out that Túrbin and Ilyín belonged to the same division. They took to one another at once, clinked glasses, drank champagne together, and were on intimate terms in five minutes. The count seemed to like Ilyín very much; he looked smilingly at him and teased him about his youth.

'There's an uhlan of the right sort!' he said. 'What moustaches! Dear me, what moustaches!'

Even what little down there was on Ilyín's lip was quite white.

'I suppose you are going to play?' said the count: 'Well, I wish you luck, Ilyín! I should think you are a master at it,' he added with a smile.

'Yes, they mean to start,' said Lúkhnov, tearing open a bundle of a dozen packs of cards, 'and you'll join in too, Count, won't you?'

'No, not to-day. I should clear you all out if I did. When I begin "cornering" in earnest the bank begins to crack! But I have nothing to play with – I was cleaned out at a station near Volochók. I met some infantry fellow there with rings on his fingers – a sharper I should think – and he plucked me clean.'

'Why, did you stay at that station long?' asked Ilyín.

'I sat there for twenty-two hours. I shan't forget that accursed station! And the superintendent won't forget me either...'

'How's that?'

'I drive up, you know; out rushes the superintendent looking a regular brigand. "No horses!" says he. Now I must tell you that it's my rule, if there are no horses I don't take off my fur cloak but go into the superintendent's own room – not into the public room but into his private room – and I have all the doors and windows opened on the ground that it's smoky. Well, that's just what I did there. You remember what frosts we had last month? About twenty degrees![1] The superintendent began to argue, I punched his head. There was an old woman there, and girls and other women; they kicked up a row, snatched up their pots and pans and were rushing off to the village. . . . I went to the door and said, "Let me have horses and I'll be off. If not, no one shall go out: I'll freeze you all!"'

1 Réaumur = thirteen below zero Fahrenheit.

'That's an infernally good plan!' said the puffy squire, rolling with laughter. 'It's the way they freeze out cockroaches...'

'But I didn't watch carefully enough and the superintendent got away with the women. Only one old woman remained in pawn on the top of the stove; she kept sneezing and saying her prayers. Afterwards we began negotiating: the superintendent came and from a distance began persuading me to let the old woman go, but I set Blücher at him a bit. Blücher's splendid at tackling superintendents! But still the rascal didn't let me have horses until the next morning. Meanwhile that infantry fellow came along. I joined him in another room, and we began to play. You have seen Blücher?...Blücher!...' and he gave a whistle.

Blücher rushed in, and the players condescendingly paid some attention to him though it was evident that they wished to attend to quite other matters.

'But why don't you play, gentlemen? Please don't let me prevent you. I am a chatterbox, you see,' said Túrbin. 'Play is play whether one likes it or not.'

III

LÚKHNOV drew two candles nearer to him, took out a large brown pocket-book full of paper money, and slowly, as if performing some rite, opened it on the table, took out two one-hundred ruble notes and placed them under the cards.

'Two hundred for the bank, the same as yesterday,' said he, adjusting his spectacles and opening a pack of cards.

'Very well,' said Ilyín, continuing his conversation with Túrbin without looking at Lúknov.

The game[1] started. Lúkhnov dealt the cards with machine-like precision, stopping now and then and deliberately jotting

[1] The game referred to was *shtos*. The players selected cards for themselves from packs on the table, and placed their stakes on or under their cards. The banker had a pack from which he dealt to right and left alternately. Cards dealt to the right won for him, those dealt to the left won for the players. 'Pass up' was a reminder to the players to hand up stakes due to the bank. 'Simples' were single stakes. By turning down 'corners' of his card a player

something down, or looking sternly over his spectacles and saying in low tones, 'Pass up!' The fat landowner spoke louder than anyone else, audibly deliberating with himself and wetting his plump fingers when he turned down the corner of a card. The garrison officer silently and neatly noted the amount of his stake on his card and bent down small corners under the table. The Greek sat beside the banker watching the game attentively with his sunken black eyes, and seemed to be waiting for something. Zavalshévski standing by the table would suddenly begin to fidget all over, take a red or blue bank-note[1] out of his trouser pocket, lay a card on it, slap it with his palm and say: 'Little seven, pull me through!' Then he would bite his moustache, shift from foot to foot, and keep fidgeting till his card was dealt. Ilyín sat eating veal and pickled cucumbers, which were placed beside him on the horsehair sofa, and hastily wiping his hands on his coat laid down one card after another. Túrbin, who at first was sitting on the sofa, quickly saw how matters stood. Lúkhnov did not look at or speak to Ilyín, only now and then his spectacles would turn for a moment towards the latter's hand, but most of Ilyín's cards lost.

'There now, I'd like to beat that card,' said Lúkhnov of a card the fat landowner, who was staking half-rubles, had put down.

'You beat Ilyín's, never mind me!' remarked the squire.

And indeed Ilyín's cards lost more often than any of the others. He would tear up the losing card nervously under the table and choose another with trembling fingers. Túrbin rose from the sofa and asked the Greek to let him sit by the banker. The Greek moved to another place, the count took his chair and began watching Lúkhnov's hands attentively, not taking his eyes off them.

'Ilyín!' he suddenly said in his usual voice, which quite unintentionally drowned all the others. 'Why do you keep to a routine? You don't know how to play.'

---

increased his stake two- or three-fold. A 'transport' increased it six-fold. *Shtos* has long gone out of fashion and been replaced by other forms of gambling.
1 Five-ruble notes were blue and ten-ruble notes red.

'It's all the same how one plays.'

'But you're sure to lose that way. Let me play for you.'

'No, please excuse me. I always do it myself. Play for yourself if you like.'

'I said I should not play for myself, but I should like to play for you. I am vexed that you are losing.'

'I suppose it's my fate.'

The count was silent, but leaning on his elbows he again gazed intently at the banker's hands.

'Abominable!' he suddenly said in a loud, long-drawn tone.

Lúkhnov glanced at him.

'Abominable, quite abominable!' he repeated still louder, looking straight into Lúkhnov's eyes.

The game continued.

'It is not right!' Túrbin remarked again, just as Lúkhnov beat a heavily-backed card of Ilyín's.

'What is it you don't like, Count?' inquired the banker with polite indifference.

'This! – that you let Ilyín win his simples and beat his corners. That's what's bad.'

Lúkhnov made a slight movement with his brows and shoulders, expressing the advisability of submitting to fate in everything, and continued to play.

'Blücher!' shouted the count, rising and whistling to the dog. 'At him!' he added quickly.

Blücher, bumping his back against the sofa as he leapt from under it and nearly upsetting the garrison officer, ran to his master and growled, looking round at everyone and moving his tail as if asking, 'Who is misbehaving here, eh?'

Lúkhnov put down his cards and moved his chair to one side.

'One can't play like that,' he said. 'I hate dogs. What kind of a game is it when you bring a whole pack of hounds in here?'

'Especially a dog like that. I believe they are called "leeches",' chimed in the garrison officer.

'Well, are we going to play or not, Michael Vasílich?' said Lúkhnov to their host.

'Please don't interfere with us, Count,' said Ilyín, turning to Túrbin.

'Come here a minute,' said Túrbin, taking Ilyín's arm and going behind the partition with him.

The count's words, spoken in his usual tone, were distinctly audible from there. His voice always carried across three rooms.

'Are you daft, eh? Don't you see that that gentleman in spectacles is a sharper of the first water?'

'Come now, enough! What are you saying?'

'No enough about it! Stop playing, I tell you. It's nothing to me. Another time I'd pluck you myself, but somehow I'm sorry to see you fleeced. And maybe you have Crown money too?'

'No . . . why do you imagine such things?'

'Ah, my lad, I've been that way myself so I know all those sharpers' tricks. I tell you the one in spectacles is a sharper. Stop playing! I ask you as a comrade.'

'Well then, I'll only finish this one deal.'

'I know what "one deal" means. Well, we'll see.'

They went back. In that one deal Ilyín put down so many cards and so many of them were beaten that he lost a large amount.

Túrbin put his hands in the middle of the table. 'Now stop it! Come along.'

'No, I can't. Leave me alone, do!' said Ilyín, irritably shuffling some bent cards without looking at Túrbin.

'Well, go to the devil! Go on losing for certain, if that pleases you. It's time for me to be off. Let's go to the Marshal's, Zavalshévski.'

They went out. All remained silent and Lúkhnov dealt no more cards until the sound of their steps and of Blücher's claws on the passage floor had died away.

'What a devil of a fellow!' said the landowner laughing.

'Well, he won't interfere now,' remarked the garrison officer hastily, and still in a whisper.

And the play continued.

IV

THE band, composed of some of the Marshal's serfs standing in the pantry – which had been cleared out for the occasion –

with their coat-sleeves turned up ready, had at a given signal struck up the old polonaise, 'Alexander, 'Lizabeth', and under the bright soft light of the wax-candles a Governor-General of Catharine's days, with a star on his breast, arm-in-arm with the Marshal's skinny wife, and the rest of the local grandees with their partners, had begun slowly gliding over the parquet floor of the large dancing-room in various combinations and variations, when Zavalshévski entered, wearing stockings and pumps and a blue swallow-tail coat with an immense and padded collar, and exhaling a strong smell of the frangipane with which the facings of his coat, his handkerchief, and his moustaches, were abundantly sprinkled. The handsome hussar who came with him wore tight-fitting light-blue riding-breeches and a gold-embroidered scarlet coat on which a Vladímir cross and an 1812 medal[1] were fastened. The count was not tall but remarkably well built. His clear blue and exceedingly brilliant eyes, and thick, closely curling, dark-brown hair, gave a remarkable character to his beauty. His arrival at the ball was expected, for the handsome young man who had seen him at the hotel had already prepared the Marshal for it. Various impressions had been produced by the news, for the most part not altogether pleasant.

'It's not unlikely that this youngster will hold us up to ridicule,' was the opinion of the men and of the older women. 'What if he should run away with me?' was more or less in the minds of the younger ladies, married or unmarried.

As soon as the polonaise was over and the couples after bowing to one another had separated – the women into one group and the men into another – Zavalshévski, proud and happy, introduced the count to their hostess.

The Marshal's wife, feeling an inner trepidation lest this hussar should treat her in some scandalous manner before everybody, turned away haughtily and contemptuously as she said: 'Very pleased, I hope you will dance,' and then gave him a distrustful look that said, 'Now, if you offend a woman it

---

1 That is to say, a medal gained in the defence of his country against Napoleon.

will show me that you are a perfect villain.' The count however soon conquered her prejudices by his amiability, attentive
manner, and handsome gay appearance, so that five minutes
later the expression on the face of the Marshal's wife told the
company: 'I know how to manage such gentlemen. He immediately understood with whom he had to deal, and now he'll
be charming to me for the rest of the evening.' Moreover at
that moment the governor of the town, who had known the
count's father, came up to him and very affably took him aside
for a talk, which still further calmed the provincial public and
raised the count in its estimation. After that Zavalshévski
introduced the count to his sister, a plump young widow
whose large black eyes had not left the count from the
moment he entered. The count asked her to dance the waltz
the band had just commenced, and the general prejudice was
finally dispersed by the masterly way in which he danced.

'What a splendid dancer!' said a fat landed proprietress,
watching his legs in their blue riding-breeches as they flitted
across the room, and mentally counting 'one, two, three –
one, two, three – splendid!'

'There he goes – jig, jig, jig,' said another, a visitor in the
town whom local society did not consider genteel. 'How does
he manage not to entangle his spurs? Wonderfully clever!'

The count's artistic dancing eclipsed the three best dancers
of the province: the tall fair-haired adjutant of the governor,
noted for the rapidity with which he danced and for holding
his partner very close to him; the cavalryman, famous for the
graceful swaying motion with which he waltzed and for the
frequent but light tapping of his heels; and a civilian, of whom
everybody said that though he was not very intellectual he was
a first-rate dancer and the soul of every ball. In fact, from its
very commencement this civilian would ask all the ladies in
turn to dance, in the order in which they were sitting,[1] and
never stopped for a moment except occasionally to wipe the

1 The custom was, not to dance a whole dance with one lady but to take a
few turns round the room, conduct her to her seat, bow to her, thank her,
and seek a fresh partner.

perspiration from his weary but cheerful face with a very wet
cambric handkerchief. The count eclipsed them all and danced
with the three principal ladies: the tall one, rich, handsome,
stupid; the one of middle height, thin and not very pretty but
splendidly dressed; and the little one, who was plain but very
clever. He danced with others too – with all the pretty ones,
and there were many of these – but it was Zavalshévski's sister,
the little widow, who pleased him best. With her he danced a
quadrille, an *écossaise*, and a mazurka. When they were sitting
down during the quadrille he began paying her many compliments; comparing her to Venus and Diana, to a rose, and to
some other flower. But all these compliments only made the
widow bend her white neck, lower her eyes and look at her
white muslin dress, or pass her fan from hand to hand. But
when she said: 'Don't, you're only joking, Count,' and other
words to that effect, there was a note of such naïve simplicity
and amusing silliness in her slightly guttural voice, that looking
at her it really seemed that this was not a woman but a flower,
and not a rose, but some gorgeous scentless rosy-white wild
flower that had grown all alone out of a snowdrift in some very
remote land.

This combination of naïveté and unconventionality with
her fresh beauty created such a peculiar impression on the
count that several times during the intervals of conversation,
when gazing silently into her eyes or at the beautiful outline of
her neck and arms, the desire to seize her in his arms and cover
her with kisses assailed him with such force that he had to
make a serious effort to resist it. The widow noticed with
pleasure the effect she was producing, yet something in the
count's behaviour began to frighten and excite her, though the
young hussar, despite his insinuating amiability, was respectful
to a degree that in our days would be considered cloying. He
ran to fetch almond-milk for her, picked up her handkerchief,
snatched a chair from the hands of a scrofulous young squire
who danced attendance on her, to hand it her more quickly,
and so forth.

When he noticed that the society attentions of the day had
little effect on the lady he tried to amuse her by telling her

funny stories and assured her that he was ready to stand on his head, to crow like a cock, to jump out of the window or plunge into the water through a hole in the ice, if she ordered him to do so. This proved quite a success. The widow brightened up and burst into peals of laughter, showing lovely white teeth, and was quite satisfied with her cavalier. The count liked her more and more every minute, so that by the end of the quadrille he was seriously in love with her.

When, after the quadrille, her eighteen-year-old adorer of long standing came up to the widow (he was the same scrofulous young man from whom Túrbin had snatched the chair – a son of the richest local landed proprietor and not yet in government service) she received him with extreme coolness and did not show one-tenth of the confusion she had experienced with the count.

'Well, you are a fine fellow!' she said, looking all the time at Túrbin's back and unconsciously considering how many yards of gold cord it had taken to embroider his whole jacket. 'You are a good one! You promised to call and fetch me for a drive and bring me some comfits.'

'I did come, Anna Fëdorovna, but you had already gone, and I left some of the very best comfits for you,' said the young man, who – despite his tallness – spoke in a very high-pitched voice.

'You always find excuses! . . . I don't want your bonbons. Please don't imagine —'

'I see, Anna Fëdorovna, that you have changed towards me and I know why. But it's not right,' he added, evidently unable to finish his speech because a strong inward agitation caused his lips to quiver in a very strange and rapid manner.

Anna Fëdorovna did not listen to him, but continued to follow Túrbin with her eyes.

The master of the house, the stout, toothless, stately old Marshal, came up to the count, took him by the arm, and invited him into the study for a smoke and a drink. As soon as Túrbin left the room Anna Fëdorovna felt that there was absolutely nothing to do there and went out into the dressing-room arm-in-arm with a friend of hers, a bony, elderly, maiden lady.

'Well, is he nice?' asked the maiden lady.

'Only he bothers so!' Anna Fëdorovna replied walking up to the mirror and looking at herself.

Her face brightened, her eyes laughed, she even blushed, and suddenly, imitating the ballet-dancers she had seen during the elections, she twirled round on one foot, then laughed her guttural but pleasant laugh and even bent her knees and gave a jump.

'Just fancy, what a man! He actually asked me for a keep-sake,' she said to her friend, 'but he will get no-o-o-thing.' She sang the last word and held up one finger in her kid glove which reached to her elbow.

In the study, where the Marshal had taken Túrbin, stood bottles of different sorts of vodka, liqueurs, champagne, and *zakúska*.[1] The nobility, walking about or sitting in a cloud of tobacco smoke, were talking about the elections.

'When the whole worshipful society of our nobility has honoured him by their choice,' said the newly elected Captain of Police who had already imbibed freely, 'he should on no account transgress in the face of the whole society – he ought never...'

The count's entrance interrupted the conversation. Everybody wished to be introduced to him and the Captain of Police especially kept pressing the count's hand between his own for a long time, and repeatedly asked him not to refuse to accompany him to the new restaurant where he was going to treat the gentlemen after the ball, and where the gipsies were going to sing. The count promised to come without fail, and drank some glasses of champagne with him.

'But why are you not dancing, gentlemen?' said the count, as he was about to leave the room.

'We are not dancers,' replied the Captain of Police, laughing. 'Wine is more in our line, Count. . . . And besides, I have

---

1 The *zakúska* ('little bite') consists of a choice of snacks: caviare, salt-fish, cheese, radishes, or what not, with small glasses of vodka or other spirits. It is sometimes served alone, but usually forms an appetizer laid out on a side table and partaken of immediately before dinner or supper. It answers somewhat to the *hors-d'œuvre* of an English dinner.

seen all those young ladies grow up, Count! But I can walk through an *écossaise* now and then, Count . . . I can do it, Count.'

'Then come and walk through one now,' said Túrbin. 'It will brighten us up before going to hear the gipsies.'

'Very well, gentlemen! Let's come and gratify our host.'

And three or four of the noblemen who had been drinking in the study since the commencement of the ball, put on gloves of black kid or knitted silk, and with red faces were just about to follow the count into the ball-room when they were stopped by the scrofulous young man who, pale and hardly able to restrain his tears, accosted Túrbin.

'You think that because you are a count you can jostle people about as if you were in the market-place,' he said, breathing with difficulty, 'but that is impolite . . .'

And again, do what he would, his quivering lips checked the flow of his words.

'What?' cried Túrbin, suddenly frowning. 'What? . . . You brat!' he cried, seizing him by the arms and squeezing them so that the blood rushed to the young man's head not so much from vexation as from fear. 'What? Do you want to fight? I am at your service!'

Hardly had Túrbin released the arms he had been squeezing so hard, than two nobles caught hold of them and dragged the young man towards the back door.

'What! Are you out of your mind? You must be tipsy! Suppose we were to tell your papa! What's the matter with you?' they said to him.

'No, I'm not tipsy, but he jostles one and does not apologize. He's a swine, that's what he is!' squealed the young man, now quite in tears.

But they did not listen to him and someone took him home.

On the other side the Captain of Police and Zavalshévski were exhorting Túrbin: 'Never mind him, Count, he's only a child. He still gets whipped, he's only sixteen. . . . What can have happened to him? What bee has stung him? And his father such a respectable man – and our candidate.'

'Well, let him go to the devil if he does not wish . . .'

And the count returned to the ball-room and danced the *écossaise* with the pretty widow as gaily as before, laughed with all his heart as he watched the steps performed by the gentlemen who had come with him out of the study, and burst into peals of laughter that rang across the room when the Captain of Police slipped and measured his full length in the midst of the dancers.

V

WHILE the count was in the study Anna Fëdorovna had approached her brother, and supposing that she ought to pretend to be very little interested in the count began by asking:

'Who is that hussar who was dancing with me? Can you tell me, brother?'

The cavalryman explained to his sister as well as he could what a great man the hussar was, and told her at the same time that the count was only stopping in the town because his money had been stolen on the way, and that he himself had lent him a hundred rubles, but that that was not enough, so that perhaps 'sister' would lend another couple of hundred. Only Zavalshévski asked her on no account to mention the matter to anyone – especially not to the count. Anna Fëdorovna promised to send her brother the money that very day and to keep the affair secret, but somehow during the *écossaise* she felt a great longing herself to offer the count as much money as he wanted. She took a long time making up her mind, and blushed, but at last with a great effort broached the subject as follows:

'My brother tells me that a misfortune befell you on the road, Count, and that you have no money by you. If you need any, won't you take it from me? I should be so glad.'

But having said this, Anna Fëdorovna suddenly felt frightened of something and blushed. All gaiety instantly left the count's face.

'Your brother is a fool!' he said abruptly. 'You know when a man insults another man they fight; but when a woman insults a man, what does he do then – do you know?'

Poor Anna Fëdorovna's neck and ears grew red with confusion. She lowered her eyes and said nothing.

'He kisses the woman in public,' said the count in a low voice, leaning towards her ear. 'Allow me at least to kiss your little hand,' he added in a whisper after a prolonged silence, taking pity on his partner's confusion.

'But not now!' said Anna Fëdorovna, with a deep sigh.

'When then? I am leaving early to-morrow and you owe it me.'

'Well then it's impossible,' said Anna Fëdorovna with a smile.

'Only allow me a chance to meet you to-night to kiss your hand. I shall not fail to find an opportunity.'

'How can you find it?'

'That is not your business. In order to see you everything is possible. . . . It's agreed?'

'Agreed.'

The *écossaise* ended. After that they danced a mazurka and the count was quite wonderful: catching handkerchiefs, kneeling on one knee, striking his spurs together in a quite special Warsaw manner, so that all the old people left their game of boston and flocked into the ball-room to see, and the cavalryman, their best dancer, confessed himself eclipsed. Then they had supper after which they danced the 'Grandfather', and the ball began to break up. The count never took his eyes off the little widow. It was not pretence when he said he was ready to jump through a hole in the ice for her sake. Whether it was whim, or love, or obstinacy, all his mental powers that evening were concentrated on the one desire – to meet and love her. As soon as he noticed that Anna Fëdorovna was taking leave of her hostess he ran out to the footmen's room, and thence – without his fur cloak – into the courtyard to the place where the carriages stood.

'Anna Fëdorovna Záytseva's carriage!' he shouted.

A high four-seated closed carriage with lamps burning moved from its place and approached the porch.

'Stop!' he called to the coachman, and plunging knee-deep into the snow ran to the carriage.

'What do you want?' said the coachman.

'I want to get into the carriage,' replied the count opening the door and trying to get in while the carriage was moving. 'Stop, I tell you, you fool!'

'Stop, Váska!' shouted the coachman to the postilion, and pulled up the horses. 'What are you getting into other people's carriages for? This carriage belongs to my mistress, to Anna Fëdorovna, and not to your honour.'

'Shut up, you blockhead! Here's a ruble for you; get down and close the door,' said the count. But as the coachman did not stir he lifted the steps himself and, lowering the window, managed somehow to close the door. In the carriage, as in all old carriages, especially in those in which yellow galloon is used, there was a musty odour something like the smell of decayed and burnt bristles. The count's legs were wet with snow up to the knees and felt very cold in his thin boots and riding-breeches; in fact the winter cold penetrated his whole body. The coachman grumbled on the box and seemed to be preparing to get down. But the count neither heard nor felt anything. His face was aflame and his heart beat fast. In his nervous tension he seized the yellow window strap and leant out of the side window, and all his being merged into one feeling of expectation.

This expectancy did not last long. Someone called from the porch: 'Záytseva's carriage!' The coachman shook the reins, the body of the carriage swayed on its high springs, and the illuminated windows of the house ran one after another past the carriage windows.

'Mind, fellow,' said the count to the coachman, putting his head out of the front window, 'if you tell the footman I'm here, I'll thrash you, but hold your tongue and you shall have another ten rubles.'

Hardly had he time to close the window before the body of the carriage shook more violently and then stopped. He pressed close into the corner, held his breath, and even shut his eyes, so terrified was he lest anything should balk his passionate expectation. The door opened, the carriage steps fell noisily one after the other, he heard the rustle of a woman's dress, a smell of frangipane perfume filled the musty carriage, quick little feet ran up the carriage steps, and Anna Fëdorovna, brushing the count's leg with the skirt of her cloak which had come open, sank silently onto the seat beside him breathing heavily.

Whether she saw him or not no one could tell, not even Anna Fëdorovna herself, but when he took her hand and said: 'Well, now I will kiss your little hand,'[1] she showed very little fear, gave no reply, but yielded her arm to him, which he covered much higher than the top of her glove with kisses. The carriage started.

'Say something! Art thou angry?' he said.

She silently pressed into her corner, but suddenly something caused her to burst into tears and of her own accord she let her head fall on his breast.

VI

THE newly elected Captain of Police and his guests the cavalryman and other nobles had long been listening to the gipsies and drinking in the new restaurant when the count, wearing a blue cloth cloak lined with bearskin which had belonged to Anna Fëdorovna's late husband, joined them.

'Sure, your excellency, we have been awaiting you impatiently!' said a dark cross-eyed gipsy, showing his white teeth, as he met the count at the very entrance and rushed to help him off with his cloak. 'We have not seen you since the fair at Lebedyáni ... Stëshka is quite pining away for you.'

Stëshka, a young, graceful little gipsy with a brick-red glow on her brown face and deep, sparkling black eyes shaded by long lashes, also ran out to meet him.

'Ah, little Count! Dearest! Jewel! This is a joy!' she murmured between her teeth, smiling merrily.

Ilyúshka himself ran out to greet him, pretending to be very glad to see him. The old women, matrons, and maids, jumped

---

1 The same word (ruká) stands for hand or arm in Russian.

from their places and surrounded the guest, some claiming him as a fellow god-father, some as brother by baptism.[1]

Túrbin kissed all the young gipsy girls on their lips; the old women and the men kissed him on his shoulder or hand. The noblemen were also glad of their visitor's arrival, especially as the carousal, having reached its zenith, was beginning to flag, and everyone was beginning to feel satiated. The wine having lost its stimulating effect on the nerves merely weighed on the stomach. Each one had already let off his store of swagger, and they were getting tired of one another; the songs had all been sung and had got mixed in everyone's head, leaving a noisy, dissolute impression behind. No matter what strange or dashing thing anyone did, it began to occur to everyone that there was nothing agreeable or funny in it. The Captain of Police, who lay in a shocking state on the floor at the feet of an old woman, began wriggling his legs and shouting: 'Champagne!... The count's come!... Champagne!... He's come ... now then, champagne!... I'll have a champagne bath and bathe in it! Noble gentlemen!... I love the society of our brave old nobility... Stёshka, sing *The Pathway*.'

The cavalryman was also rather tipsy, but in another way. He sat on a sofa in the corner very close to a tall handsome gipsy girl, Lyubásha; and feeling his eyes misty with drink he kept blinking and shaking his head and, repeating the same words over and over again in a whisper, besought the gipsy to fly with him somewhere. Lyubásha, smiling and listening as if what he said were very amusing and yet rather sad, glanced occasionally at her husband – the cross-eyed Sáshka who was standing behind the chair opposite her – and in reply to the cavalryman's declarations of love, stooped and whispering in his ear asked him to buy her some scent and ribbons on the quiet, so that the others should not notice.

'Hurrah!' cried the cavalryman when the count entered.

The handsome young man was pacing up and down the room with laboriously steady steps and a careworn expression on his face, warbling an air from *Il Seraglio*.

1 In Russia god-parents and their god-children, and people having the same god-father or god-mother, were considered to be related.

An elderly paterfamilias, who had been tempted by the persistent entreaties of the nobles to come and hear the gipsies, as they said that without him the thing would be worthless and it would be better not to go at all, was lying on a sofa where he had sunk as soon as he arrived, and no one was taking any notice of him. Some official or other who was also there had taken off his swallow-tail coat and was sitting up on the table, feet and all, ruffling his hair, and thereby showing that he was very much on the spree. As soon as the count entered, this official unbuttoned the collar of his shirt and got still farther onto the table. In general on Túrbin's arrival the carousal revived.

The gipsy girls, who had been wandering about the room, again gathered and sat down in a circle. The count took Stëshka, the leading singer, on his knee, and ordered more champagne.

Ilyúshka came and stood in front of Stëshka with his guitar, and the 'dance' commenced, i.e. the gipsy songs, *When you go along the Street, O Hussars!, Do you hear, do you know?*, and so on in a definite order. Stëshka sang admirably. The flexible sonorous contralto that flowed from her very chest, her smiles while singing, her laughing passionate eyes, and her foot that moved involuntarily in measure with the song, her wild shriek at the commencement of the chorus – all touched some powerful but rarely-reached chord. It was evident that she lived only in the song she was singing. Ilyúshka accompanied her on the guitar – his back, legs, smile, and whole being, expressing sympathy with the song – and eagerly watching her, raised and lowered his head as attentive and engrossed as though he heard the song for the first time. Then at the last melodious note he suddenly drew himself up, and as if feeling himself superior to everyone in the world, proudly and resolutely threw up his guitar with his foot, twirled it about, stamped, tossed back his hair, and looked round at the choir with a frown. His whole body from neck to heels began dancing in every muscle – and twenty energetic, powerful voices each trying to chime in more strongly and more strangely than the rest, rang through the air. The old women bobbed up and down on their chairs waving their handkerchiefs, showing their teeth, and vying with one another in their harmonious and measured shouts. The basses with strained necks and heads bent to one side boomed while standing behind the chairs.

When Stëshka took a high note Ilyúshka brought his guitar closer to her as if wishing to help her, and the handsome young man screamed with rapture, saying that now they were beginning the *bémols.*[1]

When a dance was struck up and Dunyásha, advancing with quivering shoulders and bosom, twirled round in front of the count and glided onwards, Túrbin leapt up, threw off his jacket, and in his red shirt stepped jauntily with her in precise and measured step, accomplishing such things with his legs that the gipsies smiled with approval and glanced at one another.

The Captain of Police sat down like a Turk, beat his breast with his fist, and cried '*vivat!*' and then, having caught hold of the count's leg, began to tell him that of two thousand rubles he now had only five hundred left, but that he could do anything he liked if only the count would allow it. The elderly paterfamilias awoke and wished to go away, but was not allowed to do so. The handsome young man began persuading a gipsy to waltz with him. The cavalryman, wishing to show off his intimacy with the count, rose and embraced Túrbin. 'Ah, my dear fellow,' he said, 'why didst thou leave us, eh?' The count was silent, evidently thinking of something else. 'Where did you go to? Ah, you rogue of a count, I know where you went to!'

For some reason this familiarity displeased Túrbin. Without a smile he looked silently into the cavalryman's face and suddenly launched at him such terrible and rude abuse that the cavalryman was pained, and for a while could not make up his mind whether to take the offence as a joke or seriously. At last he decided to take it as a joke, smiled, and went back to his gipsy, assuring her that he would certainly marry her after

---

1 *Bémol* is French for a flat; but in Russia many people knowing nothing of musical technicalities imagined it to have something to do with excellence in music.

Easter. They sang another song and another, danced again, and 'hailed the guests', and everyone continued to imagine that he was enjoying it. There was no end to the champagne. The count drank a great deal. His eyes seemed to grow moist, but he was not unsteady. He danced even better than before, spoke firmly, even joined in the chorus extremely well, and chimed in when Stëshka sang *Friendship's Tender Emotions*. In the midst of a dance the landlord came in to ask the guests to return to their homes as it was getting on for three in the morning.

The count seized the landlord by the scruff of his neck and ordered him to dance the Russian dance. The landlord refused. The count snatched up a bottle of champagne and having stood the landlord on his head and had him held in that position, amidst general laughter, slowly emptied the bottle over him.

It was beginning to dawn. Everyone looked pale and exhausted except the count.

'Well, I must be starting for Moscow,' said he, suddenly rising. 'Come along, all of you! Come and see me off... and we'll have some tea together.'

All agreed except the paterfamilias (who was left behind asleep), and crowding into three large sledges that stood at the door, they all drove off to the hotel.

VII

'GET horses ready!' cried the count as he entered the saloon of his hotel followed by the guests and gipsies. 'Sáshka! – not gipsy Sáshka but my Sáshka – tell the superintendent I'll thrash him if he gives me bad horses. And get us some tea. Zavalshévski, look after the tea: I'm going to have a look at Ilyín and see how he's getting on...' added Túrbin, and went along the passage towards the uhlan's room.

Ilyín had just finished playing, and having lost his last kopék was lying face downwards on the sofa, pulling one hair after another from its torn horsehair cover, putting them in his mouth, biting them in two and spitting them out again.

Two tallow candles, one of which had burnt down to the paper in the socket, stood on the card-strewn table and feebly wrestled with the morning light that crept in through the window. There were no ideas in Ilyín's head: a dense mist of gambling passion shrouded all his faculties, he did not even feel penitent. He made one attempt to think of what he should do now: how being penniless he could get away, how he could repay the fifteen thousand rubles of Crown money, what his regimental commander would say, what his mother and his comrades would say, and he felt such terror and disgust with himself that wishing to forget himself he rose and began pacing up and down the room trying to step only where the floor-boards joined, and began, once more, vividly to recall every slightest detail of the course of play. He vividly imagined how he had begun to win back his money, how he withdrew a nine and placed the king of spades over two thousand rubles. A queen was dealt to the right, an ace to the left, then the king of diamonds to the right and all was lost; but if, say, a six had been dealt to the right and the king of diamonds to the left, he would have won everything back, would have played once more double or quits, would have won fifteen thousand rubles, and would then have bought himself an ambler from his regimental commander and another pair of horses besides, and a phaeton. Well, and what then? – Well it would have been a splendid, splendid thing!

And he lay down on the sofa again and began chewing the horsehair.

'Why are they singing in No. 7?' thought he. 'There must be a spree on at Túrbin's. Shall I go in and have a good drink?'

At this moment the count entered.

'Well, old fellow, cleaned out, are you? Eh?' cried he.

'I'll pretend to be asleep,' thought Ilyín, 'or else I shall have to speak to him, and I want to sleep.'

Túrbin, however, came up and stroked his head.

'Well, my dear friend, cleaned out – lost everything? Tell me.'

Ilyín gave no answer.

The count pulled his arm.

'I have lost. But what is that to you?' muttered Ilyín in a sleepy, indifferent, discontented voice, without changing his position.

'Everything?'

'Well – yes. What of it? Everything. What is it to you?'

'Listen. Tell me the truth as to a comrade,' said the count, inclined to tenderness by the influence of the wine he had drunk and continuing to stroke Ilyín's hair. 'I have really taken a liking to you. Tell me the truth. If you have lost Crown money I'll get you out of your scrape: it will soon be too late.... Had you Crown money?'

Ilyín jumped up from the sofa.

'Well then, if you wish me to tell you, don't speak to me, because ... please don't speak to me.... To shoot myself is the only thing!' said Ilyín, with real despair, and his head fell on his hands and he burst into tears, though but a moment before he had been calmly thinking about amblers.

'What pretty girlishness! Where's the man who has not done the like? It's not such a calamity; perhaps we can mend it. Wait for me here.'

The count left the room.

'Where is Squire Lúkhnov's room?' he asked the boots.

The boots offered to show him the way. In spite of the valet's remark that his master had only just returned and was undressing, the count went in. Lúkhnov was sitting at a table in his dressing-gown counting several packets of paper money that lay before him. A bottle of Rhine wine, of which he was very fond, stood on the table. After winning he permitted himself that pleasure. Lúkhnov looked coldly and sternly through his spectacles at the count as though not recognizing him.

'You don't recognize me, I think?' said the count, resolutely stepping up to the table.

Lúkhnov made a gesture of recognition, and said: 'What is it you want?'

'I should like to play with you,' said Túrbin, sitting down on the sofa.

'Now?'

'Yes.'

'Another time with pleasure, Count! But now I am tired and am going to bed. Won't you have a glass of wine? It is famous wine.'

'But I want to play a little – now.'

'I don't intend to play any more to-night. Perhaps some of the other gentlemen will, but I won't. You must please excuse me, Count.'

'Then you won't?'

Lúkhnov shrugged his shoulders to express his regret at his inability to comply with the count's desire.

'Not on any account?'

The same shrug.

'But I particularly request it. . . . Well, will you play?'

Silence.

'Will you play?' the count asked again. 'Mind!'

The same silence and a rapid glance over the spectacles at the count's face which was beginning to frown.

'Will you play?' shouted the count very loud, striking the table with his hand so that the bottle toppled over and the wine was spilt. 'You know you did not win fairly. . . . Will you play? I ask you for the third time.'

'I said I would not. This is really strange, Count! And it is not at all proper to come and hold a knife to a man's throat,' remarked Lúkhnov, not raising his eyes. A momentary silence followed during which the count's face grew paler and paler. Suddenly a terrible blow on the head stupefied Lúkhnov. He fell on the sofa trying to seize the money and uttered such a piercingly despairing cry as no one could have expected from so calm and imposing a person. Túrbin gathered up what money lay on the table, pushed aside the servant who ran in to his master's assistance, and left the room with rapid strides.

'If you want satisfaction I am at your service! I shall be in my room for another half-hour,' said the count, returning to Lúkhnov's door.

'Thief! Robber! I'll have the law on you . . .' was all that was audible from the room.

Ilýín, who had paid no attention to the count's promise to help him, still lay as before on the sofa in his room choking with tears of despair. Consciousness of what had really happened, which the count's caresses and sympathy had evoked from behind the strange tangle of feelings, thoughts, and memories filling his soul, did not leave him. His youth, rich with hope, his honour, the respect of society, his dreams of love and friendship – all were utterly lost. The source of his tears began to run dry, a too passive feeling of hopelessness overcame him more and more, and thoughts of suicide, no longer arousing revulsion or horror, claimed his attention with increasing frequency. Just then the count's firm footsteps were heard.

In Túrbin's face traces of anger could still be seen, his hands shook a little, but his eyes beamed with kindly merriment and self-satisfaction.

'Here you are, it's won back!' he said, throwing several bundles of paper money on the table. 'See if it's all there and then make haste and come into the saloon. I am just leaving,' he added, as though not noticing the joy and gratitude and extreme agitation on Ilyín's face, and whistling a gipsy song he left the room.

VIII

S Á S H K A , with a sash tied round his waist, announced that the horses were ready, but insisted that the count's cloak, which, he said, with its fur collar was worth three hundred rubles, should be recovered, and the shabby blue one returned to the rascal who had changed it for the count's at the Marshal's; but Túrbin told him there was no need to look for the cloak, and went to his room to change his clothes.

The cavalryman kept hiccoughing as he sat silent beside his gipsy girl. The Captain of Police called for vodka, and invited everyone to come at once and have breakfast with him, promising that his wife would certainly dance with the gipsies. The handsome young man was profoundly explaining to Ilyúshka that there is more soulfulness in pianoforte music, and that it is not possible to play *bémols* on a guitar. The official sat in a corner sadly drinking his tea, and in the daylight seemed ashamed of his debauchery. The gipsies were disputing among themselves in their own tongue as to 'hailing the guests' again, which Stëshka opposed, saying that the *baroráy* (in gipsy language count or prince or, more literally, 'great gentleman') would be angry. In general the last embers of the debauch were dying down in everyone.

'Well, one farewell song, and then off home!' said the count, entering the parlour in travelling dress, fresh, merry, and handsomer than ever.

The gipsies again formed their circle and were just ready to begin when Ilyín entered with a packet of paper money in his hand and took the count aside.

'I only had fifteen thousand rubles of Crown money and you have given me sixteen thousand three hundred,' he said, 'so this is yours.'

'That's a good thing. Give it here!'

Ilyín gave him the money and, looking timidly at the count, opened his lips to say something, but only blushed till tears came into his eyes and seizing the count's hand began to press it.

'You be off!...Ilyúshka! Listen! Here's some money for you, but you must accompany me out of the town with songs!' and he threw onto the guitar the thirteen hundred rubles Ilyín had brought him. But the count quite forgot to repay the hundred rubles he had borrowed of the cavalryman the day before.

It was already ten o'clock in the morning. The sun had risen above the roofs of the houses. People were moving about in the streets. The tradesmen had long since opened their shops. Noblemen and officials were driving through the streets and ladies were shopping in the bazaar, when the whole gipsy band, with the Captain of Police, the cavalryman, the handsome young man, Ilyín, and the count in the blue bearskin cloak, came out into the hotel porch.

It was a sunny day and a thaw had set in. The large post-sledges, each drawn by three horses with their tails tied up tight, drove up to the porch splashing through the mud and the whole lively party took their places. The count, Ilyín, Stëshka, and Ilyúshka, with Sáshka the count's orderly, got into the first sledge. Blücher was beside himself, and wagged his tail, barking at the shaft-horse. The other gentlemen got into the two other sledges with the rest of the gipsy men and women. The tróykas got abreast as they left the hotel and the gipsies struck up in chorus.

The tróykas with their songs and bells − forcing every vehicle they met right onto the pavements − dashed through the whole town right to the town gates.

The tradesmen and passers-by who did not know them, and especially those who did, were not a little astonished when they saw the noblemen driving through the streets in broad daylight with gipsy girls and tipsy gipsy men, singing.

When they had passed the town gates the tróykas stopped and everyone began bidding the count farewell.

Ilyín, who had drunk a good deal at the leave-taking and had himself been driving the sledge all the way, suddenly became very sad, begged the count to stay another day, and when he found that this was not possible, rushed quite un-expectedly at his new friend, kissed him and promised with tears to try to exchange into the hussar regiment the count was serving in as soon as he got back. The count was particularly gay; he tumbled the cavalryman, who had become very famil-iar in the morning, into a snowdrift; set Blücher at the Captain of Police, took Stëshka in his arms and wished to carry her off to Moscow, and finally jumped into his sledge and made Blücher, who wanted to stand up in the middle, sit down by his side. Sáshka jumped on the box after having again asked the cavalryman to recover the count's cloak from *them*, and to send it on. The count cried, 'Go!', took off his cap, waved it over his head, and whistled to the horses like a post-boy. The tróykas drove off in their different directions.

A monotonous snow-covered plain stretched far in front with a dirty yellowish road winding through it. The bright sunshine − playfully sparkling on the thawing snow which was coated with a transparent crust of ice − was pleasantly warm to one's face and back. Steam rose thickly from the sweating horses. The bell tinkled merrily. A peasant, with a loaded sledge that kept gliding to the side of the road, got hurriedly out of the way, jerking his rope reins and plashing with his wet bast shoes as he ran along the thawing road. A fat red-faced peasant woman, with a baby wrapped in the bosom of her sheepskin cloak, sat in another laden sledge, urging on a thin-tailed, jaded white horse with the ends of the reins. The count suddenly thought of Anna Fëdorovna.

'Turn back!' he shouted.

The driver did not at once understand.

'Turn back! Back to town! Be quick!'

The tróyka passed the town gates once more, and drove briskly up to the wooden porch of Anna Fëdorovna's house. The count ran quickly up the steps, passed through the vestibule and the drawing-room, and having found the widow still asleep, took her in his arms, lifted her out of bed, kissed her sleepy eyes, and ran quickly back. Anna Fëdorovna, only half awake, licked her lips and asked, 'What has happened?' The count jumped into his sledge, shouted to the driver, and with no further delay and without even a thought of Lúkhnov, or the widow, or Stëshka, but only of what awaited him in Moscow, left the town of K— for ever.

* * *

IX

MORE than twenty years had gone by. Much water had flowed away, many people had died, many been born, many had grown up or grown old; still more ideas had been born and had died, much that was old and beautiful and much that was old and bad had perished; much that was beautiful and new had grown up and still more that was immature, monstrous, and new, had come into God's world.

Count Fëdor Túrbin had been killed long ago in a duel by some foreigner he had horse-whipped in the street. His son, physically as like him as one drop of water to another, was a handsome young man already twenty-three years old and serving in the Horse Guards. But morally the young Túrbin did not in the least resemble his father. There was not a shade of the impetuous, passionate and, to speak frankly, depraved propensities of the past age. Together with his intelligence, culture, and the gifted nature he had inherited a love of propriety and the comforts of life; a practical way of looking at men and affairs, reasonableness and prudence were his distinguishing characteristics. The young count had got on well in the service and at twenty-three was already a lieutenant. At the commencement of the war he made up his mind that he would be more likely to secure promotion if he exchanged into the active army, and so he entered an hussar regiment as captain and was soon in command of a squadron.

In May 1848[1] the S— hussar regiment was marching to the campaign through the province of K—, and the very squadron young Count Túrbin commanded had to spend the night in the village of Morózovka, Anna Fëdorovna's estate.

Anna Fëdorovna was still living, but was already so far from young that she did not even consider herself young, which means a good deal for a woman. She had grown very fat, which is said to make a woman look younger, but deep soft wrinkles were apparent on her white plumpness. She never went to town now, it was an effort for her even to get into her carriage, but she was still just as kind-hearted and as silly as ever (now that her beauty no longer biases one, the truth may be told). With her lived her twenty-three-year-old daughter Lisa, a Russian country belle, and her brother – our acquaintance the cavalryman – who had good-naturedly squandered the whole of his small fortune and had found a home for his old age with Anna Fëdorovna. His hair was quite grey and his upper lip had fallen in, but the moustache above it was still carefully blackened. His back was bent, and not only his forehead and cheeks but even his nose and neck were wrinkled, yet in the movements of his feeble crooked legs the manner of a cavalryman was still perceptible.

The family and household sat in the small drawing-room of the old house, with an open door leading out onto the

---

1 Tolstóy seems here to antedate Russia's intervention in the Hungarian insurrection. The Russian army did not enter Hungary till May 1849 and the war lasted till the end of September that year.

verandah, and open windows overlooking the ancient star-shaped garden with its lime trees. Grey-haired Anna Fëdorovna, wearing a lilac jacket, sat on the sofa laying out cards on a round mahogany table. Her old brother in his clean white trousers and a blue coat had settled himself by the window and was plaiting a cord out of white cotton with the aid of a wooden fork – a pastime his niece had taught him and which he liked very much, as he could no longer do anything and his eyes were too weak for newspaper reading, his favourite occupation. Pímochka, Anna Fëdorovna's ward, sat by him learning a lesson – Lisa helping her and at the same time making a goat's-wool stocking for her uncle with wooden knitting needles. The last rays of the setting sun, as usual at that hour, shone through the lime-tree avenue and threw slanting gleams on the farthest window and the what-not standing near it. It was so quiet in the garden and the room that one could hear the swift flutter of a swallow's wings outside the window, and Anna Fëdorovna's soft sigh or the old man's slight groan as he crossed his legs.

'How do they go? Show me, Lisa! I always forget,' said Anna Fëdorovna, at a standstill in laying out her cards for patience.

Without stopping her work Lisa went to her mother and glanced at the cards:

'Ah, you've muddled them all, mamma dear!' she said, rearranging them. 'That's the way they should go. And what you are trying your fortune about will still come true,' she added, withdrawing a card so that it was not noticed.

'Ah yes, you always deceive me and say it has come out.'

'No really, it means . . . you'll succeed. It has come out.'

'All right, all right, you sly puss! But isn't it time we had tea?'

'I have ordered the samovar to be lit. I'll see to it at once. Do you want to have it here? . . . Be quick and finish your lesson, Pímochka, and let's have a run.'

And Lisa went to the door.

'Lisa, Lizzie!' said her uncle, looking intently at his fork. 'I think I've dropped a stitch again – pick it up for me, there's a dear.'

'Directly, directly! But I must give out a loaf of sugar to be broken up.'

And really, three minutes later she ran back, went to her uncle and pinched his ear.

'That's for dropping your stitches!' she said laughing, 'and you haven't done your task!'

'Well, well, never mind, never mind. Put it right – there's a little knot or something.'

Lisa took the fork, drew a pin out of her tippet – which thereupon the breeze coming in at the door blew slightly open – and managing somehow to pick up the stitch with the pin, pulled two loops through, and returned the fork to her uncle.

'Now give me a kiss for it,' she said, holding out her rosy cheek to him and pinning up her tippet. 'You shall have rum with your tea to-day. It's Friday, you know.'

And she again went into the tea-room.

'Come here and look, uncle, the hussars are coming!' she called from there in her clear voice.

Anna Fëdorovna came with her brother into the tea-room, the windows of which overlooked the village, to see the hussars. Very little was visible from the windows – only a crowd moving in a cloud of dust.

'It's a pity we have so little room, sister, and that the wing is not yet finished,' said the old man to Anna Fëdorovna. 'We might have invited the officers. Hussar officers are such splendid, gay young fellows, you know. It would have been good to see something of them.'

'Why of course, I should have been only too glad, brother; but you know yourself we have no room. There's my bedroom, Lisa's room, the drawing-room, and this room of yours, and that's all. Really now, where could we put them? The village elder's hut has been cleaned up for them: Michael Matvéev says it's quite clean now.'

'And we could have chosen a bridegroom for you from among them, Lizzie – a fine hussar!'

'I don't want an hussar; I'd rather have an uhlan. Weren't you in the uhlans, uncle? ... I don't want to have anything to do with these hussars. They are all said to be desperate fellows.' And Lisa blushed a little but again laughed her musical laugh.

'Here comes Ustyúshka running; we must ask her what she has seen,' she added.

Anna Fëdorovna told her to call Ustyúshka.

'It's not in you to keep to your work, you must needs run off to see the soldiers,' said Anna Fëdorovna. 'Well, where have the officers put up?'

'In Erómkin's house, mistress. There are two of them, such handsome ones. One's a count, they say!'

'And what's his name?'

'Kazárov or Turbínov.... I'm sorry – I've forgotten.'

'What a fool; can't so much as tell us anything. You might at least have found out the name.'

'Well, I'll run back.'

'Yes, I know you're first-rate at that sort of thing.... No, let Daniel go. Tell him to go and ask whether the officers want anything, brother. One ought to show them some politeness after all. Say the mistress sent to inquire.'

The old people again sat down in the tea-room and Lisa went to the servants' room to put into a box the sugar that had been broken up. Ustyúshka was there telling about the hussars.

'Darling miss, what a handsome man that count is!' she said. 'A regular cherubim with black eyebrows. There now, if you had a bridegroom like that you would be a couple of the right sort.'

The other maids smiled approvingly; the old nurse sighed as she sat knitting at a window and even whispered a prayer, drawing in her breath.

'So you liked the hussars very much?' said Lisa. 'And you're a good one at telling what you've seen. Go, please, and bring some of the cranberry juice, Ustyúshka, to give the hussars something sour to drink.'

And Lisa, laughing, went out with the sugar basin in her hands.

'I should really like to have seen what that hussar is like,' she thought, 'brown or fair? And he would have been glad to make our acquaintance I should think.... And if he goes away he'll never know that I was here and thought about him. And how many such have already passed me by? Who sees me here except uncle and Ustyúshka? Whichever way I do my hair, whatever sleeves I put on, no one looks at me with pleasure,' she thought with a sigh as she looked at her plump white arm. 'I suppose he is tall, with large eyes, and certainly small black moustaches. . . . Here am I, more than twenty-two, and no one has fallen in love with me except pock-marked Iván Ipátich, and four years ago I was even prettier. . . . And so my girlhood has passed without gladdening anyone. Oh, poor, poor country lass that I am!'

Her mother's voice, calling her to pour out tea, roused the country lass from this momentary meditation. She lifted her head with a start and went into the tea-room.

The best results are often obtained accidentally, and the more one tries the worse things turn out. In the country, people rarely try to educate their children and therefore unwittingly usually give them an excellent education. This was particularly so in Lisa's case. Anna Fëdorovna, with her limited intellect and careless temperament, gave Lisa no education – did not teach her music or that very useful French language – but having accidentally borne a healthy pretty child by her deceased husband she gave her little daughter over to a wet-nurse and a dry-nurse, fed her, dressed her in cotton prints and goat-skin shoes, sent her out to walk and gather mushrooms and wild berries, engaged a student from the seminary to teach her reading, writing, and arithmetic, and when sixteen years had passed she casually found in Lisa a friend, an ever-kind-hearted, ever-cheerful soul, and an active housekeeper. Anna Fëdorovna, being kind-hearted, always had some children to bring up – either serf children or foundlings. Lisa began looking after them when she was ten years old: teaching them, dressing them, taking them to church, and checking them when they played too many pranks. Later on the decrepit kindly uncle, who had to be tended like a child, appeared on the scene. Then the servants and peasants came to the young lady with various requests and with their ailments, which latter she treated with elderberry, peppermint, and camphorated spirits. Then there was the household management which all fell on her shoulders of itself. Then an

unsatisfied longing for love awoke and found its outlet only in
Nature and religion. And Lisa accidentally grew into an active,
good-natured, cheerful, self-reliant, pure, and deeply religious
woman. It is true that she suffered a little from vanity when she
saw neighbours standing by her in church wearing fashionable
bonnets brought from K—, and sometimes she was vexed to
tears by her old mother's whims and grumbling. She had
dreams of love, too, in most absurd and sometimes crude
forms, but these were dispersed by her useful activity which
had grown into a necessity, and at the age of twenty-two there
was not one spot or sting of remorse in the clear calm soul of
the physically and morally beautifully developed maiden. Lisa
was of medium height, plump rather than thin, her eyes were
hazel, not large, and had slight shadows on the lower lids, and
she had a long light-brown plait of hair. She walked with big
steps and with a slight sway – a 'duck's waddle' as the saying is.
Her face, when she was occupied and not agitated by anything
in particular, seemed to say to everyone who looked into it: 'It
is a joy to live in the world when one has someone to love and
a clear conscience.' Even in moments of vexation, perplexity,
alarm, or sorrow, in spite of herself there shone – through the
tear in her eye, her frowning left eyebrow and her compressed
lips – a kind straightforward spirit unspoilt by the intellect; it
shone in the dimples of her cheeks, in the corners of her
mouth, and in her beaming eyes accustomed to smile and to
rejoice in life.

X

THE air was still hot though the sun was setting when the
squadron entered Morózovka. In front of them along the dusty
village street trotted a brindled cow separated from its herd,
looking round and now and then stopping and lowing, but
never suspecting that all she had to do was to turn aside. The
peasants – old men, women, and children, and the servants
from the manor-house, crowded on both sides of the street
and eagerly watched the hussars as the latter rode through a
thick cloud of dust, curbing their horses which occasionally

stamped and snorted. On the right of the squadron were two officers who sat their fine black horses carelessly. One was Count Túrbin, the commander, the other a very young man recently promoted from cadet, whose name was Pólozov.

An hussar in a white linen jacket came out of the best of the huts, raised his cap, and went up to the officers.

'Where are the quarters assigned us?'

'For your Excellency?' answered the quartermaster-sergeant, with a start of his whole body. 'The village elder's hut has been cleaned out. I wanted to get quarters at the manor-house, but they say there is no room there. The proprietress is such a vixen.'

'All right!' said the count, dismounting and stretching his legs as he reached the village elder's hut. 'And has my phaeton arrived?'

'It has deigned to arrive, your Excellency!' answered the quartermaster-sergeant, pointing with his cap to the leather body of a carriage visible through the gateway, and rushing forward to the entrance of the hut, which was thronged with members of the peasant family collected to look at the officer. He even pushed one old woman over as he briskly opened the door of the freshly cleaned hut and stepped aside to let the count pass.

The hut was fairly large and roomy but not very clean. The German valet, dressed like a gentleman, stood inside sorting the linen in a portmanteau after having set up an iron bedstead and made the bed.

'Faugh, what filthy lodgings!' said the count with vexation. 'Couldn't you have found anything better at some gentleman's house, Dyádenko?'

'If your Excellency desires it I will try at the manor-house,' answered the quartermaster-sergeant, 'but it isn't up to much – doesn't look much better than a hut.'

'Never mind now. Go away.'

And the count lay down on the bed and threw his arms behind his head.

'Johann!' he called to his valet. 'You've made a lump in the middle again! How is it you can't make a bed properly?'

Johann came up to put it right.

'No, never mind now. But where is my dressing-gown?' said the count in a dissatisfied tone.

The valet handed him the dressing-gown. Before putting it on the count examined the front.

'I thought so, that spot is not cleaned off. Could anyone be a worse servant than you?' he added, pulling the dressing-gown out of the valet's hands and putting it on. 'Tell me, do you do it on purpose? . . . Is the tea ready?'

'I have not had time,' said Johann.

'Fool!'

After that the count took up the French novel placed ready for him and read for some time in silence: Johann went out into the passage to prepare the samovar. The count was obviously in a bad temper, probably caused by fatigue, a dusty face, tight clothing, and an empty stomach.

'Johann!' he cried again, 'bring me the account for those ten rubles. What did you buy in the town?'

He looked over the account handed him, and made some dissatisfied remarks about the dearness of the things purchased.

'Serve rum with my tea.'

'I didn't buy any rum,' said Johann.

'That's good! . . . How many times have I told you to have rum?'

'I hadn't enough money.'

'Then why didn't Pólozov buy some? You should have got some from his man.'

'Cornet Pólozov? I don't know. He bought the tea and the sugar.'

'Idiot! . . . Get out! . . . You are the only man who knows how to make me lose my patience. . . . You know that on a march I always have rum with my tea.'

'Here are two letters for you from the staff,' said the valet.

The count opened his letters and began reading them without rising. The cornet, having quartered the squadron, came in with a merry face.

'Well, how is it, Túrbin? It seems very nice here. But I must confess I'm tired. It was hot.'

'Very nice!... A filthy stinking hut, and thanks to your lordship no rum; your blockhead didn't buy any, nor did this one. You might at least have mentioned it.'

And he continued to read his letter. When he had finished he rolled it into a ball and threw it on the floor.

In the passage the cornet was meanwhile saying to his orderly in a whisper: 'Why didn't you buy any rum? You had money enough, you know.'

'But why should we buy everything? As it is I pay for everything, while his German does nothing but smoke his pipe.'

It was evident that the count's second letter was not unpleasant, for he smiled as he read it.

'Who is it from?' asked Pólozov, returning to the room and beginning to arrange a sleeping-place for himself on some boards by the oven.

'From Mina,' answered the count gaily, handing him the letter. 'Do you want to see it? What a delightful woman she is!... Really she's much better than our young ladies.... Just see how much feeling and wit there is in that letter. Only one thing is bad – she's asking for money.'

'Yes, that's bad,' said the cornet.

'It's true I promised her some, but then this campaign came on, and besides.... However if I remain in command of the squadron another three months I'll send her some. It's worth it, really; such a charming creature, eh?' said he, watching the expression on Pólozov's face as he read the letter.

'Dreadfully ungrammatical, but very nice, and it seems as if she really loves you,' said the cornet.

'H'm... I should think so! It's only women of that kind who love sincerely when once they do love.'

'And who was the other letter from?' asked the cornet, handing back the one he had read.

'Oh, that... there's a man, a nasty beast who won from me at cards, and he's reminding me of it for the third time.... I can't let him have it at present.... A stupid letter!' said the count, evidently vexed at the recollection.

After this both officers were silent for a while. The cornet, who was evidently under the count's influence, glanced now

and then at the handsome though clouded countenance of
Túrbin – who was looking fixedly through the window – and
drank his tea in silence, not venturing to start a conversation.

'But d'you know, it may turn out capitally,' said the count,
suddenly turning to Pólozov with a shake of his head. 'Supposing we get promotions by seniority this year, and take part
in an action besides, I may get ahead of my own captains in the
Guards.'

The conversation was still on the same topic and they were
drinking their second tumblers of tea, when old Daniel
entered and delivered Anna Fëdorovna's message.

'And I was also to inquire if you are not Count Fëdor
Iványch Túrbin's son?' added Daniel on his own account,
having learnt the count's name and remembering the deceased
count's sojourn in the town of K—. 'Our mistress, Anna
Fëdorovna, was very well acquainted with him.'

'He was my father. And tell your mistress I am very much
obliged to her. We want nothing, but say we told you to ask
whether we could not have a cleaner room somewhere – in
the manor-house, or anywhere.'

'Now, why did you do that?' asked Pólozov when
Daniel had gone. 'What does it matter? Just for one night –
what does it matter? And they will be inconveniencing
themselves.'

'What an idea! I think we've had our share of smoky
huts! . . . It's easy to see you're not a practical man. Why not
seize the opportunity when we can, and live like human beings
for at least one night? And on the contrary they will be very
pleased to have us. . . . The worst of it is, if this lady really knew
my father . . .' continued the count with a smile which displayed his glistening white teeth. 'I always have to feel
ashamed of my departed papa. There is always some scandalous
story or other, or some debt he has left. That is why I hate
meeting these acquaintances of my father's. However that was
the way in those days,' he added, growing serious.

'Did I ever tell you,' said Pólozov, 'I once met an uhlan
brigade-commander, Ilyín? He was very anxious to meet you.
He is awfully fond of your father.'

'That Ilyín is an awful good-for-nothing, I believe. But the worst of it is that these good people, who assure me that they knew my father in order to make my acquaintance, while pretending to be very pleasant, relate such tales about my father as make me ashamed to listen. It is true – I don't deceive myself, but look at things dispassionately – that he had too ardent a nature and sometimes did things that were not nice. However that was the way in those times. In our days he might have turned out a very successful man, for to do him justice he had extraordinary capacities.'

A quarter of an hour later the servant came back with a request from the proprietress that they would be so good as to spend the night at her house.

XI

HAVING heard that the hussar officer was the son of Count Fëdor Túrbin, Anna Fëdorovna was all in a flutter.

'Oh, dear me! The darling boy!... Daniel, run quickly and say your mistress asks them to her house!' she began, jumping up and hurrying with quick steps to the servants' room. 'Lizzie! Ustyúshka!... Your room must be got ready, Lisa, you can move into your uncle's room. And you, brother, you won't mind sleeping in the drawing-room, will you? It's only for one night.'

'I don't mind, sister. I can sleep on the floor.'

'He must be handsome if he's like his father. Only to have a look at him, the darling.... You must have a good look at him, Lisa! The father *was* handsome.... Where are you taking that table to? Leave it here,' said Anna Fëdorovna, bustling about. 'Bring two beds – take one from the foreman's – and get the crystal candlestick, the one my brother gave me on my birthday – it's on the what-not – and put a stearine candle in it.'

At last everything was ready. In spite of her mother's interference Lisa arranged the room for the two officers her own way. She took out clean bed-clothes scented with mignonette, made the beds, had candles and a bottle of water placed on a small table near by, fumigated the servants' room with scented paper, and moved her own little bed into her uncle's room. Anna Fëdorovna quieted down a little, settled in her own place, and even took up the cards again, but instead of laying them out she leaned her plump elbow on the table and grew thoughtful.

'Ah, time, time, how it flies!' she whispered to herself. 'Is it so long ago? It is as if I could see him now. Ah, he was a madcap! . . .' and tears came into her eyes. 'And now there's Lizzie . . . but still, she's not what I was at her age – she's a nice girl but she's not like that . . .'

'Lisa, you should put on your *mousseline-de-laine* dress for the evening.'

'Why, mother, you are not going to ask them in to see us? Better not,' said Lisa, unable to master her excitement at the thought of meeting the officers: 'Better not, mamma!'

And really her desire to see them was less strong than her fear of the agitating joy she imagined awaited her.

'Maybe they themselves will wish to make our acquaintance, Lizzie!' said Anna Fëdorovna, stroking her head and thinking: 'No, her hair is not what mine was at her age. . . . Oh, Lizzie, how I should like you to. . . .' And she really did very earnestly desire something for her daughter. But she could not imagine a marriage with the count, and she could not desire for her daughter relations such as she had had with the father; but still she did desire something very much. She may have longed to relive in the soul of her daughter what she had experienced with him who was dead.

The old cavalryman was also somewhat excited by the arrival of the count. He locked himself into his room and emerged a quarter of an hour later in a Hungarian jacket and pale-blue trousers, and entered the room prepared for the visitors with the bashfully pleased expression of a girl who puts on a ball-dress for the first time in her life.

'I'll have a look at the hussars of to-day, sister! The late count was indeed a true hussar. I'll see, I'll see!'

The officers had already reached the room assigned to them through the back entrance.

'There, you see! Isn't this better than that hut with the cockroaches?' said the count, lying down as he was, in his dusty boots, on the bed that had been prepared for him.

'Of course it's better; but still, to be indebted to the proprietress...'

'Oh, what nonsense! One must be practical in all things. They're awfully pleased, I'm sure... Eh, you there!' he cried. 'Ask for something to hang over this window, or it will be draughty in the night.'

At this moment the old man came in to make the officers' acquaintance. Of course, though he did it with a slight blush, he did not omit to say that he and the old count had been comrades, that he had enjoyed the count's favour, and he even added that he had more than once been under obligations to the deceased. What obligations he referred to, whether it was the count's omission to repay the hundred rubles he had borrowed, or his throwing him into a snow-heap, or swearing at him, the old man quite omitted to explain. The young count was very polite to the old cavalryman and thanked him for the night's lodging.

'You must excuse us if it is not luxurious, Count' (he very nearly said 'your Excellency', so unaccustomed had he become to conversing with important persons), 'my sister's house is so small. But we'll hang something up there directly and it will be all right,' added the old man, and on the plea of seeing about a curtain, but mainly because he was in a hurry to give an account of the officers, he bowed and left the room.

The pretty Ustyúshka came in with her mistress's shawl to cover the window, and besides, the mistress had told her to ask if the gentlemen would not like some tea.

The pleasant surroundings seemed to have a good influence on the count's spirits. He smiled merrily, joked with Ustyúshka in such a way that she even called him a scamp, asked whether her young lady was pretty, and in answer to her question whether they would have any tea he said she might bring them some tea, but the chief thing was that, their own supper not being ready yet, perhaps they might have some vodka and something to eat, and some sherry if there was any.

The uncle was in raptures over the young count's politeness, and praised the new generation of officers to the skies, saying that the present men were incomparably superior to the former generation.

Anna Fëdorovna did not agree – no one could be superior to Count Fëdor Iványch Túrbin – and at last she grew seriously angry and drily remarked, 'The one who has last stroked you, brother, is always the best. . . . Of course people are cleverer nowadays, but Count Fëdor Iványch danced the *écossaise* in such a way and was so amiable that everybody lost their heads about him, though he paid attention to no one but me. So you see, there were good people in the old days too.'

Here came the news of the demand for vodka, light refreshments, and sherry.

'There now, brother, you never do the right thing; you should have ordered supper,' began Anna Fëdorovna. 'Lisa, see to it, dear!'

Lisa ran to the larder to get some pickled mushrooms and fresh butter, and the cook was ordered to make rissoles.

'But how about sherry? Have you any left, brother?'

'No, sister, I never had any.'

'How's that? Why, what is it you take with your tea?'

'That's rum, Anna Fëdorovna.'

'Isn't it all the same? Give them some of that – it's all the same. But wouldn't it after all be best to ask them in here, brother? You know all about it – I don't think they would take offence.'

The cavalryman declared he would warrant that the count was too good-natured to refuse and that he would certainly fetch them. Anna Fëdorovna went and put on a silk dress and a new cap for some reason, but Lisa was so busy that she had no time to change her pink gingham dress with the wide sleeves. Besides, she was terribly excited; she felt as if something wonderful was awaiting her and as if a low black cloud hung over her soul. It seemed to her that this handsome hussar count must be a perfectly new, incomprehensible, but beautiful being. His character, his habits, his speech, must all be so unusual, so different from anything she had ever met. All he

thinks or says must be wise and right, all he does must be
honourable, his whole appearance must be beautiful. She
never doubted that. Had he asked not merely for refreshments
and sherry, but for a bath of sage-brandy and perfume, she
would not have been surprised and would not have blamed
him, but would have been firmly convinced that it was right
and necessary.

The count at once agreed when the cavalryman informed
them of his sister's wish. He brushed his hair, put on his
uniform, and took his cigar-case.

'Come along,' he said to Pólozov.

'Really it would be better not to go,' answered the cornet.
'*Ils feront des frais pour nous recevoir.*'[1]

'Nonsense, they will be only too happy! Besides, I have
made some inquiries: there is a pretty daughter.... Come
along!' said the count, speaking in French.

'*Je vous en prie, messieurs!*'[2] said the cavalryman, merely to
make the officers feel that he also knew French and had
understood what they had said.

XII

LISA, afraid to look at the officers, blushed and cast down her
eyes and pretended to be busy filling the teapot when they
entered the room. Anna Fëdorovna on the contrary jumped
up hurriedly, bowed, and not taking her eyes off the count,
began talking to him – now saying how unusually like his
father he was, now introducing her daughter to him, now
offering him tea, jam, or home-made sweetmeats. No one
paid any attention to the cornet because of his modest appearance, and he was very glad of it, for he was, as far as propriety
allowed, gazing at Lisa and minutely examining her beauty
which evidently took him by surprise. The uncle, listening to
his sister's conversation with the count, awaited, with the
words ready on his lips, an opportunity to narrate his cavalry

1 'They will be putting themselves to expense on our account.'
2 'If you please, gentlemen.'

reminiscences. During tea the count lit a cigar and Lisa found it difficult to prevent herself from coughing. He was very talkative and amiable, at first slipping his stories into the intervals of Anna Fëdorovna's ever-flowing speech, but at last monopolizing the conversation. One thing struck his hearers as strange; in his stories he often used words not considered improper in the society he belonged to, but which here sounded rather too bold and somewhat frightened Anna Fëdorovna and made Lisa blush to her ears; but the count did not notice it and remained calmly natural and amiable.

Lisa silently filled the tumblers, which she did not give into the visitors' hands but placed on the table near them, not having quite recovered from her excitement, and she listened eagerly to the count's remarks. His stories, which were not very deep, and the hesitation in his speech gradually calmed her. She did not hear from him the very clever things she had expected, nor did she see that elegance in everything which she had vaguely expected to find in him. At the third glass of tea, after her bashful eyes had once met his and he had not looked down but had continued to look at her too quietly and with a slight smile, she even felt rather inimically disposed towards him, and soon found that not only was there nothing especial about him but that he was in no wise different from other people she had met, that there was no need to be afraid of him though his nails were long and clean, and that there was not even any special beauty in him. Lisa suddenly relinquished her dream, not without some inward pain, and grew calmer, and only the gaze of the taciturn cornet which she felt fixed upon her, disquieted her.

'Perhaps it's not this one, but that one!' she thought.

XIII

AFTER tea the old lady asked the visitors into the drawing-room and again sat down in her old place.

'But wouldn't you like to rest, Count?' she asked, and after receiving an answer in the negative continued: 'What can I do to entertain our dear guests? Do you play cards,

Count? There now, brother, you should arrange something; arrange a set —'

'But you yourself play *préférence*,'[1] answered the cavalryman. 'Why not all play? Will you play, Count? And you too?'

The officers expressed their readiness to do whatever their kind hosts desired.

Lisa brought her old pack of cards which she used for divining when her mother's swollen face would get well, whether her uncle would return the same day when he went to town, whether a neighbour would call to-day, and so on. These cards, though she had used them for a couple of months, were cleaner than those Anna Fëdorovna used to tell fortunes.

'But perhaps you won't play for small stakes?' inquired the uncle. 'Anna Fëdorovna and I play for half-kopeks. . . . And even so she wins all our money.'

'Oh, any stakes you like – I shall be delighted,' replied the count.

'Well then, one kopek "assignats"[2] just for once, in honour of our dear visitors! Let them beat me, an old woman!' said Anna Fëdorovna, settling down in her arm-chair and arranging her mantilla. 'And perhaps I'll win a ruble or so from them,' thought she, having developed a slight passion for cards in her old age.

1 In *préférence* partners play together as in whist. There is a method of scoring 'with tables' which increases the gains and losses of the players. The players compete in declaring the number of tricks the cards they hold will enable them to make. The highest bidder decides which suit is to be trumps and has to make the number of tricks he has declared, or be fined. A player declaring *misère* undertakes to make no tricks, and is fined (puts on a *remise*) for each trick he or she takes. 'Ace and king blank' means that a player holds the two highest cards and no others of a given suit.
2 At the time of this story two currencies were in use simultaneously – the depreciated 'assignats' and the 'silver rubles', which like the 'assignats' were usually paper. The assignats had been introduced in Russia in 1768 and by the end of the Napoleonic wars were much depreciated. They fluctuated till 1841, when a new 'silver ruble' was introduced, the value of which was about 38 pence. Paper 'silver rubles' were exchangeable for coin at par, and it was decreed that the assignats would be redeemed at the rate of 3½ assignats for one 'silver ruble'. In out-of-the-way provincial districts the assignats were still in general use.

'If you like, I'll teach you to play with "tables" and "*misère*",' said the count. 'It is capital.'

Everyone liked the new Petersburg way. The uncle was even sure he knew it; it was just the same as 'boston' used to be, only he had forgotten it a bit. But Anna Fëdorovna could not understand it at all, and failed to understand it for so long that at last, with a smile and a nod of approval, she felt herself obliged to assert that now she understood it and that all was quite clear to her. There was not a little laughter during the game when Anna Fëdorovna, holding ace and king blank, declared *misère*, and was left with six tricks. She even became confused and began to smile shyly and hurriedly explain that she had not got quite used to the new way. But they scored against her all the same, especially as the count, being used to playing a careful game for high stakes, was cautious, skilfully played through his opponents' hands, and refused to understand the shoves the cornet gave him under the table with his foot, or the mistakes the latter made when they were partners.

Lisa brought more sweets, three kinds of jam, and some specially prepared apples that had been kept since last season, and stood behind her mother's back watching the game and occasionally looking at the officers and especially at the count's white hands with their rosy well-kept nails, which threw the cards and took up the tricks in so practised, assured, and elegant a manner.

Again Anna Fëdorovna, rather irritably outbidding the others, declared seven tricks, made only four, and was fined accordingly, and having very clumsily noted down, on her brother's demand, the points she had lost, became quite confused and fluttered.

'Never mind, mamma, you'll win it back!' smilingly remarked Lisa, wishing to help her mother out of the ridiculous situation. 'Let uncle make a forfeit, and then he'll be caught.'

'If you would only help me, Lisa dear!' said Anna Fëdorovna, with a frightened glance at her daughter. 'I don't know how this is . . . '

'But I don't know this way either,' Lisa answered, mentally reckoning up her mother's losses. 'You will lose a lot that way, mamma! There will be nothing left for Pímochka's new dress,' she added in jest.

'Yes, this way one may easily lose ten silver rubles,' said the cornet looking at Lisa and anxious to enter into conversation with her.

'Aren't we playing for "assignats"?' said Anna Fëdorovna, looking round at them all.

'I don't know how we are playing, but I can't reckon in "assignats",' said the count. 'What is it? I mean, what are "assignats"?'

'Why, nowadays nobody counts in "assignats" any longer,' remarked the uncle who had played very cautiously and had been winning.

The old lady ordered some sparkling home-made wine to be brought, drank two glasses, became very red, and seemed to resign herself to any fate. A lock of her grey hair escaped from under her cap and she did not even put it right. No doubt it seemed to her as if she had lost millions and it was all up with her. The cornet touched the count with his foot more and more often. The count scored down the old lady's losses. At last the game ended, and in spite of Anna Fëdorovna's wicked attempts to add to her score by pretending to make mistakes in adding it up, in spite of her horror at the amount of her losses, it turned out at last that she had lost 920 points. 'That's nine "assignats"?' she asked several times, and did not comprehend the full extent of her loss until her brother told her, to her horror, that she had lost more than thirty-two 'assignats' and that she must certainly pay.

The count did not even add up his winnings, but rose immediately the game was over, went over to the window at which Lisa was arranging the *zakúshka* and turning pickled mushrooms out of a jar onto a plate for supper, and there quite quietly and simply did what the cornet had all that evening so longed, but failed, to do – entered into conversation with her about the weather.

Meanwhile the cornet was in a very unpleasant position. In the absence of the count, and more especially of Lisa, who had been keeping her in good humour, Anna Fëdorovna became frankly angry.

'Really, it's too bad that we should win from you like this,' said Pólozov in order to say something. 'It is a real shame!'

'Well, of course, if you go and invent some kind of "tables" and "*misères*" and I don't know how to play them. . . . Well then, how much does it come to in "assignats"?' she asked.

'Thirty-two rubles, thirty-two and a quarter,' repeated the cavalryman who under the influence of his success was in a playful mood. 'Hand over the money, sister; pay up!'

'I'll pay it all, but you won't catch me again. No! . . . I shall not win this back as long as I live.'

And Anna Fëdorovna went off to her room, hurriedly swaying from side to side, and came back bringing nine 'assignats'. It was only on the old man's insistent demand that she eventually paid the whole amount.

Pólozov was seized with fear lest Anna Fëdorovna should scold him if he spoke to her. He silently and quietly left her and joined the count and Lisa who were talking at the open window.

On the table spread for supper stood two tallow candles. Now and then the soft fresh breath of the May night caused the flames to flicker. Outside the window, which opened onto the garden, it was also light but it was a quite different light. The moon, which was almost full and already losing its golden tinge, floated above the tops of the tall lindens and more and more lit up the thin white clouds which veiled it at intervals. Frogs were croaking loudly by the pond, the surface of which, silvered in one place by the moon, was visible through the avenue. Some little birds fluttered slightly or lightly hopped from bough to bough in a sweet-scented lilac-bush whose dewy branches occasionally swayed gently close to the window.

'What wonderful weather!' the count said as he approached Lisa and sat down on the low window-sill. 'I suppose you walk a good deal?'

'Yes,' said Lisa, not feeling the least shyness in speaking with the count. 'In the morning about seven o'clock I look after what has to be attended to on the estate and take my mother's ward, Pímochka, with me for a walk.'

'It is pleasant to live in the country!' said the count, putting his eye-glass to his eye and looking now at the garden now at Lisa. 'And don't you ever go out at night, by moonlight?'

'No. But two years ago uncle and I used to walk every moonlight night. He was troubled with a strange complaint – insomnia. When there was a full moon he could not fall asleep. His little room – that one – looks straight out into the garden, the window is low but the moon shines straight into it.'

'That's strange: I thought that was your room,' said the count.

'No, I only sleep there to-night. You have my room.'

'Is it possible? Dear me, I shall never forgive myself for having disturbed you in such a way!' said the count letting the monocle fall from his eye in proof of the sincerity of his feelings. 'If I had known that I was troubling you . . .'

'It's no trouble! On the contrary I am very glad: uncle's is such a charming room, so bright, and the window is so low. I shall sit there till I fall asleep, or else I shall climb out into the garden and walk about a bit before going to bed.'

'What a splendid girl!' thought the count, replacing his eye-glass and looking at her and trying to touch her foot with his own while pretending to seat himself more comfortably on the window-sill. 'And how cleverly she has let me know that I may see her in the garden at the window if I like!' Lisa even lost much of her charm in his eyes – the conquest seemed so easy.

'And how delightful it must be,' he said, looking thoughtfully at the dark avenue of trees, 'to spend a night like this in the garden with a beloved one.'

Lisa was embarrassed by these words and by the repeated, seemingly accidental, touch of his foot. Anxious to hide her confusion she said without thinking: 'Yes, it is nice to walk in the moonlight.' She was beginning to feel rather uncomfortable. She had tied up the jar out of which she had taken the mushrooms, and was going away from the window, when the cornet joined them and she felt a wish to see what kind of man he was.

'What a lovely night!' he said.

'Why, they talk of nothing but the weather,' thought Lisa.

'What a wonderful view!' continued the cornet. 'But I suppose you are tired of it,' he added, having a curious propensity to say rather unpleasant things to people he liked very much.

'Why do you think so? The same kind of food or the same dress one may get tired of, but not of a beautiful garden if one is fond of walking – especially when the moon is still higher. From uncle's window the whole pond can be seen. I shall look at it to-night.'

'But I don't think you have any nightingales?' said the count, much dissatisfied that the cornet had come and prevented his ascertaining more definitely the terms of the rendezvous.

'No, but there always were until last year when some sportsman caught one, and this year one began to sing beautifully only last week but the police-officer came here and his carriage-bells frightened it away. Two years ago uncle and I used to sit in the covered alley and listen to them for two hours or more at a time.'

'What is this chatterbox telling you?' said her uncle coming up to them. 'Won't you come and have something to eat?'

After supper, during which the count by praising the food and by his appetite had somewhat dispelled the hostess's ill humour, the officers said good-night and went into their room. The count shook hands with the uncle and to Anna Fëdorovna's surprise shook her hand also without kissing it, and even shook Lisa's looking straight into her eyes the while and slightly smiling his pleasant smile. This look again abashed the girl.

'He is very good-looking,' she thought, 'but he thinks too much of himself.'

XIV

'I SAY, aren't you ashamed of yourself?' said Pólozov when they were in their room. 'I purposely tried to lose, and kept touching you under the table. Aren't you ashamed? The old lady was quite upset, you know.'

The count laughed very heartily.

'She was awfully funny, that old lady. . . . How offended she was! . . . '

And he again began laughing so merrily that even Johann, who stood in front of him, cast down his eyes and turned away with a slight smile.

'And with the son of a friend of the family! Ha-ha-ha! . . . ' the count continued to laugh.

'No, really it was too bad. I was quite sorry for her,' said the cornet.

'What nonsense! How young you still are! Why, did you wish me to lose? Why should one lose? I used to lose before I knew how to play! Ten rubles may come in useful, my dear fellow. You must look at life practically or you'll always be left in the lurch.'

Pólozov was silenced; besides, he wished to be quiet and to think about Lisa who seemed to him an unusually pure and beautiful creature. He undressed and lay down in the soft clean bed prepared for him.

'What nonsense all this military honour and glory is!' he thought, looking at the window curtained by the shawl through which the white moonbeams stole in. 'It would be happiness to live in a quiet nook with a dear, wise, simple-hearted wife – yes, that is true and lasting happiness!'

But for some reason he did not communicate these reflections to his friend and did not even refer to the country lass, though he was convinced that the count too was thinking of her.

'Why don't you undress?' he asked the count who was walking up and down the room.

'I don't feel sleepy yet, somehow. You can put out the candle if you like. I shall lie down as I am.'

And he continued to pace up and down.

'Don't feel sleepy yet somehow,' repeated Pólozov, who after this last evening felt more dissatisfied than ever with the count's influence over him and was inclined to rebel against it. 'I can imagine,' he thought, addressing himself mentally to Túrbin, 'what is now passing through that well-brushed head of yours! I saw how you admired her. But you are not capable of understanding such a simple honest creature: you want a Mina and a colonel's epaulettes . . . I really must ask him how he liked her.'

And Pólozov turned towards him – but changed his mind. He felt he would not be able to hold his own with the count, if the latter's opinion of Lisa were what he supposed it to be, and that he would even be unable to avoid agreeing with him so accustomed was he to bow to the count's influence, which he felt more and more every day to be oppressive and unjust.

'Where are you going?' he asked, when the count put on his cap and went to the door.

'I'm going to see if things are all right in the stables.'

'Strange!' thought the cornet, but put out the candle and turned over on his other side, trying to drive away the absurdly jealous and hostile thoughts that crowded into his head concerning his former friend.

Anna Fëdorovna meanwhile, having as usual kissed her brother, daughter, and ward, and made the sign of the cross over each of them, had also retired to her room. It was long since the old lady had experienced so many strong impressions in one day and she could not even pray quietly: she could not rid herself of the sad and vivid memories of the deceased count and of the young dandy who had plundered her so unmercifully. However she undressed as usual, drank half a tumbler of kvas[1] that stood ready for her on a little table by her bed, and lay down. Her favourite cat crept softly into the room. Anna Fëdorovna called her up and began to stroke her and listened to her purring, but could not fall asleep.

'It's the cat that keeps me awake,' she thought and drove her away. The cat fell softly on the floor and gently moving her bushy tail leapt onto the stove. And now the maid, who always slept in Anna Fëdorovna's room, came and spread the piece of felt that served her for a mattress, put out the candle, and lit the lamp before the icon. At last the maid began to snore, but still

1 Kvas is a non-intoxicating drink usually made from rye-malt and rye-flour.

sleep would not come to soothe Anna Fëdorovna's excited imagination. When she closed her eyes the hussar's face appeared to her, and she seemed to see it in the room in various guises when she opened her eyes and by the dim light of the lamp looked at the chest of drawers, the table, or a white dress that was hanging up. Now she felt very hot on the feather bed, now her watch ticked unbearably on the little table, and the maid snored unendurably through her nose. She woke her up and told her not to snore. Again thoughts of her daughter, of the old count and the young one, and of the *préference*, became curiously mixed in her head. Now she saw herself waltzing with the old count, saw her own round white shoulders, felt someone's kisses on them, and then saw her daughter in the arms of the young count. Ustyúshka again began to snore.

'No, people are not the same nowadays. The other one was ready to leap into the fire for me – and not without cause. But this one is sleeping like a fool, no fear, glad to have won – no love-making about him. . . . How the other one said on his knees, "What do you wish me to do? I'll kill myself on the spot, or do anything you like!" And he would have killed himself had I told him to.'

Suddenly she heard a patter of bare feet in the passage and Lisa, with a shawl thrown over her, ran in pale and trembling and almost fell onto her mother's bed.

After saying good-night to her mother that evening Lisa had gone alone to the room her uncle generally slept in. She put on a white dressing-jacket and covering her long thick plait with a kerchief, extinguished the candle, opened the window, and sat down on a chair, drawing her feet up and fixing her pensive eyes on the pond now all glittering in the silvery light.

All her accustomed occupations and interests suddenly appeared to her in a new light: her capricious old mother, uncritical love for whom had become part of her soul; her decrepit but amiable old uncle; the domestic and village serfs who worshipped their young mistress; the milch cows and the calves, and all this Nature which had died and been renewed so many times and amid which she had grown up loving and beloved – all this that had given such light and pleasant tranquillity to her soul suddenly seemed unsatisfactory; it seemed dull and unnecessary. It was as if someone had said to her: 'Little fool, little fool, for twenty years you have been trifling, serving someone without knowing why, and without knowing what life and happiness are!' As she gazed into the depths of the moonlit, motionless garden she thought this more intensely, far more intensely, than ever before. And what caused these thoughts? Not any sudden love for the count as one might have supposed. On the contrary she did not like him. She could have been interested in the cornet more easily, but he was plain, poor fellow, and silent. She kept involuntarily forgetting him and recalling the image of the count with anger and annoyance. 'No, that's not it,' she said to herself. Her ideal had been so beautiful. It was an ideal that could have been loved on such a night amid this Nature without impairing its beauty – an ideal never abridged to fit it to some coarse reality.

Formerly, solitude and the absence of anyone who might have attracted her attention had caused the power of love, which Providence has given impartially to each of us, to rest intact and tranquil in her bosom, and now she had lived too long in the melancholy happiness of feeling within her the presence of this something, and of now and again opening the secret chalice of her heart to contemplate its riches, to be able to lavish its contents thoughtlessly on anyone. God grant she may enjoy to her grave this chary bliss! Who knows whether it be not the best and strongest, and whether it is not the only true and possible happiness?

'O Lord my God,' she thought, 'can it be that I have lost my youth and happiness in vain and that it will never be . . . never be? Can that be true?' And she looked into the depths of the sky lit up by the moon and covered by light fleecy clouds that, veiling the stars, crept nearer to the moon. 'If that highest white cloudlet touches the moon it will be a sign that it is true,' thought she. The mist-like smoky strip ran across the bottom half of the bright disk and little by little the light on the grass, on the tops of the limes, and on the pond, grew dimmer and the black shadows of the trees grew less distinct. As if to harmonize with the gloomy shadows that spread over the world outside, a light wind ran through the leaves and brought to the window the odour of dewy leaves, of moist earth, and of blooming lilacs.

'But it is not true,' she consoled herself. 'There now, if the nightingale sings to-night it will be a sign that what I'm thinking is all nonsense, and that I need not despair,' thought she. And she sat a long while in silence waiting for something, while again all became bright and full of life and again and again the cloudlets ran across the moon making everything dim. She was beginning to fall asleep as she sat by the window, when the quivering trills of a nightingale came ringing from below across the pond and awoke her. The country maiden opened her eyes. And once more her soul was renewed with fresh joy by its mysterious union with Nature which spread out so calmly and brightly before her. She leant on both arms. A sweet, languid sensation of sadness oppressed her heart, and tears of pure wide-spreading love, thirsting to be satisfied – good comforting tears – filled her eyes. She folded her arms on the window-sill and laid her head on them. Her favourite prayer rose to her mind and she fell asleep with her eyes still moist.

The touch of someone's hand aroused her. She awoke. But the touch was light and pleasant. The hand pressed hers more closely. Suddenly she became alive to reality, screamed, jumped up, and trying to persuade herself that she had not recognized the count who was standing under the window bathed in the moonlight, she ran out of the room. . . .

XV

AND it really was the count. When he heard the girl's cry and a husky sound from the watchman behind the fence, who had been roused by that cry, he rushed headlong across the wet dewy grass into the depths of the garden feeling like a detected thief. 'Fool that I am!' he repeated unconsciously, 'I frightened her. I ought to have roused her gently by speaking to her. Awkward brute that I am!' He stopped and listened: the watchman came into the garden through the gateway, dragging his stick along the sandy path. It was necessary to hide and the count went down by the pond. The frogs made him start as they plumped from beneath his feet into the water. Though his boots were wet through, he squatted down and began to recall all he had done: how he had climbed the fence, looked for her window, and at last espied a white shadow; how, listening to the faintest rustle, he had several times approached the window and gone back again: how at one moment he felt sure she was waiting, vexed at his tardiness, and the next, that it was impossible she should so readily have agreed to a rendez-vous: how at last, persuading himself that it was only the bashfulness of a country-bred girl that made her pretend to be asleep, he went up resolutely and distinctly saw how she sat, but then for some reason ran away again and only after severely taunting himself for cowardice boldly drew near to her and touched her hand.

The watchman again made a husky sound and the gate creaked as he left the garden. The girl's window was slammed to and a shutter fastened from inside. This was very provoking. The count would have given a good deal for a chance to begin all over again; he would not have acted so stupidly now.... 'And she is a wonderful girl – so fresh – quite charming! And I have let her slip through my fingers.... Awkward fool that I am!' He did not want to sleep now and went at random, with the firm tread of one who has been crossed, along the covered lime-tree avenue.

And here the night brought to him also its peaceful gifts of soothing sadness and the need of love. The straight pale beams of the moon threw spots of light through the thick foliage of the limes onto the clay path, where a few blades of grass grew, or a dead branch lay here and there. The light falling on one side of a bent bough made it seem as if covered with white moss. The silvered leaves whispered now and then. There were no lights in the house and all was silent; the voice of the nightingale alone seemed to fill the bright, still, limitless space. 'O God, what a night! What a wonderful night!' thought the count, inhaling the fragrant freshness of the garden. 'Yet I feel a kind of regret – as if I were discontented with myself and with others, discontented with life generally. A splendid, sweet girl! Perhaps she was really hurt. . . .' Here his dreams became mixed: he imagined himself in this garden with the country-bred girl in various extraordinary situations. Then the role of the girl was taken by his beloved Mina. 'Eh, what a fool I was! I ought simply to have caught her round the waist and kissed her.' And regretting that he had not done so, the count returned to his room.

The cornet was still awake. He at once turned in his bed and faced the count.

'Not asleep yet?' asked the count.

'No.'

'Shall I tell you what has happened?'

'Well?'

'No, I'd better not, or . . . all right, I'll tell you – draw in your legs.'

And the count having mentally abandoned the intrigue that had miscarried, sat down on his comrade's bed with an animated smile.

'Would you believe it, that young lady gave me a rendezvous!'

'What are you saying?' cried Pólozov, jumping out of bed.

'No, but listen.'

'But how? When? It's impossible!'

'Why, while you were adding up after we had played *préférence*, she told me she would sit at the window in the night and that one could get in at the window. There, you see what it is to be practical! While you were calculating with the old woman, I arranged that little matter. Why, you heard her say in your presence that she would sit by the window to-night and look at the pond.'

'Yes, but she didn't mean anything of the kind.'

'Well, that's just what I can't make out: did she say it intentionally or not? Maybe she didn't really wish to agree so suddenly, but it looked very like it. It turned out horribly. I quite played the fool,' he added, smiling contemptuously at himself.

'What do you mean? Where have you been?'

The count, omitting his manifold irresolute approaches, related everything as it had happened.

'I spoilt it myself: I ought to have been bolder. She screamed and ran from the window.'

'So she screamed and ran away,' said the cornet, smiling uneasily in answer to the count's smile, which for such a long time had had so strong an influence over him.

'Yes, but it's time to go to sleep.'

The cornet again turned his back to the door and lay silent for about ten minutes. Heaven knows what went on in his soul, but when he turned again, his face bore an expression of suffering and resolve.

'Count Túrbin!' he said abruptly.

'Are you delirious?' quietly replied the count. ' . . . What is it, Cornet Pólozov?'

'Count Túrbin, you are a scoundrel!' cried Pólozov, and again jumped out of bed.

XVI

THE squadron left next day. The two officers did not see their hosts again and did not bid them farewell. Neither did they speak to one another. They intended to fight a duel at the first halting-place. But Captain Schulz, a good comrade and splendid horseman, beloved by everyone in the regiment and chosen by the count to act as his second, managed to settle the affair so well that not only did they not fight but no one in the regiment knew anything about the matter, and Túrbin and Pólozov, though no longer on the old friendly footing, still continued to speak in familiar terms to one another and to meet at dinners and card-parties.

A LANDLORD'S
MORNING
(PART OF AN UNFINISHED NOVEL
'A RUSSIAN LANDLORD')

Chapter I

PRINCE NEKHLYÚDOV was nineteen years old when, at the end of his Third Course at the University, he came to his estate for the summer vacation and spent the whole summer there by himself. That autumn, in his unformed boyish hand, he wrote the following letter to his aunt, Countess Belorétski, whom he considered to be his best friend and the cleverest woman in the world. It was in French, and ran as follows:

'My dear Aunt,

'I have made a resolution which will affect my destiny for life. I am leaving the university to devote myself to life on my estate, because I feel that I was born for it. For heaven's sake, dear Aunt, don't laugh at me. You will say that I am young; perhaps I really am still a child, but that does not prevent me from feeling my vocation – from wishing to do good, and from loving goodness.

'As I wrote you before, I found affairs here in indescribable disorder. Wishing to put them in order and understand them, I discovered that the chief evil lies in the very pitiable and impoverished condition of the peasants, and that this is an evil that can be remedied only by work and patience. If you could only see two of my peasants, David and Iván, and the way they and their families live, I am sure that the mere sight of those two unfortunates would do more to convince you than anything I can say to explain my intention. Is it not my sacred and direct duty to care for the welfare of these seven hundred men for whom I must be responsible to God? Would it not be a sin, for the sake of pleasure or ambition, to abandon them to the caprice of harsh elders and stewards? And why should I seek other opportunities of being useful and doing good, when such a noble, brilliant, and immediate duty lies at hand? I feel that I am capable of being a good landlord; and to be so, as I understand the word, one needs neither university diplomas nor official rank, such as you desire for me. Dear Aunt, don't make ambitious plans for me; accustom yourself to the thought that I have chosen quite a special path, but a good one which I feel will yield me happiness. I have thought much, very much, about my future duties, and have written down rules of conduct for myself; and if God only grants me life and strength, I shall succeed in my undertaking.

'Don't show my brother Vásya this letter: I am afraid of his ridicule. He is accustomed to domineer over me and I am accustomed to submit to him. Ványa even if he does not approve of my intentions will at least understand them.'

The countess answered with the following letter, which is here also translated from the French:

'Your letter, my dear Dmítri, proved nothing to me except that you have an admirable heart, of which I was always convinced. But, my dear boy, our good qualities do us more harm in life than our bad ones. I must not tell you that you are doing a foolish thing and that your action grieves me; I will try to influence you only by persuasion. Let us consider the matter, my dear. You say you feel a vocation for country life, that you wish to make your serfs happy, and hope to be a good proprietor. I must tell you: first, that we feel our vocation only after we have once mistaken it: secondly, that it is easier to make oneself happy than others, and thirdly, that to be a good landlord one must be a cold and austere man, which you will scarcely be, though you may try to make believe that you are.

'You think your arguments irrefutable and even accept them as rules for the conduct of life, but at my age, my dear, one does not believe in arguments and rules but only in experience; and experience tells me that your plans are child-ish. I am getting on for fifty and have known many fine men, but have never heard of a young man of good family and ability burying himself in the country in order to do good. You always wished to appear original, but your originality is really nothing but excessive self-esteem. Believe me, my dear, it is better to choose the trodden paths. They lead more easily to success, and success, even if you don't want it for yourself, is indispensable to enable you to do the good you desire.

'The poverty of some peasants is an unavoidable evil or one which can be remedied without forgetting all your obligations to society, to your relations, and to yourself. With your intelligence, your heart, and your love of goodness, there is no career in which you would not obtain success; but choose at any rate one worthy of you and which will bring you honour.

'I believe in your sincerity when you say you are free from ambition, but you are deceiving yourself. At your age and with your capacity ambition is a virtue, though it becomes a defect and a vulgarity when a man is no longer able to satisfy that passion, and you will experience this if you do not change your intention.

'Goodbye, dear Dmítri. It seems to me that I love you more than ever for your absurd, but noble and magnanimous plan. Do as you think best, but I confess that I cannot agree with you.'

Having received this letter the young man considered it for a long time, and at last, having come to the conclusion that even the cleverest woman may make mistakes, sent in his petition for discharge from the university, and settled down on his estate.

Chapter II

THE young landowner, as he had written to his aunt, had drawn up rules for his estate management and for his life in general, and had allotted his hours, days, and months to different occupations. Sundays were fixed for receiving petitioners – the domestic and other serfs – for visiting the allotments of the poorest peasants and giving them assistance with the assent of the village Commune (the *mir*) which met each Sunday evening and decided how much help should be distributed and to whom.

More than a year had passed in such activities and the young man was no longer quite a novice either in practical or theoretical knowledge of estate management.

It was a bright Sunday in June when Nekhlyúdov, having drunk his coffee and glanced through a chapter of *Maison Rustique*, put a note-book and a packet of ruble notes in the pocket of his light overcoat, and started out from the large wooden house with its colonnades and verandas, in which he occupied one small room downstairs, and went along the unswept weed-grown paths of the old English garden, towards the village which lay along both sides of the high road. Nekhlyúdov was a tall well-knit young man, with a mass of thick curly brown hair, a bright sparkle in his dark eyes, a fresh complexion, and rosy lips above which the first down of young manhood was just appearing. Youthful strength, energy, and good-natured self-satisfaction were apparent in his gait and every movement. The peasants, dressed in their Sunday best, were returning from church in motley groups – old men, maidens, children, and women with babies in their arms – and dispersing into their homes, bowing low to the master and stepping out of his way. After going some way along the street Nekhlyúdov stopped, took out his note-book, and looked at the last page, on which in his unformed hand he had written the names of several peasants, with comments: 'Iván Chúris asks for props', he read, and went up to the gate of the second hut on his right.

The Chúrises' domicile consisted of a half-rotten log building, mouldy at the corners, sloping to one side, and so sunk in the ground that a small, broken sash window, with its shutter half torn off, and a still smaller casement window stopped up with tow, were only just above the manure heap. Attached to the principal hut were a boarded passage with a low door and a rotten threshold, another small building, still older, and even lower than the passage, a gate, and a wattled shed. All this had once been covered by one irregular roof, but the thick, black, rotting thatch now hung only over the eaves, so that in places the rafters and laths were visible. In the front of the yard was a well with dilapidated sides and the remains of a post and pulley, and a dirty cattle-trampled puddle in which ducks were splashing. Near the well stood two ancient willows that were split and had scanty pale-green shoots. Under one of these willows, which witnessed to the fact that there had been a time when someone had cared to beautify the place, sat a fair-haired little girl, about eight years old, making a two-year-old baby girl crawl round her. A puppy playing beside them, seeing Nekhlyúdov, rushed headlong under the gate and burst into frightened, quivering barking.

'Is Iván at home?' asked Nekhlyúdov.

The elder girl seemed petrified by the question and opened her eyes wider and wider without answering. The younger one opened her mouth and prepared to cry. A little, old-looking woman in a tattered check gown with an old red girdle tied low down, looked out from behind the door, but did not answer either. Nekhlyúdov went up to the door and repeated his question.

'He is, master,' said the old woman in a tremulous voice, bowing low and growing more and more frightened and agitated.

When Nekhlyúdov, having greeted her, passed through the passage into the narrow yard, the old woman went up to the door and, resting her chin on her hand and not taking her eyes off the master, began slowly to shake her head.

The yard was a wretched place. Here and there lay old blackened manure left after carting, and on this lay in disorder a rotting block, a pitchfork, and two harrows. The penthouse round the yard had almost no thatch left on the roof, and one side had fallen in so that the rafters no longer lay on the fork-posts but on the manure. On the other side stood a wooden plough, a cart lacking a wheel, and a heap of empty, useless beehives piled one on another. Chúris, with the edge and head of his axe, was getting the wattle wall clear from the roof which had crushed it. Iván Chúris was a peasant of about fifty, below the average height. His tanned, oval face, sur-rounded by a dark brown beard streaked with grey and thick hair of the same colour, was handsome and expressive. His dark blue half-closed eyes were intelligent and carelessly good-natured, and when he smiled his small regular mouth, sharply defined under his scanty brown moustache, expressed calm self-confidence and a certain ironical indifference to his surroundings. The coarseness of his skin, his deep wrinkles, the sharply marked sinews of his neck, face, and arms, the unnatural stoop of his shoulders, and his crooked bandy legs, showed that his life had been spent in labour beyond his strength. He wore thick white hempen trousers patched with blue on the knees, a dirty shirt of the same material torn at the back and arms, and a low girdle of tape, from which hung a brass key.

'Good-day,' said Nekhlyúdov as he entered the yard.

Chúris looked round and then continued his work, and only when he had cleared the wattle from under the roof by an energetic effort did he stick his axe into a log, adjust his girdle, and come out into the middle of the yard.

'A pleasant holiday, your honour!' he said, bowing low and then shaking back his hair.

'Thank you, friend. You see I've come to look at your allotment,' said Nekhlyúdov, looking at the peasant's garb with boyish friendliness and timidity. 'Let me see why you want those props you asked me for at the meeting of the Commune.'

'The props? Why, you know what props are for, your honour! I'd like to prop things up a bit: there, please see for yourself. Only the other day this corner fell in — but thank God the cattle were not inside at the time. Things hardly hold together,' said Chúris, looking contemptuously at his unthatched, crooked, and dilapidated sheds. 'The rafters, gable-ends, and cross-pieces now, if you only touch them you won't find a single piece of timber that's any use. And where's a man to get timber from nowadays — you know yourself.'

'Then what use would five props be to you, when one shed has fallen in and the others will soon do so? You don't need props, but new rafters, cross-pieces, and uprights,' said the master, evidently parading his knowledge of the subject.

Chúris was silent.

'So what you need is timber and not props. You should have said so.'

'Of course I want timber, but there's nowhere to get it. It won't do to keep going to the master's house! If the likes of us were allowed to get into the habit of coming to your honour's house for everything we need, what sort of serfs should we be? But if you will be merciful concerning the oak posts that are lying unused on your threshing-floor,' he added, bowing and shifting from foot to foot, 'I might be able to change some of the pieces, cut away others, and fix things up somehow with the old stuff.'

'With the old stuff? Don't you yourself say that it's all old and rotten? To-day this corner falls in, to-morrow that, the day after a third: so if you are to do anything you must rebuild it altogether that the work may not be wasted. Tell me, do you think your place could stand through this winter or not?'

'Who can tell?'

'But what do you think? Will it fall in or not?'

Chúris considered.

'It will all fall in,' he said suddenly.

'There, you see you should have said at the meeting that you need to rebuild the whole homestead, and not only put in a few props. You know I should be glad to help you . . .'

'We're very grateful for your favour,' Chúris replied suspiciously, and without looking at the master. 'If you would only favour me with four beams and some props I could perhaps fix things up myself; and the rotten wood I'd take out and use for supports in the hut.'

'Then is your hut in a bad state too?'

'My old woman and I are expecting from day to day that it will crush someone,' Chúris remarked indifferently. 'The other day she did get crushed by a strut from the ceiling.'

'Crushed? What do you mean?'

'Why, your honour, it hit her on the back so that she lay more dead than alive till night-time.'

'Well, and has she recovered?'

'Yes, she's recovered, but she's always ailing. It's true that she's been sickly since her birth.'

'What, are you ill?' Nekhlyúdov asked the woman who was still standing in the doorway and had begun groaning as soon as her husband mentioned her.

'Just here it never leaves me,' she said, pointing to her dirty emaciated chest.

'Again!' said Nekhlyúdov, shrugging his shoulders with vexation. 'Why don't you go to the dispensary when you're ill? That's what the dispensary is for. Haven't you been told of it?'

'We have, master, but I've no time. There's the obligatory work on the estate, our own work, and the children, and I'm all alone. We are lone people.'

Chapter III

NEKHLYÚDOV went into the hut. The uneven smoke-begrimed walls of one end of the room had all sorts of rags and clothing hanging up on them, and the best corner was literally covered with reddish cockroaches that had collected round the icon and the benches. In the middle of the black, smelly, fourteen-foot-square hovel, there was a large crack in the ceiling, which though propped up in two places was bulging so that it threatened to collapse at any moment.

'Yes, the hut is very bad,' said Nekhlyúdov, looking straight at Chúris, who did not seem inclined to begin speaking about this state of things.

'It will crush us and will crush the children,' muttered the woman in a tearful voice, leaning against the brick oven under the bunks.

'Don't you talk,' Chúris said sternly, and with a subtle smile showing slightly under his moustache he turned to the master. 'I can't think what could be done to it, your honour – to the hut. I have put up props and boards, but nothing can be done.'

'How are we to live through the winter here? Oh, oh, oh!' said the woman.

'If we put up some more props and new struts,' her husband interrupted her with a quiet business-like expression, 'and changed one of the rafters, we might somehow get through the winter. We might get along – only the props will crowd the hut, that's all. But if we touch it, there won't be a sound bit left. It's only as long as it's not touched that it holds together,' he concluded, evidently well pleased to have realized that fact.

Nekhlyúdov was vexed and grieved that Chúris had let himself come to such a pass and had not applied to him sooner, for ever since his arrival he had never refused help to a peasant, and only tried to get them to come straight to him with their troubles. He even felt a sort of animosity against Chúris, and angrily shrugged his shoulders and frowned; but the sight of the wretchedness around him and Chúris's quiet, self-satisfied appearance in the midst of it, changed his vexation into a melancholy feeling of hopelessness.

'Now why didn't you tell me sooner, Iván?' he said reproachfully, sitting down on the dirty crooked bench.

'I daren't, your honour,' Chúris replied with the same barely perceptible smile, shifting from one dirty bare foot to the other on the uneven earth floor, but he said this so boldly and calmly that it was hard to believe that he had not dared to apply to his master.

'We are only peasants: how can we dare . . .' began the woman with a sob.

'Hold your jabber,' Chúris addressed her again.

'It's impossible for you to live in this hut. It's nonsense!' said Nekhlyúdov after a pause. 'Now this is what we'll do, friend . . .'

'Yes, sir,' Chúris replied.

'You've seen those brick cottages with hollow walls that I have been building in the new village?'

'Of course I have,' answered Chúris, showing his still sound and white teeth in a smile. 'We were quite surprised at the way they were laid. Tricky cottages! The children were laughing and asked if they were going to be store-houses, and the walls filled in to keep the rats out. . . . Grand cottages!' he finished, shaking his head with a look of ironical perplexity. 'Just like jails!'

'Yes, they are fine cottages, warm and dry, and not so likely to catch on fire,' said the master with a frown on his young face, evidently annoyed by the peasant's irony.

'No gainsaying, your honour – grand cottages!'

'Well then, one of them is quite ready. It is twenty-three feet square, with a passage and a larder, and is quite ready. I might let you have it at cost price and you could pay me when you can,' said the master with a self-satisfied smile which he could not control at the thought of his benevolence. 'You can pull down this old one and use it to build a granary, and we will move the yard buildings too. There is good water there. I will allot you fresh land for your vegetable plots and you will have arable land quite close. You'll soon live well. Now, don't you like it?' he added, noticing that as soon as he spoke of settling somewhere else, Chúris stood quite motionless and looked at the ground no longer smiling.

'It's as your honour pleases,' he said without looking up.

The old woman came forward as if touched to the quick, and prepared to say something, but her husband forestalled her.

'It's as your honour pleases,' he replied, firmly and yet submissively, looking up at his master and tossing back his hair, 'but it won't do for us to live in the new village.'

'Why not?'

'No, your honour. If you move us there – we're in a bad way as it is, but there we should never be proper peasants. What sort of peasants should we be there? Why, a man couldn't possibly live there . . . but just as you please.'

'Why not?'

'We should be quite ruined, your honour.'

'But why couldn't a man live there?'

'What kind of life would it be? Just think. The place has never been lived in, the water not tested, and there's no pasture. Our hemp plots here have been manured from olden times, but what is there there? There's nothing! All bare! No wattles, no corn-kilns, no sheds – nothing at all. We shall be ruined, your honour, if you drive us there, we shall be ruined completely. The place is new, unknown . . . ' he repeated thoughtfully but shaking his head decisively.

Nekhlyúdov began to argue that the change would on the contrary be very advantageous for him, that wattles and sheds would be erected, that the water was good there, and so on;

but Chúris's dull silence confused him and he felt he was not saying the right things. Chúris did not reply, but when his master stopped, remarked with a slight smile that it would be better to house the old domestic serfs and Alëshka, the fool, in the new village, to watch over the grain there.

'That would be fine,' he remarked, and laughed calmly. 'No, it's a hopeless business, your honour!'

'Well, what if the place *is* uninhabited?' Nekhlyúdov insisted patiently. 'This place was uninhabited once, but now people live here; and you will be the first to settle in the new village and will bring luck.... You must certainly settle there...'

'Oh sir, your honour, how can they be compared?' said Chúris with animation, as if afraid the master might take a definite decision. 'Here we are in the Commune – it's lively, and we're accustomed to it. We have the road, and the pond here for the wife to wash the clothes and water the cattle, and our whole peasant establishment here from days of old: the threshing-floor and little vegetable plot, and these willows that my parents planted. My grandfather and father breathed their last here and if only I can end my days here, your honour, I don't ask anything more. If you will have the goodness to let my hut be mended, we shall be very grateful for your kindness. If not, we'll manage to live somehow in the old one to the end of our days. Let us pray for you all our lives,' he continued, bowing low. 'Don't turn us from our nest, master....'

While Chúris was speaking, louder and louder sobs came from the place under the bunks where his wife stood, and when her husband said 'master' she unexpectedly sprang forward and threw herself on her knees at Nekhlyúdov's feet, weeping bitterly.

'Don't ruin us, benefactor! You are like father and mother to us! How could we move? We are old, lonely people. As God, so you...' and she began her lamentations again.

Nekhlyúdov jumped up from the bench to raise the old woman, but she beat her head on the earthen floor in a kind of passionate despair and pushed away his hand.

'What are you doing? Please get up. If you don't wish to go, you needn't. I won't force you,' he said, waving his arms and stepping towards the door.

When Nekhlyúdov had again sat down on the bench and the silence in the hut was only interrupted by the wailing of the woman who had retired under the bunk and stood there wiping her tears with the sleeve of her smock, he realized for the first time what the tumble-down hovel, the broken-down well with the muddy puddle, the rotting sheds and outhouse, and the broken willows which he saw through the crooked window, meant to Chúris and his wife, and he felt depressed, sad, and without knowing why, ashamed.

'Why didn't you tell the Commune last Sunday that you needed a cottage, Iván? I don't know now how to help you. I told you all at the first meeting that I have settled on the estate to devote my life to you; and I was ready to deprive myself of everything to make you contented and happy, and I swear before God that I will keep my word,' said the young proprietor, ignorant of the fact that outpourings of that kind are ill adapted to arouse faith in anyone, and least of all in a Russian, who likes not words but deeds, and dislikes the expression of feelings however fine.

But the simple-hearted young man was so pleased with the feeling he experienced that he could not help pouring it out.

Chúris bent his head to one side, and blinking slowly listened to his master with forced attention, as to one who had to be listened to though he was saying things that were not very nice, and did not at all concern 'us'.

'But I can't give everybody all I am asked for. If I did not refuse some who ask me for timber, I should soon not have any left myself and should be unable to give to those who really need it. That is why I gave the "Crown wood" for the betterment of the peasants' buildings, and handed it over completely to the Commune. That wood is now not mine, but belongs to you peasants. I can no longer dispose of it, but the Commune does what it sees fit with it. Come to the meeting to-night. I will tell them of your request, and if they resolve to give you wood for a new hut it will be all right, but

I have no timber now. I wish to help you with all my heart, but if you don't want to move, the matter is not in my hands but rests with the Commune. Do you understand me?'

'We are very grateful for your kindness, your honour,' answered Chúris, abashed. 'If you will oblige us with the timber for the building, we will get straight that way. . . . Anyhow, what's the Commune? Everybody knows. . . . '

'No, you must come.'

'Yes, I'll come. Why not? But all the same I won't beg of the Commune.'

Chapter IV

THE young landlord evidently wished to ask the couple something more; he did not rise from the bench but looked hesitatingly now at Chúris and now at the empty unheated brick oven.

'Have you had dinner?' he asked at last.

A mocking smile showed under Chúris's moustache, as if it amused him that the master should ask such a silly question, and he did not answer.

'What dinner, benefactor?' said the woman with a deep sigh. 'We've eaten bread – that's our dinner. We had no time to get sorrel to-day, so I had nothing to make soup of, and what kvas there was I gave the children.'

'To-day we have a strict fast, your honour,' said Chúris, explaining his wife's words. 'Bread and onions – that's our peasant food. Thank the Lord we have grain, by your honour's kindness – for many of our peasants haven't even that. The onions failed everywhere this year. Michael the gardener asked two kopéks[1] a bunch when we sent to him the other day, so there's nowhere the likes of us can buy any. Since Easter we haven't been to church. We can't even afford a candle to put in front of St Nicholas's icon.'

Nekhlyúdov had long known, not by hearsay or by trusting to other people's words, but by personal observation, the

1 Two kopéks were about a halfpenny.

extreme poverty in which his serfs lived; but that reality was in such contrast with his whole upbringing, his bent of mind, and the course of his life, that he involuntarily kept forgetting it, and whenever he was forcibly reminded of it, as now, he felt intolerably depressed and sad, as though he were tormented by a reminder of some crime committed and unatoned for.

'Why are you so poor?' he asked, involuntarily uttering his thought.

'What else could we be but poor, master, your honour? What is our land like? As you know, it's clay and mounds, and we must have angered God, for since the cholera year the crops won't grow. And we have less meadow and less arable land now; some have been taken into the owner's farm and some added to his fields. I am a lonely man and old. . . . I'd be glad to bestir myself but I haven't the strength. My wife is ailing, and hardly a year passes without another girl baby, and they all have to be fed. Here am I working alone, and there are seven of us at home. I often sin before God, thinking that if He took some of them soon, things would be easier, and it would be better for them than suffering here. . . . '

'O-oh!' the woman sighed aloud, as if confirming her husband's words.

'Here's all the help I have,' Chúris continued, pointing to an unkempt flaxen-haired boy of seven with an enormous belly, who had just then come in timidly, making the door creak, and who now, holding onto his father's shirt with both his little hands, stood gazing with astonished eyes from under his brow at the master. 'All the help I have is this,' Chúris continued in his deep voice, stroking the child's flaxen hair with his rough hand. 'How long shall I have to wait for him? The work is getting beyond me. It's not so much my age as the rupture that is getting the best of me. In bad weather I'm ready to scream, and by rights I ought to be released from serf-labour on account of my age.[1] There's Dútlov, Dëmkin, Zyábrev – all younger than me – who have long since stopped working on

---

1 Under serfdom a man and his wife had to work some days each week for the owner, and they were reckoned as one unit.

the land. But I have no one to work for me – that's the trouble. We have to eat, so I am struggling on, your honour.'

'I should really be glad to help you. But what can I do?' said the young master, looking compassionately at the serf.

'How can it be helped? Of course if a man holds land he must work for his master – we know that well enough. I'll have somehow to wait for my lad to grow up. Only, if you'll be so good, excuse him from school! The other day the clerk came round and said that your honour ordered him to go to school. Do let him off, your honour. What sense has he got? He's too young to understand anything.'

'Oh, no, friend. Say what you will, your boy can understand,' replied Nekhlyúdov, 'and it's time for him to be learning. I'm saying it for your own good. Just think: when he grows up and is head of the house he'll be able to read and write, and to read in church too – with God's help everything will go right in the home,' he added, trying to express himself so as to be understood, but yet blushing and hesitating without knowing why.

'There's no denying it, your honour, you don't wish us any harm, but there's no one to stay at home when my wife and I go to work on the owner's land; of course he's small, but still he's useful to drive in the cattle and water the horses. Such as he is, still he's a peasant,' and Chúris smiled and took hold of the child's nose with his thick fingers and blew it for him.

'All the same, send him when you are at home and he has time. Do you hear? Be sure to send him.'

Chúris sighed deeply and gave no reply.

Chapter V

'YES, and I wanted to ask why your manure has not been carted,' continued Nekhlyúdov.

'What manure have I got, sir, your honour? There's nothing to cart. What live-stock have I got? I have a little mare and a foal. The heifer I sold to the inn-keeper as a calf last autumn. That's all the live-stock I have.'

'How is that? You haven't enough cattle, yet you sold a heifer as a calf?' the master asked with surprise.

'But what could I feed it on?'

'Haven't you enough straw to feed a cow? Others have enough.'

'Others have manured land, but mine is nothing but clay. I can't do anything with it.'

'Well then dress it, so that it should not be all clay, then it will yield grain and there'll be something to feed the cattle on.'

'But I have no cattle, so how can there be any manure?'

'This is a strange vicious circle,' thought Nekhlyúdov, but could not imagine how to advise the peasant.

'And then again, your honour,' Chúris went on, 'it is not manure that makes the corn grow, but only God. Last year I got six ricks from an unmanured plot, but from the manured land we got almost nothing. It's only God!' he added with a sigh. 'And then cattle do not thrive in our yard. This is the sixth year they have died. Last year one calf died, the other I sold, as we had nothing to live on, and the year before last a fine cow perished: she was driven home from the pasture all right, then suddenly she staggered and staggered and died. Just my bad luck!'

'Well friend, so that you should not say you have no cattle because you have no fodder, and no fodder because you have no cattle, here's something to buy a cow with,' said Nekhlyúdov, blushing as he took some crumpled paper money out of his trouser pocket and began sorting it. 'Buy yourself a cow, and I wish you luck; and you can have fodder from the threshing ground; I'll give orders. Mind you have a cow by next Sunday. I'll look in.'

Chúris stood so long smiling and shifting from foot to foot without stretching out his hand for the money, that Nekhlyúdov at last put it on the table, blushing still more.

'We are greatly satisfied with your kindness,' Chúris said with his usual rather sarcastic smile.

His wife stood under the bunks sighing heavily, and seemed to be saying a prayer.

The young master felt embarrassed; he hurriedly rose from his seat, went out into the passage, and called Chúris to follow. The sight of the man he was befriending was so pleasant that he did not wish to part from him at once.

'I am glad to help you,' he said, stopping by the well. 'I can help you because I know you are not lazy. If you take pains I'll help you, and with God's aid you'll get straight.'

'It's not a case of getting straight, your honour,' said Chúris, his face suddenly assuming a serious and even stern expression as if quite dissatisfied that the master should suppose he could get straight. 'In my father's time I lived with my brothers and we did not know any want, but when he died and we broke up, everything went from bad to worse. It's all from being alone!'

'Why did you separate?'

'All because of our wives, your honour. Your grandfather was not living then. In his time we should not have dared to, there used to be real order then. Like yourself he looked into everything, and we should not have dared to think of separating. Your grandfather did not like to let the peasants get into bad ways. But after him Andrew Ilých managed us. God forgive him! He's left different memories behind – he was a drunken and unreliable man. We went to ask him once and again. "The women make life impossible," we said, "allow us to separate." Well he had us thrashed once and again, but in the end the women got their way and the families separated and lived apart. Of course everyone knows what a one-man home is! Besides there was no kind of order. Andrew Ilých ruled us as he pleased. "See that you have everything that's needed," – but how a peasant was to get it he didn't ask. Then the poll-tax was increased, and more provisions were requisitioned and we had less land, and the crops began to fail. And when the time came for re-allotting the land, he took away from our manured land to add to the owner's – the rascal – and did for us altogether. We might as well die! Your father – the kingdom of heaven be his! – was a kind master, but we rarely had sight of him; he always lived in Moscow, and of course we had to cart more produce there. Sometimes when a thaw set in and the roads were impassable and we had no fodder left we still had to cart! The master could not do without it. We dare not complain of that, but there was no order. Now that your honour lets every peasant come to you, we are a different people and the steward is a different man. At least we know now that we have a master. And it's impossible to say how grateful the peasants are to your honour! During the time you were under guardianship we had no real master. Everybody was master – your guardian and Ilých, and his wife was mistress, and the clerk from the police-office was a master too. At that time we peasants suffered a great deal – oh God! How much sorrow!'

Again Nekhlyúdov experienced something like shame or remorse. He raised his hat and went his way.

Chapter VI

'Epifán Wiseman wishes to sell a horse,' Nekhlyúdov read in his note-book, and he crossed the street to Epifán's home.

This hut was carefully thatched with straw from the threshing-floor of the estate, and was built of light grey aspen timber – also from the master's forest. It had two red painted shutters to each window, a little roofed porch, and board railings with fancy patterns cut in them. The passage and unheated portion of the house were also sound; but the general look of well-being and sufficiency was rather marred by a shed with an unfinished wattle wall and unthatched roof adjoining the gateway. Just as Nekhlyúdov reached the porch from one side, two women came up from the other carrying between them a full tub slung from a pole. One was Epifán Wiseman's wife, the other his mother. The former was a sturdy red-cheeked woman with a very fully developed bosom and broad fleshy cheeks. She wore a clean smock with embroidered sleeves and collar, an apron with similar embroidery, a new linen skirt, shoes, glass beads and a smart square head-dress embroidered with red cotton and spangles.

The end of the pole did not sway but lay firmly on her broad solid shoulder. The easy effort noticeable in her red face, in the curve of her back, and the measured movement of her arms and legs, indicated excellent health and extraordinary masculine strength.

Epifán's mother who carried the other end of the pole was, on the contrary, one of those elderly women who seem to have reached the utmost limit of age and decrepitude possible to a living person. Her bony figure, clad in a dirty torn smock and discoloured skirt, was so bent that the pole rested rather on her back than on her shoulder. Her hands were of a dark red-brown colour, with crooked fingers which seemed unable to unbend and with which she seemed to clutch the pole for support. Her drooping head, wrapped in some clout, bore the unsightly evidence of want and great age. From under her low forehead, furrowed in all directions by deep wrinkles, her two red, lashless eyes looked dimly on the ground. One yellow tooth protruded from under her sunken upper lip and, constantly moving, touched at times her pointed chin. The folds on the lower part of her face and throat were like bags that swung with every movement. She breathed heavily and hoarsely, but her bare deformed feet, though they dragged along the ground with effort, moved evenly one after the other.

Chapter VII

HAVING almost collided with the master, the young woman looked abashed, briskly set down the tub, bowed, glanced at him with sparkling eyes from under her brow, and clattering with her shoes ran up the steps, trying to hide a slight smile with the embroidered sleeve of her smock.

'You go and take the yoke back to Aunt Nastásya, mother,' she said to the old woman, pausing at the door.

The modest young man looked attentively but sternly at the rosy-faced woman, frowned, and turned to the old one, who having disengaged the yoke from the tub with her rough hands and lifted it onto her shoulders, was submissively directing her steps towards the neighbouring hut.

'Is your son at home?' the master asked.

The old woman, bending still lower, bowed and was about to speak, but lifting her hand to her mouth began coughing so that Nekhlyúdov did not wait, but went into the hut.

Epifán, who was sitting on the bench in the best corner, rushed to the oven when he saw his master, as if trying to hide from him, hurriedly shoved something onto the bunk, and with mouth and eyes twitching, pressed himself against the wall as if to make way for the master.

Epifán was a man of about thirty; slender, well set, with brown hair and a young pointed beard, he would have been rather good-looking had it not been for the evasive little brown eyes that looked unpleasantly from under his puckered brows, and for the absence of two front teeth, which at once caught the eye as his lips were short and constantly moving. He had on a holiday shirt with bright red gussets, striped cotton trousers, and heavy boots with wrinkled legs. The interior of his hut was not so crowded and gloomy as Chúris's, though it was also stuffy, smelt of smoke and sheepskin coats, and was littered in the same untidy way with peasant garments and implements. Two things struck one as strange: a small dented samovar which stood on a shelf, and the portrait of an archimandrite with a red nose and six fingers, that hung near the icon with its brass facings, in a black frame with the remnant of a dirty piece of glass. Nekhlyúdov looked with dissatisfaction at the samovar, the archimandrite's portrait, and the bunk where the end of a brass-mounted pipe protruded from under some rags, and addressed the peasant.

'Good morning, Epifán,' he said, looking into his eyes.

Epifán bowed and muttered, 'Hope you're well, y'r Ex'cency,' pronouncing the last word with peculiar tenderness while his eyes ran rapidly over his master's whole figure, the hut, the floor, and the ceiling, not resting on anything. Then he hurriedly went to the bunk and pulled down from it a coat which he began putting on.

'Why are you doing that?' said Nekhlyúdov, sitting down on the bench and trying to look at Epifán as sternly as possible.

'What else could I do, y'r Ex'cency? I think we know our place....'

'I have come to ask what you need to sell a horse for, and how many horses you have, and which horse you want to sell,' said Nekhlyúdov drily, evidently repeating questions he had prepared.

'We are very pleased that y'r Ex'cency deigns to come to peasants like us,' replied Epifán with a rapid glance at the archimandrite's portrait, at the oven, at Nekhlyúdov's boots, and at everything except his master's face. 'We always pray God for y'r Ex'cency. . . .'

'Why must you sell a horse?' Nekhlyúdov repeated, raising his voice and clearing his throat.

Epifán sighed, shook back his hair, his glance again roving over the whole hut, and noticing a cat that lay quietly purring on the bench, shouted to it, 'Sss, get away, beast!' and hurriedly turned to the master.

'It's a horse, y'r Ex'cency, that's no good. . . . If it were a good beast I wouldn't sell it, y'r Ex'cency.'

'And how many horses have you?'

'Three horses, y'r Ex'cency.'

'And no foals?'

'Why certainly, y'r Ex'cency, I have a foal too.'

Chapter VIII

'COME, let me see your horses. Are they in the yard?'

'Exactly so, y'r Ex'cency. I have done as I was ordered, y'r Ex'cency. As if we could disobey y'r Ex'cency! Jacob Alpátych told me not to let the horses out into the field. "The prince will look at them," he said, so we did not let them out. We dare not disobey y'r Ex'cency.'

As Nekhlyúdov was passing out of the hut, Epifán snatched his pipe from the bunk and shoved it behind the oven; his lips continued to move restlessly even when the master was not looking at him.

A lean little grey mare was rummaging among some rotten straw under the penthouse, and a two-months-old long-legged foal of some nondescript colour, with bluish legs and muzzle, kept close to her thin tail which was full of burrs. In the middle of the yard, with its eyes shut and pensively hanging its head, stood a thick-bellied sorrel gelding – by his appearance a good peasant horse.

'Are these all the horses you have?'

'No, sir, y'r Ex'cency, there's also the mare and the foal,' Epifán said, pointing to the horses which his master could not have helped seeing.

'I see. And which of them do you want to sell?'

'Why, this one, y'r Ex'cency,' replied Epifán, shaking the skirt of his coat towards the drowsy gelding and continually blinking and twitching his lips. The gelding opened its eyes and lazily turned its tail to him.

'He doesn't look old and is a sturdy horse,' said Nekhlyúdov. 'Just catch him, and let me see his teeth. I can tell if he is old.'

'It's impossible for one person to catch him, Ex'cency. The beast is not worth a penny and has a temper – he bites and kicks, Ex'cency,' replied Epifán, smiling gaily and letting his eyes rove in all directions.

'What nonsense! Catch him, I tell you.'

Epifán smiled for a long time, shuffling from foot to foot, and only when Nekhlyúdov cried angrily: 'Well, what are you about?' did he rush under the penthouse, bring out a halter, and begin running after the horse, frightening it and following it.

The young master was evidently weary of seeing this, and perhaps wished to show his skill.

'Let me have the halter!' he said.

'I beg your pardon, how can y'r Ex'cency? Please don't....'

But Nekhlyúdov went up to the horse's head and suddenly seized it by the ears with such force that the gelding, which was after all a very quiet peasant horse, swayed and snorted, trying to get away. When Nekhlyúdov noticed that it was quite unnecessary to use such force, and looked at Epifán who continued to smile, the idea – most humiliating to one of his age – occurred to him that Epifán was making fun of him and regarded him as a child. He flushed, let go of the horse's ears, and without making use of the halter opened its mouth and examined its teeth: the eye-teeth were sound and the double teeth full – which the young master knew the meaning of. Of course the horse was a young one.

Meanwhile Epifán had gone to the penthouse, and noticing that a harrow was not lying in its place, moved it and stood it up against the wattle wall.

'Come here!' cried Nekhlyúdov with an expression of childish annoyance on his face and a voice almost tearful with vexation and anger. 'Now, is this horse old?'

'Please, y'r Ex'cency, very old. It must be twenty. . . . Some horses . . .'

'Silence! You're a liar and a good-for-nothing! A decent peasant does not lie – he has no need to!' said Nekhlyúdov, choking with angry tears. He stopped, in order not to disgrace himself by bursting into tears before the peasant. Epifán too was silent, and looking as if he would begin to cry at any moment, sniffed and slightly jerked his head.

'Tell me, what will you plough with if you sell this horse?' Nekhlyúdov went on when he had calmed down sufficiently to speak in his ordinary tone. 'You are being sent to do work on foot so as to let your horses be in better condition for the ploughing, and you want to sell your last one? And above all, why do you tell lies?'

As soon as his master grew calm Epifán quieted down too. He stood straight, still twitching his lips and his eyes roaming from one object to another.

'We'll come out to work for y'r Ex'cy no worse than the others.'

'But what will you plough with?'

'Don't trouble about that, we'll get y'r Ex'cency's work done!' said Epifán, shooing at the horse and driving it away. 'If I didn't need the money would I sell him?'

'What do you need the money for?'

'We have no flour left, y'r Ex'cency, and I must pay my debts to other peasants, y'r Ex'cency.'

'No flour? How is it that others with families still have flour, while you without a family have none? What have you done with it?'

'Eaten it up, y'r Ex'cency, and now there's none left at all. I'll buy a horse before the autumn, y'r Ex'cency.'

'Don't dare to think of selling the horse!'

'But if I don't sell it, y'r Ex'cency, what kind of a life will ours be, when we've no flour and daren't sell anything...' replied Epifán turning aside, twitching his lips, and suddenly casting an insolent look at his master's face – 'it means we're to starve!'

'Mind, my man!' Nekhlyúdov shouted, pale with anger and experiencing a feeling of personal animosity towards the peasant. 'I won't keep such peasants as you. It will go ill with you.'

'That's as you wish, if I've not satisfied y'r Ex'cency,' replied Epifán, closing his eyes with an expression of feigned humility, 'but it seems that no fault has been noticed in me. Of course if y'r Ex'cency doesn't like me, it's all in your power: but I don't know what I am to be punished for.'

'For this: that your sheds are not thatched, your wattle walls are broken, your manure is not ploughed in, and you sit at home smoking a pipe and not working; and because you don't give your mother, who turned the whole farm over to you, a bit of bread, but let your wife beat her so that she has to come to me with complaints.'

'Oh no, y'r Ex'cency, I don't even know what a pipe is!' replied Epifán in confusion, apparently hurt most of all by being accused of smoking a pipe. 'It is possible to say anything about a man...'

'There you are, lying again! I saw it myself.'

'How should I dare to lie to y'r Ex'cency?'

Nekhlyúdov bit his lip silently and began pacing up and down the yard. Epifán stood in one spot and without lifting his eyes watched his master's feet.

'Listen, Epifán!' said Nekhlyúdov suddenly in a voice of childlike gentleness, stopping in front of the peasant and trying to conceal his excitement. 'You can't live like that – you will ruin your life. Bethink yourself. If you want to be a good peasant change your way of life, give up your bad habits, stop lying, don't get drunk, and respect your mother. You see I know all about you. Attend to your allotment, don't steal from the Crown forest, and stop going to the tavern. What good is all that? – just think. If you need anything come to me and ask straight out for what you want, and tell me why you want it. Don't lie, but tell the whole truth, and then I shan't refuse anything I can do for you.'

'Excuse me, y'r Ex'cency, I think we can understand y'r Ex'cency!' Epifán replied smiling, as if he quite understood the excellence of the master's joke.

That smile and that reply completely disillusioned Nekhlyúdov of his hope of touching Epifán and bringing him to the right path by persuasion. Moreover he felt all the time as if it were indecorous for him, who had authority, to persuade his own serf, as if all that he had said was not at all what he ought to have said. He sadly bowed his head and went into the passage. The old woman was sitting on the threshold groaning aloud, as if to show her sympathy with the master's words which she had overheard.

'Here is something to buy yourself bread with,' Nekhlyúdov whispered, giving her a ruble note. 'But buy it yourself, and don't give it to Epifán or he will drink it.'

The old woman took hold of the door-post with her bony hand, trying to rise and thank the master, but her head began shaking, and Nekhlyúdov had already crossed the road before she had got to her feet.

Chapter IX

'WHITE DAVID wants grain and posts,' was the next entry in Nekhlyúdov's note-book.

After passing several homesteads, he met his steward, Jacob Alpátych, at the corner of the lane. The latter having seen his master in the distance had removed his oilskin cap, produced a foulard kerchief, and begun wiping his fat red face.

'Put on your cap, Jacob! Put it on I tell you. . . .'

'Where has your Excellency been pleased to go?' said Jacob, holding up his cap to shade the sun, but not putting it on.

'I've been to see Wiseman. Now tell me, why has he become like that?' asked the master continuing on his way.

'Like what, your Excellency?' replied the steward, who followed his master at a respectful distance and having put on his cap was smoothing his moustache.

'What indeed! He is a perfect scamp – lazy, a thief, a liar, ill-treats his mother, and seems to be such a confirmed good-for-nothing that there is no reforming him.'

'I don't know, your Excellency, why he has displeased you so. . . .'

'And his wife too,' his master interrupted him, 'seems to be a horrid creature. The mother is dressed worse than any beggar and has nothing to eat, but the wife is all dressed up, and so is he. I don't at all know what to do with him.'

Jacob grew visibly confused when Nekhlyúdov mentioned Epifán's wife.

'Well if he has let himself go like that,' he began, 'we ought to take measures. It's true he's poor, like all one-man house-holders, but unlike some others he does keep himself in hand a bit. He's intelligent, can read and write, and seems pretty honest. He is always sent round to collect the poll-tax, and he has been village elder for three years while I have been here, and nothing wrong has been noticed. Three years ago it pleased your guardian to dismiss him, but he was all right also when he worked on the estate. Only he has taken rather to drink, having lived at the Post Station in town, so measures should be taken against that. When he misbehaved in the past we used to threaten him with a flogging and he'd come to his senses, and it was good for him and there was peace in the family; but as you don't approve of such measures, I really don't know what we are to do with him. I know he has let himself go pretty badly. He can't be sent as a soldier because he has lost two teeth, as you will have noticed. He knocked them out purposely a long time ago.[1] But he is not the only one, if I may take the liberty of reporting to your Excellence, who has got quite out of hand.'

---

1 The proprietors had to send a certain proportion of their serfs to serve in the army, but they had to be fit men with sound teeth.

'Let that matter alone, Jacob!' said Nekhlyúdov with a slight smile. 'We have discussed it over and over again. You know what I think about it, and say what you will I shall still not change my mind....'[1]

'Of course your Excellence knows best,' said Jacob, shrugging his shoulders and gazing at his master from behind as if what he saw boded no good. 'As to the old woman, you are pleased to trouble about her needlessly,' he continued. 'It's true she brought up her fatherless children, and raised Epifán and married him off and all that; but among the peasants it is the custom, when a mother or father hands over the homestead to a son, that the son and his wife become the masters and the old woman has to earn her bread as best she can. Of course they have no delicate feelings, but it is the usual way among the peasants. So I make bold to say that the old woman has troubled you needlessly. She is an intelligent woman and a good housekeeper, but why trouble the master about every trifle? Well, she had a dispute with her daughter-in-law, and the daughter-in-law may have pushed her – those are women's affairs! They might have made it up again instead of troubling you. And besides, you take it all too much to heart,' added the steward, looking with fatherly tenderness and condescension at his master who was walking silently up the street before him with long strides.

'Are you going home, sir?' he asked.

'No, to see White David, or the Goat ... how is he called?'

'Now that's another sluggard, let me tell you. The whole Goat family are like that. Whatever you may do with him nothing helps. I drove over the peasant fields yesterday, and he has not even sown his buckwheat. What is one to do with such people? If only the old man at least taught his son, but he is just such a sluggard himself – whether it's for himself or for the owner he always bungles it.... Both your guardian and I – what have we not done to them? He's been sent to the police-station, and been flogged at home – which is what you are pleased to disapprove of....'

---

1 As to the desirability of flogging the peasants.

'Who? Surely not the old man?'

'The old man, sir. Your guardian has many a time had him flogged before the whole Commune. But would your Excellence believe it, it had no effect! He would give himself a shake, go home, and behave just the same. And I must admit that David is a quiet peasant and not stupid; he doesn't smoke or drink, that is,' Jacob explained, 'but yet you see he's worse than some drunkards. The only thing would be to conscript him, or exile him – nothing else can be done. The whole Goat family are like that. Matryúshka, who lives in that hovel, is of the same family and is a damned sluggard too. But your Excellence does not require me?' added the steward, noticing that his master was not listening to him.

'No, you may go,' replied Nekhlyúdov absent-mindedly, and went on towards White David's hut.

David's hut stood crooked and solitary at the end of the village. It had no yard, no kiln, and no barn; only some dirty cattle sheds clung to one side of it while on the other brushwood and beams, prepared for outbuildings, lay all in a heap. Tall green grass was growing where there had once been a yard. There was not a living being near the hut, except a pig that lay grunting in a puddle by the threshold.

Nekhlyúdov knocked at a broken window, but as no one answered he went into the entry and shouted, 'Hullo there!' but got no reply to this either. He entered the passage, looked into the empty cattle stalls, and entered the open door of the hut. An old red cock and two hens, jerking their crops and clattering with their claws, were strutting about the floor and benches. Seeing a man they spread their wings and, cackling desperately, flew against the walls, one of them jumping up on the oven. The hut, which was not quite fourteen-foot square, was almost filled by the brick oven with its broken chimney, a weaving loom that had not been put away though it was summer, and a blackened table with a warped and cracked top.

Though it was dry outside there was still a dirty puddle inside near the threshold, which had been formed by a leak in the roof and ceiling during previous rain. There were no beds. It was difficult to believe that the place was inhabited – there was such an appearance of absolute neglect and disorder both within the hut and outside. Yet White David and his whole family lived there, and at that very moment, though it was a hot June day, David, wrapped head and all in his sheepskin, lay huddled in a corner on the top of the oven fast asleep. The frightened hen that had alighted there and had not yet quieted down was walking over his back without waking him.

Not seeing anyone in the hut Nekhlyúdov was about to leave, when a long-drawn slobbering sigh betrayed the sleeper's presence.

'Hullo, who's there?' shouted the master.

Another long-drawn sigh came from the oven.

'Who is there? Come here!'

Another sigh, a moan, and a loud yawn replied to the master's call.

'Well, what are you about?'

Something moved slowly on the oven. The skirt of a worn-out sheepskin coat appeared, one big foot in a tattered bast shoe came down, and then another, and finally the whole of White David appeared, sitting on the oven and lazily and discontentedly rubbing his eyes with his big fist. Slowly bending his head he looked round the hut with a yawn, and, seeing his master, began to move a little quicker than before, but still so slowly that Nekhlyúdov had time to walk some three times from the puddle to the loom and back while David was getting down from the oven.

White David was really white: his hair, body, and face were all quite white. He was tall and very stout, but stout as peasants are – that is, his whole body was stout and not only his stomach – but it was a flabby and unhealthy stoutness. His rather comely face, with pale blue quiet eyes and broad, full beard, bore the impress of ill-health: there was no vestige of sunburn or colour in it; it was all of a pale yellowish tint with a purple shadow under the eyes, and seemed swollen and bloated. His hands were puffy and yellow, like those of people suffering from dropsy, and were covered with fine white hair. He was so drowsy that he could hardly open his eyes or stand without staggering and yawning.

'How is it you are not ashamed,' Nekhlyúdov began, 'to sleep in broad daylight when you ought to be building your out-houses and when you are short of grain. . . .'

As soon as David came to his senses and began to realize that his master was standing before him, he folded his hands below his stomach, hung his head, inclining it a little on one side, and did not stir a limb. He was silent; but the expression of his face and the pose of his whole body said: 'I know, I know, it's not the first time I have heard this. Well, beat me if you must. I'll endure it.' He seemed to wish that his master would stop speaking and be quick and beat him, even beat him painfully on his plump cheeks, if having done so he would but leave him in peace. Noticing that David did not understand him, Nekhlyúdov tried by various questions to rouse the peasant from his submissively patient taciturnity.

'Why did you ask me for timber, and then leave it lying about here a whole month, and that too at the time when you have most leisure, eh?'

David remained persistently silent and did not stir.

'Come now, answer me!'

David muttered something and blinked his white eyelashes.

'You know one has to work, friend. What would there be without work? You see you have no grain now, and why? Because your land was badly ploughed, not harrowed, and sown too late – and all from laziness. You ask me for grain: well suppose I give you some, since you must not starve – but that sort of thing won't do. Whose grain am I to give you? Whose do you think? Come, answer me! Whose grain am I to give you?' Nekhlyúdov insisted.

'The proprietor's,' muttered David, raising his eyes timidly and questioningly.

'But where does the proprietor's grain come from? Think of it. Who ploughed and harrowed the land? Who sowed and reaped it? The peasants. Is that not so? Then you see if I am to give away the grain, I ought to give more to those who worked most to produce it, and you have worked least. They complain about your work on the estate too. You work least, but ask for your master's grain more than anyone.

Why should I give it to you and not to others? You know if everybody lay on their backs as you do, we should all have starved long ago. One must work, friend. This sort of thing is wrong. Do you hear me, David?'

'I hear, sir,' muttered David slowly through his teeth.

Chapter X

JUST then the head of a peasant woman carrying linen hung on a wooden yoke was seen through the window, and a moment later David's mother, a tall, very fresh-looking and active woman of about fifty, entered the hut. Her pock-marked and wrinkled face was not handsome, but her straight firm nose, her thin compressed lips and keen grey eyes, expressed intelligence and energy. The squareness of her shoulders and flatness of her bosom, the leanness of her arms and the solid muscles of her dark bare legs, bore witness to the fact that she had long since ceased to be a woman and had become simply a labourer. She hurried into the hut, closed the door, pulled down her skirt, and looked angrily at her son. Nekhlyúdov was about to speak to her, but she turned her back on him and began crossing herself before a grimy icon that was visible behind the loom. Having finished doing this, she adjusted the dirty checked kerchief she wore on her head and bowed low to her master.

'A pleasant Lord's day to your Excellency,' she said. 'God bless you, our father. . . . '

When David saw his mother he evidently became confused, and stooped and hung his head still more.

'Thanks, Arína,' replied Nekhlyúdov. 'I've just been speaking to your son about your household.'

'Arína the barge-hauler', as the peasants had called her since she was a girl, rested her chin on her right fist, supporting that elbow on the palm of her left hand, and without waiting for the master to finish began to speak in such a shrill and ringing tone that her voice filled the whole hut, and from outside it might have seemed as if several women were talking together.

'What's the use of talking to him, dear sir? He can't even speak like a man. There he stands, the lout!' she continued, contemptuously wagging her head at David's pathetic massive figure. 'What's my household, sir, your Excellency? We're paupers. You've got none worse than us in the whole village! We can't do anything for ourselves or for the estate – it's a disgrace! And it's him that's brought us to it. I bore, fed, and reared him, and could scarcely wait for him to grow up, and now this is what we've got at last! He eats the bread, but we get no more work out of him than from that rotten log. All he does is to lie on the oven, or stand like that and scratch his empty pate,' she went on, mimicking him. 'If only you would frighten him a bit, sir! I ask it myself – punish him for God's sake, or send him to the army. There's no other way out. I can do nothing with him – that's how it is.'

'Now isn't it a sin for you to bring your mother to this, David?' said Nekhlyúdov reproachfully, turning to the peasant.

David did not budge.

'If he were sickly now,' Arína continued with the same animated gestures, 'but look at him, he's as big as the mill chimney! You would think there'd be enough of him to do some work, the lubberly lout; but no, he's taking a rest on the oven, the sluggard. And if he does start on anything my eyes grow tired of looking at him before he's had time to get up, turn round, and get anything done!' she added in a drawling tone, turning her square shoulders awkwardly from side to side. 'To-day, for instance, my old man himself went to fetch brushwood from the forest and told him to dig holes for the posts: but not he, didn't so much as take the spade in his hands. . . .' She paused for a moment. 'He's done for me, lone woman that I am!' she suddenly shrieked, flourishing her arms and going up to her son with a threatening gesture. 'You fat lazy mug! God forgive me. . . .'

She turned contemptuously and yet with desperation from him, spat, and with tears in her eyes again addressed her master with the same animation, still waving her arms. 'I'm all alone, benefactor! My old man is ill, old, and there's not much good in him either, and I have always to do everything alone. It's enough to crush a stone. To die would be better, that would end it. He has worn me out, the wretch! Really, father, I'm at the end of my tether! My daughter-in-law died of overwork, and so shall I.'

Chapter XI

'DIED of what?' Nekhlyúdov asked incredulously.

'From overwork, benefactor, as God is holy, she was used up. We took her from Babúrino the year before last,' continued Arína, and her angry expression suddenly changed to a sad and tearful one. 'She was a quiet, fresh-looking young woman, dear sir. She had lived in comfort as a girl at her father's and had not known want; but when she came to us and knew what our work was – work on the master's estate and at home and everywhere. . . . She and I alone to do it. It is nothing to me! I'm used to it. But she was with child, dear sir, and began to suffer pain, and was always working beyond her strength, and she overdid it poor thing. A year ago, during St Peter's Fast,[1] to her misfortune, she bore a son. We had no bread: we had to eat anything, just anything, and there was urgent work to be done – and her milk dried up. It was her first baby, we had no cow, and how can we peasants rear a baby by hand? Well, she was a woman and foolish – that made her grieve still more. And when the baby died she wept and wept for him, lamented and lamented, and there was want and the work had to be done, and things got worse and worse: she was so worn out in the summer that at the Feast of the Intercession[2] she herself died. It was he who destroyed her – the beast!' she repeated, turning with despairing anger to her son. 'What I wanted to ask of your Excellence . . . ' she went on after a pause, lowering her voice and bowing.

'What is it?' Nekhlyúdov asked absent-mindedly, still agitated by her story.

'You see he is still a young man. What work can be expected from me? I'm alive to-day but shall be dead to-morrow.

1 The feast of St Peter and St Paul is June 9th, o.s.
2 October 1st, o.s.

How is he to get on without a wife? He won't be a worker for you.... Think of something for us. You are as a father to us.'

'You mean you want to get him married? Well, all right.'

'Be merciful, you who are a father and mother to us!' and on her making a sign to her son, they both dropped on their knees at their master's feet.

'Why do you bow in such a way?' Nekhlyúdov said irritably, raising her by the shoulder. 'Can't you say what you want to say simply? You know I don't like grovellings. Get your son married if you like. I shall be very glad if you know of a wife for him.'

The old woman rose and began rubbing her dry eyes with her sleeve. David followed her example and having rubbed his eyes with his puffy fist continued to stand in the same patiently meek attitude listening to what Arína said.

'There are girls – of course there are. There's Váska Mikháy's girl, she's all right, but she won't consent unless it's your wish.'

'Doesn't she agree?'

'No, benefactor, not if she's to marry by consent.'

'Then what's to be done? I can't compel her. Look out for someone else – if not one of ours, one from another village. I'll buy her out if she comes willingly, but I won't force her to marry. There is no law that allows that, and it would be a great sin.'

'Eh, eh, benefactor! Is it likely, seeing what our life is and our poverty, that any girl would come of her own accord? Even the poorest soldier's wife wouldn't agree to such poverty. What peasant will give his girl into a house like this? A desperate man wouldn't do it. Why, we're paupers, beggars. They'd say that we have starved one to death and that the same would happen to their daughter. Who would give his girl?' she added, shaking her head dubiously. 'Just consider, your Excellency.'

'But what can I do?'

'Think of something for us, dear sir,' Arína repeated earnestly. 'What are we to do?'

'But what can I contrive? I can't do anything at all in such a case.'

'Who is to arrange it for us if not you?' said Arína, hanging down her head and spreading her arms out in mournful perplexity.

'As to the grain you asked for, I'll give orders that you shall have some —' said the master after a pause, during which Arína kept sighing and David echoed her. 'I can't do anything more.'

And Nekhlyúdov went out into the passage. The mother and son followed him, bowing.

Chapter XII

'Oh, what a life mine is!' Arína said, sighing deeply.

She stopped and looked angrily at her son. David at once turned and clumsily lifting his thick foot in its enormous and dirty bast shoe heavily over the threshold, disappeared through the door.

'What am I to do with him, master?' Arína went on. 'You see yourself what he is like. He is not a bad man, doesn't drink, is gentle, and wouldn't harm a child – it would be a sin to say otherwise. There's nothing bad in him, and God only knows what has happened to make him his own enemy. He himself is sad about it. Would you believe it, sir, my heart bleeds when I look at him and see how he suffers. Whatever he may be, I bore him and pity him – oh, how I pity him! . . . You see it's not as if he went against me, or his father, or the authorities. He's timid – like a little child, so to say. How can he live a widower? Arrange something for us, benefactor!' she said again, evidently anxious to remove the bad impression her bitter words might have produced on the master. 'Do you know, sir, your Excellence,' she went on in a confidential whisper, 'I have thought one thing and another and can't imagine why he is like that. It can only be that bad folk have bewitched him.'

She remained silent for a while.

'If I could find the right man, he might be cured.'

'What nonsense you talk, Arína. How can a man be bewitched?'

'Oh, my dear sir, a man can be so bewitched that he's never again a man! As if there were not many bad people in the world! Out of spite they'll take a handful of earth from a man's footprints . . . or something of that sort . . . and he is no longer a man. Is evil far from us? I've been thinking – shouldn't I go to old Dundúk, who lives in Vorobëvka? He knows all sorts of charms and herbs, and removes spells and makes water flow from a cross. Perhaps he would help!' said the old woman. 'Maybe he would cure him.'

'Now there is poverty and ignorance!' thought the young master as he strode with big steps through the village, sorrowfully hanging his head. 'What am I to do with him? It's impossible to leave him like that, both for my own sake and on account of the example to others, as well as for himself,' he said, counting off these different reasons on his fingers. 'I can't bear to see him in such a state, but how am I to get him out of it? He ruins all my best plans for the estate. . . . As long as there are peasants like that my dreams will never be realized,' he reflected, experiencing vexation and anger against White David for ruining his plans. 'Shall I have him sent to Siberia, as Jacob suggests, since he doesn't want to get on; or send him to be a soldier? I should at least be rid of him and should save another and better peasant from being conscripted,' he argued to himself.

He thought of this with satisfaction; but at the same time a vague consciousness told him that he was thinking with only one side of his mind and that it was not right. He stopped. 'Wait a bit, what was I thinking about?' he asked himself. 'Oh yes, into the army or to exile. But what for? He is a good man, better than many others – and besides what do I know. . . . Shall I set him free?' he thought, not now considering the question with only one side of his mind as previously. 'That would be unfair and impossible.' But suddenly a thought occurred to him which pleased him very much, and he smiled with the expression of a man who has solved a difficult problem. 'Take him into my house,' he reflected, 'observe him myself and get him used to work and reform him by kindness, persuasion, and a proper choice of occupation.'

Chapter XIII

'THAT's what I will do,' said Nekhlyúdov to himself with cheerful self-satisfaction, and remembering that he still had to see the rich peasant Dútlov he turned towards a tall roomy homestead with two chimneys, that stood in the middle of the village. As he drew near it he met at the neighbouring hut a plainly dressed woman of about forty coming to meet him.

'A pleasant holiday, sir!' said she without any sign of timidity, stopping beside him, smiling pleasantly and bowing.

'Good morning, nurse,' he replied. 'How are you? I am going to see your neighbour.'

'Yes, your Excellence, that's a good thing. But won't you please come in? My old man would be so glad!'

'Well, I'll come in and we'll have a talk, nurse. Is this your hut?'

'That's it, sir.'

The woman, who had been his wet-nurse, ran on in front. Following her into the entry Nekhlyúdov sat down on a barrel and lit a cigarette.

'It's hot in there. Let's sit out here and have a chat,' he said in answer to his nurse's invitation to enter the hut. The nurse was still a fresh-looking and handsome woman. Her features, and especially her large dark eyes, much resembled those of her master. She folded her arms under her apron and looking fearlessly at Nekhlyúdov, and continually moving her head, began to talk.

'Why are you pleased to honour Dútlov with a visit, sir?'

'I want him to rent land from me, about thirty desyatíns,[1] and start a farm, and also buy a forest jointly with me. You see he has money, so why should it lie idle? What do you think of it, nurse?'

---

1 A desyatín is nearly two and three-quarter acres.

'Well, why not? Of course, sir, everyone knows that the Dútlovs are strong people. I reckon he's the leading peasant on the whole estate,' the nurse answered, swaying her head. 'Last year they put up another building with their own timber, without troubling you. They must have at least eighteen horses, apart from foals and colts, and as to cattle and sheep – when the women go out into the street to drive them in it's a sight to see how they crowd the gateway, and they must also have two hundred hives of bees if not more. Dútlov is a very strong peasant and must have money.'

'Do you think he has much money?' asked Nekhlyúdov.

'People say – it may be their spite – that the old man has a good lot of money. Naturally he won't talk about it or tell his sons, but he must have. Why shouldn't he be interested in a forest? Unless he may be afraid of the talk spreading of his having money. Some five years back he took up meadows in a small way, in shares with Shkálik, the inn-keeper, but either Shkálik swindled him or something happened, and the old man lost some three hundred rubles and since then he has given it up. How can they help being well-to-do, your Excellency?' the nurse went on. 'They have three allotments of lands, a big family all of them workers, and the old man himself – there's no denying it – is a capital manager. He has such luck everywhere that people all wonder; what with his grain, his horses, and cattle, and bees, and his sons. He's got them all married now. He used to find wives for them among our own people, but now he's got Ilyúshka married to a free girl – he paid for her emancipation himself – and she, too, has turned out well.'

'And do they live peaceably?'

'Where there's a real head to a house there's always peace. Take the Dútlovs – of course the daughters-in-law have words behind the oven, but with their father at the head the sons live in unity all the same.'

The nurse paused a little.

'It seems that the old man wants to make his eldest son Karp head of the house now. "I am getting old," he says. "My place is to see to the bees." Well, Karp is a good peasant, a careful peasant, but all the same he won't be anything like the old man was as a manager – he hasn't the same sense.'

'Then Karp may like to take up the land and the forest. What do you think?' Nekhlyúdov asked, wishing to get from his nurse all that she knew about her neighbours.

'Scarcely, sir,' she replied. 'The old man hasn't told his son anything about his money. As long as he lives and the money is in his house, the old man will control things; besides, they go in chiefly for carting.'

'And you think the old man won't consent?'

'He will be afraid.'

'But what of?'

'But how can a serf belonging to a master let it be known what he has got, sir? In a hapless hour he might lose all his money! When he went into business with the inn-keeper and made a mistake, how could he go to law with him? So the money was lost. And with his proprietor he'd get settled at once.'

'Oh, is that it? . . .' said Nekhlyúdov flushing. 'Well, good-bye nurse.'

'Good-bye, dear sir, your Excellence. Thank you kindly.'

Chapter XIV

'HADN'T I better go home?' thought Nekhlyúdov as he approached Dútlov's gate, feeling an indefinite sadness and moral weariness.

But at that moment the new plank gates opened before him with a creak, and in the gateway appeared a handsome, ruddy, fair-haired lad of eighteen dressed as a stage-coach-driver and leading three strong-limbed shaggy horses, which were still perspiring. Briskly shaking back his flaxen hair he bowed to the master.

'Is your father at home, Ilyá?' asked Nekhlyúdov.

'He's in the apiary at the back of the yard,' replied the lad, leading one horse after the other out through the half-open gate.

'No, I'll keep to my intention and make him the offer, and do what depends on me,' Nekhlyúdov thought, and letting the horses pass out he entered Dútlov's large yard. He could see that the manure had recently been carted away: the earth was still dark and damp, and here and there, especially by the gateway, lay bits of reddish, fibrous manure. In the yard and under the high penthouse stood many carts, ploughs, sledges, troughs, tubs, and peasant property of all kinds, in good order. Pigeons flew about and cooed in the shade under the broad strong rafters. There was a smell of manure and tar in the place. In one corner Karp and Ignát were fixing a new transom under a large iron-bound three-horse cart. Dútlov's three sons all bore a strong family resemblance. The youngest, Ilyá, whom Nekhlyúdov had met by the gate, had no beard and was shorter, ruddier, and more smartly dressed than the others. The second, Ignát, was taller, darker, had a pointed beard, and though also wearing boots, a driver's shirt, and a felt hat, had not such a festive and carefree appearance as his younger brother. The eldest, Karp, was still taller, and was wearing bast shoes, a grey coat, and a shirt without gussets. He had a large red beard and looked not only serious but almost gloomy.

'Shall I send father to you, your Excellency?' he asked, coming up to his master and awkwardly making a slight bow.

'No, I'll go myself to the apiary and see his arrangements there . . . but I want to speak to you,' said Nekhlyúdov stepping to the opposite side of the yard so that Ignát should not hear what he was about to say to Karp.

The self-confidence of these two peasants and a certain pride in their deportment, as well as what his nurse had told him, so embarrassed the young master that he did not find it easy to speak of the business he had in mind. He had a sort of guilty feeling and it seemed to him easier to speak to one brother out of hearing of the others. Karp seemed surprised that the master should take him aside, but followed him.

'This is what it is,' Nekhlyúdov began hesitatingly. 'I wanted to ask, have you many horses?'

'We can muster five tróyka teams, and there are some foals too,' Karp answered readily, scratching his back.

'Do your brothers drive the stage-coach?'

'We drive stage-coaches with three tróykas, and Ilyá has been away carting; he's only just back.'

'And does that pay? What do you earn by it?'

'Earnings, your Excellence? At most we feed ourselves and the horses — and thank God for that.'

'Then why don't you take up something else? You might buy some forest or rent land.'

'Of course, your Excellence, we might rent land if there were any handy.'

'That is what I want to propose to you. Instead of the carting business that does no more than keep you, why not rent some thirty desyatíns of land from me? I'll let you have that whole strip beyond Sápov and you could start your own farming on a large scale.'

And Nekhlyúdov, carried away by the plan for a peasant farm which he had repeatedly thought out and considered, went on to explain his offer, no longer hesitatingly. Karp listened very attentively to his master's words.

'We are very grateful to your honour,' he said when Nekhlyúdov, having finished, looked at him inquiringly expecting an answer. 'Of course it is not a bad plan. It's better for a peasant to work on the land than to drive with a whip in his hand. Getting among strangers and seeing all sorts of people, the likes of us get spoilt. There is nothing better for a peasant than to work the land.'

'Then what do you think of it?'

'As long as father is alive what can I think, your Excellence? It is as he pleases.'

'Take me to the apiary. I'll talk to him.'

'This way, please,' said Karp, walking slowly towards the barn at the back. He opened a low door that led to the apiary, and having let his master pass, and shut the door behind him, returned to Ignát and silently resumed his interrupted work.

Chapter XV

NEKHLYÚDOV, stooping, passed from under the shade of the penthouse through the low doorway to the apiary beyond the

yard. Symmetrically placed hives covered with pieces of board
stood in a small space surrounded by a loosely-woven fence of
straw and wattle. Golden bees circled noisily round the hives,
and the place was flooded by the hot brilliant beams of the
June sun. From the door a trodden path led to a wooden shrine
on which stood a small tinsel-faced icon which glittered in the
sunlight. Several graceful young lime trees, stretching their
curly crowns above the thatch of the neighbouring building,
mingled the just audible rustle of their fresh dark-green foliage
with the humming of the bees. On the fine curly grass that
crept in between the hives lay black and sharply defined
shadows of the roofed fence, of the lime trees, and of the
hives with their board roofs. At the door of a freshly-thatched
wooden shed that stood among the limes could be seen the
short, bent figure of an old man whose uncovered grey head,
with a bald patch, shone in the sun. On hearing the creak of
the door the old man turned and, wiping his perspiring sunburnt face with the skirt of his smock, came with a mild and
pleasant smile to meet his master.

It was so cosy, pleasant, and quiet in the sun-lit apiary; the
grey-haired old man with the fine, close wrinkles radiating
from his eyes who, with large shoes on his bare feet, came
waddling and smiling with good-natured self-satisfaction to
welcome his master to his own private domain, was so simple-
hearted and kind that Nekhlyúdov immediately forgot the
unpleasant impressions he had received that morning, and his
cherished dream vividly recurred to him. He saw all his peasants as well off and kindly as old Dútlov, and all smiling happily
and affectionately at him because they were indebted to him
alone for their wealth and happiness.

'Wouldn't you like a net, your Excellency? The bees are
angry now, and sting,' said the old man, taking down from the
fence a dirty linen bag attached to a bark hoop and smelling of
honey, and offering it to his master. 'The bees know me and
don't sting me,' he added with the mild smile that seldom left
his handsome sunburnt face.

'Then I don't want it either. Are they swarming yet?'
Nekhlyúdov asked, also smiling, without knowing why.

'Hardly swarming, sir, Dmítri Nikoláevich,' replied the old man, expressing a special endearment by addressing his master by his Christian name and patronymic. 'Why, they've only just begun to be active. You know what a cold spring it has been.'

'I have been reading in a book,' Nekhlyúdov began, driving off a bee which had got into his hair and buzzed just above his ear, 'that if the combs are placed straight up, fixed to little laths, the bees swarm earlier. For this purpose hives are made of boards with cross-pieces. . . .'

'Please don't wave your arm about, it makes them worse,' said the old man. 'Hadn't you better have the net?'

Nekhlyúdov was in pain; but a certain childish vanity made him reluctant to own it, and so he again declined the net and continued to tell the old man about the construction of bee-hives of which he had read in *Maison Rustique* and in which, he believed, there would be twice as many swarms; but a bee stung him on the neck and he grew confused and hesitated in the midst of his description.

'It's true, sir, Dmítri Nikoláevich,' said the old man, looking with fatherly condescension at his master, 'people do write in books. But it may be that it is written wrongly. Perhaps they say "He'll do as we advise, and then we'll laugh at him." That does happen! How can one teach the bees where to build their comb? They do it themselves according to the hive, sometimes across it and sometimes lengthways. There, please look in,' he added, opening one of the nearest hives and looking into the opening where buzzing bees were crawling about on the crooked combs. 'These are young ones: they have their mind on the queen bee, but they make the comb straight or to one side as best fits the hive,' continued the old man, evidently carried away by his favourite subject and not notic-ing his master's condition. 'See, they're coming in laden to-day. It's a warm day and everything can be seen,' he added, closing the opening and pressing a crawling bee with a rag and then with his hand brushing several from his wrinkled neck. The bees did not sting him, but Nekhlyúdov could hardly refrain from running away from the apiary: they had stung him in three places and were buzzing all round his head and neck.

'How many hives have you?' he asked, stepping back towards the door.

'As many as God has given,' replied Dútlov laughingly. 'One mustn't count them, sir. The bees don't like it. There now, your Excellence, I wanted to ask your honour something,' he continued, pointing to some narrow hives standing near the fence. 'It's about Ósip, your nurse's husband – if you would only speak to him. It's wrong to act so to a neighbour in one's own village.'

'What is bad? . . . Oh, but they do sting!' said the master, with his hand already on the door-handle.

'Well, you see, every year he lets his bees out among my young ones. They ought to have a chance to improve, but the strange bees enter the combs and take the wax from them,' said the old man, not noticing his master's grimaces.

'All right . . . afterwards . . . in a moment . . .' muttered Nekhlyúdov, and unable to bear the pain any longer he ran quickly through the door waving both hands.

'Rub it with earth and it will be all right,' said the old man, following the master into the yard. The master rubbed the places that had been stung with earth, flushed as he gave a quick glance at Karp and Ignát, who were not looking at him, and frowned angrily.

Chapter XVI

'WHAT I wanted to ask your Excellency,' . . . said the old man, pretending not to notice or really not noticing his master's angry look.

'What?'

'Well, you see, we are well off for horses, thank God, and have a labourer, so that the owner's work will not be neglected by us.'

'Well, what about it?'

'If you would be so kind as to accept quit-rent and excuse my lads from service, Ilyá and Ignát could go carting all summer with three teams of horses, and might earn something.'

'Where would they go?'

'Well, that all depends,' interposed Ilyá who had tied the horses under the penthouse and came up to his father. 'The Kadmínski lads went to Rómen with eight tróykas and earned their keep and brought back about thirty rubles for each tróyka; or there's Odessa where they say fodder is cheap.'

'That's what I wanted to talk to you about,' said the master, turning to the old man and trying tactfully to introduce the question of farming. 'Tell me, is it more profitable to go carting than to farm at home?'

'Much more profitable, your Excellence,' Ilyá again broke in, vigorously shaking back his hair. 'At home we've no fodder for the horses.'

'And how much will you earn in a summer?'

'Well, after the spring – though fodder was dear – we carted goods to Kiev and loaded up grits for Moscow in Kursk, and kept ourselves, fed the horses well, and brought fifteen rubles home.'

'There's no harm in working at an honest job be it what it may,' said the master, again addressing the old man, 'but it seems to me that other work might be found. This carting work makes a young fellow go anywhere and see all sorts of people and he may get spoilt,' he added, repeating Karp's words.

'What are we peasants to take up, if not carting?' rejoined the old man, with a mild smile. 'On a good carting job a man has enough to eat himself, and the horses have enough. As to getting spoilt, it's not the first time the lads have been carting, and I used to go myself and got nothing bad from anyone – nothing but good.'

'There's plenty of work you could do at home: land, meadows...'

'How could we, your Excellency?' Ilyá interrupted with animation. 'We are born to this, we know all about it, it's suitable work for us: the pleasantest work for us, your Excellence, is carting.'

'May we ask your Excellence to do us the honour to come to the hut? You have not been there since our house-warming,' said the old man, bowing low and making a sign to his

son. Ilyá raced into the hut and the old man followed with
Nekhlyúdov.

Chapter XVII

ON entering the hut the old man bowed again, dusted the
front bench with the skirt of his smock, and asked with a smile:

'What may I offer your Excellency?'

The hut was clean and roomy, with sleeping places near
the ceiling, and bunks. It also had a chimney. The fresh aspen
logs, between which the moss-caulking could be seen, had not
yet turned dark; the new benches and sleeping places had
not yet worn smooth, and the earthen floor was not yet
trodden hard. Ilyá's wife, a thin young peasant woman with
a dreamy oval face, sat on a bunk and rocked a cradle that hung
by a long pole from the ceiling. In the cradle, breathing softly,
lay an infant with eyes closed and outstretched limbs. Karp's
wife, a plump, red-cheeked woman, stood by the oven shred-
ding onions over a wooden bowl, her sleeves turned up above
her elbows, showing her hands and arms tanned to above her
wrists. A pock-marked pregnant woman stood beside the oven
hiding her face with her sleeve. It was hot in the hut, for
besides the heat of the sun there was the heat of the oven, and
there was a strong smell of freshly-baked bread. From the
sleeping places aloft two fair-haired little boys and a girl,
who had climbed up there while awaiting dinner, looked
down with curiosity on the master.

The sight of this prosperity pleased Nekhlyúdov and yet he
felt embarrassed in the presence of these women and children,
who were all looking at him. He sat down on the bench,
blushing.

'Give me a bit of hot bread, I like it,' he said, and flushed still
more.

Karp's wife cut off a big bit, and handed it to the master on a
plate. Nekhlyúdov said nothing, not knowing what to say; the
women were also silent, and the old man kept mildly smiling.

'Really now, what am I ashamed of – just as if I had done
something wrong?' thought Nekhlyúdov. 'Why shouldn't

I suggest their starting a farm? What stupidity . . . !' Yet he still kept silent.

'Well, sir, how about the lads? What are your orders?' said the old man.

'Well I should advise you not to let them go but to find them work here,' Nekhlyúdov said, suddenly gaining courage. 'Do you know what I have thought of for you? Join me in buying a grove in the State forest, and some land too.'

'How could I, your Excellence? Where is the money to come from?' the old man interrupted him.

'Only a small grove, you know, for about two hundred rubles,' Nekhlyúdov remarked.

The old man smiled grimly.

'If I had the money, why not buy it?' he said.

'Have you no longer that amount?' said the master reproachfully.

'Oh sir, your Excellence!' said the old man in a sorrowful voice, looking towards the door. 'I have enough to do to keep the family. It's not for us to buy groves.'

'But you have the money, why should it lie idle?' insisted Nekhlyúdov.

The old man suddenly became greatly agitated; his eyes glittered and his shoulders began to twitch.

'Maybe evil persons have said it of me,' he began in a trembling voice, 'but believe me, I say before God,' he went on, becoming more and more excited and turning towards the icon, 'may my eyes burst, may I fall through the ground here, if I have anything but the fifteen rubles Ilyá brought home and even then I have the poll-tax to pay. You know yourself we have built the cottage . . .'

'Well, all right, all right!' said the master, rising. 'Good-bye, friends.'

Chapter XVIII

'My God, my God!' thought Nekhlyúdov as he walked home with big strides through the shady avenues of his neglected garden, absent-mindedly plucking twigs and leaves on his way.

'Can it be that all my dreams of the aims and duties of my life
are mere nonsense? When I planned this path of life I fancied
that I should always experience the complete moral satisfaction
I felt when the idea first occurred to me – so why do I now feel
so depressed and sad and dissatisfied with myself?' And he
remembered with extraordinary vividness and distinctness
that happy moment a year before.

He had got up very early that May morning, before anyone
else in the house, feeling painfully agitated by the secret,
unformulated impulses of youth, and had gone first into the
garden and then into the forest, where he wandered about
alone amid the vigorous, luscious, yet peaceful works of
nature, suffering from an exuberance of vague feeling and finding
no expression for it. With all the charm of the unknown his
youthful imagination pictured to him the voluptuous form of a
woman, and it seemed to him that here it was – the fulfilment
of that unexpressed desire. But some other, deeper feeling told
him: 'Not that,' and impelled him to seek something else.
Then his inexperienced, ardent mind, rising higher and higher
into realms of abstraction, discovered, as it seemed to him, the
laws of being, and he dwelt on those thoughts with proud
delight. But again a higher feeling told him: 'Not that,' and
once more agitated him and forced him to continue his search.
Empty of thought and feeling – a condition which always
follows intensive activity – he lay on his back under a tree
and began to gaze at the translucent morning clouds drifting
across the limitless blue sky above him. Suddenly without any
reason tears filled his eyes and, Heaven knows why, a definite
thought to which he clung with delight entered his mind,
filling his whole soul – the thought that love and goodness
are truth and happiness – the only truth and the only happiness
possible in the world. And this time his deeper feeling did not
say: 'Not that,' and he rose and began to verify this new
thought. 'This is it! This! So it is!' he said to himself in ecstasy,
looking at all the phenomena of life in the light of this newly-
discovered and as it seemed to him perfectly novel truth,
which displaced his former convictions. 'What rubbish is all
I knew and loved and believed in,' he said to himself. 'Love,

self-denial — that is the only true happiness — a happiness independent of chance!' and he smiled and flourished his arms. Applying this thought to all sides of life and finding it confirmed by life as well as by the inner voice which told him, 'This is it,' he experienced a new sensation of joyful agitation and delight. 'And so, to be happy I must do good,' he thought, and his whole future presented itself to him no longer in the abstract, but in vivid pictures of a landed proprietor's life.

He saw before him an immense field of action for his whole life, which he would devote to well-doing and in which consequently he would be happy. There was no need to search for a sphere of activity: it lay ready before him; he had a direct duty — he owned serfs. . . . And what a joyful and grateful task lay before him! 'To influence this simple, receptive, unperverted class of people; to save them from poverty, give them a sufficiency, transmit to them an education which fortunately I possess, to reform their vices arising from ignorance and superstition, to develop their morality, to make them love the right. . . . What a brilliant, happy future! And I, who do it all for my own happiness, shall in return enjoy their gratitude, and see myself advancing day by day further and further towards the appointed aim. A marvellous future! How could I have failed to see it before?

'And besides all that,' he thought at the same time, 'what prevents my being happy in the love of a woman, in the joys of family life?' And his youthful imagination painted a still more enchanting future. 'I and my wife, whom I love as no one ever before loved anyone in the world, will always live amid this peaceful poetic nature, with our children and perhaps with my old aunt. We have our mutual love, our love for our children, and we both know that our aim is to do good. We help each other to move towards that goal. I shall make general arrangements, give general and just assistance, carry on the farm, a savings-bank and workshops, while she, with her pretty little head, wearing a simple white dress which she lifts above her dainty foot, walks through the mud to the peasant school, to the infirmary, to some unfortunate peasant who strictly speaking does not deserve aid, and everywhere brings consolation and help. The children, the old men, and the old women, adore her and look on her as an angel – as Providence. Then she returns, and conceals from me the fact that she has been to see the unfortunate peasant and given him some money; but I know it all and embrace her tightly, and firmly and tenderly kiss her lovely eyes, her shyly blushing cheeks, and her smiling rosy lips.'

Chapter XIX

'WHERE are those dreams?' thought the young man now as he neared his house after his visits. 'For more than a year I have been seeking happiness in that way, and what have I found? It is true I sometimes feel that I have a right to be satisfied with myself, but it is a dry, reasoning sort of satisfaction. No, that is not true, I am simply dissatisfied with myself! I am dissatisfied because I do not find happiness here, and I long for happiness so passionately. I have not only experienced no enjoyment, I have cut myself off from all that gives it. Why? What for? Who is the better for it? My aunt was right when she wrote that it is easier to find happiness for oneself than to give it to others. Have my peasants grown richer? Are they more educated or morally more developed? Not at all! They are no better off, and it grows harder for me every day. If I saw my plans succeeding, or met with any gratitude . . . but no, I see a false routine, vice, suspicion, helplessness. I am wasting the best years of my life in vain,' he thought, and remembered that he had heard from his nurse that his neighbours called him a whipper-snapper; that he had no money left in the counting-house, that his newly-introduced threshing machine, to the general amusement of the peasants, had only whistled and had not threshed anything when for the first time it was started at the threshing-floor before a large audience; and that he had to expect officials from the Land Court any day to take an inventory of his estate because, tempted by different new undertakings, he had let the payments on his mortgage lapse. And suddenly, as vividly as the walk in the forest and the dream of a landlord's life had presented themselves to his mind before, so now did his little room in Moscow, where as a student he had sat late at night, by the light of one candle, with his beloved sixteen-year-old friend and comrade. They had read and repeated some dry notes on civic law for five hours on end, and having finished them had sent for supper and gone shares in the price of a bottle of champagne, and discussed the future awaiting them. How very different the future had appeared to the young student! Then it had been full of enjoyment, of varied activities, of brilliant success, and indubitably led them both to what then seemed the greatest blessing in the world – fame!

'He is already getting on, rapidly getting on, along that road,' thought Nekhlyúdov of his friend, 'while I . . .'

But by this time he was already approaching the porch of his house, where ten or more peasant- and domestic-serfs stood awaiting him with various requests, and his dreams were replaced by realities.

There was a tattered, dishevelled, blood-stained peasant woman who complained with tears that her father-in-law wanted to kill her: there were two brothers, who for two years had been quarrelling about the division of a peasant farm between them, and now stood gazing at one another with desperate hatred: and there was an unshaven grey-headed domestic serf, with hands trembling from drunkenness, whom his son, the gardener, had brought to the master with a complaint of his depraved conduct: there was a peasant who had turned his wife out of the house because she had not worked all spring: and there was his wife, a sick woman who did not speak, but sat on the grass near the entrance, sobbing and showing an inflamed and swollen leg roughly bandaged with dirty rags. . . .

Nekhlyúdov listened to all the petitions and complaints, and having given advice to some, settled the disputes of others, and made promises to yet others, went to his room with a mixed feeling of weariness, shame, helplessness, and remorse.

Chapter XX

IN the room occupied by Nekhlyúdov – which was not a large one – there was an old leather couch studded with brass nails, several arm-chairs of a similar kind, an old-fashioned carved and inlaid card-table with a brass rim, which stood open and on which were some papers, and an open, old-fashioned English grand piano with a yellowish case and worn and warped narrow keys. Between the windows hung a large mirror in an old gilt carved frame. On the floor beside the table lay bundles of papers, books, and accounts. In general the whole room had a disorderly and characterless appearance, and this air of untidy occupancy formed a sharp contrast to the stiff, old-fashioned aristocratic arrangement of the other rooms of the large house.

On entering the room Nekhlyúdov angrily flung his hat on the table and sat down on a chair before the piano, crossing his legs and hanging his head.

'Will you have lunch, your Excellence?' asked a tall, thin, wrinkled old woman who entered the room in a cap, a print dress, and a large shawl.

Nekhlyúdov turned to look at her and was silent for a moment as if considering something.

'No, I don't want any, nurse,' he said, and again sank into thought.

The old nurse shook her head at him with vexation, and sighed.

'Eh, Dmítri Nikoláevich, why are you moping? There are worse troubles! It will pass – be sure it will ...'

'But I'm not moping. What has put that into your head, Malánya Finogénovna?' replied Nekhlyúdov trying to smile.

'How can you help moping – don't I see?' the old nurse retorted warmly. 'All alone the whole day long. And you take everything so to heart and see to everything yourself – and now you hardly eat anything. Is it reasonable? If only you went to town or visited your neighbours, but who ever saw the likes of this? You are young to trouble so about everything. ... Excuse me, master, I'll sit down,' she continued, taking a chair near the door. 'Why, you've been so indulgent with them that they're not afraid of anyone. Does a master behave like that? There is nothing good in it; you only ruin yourself and let the people get spoilt. Our people are like that: they don't understand it – really they don't. You might at least go to see your aunt. What she wrote was true. . . .' she ended admonishingly.

Nekhlyúdov grew more and more dejected. He wearily touched the keys with his right hand, his elbow resting on his knee. Some sort of chord resulted, then another, and another. . . . He drew up his chair, took his other hand out of his pocket and began to play. The chords he struck were sometimes unprepared and not even quite correct; they were often trivial and commonplace, and did not indicate that he had any musical talent, but this occupation gave him a kind of indefinite, melancholy pleasure. At every change of harmony he waited with bated breath to see how it would resolve itself, and when a fresh harmony resulted his imagination vaguely supplied what was lacking. It seemed to him that he heard hundreds of melodies: a chorus and an orchestra in conformity with his harmony. What chiefly gave him pleasure was the intensified activity of his imagination which incoherently and fragmentarily, but with amazing clearness, presented him with the most varied, confused, and absurd pictures and images of the past and the future. Now it was the plump figure of White David responding to torment and privation with patience and submission: he saw his round shoulders, his immense hands covered with white hair, and his white lashes fluttering timidly at the sight of his mother's brown sinewy fist. Then he saw his self-confident wet-nurse, emboldened by residence at the master's house, and he imagined her for some reason going about the village and preaching to the serfs that they should hide their money from the landlord, and he unconsciously repeated to himself: 'Yes, one must hide one's money from the landlord.' Then suddenly the small brown head of his future wife – for some reason in tears – presented itself to him, resting on his shoulder. Then he saw Chúris's kindly blue eyes look-ing tenderly at his pot-bellied little son. 'Yes, he sees in him not only a son, but a helper and deliverer. That is love!' whispered Nekhlyúdov to himself. Then he remembered Epifán's mother and the patient, all-forgiving expression he had noticed on her aged face in spite of her one protruding tooth and ugly features. 'Probably I am the first person in the

whole seventy years of her life to notice that,' he thought, and
whispering, 'Strange!' he unconsciously continued to touch
the keys and listen to the sounds they produced. Then he
vividly recalled his flight from the apiary and the expression
on Ignát's and Karp's faces when they obviously wanted to
laugh but pretended not to see him. He blushed, and involuntarily looked round at his nurse, who was still sitting silently
by the door gazing intently at him and occasionally shaking her
grey head. Then suddenly he seemed to see three sweating
horses, and Ilyá's fine powerful figure with his fair curls, his
merrily beaming narrow blue eyes, his fresh ruddy cheeks, and
the light-coloured down just beginning to appear on his lips
and chin. He remembered how afraid Ilyá had been that he
would not be allowed to go carting, and how warmly he had
pleaded for that favourite job; and he suddenly saw a grey,
misty early morning, a slippery highway and a long row of
three-horsed carts, loaded high and covered by bast-matting
marked with big black lettering. The strong-limbed, well-fed
horses, bending their backs, tugging at the traces and jingling
their bells, pull evenly uphill, tenaciously gripping the slippery
road with their rough-shod hoofs. Rapidly descending the hill
a mail-coach gallops towards the train of loaded carts, jingling
its bells which re-echo far into the depth of the forest that
extends along both sides of the road.

'Hey, hey, hey!' shouts the driver of the first cart in a boyish
voice. He has a brass number-plate on his felt hat and flourishes
his whip above his head.

Karp, with his red beard and gloomy looks, strides heavily in
his huge boots beside the front wheel of the first cart. From the
second cart Ilyá thrusts his handsome head out from under a
piece of matting where he has been getting pleasantly warm in
the early sunlight. Three tróykas loaded with boxes dash by
with rattling wheels, jingling bells, and shouts. Ilyá again hides
his handsome head under the matting and drops asleep. And
now it is evening, clear and warm. The boarded gates open
with a creak for the weary tróykas crowded together in the
station yard, and one after another the high, mat-covered carts
jolt over the board that lies in the gateway and come to rest

under the roomy penthouse. Ilyá gaily exchanges greetings with the fair-faced, broad-bosomed hostess, who asks, 'Have you come far? And how many of you will want supper?' and with her bright kindly eyes looks with pleasure at the handsome lad. Now having seen to his horses he goes into the hot crowded house, crosses himself, sits down before a full wooden bowl, and chats merrily with the landlady and his comrades. And here, under the penthouse, is his place for the night, where the open starry sky is visible and where he will lie on the scented hay near the horses, which changing from foot to foot and snorting pick out the fodder from the wooden mangers. He goes up to the hay, turns to the east and, crossing his broad powerful chest some thirty times and shaking back his fair curls, repeats 'Our Father' and 'Lord have mercy!' some twenty times, covers himself head and all with his coat, and falls into the healthy careless sleep of strong young manhood. And now he dreams of the towns: Kiev with its saints and throngs of pilgrims, Rómen with its traders and merchandise, Odessa and the distant blue sea with its white sails, and Tsargrad[1] with its golden houses and white-breasted, dark-browed Turkish women – and thither he flies lifted on invisible wings. He flies freely and easily further and further, and sees below him golden cities bathed in bright radiance, and the blue sky with its many stars, and the blue sea with its white sails, and it is gladsome and gay to fly on further and further. . . .

'Splendid!' Nekhlyúdov whispered to himself, and the thought came to him: 'Why am I not Ilyá?'

---

1 Constantinople.

MEETING A MOSCOW ACQUAINTANCE IN THE DETACHMENT

FROM PRINCE NEKHLYÚDOV'S CAUCASIAN MEMOIRS

LIST OF CHARACTERS IN
MEETING A MOSCOW ACQUAINTANCE

GUSKÓV, nicknamed Guskantíni, condemned for punishment to serve as a private.

PAUL DMÍTRICH, Adjutant.

NICHOLAS IVÁNICH S—, Lieutenant-Captain; a good-natured officer.

NIKÍTA, an Orderly.

MAKATYÚK, another Orderly.

ALEXÉY IVÁNICH, a Captain.

ANDRÉEV, a soldier.

WE were out with a detachment. The work in hand was almost done, the cutting through the forest was nearly finished, and we were expecting every day to receive orders from head-quarters to retire to the fort.

Our division of the battery guns was placed on the slope of a steep mountain range which stretched down to the rapid little mountain river Mechik, and we had to command the plain in front. Occasionally, especially towards evening, on this pictur-esque plain beyond the range of our guns, groups of peaceable mountaineers on horseback appeared here and there, curious to see the Russian camp. The evening was clear, quiet, and fresh, as December evenings usually are in the Caucasus. The sun was setting behind the steep spur of the mountain range to the left, and threw rosy beams on the tents scattered over the mountain side, on the moving groups of soldiers, and on our two guns, standing as if with outstretched necks, heavy and motionless, on the earthwork battery close by. The infantry picket, stationed on a knoll to our left, was sharply outlined against the clear light of the sunset, with its piles of arms, the figure of its sentry, its group of soldiers, and the smoke of its dying camp-fire. To right and to left, half-way down the hill, white tents gleamed on the trodden black earth, and beyond the tents loomed the bare black trunks of the plane forest, where axes continually rang, fires crackled, and trees fell crashing down. On all sides the pale bluish smoke rose in columns towards the frosty blue sky. Beyond the tents, and on the low ground by the stream, Cossacks, dragoons, and artillery drivers trailed along, returning from watering their stamping and snorting horses. It was beginning to freeze; all

389

sounds were heard with unusual distinctness, and one could see far into the plain through the clear rarefied air. The groups of natives, no longer exciting the curiosity of our men, rode quietly over the light-yellow stubble of the maize-fields. Here and there through the trees could be seen the tall posts of Tartar cemeteries, and the smoke of their *aouls*.

Our tent was pitched near the guns, on a dry and elevated spot whence the view was specially extensive. By the tent, close to the battery, we had cleared a space for the games of Gorodki[1] or Choushki. Here the attentive soldiers had erected for us rustic seats and a small table. Because of all these conveniences our comrades the artillery officers, and some of the infantry, liked to assemble at our battery, and called this place 'The Club'.

It was a beautiful evening, the best players had come, and we were playing Gorodki. I, Ensign D., and Lieutenant O. lost two games running, and to the general amusement and laughter of the onlooking officers, and of soldiers and orderlies who were watching us from their tents, we twice carried the winners pick-a-back from one end of the ground to the other. Specially amusing was the position of the enormous, fat Lieutenant-Captain S., who puffing and smiling good-humouredly, with his feet trailing on the ground, rode on the back of the small and puny Lieutenant O. But it was growing late. The orderlies brought three tumblers of tea without any saucers for the whole six of us, and having finished our game we came to the rustic seats. Near them stood a short, bandy-legged man whom we did not know, dressed in a sheepskin coat and with a large, white, long-woolled sheepskin cap on his head. As soon as we approached him he hesitatingly took off and put on his cap several times and repeatedly seemed on the point of coming up to us, but then stopped again. But probably having decided that he could

---

1 Gorodki is a game in which short, thick sticks are arranged in certain figures within squares. Each side has its own square, and each player in turn throws a stick to try to clear out the enemy's square. The side wins which first accomplishes this with the six figures in which the sticks are successively arranged.

no longer remain unnoticed, this stranger again raised his cap, and passing round us approached Lieutenant-Captain S.

'Ah, Guskantini! Well, what is it, old chap?' said S., still continuing to smile good-humouredly after his ride.

Guskantini, as S. called him, put on his cap at once, and made as if to put his hands in the pockets of his sheepskin coat; but on the side turned to me I could see it had no pocket, so that his little red hand remained in an awkward position. I tried to make up my mind what this man could be (a cadet or an officer reduced to the ranks?), and without noticing that my attention (the attention of an unknown officer) confused him, I looked intently at his clothing and general appearance. He seemed to be about thirty. His small round grey eyes seemed to look sleepily and yet anxiously from under the dirty white wool which hung over his face from his shaggy cap. The thick irregular nose between the sunken cheeks accentuated his sickly, unnatural emaciation. His lips, only slightly covered by thin light-coloured moustaches, were continually in motion, as if trying to put on now one, now another expression. But all these expressions seemed unfinished; his face still kept its one predominant expression of mingled fear and hurry. His thin scraggy neck was enveloped in a green woollen scarf, partly hidden under his sheepskin coat. The coat was worn bare and was short; it was trimmed with dog's fur round the collar and at the false pockets. He had greyish check trousers on, and soldier's boots with short unblacked tops.

'Please don't trouble,' said I, when he again raised his cap, looking timidly at me.

He bowed with a grateful look, put on his cap, and taking from his trouser pocket a dirty calico tobacco-pouch tied with a cord, began to make a cigarette.

It was not long since I myself had been a cadet; an old cadet who could no longer act the good-humoured attentive younger comrade to the officers, and a cadet without means. Understanding, therefore, all the wretchedness of such a position for a proud man no longer young, I felt for all who were in that state, and tried to discern their characters and the degree and direction of their mental capacities, in order to be able to judge the extent of their moral suffering. This cadet, or degraded officer, judging by his restless look and the purposely varying expression of his face, seemed to be far from stupid, but very self-conscious, and therefore very pitiable.

Lieutenant-Captain S. proposed another game of Gorodki, the losers, besides carrying the winners pick-a-back, to stand a couple of bottles of claret, with rum, sugar, cinnamon, and cloves, to make mulled wine, which was very popular in our detachment that winter because of the cold weather. Guskantini, as S. again called him, was also asked to join, but before beginning, evidently wavering between the pleasure this invitation gave him and fear of some kind, he led Lieutenant-Captain S. aside and whispered something into his ear. The good-natured Lieutenant-Captain slapped him on the stomach with the palm of his big fat hand, and answered aloud, 'Never mind, old chap, I'll give you credit!'

When the game was finished, and when, the side of the lower-grade stranger having won, he should have ridden on one of our officers, Ensign D., the latter blushed, turned aside to the seats, and offered the stranger some cigarettes by way of ransom. When the mulled wine had been ordered, and one could hear Nikita's bustling arrangements in the orderlies' tent and how he sent a messenger for cinnamon and cloves, and could then see his back, first here and then there, bulging the dirty sides of the tent, – we, the seven of us, sat down by the little table, drinking tea in turns out of the three tumblers and looking out over the plain, which began to veil itself in evening twilight, while we talked and laughed over the different incidents of the game. The stranger in the sheepskin coat took no part in the conversation, persistently refused the tea I repeatedly offered him, and, sitting on the ground Tartar-fashion, made cigarettes one after the other out of tobacco-dust, and smoked them evidently not so much for his own pleasure as to give himself an appearance of being occupied. When it was mentioned that a retreat was expected next day, and that perhaps we should have a fight, he rose to his knees and, addressing only Lieutenant-Captain S., said that he had just been at home with the Adjutant and had himself written out the order to move next day. We were all silent while he spoke, and, though he was evidently abashed, we made him repeat this communication – highly interesting to us. He repeated what he had said, adding, however, that at the time the order arrived, he was *with*, and *sat with*, the Adjutant, *with whom he lived.*

'Mind, if you are not telling us a lie, old chap, I must be off to my company to give some orders for to-morrow,' said Lieutenant-Captain S.

'No.... Why should?... Is it likely?... It is certain...' began the stranger, but stopped suddenly, having evidently determined to feel hurt, frowned unnaturally and, muttering something between his teeth, again began making cigarettes. But the dregs of tobacco-dust that he could extract from his pouch being insufficient, he asked S. to *favour him with the loan of a cigarette.* We long continued among ourselves that monotonous military chatter familiar to all who have been on campaign. We complained, ever in the same terms, of the tediousness and duration of the expedition; discussed our commanders in the same old way; and, just as often before, we praised one comrade, pitied another, were astonished that So-and-so won so much, and that So-and-so lost so much at cards, and so on and so on.

'Our Adjutant has got himself into a mess, and no mistake,' said Lieutenant-Captain S. 'He always used to win when he was on the staff – whoever he sat down with he'd pluck clean – but now these last two months he does nothing but lose. He has not hit it off in this detachment! I should think he's lost 1,000 rubles in money, and things for another 500: the carpet he won of Mukhin, Nikitin's pistols, the gold watch from Sada's that Vorontsov gave him – have all gone.'

'Serves him right,' said Lieutenant O.; 'he gulled everybody, it was impossible to play with him.'

'He gulled everybody, and now he himself is gravelled,' and Lieutenant-Captain S. laughed good-naturedly. 'Guskov, here, lives with him – the Adjutant nearly lost him one day at cards! Really! Am I not right, old chap?' he said, turning to Guskov.

Guskov laughed. It was a pitifully sickly laugh which completely changed the expression of his face. This change suggested to me the idea that I had seen and known the man before, besides, Guskov, his real name, was familiar to me. But how and when I had seen him I was quite unable to remember.

'Yes,' said Guskov, who kept raising his hand to his moustaches and letting it sink again without touching them, 'Paul Dmitrich has been very unlucky this campaign: such a *veine de malheur*,'[1] he added, in carefully spoken but good French, and I again thought I had met, and even often met, him somewhere. 'I know Paul Dmitrich well; he has great confidence in me,' continued he; 'we are old acquaintances – I mean he is fond of me,' he added, evidently alarmed at his own too bold assertion of being an old acquaintance of the Adjutant. 'Paul Dmitrich plays remarkably well, but now it is incomprehensible what has happened to him; he seems quite lost – *la chance a tourné*,'[2] he said, addressing himself chiefly to me.

At first we had listened to Guskov with condescending attention, but as soon as he uttered this second French phrase we all involuntarily turned away from him.

'I have played hundreds of times with him,' said Lieutenant O., 'and you won't deny that it is *strange*' (he put a special emphasis on the word 'strange'), 'remarkably strange, that I never once won even a twenty-kopek piece of him. How is it I win when playing with others?'

'Paul Dmitrich plays admirably: I have long known him,' said I. I had really known the Adjutant for some years; had more than once seen him playing for stakes high in proportion to the officers' means; and had admired his handsome, rather stern, and always imperturbably calm face, his slow Ukrainian pronunciation, his beautiful things, his horses, his leisurely Ukrainian disposition, and especially his ability to play with self-control – systematically and pleasantly. I confess that more than once when looking at his plump white hands with a diamond ring on the first finger as he beat my cards one after

1 Run of ill luck.
2 'The luck has turned.'

the other, I was enraged with this ring, with the white hands, with the whole person of the Adjutant, and evil thoughts concerning him rose in my mind. But on thinking matters over in cool blood I became convinced that he was simply a more sagacious player than all those with whom he happened to play. I was confirmed in this by the fact that when listening to his general reflections on gaming – how, having been lucky starting with a small stake, one should follow up one's luck; how in certain cases one ought to stop playing; that the first rule was to play for *ready-money*, &c., &c. – it was clear that he always won simply because he was cleverer and more self-possessed than the rest of us. And it now appeared that this self-possessed, strong player had, in the detachment, lost completely, not only money, but other belongings as well – which among officers indicates the lowest depth of loss.

'He was always devilish lucky when playing against me,' continued Lieutenant O.; 'I have sworn never to play with him again.'

'What a queer fellow you are, old man!' said S., winking at me so that his whole head moved while he addressed O.; 'you have lost some 300 rubles to him – lost it, haven't you?'

'More!' said the Lieutenant crossly.

'And now you've suddenly come to your senses; but it's too late, old chap! Everyone else has long known him to be the sharper of our regiment,' said S., hardly able to refrain from laughter and highly delighted at his invention.

'Here's Guskov himself – he prepares the cards for him. That is why they are friends, old chap! . . . ' And Lieutenant-Captain S. laughed good-humouredly so that he shook all over and spilt some of the mulled wine he held in his hand. A faint tinge of colour seemed to rise on Guskov's thin, yellow face; he opened his mouth repeatedly, lifted his hands to his moustache and let them drop again to the places where his pockets should have been, several times began to rise but sat down again, and at last said in an unnatural voice, turning to S.:

'This is not a joke, Nicholas Ivanich, you are saying *such things*! And in the presence of people who don't know me and who see me in a common sheepskin coat . . . because . . . ' His voice failed him, and again the little red hands with their dirty nails moved from his coat to his face, now smoothing his moustaches or hair, now touching his nose, rubbing his eye, or unnecessarily scratching his cheek.

'What's the good of talking; everyone knows it, old chap!' continued S., really enjoying his joke and not in the least noticing Guskov's excitement. Guskov again muttered something, and leaning his right elbow on his left knee in a most unnatural position, looked at S. and tried to smile contemptuously.

'Yes,' thought I, watching that smile, 'I have not only seen him before, but have spoken with him somewhere.'

'We must have met somewhere before,' I said to him when, under the influence of the general silence, S.'s laughter began to subside.

Guskov's mobile face suddenly brightened, and his eyes, taking for the first time a sincerely pleased expression, turned to me.

'Certainly; I knew you at once!' he began in French. 'In '48 I had the pleasure of meeting you rather often in Moscow at my sister's – the Ivashins.'

I apologized for not having recognized him in his present costume. He rose, approached me, and with his moist hand irresolutely and feebly pressed mine. Instead of looking at me, whom he professed to be so glad to see, he looked round in an unpleasantly boastful kind of way at the other officers. Either because he had been recognized by me who had seen him some years before in a drawing-room in a dress-coat, or because that recollection suddenly raised him in his own esteem, his face and even his movements, as it seemed to me, changed completely. They now expressed a lively intellect, childish self-satisfaction at the consciousness of that intellect, and a kind of contemptuous indifference. So that I admit, notwithstanding the pitiful position he was in, my old acquaintance no longer inspired me with sympathy, but with an almost inimical feeling.

I vividly recalled our first meeting. In 1848, during my stay in Moscow, I often visited Ivashin. We had grown up together and were old friends. His wife was a pleasant hostess and what is considered an amiable woman, but I never liked her. The winter I visited them she often spoke with ill-concealed pride of her brother, who had lately finished his studies and was, it seemed, among the best-educated and most popular young men in the best Petersburg society. Knowing by reputation Guskov's father, who was very rich and held an important position, and knowing his sister's leanings, I was prejudiced before I met Guskov. One evening, having come to see Ivashin, I found there a very pleasant-looking young man, not tall, in a black swallow-tail coat and white waistcoat and tie; but the host forgot to introduce us to one another. The young man, evidently prepared to go to a ball, stood hat in hand in front of Ivashin, hotly but politely arguing about a common acquaintance of ours who had recently distinguished himself in the Hungarian campaign. He was maintaining that this acquaintance of ours was not at all a hero or a man born for war, as was said of him, but merely a clever and well-educated man. I remember that I took part against Guskov in the dispute and went to an extreme, even undertaking to show that intelligence and education were always in inverse ratio to bravery; and I remember how Guskov pleasantly and cleverly argued that bravery is an inevitable result of intelligence and of a certain degree of development, with which view (considering myself to be intelligent and well educated) I could not help secretly agreeing. I remember also how, at the end of our conversation, Ivashin's wife introduced us to one another and how her brother, with a condescending smile, gave me his little hand on which he had not quite finished drawing a kid glove, and pressed mine in the same feeble and irresolute manner as he did now. Though prejudiced against Guskov, I could not then help doing him the justice of agreeing with his sister that he really was an intelligent and pleasant young man who ought to succeed in society. He was exceedingly neat, elegantly dressed, fresh-looking, and had self-confidently modest manners and a very youthful, almost childlike, appearance which made one unconsciously forgive the expression of self-satisfaction and of a desire to mitigate the degree of his

superiority over you, which his intelligent face, and especially
his smile, always showed. It was reported that he had great
success among the Moscow ladies that winter. Meeting him at
his sister's I could only infer the amount of truth in these
reports from the expression of pleasure and satisfaction he
always wore, and from the indiscreet stories he sometimes
told. We met some half-dozen times and talked a good deal,
or rather he talked a good deal and I listened. He usually spoke
French, in a very correct, fluent, and ornamental style, and
knew how to interrupt others in conversation politely and
gently. In general he treated me and everyone rather condescendingly; and as always happens to me with people who are
firmly convinced that I ought to be treated with condescension and whom I do not know well, I felt that he was quite
right in so doing.

   Now, when he sat down beside me and gave me his hand of
his own accord, I vividly recalled his former supercilious
expression, and thought that he, as one of inferior rank, was
making a rather unfair use of the advantage of his position by
questioning me, an officer, in an off-hand manner, as to what
I had been doing all this time and how I came to be here.
Though I answered in Russian every time, he always began
again in French, in which it was noticeable that he no longer
expressed himself as easily as formerly. About himself he only
told me in passing that after that unfortunate and stupid affair
of his (I did not know what this affair was, and he did not tell
me) he had been three months under arrest, and was afterwards
sent to the Caucasus to the N— Regiment and had now
served three years as a private.

   'You would not believe,' said he, in French, 'what I have
suffered at the hands of the officer sets! It was lucky I formerly
knew this Adjutant we have just been talking about: he is really
a good fellow,' he remarked condescendingly. 'I am living
with him, and it is after all some mitigation. *Oui, mon cher, les
jours se suivent, mais ne se ressemblent pas,*'[1] he added, but
suddenly became confused, blushed, and rose from his seat,

1 'Yes, my dear fellow, the days follow, but do not resemble one another.'

having noticed that the Adjutant we had been talking about was approaching us.

'It is such a consolation to meet a man like you,' whispered Guskov as he was leaving my side; 'there is very very much I should like to talk over with you.'

I told him I should be very glad, though I confess that in reality Guskov inspired me with an unsympathetic, painful kind of pity.

I foresaw that I should feel uncomfortable when alone with him, but I wanted to hear a good many things from him, especially how it was that, while his father was so wealthy, he was poor, as his clothes and habits showed.

The Adjutant greeted us all except Guskov, and sat down beside me where the latter had been.

Paul Dmitrich, whom I had always known as a calm, deliberate, strong gambler and a moneyed man, was now very different from what he had been in the flourishing days of his card-playing. He seemed to be in a hurry, kept looking round at everybody, and before five minutes were over he, who always used to be reluctant to play, now proposed to Lieutenant O. that the latter should start a 'bank'.

Lieutenant O. declined, under pretext of having duties to attend to; his real reason being that, knowing how little money and how few things Paul Dmitrich still possessed, he considered it unwise to risk his three hundred rubles against the hundred or less he might win.

'Is it true, Paul Dmitrich,' said the Lieutenant, evidently wishing to avoid a repetition of the request, 'that we are to leave here to-morrow?'

'I don't know,' replied Paul Dmitrich, 'but the orders are, to be ready! But really we'd better have a game: I would stake my Kabardá[1] horse.'

'No, to-day. . . .'

'The grey one. Come what may! Or else, if you like, we'll play for money. Well?'

---

1 Kabardá is a district in the Térek Territory of the Caucasus, and Kabardá horses are famous for their powers of endurance.

'Oh, but I – I would readily – you must not think —' began Lieutenant O., answering his own doubts, 'but you know, we may have an attack or a march before us to-morrow and I want to have a good sleep.'

The Adjutant rose, and putting his hands in his pockets began pacing up and down. His face assumed the usual cold and somewhat proud expression which I liked in him.

'Won't you have a glass of mulled wine?' I asked.

'I don't mind if I do,' he said, coming towards me.

But Guskov hurriedly took the tumbler out of my hand and carried it to the Adjutant, trying at the same time not to look at him. But he did not notice one of the cords with which the tent was fastened, stumbled over it, and letting the tumbler drop, fell on his hands.

'What a muff!' said the Adjutant, who had already stretched out his hand for the tumbler. Everyone burst out laughing, including Guskov, who was rubbing his bony knee which he could not have hurt in falling.

'That's the way the bear served the hermit,' continued the Adjutant. 'It's the way he serves me every day! He has wrenched out all the tent-pegs stumbling over them.' Guskov, paying no heed to him, apologized, looking at me with a scarcely perceptible, sad smile, which seemed to say that I alone could understand him. He was very pitiable, but the Adjutant, his protector, seemed for some reason to be angry with his lodger and would not let him alone.

'Oh yes, he's a sharp boy, turn him which way you will.'

'But who does not stumble over those pegs, Paul Dmitrich?' said Guskov; 'you yourself stumbled the day before yesterday.'

'I, old fellow, am not in the ranks; smartness is not expected of me.'

'He may drag his feet,' added Lieutenant-Captain S., 'but a private must skip. . . .'

'What curious jokes! . . .' said Guskov, almost in a whisper, with eyes cast down. The Adjutant evidently did not feel indifferent to his lodger, he watched keenly every word he uttered.

'He'll have to be sent to the ambuscades again,' he said, addressing S., and winking towards the degraded one.

'Well, then, tears will flow again,' said S., laughing.

Guskov no longer looked at me, but pretended to be getting tobacco from the pouch which had long been empty.

'Get ready to go to the outposts, old chap,' said S., laughing, 'the scouts have reported that the camp will be attacked to-night, so reliable lads will have to be told off.'

Guskov smiled undecidedly, as if preparing to say something, and cast several imploring looks at S.

'Well, you know I have been before, and I shall go again if I am sent,' muttered he.

'Yes, and you will be sent!'

'Well, and I'll go. What of that?'

'Yes, just as you did at Argun – ran away from the ambuscade and threw away your musket,' said the Adjutant, and turning away from him began telling us about the order for the next day.

It was true that the enemy was expected to fire at the camp in the night, and a movement of some sort was to take place next day. After talking for a while on various subjects of general interest, the Adjutant, as if he had suddenly chanced to recollect it, proposed to Lieutenant O. to have a little game. The Lieutenant quite unexpectedly accepted and they went with S. and the Ensign to the Adjutant's tent, where a green folding-table and cards were to be found. The Captain, who was commander of our division, went to his tent to sleep, the other gentlemen also went away and Guskov and I were left alone.

I had not been mistaken; I really felt uncomfortable alone with him, and I could not help rising and pacing up and down the battery. Guskov walked silently by my side, turning round hurriedly and nervously so as neither to lag behind nor pass before me.

'I am not in your way?' he said, in a meek, sad voice. As far as I could judge in the darkness his face seemed deeply thoughtful and melancholy.

'Not at all,' I answered, but as he did not begin to speak, and I did not know what to say to him, we walked a good while in silence.

The twilight was now quite replaced by the darkness of night, but over the black outlines of the mountains the sheet-lightnings so common there in the evening flashed brightly. Above our heads tiny stars twinkled in the pale-blue frosty sky, and the red flames of smoking camp-fires glared all around: the tents near us seemed grey, and the embankment of our battery a gloomy black. From the fire nearest to us, round which our orderlies sat warming themselves and talking low, a gleam now and then fell on the brass of our heavy guns and made visible the figure of the sentry, as, with his cloak thrown over his shoulders, he walked with measured steps along the embankment.

'You can't think what a relief it is to me to talk to a man like you!' said Guskov, though he had not yet spoken to me about anything. 'Only a man who has been in my position can understand it.'

I did not know what to answer, and again we were silent, though it was evident that he wished to speak out and I wished to hear him.

'For what were you.... What was the cause of your misfortune?' I asked at last, unable to think of any better way to start the conversation.

'Did you not hear about the unfortunate affair with Metenin?'

'Oh yes; a duel, I think. I heard some reference to it,' I answered. 'You see, I have been some time in the Caucasus.'

'No, not a duel, but that stupid and terrible affair! I will tell you all about it if you have not heard it. It was the same year that you and I used to meet at my sister's. I was then living in Petersburg. But first I must tell you that I then had what is called *une position dans le monde*,[1] and a tolerably lucrative if not brilliant one. *Mon père me donnait* 10,000 *par an.*[2] In '49 I was promised a place in the embassy at Turin; an uncle on my mother's side had influence and was always ready to give me a lift. It's now a thing of the past. *J'étais reçu dans la meilleure société de Pétersbourg: je pouvais prétendre*[3] to make a good match. I had

---

1 A position in the world.
2 'My father allowed me 10,000 rubles a year.'
3 'I was received in the best society of Petersburg; I could aspire ...'

learnt – as we all learn at school; so that I possessed no special education. It is true I read a good deal afterwards, *mais j'avais surtout*, you know, *ce jargon du monde*;[1] and, whatever the cause, I was considered one of the leading young men in Petersburg. What raised me most in the general estimation, *c'est cette liaison avec Mme D—*,[2] which was much talked of in Petersburg. But I was awfully young at the time and set little value on these advantages. I was simply young and foolish. What more did I need? At that time in Petersburg that fellow Metenin had a reputation. . . .' And Guskov continued in this manner to tell me the story of his misfortune, which, being quite uninteresting, I will here omit.

'Two months,' continued he, 'I was under arrest and quite alone. I don't know what did not pass through my mind in that time; but, do you know, when it was all over, when it seemed as if every link with the past was severed, it became easier for me. *Mon père, vous en avez entendu parler*[3] surely: he is a man with an iron will and firm convictions; *il m'a déshérité*[4] and ceased all intercourse with me. According to his convictions it was the proper thing to do, and I do not blame him at all; *il a été conséquent.*[5] And I also did not take a step to induce him to change his mind. My sister was abroad. Mme D— was the only one who wrote to me when letters were allowed, and she offered me help; but you will understand that I could not accept it, so that I had none of those trifles which somewhat mitigate such a position, you know – no books, no linen, no private food, nothing. Many, very many thoughts passed through my brain at that time and I began to look at everything with other eyes; for instance, all that noise and gossip about me in Petersburg society no longer interested or flattered me in the least; it all seemed ridiculous. I felt I was myself to blame; I had been careless and young and had spoilt my career, and my only thought was how to retrieve it. And I felt

1 'But in particular I spoke the society jargon.'
2 'Was that liaison with Mme D—.'
3 'My father; you will have heard him spoken of.'
4 'He disinherited me.'
5 'He has been consistent.'

I had strength and energy enough to do it. After my arrest was over, I was, as I told you, sent to the Caucasus to the N— Regiment.

'I thought that here, in the Caucasus,' he continued, growing more and more animated, '*la vie de camp*,[1] the simple, honest men with whom I should be in contact, the war, the dangers – all this would just suit my frame of mind and I thought I should begin life anew. *On me verra au feu*[2] – people would like me, would respect me not for my name only; then I should receive a cross, become a non-commissioned officer and at last be pardoned and should return, *et, vous savez, avec ce prestige du malheur!*[3] But *quel désenchantement!*[4] You can't think how I was mistaken!... You know the officer set of our regiment?' He paused for some time, probably expecting me to say that I knew how bad the society of officers here is; but I did not reply to him. I was disgusted that – on account, no doubt, of my knowing French – he should suppose that I ought to despise the officer set, which on the contrary I, having lived long in the Caucasus, had fully learnt to appreciate, and which I esteemed a thousand times more than the society Mr Guskov had left. I wished to tell him so, but his position restrained me.

'In the N— Regiment the officer set is a thousand times worse than here,' he continued – *J'espère que c'est beaucoup dire*,[5] – so that you can't imagine what it is like! Not to mention the cadets and the soldiers – it was just awful! At first I was well received, that's perfectly true, but afterwards, when they saw I couldn't help despising them – when in those scarcely noticeable everyday relations, you know, they saw that I was a totally different sort of man standing on a far higher level than they – they were exasperated with me and began to retaliate by subjecting me to all kinds of petty indignities. *Ce*

1 Camp life.
2 'I should be seen under fire.'
3 'You know, with the prestige that misfortune gives.'
4 '(But) what a disenchantment!'
5 'I hope that is saying a good deal.'

que j'ai eu à souffrir, vous ne vous faites pas une idée.[1] Then, being obliged to associate with the cadets; and above all, *avec les petits moyens que j'avais, je manquais de tout,*[2] I had only what my sister sent me. A proof of what I have suffered is that I, with my character, *avec ma fierté, j'ai écrit à mon père,*[3] imploring him to send me something, however little. . . . I can understand how after five years of such a life one may become like our cashiered officer Dromov, who drinks with the soldiers and writes notes to all the officers begging them to *lend* him three rubles, and signs himself, "*Tout à vous,* Dromov." One needs a character like mine in order not to sink quite into the mire in this terrible position.' He then walked silently by my side for a long time. '*Avez-vous un papiros?*'[4] he said at last. 'Yes, . . . where had I got to? Oh yes, I could not stand it. I don't mean physically, for although it was bad enough and I suffered from cold and hunger and lived like a soldier, yet the officers still had a sort of regard for me. I still had a kind of *prestige* in their eyes. They did not send me to do sentry duty or drill. I could not have borne that. But morally I suffered terribly, and above all I could see no escape from this position. I wrote to my uncle imploring him to transfer me to this regiment, which is at least on active duty, and I thought that here Paul Dmitrich, *qui est le fils de l'intendant de mon père,*[5] would be of use to me. My uncle did this much for me, and I was transferred. After that other regiment this seemed an assembly of courtiers. And Paul Dmitrich was here; he knew who I was, and I was capitally received—at my uncle's request. . . . Guskov, *vous savez.* But I noticed that these people, without education or culture, cannot respect a man nor show him respect when he is not surrounded by an aureole of wealth and rank. I noticed how, little by little, when they saw that I was poor, their behaviour to me became more and more careless, and at last almost contemptuous. It is dreadful, but it is perfectly true.

---

1 'You can have no idea of what I had to suffer.'
2 'With the small means I had, I lacked everything.'
3 'With my pride, I wrote to my father.'
4 'Have you a cigarette?'
5 'Who is the son of my father's steward.'

'Here I have been in action, have fought, *on m'a vu au feu*,'[1] he continued, 'but when will it end? Never, I think! And my strength and energy are beginning to fail. And then I had imagined *la guerre, la vie de camp*,[2] but it turns out to be quite different from what I expected: dressed in a sheepskin, in soldier's boots, unwashed, you are sent to the outposts and lie all night in a ditch with some Antonov or other who has been sent into the army for drunkenness, and at any moment you may be shot from behind a bush – you or Antonov, all the same. . . . That is not courage! It is horrible. *C'est affreux, ça tue.*'[3]

'Well, but you may be made a non-commissioned officer for this expedition, and next year may become an ensign,' I said.

'Yes, possibly. I was promised it, but that would be another two years and it is very doubtful. And does anyone realize what two such years mean? Just imagine the life with this Paul Dmitrich: gambling, rough jokes, dissipation. . . . You want to speak out about something that has risen in your soul, but you are not understood or you are laughed at. They talk to you not to communicate their thoughts, but to make a fool of you if possible. And it's all so vulgar, coarse, horrid; and all the time you feel you are a private – they always make you feel that. That is why you can't imagine what a pleasure it is to talk *à cœur ouvert*[4] to a man like you!'

I could not imagine what sort of a man I was supposed to be and therefore did not know how to reply to him.

'Will you have supper?' at this moment asked Nikita, who had approached unseen in the darkness, and who, I noticed, was not pleased at the presence of my visitor: 'there's nothing but dumplings and a little beef left.'

'And has the Captain had his supper?'

'He's asleep long ago,' said Nikita, crossly.

---

1 'I have been seen under fire.'
2 War, camp-life.
3 'It is dreadful, it is killing.'
4 'Quite frankly.'

On my telling him to bring us something to eat and some vodka, he muttered discontentedly and went slowly to his tent. However, after grumbling there a bit, he brought us the cellaret, on which he placed a candle (round which he first tied a piece of paper to keep the wind off), a saucepan, a pot of mustard, a tin cup with a handle, and a bottle of vodka bitters. Having arranged all this, Nikita stood some time near us and watched with evident disapproval while Guskov and I drank some of the spirit. By the dim light of the candle shining through the paper the only things one could see amid the surrounding darkness were the sealskin with which the cellaret was covered, the supper standing on it, and Guskov's face, his sheepskin coat, and the little red hands with which he took the dumplings out of the saucepan. All around was black, and only by looking intently could one discern the black battery, the equally black figure of the sentry visible over the breastwork, the camp-fires around, and the reddish stars above. Guskov smiled just perceptibly in a sad and bashful way as if it were awkward for him to look me in the eyes after his confession. He drank another cup of vodka and ate greedily, scraping out the saucepan.

'Yes, it must at any rate be some relief to you,' I remarked, in order to say something, 'to be acquainted with the Adjutant; I have heard he is a very decent fellow.'

'Yes,' he answered, 'he is a kind-hearted man, but he can't help being what he is; he can't be a man, with his education one can't expect it,' and he suddenly seemed to blush. 'You noticed his coarse jokes to-day about the ambuscades.' And Guskov, in spite of my repeated efforts to turn the conversation, began to justify himself to me and to demonstrate that he did not run away from the ambuscades, and that he was not a coward as the Adjutant and Captain S. wished to imply.

'As I told you,' he said, wiping his hands on his sheepskin, 'people of that kind can't be considerate to a man who is a private and who has but little money: that is beyond them. And these last five months, during which it has somehow happened that I have received nothing from my sister, I have noticed how they have changed towards me. This sheepskin

I bought of a soldier, and which is so worn that there is no warmth in it' (here he showed me the bare skirt of the coat), 'does not inspire him with sympathy or respect for my misfortunes, but only contempt which he is unable to conceal. However great my need, as, for instance, at the present time, when I have nothing to eat except the soldiers' buckwheat, and nothing to wear,' he continued, seemingly abashed, and pouring out for himself yet another cup of vodka, 'he does not think of offering to lend me any money, although he knows that I should certainly repay him, but he waits that I, in my position, should ask him for it. You understand what it would mean for me to have to go to him. Now, to you, for instance, I could say quite straight: *Vous êtes au-dessus de cela, mon cher, je n'ai pas le sou.*[1] And do you know,' said he, looking desperately into my eyes, 'I tell you straight, I am now in terrible difficulties; *pouvez-vous me prêter dix roubles argent?*[2] My sister must send me something by the next mail, *et mon père. . . .*'

'Oh, with pleasure,' said I, though on the contrary it was painful and vexatious, especially because, having lost at cards the day before, I myself had only a little over five rubles and they were in Nikita's possession. 'Directly,' I said, rising, 'I will go and get them from the tent.'

'No, it will do later, *ne vous dérangez pas.*'[3]

But without listening to him I crept into the closed tent where my bed stood and where the Captain lay asleep.

'Alexey Ivanich, please lend me ten rubles till our allowances are paid,' said I to the Captain, shaking him.

'What! cleared out again? And it's only yesterday you resolved not to play any more!' said the Captain, still half-asleep.

'No, I have not been playing! But I want it – please lend it me.'

---

1 'You are above that [i.e. above despising me for my misfortunes], my dear fellow, I have not a halfpenny.'
2 'Can you lend me ten rubles?'
3 'Do not trouble yourself.'

'Makatyuk!' shouted the Captain to his orderly, 'get me the money-box and bring it here.'

'Hush, not so loud,' I said, listening to Guskov's measured footsteps outside the tent.

'What! . . . Why not so loud?'

'Oh, that fellow in the ranks asked me for a loan. He's just outside.'

'If I had known that, I would not have given it you,' remarked the Captain. 'I have heard about him, he's the dirtiest young scamp.'

Still the Captain let me have the money all the same, ordered the money-box to be put away and the tent properly closed, and again repeating, 'If I had known what it was for I would not have given it you,' he wrapped himself, head and all, in his blanket. 'Remember you owe me thirty-two now!' he shouted after me.

When I came out of the tent Guskov was pacing up and down in front of the little seats, his short bandy-legged figure in the ugly cap with the long white wool disappearing in the darkness and reappearing as he passed in and out of the candle-light. He pretended not to notice me. I gave him the paper-money. He said '*Merci*,' and crumpling it up he put it in his trouser-pocket.

'I suppose play is in full swing at Paul Dmitrich's now!' he then began.

'Yes, I suppose so.'

'He plays so queerly, always *à rebours*,[1] and does not hedge. When you have luck it is all right, but when it goes against you you may lose terribly. He is a proof of it. On this expedition he has lost more than fifteen hundred rubles, counting the things he has lost. And with what self-control he used to play formerly! So that that officer of yours seemed even to doubt his honesty.'

'Oh, he did not mean anything. . . . Nikita, have we any Caucasian wine left?' I asked, very much relieved by Guskov's loquacity. Nikita grumbled again, but brought us the wine all

1 Reversing.

the same, and again crossly watched Guskov emptying his cup.
In Guskov's manner the former nonchalance again became
apparent. I wished him to go away, and thought he stopped
only because he did not like to go immediately after receiving
the money. I was silent.

'How could you, with means at your disposal and no necessity, *de gaieté de cœur*[1] make up your mind to come and serve in
the Caucasus? That is what I don't understand,' he said.

I tried to justify myself for this step that seemed to him so
strange.

'I can imagine how uncongenial the society of these officers
must be to you: men without an idea of education. It is
impossible for you and them to understand one another.
Why, you may live here for ten years, and except cards and
wine and talk about rewards and campaigns, you will see
nothing and hear nothing.'

I did not like his being so certain that I shared his opinion,
and I assured him with perfect sincerity that I was very fond of
cards and wine, and of talks about campaigns, and that I did not
wish for better comrades than those I had. But he would not
believe me.

'Oh, you do not really mean it,' he continued; 'and the
absence of women – I mean *femmes comme il faut*[2] – is not that a
terrible privation? I don't know what I wouldn't give to
transport myself into a drawing-room now, and take a peep,
though but through a crack, at a charming woman.'

He was silent a moment and drank another cup of wine.

'O God, O God! It is still possible we may some day meet
again in Petersburg among men, live with human beings, with
women.'

He emptied the bottle and said: 'Oh, *pardon*, perhaps you
would have taken some more, I am so terribly absent-minded.
And I'm afraid I have drunk too much, *et je n'ai pas la tête forte*.[3]

---

1 From light-heartedness.
2 Women of good breeding.
3 'And I have not a strong head.'

There was a time when I lived on the Morskaya[1] *au rez-de-chaussée.*[2] I had a delightful little flat and furniture – you know I had a knack for arranging things elegantly and not too expensively. It is true *mon père* gave me the crockery, and plants, and excellent silver plate. *Le matin je sortais,*[3] then calls, at five o'clock *régulièrement* I went to dine with her, and often found her alone. *Il faut avouer que c'était une femme ravissante!*[4] Did you not know her? Not at all?'

'No.'

'You know, there was so much of that womanliness about her, that tenderness, and then such love! . . . O God! I did not know how to value my happiness then. . . . Or when we returned from the theatre and had supper together. It was never dull in her company, *toujours gaie, toujours aimante.*[5] Yes, I did not then foresee how rare a joy it was. *Et j'ai beaucoup à me reprocher*[6] in regard to her. *Je l'ai fait souffrir, et souvent*[7] – I was cruel. Oh, what a delightful time it was! But I am wearying you.'

'No, not at all.'

'Then I will tell you about our evenings. I used to enter – oh, that staircase, I knew every plant-pot on it – the very door-handle – all was so nice, so familiar to me – then the ante-room, and then her room. . . . No, it will never, never, return! She writes to me even now; I can, if you like, even show you her letters. But I am no longer what I was – I am ruined, I am no longer worthy of her. . . . Yes, I am completely ruined! *Je suis cassé.*[8] I have neither energy nor pride; nothing, not even nobility. . . . Yes, I am ruined! and no one will ever understand what I have suffered. Everyone is indifferent. I am a lost man! I can never rise again, because I have sunk morally . . . sunk into the mire . . . sunk. . . .' And a real,

1 Morskaya – one of the best streets in Petersburg.
2 On the ground floor.
3 'In the morning I went out.'
4 'It must be admitted that she was a ravishing woman.'
5 'Always gay, always loving.'
6 'And I have much to reproach myself with.'
7 'I made her suffer, often.'
8 'I am broken.'

deep despair sounded in his voice at that moment; he did not look at me, but sat motionless.

'Why give way to such despair?' I said.

'Because I am vile; this life has destroyed me; all that was in me has perished. I no longer suffer proudly, but basely; I have no *dignité dans le malheur.*[1] I am insulted every moment and I bear it all, and go to meet insults half-way. The mud *a déteint sur moi.*[2] I have become coarse myself, have forgotten what I knew, I can't even speak French now, and I feel that I am base and despicable. I can't fight in these surroundings; it is impossible! I might perhaps have been a hero: give me a regiment, gold epaulettes, and trumpeters; but to march side by side with some uncivilized Antonov Bondarenko or other and to think there is no difference between him and me, it is all the same whether I get killed or he does — that is the thought that is killing me. You understand how terrible it is that some ragamuffin may kill me — a man who thinks and feels — and that he might as well kill Antonov by my side, a creature indistinguishable from a brute; and it is quite likely to happen that it is I who will be killed and not Antonov — it is always so, *une fatalité* for all that is lofty or good. I know they call me a coward. Granted that I am a coward. It is true I am a coward and cannot help it; but it is not enough that I am a coward, according to them I am also a beggar and a contemptible fellow. There, I have just begged money from you, and you have a right to despise me. No, take back your money,' and he held out to me the crumpled note; 'I want you to respect me.' He covered his face with his hands and began to cry, and I did not in the least know what to say or do.

'Don't go on like that,' said I; 'you are too sensitive; you should not take things so much to heart: don't analyse but look at things simply. You say yourself that you are a man of character; face your task, you have not much longer to suffer,' I said to him very incoherently, for I was excited both by feelings of pity and by a feeling of repentance at having

---

1 Dignity in misfortune.
2 'Has stained me.'

allowed myself to condemn a man who was truly and deeply suffering.

'Yes,' he began; 'had I but once since I came into this hell heard a single word of advice, sympathy, or friendship – a single human word such as I hear from you – I might have borne everything calmly, have faced my task, and even behaved like a soldier; but now it is terrible. . . . When I reason sanely I long for death. Why should I care for a life of dishonour, or for myself who am dead to all that is good in life? But at the least sign of danger I can't help craving for this vile life and guarding it as if it were something very precious, and I can't, *je ne puis pas*,[1] master myself. . . . That is, I can,' he continued, after a moment's pause; 'but it costs me too great an effort, a tremendous effort when I am alone. When others are present, and in ordinary circumstances when going into action, I am brave enough – *j'ai fait mes preuves*,[2] – because I have self-love and am proud – that is my fault – and in the presence of others . . . I say, let me spend the night with you – they'll be playing all night in our tent. I can sleep anywhere – on the ground.'

While Nikita was making up a bed we rose, and again, in the dark, began walking up and down the battery. Guskov must really have had a very weak head, for after only two cups of vodka and two glasses of wine he was unsteady on his feet. When we had walked away from the candle I noticed that he put the ten-ruble note, which he had held in his hand all through the foregoing conversation, back into his pocket, trying not to let me see it. He continued to say that he felt he might yet rise if he had a man like myself to take an interest in him.

We were about to enter the tent to go to bed when suddenly a cannon-ball whistled over us and struck into the ground not far off. It was very strange: the quiet, sleeping camp, our conversation – and suddenly the enemy's ball flying, God knows whence, right in among our tents: so

1 'I cannot.'
2 'I have shown it.'

strange that it was some time before I could realize what had happened. But one of our soldiers, Andreev, who was pacing up and down the battery on guard, came towards me.

'He's sneaked within range. There's the place he fired from,' remarked he.

'The Captain must be roused,' said I, and glanced at Guskov.

He had crouched nearly to the earth and stammered, trying to say something, 'This . . . this . . . is unple . . . this is . . . most . . . absurd.' He said no more, and I did not see how and where he suddenly vanished.

In the Captain's tent a candle was lit and we heard him coughing, as he always did on waking; but he soon appeared, demanding the linstock to light his little pipe with.

'What's the matter, old man?' said he, smiling. 'It seems I am to have no sleep to-night; first you come with your "fellow from the ranks", and now it's Shamyl. What are we going to do? Shall we reply or not? Nothing was mentioned about it in the orders?'

'Nothing at all. There he is again,' said I; 'and this time with two guns.'

And, in fact, before us, a little to the right, two fires were seen in the darkness like a pair of eyes, and then a ball flew past, as well as an empty shell, probably one of our own returned to us – which gave a loud and shrill whistle. The soldiers crept out of the neighbouring tents and could be heard clearing their throats, stretching themselves, and talking.

'Hear him a-whistling through the fuse-hole just like a nightingale!' remarked an artilleryman.

'Call Nikita!' said the Captain, with his usual kindly banter. 'Nikita, don't go hiding yourself; come and listen to the mountain nightingales.'

'Why not, y'r honour?' said Nikita, as he came up and stood by the Captain. 'I have seen them nightingales and am not afraid of 'em; but there's that guest who was here a moment ago drinking your wine, he cut his sticks soon enough when he heard 'em; went past our tent like a ball, doubled up like some animal.'

'Well, someone must ride over to the Chief of Artillery,' said the Captain to me in a grave and authoritative tone, 'to ask whether we are to reply to the shots or not. We can't hit anything, but we can shoot for all that. Be so good as to go and ask. Order a horse to be saddled, you'll get there quicker; take my Polkan, if you like.'

Five minutes later the horse was brought, and I started to find the Chief of Artillery.

'Mind, the watchword is *pole*,' whispered the careful Captain, 'or you won't be allowed to pass the cordon.'

It was barely half a mile to where the Chief of Artillery was stationed. The whole way lay among tents. As soon as I had left the light of our own camp-fires behind, it was so dark that I could not even see my horse's ears – only the camp-fires, which seemed now very near, now very far away, flickered before my eyes. Having given the horse the rein and let him take his own course for a little, I began to distinguish the white four-cornered tents, and then the black ruts of the road. Half an hour later, after having asked my way some three or four times, twice stumbled over tent-pegs and been sworn at each time from within the tent, and after having been twice stopped by sentries, I reached the Chief of Artillery at last.

While on my way I heard two more shots fired at our camp, but they did not reach the place where the staff was stationed. The Chief of Artillery ordered not to fire, especially now that the enemy had ceased firing; so I returned, leading my horse and making my way on foot among the infantry tents. More than once, while passing a soldier's tent in which I saw a light, I slackened my pace to listen to a tale told by some wag, or to a book read out by some 'literate' person, to whom a whole company listened, tightly packed inside and crowding outside the tent and now and then interrupting the reader with their remarks, or I caught merely some scrap of conversation about an expedition, about home, or about the officers.

Passing one of the tents of the 3rd Battalion, I heard Guskov's loud voice speaking very merrily and confidently. He was answered by young voices, not of privates but of gentlemen, as merry as his own. This was evidently a cadet's or sergeant-major's tent. I stopped.

'I have long known him,' Guskov was saying. 'When I was in Petersburg he often came to see me and I visited him. He belonged to very good society.'

'Whom are you talking about?' asked a tipsy voice.

'About the prince,' answered Guskov. 'We are related, you know; more than that, we are old friends. You know, gentlemen, it is a good thing to have such an acquaintance. He is awfully rich, you see. A hundred rubles is nothing to him; so I've taken a little off him till my sister sends me some.'

'Well, then send . . .'

'All right! . . . Savelich, old boy!' came Guskov's voice from the tent as he drew near to the entrance; 'here are ten rubles, go to the canteen and get two bottles of Kahetinsky. . . . What else, gentlemen? Speak up!' and Guskov, bare-headed and with hair dishevelled, reeled out of the tent. Throwing open his sheepskin and thrusting his hands into the pockets of his greyish trousers, he stopped at the entrance. Though he was in the light and I in the dark, I trembled with fear lest he should see me, and moved on, trying not to make a noise.

'Who's there?' shouted Guskov at me in a perfectly tipsy voice. The cold air evidently had an effect on him. 'What devil is prowling about there with a horse?'

I did not reply, and silently found my way out on to the road.

LUCERNE
FROM PRINCE NEKHLYÚDOV'S MEMOIRS

LUCERNE

8th July, 1857.

LAST night I arrived at Lucerne, and put up at the Schweizerhof, the best hotel.

Lucerne, an ancient town and the capital of the canton, situated on the shore of the Lake of Lucerne, says Murray, is one of the most romantic places in Switzerland: here three important high roads meet, and it is only one hour by steamboat to Mount Rigi, from which one of the most magnificent views in the world can be seen.

Whether this be right or not, other guide-books say the same, and so tourists of all nationalities, especially the English, flock there.

The magnificent five-storeyed Schweizerhof Hotel has been recently erected on the quay, close to the lake at the very place where of old there was a roofed and crooked bridge[1] with chapels at its corners and carvings on its beams. Now, thanks to the enormous influx of English people, their needs, their tastes, and their money, the old bridge has been torn down and a granite quay, as straight as a stick, erected, on which straight, rectangular, five-storeyed houses have been built, in front of which two rows of little lindens with stakes to them have been planted, between which the usual small green benches have been placed. This is a promenade, and here Englishwomen wearing Swiss straw hats, and Englishmen in stout and comfortable clothes, walk about enjoying the work they have inspired. Perhaps such quays and houses and lime trees and Englishmen are all very well in some places, but

1 The Hofbrücke, removed in 1852.

not here amid this strangely majestic and yet inexpressibly genial and harmonious Nature.

When I went up to my room and opened the window facing the lake I was at first literally blinded and shaken by the beauty of that water, those mountains, and the sky. I felt an inward restlessness and a need to find expression for the emotion that filled my soul to overflowing. At that moment I felt a wish to embrace someone, to hug him closely, to tickle and pinch him – in a word to do something extraordinary to myself and to him.

It was past six and had rained all day, but was now beginning to clear up. The lake, light-blue like burning sulphur, and dotted with little boats which left vanishing tracks behind them, spread out before my windows motionless, smooth, and apparently convex between its variegated green shores, then passed into the distance where it narrowed between two enormous promontories, and, darkening, leaned against and disappeared among the pile of mountains, clouds, and glaciers, that towered one above the other. In the foreground were the moist, fresh-green, far-stretching shores with their reeds, meadows, gardens, and chalets; further off were dark-green wooded promontories crowned by ruined castles; in the background was the rugged, purple-white distance with its fantastic, rocky, dull-white, snow-covered mountain crests, the whole bathed in the delicate, transparent azure of the air and lit up by warm sunset rays that pierced the torn clouds. Neither on the lake nor on the mountains, nor in the sky, was there a single precise line, or one precise colour, or one unchanging moment: everywhere was motion, irregularity, fantastic shapes, an endless intermingling and variety of shades and lines, and over it all lay tranquillity, softness, unity, and inevitable beauty. And here, before my very window, amid this undefined, confused, unfettered beauty, the straight white line of the quay stretched stupidly and artificially, with its lime trees, their supports, and the green benches – miserable, vulgar human productions which did not blend with the general harmony and beauty as did the distant chalets and ruins, but on the contrary clashed coarsely with it. My eyes continually encountered that dreadfully straight quay, and I felt a desire to push it away or demolish it, as one would wipe off a black smudge that disfigured the nose just under one's eye. But the embankment with the English people walking about on it remained where it was, and I instinctively tried to find a point of view from which it would not be visible. I found a way to do this, and sat till dinner-time all alone, enjoying the incomplete, but all the more tormentingly sweet feeling one experiences when one gazes in solitude on the beauty of Nature.

At half-past seven I was called to dinner. In the large, splendidly decorated room on the ground floor two tables were laid for at least a hundred persons. For about three minutes the silent movement of assembling visitors continued – the rustle of women's dresses, light footsteps, whispered discussions with the very polite and elegant waiters – but at last all the seats were occupied by men and women very well and even richly and generally most immaculately dressed. As usual in Switzerland the majority of the visitors were English, and therefore the chief characteristic of the common table was the strict decorum they regard as an obligation – a reserve not based on pride, but on the absence of any necessity for social intercourse, and on content with the comfortable and agreeable satisfaction of their requirements. On all sides gleamed the whitest of laces, the whitest of collars, the whitest of teeth – natural or artificial – and the whitest of complexions and hands. But the faces, many of them very handsome, expressed only a consciousness of their own well-being and a complete lack of interest in all that surrounded them unless it directly concerned themselves; and the whitest of hands in rings and mittens moved only to adjust a collar, to cut up beef, or to lift a wine glass: no mental emotion was reflected in their movements. Occasionally families would exchange a few words among themselves in subdued voices about the pleasant flavour of this or that dish or wine, or the lovely view from Mount Rigi. Individual tourists, men and women, sat beside one another not even exchanging a look. If occasionally some two among these hundred people spoke to one another it was sure to be about the weather and the ascent of Mount Rigi. Knives and forks moved on the plates with scarcely any sound, food was taken a little at a time, peas and other vegetables were invariably eaten with a fork. The waiters, involuntarily subdued by the general silence, asked in a whisper what wine you would take. At such dinners I always feel depressed, uncomfortable, and at last melancholy. I always feel as if I were guilty of something and am being punished, as I used to be when, as a child, I was put in a chair when I had been naughty, and ironically told: 'Rest yourself, my dear!' while my youthful blood surged in my veins and I heard the merry shouts of my brothers in the next room. Formerly I tried to rebel against the feeling of oppression I experienced during such dinners, but in vain: all those inanimate countenances have an insuperable effect on me and I become similarly inanimate myself. I wish nothing, think nothing, and cease even to observe what is going on. At first I used to try to talk to my neighbours; but except for phrases apparently repeated a hundred thousand times in the same place and by the same people I got no response. And yet not all these frozen people are stupid and unfeeling, on the contrary many of them, no doubt, have an inner life just such as my own, and in many of them it may be much more complex and interesting. Then why do they deprive themselves of one of life's greatest pleasures – the enjoyment that comes from the intercourse of man with man?

How different it was in our Paris *pension*, where some twenty of us, of various nationalities, professions, and dispositions, under the influence of French sociability used to meet at the common table as at a game! There, from one end of the table to the other, conversation, interspersed with jests and puns, even if in broken language, at once became general. There everyone, not troubling how it would sound, said anything that came into his head. There we had our philosopher, our debater, our *bel esprit*, and our butt, all in common. There immediately after dinner we pushed away the table and, in time and out, danced the polka on the dusty carpet till late in the evening. There, even if we were inclined to flirt and were not very clever or respectable, we were human beings. The Spanish countess with her romantic adventures, the Italian abbé who declaimed the *Divine Comedy* after dinner, the American doctor who had the entrée to the Tuileries, the young playwright with long hair, and the pianist who, according to her account, had composed the best polka in the world, the unhappy widow who was a beauty and had three rings on every finger – we all treated one another like human beings, in a friendly if superficial manner, and carried away, some of us light, and others sincere and cordial, memories. But of these English at the *table d'hôte*, I often think as I look at all these silk dresses, laces, ribbons, rings, and pommaded locks, how many live women would be happy and make others happy with these adornments. It is strange to think how many potential friends and lovers – very happy friends and lovers – may be sitting there side by side without knowing it, and, God knows why, will never know it and never give one another the happiness they desire so much and which they might so easily give.

I began to feel depressed, as always after such a dinner, and without finishing my dessert went in very low spirits to stroll about the town. The narrow, dirty, unlighted streets, the shops closing, the encounters I had with tipsy workmen and with women going bareheaded to fetch water, or others wearing hats who flitted along the walls of the side-streets and continually glanced round, not only did not dispel my ill-humour but even increased it. It had already grown quite dark in the streets when, without looking around me and without any thought in my head, I turned back to the hotel hoping by sleep to rid myself of my dismal frame of mind. I was feeling terribly chilled at heart, lonely and depressed, as sometimes happens without cause to those who have just arrived at a new place.

Looking at nothing but the ground at my feet I walked along the quay towards the Schweizerhof, when I was suddenly struck by the sound of some strange but exceedingly sweet and agreeable music. These sounds had an immediately vivifying effect on me, as if a bright cheerful light had penetrated my soul. I felt myself happy and cheerful. My dormant attention was again alive to all the objects surrounding me. The beauty of the night and of the lake, to which I had been feeling indifferent, suddenly struck me joyfully like a novelty. In an instant I involuntarily noticed both the heavy grey patches of cloud on the dark blue of the sky lit up by the rising moon, the smooth dark-green lake with the little lights reflected on it, and the mist-covered mountains in the distance; I heard the croaking of the frogs from Freschenburg, and the fresh limpid whistle of quails on the opposite shore. But directly in front of me, on the spot whence the sounds to which my attention was chiefly directed came, I saw amid the semi-darkness a throng of people collected in a half-circle in the middle of the road, and at some short distance from them a tiny man in black clothes. Behind the people and the man the black poplars in the garden were gracefully silhouetted on the dark grey and blue ragged sky, and the severe spires on each side of the ancient cathedral towered majestically.

I drew nearer, the sounds became more distinct, and at some distance I could clearly distinguish the full chords of a guitar which vibrated sweetly in the evening air and several voices, which intercepting one another did not actually sing the melody but indicated it by chiming in at the chief passages. The tune was something in the nature of a charming and graceful mazurka. The voices sometimes seemed nearer and sometimes farther away; now you could hear a tenor, now a bass, and now a guttural falsetto with a warbling Tyrolese yodel. It was not a song, but the light, masterly sketch of a song. I could not make out what it was, but it was beautiful. The passionate soft chords of the guitar, that sweet gentle melody, and the lonely little figure of the man in black against the fantastic background of the dark lake, the gleaming moon, the two tall spires silently stretching upwards, and the black poplars in the garden, were all strangely but inexpressibly beautiful, or so it seemed to me.

All the confused and arbitrary impressions of life suddenly received meaning and charm. It was as if a fresh and fragrant flower had bloomed within me. Instead of the weariness, dullness, and indifference towards everything in the world that I had felt a moment before, I suddenly experienced a need of love, a fullness of hope, and a spontaneous joy in life. 'What can I possibly want, what desire?' I involuntarily thought. 'Here it is all around me – beauty, poetry. Inhale full deep draughts of it with all the strength that is in you, enjoying it. What more do you need? It is all yours, and all good...'

I went nearer. The little man seemed to be an itinerant singer from the Tyrol. He stood before the windows of the hotel with one foot advanced, his head thrown back, and while thrumming his guitar was singing his graceful song in those different voices. I immediately felt an affection for him, and gratitude for the change he had brought about in me. As far as I could see, he was dressed in an old black coat, had short black hair, and wore a very ordinary old cap on his head. There was nothing artistic about his attire, but his jaunty, childishly merry pose and movements, with his diminutive stature, produced a touching yet amusing effect. On the steps, at the windows, and on the balconies of the brilliantly lighted hotel, stood ladies resplendent in full-skirted dresses, gentlemen with the whitest of collars, a porter and footmen in gold-embroidered liveries; in the street, in the semicircle of the crowd, and farther along the boulevard among the lime-trees, elegantly dressed waiters, cooks in the whitest of caps and blouses, girls with their arms around one another, and passers-by, had gathered and stopped. They all seemed to experience the same sensation that I did, and stood in silence round the singer, listening attentively. All were quiet, only at intervals in the singing, from far away across the water came the rhythmic sound of a hammer, and from the Freschenburg shore the staccato trills of the frogs intermingling with the fresh, monotonous whistle of the quails.

In the darkness of the street the little man warbled like a nightingale, couplet after couplet and song after song. Though I had drawn close to him, his singing continued to give me great pleasure. His small voice was extremely pleasing, and the delicacy, the taste, and the sense of proportion with which he managed that voice were extraordinary, and showed immense natural gifts. He sang the refrain differently after each couplet and it was evident that all these graceful variations came to him freely and instantaneously.

Among the throng, above in the Schweizerhof and below on the boulevard, appreciative whispers could often be heard, and a respectful silence reigned. The balconies and windows kept filling, and by the hotel lights more and more elegantly dressed men and women could be seen leaning out picturesquely. The passers-by stopped and everywhere in the shadows on the embankment groups of men and women stood under the lime-trees. Near me, separated from the rest of the crowd and smoking cigars, stood an aristocratic waiter and the chef. The chef seemed to feel the charm of the music strongly and at every high falsetto note rapturously winked, nodded, and nudged the waiter in ecstatic perplexity, with a look that said: 'How he sings, eh?' The waiter, by whose broad smile I detected the pleasure the singing gave him, replied to the chef's nudgings by shrugging his shoulders to show that it was hard to surprise him, and that he had heard much better things than this.

In an interval of the singing, while the singer was clearing his throat, I asked the waiter who the man was and whether he came there often.

'Well, he comes about twice a summer,' replied the waiter. 'He is from Aargau – just a beggar.'

'And are there many like him about?' I asked.

'Oh, yes,' replied the man not having at first understood what I was asking, but having afterwards made it out, he added: 'Oh no, he is the only one I know of. There are no others.'

Just then the little man, having finished his first song, briskly turned his guitar over and said something in his German patois, which I could not understand but which caused the crowd to laugh.

'What did he say?' I asked.

'He says his throat is dry and he would like some wine,' replied the waiter near me.

'Well, I suppose he is fond of drink.'

'Yes, such people are all like that,' answered the waiter with a depreciatory gesture of his hand.

The singer raised his cap and with a flourish of the guitar went up to the hotel. Throwing back his head he addressed the gentlefolk at the windows and on the balconies: '*Messieurs et Mesdames*,' he said with a half-Italian and half-German accent and the intonation conjurors employ when addressing their audience: '*Si vous croyez que je gagne quelque chose, vous vous trompez; je ne suis qu'un pauvre tiable.*'[1] He paused and waited a moment in silence, but as no one gave him anything, he again jerked his guitar and said: '*A présent, messieurs et mesdames, je vous chanterais l'air du Righi.*'[2]

The audience up above kept silent, but continued to stand in expectation of the next song; below, among the throng, there was laughter, probably because he expressed himself so queerly and because no one had given him anything. I gave him a few centimes, which he threw nimbly from one hand to the other, and put into his waistcoat pocket. Then putting on his cap again he began to sing a sweet and graceful Tyrolese song which he called '*l'air du Righi*'. This song, which he had left to the last, was even better than the others, and on all sides among the now increased crowd one heard sounds of appreciation. He finished the song. Again he flourished his guitar, took off his cap, held it out, made two steps towards the windows, and again repeated his incomprehensible phrase: '*Messieurs et Mesdames, si vous croyez que je gagne quelque chose* —' which he evidently considered very smart and witty, but in his voice and movements I now detected a certain hesitation and childlike timidity which were the more noticeable on account of his small figure. The elegant audience still stood just as picturesquely grouped in the windows and on the balconies, the lights shining on their rich attire. A few of them talked in decorously subdued voices, apparently about the singer who was standing before them with outstretched hand, others looked with attentive curiosity down at the little

1 'If you think I earn anything you are mistaken. I am only a poor devil.'
2 'Now, gentlemen and ladies, I will sing you the Rigi song.'

black figure; on one balcony could be heard a young girl's merry laughter.

In the crowd below the talking and laughter grew louder and louder. The singer repeated his phrase a third time, in a still feebler voice, and this time he did not even finish it, but again held out his cap, and then drew it back immediately. And for the second time not one of those hundreds of brilliantly dressed people who had come to hear him threw him a single penny. The crowd laughed unmercifully. The little singer seemed to me to shrink still more into himself. He took the guitar in his other hand, lifted his cap above his head, and said: '*Messieurs et Mesdames, je vous remercie, et je vous souhaite une bonne nuit.*'[1] Then he replaced his cap. The crowd roared with merry laughter. The handsome men and women, quietly conversing, gradually disappeared from the balconies. The strolls on the boulevard were resumed. The street that had been quiet during the singing again became animated, only a few persons looked at the singer from a distance and laughed. I heard the little man mutter something to himself. He turned and, seeming to grow still smaller, went quickly towards the town. The merry strollers, still watching him, followed him at a certain distance, and laughed.

My mind was in a whirl. I was at a loss to understand what it all meant, and without moving from the spot where I had been, I senselessly gazed into the darkness after the tiny retreating figure of the man as he went striding rapidly towards the town and at the laughing strollers who followed him. I felt pained, grieved, and above all ashamed for the little man, for the crowd, and for myself, as if it were I who had been asking for money and had received nothing, and had been laughed at. I, too, without looking back and with an aching heart, moved off with rapid steps and went to the entrance of the Schweizerhof. I could not yet account for my emotions, but only knew that something heavy and unsolved filled my heart and oppressed me.

---

1 'Thank you, ladies and gentlemen. I wish you good-night.'

At the brilliantly lit entrance I met the hall porter who politely stepped aside, and an English family. A tall, portly, handsome man with black side-whiskers worn in the English fashion, a black hat on his head, a plaid over his arm, and an expensive cane in his hand, was walking with lazy self-confidence arm in arm with a lady in a grey silk gown, and a cap trimmed with bright ribbons and exquisite lace. Beside them walked a pretty, fresh-complexioned girl wearing a graceful Swiss hat trimmed with a feather *à la Mousquetaire*, and with charming long soft flaxen curls that fell over her fair face. In front of them skipped a ten-year-old girl with rosy cheeks, and plump white knees showing from under the finest embroideries.

'A lovely night!' said the lady in a tender, happy voice, just as I passed them.

'Ohe!' lazily muttered the Englishman, for whom life was so comfortable that he did not even feel like talking. To all of them life in this world was so comfortable, convenient, clean, and easy; their movements and faces expressed such indifference to any other kind of life than their own, such assurance that the porter would step aside for them and bow, and that on returning they would find comfortable rooms and beds, that it all must be so and that they had a right to it all, that I involuntarily contrasted them with the vagrant singer who, tired and perhaps hungry, was escaping ashamed from the laughing crowd, and I realized what it was that weighed on my heart like a stone, and I felt indescribable anger against these people. Twice I walked to and fro past the Englishman, and each time with inexpressible pleasure avoided making way for him and pushed him with my elbow; then darting down the steps I hastened through the darkness in the direction of the town, where the little man had disappeared.

Having overtaken three men who were walking together, I asked them where the singer was. They laughed and pointed straight ahead. He was walking quickly, by himself. No one went near him, and he seemed to me to be angrily muttering something to himself. I caught him up and proposed to him to go somewhere and drink a bottle of wine. He went on walking just as fast and looked disconsolately at me, but when he had made out what I wanted, he stopped.

'Well, I won't refuse it, if you are so kind,' he said. 'There is a small café here, we could go in there. It's a plain place,' he added, pointing to a drink shop which was still open.

The word 'plain' involuntarily suggested to me the idea of not going to the plain café but to the Schweizerhof, where the people were who had listened to him. Though in timid agitation he several times declined to go to the Schweizerhof, saying that it was too fine there, I insisted on it and he walked back along the quay with me pretending not to be at all abashed, and gaily swinging his guitar. Several idle strollers drew near as soon as I went up to the singer and listened to what I was saying: and now, after arguing among themselves, they followed us to the hotel entrance, probably expecting some further performance from the Tyrolese.

I met a waiter in the vestibule and asked him for a bottle of wine, but he merely looked at us with a smile and ran past. The head waiter, to whom I addressed the same request, listened to me seriously, and having scanned the tiny figure of the timid singer from head to foot, sternly told the porter to take us to the room on the left. This room was a bar for common people, the whole furniture consisted of bare wooden tables and benches, and a hunchbacked woman was washing up dishes in a corner. The waiter who came to take our order looked at us with a mildly supercilious smile and, thrusting his hands in his pockets, exchanged remarks with the hunchbacked dish-washer. He evidently wished to let us know that, feeling himself immeasurably superior to the singer in social standing as well as on his own merits, he was not at all offended, but even quite amused, to be waiting on us.

'Will you have *vin ordinaire*?' he asked with a knowing look, winking towards my companion and shifting his napkin from one arm to the other.

'Champagne, and your very best!' said I, trying to assume a haughty and imposing air. But neither the champagne nor my endeavour to look haughty and imposing had any effect on the waiter: he grinned, stood awhile gazing at us, looked deliberately at his gold watch, and went leisurely and with soft steps out of the room as if he were out for a stroll. He soon returned with the wine and with two other waiters. The two waiters sat down near the dish-washer and gazed at us with the amused attention and bland smiles with which parents watch their dear children when they play nicely. Only the hunchbacked dish-washer seemed to look at us with sympathy rather than irony. Though I felt it very uncomfortable and awkward to talk with the singer and entertain him under the fire of those eyes, I tried to do my part with as little constraint as possible. In the lighted room I could see him better. He was a tiny, well-proportioned, wiry man, almost a midget, with bristly black hair, large tearful black eyes without lashes, and a thoroughly pleasant and attractively shaped little mouth. He had short side-whiskers, rather short hair, and his clothes were simple and poor. He was dingy, tattered, sunburnt, and had in general the look of a labourer. He was more like a poor pedlar than an artist. Only in his humid, shining eyes and puckering mouth was there something original and touching. Judging by his appearance he might have been anything from twenty-five to forty years old; he was really thirty-eight.

This is what he told me, with good-natured readiness and evident sincerity, about his life. He was from Aargau. While still a child he had lost his father and mother and had no other relations. He had never had any means of his own. He had been apprenticed to a joiner, but twenty-two years ago a bone of his finger had begun to decay, which made it impossible for him to work. He had been fond of music from his childhood, and began to go round singing. Foreigners occasionally gave him money. He made a profession of it, bought a guitar, and for eighteen years had wandered through Switzerland and Italy singing in front of hotels. His whole belongings were the guitar and a purse, in which he now had only a franc and a half, which he would have to spend that night on food and lodging. He had gone every year to all the best and most frequented places in Switzerland: Zurich, Lucerne, Interlaken, Chamonix, and so on; and was now going round for the eighteenth time. He passed over the St Bernard into Italy

and returned by St Gotthard or through Savoy. It was getting
hard for him to walk now, because a pain in his feet which he
called *Gliederzucht* (rheumatism) got worse every year when he
caught cold, and his eyes and his voice were growing weaker.
In spite of this he was now on his way to Interlaken, Aix-les-
Bains, and over the little St Bernard to Italy, of which country
he was particularly fond; in general he seemed to be very well
satisfied with his life. When I asked him why he was going
home and whether he had any relations there, or a house and
land, his mouth puckered into a merry smile and he replied:
'*Oui, le sucre est bon, il est doux pour les enfants!*'[1] and winked at
the waiters.

I did not understand what he meant, but the group of
waiters burst out laughing.

'I've got nothing, or would I be going about like this?' he
explained. 'I go home because, after all, something draws me
back to my native land.'

And he again repeated, with a sly self-satisfied smile, the
phrase: '*Oui, le sucre est bon!*' and laughed good-naturedly.
The waiters were very pleased and laughed heartily. Only
the hunchbacked dish-washer looked at the little man seriously
with her large kindly eyes and picked up the cap he had
dropped from the bench during our conversation. I had
noticed that wandering singers, acrobats, and even jugglers,
like to call themselves artists, and so I hinted several times to
my companion that he was an artist; but he did not at all
acknowledge that quality in himself, and considered his occupation simply as a means of subsistence. When I asked him
whether he did not himself compose the songs he sang, he was
surprised at so strange a question, and answered: 'How could I?
They are all old Tyrolese songs.'

'But what about the Rigi song – that is not old, is it?' I said.

'No, that was composed about fifteen years ago,' he said.
'There was a German in Basle, a very clever man. He composed it. It's a splendid song! You see, he composed it for the
tourists.'

1 'Yes, sugar is good: it is sweet for children.'

And, translating them into French as he went along, he began repeating to me the words of the Rigi song, which he liked so much:

> 'If you would go up the Rigi
> You need no shoes as far as Weggis
>   (Because you go that far by steamer)
> But in Weggis take a big stick,
> And upon your arm a maiden.
> Drink a glass of wine at starting,
>   Only do not drink too much.
> For he who wants to have a drink
>   Should first have earned . . .

'Oh, it's a splendid song!' he said, as he finished.

The waiters, too, probably considered the song very good, for they came nearer to us.

'Yes, but who composed the music?' I asked.

'Oh, nobody! It comes of itself, you know – one must have something new to sing to the foreigners.'

When the ice was brought and I had poured out a glass of champagne for my companion, he seemed to feel ill at ease, and glancing round at the waiters shifted uneasily in his seat. We clinked glasses to the health of artists; he drank half a glass, and then found it necessary to raise his eyebrows in profound thought.

'It's a long time since I drank such wine, *je ne vous dis que ça.*[1] In Italy the d'Asti wine is good, but this is better still. Ah, Italy! It's splendid to be there!' he added.

'Yes, there they know how to appreciate music and artists,' I said, wishing to lead him back to the subject of his failure that evening before the Schweizerhof.

'No,' he replied. 'There, as far as music is concerned, I cannot give anyone pleasure. The Italians are themselves musicians like none others in the world: I sing only Tyrolese songs – that at any rate is a novelty for them.'

---

1 'I only say that to you.'

'And are the gentlefolk more generous there?' I went on, wishing to make him share my resentment against the guests at the Schweizerhof. 'It couldn't happen there, could it, as it did here, that in an immense hotel frequented by rich people, out of a hundred who listen to an artist not one gives him anything?'

My question had quite a different effect on him from what I had expected. It did not enter his head to be indignant with them: on the contrary he detected in my remark a reflection on his talent, which had failed to elicit any reward, and he tried to justify himself to me.

'One does not get much every time,' he replied. 'Sometimes my voice fails or I am tired. To-day, you know, I have been walking for nine hours and singing almost all the time. That is hard. And the great people, the aristocrats, don't always care to hear Tyrolese songs.'

'But still, how could they give nothing at all?' I insisted.

He did not understand my remark.

'It's not that,' he said, 'the chief thing here is, *on est très serré pour la police*,[1] that's where the trouble is. Here under their republican laws you are not allowed to sing, but in Italy you may go about as much as you please, and no one will say a word to you. Here they allow it only when they please, and if they don't please, they may put you in prison.'

'How is that? Is it possible?'

'Yes, if they caution you once and you sing again they may imprison you. I was there for three months,' he said smiling, as though this were one of his pleasantest recollections.

'Oh, that's dreadful!' I said. 'What for?'

'That is so under the new republican laws,' he continued, growing animated. 'They don't want to understand that a poor fellow must live somehow. If I were not a cripple, I would work. But does my singing hurt anyone? What does it mean? The rich can live as they please, but *un pauvre tiable* like myself mayn't even live. Are these the laws a republic should have? If so, we don't want a republic — isn't that so, dear sir? We don't

---

1 'One is much cramped by the police.'

want a republic, but we want – we simply want . . . we want' –
he hesitated awhile – 'we want natural laws.'

I filled up his glass.

'You are not drinking,' I said to him.

He took the glass in his hand and bowed to me.

'I know what you want,' he said, screwing up his eyes
and shaking his finger at me. 'You want to make me drunk,
so as to see what will happen to me; but no, you won't
succeed!'

'Why should I want to make you drunk?' I said. 'I only want
to give you pleasure.'

Probably he was sorry to have offended me by interpreting
my intention wrongly, for he grew confused, got up, and
pressed my elbow.

'No, no, I was only joking!' he said, looking at me with a
beseeching expression in his moist eyes.

Then he uttered some fearfully intricate, complicated sentence intended to imply that I was a good fellow after all.

'*Je ne vous dis que ça!*' he concluded.

So we continued drinking and talking and the waiters
continued to watch us unceremoniously and, as it seemed,
to make fun of us. Despite my interest in our conversation
I could not help noticing them and, I confess, I grew more and
more angry. One of them got up, came over to the little man,
looked down on the crown of his head, and began to smile.
I had accumulated a store of anger for the guests at the
Schweizerhof which I had not yet been able to vent on anyone, and I own that this audience of waiters irritated me
beyond endurance. Then the porter came in and, leaning his
elbows on the table without taking off his hat, sat down beside
me. This last circumstance stung my self-esteem or vanity, and
finally caused the oppressive rage that had been smouldering in
me all the evening to explode. 'Why when I was alone at the
entrance did he humbly bow to me, and now that I am sitting
with an itinerant singer, sprawls near me so rudely?' I was filled
with a boiling rage of indignation which I like in myself and
even stimulate when it besets me, because it has a tranquillizing effect, and gives, at least for a short time, an unusual

suppleness, energy, and power to all my physical and mental faculties.

I jumped up.

'What are you laughing at?' I shouted at the waiter, feeling that I was growing pale and that my lips were involuntarily twitching.

'I am not laughing; it's nothing!' said the waiter stepping back.

'No, you are laughing at this gentleman. . . . And what right have you to be here and to be sitting down, when there are visitors here? Don't dare to sit here!' I cried turning to the porter.

He got up with a growl and moved towards the door.

'What right have you to laugh at this gentleman and to sit near him, when he is a visitor and you are a lackey? Why didn't you laugh at me or sit beside me at dinner this evening? Is it because he is poorly dressed and sings in the street? Is it? While I wear good clothes? He is poor, but I am convinced that he is a thousand times better than you, for he insults no one, while you are insulting him!'

'But I am not doing anything!' replied my enemy the waiter, timidly. 'Do I prevent his sitting here?'

The waiter did not understand me and my German speech was lost on him. The rude porter tried to take the waiter's part, but I attacked him so vehemently that he pretended that he, too, did not understand me, and waved his arm. The hunch-backed dish-washer, either noticing my heated condition and afraid of a scandal, or because she really shared my views, took my part and, trying to interpose between me and the porter, began to persuade him to be quiet, saying that I was right and asking me to calm myself. '*Der Herr hat recht; Sie haben recht!*'[1] she said firmly. The singer presented a most piteous, frightened appearance and, evidently without understanding why I was excited or what I was aiming at, begged me to go away quickly. But my angry loquacity burned stronger and stronger in me. I recalled everything: the crowd that had laughed at

---

1 'The gentleman is right; you are right.'

him, and the audience that had given him nothing – and I would not quiet down on any account. I think that if the waiters and the porter had not been so yielding I should have enjoyed a fight with them, or could have whacked the defenceless young English lady on the head with a stick. Had I been at Sevastopol at that moment I would gladly have rushed into an English trench to hack and slash at them.

'And why did you show me and this gentleman into this room, and not the other, eh?' I asked the porter, seizing his arm to prevent his going away. 'What right had you to decide from his appearance that this gentleman must be in this and not in the other room? Are not all who pay on an equal footing in an hotel – not only in a republic, but all over the world? Yours is a scurvy republic! ... This is your equality! You dare not show those English people into this room – the very Englishmen who listened to this gentleman without paying him – that is, who each stole from him the few centimes they ought to have given him. How dared you show us in here?'

'The other room is closed,' replied the porter.

'No!' I cried. 'That's not true – it's not closed.'

'You know better then.'

'I know! I know that you are lying.'

The porter turned his shoulder towards me.

'What is the use of talking?' he muttered.

'No, not "what is the use ..."' I shouted. 'Take us to the other room at once!'

Despite the hunchbacked woman's and the singer's entreaties that we should go away, I had the head waiter called and went into the other room with my companion. When the head waiter heard my angry voice and saw my excited face he did not argue with me, but told me with contemptuous civility that I might go where I liked. I could not convict the porter of his lie, as he had disappeared before I went into the other room.

The room was really open and lighted up, and at one of the tables the Englishman with the lady was having supper. Though we were shown to another table, I sat down with the dirty singer close to the Englishman, and ordered the unfinished bottle to be brought me.

The Englishman and the lady looked first with surprise and then with anger at the little man who sat beside me more dead than alive. They exchanged some words, and the lady pushed away her plate, and rustled her silk dress as they went away. Through the panes in the door I could see the Englishman speaking angrily to the waiter, pointing in our direction all the time. The waiter thrust his head in at the door and looked towards us. I waited with pleasure for them to come to turn us out, and to be able at last to vent my whole indignation on them – but fortunately, though I then regretted it, they left us in peace.

The singer, who had before refused the wine, now hastened to empty the bottle in order to get away as soon as possible. However, he thanked me, feelingly I thought, for his entertainment. His moist eyes became still more tearful and shining, and he expressed his gratitude in a most curious and confused little speech. But that speech, in which he said that if everyone respected artists as I did he would be well off, and that he wished me all happiness, was very pleasant to me. We went out into the vestibule. The waiters were there and my enemy the porter who seemed to be complaining of me to them. They all looked on me, I think, as insane. I let the little man come up to them all, and then, with all the respect I could show, I took off my hat and pressed his hand with its ossified and withered finger. The waiters made a show of not taking any notice of me, but one of them burst into a sardonic laugh.

After bowing to me, the singer disappeared into the darkness, and I went up to my room, wishing to sleep off all these impressions and the foolish, childish anger which had so unexpectedly beset me. Feeling too agitated however for sleep, I went out again into the street to walk about till I should have calmed down, and also I must admit with a vague hope of finding an opportunity to come across the porter, the waiter, or the Englishman, to prove to them how cruel and above all how unjust they had been. But I met no one except the porter, who turned his back on seeing me, and I paced up and down the embankment all alone.

'This is the strange fate of art!' I reflected, having grown a little calmer. 'All seek it and love it – it is the one thing

everybody wants and tries to find in life, yet nobody acknow-
ledges its power, nobody values this greatest blessing in the
world, nor esteems or is grateful to those who give it to
mankind. Ask anyone you like of all these guests at the
Schweizerhof what is the greatest blessing in the world, and
everyone, or ninety-nine out of a hundred, assuming a sardonic expression, will say that the best thing in the world is
money! "Maybe this idea does not please you and does not
conform to your lofty ideas," he will tell you, "but what is to
be done if human life is so constituted that money alone gives
people happiness? I cannot help letting my reason see the
world as it is," he will add, "that is – see the truth."

'Pitiful is your reason, pitiful the happiness you desire, and
you are a miserable being who does not know what you
want. . . . Why have you all left your country, your relations,
your occupations, and your financial affairs, and congregated
here in this small Swiss town of Lucerne? Why did you all
come out onto the balcony this evening and listen in respectful
silence to the songs of that poor little mendicant? And had he
chosen to go on singing you would still have remained silent
and listened. What money, even millions of it, could have
driven you all from your country and assembled you in this
little corner, Lucerne? Could money have gathered you all on
those balconies and made you stand for half an hour silent and
motionless? No! One thing alone causes you to act, and will
always influence you more strongly than any other motive
power in life, and that is the need for art, which you do not
acknowledge, but which you feel and will always feel as long as
there is anything human left in you. The word "art" seems
ridiculous to you. You use it as a scornful reproach; you
perhaps allow love of the poetic in children and in silly girls,
but even then you laugh at them; but for yourselves you
require something positive. But children see life healthily,
they love and know what men should love, and what gives
happiness, but life has so enmeshed and depraved you that you
laugh at the one thing you love, and seek only that which you
hate and which causes you unhappiness. You are so enmeshed
that you do not understand your obligation to this poor

Tyrolese who has afforded you a pure enjoyment, yet you feel yourselves bound to humble yourselves gratuitously before a lord, without advantage or pleasure, and for some reason sacrifice for him your comfort and convenience. What nonsense! What incomprehensible senselessness! But it was not this that struck me most this evening. This ignorance of what gives happiness, this unconsciousness of poetic enjoyment, I almost understand, or have become used to, having often met it in my life; nor was the coarse, unconscious cruelty of the crowd new to me. Whatever the advocates of the popular spirit may say, a crowd is a combination possibly of good people, but of people who have come in touch merely on their base, animal sides, and it expresses only the weakness and cruelty of human nature. How could you, children of a free, humane nation, as Christians or simply as human beings, respond with coldness and ridicule to the pleasure afforded you by an unfortunate mendicant? But no, in your country there are institutions for the needy. There are no beggars and must be none, nor must there be any compassion, on which mendicancy is based. But this man had laboured, he gave you pleasure, he implored you to give him something from your superabundance for his pains, of which you availed yourselves. But you, from your lofty, brilliant palace, regarded him with a cold smile and there was not one among you hundred, happy, rich people who threw him anything. He went away humiliated, and the senseless crowd followed him laughing, and insulted not you but him, because you were cold, cruel, and dishonest; because you stole the pleasure he had afforded you, they insulted *him*.'

'*On the seventh of July 1857, in Lucerne, in front of the Hotel Schweizerhof in which the richest people stay, an itinerant beggar singer sang and played the guitar for half an hour. About a hundred people listened to him. The singer asked them all three times to give him something. Not one of them gave him anything, and many people laughed at him.*'

This is not fiction, but a positive fact, which can be verified by anyone who likes from the permanent residents at the Hotel Schweizerhof, after ascertaining from the papers who the foreigners were who were staying at the Schweizerhof on the 7th of July.

Here is an occurrence the historians of our time ought to record in indelible letters of fire. This incident is more significant, more serious, and has a profounder meaning, than the facts usually printed in newspapers and histories. That the English have killed another thousand Chinamen because the Chinese buy nothing for money while their country absorbs metal coins, that the French have killed another thousand Arabs because corn grows easily in Africa and constant warfare is useful for training armies; that the Turkish Ambassador in Naples must not be a Jew, and that the Emperor Napoleon walks on foot at Plombières and assures the people in print that he reigns only by the will of the whole nation – all these are words that conceal or reveal what has long been known; but what happened at Lucerne on July the 7th appears to me to be something quite new and strange, and relates not to the eternally evil side of human nature, but to a certain epoch in social evolution. This is a fact not for the history of human actions, but for the history of progress and civilization.

Why is this inhuman occurrence, which would be impossible in any German, French, or Italian village, possible here where civilization, liberty, and equality have been brought to the highest point, and where the most civilized travellers from the most civilized nations congregate? Why have these developed, humane people, who collectively are capable of any honourable and humane action, no human, cordial inclination to perform a kindly personal action? Why do these people – who in their parliaments, meetings, and societies are warmly concerned about the condition of the celibate Chinese in India, about propagating Christianity and education in Africa, about the establishment of societies for the betterment of the whole human race – not find in their souls the simple elemental feeling of human sympathy? Is it possible that they do not possess that feeling, and that its place has been occupied by the vanity, ambition, and cupidity governing these men in their parliaments, meetings, and societies? Can it be that the spread of the sensible and selfish association of men called civilization, destroys and contradicts the need for instinctive, loving association? And is it possible that this is the equality for which so much innocent blood has been shed and so many crimes committed? Is it possible that nations, like children, can be made happy by the mere sound of the word equality?

'Equality before the law?' But does the whole life of man take place in the sphere of law? Only a thousandth part of it depends on law, the rest takes place outside, in the sphere of social customs and conceptions. In this society the waiter is better dressed than the singer and insults him with impunity. I am better dressed than the waiter and insult him with impunity. The porter regards me as superior, and the singer as inferior, to himself; when I joined the singer he considered himself our equal and became rude. I grew insolent to the porter and he felt himself inferior to me. The waiter was insolent to the singer and the latter felt himself inferior to him. Can this be a free country – 'positively free' as people say – in which there is a single citizen who, without having caused harm to anyone, is put in prison for doing the only thing he can do to save himself from starvation?

What an unfortunate, pitiful creature is man, with his desire for positive decisions, thrown into this ever moving, limitless ocean of good and evil, of facts, conceptions, and contradictions! For ages men have struggled and laboured to place good on one side and evil on the other. Centuries pass, and whenever an impartial mind places good and evil on the scales, the balance remains even, and the proportion of good and evil remains unaltered. If only man would learn not to judge, not to think sharply and positively, and not to answer questions presented to him only because they are for ever unanswerable! If only he understood that every thought is both false and true! False by one-sidedness resulting from man's inability to embrace the whole of truth, and true as an expression of one fact of human endeavour.

Men have made subdivisions for themselves in this eternally moving, unending, intermingled chaos of good and evil; they have traced imaginary lines on that ocean, and expect the ocean to divide itself accordingly, as if there were not millions of other subdivisions made from quite other points of view on another plane. It is true that fresh subdivisions are worked out from century to century, but millions of centuries have passed and millions more will pass. 'Civilization is good, barbarianism is bad. Freedom is good, subjection is bad.' This imaginary knowledge destroys the instinctive, beatific, primitive demand for kindliness in human nature. And who will define for me what is freedom, what is despotism, what is civilization, and what barbarianism? Where does the boundary lie between the one and the other? Whose soul possesses so absolute a standard of good and evil that he can measure all the confused and fleeting facts? Whose mind is so great that it can comprehend and measure even the facts of the stationary past? And who has seen a condition in which good and evil did not exist together? And how do I know that it is not my point of view which decides whether I see more of the one than of the other? Who is capable, even for a moment, of severing himself so completely from life as to look down on it with complete detachment? We have one unerring guide, and only one – the universal Spirit which inspiring each and all of us, implants in every individual a craving for what ought to be; that same Spirit which causes the tree to grow towards the sun, the flower to shed its seeds in the autumn, and bids us instinctively draw closer together.

And it is that one blissful and impeccable voice that the noisy, hasty development of civilization stifles. Who is more a man and less a barbarian: that lord who, seeing the threadbare clothes of the singer, angrily left the table, and for his efforts did not give him a millionth part of his wealth, and who now sits, well fed, in a bright comfortable room, calmly discussing the affairs in China and finding the massacres committed there quite justified – or the little singer, who risking imprisonment and with a franc in his pocket has for twenty years been going over mountains and valleys doing no one any harm, but bringing consolation to them by his singing, and who was to-day insulted and almost driven out and, tired, hungry, and humiliated, has gone to sleep somewhere on rotting straw?

At that moment, in the dead stillness of the night, I heard somewhere in the far distance the little man's guitar and voice.

'No,' I said to myself involuntarily, 'you have no right to pity him and to be indignant at the lord's well-being. Who has weighed the inner happiness to be found in the soul of each of them? He is now sitting somewhere on a dirty door-step, gazing at the gleaming moonlit sky and gaily singing in the calm of the fragrant night; in his heart there is no reproach, or malice, or regret. And who knows what is now going on in the souls of all the people within these palatial walls? Who can tell whether among them all there is as much carefree benign joy in life and harmony with the world as lives in the soul of that little man? Endless is the mercy and wisdom of Him who has allowed and ordained that all these contradictions should exist. Only to you, insignificant worm, who rashly and wrongly try to penetrate His laws and His intentions – only to you do they seem contradictions. He looks down benignly from His bright immeasurable height and rejoices in the infinite harmony into which all your endless contradictory movements resolve themselves.

'In your pride you thought you could separate yourself from the universal law. But you, too, with your mean and petty indignation at the waiters, have been playing your necessary part in the eternal and infinite harmony.'

ALBERT

A TALE

I

F I V E wealthy young men had come, after two in the morning, to amuse themselves at a small Petersburg party.

Much champagne had been drunk, most of the men were very young, the girls were pretty, the piano and violin indefatigably played one polka after another, and dancing and noise went on unceasingly: yet for some reason it was dull and awkward, and, as often happens, everybody felt that it was all unnecessary and was not the thing.

Several times they tried to get things going, but forced merriment was worse even than boredom.

One of the five young men, more dissatisfied than the others with himself, with the others, and with the whole evening, rose with a feeling of disgust, found his hat, and went out quietly, intending to go home.

There was no one in the ante-room, but in the adjoining room he heard two voices disputing. The young man stopped to listen.

'You can't, there are guests there,' said a woman's voice.

'Let me in, please. I'm all right!' a man's weak voice entreated.

'No, I won't let you in without Madame's permission,' said the woman. 'Where are you going? Ah! What a man you are!'

The door burst open and a strange figure of a man appeared on the threshold. The servant on seeing a visitor no longer protested, and the strange figure, bowing timidly, entered the room, swaying on his bent legs. He was of medium height, with a narrow, stooping back, and long tangled hair. He wore a short overcoat, and narrow torn trousers over a pair of rough uncleaned boots. A necktie, twisted into a cord, was fastened

447

round his long white neck. A dirty shirt showed from under his coat and hung over his thin hands. Yet despite the extreme emaciation of his body, his face was white and delicate, and freshness and colour played on his cheeks above his scanty black beard and whiskers. His unkempt hair, thrown back, revealed a rather low and extremely clear forehead. His dark languid eyes looked softly, imploringly, and yet with dignity, before him. Their expression corresponded alluringly with that of the fresh lips, curved at the corners, which showed from under his thin moustache.

Having advanced a few steps he stopped, turned to the young man, and smiled. He seemed to smile with difficulty, but when the smile lit up his face the young man – without knowing why – smiled too.

'Who is that?' he whispered to the servant, when the strange figure had passed into the room from which came the sounds of a dance.

'A crazy musician from the theatre,' replied the maid. 'He comes sometimes to see the mistress.'

'Where have you been, Delésov?' someone just then called out, and the young man, who was named Delésov, returned to the ball-room.

The musician was standing at the door and, looking at the dancers, showed by his smile, his look, and the tapping of his foot, the satisfaction the spectacle afforded him.

'Come in and dance yourself,' said one of the visitors to him.

The musician bowed and looked inquiringly at the hostess.

'Go, go . . . Why not, when the gentlemen ask you to?' she said.

The thin, weak limbs of the musician suddenly came into active motion, and winking, smiling, and twitching, he began to prance awkwardly and heavily about the room. In the middle of the quadrille a merry officer, who danced very vivaciously and well, accidentally bumped into the musician with his back. The latter's weak and weary legs did not maintain their balance and after a few stumbling steps aside, he fell full length on the floor. Notwithstanding the dull thud produced by his fall, at first nearly everyone burst out laughing.

But the musician did not get up. The visitors grew silent and even the piano ceased. Delésov and the hostess were the first to run up to the fallen man. He was lying on his elbow, staring with dull eyes at the floor. When they lifted him and seated him on a chair, he brushed the hair back from his forehead with a quick movement of his bony hand and began to smile without answering their questions.

'Mr Albert! Mr Albert!' said the hostess. 'Have you hurt yourself? Where? There now, I said you ought not to dance. He is so weak,' she continued, addressing her guests, ' – he can hardly walk. How could he dance?'

'Who is he?' they asked her.

'A poor man – an artist. A very good fellow, but pitiable, as you see.'

She said this unembarrassed by the presence of the musician. He suddenly came to himself and, as if afraid of something, shrank into a heap and pushed those around him away.

'It's all nothing!' he suddenly said, rising from his chair with an obvious effort.

And to show that he was not at all hurt he went into the middle of the room and tried to jump about, but staggered and would have fallen down again had someone not supported him.

Everyone felt awkward, and looking at him they all became silent.

The musician's eyes again grew dim, and evidently oblivious of everyone he began rubbing his knee with his hand. Suddenly he raised his head, advanced a trembling leg, threw back his hair with the same heedless movement as before, and going up to the violinist took his violin from him.

'It's nothing!' he said once more, flourishing the violin. 'Gentlemen, let's have some music!'

'What a strange person!' the visitors remarked to one another.

'Perhaps a fine talent is perishing in this unfortunate creature,' said one of the guests.

'Yes, he's pitiable, pitiable!' said a third.

'What a beautiful face! . . . There is something extraordinary about him,' said Delésov. 'Let us see . . .'

II

ALBERT meanwhile, paying no attention to anyone, pressed the violin to his shoulder and paced slowly up and down by the piano tuning it. His lips took on an impassive expression, his eyes could not be seen, but his narrow bony back, his long white neck, his crooked legs and shaggy black head, presented a queer – but for some reason not at all ridiculous – spectacle. Having tuned the violin he briskly struck a chord, and throwing back his head turned to the pianist who was preparing to accompany him.

'Mélancolie G-dur!' he said, addressing the pianist with a gesture of command.

Then, as if begging forgiveness for that gesture, he smiled meekly, and glanced round at the audience with that same smile. Having pushed back his hair with the hand in which he held the bow, he stopped at the corner of the piano, and with a smooth and easy movement drew the bow across the strings. A clear melodious sound was borne through the room and complete silence ensued.

After that first note the theme flowed freely and elegantly, suddenly illumining the inner world of every listener with an unexpectedly clear and tranquillizing light. Not one false or exaggerated sound impaired the acquiescence of the listeners: the notes were all clear, elegant, and significant. Everyone silently followed their development with tremulous expectation. From the state of dullness, noisy distraction and mental torpor in which they had been, these people were suddenly and imperceptibly carried into another quite different world that they had forgotten. Now a calm contemplation of the past arose in their souls, now an impassioned memory of some past happiness, now a boundless desire for power and splendour, now a feeling of resignation, of unsatisfied love and sadness. Sounds now tenderly sad, now vehemently despairing, mingled freely, flowing and flowing one after the other so elegantly, so strongly, and so unconsciously, that the sounds themselves were not noticed, but there flowed of itself into the soul a beautiful torrent of poetry, long familiar but only now expressed. At each note Albert grew taller and taller. He was far from appearing misshapen or strange. Pressing the violin with his chin and listening to his notes with an expression of passionate attention, he convulsively moved his feet. Now he straightened himself to his full height, now he strenuously bent his back. His left arm seemed to have become set in the bent position to which he had strained it and only the bony fingers moved convulsively: the right arm moved smoothly, elegantly, and almost imperceptibly. His face shone with uninterrupted, ecstatic joy; his eyes burnt with a bright, dry brilliance, his nostrils expanded, his red lips opened with delight.

Sometimes his head bent closer to the violin, his eyes closed, and his face, half covered by his hair, lit up with a smile of mild rapture. Sometimes he drew himself up rapidly, advancing one foot, and his clear brow and the beaming look he cast round the room gleamed with pride, dignity, and a consciousness of power. Once the pianist blundered and struck a wrong chord. Physical suffering was apparent in the whole face and figure of the musician. He paused for an instant and stamping his foot with an expression of childish anger, cried: '*Moll, ce moll!*' The pianist recovered himself. Albert closed his eyes, smiled, and again forgetting himself, the others, and the whole world, gave himself up rapturously to his task.

All who were in the room preserved a submissive silence while Albert was playing, and seemed to live and breathe only in his music.

The merry officer sat motionless on a chair by a window, directing a lifeless gaze upon the floor and breathing slowly and heavily. The girls sat in complete silence along the walls, and only occasionally threw approving and bewildered glances at one another. The hostess's fat smiling face expanded with pleasure. The pianist riveted his eyes on Albert's face and, with a fear of blundering which expressed itself in his whole taut figure, tried to keep up with him. One of the visitors who had drunk more than the others lay prone on the sofa, trying not to move for fear of betraying his agitation. Delésov experienced an unaccustomed sensation. It was as if a cold circle, now expanding, now contracting, held his head in a vice. The roots of his hair became sensitive, cold shivers ran up his spine, something rising higher and higher in his throat pricked his nose and palate as if with fine needles, and tears involuntarily wetted his cheeks. He shook himself, tried to restrain them and wipe them unperceived, but others rose and ran down his cheeks. By some strange concatenation of impressions the first sounds of Albert's violin carried Delésov back to his early youth. Now no longer very young, tired of life and exhausted, he suddenly felt himself a self-satisfied, good-looking, blissfully foolish and unconsciously happy lad of seventeen. He remembered his first love – for his cousin in a little pink dress; remembered his first declaration of love made in a linden avenue; remembered the warmth and incomprehensible delight of a spontaneous kiss, and the magic and undivined mystery of the Nature that then surrounded him. In the memories that returned to him *she* shone out amid a mist of vague hopes, uncomprehended desires, and questioning faith in the possibility of impossible happiness. All the unappreciated moments of that time arose before him one after another, not as insignificant moments of a fleeting present, but as arrested, growing, reproachful images of the past. He contemplated them with joy, and wept – wept not because the time was past that he might have spent better (if he had it again he would not have undertaken to employ it better), but merely because it was past and would never return. Memories rose up of themselves, and Albert's violin repeated again and again: 'For you that time of vigour, love, and happiness has passed for ever, and will not return. Weep for it, shed all your tears, die weeping for that time – that is the best happiness left for you.'

Towards the end of the last variation Albert's face grew red, his eyes burnt and glowed, and large drops of perspiration ran down his cheeks. The veins of his forehead swelled up, his whole body came more and more into motion, his pale lips no longer closed, and his whole figure expressed ecstatic eagerness for enjoyment.

Passionately swaying his whole body and tossing back his hair he lowered the violin, and with a smile of proud dignity and happiness surveyed the audience. Then his back sagged, his head hung down, his lips closed, his eyes grew dim, and he timidly glanced round as if ashamed of himself, and made his way stumblingly into the other room.

III

SOMETHING strange occurred with everyone present and something strange was felt in the dead silence that followed Albert's playing. It was as if each would have liked to express what all this meant, but was unable to do so. What did it mean – this bright hot room, brilliant women, the dawn in the windows, excitement in the blood, and the pure impression left by sounds that had flowed past? But no one even tried to say what it all meant: on the contrary everyone, unable to dwell in those regions which the new impression had revealed to them, rebelled against it.

'He really plays well, you know!' said the officer.

'Wonderfully!' replied Delésov, stealthily wiping his cheek with his sleeve.

'However, it's time for us to be going,' said the man who was lying on the sofa, having somewhat recovered. 'We must give him something. Let's make a collection.'

Meanwhile Albert sat alone on a sofa in the next room. Leaning his elbows on his bony knees he stroked his face and ruffled his hair with his moist and dirty hands, smiling happily to himself.

They made a good collection, which Delésov offered to hand to Albert.

Moreover it had occurred to Delésov, on whom the music had made an unusual and powerful impression, to be of use to this man. It occurred to him to take him home, dress him, get him a place somewhere, and in general rescue him from his sordid condition.

'Well, are you tired?' he asked, coming up to him.

Albert smiled.

'You have real talent. You ought to study music seriously and give public performances.'

'I'd like to have something to drink,' said Albert, as if just awake.

Delésov brought some wine, and the musician eagerly drank two glasses.

'What excellent wine!' he said.

'What a delightful thing that *Mélancolie* is!' said Delésov.

'Oh, yes, yes!' replied Albert with a smile – 'but excuse me: I don't know with whom I have the honour of speaking, maybe you are a count, or a prince: could you, perhaps, lend me a little money?' He paused a little. 'I have nothing . . . I am a poor man. I couldn't pay it back.'

Delésov flushed: he felt awkward, and hastily handed the musician the money that had been collected.

'Thank you very much!' said Albert, seizing the money. 'Now let's have some music. I'll play for you as much as you like – only let me have a drink of something, a drink . . . ' he added, rising.

Delésov brought him some more wine and asked him to sit beside him.

'Excuse me if I am frank with you,' he said, 'your talent interests me so much. It seems to me you are not in good circumstances.'

Albert looked now at Delésov and now at his hostess who had entered the room.

'Allow me to offer you my services,' continued Delésov. 'If you are in need of anything I should be glad if you would stay with me for a time. I am living alone and could perhaps be of use to you.'

Albert smiled and made no reply.

'Why don't you thank him?' said the hostess. 'Of course it is a godsend for you. Only I should not advise you to,' she continued, turning to Delésov and shaking her head disapprovingly.

'I am very grateful to you!' said Albert, pressing Delésov's hand with his own moist ones – 'Only let us have some music now, please.'

But the other visitors were preparing to leave, and despite Albert's endeavours to persuade them to stay they went out into the hall.

Albert took leave of the hostess, put on his shabby broad-brimmed hat and old summer cloak, which was his only winter clothing, and went out into the porch with Delésov.

When Delésov had seated himself with his new acquaintance in his carriage, and became aware of the unpleasant odour of drunkenness and uncleanness which emanated so strongly from the musician, he began to repent of his action and blamed himself for childish soft-heartedness and imprudence. Besides, everything Albert said was so stupid and trivial, and the fresh air suddenly made him so disgustingly drunk that Delésov was repelled. 'What am I to do with him?' he thought.

When they had driven for a quarter of an hour Albert grew silent, his hat fell down at his feet, and he himself tumbled into a corner of the carriage and began to snore. The wheels continued to creak monotonously over the frozen snow; the feeble light of dawn hardly penetrated the frozen windows.

Delésov turned and looked at his companion. The long body covered by the cloak lay lifelessly beside him. The long head with its big black nose seemed to sway on that body, but looking closer Delésov saw that what he had taken for nose and face was hair, and that the real face hung lower. He stooped and was able to distinguish Albert's features. Then the beauty of the forehead and calmly closed lips struck him again.

Under the influence of tired nerves, restlessness from lack of sleep at that hour of the morning, and of the music he had heard, Delésov, looking at that face, let himself again be carried back to the blissful world into which he had glanced that night; he again recalled the happy and magnanimous days of his youth and no longer repented of what he had done. At that moment he was sincerely and warmly attached to Albert, and firmly resolved to be of use to him.

IV

NEXT morning when he was awakened to go to his office, Delésov with a feeling of unpleasant surprise saw around him his old screen, his old valet, and his watch lying on the small side-table. 'But what did I expect to see if not what is always around me?' he asked himself. Then he remembered the musician's black eyes and happy smile, the motif of *Mélancolie*, and all the strange experiences of the previous night passed through his mind.

He had no time however to consider whether he had acted well or badly by taking the musician into his house. While dressing he mapped out the day, took his papers, gave the necessary household orders, and hurriedly put on his overcoat and overshoes. Passing the dining-room door he looked in. Albert, after tossing about, had sunk his face in the pillow, and lay in his dirty ragged shirt, dead asleep on the leather sofa where he had been deposited unconscious the night before. 'There's something wrong!' thought Delésov involuntarily.

'Please go to Boryuzóvski and ask him to lend me a violin for a couple of days,' he said to his manservant. 'When he wakes up, give him coffee and let him have some undercloth-ing and old clothes of mine. In general, make him comfortable – please!'

On returning late in the evening Delésov was surprised not to find Albert.

'Where is he?' he asked his man.

'He went away immediately after dinner,' replied the ser-vant. 'He took the violin and went away. He promised to be back in an hour, but he's not here yet.'

'Tut, tut! How provoking!' muttered Delésov. 'Why did you let him go, Zakhár?'

Zakhár was a Petersburg valet who had been in Delésov's service for eight years. Delésov, being a lonely bachelor, could not help confiding his intentions to him, and liked to know his opinion about all his undertakings.

'How could I dare not to let him?' Zakhár replied, toying with the fob of his watch. 'If you had told me to keep him in I might have amused him at home. But you only spoke to me about clothes.'

'Pshaw! How provoking! Well, and what was he doing here without me?'

Zakhár smiled.

'One can well call him an "artist",[1] sir. As soon as he woke he asked for Madeira, and then he amused himself with the cook and with the neighbour's manservant. He is so funny. However, he is good-natured. I gave him tea and brought him dinner. He would not eat anything himself, but kept inviting me to do so. But when it comes to playing the violin, even Izler has few artists like him. One may well befriend such a man. When he played *Down the Little Mother Vólga* to us it was as if a man were weeping. It was too beautiful. Even the servants from all the flats came to our back-entrance to hear him.'

'Well, and did you get him dressed?' his master interrupted him.

'Of course. I gave him a nightshirt of yours and put my own paletot on him. A man like that is worth helping – he really is a dear fellow!' Zakhár smiled.

'He kept asking me what your rank is, whether you have influential acquaintances, and how many serfs you own.'

'Well, all right, but now he must be found, and in future don't let him have anything to drink, or it'll be worse for him.'

'That's true,' Zakhár interjected. 'He is evidently feeble; our old master had a clerk like that . . .'

But Delésov, who had long known the story of the clerk who took hopelessly to drink, did not let Zakhár finish, and telling him to get everything ready for the night, sent him out to find Albert and bring him back.

He then went to bed and put out the light, but could not fall asleep for a long time, thinking about Albert. 'Though it may seem strange to many of my acquaintances,' he thought, 'yet one so seldom does anything for others that one ought to thank God when such an opportunity presents itself, and I will not miss it. I will do anything – positively anything in my power – to help him. He may not be mad at all, but only under the influence of drink. It won't cost me very much.

---

1 In addition to its proper meaning, the word 'artist' was used in Russian to denote a thief, or a man dexterous at anything, good or bad.

Where there's enough for one there's enough for two. Let him live with me a while, then we'll find him a place or arrange a concert for him and pull him out of the shallows, and then see what happens.'

He experienced a pleasant feeling of self-satisfaction after this reflection.

'Really I'm not altogether a bad fellow,' he thought. 'Not at all bad even – when I compare myself with others.'

He was already falling asleep when the sound of opening doors and of footsteps in the hall roused him.

'Well, I'll be stricter with him,' he thought, 'that will be best; and I must do it.'

He rang.

'Have you brought him back?' he asked when Zakhár entered.

'A pitiable man, sir,' said Zakhár, shaking his head significantly and closing his eyes.

'Is he drunk?'

'He is very weak.'

'And has he the violin?'

'I've brought it back. The lady gave it me.'

'Well, please don't let him in here now. Put him to bed, and to-morrow be sure not to let him leave the house on any account.'

But before Zakhár was out of the room Albert entered it.

V

'Do you want to sleep already?' asked Albert with a smile. 'And I have been at Anna Ivánovna's and had a very pleasant evening. We had music, and laughed, and there was delightful company. Let me have a glass of something,' he added, taking hold of a water-bottle that stood on a little table, ' – but not water.'

Albert was just the same as he had been the previous evening: the same beautiful smile in his eyes and on his lips, the same bright inspired forehead, and the same feeble limbs. Zakhár's paletot fitted him well, and the clean wide unstarched

collar of the nightshirt encircled his thin white neck picturesquely, giving him a particularly childlike and innocent
look. He sat down on Delésov's bed and looked at him silently
with a happy and grateful smile. Delésov looked into his
eyes, and again suddenly felt himself captivated by that smile.
He no longer wanted to sleep, he forgot that it was his duty to
be stern: on the contrary he wished to make merry, to hear
music, and to chat amicably with Albert till morning. He told
Zakhár to bring a bottle of wine, some cigarettes, and the
violin.

'There, that's splendid!' said Albert. 'It's still early, and we'll
have some music. I'll play for you as much as you like.'

Zakhár, with evident pleasure, brought a bottle of Lafitte,
two tumblers, some mild cigarettes such as Albert smoked, and
the violin. But instead of going to bed as his master told him
to, he himself lit a cigar and sat down in the adjoining room.

'Let us have a talk,' said Delésov to the musician, who was
about to take up the violin.

Albert submissively sat down on the bed and again smiled
joyfully.

'Oh yes!' said he, suddenly striking his forehead with his
hand and assuming an anxiously inquisitive expression. (A
change of expression always preceded anything he was about
to say.) – 'Allow me to ask —' he made a slight pause – 'that
gentleman who was there with you last night – you called him
N—, isn't he the son of the celebrated N—?'

'His own son,' Delésov answered, not at all understanding
how that could interest Albert.

'Exactly!' said Albert with a self-satisfied smile. 'I noticed at
once something particularly aristocratic in his manner. I love
aristocrats: there is something particularly beautiful and elegant
in an aristocrat. And that officer who dances so well?' he asked.
'I liked him very much too: he is so merry and so fine. Isn't he
Adjutant N. N.?'

'Which one?' asked Delésov.

'The one who bumped against me when we were dancing.
He must be an excellent fellow.'

'No, he's a shallow fellow,' Delésov replied.

'Oh, no!' Albert warmly defended him. 'There is something very, very pleasant about him. He is a capital musician,' he added. 'He played something there out of an opera. It's a long time since I took such a liking to anyone.'

'Yes, he plays well, but I don't like his playing,' said Delésov, wishing to get his companion to talk about music. 'He does not understand classical music – Donizetti and Bellini, you know, are not music. You think so too, no doubt?'

'Oh, no, no, excuse me!' began Albert with a gentle, pleading look. 'The old music is music, and the new music is music. There are extraordinary beauties in the new music too. Sonnambula,[1] and the finale of Lucia,[2] and Chopin, and Robert![3] I often think —' he paused, evidently collecting his thoughts – 'that if Beethoven were alive he would weep with joy listening to Sonnambula. There is beauty everywhere. I heard Sonnambula for the first time when Viardot[4] and Rubini[5] were here. It was like this...' he said, and his eyes glistened as he made a gesture with both arms as though tearing something out of his breast. 'A little more and it would have been impossible to bear it.'

'And what do you think of the opera at the present time?' asked Delésov.

'Bosio[6] is good, very good,' he said, 'extraordinarily exquisite, but she does not touch one here,' – pointing to his sunken chest. 'A singer needs passion, and she has none. She gives pleasure but does not torment.'

'How about Lablache?'[7]

'I heard him in Paris in the Barbier de Séville. He was unique then, but now he is old: he cannot be an artist, he is old.'

---

1 Opera by Bellini, produced in 1831.
2 Lucia di Lammermoor, an opera by Donizetti, produced in 1835.
3 Robert the Devil, an opera by Meyerbeer, produced in 1831, or possibly the allusion may be to Roberto Devereux by Donizetti.
4 Pauline Viardot-Garcia. A celebrated operatic singer with whom Turgenev had a close friendship for many years.
5 Rubini. An Italian tenor who had great success in Russia in the 1840s.
6 Angidina Bosio, an Italian singer, who was in Petersburg in 1856–9.
7 Luigi Lablache. He was regarded as the chief basso of his time.

'Well, what if he is old? He is still good in *morceaux d'en-semble*,' said Delésov, who was in the habit of saying that of Lablache.

'How "what if he is old?"' rejoined Albert severely. 'He should not be old. An artist should not be old. Much is needed for art, but above all, fire!' said he with glittering eyes and stretching both arms upwards.

And a terrible inner fire really seemed to burn in his whole body.

'O my God!' he suddenly exclaimed. 'Don't you know Petróv, the artist?'

'No, I don't,' Delésov replied, smiling.

'How I should like you to make his acquaintance! You would enjoy talks with him. How well he understands art, too! I used often to meet him at Anna Ivánovna's, but now she is angry with him for some reason. I should very much like you to know him. He has great talent, great talent!'

'Does he paint now?' Delésov asked.

'I don't know, I think not, but he was an Academy artist. What ideas he has! It's wonderful when he talks sometimes. Oh, Petróv has great talent, only he leads a very gay life . . . that's a pity,' Albert added with a smile. After that he got off the bed, took the violin, and began tuning it.

'Is it long since you were at the opera?' Delésov asked.

Albert looked round and sighed.

'Ah, I can't go there any more!' he said. 'I will tell you!' And clutching his head he again sat down beside Delésov and muttered almost in a whisper: 'I can't go there. I can't play there – I have nothing – nothing! No clothes, no home, no violin. It is a miserable life! A miserable life!' he repeated several times. 'And why should I go there? What for? No need!' he said, smiling. 'Ah! *Don Juan* . . .'

He struck his head with his hand.

'Then let us go there together sometime,' said Delésov.

Without answering, Albert jumped up, seized the violin, and began playing the finale of the first act of *Don Juan*, telling the story of the opera in his own words.

Delésov felt the hair stir on his head as Albert played the voice of the dying commandant.

'No!' said Albert, putting down the violin. 'I cannot play to-day. I have had too much to drink.'

But after that he went up to the table, filled a tumbler with wine, drank it at a gulp, and again sat down on Delésov's bed.

Delésov looked at Albert, not taking his eyes off him. Occasionally Albert smiled, and so did Delésov. They were both silent; but their looks and smiles created more and more affectionate relations between them. Delésov felt himself growing fonder of the man, and experienced an incomprehensible joy.

'Have you ever been in love?' he suddenly asked.

Albert thought for a few seconds, and then a sad smile lit up his face. He leaned over to Delésov and looked attentively in his eyes.

'Why have you asked me that?' he whispered. 'I will tell you everything, because I like you,' he continued, after looking at him for awhile and then glancing round. 'I won't deceive you, but will tell you everything from the beginning, just as it happened.' He stopped, his eyes wild and strangely fixed. 'You know that my mind is weak,' he suddenly said. 'Yes, yes,' he went on. 'Anna Ivánovna is sure to have told you. She tells everybody that I am mad! That is not true; she says it as a joke, she is a kindly woman, and I have really not been quite well for some time.' He stopped again and gazed with fixed wide-open eyes at the dark doorway. 'You asked whether I have been in love? . . . Yes, I have been in love,' he whispered, lifting his brows. 'It happened long ago, when I still had my job in the theatre. I used to play second violin at the Opera, and she used to have the lower-tier box next the stage, on the left.'

He got up and leaned over to Delésov's ear.

'No, why should I name her?' he said. 'You no doubt know her – everybody knows her. I kept silent and only looked at her; I knew I was a poor artist, and she an aristocratic lady. I knew that very well. I only looked at her and planned nothing . . .'

Albert reflected, trying to remember.

'How it happened I don't remember; but I was once called in to accompany her on the violin. . . . But what was I, a poor artist?' he said, shaking his head and smiling. 'But no, I can't tell it . . .' he added, clutching his head. 'How happy I was!'

'Yes? And did you often go to her house?' Delésov asked.

'Once! Once only . . . but it was my own fault. I was mad! I was a poor artist, and she an aristocratic lady. I ought not to have said anything to her. But I went mad and acted like a fool. Since then all has been over for me. Petróv told the truth, that it would have been better for me to have seen her only at the theatre . . .'

'What was it you did?' asked Delésov.

'Ah, wait! Wait! I can't speak of that!'

With his face hidden in his hands he remained silent for some time.

'I came late to the orchestra. Petróv and I had been drinking that evening, and I was distracted. She was sitting in her box talking to a general. I don't know who that general was. She sat at the very edge of the box, with her arm on the ledge; she had on a white dress and pearls round her neck. She talked to him and looked at me. She looked at me twice. Her hair was done like this. I was not playing, but stood near the basses and looked at her. Then for the first time I felt strange. She smiled at the general and looked at me. I felt she was speaking about me, and I suddenly saw that I was not in the orchestra, but in the box beside her and holding her arm, just there. . . . How was that?' Albert asked after a short silence.

'That was vivid imagination,' said Delésov.

'No, no! . . . but I don't know how to tell it,' Albert replied, frowning. 'Even then I was poor and had no lodging, and when I went to the theatre I sometimes stayed the night there.'

'What, at the theatre? In that dark, empty place?'

'Oh, I am not afraid of such nonsense. Wait a bit. . . . When they had all gone away I would go to the box where she had been sitting and sleep there. That was my one delight. What nights I spent there! But once it began again. Many things appeared to me in the night, but I can't tell you much.' Albert glanced at Delésov with downcast eyes. 'What was it?' he asked.

'It is strange!' said Delésov.

'No, wait, wait!' he continued, whispering in Delésov's ear. 'I kissed her hand, wept there beside her, and talked much with her. I inhaled the scent of her perfume and heard her voice. She told me much in one night. Then I took my violin and played softly; and I played splendidly. But I felt frightened. I am not afraid of those foolish things and don't believe in them, but I was afraid for my head,' he said, touching his forehead with an amiable smile. 'I was frightened for my poor wits. It seemed to me that something had happened to my head. Perhaps it's nothing. What do you think?'

Both were silent for some minutes.

> *'Und wenn die Wolken sie verhüllen*
> *Die Sonne bleibt doch ewig klar.'*[1]

Albert sang with a soft smile. 'Is not that so?' he added.

> *'Ich auch habe gelebt und genossen . . .'*[2]

'Ah, how well old Petróv would have explained it all to you!'

Delésov looked silently and in terror at the pale and agitated face of his companion.

'Do you know the "*Juristen-Waltzer*"?' Albert suddenly exclaimed, and without awaiting an answer he jumped up, seized the violin, and began to play the merry waltz tune, forgetting himself completely, and evidently imagining that a whole orchestra was playing with him. He smiled, swayed, shifted his feet, and played superbly.

'Eh! Enough of merrymaking!' he said when he had finished, and flourished the violin.

'I am going,' he said, after sitting silently for awhile – 'won't you come with me?'

---

1 'And even if the clouds do hide it
  The sun remains for ever clear.'
2 'I, too, have lived and enjoyed.'

'Where to?' Delésov asked in surprise.

'Let's go to Anna Ivánovna's again. It's gay there – noise, people, music!'

At first Delésov almost consented, but bethinking himself he tried to persuade Albert not to go that night.

'Only for a moment.'

'No really, you'd better not!'

Albert sighed and put down the violin.

'So I must stay here?'

And looking again at the table (there was no wine left) he said good-night and left the room.

Delésov rang.

'See that you don't let Mr Albert go anywhere without my permission,' he said to Zakhár.

VI

THE next day was a holiday. Delésov was already awake and sitting in his drawing-room drinking coffee and reading a book. Albert had not yet stirred in the next room.

Zakhár cautiously opened the door and looked into the dining-room.

'Would you believe it, sir? He is asleep on the bare sofa! He wouldn't have anything spread on it, really. Like a little child. Truly, an artist.'

Towards noon groaning and coughing were heard through the door.

Zakhár again went into the dining-room, and Delésov could hear his kindly voice and Albert's weak, entreating one.

'Well?' he asked, when Zakhár returned.

'He's fretting, sir, won't wash, and seems gloomy. He keeps asking for a drink.'

'No. Having taken this matter up I must show character,' said Delésov to himself.

He ordered that no wine should be given to Albert and resumed his book, but involuntarily listened to what was going on in the dining-room. There was no sound of movement there and an occasional deep cough and spitting was all that could be heard. Two hours passed. Having dressed, Delésov decided to look in at his visitor before going out. Albert was sitting motionless at the window, his head resting on his hand. He looked round. His face was yellow, wrinkled, and not merely sad but profoundly miserable. He tried to smile by way of greeting, but his face took on a still more sorrowful expression. He seemed ready to cry. He rose with difficulty and bowed.

'If I might just have a glass of simple vodka!' he said with a look of entreaty. 'I am so weak – please!'

'Coffee will do you more good. Have some of that instead.'

Albert's face suddenly lost its childlike expression; he looked coldly, dim-eyed, out of the window, and sank feebly onto his chair.

'Or would you like some lunch?'

'No thank you, I have no appetite.'

'If you wish to play the violin you will not disturb me,' said Delésov, laying the violin on the table.

Albert looked at the violin with a contemptuous smile.

'No,' he said. 'I am too weak, I can't play,' and he pushed the instrument away from him.

After that, whatever Delésov might say, offering to go for a walk with him, and to the theatre in the evening, he only bowed humbly and remained stubbornly silent. Delésov went out, paid several calls, dined with friends, and before going to the theatre returned home to change and to see what the musician was doing. Albert was sitting in the dark hall, leaning his head in his hands and looking at the heated stove. He was neatly dressed, washed, and his hair was brushed; but his eyes were dim and lifeless, and his whole figure expressed weakness and exhaustion even more than in the morning.

'Have you dined, Mr Albert?' asked Delésov.

Albert made an affirmative gesture with his head and, after a frightened look at Delésov, lowered his eyes. Delésov felt uncomfortable.

'I spoke to the director of the theatre about you to-day,' he said, also lowering his eyes. 'He will be very glad to receive you if you will let him hear you.'

'Thank you, I cannot play!' muttered Albert under his breath, and went into his room, shutting the door behind him very softly.

A few minutes later the door-knob was turned just as gently, and he came out of the room with the violin. With a rapid and hostile glance at Delésov he placed the violin on a chair and disappeared again.

Delésov shrugged his shoulders and smiled.

'What more am I to do? In what am I to blame?' he thought.

'Well, how is the musician?' was his first question when he returned home late that evening.

'Bad!' said Zakhár, briefly and clearly. 'He has been sighing and coughing and says nothing, except that he started begging for vodka four or five times. At last I gave him one glass – or else we might finish him off, sir. Just like the clerk . . .'

'Has he not played the violin?'

'Didn't even touch it. I took it to him a couple of times, but he just took it up gently and brought it out again,' Zakhár answered with a smile. 'So your orders are not to give him any drink?'

'No, we'll wait another day and see what happens. And what's he doing now?'

'He has locked himself up in the drawing-room.'

Delésov went into his study and chose several French books and a German Bible. 'Put these books in his room to-morrow, and see that you don't let him out,' he said to Zakhár.

Next morning Zakhár informed his master that the musician had not slept all night: he had paced up and down the rooms, and had been into the pantry, trying to open the cupboard and the door, but he (Zakhár) had taken care to lock everything up. He said that while he pretended to be asleep he had heard Albert in the dark muttering something to himself and waving his arms about.

Albert grew gloomier and more taciturn every day. He seemed to be afraid of Delésov, and when their eyes met his face expressed sickly fear. He did not touch the books or the violin, and did not reply to questions put to him.

On the third day of the musician's stay Delésov returned home late, tired and upset. He had been driving about all day attending to a matter that had promised to be very simple and easy but, as often happens, in spite of strenuous efforts he had been quite unable to advance a single step with it. Besides that he had called in at his club and had lost at whist. He was in bad spirits.

'Well, let him go his way!' he said to Zakhár, who told him of Albert's sad plight. 'To-morrow I'll get a definite answer out of him, whether he wants to stay here and follow my advice, or not. If not, he needn't! It seems to me that I have done all I could.'

'There now, try doing good to people!' he thought to himself. 'I put myself out for him, I keep that dirty creature in my house, so that I can't receive a visitor in the morning. I bustle and run about, and he looks on me as if I were a villain who for his own pleasure has locked him up in a cage. And above all, he won't take a single step to help himself. They are all like that.' (The 'they' referred to people in general, and especially to those with whom he had had business that day.) 'And what is the matter with him now? What is he thinking about and pining for? Pining for the debauchery from which I have dragged him? For the humiliation in which he was? For the destitution from which I have saved him? Evidently he has fallen so low that it hurts him to see a decent life . . .

'No, it was a childish act,' Delésov concluded. 'How can I improve others, when God knows whether I can manage myself?' He thought of letting Albert go at once, but after a little reflection put it off till the next day.

During the night he was roused by the sound of a table falling in the hall, and the sound of voices and footsteps. He lighted a candle and listened in surprise.

'Wait a bit. I'll tell my master,' Zakhár was saying; Albert's voice muttered something incoherently and heatedly. Delésov jumped up and ran into the hall with the candle. Zakhár stood against the front door in his night attire, and Albert, with his hat and cloak on, was pushing him aside and shouting in a tearful voice:

'You can't keep me here! I have a passport,[1] and have taken nothing of yours. You may search me. I shall go to the chief of police! . . .'

'Excuse me, sir!' Zakhár said, addressing his master while continuing to guard the door with his back. 'He got up during the night, found the key in my overcoat pocket, and drank a whole decanter of liqueur vodka. Is that right? And now he wants to go away. You ordered me not to let him out, so I dare not let him go.'

On seeing Delésov Albert made for Zakhár still more excitedly.

'No one dare hold me! No one has a right to!' he shouted, raising his voice more and more.

'Step aside, Zakhár!' said Delésov. 'I can't and don't want to keep you, but I advise you to stay till the morning,' he said to Albert.

'No one can keep me! I'll go to the chief of police!' Albert cried louder and louder, addressing himself to Zakhár alone and not looking at Delésov. 'Help!' he suddenly screamed in a furious voice.

'What are you screaming like that for? Nobody is keeping you!' said Zakhár, opening the door.

Albert stopped shouting. 'You didn't succeed, did you? Wanted to do for me – did you!' he muttered to himself, putting on his goloshes. Without taking leave, and continuing to mutter incoherently, he went out. Zakhár held a light for him as far as the gate, and then came back.

'Well, God be thanked, sir!' he said to his master. 'Who knows what might happen? As it is I must count the silver plate . . .'

Delésov merely shook his head and did not reply. He vividly recalled the first two evenings he had spent with the musician, and recalled the last sad days which by his fault Albert had spent there, and above all he recalled that sweet, mixed feeling of surprise, affection and pity, which that strange man had

---

[1] To be free to go from place to place it was necessary to have a properly stamped passport from the police.

aroused in him at first sight, and he felt sorry for him. 'And what will become of him now?' he thought. 'Without money, without warm clothing, alone in the middle of the night...' He was about to send Zakhár after him, but it was too late.

'Is it cold outside?' he inquired.

'A hard frost, sir,' replied Zakhár. 'I forgot to inform you, but we shall have to buy more wood for fuel before the spring.'

'How is that? You said that we should have some left over.'

VII

IT was indeed cold outside, but Albert, heated by the liquor he had drunk and by the dispute, did not feel it. On reaching the street he looked round and rubbed his hands joyfully. The street was empty, but the long row of lamps still burned with ruddy light; the sky was clear and starry. 'There now!' he said, addressing the lighted window of Delésov's lodging, thrusting his hands into his trouser pockets under his cape, and stooping forward. He went with heavy, uncertain steps down the street to the right. He felt an unusual weight in his legs and stomach, something made a noise in his head, and some invisible force was throwing him from side to side, but he still went on in the direction of Anna Ivánovna's house. Strange, incoherent thoughts passed through his mind. Now he remembered his last altercation with Zakhár, then for some reason the sea and his first arrival in Russia by steamboat, then a happy night he had passed with a friend in a small shop he was passing, then suddenly a familiar motif began singing itself in his imagination, and he remembered the object of his passion and the dreadful night in the theatre. Despite their incoherence all these memories presented themselves so clearly to his mind that, closing his eyes, he did not know which was the more real: what he was doing, or what he was thinking. He did not realize or feel how his legs were moving, how he swayed and bumped against the wall, how he looked around him, or passed from street to street. He realized and felt only the things that, intermingling and fantastically following one another, rose in his imagination.

Passing along the Little Morskáya Street, Albert stumbled and fell. Coming to his senses for a moment he saw an immense and splendid building before him and went on. In the sky no stars, nor moon, nor dawn, were visible, nor were there any street lamps, but everything was clearly outlined. In the windows of the building that towered at the end of the street lights were shining, but those lights quivered like reflections. The building stood out nearer and nearer and clearer and clearer before him. But the lights disappeared directly he entered the wide portals. All was dark within. Solitary footsteps resounded under the vaulted ceiling, and some shadows slid rapidly away as he approached. 'Why have I come here?' thought he; but some irresistible force drew him on into the depths of the immense hall. There was some kind of platform, around which some small people stood silently. 'Who is going to speak?' asked Albert. No one replied, except that someone pointed to the platform. A tall thin man with bristly hair and wearing a parti-coloured dressing-gown was already standing there, and Albert immediately recognized his friend Petróv. 'How strange that he should be here!' thought he. 'No, brothers!' Petróv was saying, pointing to someone. 'You did not understand a man living among you; you have not understood him! He is not a mercenary artist, not a mechanical performer, not a lunatic or a lost man. He is a genius – a great musical genius who has perished among you unnoticed and unappreciated!' Albert at once understood of whom his friend was speaking, but not wishing to embarrass him he modestly lowered his head.

'The holy fire that we all serve has consumed him like a blade of straw!' the voice went on, 'but he has fulfilled all that God implanted in him and should therefore be called a great man. You could despise, torment, humiliate him,' the voice continued, growing louder and louder – 'but he was, is, and will be, immeasurably higher than you all. He is happy, he is kind. He loves or despises all alike, but serves only that which was implanted in him from above. He loves but one thing – beauty, the one indubitable blessing in the world. Yes, such is the man! Fall prostrate before him, all of you! On your knees!' he cried aloud.

But another voice came mildly from the opposite corner of the hall: 'I do not wish to bow my knees before him,' said the voice, which Albert immediately recognized as Delésov's. 'Wherein is he great? Why should we bow before him? Did he behave honourably and justly? Has he been of any use to society? Don't we know how he borrowed money and did not return it, and how he carried away his fellow-artist's violin and pawned it? . . .' ('O God, how does he know all that?' thought Albert, hanging his head still lower.) 'Do we not know how he flattered the most insignificant people, flattered them for the sake of money?' Delésov continued – 'Don't we know how he was expelled from the theatre? And how Anna Ivánovna wanted to send him to the police?' ('O God! That is all true, but defend me, Thou who alone knowest why I did it!' muttered Albert.)

'Cease, for shame!' Petróv's voice began again. 'What right have you to accuse him? Have you lived his life? Have you experienced his rapture?' ('True, true!' whispered Albert.) 'Art is the highest manifestation of power in man. It is given to a few of the elect, and raises the chosen one to such a height as turns the head and makes it difficult for him to remain sane. In Art, as in every struggle, there are heroes who have devoted themselves entirely to its service and have perished without having reached the goal.' Petróv stopped, and Albert raised his head and cried out: 'True, true!' but his voice died away without a sound.

'It does not concern you,' said the artist Petróv, turning to him severely. 'Yes, humiliate and despise him,' he continued, 'but yet he is the best and happiest of you all.'

Albert, who had listened to these words with rapture in his soul, could not restrain himself, and went up to his friend wishing to kiss him.

'Go away! I do not know you!' Petróv said. 'Go your way, or you won't get there.'

'Just see how the drink's got hold of you! You won't get there,' shouted a policeman at the crossroad.

Albert stopped, collected his strength and, trying not to stagger, turned into the side street.

Only a few more steps were left to Anna Ivánovna's door. From the hall of her house the light fell on the snow in the courtyard, and sledges and carriages stood at the gate.

Holding onto the banister with his numbed hands, he ran up the steps and rang. The sleepy face of a maid appeared in the opening of the doorway, and she looked angrily at Albert. 'You can't!' she cried. 'The orders are not to let you in,' and she slammed the door to. The sound of music and of women's voices reached the steps. Albert sat down, leaned his head against the wall, and closed his eyes. Immediately a throng of disconnected but kindred visions beset him with renewed force, engulfed him in their waves, and bore him away into the free and beautiful realm of dreams. 'Yes, he was the best and happiest!' ran involuntarily through his imagination. The sounds of a polka came through the door. These sounds also told him that he was the best and happiest. The bells in the nearest church rang out for early service, and these bells also said: 'Yes, he is the best and happiest!' . . . 'I will go back to the hall,' thought Albert. 'Petróv must tell me much more.' But there was no one in the hall now, and instead of the artist Petróv, Albert himself stood on the platform and played on the violin all that the voice had said before. But the violin was of strange construction; it was made of glass and it had to be held in both hands and slowly pressed to the breast to make it produce sounds. The sounds were the most delicate and delightful Albert had ever heard. The closer he pressed the violin to his breast the more joyful and tender he felt. The louder the sounds grew the faster the shadows dispersed and the brighter the walls of the hall were lit up by transparent light. But it was necessary to play the violin very warily so as not to break it. He played the glass instrument very carefully and well. He played such things as he felt no one would ever hear again. He was beginning to grow tired when another distant, muffled sound distracted his attention. It was the sound of a bell, but it spoke words: 'Yes,' said the bell, droning somewhere high up and far away, 'he seems to you pitiful, you despise him, yet he is the best and happiest of men! No one will ever again play that instrument.'

These familiar words suddenly seemed so wise, so new, and so true, to Albert that he stopped playing and, trying not to move, raised his arms and eyes to heaven. He felt that he was beautiful and happy. Although there was no one else in the hall he expanded his chest and stood on the platform with head proudly erect so that all might see him. Suddenly someone's hand lightly touched his shoulder; he turned and saw a woman in the faint light. She looked at him sadly and shook her head deprecatingly. He immediately realized that what he was doing was bad, and felt ashamed of himself. 'Whither?' he asked her. She again gave him a long fixed look and sadly inclined her head. It was she – none other than she whom he loved, and her garments were the same; on her full white neck a string of pearls, and her superb arms bare to above the elbow. She took his hand and led him out of the hall. 'The exit is on the other side,' said Albert, but without replying she smiled and led him out. At the threshold of the hall Albert saw the moon and some water. But the water was not below as it usually is, nor was the moon a white circle in one place up above as it usually is. Moon and water were together and everywhere – above, below, at the sides, and all around them both. Albert threw himself with her into the moon and the water, and realized that he could now embrace her, whom he loved more than anything in the world. He embraced her and felt unutterable happiness. 'Is this not a dream?' he asked himself. But no! It was more than reality: it was reality and recollection combined. Then he felt that the unutterable bliss he had at that moment enjoyed had passed and would never return. 'What am I weeping for?' he asked her. She looked at him silently and sadly. Albert understood what she meant by that. 'But how can it be, since I am alive?' he muttered. Without replying or moving she looked straight before her. 'This is terrible! How can I explain to her that I am alive?' he thought with horror. 'O Lord! I am alive, do understand me!' he whispered.

'He is the best and happiest!' a voice was saying. But something was pressing more and more heavily on Albert. Whether it was the moon and the water, her embraces, or his tears, he did not know, but he felt he would not be able to say all that was necessary, and that soon all would be over.

Two visitors, leaving Anna Ivánovna's house, stumbled over Albert, who lay stretched out on the threshold. One of them went back and called the hostess.

'Why, this is inhuman!' he said. 'You might let a man freeze like that!'

'Ah, that Albert! I'm sick to death of him!' replied the hostess. 'Ánnushka, lay him down somewhere in a room,' she said to the maid.

'But I am alive – why bury me?' muttered Albert, as they carried him insensible into the room.

FAMILY HAPPINESS

A NOVEL

Translated by J. D. Duff

PART I

Chapter I

WE were in mourning for my mother, who had died in the autumn, and I spent all that winter alone in the country with Kátya and Sónya.

Kátya was an old friend of the family, our governess who had brought us all up, and I had known and loved her since my earliest recollections. Sónya was my younger sister. It was a dark and sad winter which we spent in our old house of Pokróvskoe. The weather was cold and so windy that the snowdrifts came higher than the windows; the panes were almost always dimmed by frost, and we seldom walked or drove anywhere throughout the winter. Our visitors were few, and those who came brought no addition of cheerfulness or happiness to the household. They all wore sad faces and spoke low, as if they were afraid of waking someone; they never laughed, but sighed and often shed tears as they looked at me and especially at little Sónya in her black frock. The feeling of death clung to the house; the air was still filled with the grief and horror of death. My mother's room was kept locked; and whenever I passed it on my way to bed, I felt a strange uncomfortable impulse to look into that cold empty room.

I was then seventeen; and in the very year of her death my mother was intending to move to Petersburg, in order to take me into society. The loss of my mother was a great grief to me; but I must confess to another feeling behind that grief – a feeling that though I was young and pretty (so everybody told me), I was wasting a second winter in the solitude of the country. Before the winter ended, this sense of dejection, solitude, and simple boredom increased to such an extent that

479

I refused to leave my room or open the piano or take up a book. When Kátya urged me to find some occupation, I said that I did not feel able for it; but in my heart I said, 'What is the good of it? What is the good of doing anything, when the best part of my life is being wasted like this?' And to this question, tears were my only answer.

I was told that I was growing thin and losing my looks; but even this failed to interest me. What did it matter? For whom? I felt that my whole life was bound to go on in the same solitude and helpless dreariness, from which I had myself no strength and even no wish to escape. Towards the end of winter Kátya became anxious about me and determined to make an effort to take me abroad. But money was needed for this, and we hardly knew how our affairs stood after my mother's death. Our guardian, who was to come and clear up our position, was expected every day.

In March he arrived.

'Well, thank God!' Kátya said to me one day, when I was walking up and down the room like a shadow, without occupation, without a thought, and without a wish. 'Sergéy Mikháylych has arrived; he has sent to inquire about us and means to come here for dinner. You must rouse yourself, dear Máshechka,' she added, 'or what will he think of you? He was so fond of you all.'

Sergéy Mikháylych was our near neighbour, and, though a much younger man, had been a friend of my father's. His coming was likely to change our plans and to make it possible to leave the country; and also I had grown up in the habit of love and regard for him; and when Kátya begged me to rouse myself, she guessed rightly that it would give me especial pain to show to disadvantage before him, more than before any other of our friends. Like everyone in the house, from Kátya and his god-daughter Sónya down to the helper in the stables, I loved him from old habit; and also he had a special significance for me, owing to a remark which my mother had once made in my presence. 'I should like you to marry a man like him,' she said. At the time this seemed to me strange and even unpleasant. My ideal husband was quite different: he was to be thin, pale, and sad; and Sergéy Mikháylych was middle-aged, tall, robust, and always, as it seemed to me, in good spirits. But still my mother's words stuck in my head; and even six years before this time, when I was eleven, and he still said 'thou' to me, and played with me, and called me by the pet-name of 'violet' – even then I sometimes asked myself in a fright, 'What *shall* I do, if he suddenly wants to marry me?'

Before our dinner, to which Kátya made an addition of sweets and a dish of spinach, Sergéy Mikháylych arrived. From the window I watched him drive up to the house in a small sleigh; but as soon as it turned the corner, I hastened to the drawing-room, meaning to pretend that his visit was a complete surprise. But when I heard his tramp and loud voice and Kátya's footsteps in the hall, I lost patience and went to meet him myself. He was holding Kátya's hand, talking loud, and smiling. When he saw me, he stopped and looked at me for a time without bowing. I was uncomfortable and felt myself blushing.

'Can this be really you?' he said in his plain decisive way, walking towards me with his arms apart. 'Is so great a change possible? How grown-up you are! I used to call you "violet", but now you are a rose in full bloom!'

He took my hand in his own large hand and pressed it so hard that it almost hurt. Expecting him to kiss my hand, I bent towards him, but he only pressed it again and looked straight into my eyes with the old firmness and cheerfulness in his face.

It was six years since I had seen him last. He was much changed – older and darker in complexion; and he now wore whiskers which did not become him at all; but much remained the same – his simple manner, the large features of his honest open face, his bright intelligent eyes, his friendly, almost boyish, smile.

Five minutes later he had ceased to be a visitor and had become the friend of us all, even of the servants, whose visible eagerness to wait on him proved their pleasure at his arrival.

He behaved quite unlike the neighbours who had visited us after my mother's death. They had thought it necessary to be silent when they sat with us, and to shed tears. He, on the contrary, was cheerful and talkative, and said not a word about my mother, so that this indifference seemed strange to me at first and even improper on the part of so close a friend. But I understood later that what seemed indifference was sincerity, and I felt grateful for it. In the evening Kátya poured out tea, sitting in her old place in the drawing-room, where she used to sit in my mother's lifetime; Sónya and I sat near him; our old butler Grigóri had hunted out one of my father's pipes and brought it to him; and he began to walk up and down the room as he used to do in past days.

'How many terrible changes there are in this house, when one thinks of it all!' he said, stopping in his walk.

'Yes,' said Kátya with a sigh; and then she put the lid on the samovar and looked at him, quite ready to burst out crying.

'I suppose you remember your father?' he said, turning to me.

'Not clearly,' I answered.

'How happy you would have been together now!' he added in a low voice, looking thoughtfully at my face above the eyes. 'I was very fond of him,' he added in a still lower tone, and it seemed to me that his eyes were shining more than usual.

'And now God has taken her too!' said Kátya; and at once she laid her napkin on the teapot, took out her handkerchief, and began to cry.

'Yes, the changes in this house are terrible,' he repeated, turning away. 'Sónya, show me your toys,' he added after a little and went off to the parlour. When he had gone, I looked at Kátya with eyes full of tears.

'What a splendid friend he is!' she said. And, though he was no relation, I did really feel a kind of warmth and comfort in the sympathy of this good man.

I could hear him moving about in the parlour with Sónya, and the sound of her high childish voice. I sent tea to him there; and I heard him sit down at the piano and strike the keys with Sónya's little hands.

Then his voice came – 'Márya Alexándrovna, come here and play something.'

I liked his easy behaviour to me and his friendly tone of command; I got up and went to him.

'Play this,' he said, opening a book of Beethoven's music at the *adagio* of the Moonlight Sonata. 'Let me hear how you play,' he added, and went off to a corner of the room, carrying his cup with him.

I somehow felt that with him it was impossible to refuse or to say beforehand that I played badly: I sat down obediently at the piano and began to play as well as I could; yet I was afraid of criticism, because I knew that he understood and enjoyed music. The *adagio* suited the remembrance of past days evoked by our conversation at tea, and I believe that I played it fairly well. But he would not let me play the *scherzo*. 'No,' he said, coming up to me; 'you don't play that right; don't go on; but the first movement was not bad; you seem to be musical.' This moderate praise pleased me so much that I even reddened. I felt it pleasant and strange that a friend of my father's, and his contemporary, should no longer treat me like a child but speak to me seriously. Kátya now went upstairs to put Sónya to bed, and we were left alone in the parlour.

He talked to me about my father, and about the beginning of their friendship and the happy days they had spent together, while I was still busy with lesson-books and toys; and his talk put my father before me in quite a new light, as a man of simple and delightful character. He asked me too about my tastes, what I read and what I intended to do, and gave me advice. The man of mirth and jest who used to tease me and make me toys had disappeared; here was a serious, simple, and affectionate friend, for whom I could not help feeling respect and sympathy. It was easy and pleasant to talk to him; and yet I felt an involuntary strain also. I was anxious about each word I spoke: I wished so much to earn for my own sake the love which had been given me already merely because I was my father's daughter.

After putting Sónya to bed, Kátya joined us and began to complain to him of my apathy, about which I had said nothing.

'So she never told me the most important thing of all!' he said, smiling and shaking his head reproachfully at me.

'Why tell you?' I said. 'It is very tiresome to talk about, and it will pass off.' (I really felt now, not only that my dejection would pass off, but that it had already passed off, or rather had never existed.)

'It is a bad thing,' he said, 'not to be able to stand solitude. Can it be that you are a young lady?'

'Of course, I am a young lady,' I answered, laughing.

'Well, I can't praise a young lady who is alive only when people are admiring her, but as soon as she is left alone, collapses and finds nothing to her taste – one who is all for show and has no resources in herself.'

'You have a flattering opinion of me!' I said, just for the sake of saying something.

He was silent for a little. Then he said: 'Yes; your likeness to your father means something. There is something in you . . .' and his kind attentive look again flattered me and made me feel a pleasant embarrassment.

I noticed now for the first time that his face, which gave one at first the impression of high spirits, had also an expression peculiar to himself – bright at first and then more and more attentive and rather sad.

'You ought not to be bored and you cannot be,' he said; 'you have music, which you appreciate, books, study; your whole life lies before you, and now or never is the time to prepare for it and save yourself future regrets. A year hence it will be too late.'

He spoke to me like a father or an uncle, and I felt that he kept a constant check upon himself, in order to keep on my level. Though I was hurt that he considered me as inferior to himself, I was pleased that for me alone he thought it necessary to try to be different.

For the rest of the evening he talked about business with Kátya.

'Well, good-bye, dear friends,' he said. Then he got up, came towards me, and took my hand.

'When shall we see you again?' asked Kátya.

'In spring,' he answered, still holding my hand. 'I shall go now to Danílovka' (this was another property of ours), 'look into things there and make what arrangements I can; then I go to Moscow on business of my own; and in summer we shall meet again.'

'Must you really be away so long?' I asked, and I felt terribly grieved. I had really hoped to see him every day, and I felt a sudden shock of regret, and a fear that my depression would return. And my face and voice must have made this plain.

'You must find more to do and not get depressed,' he said; and I thought his tone too cool and unconcerned. 'I shall put you through an examination in spring,' he added, letting go my hand and not looking at me.

When we saw him off in the hall, he put on his fur coat in a hurry and still avoided looking at me. 'He is taking a deal of trouble for nothing!' I thought. 'Does he think me so anxious that he should look at me? He is a good man, a very good man; but that's all.'

That evening, however, Kátya and I sat up late, talking, not about him but about our plans for the summer, and where we should spend next winter and what we should do then. I had ceased to ask that terrible question – what is the good of it all? Now it seemed quite plain and simple: the proper object of life was happiness, and I promised myself much happiness ahead. It seemed as if our gloomy old house had suddenly become full of light and life.

Chapter II

MEANWHILE spring arrived. My old dejection passed away and gave place to the unrest which spring brings with it, full of dreams and vague hopes and desires. Instead of living as I had done at the beginning of winter, I read and played the piano and gave lessons to Sónya; but also I often went into the garden and wandered for long alone through the avenues, or sat on a bench there; and Heaven knows what my thoughts and wishes and hopes were at such times. Sometimes at night, especially if there was a moon, I sat by my bedroom window till dawn; sometimes, when Kátya was not watching, I stole out into the garden wearing only a wrapper and ran through the dew as far as the pond; and once I went all the way to the open fields and walked right round the garden alone at night.

I find it difficult now to recall and understand the dreams which then filled my imagination. Even when I *can* recall them, I find it hard to believe that my dreams were just like that: they were so strange and so remote from life.

Sergéy Mikháylych kept his promise: he returned from his travels at the end of May.

His first visit to us was in the evening and was quite unexpected. We were sitting in the veranda, preparing for tea. By this time the garden was all green, and the nightingales had taken up their quarters for the whole of St Peter's Fast in the leafy borders. The tops of the round lilac bushes had a sprinkling of white and purple – a sign that their flowers were ready to open. The foliage of the birch avenue was all transparent in the light of the setting sun. In the veranda there was shade and freshness. The evening dew was sure to be heavy on the grass. Out of doors beyond the garden the last sounds of day were audible, and the noise of the sheep and cattle, as they were driven home. Níkon, the half-witted boy, was driving his water-cart along the path outside the veranda, and a cold stream of water from the sprinkler made dark circles on the mould round the stems and supports of the dahlias. In our veranda the polished samovar shone and hissed on the white table-cloth; there were cracknels and biscuits and cream on the table. Kátya was busy washing the cups with her plump hands. I was too hungry after bathing to wait for tea, and was eating bread with thick fresh cream. I was wearing a gingham blouse with loose sleeves, and my hair, still wet, was covered with a kerchief. Kátya saw him first, even before he came in.

'You, Sergéy Mikháylych!' she cried. 'Why, we were just talking about you.'

I got up, meaning to go and change my dress, but he caught me just by the door.

'Why stand on such ceremony in the country?' he said, looking with a smile at the kerchief on my head. 'You don't mind the presence of your butler, and I am really the same to you as Grigóri is.' But I felt just then that he was looking at me in a way quite unlike Grigóri's way, and I was uncomfortable.

'I shall come back at once,' I said, as I left them.

'But what is wrong?' he called out after me; 'it's just the dress of a young peasant woman.'

'How strangely he looked at me!' I said to myself as I was quickly changing upstairs. 'Well, I'm glad he has come; things will be more lively.' After a look in the glass I ran gaily downstairs and into the veranda; I was out of breath and did not disguise my haste. He was sitting at the table, talking to Kátya about our affairs. He glanced at me and smiled; then he went on talking. From what he said it appeared that our affairs were in capital shape: it was now possible for us, after spending the summer in the country, to go either to Petersburg for Sónya's education, or abroad.

'If only you would go abroad with us —' said Kátya; 'without you we shall be quite lost there.'

'Oh, I should like to go round the world with you,' he said, half in jest and half in earnest.

'All right,' I said; 'let us start off and go round the world.'

He smiled and shook his head.

'What about my mother? What about my business?' he said. 'But that's not the question just now: I want to know how you have been spending your time. Not depressed again, I hope?'

When I told him that I had been busy and not bored during his absence, and when Kátya confirmed my report, he praised me as if he had a right to do so, and his words and looks were kind, as they might have been to a child. I felt obliged to tell him, in detail and with perfect frankness, all my good actions, and to confess, as if I were in church, all that he might disapprove of. The evening was so fine that we stayed in the veranda after tea was cleared away; and the conversation interested me so much that I did not notice how we ceased by degrees to hear any sound of the servants indoors. The scent of flowers grew stronger and came from all sides; the grass was drenched with dew; a nightingale struck up in a lilac bush close by and then stopped on hearing our voices; the starry sky seemed to come down lower over our heads.

It was growing dusk, but I did not notice it till a bat suddenly and silently flew in beneath the veranda awning and began to flutter round my white shawl. I shrank back against the wall and nearly cried out; but the bat as silently and swiftly dived out from under the awning and disappeared in the half-darkness of the garden.

'How fond I am of this place of yours!' he said, changing the conversation; 'I wish I could spend all my life here, sitting in this veranda.'

'Well, do then!' said Kátya.

'That's all very well,' he said, 'but life won't sit still.'

'Why don't you marry?' asked Kátya; 'you would make an excellent husband.'

'Because I like sitting still?' and he laughed. 'No, Katerína Kárlovna, too late for you and me to marry. People have long ceased to think of me as a marrying man, and I am even surer of it myself; and I declare I have felt quite comfortable since the matter was settled.'

It seemed to me that he said this in an unnaturally persuasive way.

'Nonsense!' said Kátya; 'a man of thirty-six makes out that he is too old!'

'Too old indeed,' he went on, 'when all one wants is to sit still. For a man who is going to marry that's not enough. Just you ask her,' he added, nodding at me; 'people of her age should marry, and you and I can rejoice in their happiness.'

The sadness and constraint latent in his voice were not lost upon me. He was silent for a little, and neither Kátya nor I spoke.

'Well, just fancy,' he went on, turning a little on his seat; 'suppose that by some mischance I married a girl of seventeen, Másha, if you like – I mean, Márya Alexándrovna. The instance is good; I am glad it turned up; there could not be a better instance.'

I laughed; but I could not understand why he was glad, or what it was that had turned up.

'Just tell me honestly, with your hand on your heart,' he said, turning as if playfully to me, 'would it not be a misfortune for you to unite your life with that of an old worn-out man who only wants to sit still, whereas Heaven knows what wishes are fermenting in that heart of yours?'

I felt uncomfortable and was silent, not knowing how to answer him.

'I am not making you a proposal, you know,' he said, laughing; 'but am I really the kind of husband you dream of when walking alone in the avenue at twilight? It would be a misfortune, would it not?'

'No, not a misfortune,' I began.

'But a bad thing,' he ended my sentence.

'Perhaps; but I may be mistaken . . .' He interrupted me again.

'There, you see! She is quite right, and I am grateful to her for her frankness, and very glad to have had this conversation. And there is something else to be said' – he added: 'for me too it would be a very great misfortune.'

'How odd you are! You have not changed in the least,' said Kátya, and then left the veranda, to order supper to be served.

When she had gone, we were both silent and all was still around us, but for one exception. A nightingale, which had sung last night by fitful snatches, now flooded the garden with a steady stream of song, and was soon answered by another from the dell below, which had not sung till that evening. The nearer bird stopped and seemed to listen for a moment, and then broke out again still louder than before, pouring out his song in piercing long-drawn cadences. There was a regal calm in the birds' voices, as they floated through the realm of night which belongs to those birds and not to man. The gardener walked past to his sleeping-quarters in the greenhouse, and the noise of his heavy boots grew fainter and fainter along the path. Someone whistled twice sharply at the foot of the hill; and then all was still again. The rustling of leaves could just be heard; the veranda awning flapped; a faint perfume, floating in the air, came down on the veranda and filled it. I felt silence awkward after what had been said, but what to say I did not know. I looked at him. His eyes, bright in the half-darkness, turned towards me.

'How good life is!' he said.

I sighed, I don't know why.

'Well?' he asked.

'Life is good,' I repeated after him.

Again we were silent, and again I felt uncomfortable. I could not help fancying that I had wounded him by agreeing that he was old; and I wished to comfort him but did not know how.

'Well, I must be saying good-bye,' he said, rising; 'my mother expects me for supper; I have hardly seen her all day.'

'I meant to play you the new sonata,' I said.

'That must wait,' he replied; and I thought that he spoke coldly.

'Good-bye.'

I felt still more certain that I had wounded him, and I was sorry. Kátya and I went to the steps to see him off and stood for a while in the open, looking along the road where he had disappeared from view. When we ceased to hear the sound of his horse's hoofs, I walked round the house to the veranda, and again sat looking into the garden; and all I wished to see and hear, I still saw and heard for a long time in the dewy mist filled with the sounds of night.

He came a second time, and a third; and the awkwardness arising from that strange conversation passed away entirely, never to return. During that whole summer he came two or three times a week; and I grew so accustomed to his presence, that, when he failed to come for some time, I missed him and felt angry with him, and thought he was behaving badly in deserting me. He treated me like a boy whose company he liked, asked me questions, invited the most cordial frankness on my part, gave me advice and encouragement, or sometimes scolded and checked me. But in spite of his constant effort to keep on my level, I was aware that behind the part of him which I could understand there remained an entire region of mystery, into which he did not consider it necessary to admit me; and this fact did much to preserve my respect for him and his attraction for me. I knew from Kátya and from our neighbours that he had not only to care for his old mother with whom he lived, and to manage his own estate and our affairs, but was also responsible for some public business which was the source of serious worries; but what view he took of all this, what were his convictions, plans, and hopes, I could not in the least find out from him. Whenever I turned the conversation to his affairs, he frowned in a way peculiar to himself and seemed to imply, 'Please stop! That is no business of yours'; and then he changed the subject. This hurt me at first; but I soon grew accustomed to confining our talk to my affairs, and felt this to be quite natural.

There was another thing which displeased me at first and then became pleasant to me. This was his complete indifference and even contempt for my personal appearance. Never by word or look did he imply that I was pretty; on the contrary, he frowned and laughed, whenever the word was applied to me in his presence. He even liked to find fault with my looks and tease me about them. On special days Kátya liked to dress me out in fine clothes and to arrange my hair effectively; but my finery met only with mockery from him, which pained kind-hearted Kátya and at first disconcerted me. She had made up her mind that he admired me; and she could not understand how a man could help wishing a woman whom he admired to appear to the utmost advantage. But I soon understood what he wanted. He wished to make sure that I had not a trace of affectation. And when I understood this I was really quite free from affectation in the clothes I wore, or the arrangement of my hair, or my movements; but a very obvious form of affectation took its place – an affectation of simplicity, at a time when I could not yet be really simple. That he loved me, I knew; but I did not yet ask myself whether he loved me as a child or as a woman. I valued his love; I felt that he thought me better than all other young women in the world, and I could not help wishing him to go on being deceived about me. Without wishing to deceive him, I did deceive him, and I became better myself while deceiving him. I felt it a better and worthier course to show him the good points of my heart and mind than of my body. My hair, hands, face, ways – all these, whether good or bad, he had appraised at once and knew so well, that I could add nothing to my external appearance except the wish to deceive him. But my mind and heart he did not know, because he loved them, and because they were in the very process of growth and development; and on this point I could and did deceive him. And how easy I felt in his company, once I understood this clearly! My causeless bashfulness and awkward movements completely disappeared. Whether he saw me from in front, or in profile, sitting or standing, with my hair up or my hair down, I felt that he knew me from head to foot, and I fancied, was satisfied with me as I was. If, contrary to his habit, he had suddenly said to me as other people did, that I had a pretty face, I believe that I should not have liked it at all. But, on the other hand, how light and happy my heart was when, after I had said something, he looked hard at me and said, hiding emotion under a mask of raillery:

'Yes, there *is* something in you! you are a fine girl – that I must tell you.'

And for what did I receive such rewards, which filled my heart with pride and joy? Merely for saying that I felt for old Grigóri in his love for his little granddaughter; or because the reading of some poem or novel moved me to tears; or because I liked Mozart better than Schulhof. And I was surprised at my own quickness in guessing what was good and worthy of love, when I certainly did not know then what *was* good and worthy to be loved. Most of my former tastes and habits did not please him; and a mere look of his, or a twitch of his eyebrow was enough to show that he did not like what I was trying to say; and I felt at once that my own standard was changed. Sometimes, when he was about to give me a piece of advice, I seemed to know beforehand what he would say. When he looked in my face and asked me a question, his very look would draw out of me the answer he wanted. All my thoughts and feelings of that time were not really mine: they were his thoughts and feelings, which had suddenly become mine and passed into my life and lighted it up. Quite unconsciously

I began to look at everything with different eyes – at Kátya and the servants and Sónya and myself and my occupations. Books, which I used to read merely to escape boredom, now became one of the chief pleasures of my life, merely because he brought me the books and we read and discussed them together. The lessons I gave to Sónya had been a burdensome obligation which I forced myself to go through from a sense of duty; but, after he was present at a lesson, it became a joy to me to watch Sónya's progress. It used to seem to me an impossibility to learn a whole piece of music by heart; but now, when I knew that he would hear it and might praise it, I would play a single movement forty times over without stopping, till poor Kátya stuffed her ears with cotton-wool, while I was still not weary of it. The same old sonatas seemed quite different in their expression, and came out quite changed and much improved. Even Kátya, whom I knew and loved like a second self, became different in my eyes. I now understood for the first time that she was not in the least bound to be the mother, friend, and slave that she was to us. Now I appreciated all the self-sacrifice and devotion of this affectionate creature, and all my obligations to her; and I began to love her even better. It was he too who taught me to take quite a new view of our serfs and servants and maids. It is an absurd confession to make – but I had spent seventeen years among these people and yet knew less about them than about strangers whom I had never seen; it had never once occurred to me that they had their affections and wishes and sorrows, just as I had. Our garden and woods and fields, which I had known so long, became suddenly new and beautiful to me. He was right in saying that the only certain happiness in life is to live for others. At the time his words seemed to me strange, and I did not understand them; but by degrees this became a conviction with me, without thinking about it. He revealed to me a whole new world of joys in the present, without changing anything in my life, without adding anything except himself to each impression in my mind. All that had surrounded me from childhood without saying anything to me, suddenly came to life. The mere sight of him made everything begin to speak and press for admittance to my heart, filling it with happiness.

Often during that summer, when I went upstairs to my room and lay down on my bed, the old unhappiness of spring with its desires and hopes for the future gave place to a passionate happiness in the present. Unable to sleep, I often got up and sat on Kátya's bed, and told her how perfectly happy I was, though I now realize that this was quite unnecessary, as she could see it for herself. But she told me that she was quite content and perfectly happy, and kissed me. I believed her – it seemed to me so necessary and just that everyone should be happy. But Kátya could think of sleep too; and sometimes, pretending to be angry, she drove me from her bed and went to sleep, while I turned over and over in my mind all that made me so happy. Sometimes I got up and said my prayers over again, praying in my own words and thanking God for all the happiness he had given me.

All was quiet in the room; there was only the even breathing of Kátya in her sleep, and the ticking of the clock by her bed, while I turned from side to side and whispered words of prayer, or crossed myself and kissed the cross round my neck. The door was shut and the windows shuttered; perhaps a fly or gnat hung buzzing in the air. I felt a wish never to leave that room – a wish that dawn might never come, that my present frame of mind might never change. I felt that my dreams and thoughts and prayers were live things, living there in the dark with me, hovering about my bed, and standing over me. And every thought was his thought, and every feeling his feeling. I did not know yet that this was love; I thought that things might go on so for ever, and that this feeling involved no consequences.

Chapter III

ONE day when the corn was being carried, I went with Kátya and Sónya to our favourite seat in the garden, in the shade of the lime-trees and above the dell, beyond which the fields and

woods lay open before us. It was three days since Sergéy
Mikháylych had been to see us; we were expecting him, all
the more because our bailiff reported that he had promised to
visit the harvest-field. At two o'clock we saw him ride on to
the rye-field. With a smile and a glance at me, Kátya ordered
peaches and cherries, of which he was very fond, to be
brought; then she lay down on the bench and began to doze.
I tore off a crooked flat lime-tree branch, which made my
hand wet with its juicy leaves and juicy bark. Then I fanned
Kátya with it and went on with my book, breaking off from
time to time, to look at the field-path along which he
must come. Sónya was making a dolls' house at the root of
an old lime-tree. The day was sultry, windless, and steaming;
the clouds were packing and growing blacker; all morning
a thunderstorm had been gathering, and I felt restless, as
I always did before thunder. But by afternoon the clouds
began to part, the sun sailed out into a clear sky, and only in
one quarter was there a faint rumbling. A single heavy cloud,
louring above the horizon and mingling with the dust from the
fields, was rent from time to time by pale zigzags of lightning
which ran down to the ground. It was clear that for to-day the
storm would pass off, with us at all events. The road beyond
the garden was visible in places, and we could see a procession
of high creaking carts slowly moving along it with their load of
sheaves, while the empty carts rattled at a faster pace to meet
them, with swaying legs and shirts fluttering in them. The
thick dust neither blew away nor settled down – it stood still
beyond the fence, and we could see it through the transparent
foliage of the garden trees. A little farther off, in the stack-yard,
the same voices and the same creaking of wheels were audible;
and the same yellow sheaves that had moved slowly past the
fence were now flying aloft, and I could see the oval stacks
gradually rising higher, and their conspicuous pointed tops,
and the labourers swarming upon them. On the dusty field in
front more carts were moving and more yellow sheaves were
visible; and the noise of the carts, with the sound of talking and
singing, came to us from a distance. At one side the bare
stubble, with strips of fallow covered with wormwood, came

more and more into view. Lower down, to the right, the gay
dresses of the women were visible, as they bent down and
swung their arms to bind the sheaves. Here the bare stubble
looked untidy; but the disorder was cleared by degrees, as the
pretty sheaves were ranged at close intervals. It seemed as if
summer had suddenly turned to autumn before my eyes. The
dust and heat were everywhere, except in our favourite nook
in the garden; and everywhere, in this heat and dust and under
the burning sun, the labourers carried on their heavy task with
talk and noise.

Meanwhile Kátya slept so sweetly on our shady bench,
beneath her white cambric handkerchief, the black juicy
cherries glistened so temptingly on the plate, our dresses
were so clean and fresh, the water in the jug was so bright
with rainbow colours in the sun, and I felt so happy! 'How can
I help it?' I thought; 'am I to blame for being happy? And how
can I share my happiness? How and to whom can I surrender
all myself and all my happiness?'

By this time the sun had sunk behind the tops of the birch
avenue, the dust was settling on the fields, the distance became
clearer and brighter in the slanting light. The clouds had
dispersed altogether; I could see through the trees the thatch
of three new corn-stacks. The labourers came down off the
stacks; the carts hurried past, evidently for the last time, with a
loud noise of shouting; the women, with rakes over their
shoulders and straw-bands in their belts, walked home past
us, singing loudly; and still there was no sign of Sergéy
Mikháylych, though I had seen him ride down the hill long
ago. Suddenly he appeared upon the avenue, coming from a
quarter where I was not looking for him. He had walked
round by the dell. He came quickly towards me, with his hat
off and radiant with high spirits. Seeing that Kátya was asleep,
he bit his lip, closed his eyes, and advanced on tiptoe; I saw at
once that he was in that peculiar mood of causeless merriment
which I always delighted to see in him, and which we called
'wild ecstasy'. He was just like a schoolboy playing truant; his
whole figure, from head to foot, breathed content, happiness,
and boyish frolic.

'Well, young violet, how are you? All right?' he said in a whisper, coming up to me and taking my hand. Then, in answer to my question, 'Oh, I'm splendid to-day, I feel like a boy of thirteen – I want to play at horses and climb trees.'

'Is it wild ecstasy?' I asked, looking into his laughing eyes, and feeling that the 'wild ecstasy' was infecting me.

'Yes,' he answered, winking and checking a smile. 'But I don't see why you need hit Katerína Kárlovna on the nose.'

With my eyes on him I had gone on waving the branch, without noticing that I had knocked the handkerchief off Kátya's face and was now brushing her with the leaves. I laughed.

'She will say she was awake all the time,' I whispered, as if not to awake Kátya; but that was not my real reason – it was only that I liked to whisper to him.

He moved his lips in imitation of me, pretending that my voice was too low for him to hear. Catching sight of the dish of cherries, he pretended to steal it, and carried it off to Sónya under the lime-tree, where he sat down on her dolls. Sónya was angry at first, but he soon made his peace with her by starting a game, to see which of them could eat cherries faster.

'If you like, I will send for more cherries,' I said; 'or let us go ourselves.'

He took the dish and set the dolls on it, and we all three started for the orchard. Sónya ran behind us, laughing and pulling at his coat, to make him surrender the dolls. He gave them up and then turned to me, speaking more seriously.

'You really are a violet,' he said, still speaking low, though there was no longer any fear of waking anybody; 'when I came to you out of all that dust and heat and toil, I positively smelt violets at once. But not the sweet violet – you know, that early dark violet that smells of melting snow and spring grass.'

'Is harvest going on well?' I asked, in order to hide the happy agitation which his words produced in me.

'First-rate! Our people are always splendid. The more you know them, the better you like them.'

'Yes,' I said; 'before you came I was watching them from the garden, and suddenly I felt ashamed to be so comfortable myself while they were hard at work, and so . . .'

He interrupted me, with a kind but grave look: 'Don't talk like that, my dear; it is too sacred a matter to talk of lightly. God forbid that you should use fine phrases about that!'

'But it is only to *you* I say this.'

'All right, I understand. But what about those cherries?'

The orchard was locked, and no gardener to be seen: he had sent them all off to help with the harvest. Sónya ran to fetch the key. But he would not wait for her: climbing up a corner of the wall, he raised the net and jumped down on the other side.

His voice came over the wall – 'If you want some, give me the dish.'

'No,' I said; 'I want to pick for myself. I shall fetch the key; Sónya won't find it.'

But suddenly I felt that I must see what he was doing there and what he looked like – that I must watch his movements while he supposed that no one saw him. Besides I was simply unwilling just then to lose sight of him for a single minute. Running on tiptoe through the nettles to the other side of the orchard where the wall was lower, I mounted on an empty cask, till the top of the wall was on a level with my waist, and then leaned over into the orchard. I looked at the gnarled old trees, with their broad dented leaves and the ripe black cherries hanging straight and heavy among the foliage; then I pushed my head under the net, and from under the knotted bough of an old cherry-tree I caught sight of Sergéy Mikháylych. He evidently thought that I had gone away and that no one was watching him. With his hat off and his eyes shut, he was sitting on the fork of an old tree and carefully rolling into a ball a lump of cherry-tree gum. Suddenly he shrugged his shoulders, opened his eyes, muttered something, and smiled. Both words and smile were so unlike him that I felt ashamed of myself for eavesdropping. It seemed to me that he had said, 'Másha!' 'Impossible,' I thought. 'Darling Másha!' he said again, in a lower and more tender tone. There was no possible doubt about the two words this time. My heart beat hard, and such a passionate joy – illicit joy, as I felt – took hold of me, that I clutched at the wall, fearing to fall and betray myself. Startled by the sound of my movement, he looked round – he dropped his eyes instantly, and his face turned red, even scarlet, like a child's. He tried to speak, but in vain; again and again his face positively flamed up. Still he smiled as he looked at me, and I smiled too. Then his whole face grew radiant with happiness. He had ceased to be the old uncle who spoiled or scolded me; he was a man on my level, who loved and feared me as I loved and feared him. We looked at one another without speaking. But suddenly he frowned; the smile and light in his eyes disappeared, and he resumed his cold paternal tone, just as if we were doing something wrong and he was repenting and calling on me to repent.

'You had better get down, or you will hurt yourself,' he said; 'and do put your hair straight; just think what you look like!'

'What makes him pretend? what makes him want to give me pain?' I thought in my vexation. And the same instant brought an irresistible desire to upset his composure again and test my power over him.

'No,' I said; 'I mean to pick for myself.' I caught hold of the nearest branch and climbed to the top of the wall; then, before he had time to catch me, I jumped down on the other side.

'What foolish things you do!' he muttered, flushing again and trying to hide his confusion under a pretence of annoyance; 'you might really have hurt yourself. But how do you mean to get out of this?'

He was even more confused than before, but this time his confusion frightened rather than pleased me. It infected me too and made me blush; avoiding his eye and not knowing what to say, I began to pick cherries though I had nothing to put them in. I reproached myself, I repented of what I had done, I was frightened; I felt that I had lost his good opinion for ever by my folly. Both of us were silent and embarrassed. From this difficult situation Sónya rescued us by running back with the key in her hand. For some time we both addressed our conversation to her and said nothing to each other. When we returned to Kátya, who assured us that she had never been asleep and was listening all the time, I calmed down, and he tried to drop into his fatherly patronizing manner again, but I was not taken in by it. A discussion which we had had some days before came back clear before me.

Kátya had been saying that it was easier for a man to be in love and declare his love than for a woman.

'A man may say that he is in love, and a woman can't,' she said.

'I disagree,' said he; 'a man has no business to say, and can't say, that he is in love.'

'Why not?' I asked.

'Because it never can be true. What sort of a revelation is that, that a man is in love? A man seems to think that whenever he says the word, something will go pop! – that some miracle will be worked, signs and wonders, with all the big guns firing at once! In my opinion,' he went on, 'whoever solemnly brings out the words "I love you" is either deceiving himself or, which is even worse, deceiving others.'

'Then how is a woman to know that a man is in love with her, unless he tells her?' asked Kátya.

'That I don't know,' he answered; 'every man has his own way of telling things. If the feeling exists, it will out somehow. But when I read novels, I always fancy the crestfallen look of Lieut. Strélsky or Alfred, when he says, "I love you, Eleanora", and expects something wonderful to happen at once, and no change at all takes place in either of them – their eyes and their noses and their whole selves remain exactly as they were.'

Even then I had felt that this banter covered something serious that had reference to myself. But Kátya resented his disrespectful treatment of the heroes in novels.

'You are never serious,' she said; 'but tell me truthfully, have you never yourself told a woman that you loved her?'

'Never, and never gone down on one knee,' he answered, laughing; 'and never will.'

This conversation I now recalled, and I reflected that there was no need for him to tell me that he loved me. 'I know that he loves me,' I thought, 'and all his endeavours to seem indifferent will not change my opinion.'

He said little to me throughout the evening, but in every word he said to Kátya and Sónya and in every look and movement of his I saw love and felt no doubt of it. I was only vexed and sorry for him, that he thought it necessary still to hide his feelings and pretend coldness, when it was all so clear, and when it would have been so simple and easy to be boundlessly happy. But my jumping down to him in the orchard weighed on me like a crime. I kept feeling that he would cease to respect me and was angry with me.

After tea I went to the piano, and he followed me.

'Play me something – it is long since I heard you,' he said, catching me up in the parlour.

'I was just going to,' I said. Then I looked straight in his face and said quickly, 'Sergéy Mikháylych, you are not angry with me, are you?'

'What for?' he asked.

'For not obeying you this afternoon,' I said, blushing.

He understood me: he shook his head and made a grimace, which implied that I deserved a scolding but that he did not feel able to give it.

'So it's all right, and we are friends again?' I said, sitting down at the piano.

'Of course!' he said.

In the drawing-room, a large lofty room, there were only two lighted candles on the piano, the rest of the room remaining in half-darkness. Outside the open windows the summer night was bright. All was silent, except when the sound of Kátya's footsteps in the unlighted parlour was heard occasionally, or when his horse, which was tied up under the window, snorted or stamped his hoof on the burdocks that grew there. He sat behind me, where I could not see him; but everywhere – in the half-darkness of the room, in every sound, in myself – I felt his presence. Every look, every movement of his, though I could not see them, found an echo in my heart. I played a sonata of Mozart's which he had brought me and which I had learnt in his presence and for him. I was not thinking at all of what I was playing, but I believe that I played it well, and I thought that he was pleased. I was conscious of his pleasure, and conscious too, though I never looked at him, of the gaze fixed on me from behind. Still moving my fingers mechanically, I turned round quite involuntarily and looked at him. The night had grown brighter, and his head stood out on a background of darkness. He was sitting with his head propped on his hands, and his eyes shone as they gazed at me. Catching his look, I smiled and stopped playing. He smiled too and shook his head reproachfully at the music, for me to go on. When I stopped, the moon had grown brighter and was riding high in the heavens; and the faint light of the candles was supplemented by a new silvery light which came in through the windows and fell on the floor. Kátya called out that it was really too bad – that I had stopped at the best part of the piece, and that I was playing badly. But he declared that I had never played so well; and then he began to walk about the rooms – through the drawing-room to the unlighted parlour and back again to the drawing-room, and each time he looked at me and smiled. I smiled too; I wanted even to laugh with no reason; I was so happy at something that had happened that very day. Kátya and I were standing by the piano; and each time that he vanished through the drawing-room door, I started kissing her in my favourite place, the soft part of her neck under the chin; and each time he came back, I made a solemn face and refrained with difficulty from laughing.

'What is the matter with her to-day?' Kátya asked him.

He only smiled at me without answering; he knew what was the matter with me.

'Just look what a night it is!' he called out from the parlour, where he had stopped by the open French window looking into the garden.

We joined him; and it really was such a night as I have never seen since. The full moon shone above the house and behind us, so that we could not see it, and half the shadow, thrown by the roof and pillars of the house and by the veranda awning, lay slanting and foreshortened on the gravel-path and the strip of turf beyond. Everything else was bright and saturated with the silver of the dew and the moonlight. The broad garden-path, on one side of which the shadows of the dahlias and their supports lay aslant, all bright and cold, and shining on the inequalities of the gravel, ran on till it vanished in the mist. Through the trees the roof of the greenhouse shone bright, and a growing mist rose from the dell. The lilac-bushes, already partly leafless, were all bright to the centre. Each flower was distinguishable apart, and all were drenched with dew. In the avenues light and shade were so mingled that they looked, not like paths and trees but like transparent houses, swaying and moving. To our right, in the shadow of the house, everything was black, indistinguishable, and uncanny. But all the brighter for the surrounding darkness was the top of a poplar, with a fantastic crown of leaves, which for some strange reason remained there close to the house, towering into the bright light, instead of flying away into the dim distance, into the retreating dark-blue of the sky.

'Let us go for a walk,' I said.

Kátya agreed, but said I must put on goloshes.

'I don't want them, Kátya,' I said; 'Sergéy Mikháylych will give me his arm.'

As if that would prevent me from wetting my feet! But to us three this seemed perfectly natural at the time. Though he never used to offer me his arm, I now took it of my own accord, and he saw nothing strange in it. We all went down from the veranda together. That whole world, that sky, that garden, that air, were different from those that I knew.

We were walking along an avenue, and it seemed to me, whenever I looked ahead, that we could go no farther in the same direction, that the world of the possible ended there, and that the whole scene must remain fixed for ever in its beauty. But we still moved on, and the magic wall kept parting to let us in; and still we found the familiar garden with trees and paths and withered leaves. And we were really walking along the paths, treading on patches of light and shade; and a withered leaf was really crackling under my foot, and a live twig brushing my face. And that was really he, walking steadily and slowly at my side, and carefully supporting my arm; and that was really Kátya walking beside us with her creaking shoes. And that must be the moon in the sky, shining down on us through the motionless branches.

But at each step the magic wall closed up again behind us and in front, and I ceased to believe in the possibility of advancing farther – I ceased to believe in the reality of it all.

'Oh, there's a frog!' cried Kátya.

'Who said that? and why?' I thought. But then I realized it was Kátya, and that she was afraid of frogs. Then I looked at the ground and saw a little frog which gave a jump and then stood still in front of me, while its tiny shadow was reflected on the shining clay of the path.

'You're not afraid of frogs, are you?' he asked.

I turned and looked at him. Just where we were there was a gap of one tree in the lime-avenue, and I could see his face clearly – it was so handsome and so happy!

Though he had spoken of my fear of frogs, I knew that he meant to say, 'I love you, my dear one!' 'I love you, I love you' was repeated by his look, by his arm; the light, the shadow, and the air all repeated the same words.

We had gone all round the garden. Kátya's short steps had kept up with us, but now she was tired and out of breath. She said it was time to go in; and I felt very sorry for her. 'Poor thing!' I thought; 'why does not she feel as we do? why are we not all young and happy, like this night and like him and me?'

We went in, but it was a long time before he went away, though the cocks had crowed, and everyone in the house was asleep, and his horse, tethered under the window, snorted continually and stamped his hoof on the burdocks. Kátya never reminded us of the hour, and we sat on talking of the merest trifles and not thinking of the time, till it was past two. The cocks were crowing for the third time and the dawn was breaking when he rode away. He said good-bye as usual and made no special allusion; but I knew that from that day he was mine, and that I should never lose him now. As soon as I had confessed to myself that I loved him, I took Kátya into my confidence. She rejoiced in the news and was touched by my telling her; but she was actually able – poor thing! – to go to bed and sleep! For me, I walked for a long, long time about the veranda; then I went down to the garden, where, recalling each word, each movement, I walked along the same avenues through which I had walked with him. I did not sleep at all that night, and saw sunrise and early dawn for the first time in my life. And never again did I see such a night and such a morning. 'Only why does he not tell me plainly that he loves me?' I thought; 'what makes him invent obstacles and call himself old, when all is so simple and so splendid? What makes him waste this golden time which may never return? Let him say "I love you" – say it in plain words; let him take my hand in his and bend over it and say "I love you". Let him blush and look down before me; and then I will tell him all. No! not tell him, but throw my arms round him and press close to him and weep.' But then a thought came to me – 'What if I am mistaken and he does not love me?'

I was startled by this fear – God knows where it might have led me. I recalled his embarrassment and mine, when I jumped down to him in the orchard; and my heart grew very heavy. Tears gushed from my eyes, and I began to pray. A strange thought occurred to me, calming me and bringing hope with it. I resolved to begin fasting on that day, to take the Communion on my birthday, and on that same day to be betrothed to him.

How this result would come to pass I had no idea; but from that moment I believed and felt sure it would be so. The dawn had fully come and the labourers were getting up when I went back to my room.

Chapter IV

THE Fast of the Assumption falling in August, no one in the house was surprised by my intention of fasting.

During the whole of the week he never once came to see us; but, far from being surprised or vexed or made uneasy by his absence, I was glad of it – I did not expect him until my birthday. Each day during the week I got up early. While the horses were being harnessed, I walked in the garden alone, turning over in my mind the sins of the day before, and considering what I must do to-day, so as to be satisfied with my day and not spoil it by a single sin. It seemed so easy to me then to abstain from sin altogether; only a trifling effort seemed necessary. When the horses came round, I got into the carriage with Kátya or one of the maids, and we drove to the church two miles away. While entering the church, I always recalled the prayer for those who 'come unto the Temple in the fear of God', and tried to get just that frame of mind when mounting the two grass-grown steps up to the building. At that hour there were not more than a dozen worshippers – household servants or peasant women keeping the Fast. They bowed to me, and I returned their bows with studied humility. Then, with what seemed to me a great effort of courage, I went myself and got candles from the man who kept them, an old soldier and an Elder; and I placed the candles before the icons. Through the central door of the altar-screen I could see the altar-cloth which my mother had worked; on the screen were the two angels which had seemed so big to me when I was little, and the dove with a golden halo which had fascinated me long ago. Behind the choir stood the old battered font, where I had been christened myself and had stood godmother to so many of the servants' children. The old priest came out, wearing a cope made of the pall that had covered my father's coffin, and began to read in the same voice that I had heard all my life – at services held in our house, at Sónya's christening, at memorial services for my father, and at my mother's funeral. The same old quavering voice of the deacon rose in the choir; and the same old woman, whom I could remember at every service in that church, crouched by the wall, fixing her streaming eyes on an icon in the choir, pressing her folded fingers against her faded kerchief, and muttering with her toothless gums. And these objects were no longer merely curious to me, merely interesting from old recollections – each had become important and sacred in my eyes and seemed charged with profound meaning. I listened to each word of the prayers and tried to suit my feeling to it; and if I failed to understand, I prayed silently that God would enlighten me, or made up

a prayer of my own in place of what I had failed to catch.
When the penitential prayers were repeated, I recalled my past
life, and that innocent childish past seemed to me so black
when compared to the present brightness of my soul, that
I wept and was horrified at myself; but I felt too that all
those sins would be forgiven, and that if my sins had been
even greater, my repentance would be all the sweeter. At the
end of the service when the priest said, 'The blessing of the
Lord be upon you!' I seemed to feel an immediate sensation of
physical well-being, of a mysterious light and warmth that
instantly filled my heart. The service over, the priest came
and asked me whether he should come to our house to say
Mass, and what hour would suit me; and I thanked him for the
suggestion, intended, as I thought, to please me, but said that
I would come to church instead, walking or driving.

'Is that not too much trouble?' he asked. And I was at a loss
for an answer, fearing to commit a sin of pride.

After the Mass, if Kátya was not with me, I always sent the
carriage home and walked back alone, bowing humbly to all
who passed, and trying to find an opportunity of giving help or
advice. I was eager to sacrifice myself for someone, to help in
lifting a fallen cart, to rock a child's cradle, to give up the path
to others by stepping into the mud. One evening I heard the
bailiff report to Kátya that Simon, one of our serfs, had come
to beg some boards to make a coffin for his daughter, and
a ruble to pay the priest for the funeral; the bailiff had given
what he asked. 'Are they as poor as that?' I asked. 'Very poor,
Miss,' the bailiff answered; 'they have no salt to their food.'
My heart ached to hear this, and yet I felt a kind of pleasure
too. Pretending to Kátya that I was merely going for a walk,
I ran upstairs, got out all my money (it was very little but it was
all I had), crossed myself, and started off alone, through the
veranda and the garden, on my way to Simon's hut. It stood at
the end of the village, and no one saw me as I went up to the
window, placed the money on the sill, and tapped on the pane.
Someone came out, making the door creak, and hailed me;
but I hurried home, cold and shaking with fear like a criminal.
Kátya asked where I had been and what was the matter with

me; but I did not answer, and did not even understand what she was saying. Everything suddenly seemed to me so petty and insignificant. I locked myself up in my own room, and walked up and down alone for a long time, unable to do anything, unable to think, unable to understand my own feelings. I thought of the joy of the whole family, and of what they would say of their benefactor; and I felt sorry that I had not given them the money myself. I thought too of what Sergéy Mikháylych would say, if he knew what I had done; and I was glad to think that no one would ever find out. I was so happy, and I felt myself and everyone else so bad, and yet was so kindly disposed to myself and to all the world, that the thought of death came to me as a dream of happiness. I smiled and prayed and wept, and felt at that moment a burning passion of love for all the world, myself included. Between services I used to read the Gospel; and the book became more and more intelligible to me, and the story of that divine life simpler and more touching; and the depths of thought and feeling I found in studying it became more awful and impene- trable. On the other hand, how clear and simple everything seemed to me when I rose from the study of this book and looked again on life around me and reflected on it! It was so difficult, I felt, to lead a bad life, and so simple to love everyone and be loved. All were so kind and gentle to me; even Sónya, whose lessons I had not broken off, was quite different – trying to understand and please me and not to vex me. Everyone treated me as I treated them. Thinking over my enemies, of whom I must ask pardon before confession, I could only remember one – one of our neighbours, a girl, whom I had made fun of in company a year ago, and who had ceased to visit us. I wrote to her, confessing my fault and asking her forgiveness. She replied that she forgave me and wished me to forgive her. I cried for joy over her simple words, and saw in them, at the time, a deep and touching feeling. My old nurse cried, when I asked her to forgive me. 'What makes them all so kind to me? what have I done to deserve their love?' I asked myself. Sergéy Mikháylych would come into my mind, and I thought for long about him. I could not help it, and I did not consider these thoughts sinful. But my thoughts of him were quite different from what they had been on the night when I first realized that I loved him: he seemed to me now like a second self, and became a part of every plan for the future. The inferiority which I had always felt in his presence had vanished entirely: I felt myself his equal, and could understand him thoroughly from the moral elevation I had reached. What had seemed strange in him was now quite clear to me. Now I could see what he meant by saying that to live for others was the only true happiness, and I agreed with him perfectly. I believed that our life together would be endlessly happy and untroubled. I looked forward, not to foreign tours or fashionable society or display, but to a quite different scene – a quiet family life in the country, with constant self-sacrifice, constant mutual love, and constant recognition in all things of the kind hand of Providence.

I carried out my plan of taking the Communion on my birthday. When I came back from church that day, my heart was so swelling with happiness that I was afraid of life, afraid of any feeling that might break in on that happiness. We had hardly left the carriage for the steps in front of the house, when there was a sound of wheels on the bridge, and I saw Sergéy Mikháylych drive up in his well-known trap. He congratulated me,[1] and we went together to the parlour. Never since I had known him had I been so much at my ease with him and so self-possessed as on that morning. I felt in myself a whole new world, out of his reach and beyond his comprehension. I was not conscious of the slightest embarrassment in speaking to him. He must have understood the cause of this feeling; for he was tender and gentle beyond his wont and showed a kind of reverent consideration for me. When I made for the piano, he locked it and put the key in his pocket.

'Don't spoil your present mood,' he said, 'you have the sweetest of all music in your soul just now.'

1 It is the custom in Russia to congratulate anyone on his or her birthday, and also on receiving Communion.

I was grateful for his words, and yet I was not quite pleased at his understanding too easily and clearly what ought to have been an exclusive secret in my heart. At dinner he said that he had come to congratulate me and also to say good-bye; for he must go to Moscow to-morrow. He looked at Kátya as he spoke; but then he stole a glance at me, and I saw that he was afraid he might detect signs of emotion on my face. But I was neither surprised nor agitated; I did not even ask whether he would be long away. I knew he would say this, and I knew that he would not go. How did I know? I cannot explain that to myself now; but on that memorable day it seemed that I knew everything that had been and that would be. It was like a delightful dream, when all that happens seems to have happened already and to be quite familiar, and it will all happen over again, and one knows that it will happen.

He meant to go away immediately after dinner; but, as Kátya was tired after church and went to lie down for a little, he had to wait until she woke up in order to say good-bye to her. The sun shone into the drawing-room, and we went out to the veranda. When we were seated, I began at once, quite calmly, the conversation that was bound to fix the fate of my heart. I began to speak, no sooner and no later, but at the very moment when we sat down, before our talk had taken any turn or colour that might have hindered me from saying what I meant to say. I cannot tell myself where it came from – my coolness and determination and preciseness of expression. It was as if something independent of my will was speaking through my lips. He sat opposite me with his elbows resting on the rails of the veranda; he pulled a lilac-branch towards him and stripped the leaves off it. When I began to speak, he let go the branch and leaned his head on one hand. His attitude might have shown either perfect calmness or strong emotion.

'Why are you going?' I asked, significantly, deliberately, and looking straight at him.

He did not answer at once.

'Business!' he muttered at last and dropped his eyes.

I realized how difficult he found it to lie to me, and in reply to such a frank question.

'Listen,' I said; 'you know what to-day is to me, how important for many reasons. If I question you, it is not to show an interest in your doings (you know that I have become intimate with you and fond of you) – I ask you this question, because I *must* know the answer. Why are you going?'

'It is very hard for me to tell you the true reason,' he said. 'During this week I have thought much about you and about myself, and have decided that I must go. You understand why; and if you care for me, you will ask no questions.' He put up a hand to rub his forehead and cover his eyes. 'I find it very difficult . . . But you will understand.'

My heart began to beat fast.

'I cannot understand you,' I said; 'I *cannot! you* must tell me; in God's name and for the sake of this day tell me what you please, and I shall hear it with calmness,' I said.

He changed his position, glanced at me, and again drew the lilac-twig towards him.

'Well!' he said, after a short silence in a voice that tried in vain to seem steady, 'it is a foolish business and impossible to put into words, and I feel the difficulty, but I will try to explain it to you,' he added, frowning as if in bodily pain.

'Well?' I said.

'Just imagine the existence of a man – let us call him A – who has left youth far behind, and of a woman whom we may call B, who is young and happy and has seen nothing as yet of life or of the world. Family circumstances of various kinds brought them together, and he grew to love her as a daughter, and had no fear that his love would change its nature.'

He stopped, but I did not interrupt him.

'But he forgot that B was so young, that life was still all a May-game to her,' he went on with a sudden swiftness and determination and without looking at me, 'and that it was easy to fall in love with her in a different way, and that this would amuse her. He made a mistake and was suddenly aware of another feeling, as heavy as remorse, making its way into his heart, and he was afraid. He was afraid that their old friendly relations would be destroyed, and he made up his mind to go away before that happened.' As he said this, he began again to rub his eyes, with a pretence of indifference, and to close them.

'Why was he afraid to love differently?' I asked very low; but I restrained my emotion and spoke in an even voice. He evidently thought that I was not serious; for he answered as if he were hurt.

'You are young, and I am not young. You want amusement, and I want something different. Amuse yourself, if you like, but not with me. If you do, I shall take it seriously; and then I shall be unhappy, and you will repent. That is what A said,' he added; 'however, this is all nonsense; but you understand why I am going. And don't let us continue this conversation. Please not!'

'No! no!' I said, 'we must continue it,' and tears began to tremble in my voice. 'Did he love her, or not?'

He did not answer.

'If he did not love her, why did he treat her as a child and pretend to her?' I asked.

'Yes, A behaved badly,' he interrupted me quickly; 'but it all came to an end and they parted friends.'

'This is horrible! Is there no other ending?' I said with a great effort, and then felt afraid of what I had said.

'Yes, there is,' he said, showing a face full of emotion and looking straight at me. 'There are two different endings. But, for God's sake, listen to me quietly and don't interrupt. Some say' – here he stood up and smiled with a smile that was heavy with pain – 'some say that A went off his head, fell passionately in love with B, and told her so. But she only laughed. To her it was all a jest, but to him a matter of life and death.'

I shuddered and tried to interrupt him – tried to say that he must not dare to speak for me; but he checked me, laying his hand on mine.

'Wait!' he said, and his voice shook. 'The other story is that she took pity on him, and fancied, poor child, from her ignorance of the world, that she really could love him, and so consented to be his wife. And he, in his madness, believed it – believed that his whole life could begin anew; but she saw herself that she had deceived him and that he had deceived her. . . . But let us drop the subject finally,' he ended, clearly unable to say more; and then he began to walk up and down in silence before me.

Though he had asked that the subject should be dropped, I saw that his whole soul was hanging on my answer. I tried to speak, but the pain at my heart kept me dumb. I glanced at him – he was pale and his lower lip trembled. I felt sorry for him. With a sudden effort I broke the bonds of silence which had held me fast, and began to speak in a low inward voice, which I feared would break every moment.

'There is a third ending to the story,' I said, and then paused, but he said nothing; 'the third ending is that he did not love her, but hurt her, hurt her, and thought that he was right; and he left her and was actually proud of himself. You have been pretending, not I; I have loved you since the first day we met, loved you,' I repeated, and at the word 'loved' my low inward voice changed, without intention of mine, to a wild cry which frightened me myself.

He stood pale before me, his lip trembled more and more violently, and two tears came out upon his cheeks.

'It is wrong!' I almost screamed, feeling that I was choking with angry unshed tears. 'Why do you do it?' I cried, and got up to leave him.

But he would not let me go. His head was resting on my knees, his lips were kissing my still trembling hands, and his tears were wetting them. 'My God! if I had only known!' he whispered.

'Why? why?' I kept on repeating, but in my heart there was happiness, happiness which had now come back, after so nearly departing for ever.

Five minutes later Sónya was rushing upstairs to Kátya and proclaiming all over the house that Másha intended to marry Sergéy Mikháylych.

Chapter V

THERE were no reasons for putting off our wedding, and neither he nor I wished for delay. Kátya, it is true, thought we ought to go to Moscow, to buy and order wedding-clothes; and his mother tried to insist that, before the wedding, he must set up a new carriage, buy new furniture, and re-paper the whole house. But we two together carried our point, that all these things, if they were really indispensable, should be done afterwards, and that we should be married within a fort-night after my birthday, quietly, without wedding-clothes, without a party, without best men and supper and champagne, and all the other conventional features of a wedding. He told me how dissatisfied his mother was that there should be no band, no mountain of luggage, no renovation of the whole house – so unlike her own marriage which had cost thirty thousand rubles; and he told of the solemn and secret con-fabulations which she held in her store-room with her house-keeper, Maryúshka, rummaging the chests and discussing carpets, curtains, and salvers as indispensable conditions of our happiness. At our house Kátya did just the same with my old nurse, Kuzmínichna. It was impossible to treat the matter lightly with Kátya. She was firmly convinced that he and I, when discussing our future, were merely talking the senti-mental nonsense natural to people in our position; and that our real future happiness depended on the hemming of table-cloths and napkins and the proper cutting-out and stitching of under-clothing. Several times a day secret information passed between the two houses, to communicate what was going forward in each; and though the external relations between Kátya and his mother were most affectionate, yet a slightly hostile though very subtle diplomacy was already perceptible in their dealings. I now became more intimate with Tatyána Semënovna, the mother of Sergéy Mikháylych, an old-fash-ioned lady, strict and formal in the management of her house-hold. Her son loved her, and not merely because she was his mother: he thought her the best, cleverest, kindest, and most affectionate woman in the world. She was always kind to us and to me especially, and was glad that her son should be getting married; but when I was with her after our engage-ment, I always felt that she wished me to understand that, in her opinion, her son might have looked higher, and that it would be as well for me to keep that in mind. I understood her meaning perfectly and thought her quite right.

During that fortnight he and I met every day. He came to dinner regularly and stayed on till midnight. But though he said – and I knew he was speaking the truth – that he had no life apart from me, yet he never spent the whole day with me, and tried to go on with his ordinary occupations. Our outward relations remained unchanged to the very day of our marriage: we went on saying 'you' and not 'thou' to each other; he did not even kiss my hand; he did not seek, but even avoided, opportunities of being alone with me. It was as if he feared to yield to the harmful excess of tenderness he felt. I don't know which of us had changed; but I now felt myself entirely his equal; I no longer found in him the pretence of simplicity which had displeased me earlier; and I often delighted to see in him, not a grown man inspiring respect and awe but a loving and wildly happy child. 'How mistaken I was about him!' I often thought; 'he is just such another human being as myself!' It seemed to me now, that his whole character was before me and that I thoroughly understood it. And how simple was every feature of his character, and how congenial to my own! Even his plans for our future life together were just my plans, only more clearly and better expressed in his words.

The weather was bad just then, and we spent most of our time indoors. The corner between the piano and the window was the scene of our best intimate talks. The candle-light was reflected on the blackness of the window near us; from time to time drops struck the glistening pane and rolled down. The rain pattered on the roof; the water splashed in a puddle under the spout; it felt damp near the window; but our corner seemed all the brighter and warmer and happier for that.

'Do you know, there is something I have long wished to say to you,' he began one night when we were sitting up late in our corner; 'I was thinking of it all the time you were playing.'

'Don't say it, I know all about it,' I replied.

'All right! mum's the word!'

'No! what is it?' I asked.

'Well, it is this. You remember the story I told you about A and B?'

'I should just think I did! What a stupid story! Lucky that it ended as it did!'

'Yes, I was very near destroying my happiness by my own act. You saved me. But the main thing is that I was always telling lies then, and I'm ashamed of it, and I want to have my say out now.'

'Please don't! you really mustn't!'

'Don't be frightened,' he said, smiling. 'I only want to justify myself. When I began then, I meant to argue.'

'It is always a mistake to argue,' I said.

'Yes, I argued wrong. After all my disappointments and mistakes in life, I told myself firmly when I came to the country this year, that love was no more for me, and that all I had to do was to grow old decently. So for a long time, I was unable to clear up my feeling towards you, or to make out where it might lead me. I hoped, and I didn't hope: at one time I thought you were trifling with me; at another I felt sure of you but could not decide what to do. But after that evening, you remember, when we walked in the garden at night, I got alarmed: the present happiness seemed too great to be real. What if I allowed myself to hope and then failed? But of course I was thinking only of myself, for I am disgustingly selfish.'

He stopped and looked at me.

'But it was not all nonsense that I said then. It was possible and right for me to have fears. I take so much from you and can give so little. You are still a child, a bud that has yet to open; you have never been in love before, and I . . .'

'Yes, do tell me the truth . . .' I began, and then stopped, afraid of his answer. 'No, never mind,' I added.

'Have I been in love before? is that it?' he said, guessing my thoughts at once. 'That I can tell you. No, never before – nothing at all like what I feel now.' But a sudden painful recollection seemed to flash across his mind. 'No,' he said sadly; 'in this too I need your compassion, in order to have the right to love you. Well, was I not bound to think twice before saying that I loved you? What do I give you? love, no doubt.'

'And is that little?' I asked, looking him in the face.

'Yes, my dear, it is little to give *you*,' he continued; 'you have youth and beauty. I often lie awake at night from happiness, and all the time I think of our future life together. I have lived through much, and now I think I have found what is needed for happiness. A quiet secluded life in the country, with the possibility of being useful to people to whom it is easy to do good, and who are not accustomed to have it done to them; then work which one hopes may be of some use; then rest, nature, books, music, love for one's neighbour – such is my idea of happiness. And then, on the top of all that, you for a mate, and children, perhaps – what more can the heart of man desire?'

'It should be enough,' I said.

'Enough for me whose youth is over,' he went on, 'but not for you. Life is still before you, and you will perhaps seek happiness, and perhaps find it, in something different. You think now that this is happiness, because you love me.'

'You are wrong,' I said; 'I have always desired just that quiet domestic life and prized it. And you only say just what I have thought.'

He smiled.

'So you think, my dear; but that is not enough for you. You have youth and beauty,' he repeated thoughtfully.

But I was angry because he disbelieved me and seemed to cast my youth and beauty in my teeth.

'Why do you love me then?' I asked angrily; 'for my youth or for myself?'

'I don't know, but I love you,' he answered, looking at me with his attentive and attractive gaze.

I did not reply and involuntarily looked into his eyes. Suddenly a strange thing happened to me: first I ceased to see what was around me; then his face seemed to vanish till only the eyes were left, shining over against mine; next the eyes seemed to be in my own head, and then all became confused – I could see nothing and was forced to shut my

eyes, in order to break loose from the feeling of pleasure and
fear which his gaze was producing in me ...

The day before our wedding-day, the weather cleared up
towards evening. The rains which had begun in summer gave
place to clear weather, and we had our first autumn evening,
bright and cold. It was a wet, cold, shining world, and the
garden showed for the first time the spaciousness and colour
and bareness of autumn. The sky was clear, cold, and pale.
I went to bed happy in the thought that to-morrow, our
wedding-day, would be fine. I awoke with the sun, and the
thought that this very day ... seemed alarming and surprising.
I went out into the garden. The sun had just risen and shone
fitfully through the meagre yellow leaves of the lime avenue.
The path was strewn with rustling leaves, clusters of moun-
tain-ash berries hung red and wrinkled on the boughs, with
a sprinkling of frost-bitten crumpled leaves; the dahlias were
black and wrinkled. The first rime lay like silver on the pale
green of the grass and on the broken burdock plants round the
house. In the clear cold sky there was not, and could not be,
a single cloud.

'Can it possibly be to-day?' I asked myself, incredulous of
my own happiness. 'Is it possible that I shall wake to-morrow,
not here but in that strange house with the pillars? Is it possible
that I shall never again wait for his coming and meet him, and
sit up late with Kátya to talk about him? Shall I never sit with
him beside the piano in our drawing-room? never see him off
and feel uneasy about him on dark nights?' But I remembered
that he promised yesterday to pay a last visit, and that Kátya
had insisted on my trying on my wedding-dress, and had said
'For to-morrow'. I believed for a moment that it was all real,
and then doubted again. 'Can it be that after to-day I shall be
living there with a mother-in-law, without Nadëzha or old
Grigóri or Kátya? Shall I go to bed without kissing my old
nurse good-night and hearing her say, while she signs me with
the cross from old custom, "Good-night, Miss"? Shall I never
again teach Sónya and play with her and knock through the
wall to her in the morning and hear her hearty laugh? Shall
I become from to-day someone that I myself do not know?

and is a new world, that will realize my hopes and desires, opening before me? and will that new world last for ever?' Alone with these thoughts I was depressed and impatient for his arrival. He came early, and it required his presence to convince me that I should really be his wife that very day, and the prospect ceased to frighten me.

Before dinner we walked to our church, to attend a memorial service for my father.

'If only he were living now!' I thought as we were returning and I leant silently on the arm of him who had been the dearest friend of the object of my thoughts. During the service, while I pressed my forehead against the cold stone of the chapel floor, I called up my father so vividly; I was so convinced that he understood me and approved my choice, that I felt as if his spirit were still hovering over us and blessing me. And my recollections and hopes, my joy and sadness, made up one solemn and satisfied feeling which was in harmony with the fresh still air, the silence, the bare fields and pale sky, from which the bright but powerless rays, trying in vain to burn my cheek, fell over all the landscape. My companion seemed to understand and share my feeling. He walked slowly and silently; and his face, at which I glanced from time to time, expressed the same serious mood between joy and sorrow which I shared with nature.

Suddenly he turned to me, and I saw that he intended to speak. 'Suppose he starts some other subject than that which is in my mind?' I thought. But he began to speak of my father and did not even name him.

'He once said to me in jest, "you should marry my Másha",' he began.

'He would have been happy now,' I answered, pressing closer the arm which held mine.

'You were a child then,' he went on, looking into my eyes; 'I loved those eyes then and used to kiss them only because they were like his, never thinking they would be so dear to me for their own sake. I used to call you Másha then.'

'I want you to say "thou" to me,' I said.

'I was just going to,' he answered; 'I feel for the first time that *thou art* entirely mine'; and his calm happy gaze that drew me to him rested on me.

We went on along the footpath over the beaten and trampled stubble; our voices and footsteps were the only sounds. On one side the brownish stubble stretched over a hollow to a distant leafless wood; across it at some distance a peasant was noiselessly ploughing a black strip which grew wider and wider. A drove of horses scattered under the hill seemed close to us. On the other side, as far as the garden and our house peeping through the trees, a field of winter corn, thawed by the sun, showed black with occasional patches of green. The winter sun shone over everything, and everything was covered with long gossamer spider's webs, which floated in the air round us, lay on the frost-dried stubble, and got into our eyes and hair and clothes. When we spoke, the sound of our voices hung in the motionless air above us, as if we two were alone in the whole world – alone under that azure vault, in which the beams of the winter sun played and flashed without scorching.

I too wished to say 'thou' to him, but I felt ashamed.

'Why *dost thou* walk so fast?' I said quickly and almost in a whisper; I could not help blushing.

He slackened his pace, and the gaze he turned on me was even more affectionate, gay, and happy.

At home we found that his mother and the inevitable guests had arrived already, and I was never alone with him again till we came out of church to drive to Nikólskoe.

The church was nearly empty: I just caught a glimpse of his mother standing up straight on a mat by the choir and of Kátya wearing a cap with purple ribbons and with tears on her cheeks, and of two or three of our servants looking curiously at me. I did not look at him, but felt his presence there beside me. I attended to the words of the prayers and repeated them, but they found no echo in my heart. Unable to pray, I looked listlessly at the icons, the candles, the embroidered cross on the priest's cope, the screen, and the window, and took nothing in. I only felt that something strange was being done to me. At last the priest turned to us with the cross in his hand, congratulated us, and said, 'I christened you and by God's mercy have lived to marry you.' Kátya and his mother kissed us, and Grigóri's voice was heard, calling up the carriage. But I was only frightened and disappointed: all was over, but nothing extraordinary, nothing worthy of the Sacrament I had just received, had taken place in myself. He and I exchanged kisses, but the kiss seemed strange and not expressive of our feeling. 'Is this all?' I thought. We went out of church, the sound of wheels reverberated under the vaulted roof, the fresh air blew on my face, he put on his hat and handed me into the carriage. Through the window I could see a frosty moon with a halo round it. He sat down beside me and shut the door after him. I felt a sudden pang. The assurance of his proceedings seemed to me insulting. Kátya called out that I should put something on my head; the wheels rumbled on the stone and then moved along the soft road, and we were off. Huddling in a corner, I looked out at the distant fields and the road flying past in the cold glitter of the moon. Without looking at him, I felt his presence beside me. 'Is this all I have got from the moment, of which I expected so much?' I thought; and still it seemed humiliating and insulting to be sitting alone with him, and so close. I turned to him, intending to speak; but the words would not come, as if my love had vanished, giving place to a feeling of mortification and alarm.

'Till this moment I did not believe it was possible,' he said in a low voice in answer to my look.

'But I am afraid somehow,' I said.

'Afraid of me, my dear?' he said, taking my hand and bending over it.

My hand lay lifeless in his, and the cold at my heart was painful.

'Yes,' I whispered.

But at that moment my heart began to beat faster, my hand trembled and pressed his, I grew hot, my eyes sought his in the half-darkness, and all at once I felt that I did not fear him, that this fear was love – a new love still more tender and stronger than the old. I felt that I was wholly his, and that I was happy in his power over me.

PART II

Chapter I

DAYS, weeks, two whole months, of seclusion in the country slipped by unnoticed, as we thought then; and yet those two months comprised feelings, emotions, and happiness, sufficient for a lifetime. Our plans for the regulation of our life in the country were not carried out at all in the way that we expected; but the reality was not inferior to our ideal. There was none of that hard work, performance of duty, self-sacrifice, and life for others, which I had pictured to myself before our marriage; there was, on the contrary, merely a selfish feeling of love for one another, a wish to be loved, a constant causeless gaiety and entire oblivion of all the world. It is true that my husband sometimes went to his study to work, or drove to town on business, or walked about attending to the management of the estate; but I saw what it cost him to tear himself away from me. He confessed later that every occupation, in my absence, seemed to him mere nonsense in which it was impossible to take any interest. It was just the same with me. If I read, or played the piano, or passed my time with his mother, or taught in the school, I did so only because each of these occupations was connected with him and won his approval; but whenever the thought of him was not associated with any duty, my hands fell by my sides and it seemed to me absurd to think that anything existed apart from him. Perhaps it was a wrong and selfish feeling, but it gave me happiness and lifted me high above all the world. He alone existed on earth for me, and I considered him the best and most faultless man in the world; so that I could not live for anything else than for him, and my one object was to realize his conception of me. And in his eyes I was the first and most excellent woman in the world, the possessor of all possible virtues; and I strove to be that woman in the opinion of the first and best of men.

He came to my room one day while I was praying. I looked round at him and went on with my prayers. Not wishing to interrupt me, he sat down at a table and opened a book. But I thought he was looking at me and looked round myself. He smiled, I laughed, and had to stop my prayers.

'Have you prayed already?' I asked.

'Yes. But you go on; I'll go away.'

'You do say your prayers, I hope?'

He made no answer and was about to leave the room when I stopped him.

'Darling, for my sake, please repeat the prayers with me!' He stood up beside me, dropped his arms awkwardly, and began, with a serious face and some hesitation. Occasionally he turned towards me, seeking signs of approval and aid in my face.

When he came to an end, I laughed and embraced him.

'I feel just as if I were ten! And you do it all!' he said, blushing and kissing my hands.

Our house was one of those old-fashioned country houses in which several generations have passed their lives together under one roof, respecting and loving one another. It was all redolent of good sound family traditions, which as soon as I entered it seemed to become mine too. The management of the household was carried on by Tatyána Semënovna, my mother-in-law, on old-fashioned lines. Of grace and beauty there was not much; but, from the servants down to the furniture and food, there was abundance of everything, and a general cleanliness, solidity, and order, which inspired respect. The drawing-room furniture was arranged symmetrically; there were portraits on the walls, and the floor was covered with home-made carpets and mats. In the morning-room there was an old piano, with chiffoniers of two different patterns, sofas, and little carved tables with bronze ornaments. My sitting-room, specially arranged by Tatyána Semënovna, contained the best furniture in the house, of many styles and periods, including an old pier-glass, which I was frightened to look into at first, but came to value as an old friend. Though Tatyána Semënovna's voice was never heard, the whole household went like a clock. The number of servants was far too large (they all wore soft boots with no heels, because Tatyána Semënovna had an intense dislike for stamping heels and creaking soles); but they all seemed proud of their calling, trembled before their old mistress, treated my husband and me with an affectionate air of patronage, and performed their duties, to all appearance, with extreme satisfaction. Every Saturday the floors were scoured and the carpets beaten without fail; on the first of every month there was a religious service in the house and holy water was sprinkled; on Tatyána Semënovna's name-day and on her son's (and on mine too, beginning from that autumn) an entertainment was regularly provided for the whole neighbourhood. And all this had gone on without a break ever since the beginning of Tatyána Semënovna's life.

My husband took no part in the household management, he attended only to the farm-work and the labourers, and gave much time to this. Even in winter he got up so early that I often woke to find him gone. He generally came back for early tea, which we drank alone together; and at that time, when the worries and vexations of the farm were over, he was almost always in that state of high spirits which we called 'wild ecstasy'. I often made him tell me what he had been doing in the morning, and he gave such absurd accounts that we both laughed till we cried. Sometimes I insisted on a serious account, and he gave it, restraining a smile. I watched his eyes and moving lips and took nothing in: the sight of him and the sound of his voice was pleasure enough.

'Well, what have I been saying? repeat it,' he would sometimes say. But I could repeat nothing. It seemed so absurd that *he* should talk to *me* of any other subject than ourselves. As if it mattered in the least what went on in the world outside! It was at a much later time that I began to some extent to understand and take an interest in his occupations. Tatyána Semënovna

never appeared before dinner: she breakfasted alone and said
good-morning to us by deputy. In our exclusive little world of
frantic happiness a voice from the staid orderly region in which
she dwelt was quite startling: I often lost self-control and could
only laugh without speaking, when the maid stood before me
with folded hands and made her formal report: 'The mistress
bade me inquire how you slept after your walk yesterday
evening; and about her I was to report that she had pain in
her side all night, and a stupid dog barked in the village and
kept her awake: and also I was to ask how you liked the bread
this morning, and to tell you that it was not Tarás who baked
to-day, but Nikoláshka who was trying his hand for the first
time; and she says his baking is not at all bad, especially the
cracknels: but the tea-rusks were over-baked.' Before dinner
we saw little of each other: he wrote or went out again while
I played the piano or read; but at four o'clock we all met in the
drawing-room before dinner. Tatyána Semënovna sailed out
of her own room, and certain poor and pious maiden ladies, of
whom there were always two or three living in the house,
made their appearance also. Every day without fail my husband
by old habit offered his arm to his mother, to take her in to
dinner; but she insisted that I should take the other, so that
every day, without fail, we stuck in the doors and got in each
other's way. She also presided at dinner, where the conversation, if rather solemn, was polite and sensible. The commonplace talk between my husband and me was a pleasant
interruption to the formality of those entertainments. Sometimes there were squabbles between mother and son and they
bantered one another; and I especially enjoyed those scenes,
because they were the best proof of the strong and tender love
which united the two. After dinner Tatyána Semënovna went
to the parlour, where she sat in an arm-chair and ground her
snuff or cut the leaves of new books, while we read aloud or
went off to the piano in the morning-room. We read much
together at this time, but music was our favourite and best
enjoyment, always evoking fresh chords in our hearts and as it
were revealing each afresh to the other. While I played his
favourite pieces, he sat on a distant sofa where I could hardly

see him. He was ashamed to betray the impression produced on him by the music; but often, when he was not expecting it, I rose from the piano, went up to him, and tried to detect on his face signs of emotion – the unnatural brightness and moistness of the eyes, which he tried in vain to conceal. Tatyána Semënovna, though she often wanted to take a look at us there, was also anxious to put no constraint upon us. So she always passed through the room with an air of indifference and a pretence of being busy; but I knew that she had no real reason for going to her room and returning so soon. In the evening I poured out tea in the large drawing-room, and all the household met again. This solemn ceremony of distributing cups and glasses before the solemnly shining samovar made me nervous for a long time. I felt myself still unworthy of such a distinction, too young and frivolous to turn the tap of such a big samovar, to put glasses on Nikíta's salver, saying 'For Peter Ivánovich', 'For Márya Mínichna', to ask 'Is it sweet enough?' and to leave out lumps of sugar for Nurse and other deserving persons. 'Capital! capital! Just like a grown-up person!' was a frequent comment from my husband, which only increased my confusion.

After tea Tatyána Semënovna played patience or listened to Márya Mínichna telling fortunes by the cards. Then she kissed us both and signed us with the cross, and we went off to our own rooms. But we generally sat up together till midnight, and that was our best and pleasantest time. He told me stories of his past life; we made plans and sometimes even talked philosophy; but we tried always to speak low, for fear we should be heard upstairs and reported to Tatyána Semënovna, who insisted on our going to bed early. Sometimes we grew hungry; and then we stole off to the pantry, secured a cold supper by the good offices of Nikíta, and ate it in my sitting-room by the light of one candle. He and I lived like strangers in that big old house, where the uncompromising spirit of the past and of Tatyána Semënovna ruled supreme. Not she only, but the servants, the old ladies, the furniture, even the pictures, inspired me with respect and a little alarm, and made me feel that he and I were a little out of place in that house and must always be very careful and cautious in our doings. Thinking it over now, I see that many things – the pressure of that unvarying routine, and that crowd of idle and inquisitive servants – were uncomfortable and oppressive; but at the time that very constraint made our love for one another still keener. Not I only, but he also, never grumbled openly at anything; on the contrary he shut his eyes to what was amiss. Dmítri Sídorov, one of the footmen, was a great smoker; and regularly every day, when we two were in the morning-room after dinner, he went to my husband's study to take tobacco from the jar; and it was a sight to see Sergéy Mikháylych creeping on tiptoe to me with a face between delight and terror, and a wink and a warning forefinger, while he pointed at Dmítri Sídorov, who was quite unconscious of being watched. Then, when Dmítri Sídorov had gone away without having seen us, in his joy that all had passed off successfully, he declared (as he did on every other occasion) that I was a darling, and kissed me. At times his calm connivance and apparent indifference to everything annoyed me, and I took it for weakness, never noticing that I acted in the same way myself. 'It's like a child who dares not show his will,' I thought.

'My dear! my dear!' he said once when I told him that his weakness surprised me; 'how can a man, as happy as I am, be dissatisfied with anything? Better to give way myself than to put compulsion on others; of that I have long been convinced. There is no condition in which one cannot be happy; but our life is such bliss! I simply cannot be angry; to me now nothing seems bad, but only pitiful and amusing. Above all – *le mieux est l'ennemi du bien*.[1] Will you believe it, when I hear a ring at the bell, or receive a letter, or even wake up in the morning, I'm frightened. Life must go on, something may change; and nothing can be better than the present.'

I believed him but did not understand him. I was happy; but I took that as a matter of course, the invariable experience of people in our position, and believed that there was

---

1 'The better is the enemy of the good.'

somewhere, I knew not where, a different happiness, not greater but different.

So two months went by and winter came with its cold and snow; and, in spite of his company, I began to feel lonely, that life was repeating itself, that there was nothing new either in him or in myself, and that we were merely going back to what had been before. He began to give more time to business which kept him away from me, and my old feeling returned, that there was a special department of his mind into which he was unwilling to admit me. His unbroken calmness provoked me. I loved him as much as ever and was as happy as ever in his love; but my love, instead of increasing, stood still; and another new and disquieting sensation began to creep into my heart. To love him was not enough for me after the happiness I had felt in falling in love. I wanted movement and not a calm course of existence. I wanted excitement and danger and the chance to sacrifice myself for my love. I felt in myself a super-abundance of energy which found no outlet in our quiet life. I had fits of depression which I was ashamed of and tried to conceal from him, and fits of excessive tenderness and high spirits which alarmed him. He realized my state of mind before I did, and proposed a visit to Petersburg; but I begged him to give this up and not to change our manner of life or spoil our happiness. Happy indeed I was; but I was tormented by the thought that this happiness cost me no effort and no sacrifice, though I was even painfully conscious of my power to face both. I loved him and saw that I was all in all to him; but I wanted everyone to see our love; I wanted to love him in spite of obstacles. My mind, and even my senses, were fully occupied; but there was another feeling of youth and craving for movement, which found no satisfaction in our quiet life. What made him say that, whenever I liked, we could go to town? Had he not said so I might have realized that my uncomfortable feelings were my own fault and dangerous nonsense, and that the sacrifice I desired was there before me, in the task of overcoming these feelings. I was haunted by the thought that I could escape from depression by a mere change from the country; and at the same time I felt ashamed and sorry to tear him away, out of selfish motives, from all he cared for. So time went on, the snow grew deeper, and there we remained together, all alone and just the same as before, while outside I knew there was noise and glitter and excitement, and hosts of people suffering or rejoicing without one thought of us and our remote existence. I suffered most from the feeling that custom was daily petrifying our lives into one fixed shape, that our minds were losing their freedom and becoming enslaved to the steady passionless course of time. The morning always found us cheerful; we were polite at dinner, and affectionate in the evening. 'It is all right,' I thought, 'to do good to others and lead upright lives, as he says; but there is time for that later; and there are other things, for which the time is now or never.' I wanted, not what I had got, but a life of struggle; I wanted feeling to be the guide of life, and not life to guide feeling. If only I could go with him to the edge of a precipice and say, 'One step, and I shall fall over – one movement, and I shall be lost!' then, pale with fear, he would catch me in his strong arms and hold me over the edge till my blood froze, and then carry me off whither he pleased.

This state of feeling even affected my health, and I began to suffer from nerves. One morning I was worse than usual. He had come back from the estate-office out of sorts, which was a rare thing with him. I noticed it at once and asked what was the matter. He would not tell me and said it was of no importance. I found out afterwards that the police-inspector, out of spite against my husband, was summoning our peasants, making illegal demands on them, and using threats to them. My husband could not swallow this at once; he could not feel it merely 'pitiful and amusing'. He was provoked, and therefore unwilling to speak of it to me. But it seemed to me that he did not wish to speak to me about it because he considered me a mere child, incapable of understanding his concerns. I turned from him and said no more. I then told the servant to ask Márya Mínichna, who was staying in the house, to join us at breakfast. I ate my breakfast very fast and took her to the morning-room, where I began to talk loudly to her about some trifle which did not interest me in the least. He walked about the room, glancing at us from time to time. This made me more and more inclined to talk and even to laugh; all that I said myself, and all that Márya Mínichna said, seemed to me laughable. Without a word to me he went off to his study and shut the door behind him. When I ceased to hear him, all my high spirits vanished at once: indeed Márya Mínichna was surprised and asked what was the matter. I sat down on a sofa without answering, and felt ready to cry. 'What has he got on his mind?' I wondered; 'some trifle which he thinks important; but, if he tried to tell it me, I should soon show him it was mere nonsense. But he must needs think that I won't understand, must humiliate me by his majestic composure, and always be in the right as against me. But I too am in the right when I find things tiresome and trivial,' I reflected; 'and I do well to want an active life rather than to stagnate in one spot and feel life flowing past me. I want to move forward, to have some new experience every day and every hour, whereas he wants to stand still and to keep me standing beside him. And how easy it would be for him to gratify me! He need not take me to town; he need only be like me and not put compulsion on himself and regulate his feelings, but live simply. That is the advice he gives me, but he is not simple himself. That is what is the matter.'

I felt the tears rising and knew that I was irritated with him. My irritation frightened me, and I went to his study. He was sitting at the table, writing. Hearing my step, he looked up for a moment and then went on writing; he seemed calm and unconcerned. His look vexed me: instead of going up to him, I stood beside his writing-table, opened a book, and began to look at it. He broke off his writing again and looked at me.

'Másha, are you out of sorts?' he asked.

I replied with a cold look, as much as to say, 'You are very polite, but what is the use of asking?' He shook his head and smiled with a tender timid air; but his smile, for the first time, drew no answering smile from me.

'What happened to you to-day?' I asked; 'why did you not tell me?'

'Nothing much – a trifling nuisance,' he said. 'But I might tell you now. Two of our serfs went off to the town...'

But I would not let him go on.

'Why would you not tell me, when I asked you at breakfast?'

'I was angry then and should have said something foolish.'

'I wished to know then.'

'Why?'

'Why do you suppose that I can never help you in anything?'

'Not help me!' he said, dropping his pen. 'Why, I believe that without you I could not live. You not only help me in everything I do, but you do it yourself. You are very wide of the mark,' he said, and laughed. 'My life depends on you. I am pleased with things, only because you are there, because I need you...'

'Yes, I know; I am a delightful child who must be humoured and kept quiet,' I said in a voice that astonished him, so that he looked up as if this was a new experience; 'but I don't want to be quiet and calm; that is more in your line, and too much in your line,' I added.

'Well,' he began quickly, interrupting me and evidently afraid to let me continue, 'when I tell you the facts, I should like to know your opinion.'

'I don't want to hear them now,' I answered. I did want to hear the story, but I found it so pleasant to break down his composure. 'I don't want to play at life,' I said, 'but to live, as you do yourself.'

His face, which reflected every feeling so quickly and so vividly, now expressed pain and intense attention.

'I want to share your life, to...' but I could not go on – his face showed such deep distress. He was silent for a moment.

'But what part of my life do you not share?' he asked; 'is it because I, and not you, have to bother with the inspector and with tipsy labourers?'

'That's not the only thing,' I said.

'For God's sake try to understand me, my dear!' he cried. 'I know that excitement is always painful; I have learnt that from the experience of life. I love you, and I can't but wish to save you from excitement. My life consists of my love for you; so you should not make life impossible for me.'

'You are always in the right,' I said without looking at him.

I was vexed again by his calmness and coolness while I was conscious of annoyance and some feeling akin to penitence.

'Másha, what is the matter?' he asked. 'The question is not, which of us is in the right – not at all; but rather, what grievance have you against me? Take time before you answer, and tell me all that is in your mind. You are dissatisfied with me: and you are, no doubt, right; but let me understand what I have done wrong.'

But how could I put my feeling into words? That he understood me at once, that I again stood before him like a child, that I could do nothing without his understanding and foreseeing it – all this only increased my agitation.

'I have no complaint to make of you,' I said; 'I am merely bored and want not to be bored. But you say that it can't be helped, and, as always, you are right.'

I looked at him as I spoke. I had gained my object: his calmness had disappeared, and I read fear and pain in his face.

'Másha,' he began in a low troubled voice, 'this is no mere trifle: the happiness of our lives is at stake. Please hear me out without answering. Why do you wish to torment me?'

But I interrupted him.

'Oh, I know you will turn out to be right. Words are useless; of course you are right.' I spoke coldly, as if some evil spirit were speaking with my voice.

'If you only knew what you are doing!' he said, and his voice shook.

I burst out crying and felt relieved. He sat down beside me and said nothing. I felt sorry for him, ashamed of myself, and annoyed at what I had done. I avoided looking at him. I felt that any look from him at that moment must express severity or perplexity. At last I looked up and saw his eyes: they were fixed on me with a tender gentle expression that seemed to ask for pardon. I caught his hand and said,

'Forgive me! I don't know myself what I have been saying.'

'But I do; and you spoke the truth.'

'What do you mean?' I asked.

'That we must go to Petersburg,' he said; 'there is nothing for us to do here just now.'

'As you please,' I said.

He took me in his arms and kissed me.

'You must forgive me,' he said; 'for I am to blame.'

That evening I played to him for a long time, while he walked about the room. He had a habit of muttering to himself; and when I asked him what he was muttering, he always thought for a moment and then told me exactly what it was. It was generally verse, and sometimes mere nonsense, but I could always judge of his mood by it. When I asked him now, he stood still, thought an instant, and then repeated two lines from Lérmontov:

> He in his madness prays for storms,
> And dreams that storms will bring him peace.

'He is really more than human,' I thought; 'he knows everything. How can one help loving him?'

I got up, took his arm, and began to walk up and down with him, trying to keep step.

'Well?' he asked, smiling and looking at me.

'All right,' I whispered. And then a sudden fit of merriment came over us both: our eyes laughed, we took longer and longer steps, and rose higher and higher on tiptoe. Prancing in this manner, to the profound dissatisfaction of the butler and astonishment of my mother-in-law, who was playing patience in the parlour, we proceeded through the house till we reached the dining-room; there we stopped, looked at one another, and burst out laughing.

A fortnight later, before Christmas, we were in Petersburg.

Chapter II

THE journey to Petersburg, a week in Moscow, visits to my own relations and my husband's, settling down in our new quarters, travel, new towns and new faces – all this passed before me like a dream. It was all so new, various, and delightful, so warmly and brightly lighted up by his presence and his love, that our quiet life in the country seemed to me something very remote and unimportant. I had expected to find people in society proud and cold; but to my great surprise, I was received everywhere with unfeigned cordiality and pleasure, not only by relations, but also by strangers. I seemed to be the one object of their thoughts, and my arrival the one thing they wanted, to complete their happiness. I was surprised too to discover in what seemed to me the very best society a number of people acquainted with my husband, though he had never spoken of them to me; and I often felt it odd and disagreeable to hear him now speak disapprovingly of some of these people who seemed to me so kind. I could not understand his coolness towards them or his endeavours to avoid many acquaintances that seemed to me flattering. Surely, the more kind people one knows, the better; and here everyone was kind.

'This is how we must manage, you see,' he said to me before we left the country; 'here we are little Croesuses, but in town we shall not be at all rich. So we must not stay after Easter, or go into society, or we shall get into difficulties. For your sake too I should not wish it.'

'Why should we go into society?' I asked; 'we shall have a look at the theatres, see our relations, go to the opera, hear some good music, and be ready to come home before Easter.'

But these plans were forgotten the moment we got to Petersburg. I found myself at once in such a new and delightful world, surrounded by so many pleasures and confronted by such novel interests, that I instantly, though unconsciously, turned my back on my past life and its plans. 'All that was preparatory, a mere playing at life; but here is the real thing! And there is the future too!' Such were my thoughts. The restlessness and symptoms of depression which had troubled me at home vanished at once and entirely, as if by magic. My love for my husband grew calmer, and I ceased to wonder whether he loved me less. Indeed I could not doubt his love: every thought of mine was understood at once, every feeling

shared, and every wish gratified by him. His composure, if it
still existed, no longer provoked me. I also began to realize that
he not only loved me but was proud of me. If we paid a call, or
made some new acquaintance, or gave an evening party at
which I, trembling inwardly from fear of disgracing myself,
acted as hostess, he often said when it was over: 'Bravo, young
woman! capital! you needn't be frightened; a real success!'
And his praise gave me great pleasure. Soon after our arrival
he wrote to his mother and asked me to add a postscript,
but refused to let me see his letter; of course I insisted on
reading it; and he had said: 'You would not know Másha
again, I don't myself. Where does she get that charming graceful self-confidence and ease, such social gifts with such simplicity and charm and kindliness? Everybody is delighted with
her. I can't admire her enough myself, and should be more in
love with her than ever, if that were possible.'

'Now I know what I am like,' I thought. In my joy and
pride I felt that I loved him more than before. My success
with all our new acquaintances was a complete surprise to me.
I heard on all sides, how this uncle had taken a special fancy for
me, and that aunt was raving about me; I was told by one
admirer that I had no rival among the Petersburg ladies, and
assured by another, a lady, that I might, if I cared, lead the
fashion in society. A cousin of my husband's, in particular,
a Princess D—, middle-aged and very much at home in
society, fell in love with me at first sight and paid me compliments which turned my head. The first time that she invited
me to a ball and spoke to my husband about it, he turned to me
and asked if I wished to go; I could just detect a sly smile on his
face. I nodded assent and felt that I was blushing.

'She looks like a criminal when confessing what she wishes,'
he said with a good-natured laugh.

'But you said that we must not go into society, and you
don't care for it yourself,' I answered, smiling and looking
imploringly at him.

'Let us go, if you want to very much,' he said.

'Really, we had better not.'

'Do you want to? very badly?' he asked again.

I said nothing.

'Society in itself is no great harm,' he went on; 'but unsatisfied social aspirations are a bad and ugly business. We must certainly accept, and we will.'

'To tell you the truth,' I said, 'I never in my life longed for anything as much as I do for this ball.'

So we went, and my delight exceeded all my expectations. It seemed to me, more than ever, that I was the centre round which everything revolved, that for my sake alone this great room was lighted up and the band played, and that this crowd of people had assembled to admire me. From the hairdresser and the lady's maid to my partners and the old gentlemen promenading the ball-room, all alike seemed to make it plain that they were in love with me. The general verdict formed at the ball about me and reported by my cousin, came to this: I was quite unlike the other women and had a rural simplicity and charm of my own. I was so flattered by my success that I frankly told my husband I should like to attend two or three more balls during the season, and 'so get thoroughly sick of them', I added; but I did not mean what I said.

He agreed readily; and he went with me at first with obvious satisfaction. He took pleasure in my success, and seemed to have quite forgotten his former warning or to have changed his opinion.

But a time came when he was evidently bored and wearied by the life we were leading. I was too busy, however, to think about that. Even if I sometimes noticed his eyes fixed questioningly on me with a serious attentive gaze, I did not realize its meaning. I was utterly blinded by this sudden affection which I seemed to evoke in all our new acquaintances, and confused by the unfamiliar atmosphere of luxury, refinement, and novelty. It pleased me so much to find myself in these surroundings not merely his equal but his superior, and yet to love him better and more independently than before, that I could not understand what he could object to for me in society life. I had a new sense of pride and self-satisfaction when my entry at a ball attracted all eyes, while he, as if ashamed to confess his ownership of me in public, made haste to leave my side and efface himself in the crowd of black coats. 'Wait a little!' I often said in my heart, when I identified his obscure and sometimes woebegone figure at the end of the room – 'Wait till we get home! Then you will see and understand for whose sake I try to be beautiful and brilliant, and what it is I love in all that surrounds me this evening!' I really believed that my success pleased me only because it enabled me to give it up for his sake. One danger I recognized as possible – that I might be carried away by a fancy for some new acquaintance, and that my husband might grow jealous. But he trusted me so absolutely, and seemed so undisturbed and indifferent, and all the young men were so inferior to him, that I was not alarmed by this one danger. Yet the attention of so many people in society gave me satisfaction, flattered my vanity, and made me think that there was some merit in my love for my husband. Thus I became more offhand and self-confident in my behaviour to him.

'Oh, I saw you this evening carrying on a most animated conversation with Mme N—,' I said one night on returning from a ball, shaking my finger at him. He had really been talking to this lady, who was a well-known figure in Petersburg society. He was more silent and depressed than usual, and I said this to rouse him up.

'What is the good of talking like that, for *you* especially, Másha?' he said with half-closed teeth and frowning as if in pain. 'Leave that to others; it does not suit you and me. Pretence of that sort may spoil the true relation between us, which I still hope may come back.'

I was ashamed and said nothing.

'Will it ever come back, Másha, do you think?' he asked.

'It never was spoilt and never will be,' I said; and I really believed this then.

'God grant that you are right!' he said; 'if not, we ought to be going home.'

But he only spoke like this once – in general he seemed as satisfied as I was, and I was so gay and so happy! I comforted myself too by thinking, 'If he is bored sometimes, I endured the same thing for his sake in the country. If the relation between us has become a little different, everything will be the same again in summer, when we shall be alone in our house at Nikólskoe with Tatyána Semënovna.'

So the winter slipped by, and we stayed on, in spite of our plans, over Easter in Petersburg. A week later we were preparing to start; our packing was all done; my husband, who had bought things – plants for the garden and presents for people at Nikólskoe, was in a specially cheerful and affectionate mood. Just then Princess D— came and begged us to stay till the Saturday, in order to be present at a reception to be given by Countess R—. The Countess was very anxious to secure me, because a foreign prince, who was visiting Petersburg and had seen me already at a ball, wished to make my acquaintance; indeed this was his motive for attending the reception, and he declared that I was the most beautiful woman in Russia. All the world was to be there; and, in a word, it would really be too bad, if I did not go too.

My husband was talking to someone at the other end of the drawing-room.

'So you will go, won't you, Mary?' said the Princess.

'We meant to start for the country the day after to-morrow,' I answered undecidedly, glancing at my husband. Our eyes met, and he turned away at once.

'I must persuade him to stay,' she said, 'and then we can go on Saturday and turn all heads. All right?'

'It would upset our plans; and we have packed,' I answered, beginning to give way.

'She had better go this evening and make her curtsey to the Prince,' my husband called out from the other end of the room; and he spoke in a tone of suppressed irritation which I had never heard from him before.

'I declare he's jealous, for the first time in his life,' said the lady, laughing. 'But it's not for the sake of the Prince I urge it, Sergéy Mikháylych, but for all our sakes. The Countess was so anxious to have her.'

'It rests with her entirely,' my husband said coldly, and then left the room.

I saw that he was much disturbed, and this pained me. I gave no positive promise. As soon as our visitor left, I went to my husband. He was walking up and down his room, thinking, and neither saw nor heard me when I came in on tiptoe.

Looking at him I said to myself: 'He is dreaming already of his dear Nikólskoe, our morning coffee in the bright drawing-room, the land and the labourers, our evenings in the music-room, and our secret midnight suppers.' Then I decided in my own heart: 'Not for all the balls and all the flattering princes in the world will I give up his glad confusion and tender cares.' I was just about to say that I did not wish to go to the ball and would refuse, when he looked round, saw me, and frowned. His face, which had been gentle and thoughtful, changed at once to its old expression of sagacity, penetration, and patron-izing composure. He would not show himself to me as a mere man, but had to be a demigod on a pedestal.

'Well, my dear?' he asked, turning towards me with an unconcerned air.

I said nothing. I was provoked, because he was hiding his real self from me, and would not continue to be the man I loved.

'Do you want to go to this reception on Saturday?' he asked.

'I did, but you disapprove. Besides, our things are all packed,' I said.

Never before had I heard such coldness in his tone to me, and never before seen such coldness in his eye.

'I shall order the things to be unpacked,' he said, 'and I shall stay till Tuesday. So you can go to the party, if you like. I hope you will; but I shall not go.'

Without looking at me, he began to walk about the room jerkily, as his habit was when perturbed.

'I simply can't understand you,' I said, following him with my eyes from where I stood. 'You say that you never lose self-control' (he had never really said so); 'then why do you talk to me so strangely? I am ready on your account to sacrifice this pleasure, and then you, in a sarcastic tone which is new from you to me, insist that I should go.'

'So you make a *sacrifice*!' he threw special emphasis on the last word. 'Well, so do I. What could be better? We compete in generosity – what an example of family happiness!'

Such harsh and contemptuous language I had never heard from his lips before. I was not abashed, but mortified by his contempt; and his harshness did not frighten me but made me harsh too. How could *he* speak thus, he who was always so frank and simple and dreaded insincerity in our speech to one another? And what had I done that he should speak so? I really intended to sacrifice for his sake a pleasure in which I could see no harm; and a moment ago I loved him and understood his feelings as well as ever. We had changed parts: now he avoided direct and plain words, and I desired them.

'You are much changed,' I said, with a sigh. 'How am I guilty before you? It is not this party – you have something else, some old count against me. Why this insincerity? You used to be so afraid of it yourself. Tell me plainly what you complain of.' 'What will he say?' thought I, and reflected with some complacency that I had done nothing all winter which he could find fault with.

I went into the middle of the room, so that he had to pass close to me, and looked at him. I thought, 'He will come and clasp me in his arms, and there will be an end of it.' I was even sorry that I should not have the chance of proving him wrong. But he stopped at the far end of the room and looked at me.

'Do you not understand yet?' he asked.

'No, I don't.'

'Then I must explain. What I feel, and cannot help feeling, positively sickens me for the first time in my life.' He stopped, evidently startled by the harsh sound of his own voice.

'What do you mean?' I asked, with tears of indignation in my eyes.

'It sickens me that the Prince admired you, and you therefore run to meet him, forgetting your husband and yourself and womanly dignity; and you wilfully misunderstand what your want of self-respect makes your husband feel for you: you actually come to your husband and speak of the "sacrifice" you are making, by which you mean – "To show myself to His Highness is a great pleasure to me, but I 'sacrifice' it."'

The longer he spoke, the more he was excited by the sound of his own voice, which was hard and rough and cruel. I had never seen him, had never thought of seeing him, like that. The blood rushed to my heart and I was frightened; but I felt that I had nothing to be ashamed of, and the excitement of wounded vanity made me eager to punish him.

'I have long been expecting this,' I said. 'Go on. Go on!'

'What you expected, I don't know,' he went on; 'but I might well expect the worst, when I saw you day after day sharing the dirtiness and idleness and luxury of this foolish society, and it has come at last. Never have I felt such shame and pain as now — pain for myself, when your friend thrusts her unclean fingers into my heart and speaks of my jealousy! — jealousy of a man whom neither you nor I know; and you refuse to understand me and offer to make a sacrifice for me — and what sacrifice? I am ashamed for you, for your degradation!...Sacrifice!' he repeated again.

'Ah, so this is a husband's power,' thought I: 'to insult and humiliate a perfectly innocent woman. Such may be a husband's rights, but I will not submit to them.' I felt the blood leave my face and a strange distension of my nostrils, as I said, 'No! I make no sacrifice on your account. I shall go to the party on Saturday without fail.'

'And I hope you may enjoy it. But all is over between us two!' he cried out in a fit of unrestrained fury. 'But you shall not torture me any longer! I was a fool, when I . . .', but his lips quivered, and he refrained with a visible effort from ending the sentence.

I feared and hated him at that moment. I wished to say a great deal to him and punish him for all his insults; but if I had opened my mouth, I should have lost my dignity by bursting into tears. I said nothing and left the room. But as soon as I ceased to hear his footsteps, I was horrified at what we had done. I feared that the tie which had made all my happiness might really be snapped for ever; and I thought of going back. But then I wondered: 'Is he calm enough now to understand me, if I mutely stretch out my hand and look at him? Will he realize my generosity? What if he calls my grief a mere pretence? Or he may feel sure that he is right and accept my repentance and forgive me with unruffled pride. And why, oh why, did he whom I loved so well insult me so cruelly?'

I went not to him but to my own room, where I sat for a long time and cried. I recalled with horror each word of our conversation, and substituted different words, kind words, for those that we had spoken, and added others; and then again I remembered the reality with horror and a feeling of injury. In the evening I went down for tea and met my husband in the presence of a friend who was staying with us; and it seemed to me that a wide gulf had opened between us from that day. Our friend asked me when we were to start; and before I could speak, my husband answered:

'On Tuesday,' he said; 'we have to stay for Countess R——'s reception.' He turned to me: 'I believe you intend to go?' he asked.

His matter-of-fact tone frightened me, and I looked at him timidly. His eyes were directed straight at me with an unkind and scornful expression; his voice was cold and even.

'Yes,' I answered.

When we were alone that evening, he came up to me and held out his hand.

'Please forget what I said to you to-day,' he began.

As I took his hand, a smile quivered on my lips and the tears were ready to flow; but he took his hand away and sat down on an arm-chair at some distance, as if fearing a sentimental scene. 'Is it possible that he still thinks himself in the right?' I wondered; and, though I was quite ready to explain and to beg that we might not go to the party, the words died on my lips.

'I must write to my mother that we have put off our departure,' he said; 'otherwise she will be uneasy.'

'When do you think of going?' I asked.

'On Tuesday, after the reception,' he replied.

'I hope it is not on my account,' I said, looking into his eyes; but those eyes merely looked – they said nothing, and a veil seemed to cover them from me. His face seemed to me to have grown suddenly old and disagreeable.

We went to the reception, and good friendly relations between us seemed to have been restored, but these relations were quite different from what they had been.

At the party I was sitting with other ladies when the Prince came up to me, so that I had to stand up in order to speak to him. As I rose, my eyes involuntarily sought my husband. He was looking at me from the other end of the room, and now turned away. I was seized by a sudden sense of shame and pain; in my confusion I blushed all over my face and neck under the Prince's eye. But I was forced to stand and listen, while he spoke, eyeing me from his superior height. Our conversation was soon over: there was no room for him beside me, and he, no doubt, felt that I was uncomfortable with him. We talked of the last ball, of where I should spend the summer, and so on. As he left me, he expressed a wish to make the acquaintance of my husband, and I saw them meet and begin a conversation at the far end of the room. The Prince evidently said something about me; for he smiled in the middle of their talk and looked in my direction.

My husband suddenly flushed up. He made a low bow and turned away from the Prince without being dismissed. I blushed too: I was ashamed of the impression which I and, still more, my husband must have made on the Prince. Everyone, I thought, must have noticed my awkward shyness when I was presented, and my husband's eccentric behaviour. 'Heaven knows how they will interpret such conduct? Perhaps they know already about my scene with my husband!'

Princess D— drove me home, and on the way I spoke to her about my husband. My patience was at an end, and I told her the whole story of what had taken place between us owing to this unlucky party. To calm me, she said that such differences were very common and quite unimportant, and that our quarrel would leave no trace behind. She explained to me her view of my husband's character – that he had become very stiff and unsociable. I agreed, and believed that I had learned to judge him myself more calmly and more truly.

But when I was alone with my husband later, the thought that I had sat in judgement upon him weighed like a crime

upon my conscience; and I felt that the gulf which divided us
had grown still greater.

Chapter III

FROM that day there was a complete change in our life and
our relations to each other. We were no longer as happy when
we were alone together as before. To certain subjects we gave
a wide berth, and conversation flowed more easily in the
presence of a third person. When the talk turned on life in
the country, or on a ball, we were uneasy and shrank from
looking at one another. Both of us knew where the gulf
between us lay, and seemed afraid to approach it. I was convinced that he was proud and irascible, and that I must be
careful not to touch him on his weak point. He was equally
sure that I disliked the country and was dying for social
distraction, and that he must put up with this unfortunate
taste of mine. We both avoided frank conversation on these
topics, and each misjudged the other. We had long ceased to
think each other the most perfect people in the world; each
now judged the other in secret, and measured the offender by
the standard of other people. I fell ill before we left Petersburg,
and we went from there to a house near town, from which my
husband went on alone, to join his mother at Nikólskoe. By
that time I was well enough to have gone with him, but he
urged me to stay on the pretext of my health. I knew, however, that he was really afraid we should be uncomfortable
together in the country; so I did not insist much, and he went
off alone. I felt it dull and solitary in his absence; but when he
came back, I saw that he did not add to my life what he had
added formerly. In the old days every thought and experience
weighed on me like a crime till I had imparted it to him; every
action and word of his seemed to me a model of perfection; we
often laughed for joy at the mere sight of each other. But these
relations had changed, so imperceptibly that we had not even
noticed their disappearance. Separate interests and cares,
which we no longer tried to share, made their appearance,
and even the fact of our estrangement ceased to trouble us.

The idea became familiar, and, before a year had passed, each could look at the other without confusion. His fits of boyish merriment with me had quite vanished; his mood of calm indulgence to all that passed, which used to provoke me, had disappeared; there was an end of those penetrating looks which used to confuse and delight me, an end of the ecstasies and prayers which we once shared in common. We did not even meet often: he was continually absent, with no fears or regrets for leaving me alone; and I was constantly in society, where I did not need him.

There were no further scenes or quarrels between us. I tried to satisfy him, he carried out all my wishes, and we seemed to love each other.

When we were by ourselves, which we seldom were, I felt neither joy nor excitement nor embarrassment in his company: it seemed like being alone. I realized that he was my husband and no mere stranger, a good man, and as familiar to me as my own self. I was convinced that I knew just what he would say and do, and how he would look; and if anything he did surprised me, I concluded that he had made a mistake. I expected nothing from him. In a word, he was my husband – and that was all. It seemed to me that things must be so, as a matter of course, and that no other relations between us had ever existed. When he left home, especially at first, I was lonely and frightened and felt keenly my need of support; when he came back, I ran to his arms with joy, though two hours later my joy was quite forgotten, and I found nothing to say to him. Only at moments which sometimes occurred between us of quiet undemonstrative affection, I felt something wrong and some pain at my heart, and I seemed to read the same story in his eyes. I was conscious of a limit to tenderness, which he seemingly would not, and I could not, overstep. This saddened me sometimes; but I had no leisure to reflect on anything, and my regret for a change which I vaguely realized I tried to drown in the distractions which were always within my reach. Fashionable life, which had dazzled me at first by its glitter and flattery of my self-love, now took entire command of my nature, became a habit, laid its fetters upon me, and monopolized my capacity for feeling. I could not bear solitude, and was afraid to reflect on my position. My whole day, from late in the morning till late at night, was taken up by the claims of society; even if I stayed at home, my time was not my own. This no longer seemed to me either gay or dull, but it seemed that so, and not otherwise, it always had to be.

So three years passed, during which our relations to one another remained unchanged and seemed to have taken a fixed shape which could not become either better or worse. Though two events of importance in our family life took place during that time, neither of them changed my own life. These were the birth of my first child and the death of Tatyána Semën-ovna. At first the feeling of motherhood did take hold of me with such power, and produce in me such a passion of unanti-cipated joy, that I believed this would prove the beginning of a new life for me. But, in the course of two months, when I began to go out again, my feeling grew weaker and weaker, till it passed into mere habit and the lifeless performance of a duty. My husband, on the contrary, from the birth of our first boy, became his old self again – gentle, composed, and home-loving, and transferred to the child his old tenderness and gaiety. Many a night when I went, dressed for a ball, to the nursery, to sign the child with the cross before he slept, I found my husband there and felt his eyes fixed on me with something of reproof in their serious gaze. Then I was ashamed and even shocked by my own callousness, and asked myself if I was worse than other women. 'But it can't be helped,' I said to myself; 'I love my child, but to sit beside him all day long would bore me; and nothing will make me pretend what I do not really feel.'

His mother's death was a great sorrow to my husband; he said that he found it painful to go on living at Nikólskoe. For myself, although I mourned for her and sympathized with my husband's sorrow, yet I found life in that house easier and pleasanter after her death. Most of those three years we spent in town: I went only once to Nikólskoe for two months; and the third year we went abroad and spent the summer at Baden.

I was then twenty-one; our financial position was, I believed, satisfactory; my domestic life gave me all that I asked of it; everyone I knew, it seemed to me, loved me; my health was good; I was the best-dressed woman in Baden; I knew that I was good-looking; the weather was fine; I enjoyed the atmosphere of beauty and refinement; and, in short, I was in excellent spirits. They had once been even higher at Nikólskoe, when my happiness was in myself and came from the feeling that I deserved to be happy, and from the anticipation of still greater happiness to come. That was a different state of things; but I did very well this summer also. I had no special wishes or hopes or fears; it seemed to me that my life was full and my conscience easy. Among all the visitors at Baden that season there was no one man whom I preferred to the rest, or even to our old ambassador, Prince K—, who was assiduous in his attentions to me. One was young, and another old; one was English and fair, another French and wore a beard – to me they were all alike, but all indispensable. Indistinguishable as they were, they together made up the atmosphere which I found so pleasant. But there was one, an Italian marquis, who stood out from the rest by reason of the boldness with which he expressed his admiration. He seized every opportunity of being with me – danced with me, rode with me, and met me at the casino; and everywhere he spoke to me of my charms. Several times I saw him from my windows loitering round our hotel, and the fixed gaze of his bright eyes often troubled me, and made me blush and turn away. He was young, handsome, and well-mannered; and, above all, by his smile and the expression of his brow, he resembled my husband, though much handsomer than he. He struck me by this likeness, though in general, in his lips, eyes, and long chin, there was something coarse and animal which contrasted with my husband's charming expression of kindness and noble serenity. I supposed him to be passionately in love with me, and thought of him sometimes with proud commiseration. When I tried at times to soothe him and change his tone to one of easy, half-friendly confidence, he resented the suggestion with vehemence, and continued to disquiet me by a smouldering passion which was ready at any moment to burst forth. Though I would not own it even to myself, I feared him and often thought of him against my will. My husband knew him, and treated him – even more than other acquaintances of ours who regarded him only as my husband – with coldness and disdain.

Towards the end of the season I fell ill and stayed indoors for a fortnight. The first evening that I went out again to hear the band, I learnt that Lady S—, an Englishwoman famous for her beauty, who had long been expected, had arrived in my absence. My return was welcomed, and a group gathered round me; but a more distinguished group attended the beautiful stranger. She and her beauty were the one subject of conversation around me. When I saw her, she was really beautiful, but her self-satisfied expression struck me as disagreeable, and I said so. That day everything that had formerly seemed amusing, seemed dull. Lady S— arranged an expedition to the ruined castle for the next day; but I declined to be of the party. Almost everyone else went; and my opinion of Baden underwent a complete change. Everything and everybody seemed to me stupid and tiresome; I wanted to cry, to break off my cure, to return to Russia. There was some evil feeling in my soul, but I did not yet acknowledge it to myself. Pretending that I was not strong, I ceased to appear at crowded parties; if I went out, it was only in the morning by myself, to drink the waters; and my only companion was Mme M—, a Russian lady, with whom I sometimes took drives in the surrounding country. My husband was absent: he had gone to Heidelberg for a time, intending to return to Russia when my cure was over, and only paid me occasional visits at Baden.

One day when Lady S— had carried off all the company on a hunting-expedition, Mme M— and I drove in the afternoon to the castle. While our carriage moved slowly along the winding road, bordered by ancient chestnut-trees and commanding a vista of the pretty and pleasant country round Baden, with the setting sun lighting it up, our conversation took a more serious turn than had ever happened to us before. I had known my companion for a long time; but she appeared to me now in a new light, as a well-principled and intelligent woman, to whom it was possible to speak without reserve, and whose friendship was worth having. We spoke of our private concerns, of our children, of the emptiness of life at Baden, till we felt a longing for Russia and the Russian countryside. When we entered the castle we were still under the impression of this serious feeling. Within the walls there was shade and coolness; the sunlight played from above upon the ruins. Steps and voices were audible. The landscape, charming enough but cold to a Russian eye, lay before us in the frame made by a doorway. We sat down to rest and watched the sunset in silence. The voices now sounded louder, and I thought I heard my own name. I listened and could not help overhearing every word. I recognized the voices: the speakers were the Italian marquis and a French friend of his whom I knew also. They were talking of me and of Lady S——, and the Frenchman was comparing us as rival beauties. Though he said nothing insulting, his words made my pulse quicken. He explained in detail the good points of us both. I was already a mother, while Lady S—— was only nineteen; though I had the advantage in hair, my rival had a better figure. 'Besides,' he added, 'Lady S—— is a real *grande dame*, and the other is nothing in particular, only one of those obscure Russian princesses who turn up here nowadays in such numbers.' He ended by saying that I was wise in not attempting to compete with Lady S——, and that I was completely buried as far as Baden was concerned.

'I am sorry for her – unless indeed she takes a fancy to console herself with you,' he added with a hard ringing laugh.

'If she goes away, I follow her' – the words were blurted out in an Italian accent.

'Happy man! he is still capable of a passion!' laughed the Frenchman.

'Passion!' said the other voice and then was still for a moment. 'It is a necessity to me: I cannot live without it. To make life a romance is the one thing worth doing. And with me romance never breaks off in the middle, and this affair I shall carry through to the end.'

'*Bonne chance, mon ami!*'[1] said the Frenchman.

1 'Good luck, my friend!'

They now turned a corner, and the voices stopped. Then we heard them coming down the steps, and a few minutes later they came out upon us by a side-door. They were much surprised to see us. I blushed when the marquis approached me, and felt afraid when we left the castle and he offered me his arm. I could not refuse, and we set off for the carriage, walking behind Mme M— and his friend. I was mortified by what the Frenchman had said of me, though I secretly admitted that he had only put in words what I felt myself; but the plain speaking of the Italian had surprised and upset me by its coarseness. I was tormented by the thought that, though I had overheard him, he showed no fear of me. It was hateful to have him so close to me; and I walked fast after the other couple, not looking at him or answering him and trying to hold his arm in such a way as not to hear him. He spoke of the fine view, of the unexpected pleasure of our meeting, and so on; but I was not listening. My thoughts were with my husband, my child, my country; I felt ashamed, distressed, anxious; I was in a hurry to get back to my solitary room in the Hôtel de Bade, there to think at leisure of the storm of feeling that had just risen in my heart. But Mme M— walked slowly, it was still a long way to the carriage, and my escort seemed to loiter on purpose as if he wished to detain me. 'None of that!' I thought, and resolutely quickened my pace. But it soon became unmistakable that he was detaining me and even pressing my arm. Mme M— turned a corner, and we were quite alone. I was afraid.

'Excuse me,' I said coldly and tried to free my arm; but the lace of my sleeve caught on a button of his coat. Bending towards me, he began to unfasten it, and his ungloved fingers touched my arm. A feeling new to me, half horror and half pleasure, sent an icy shiver down my back. I looked at him, intending by my coldness to convey all the contempt I felt for him; but my look expressed nothing but fear and excitement. His liquid blazing eyes, right up against my face, stared strangely at me, at my neck and breast; both his hands fingered my arm above the wrist; his parted lips were saying that he loved me, and that I was all the world to him; and those lips were coming nearer and nearer, and those hands were squeezing mine harder and harder and burning me. A fever ran through my veins, my sight grew dim, I trembled, and the words intended to check him died in my throat. Suddenly I felt a kiss on my cheek. Trembling all over and turning cold, I stood still and stared at him. Unable to speak or move, I stood there, horrified, expectant, even desirous. It was over in a moment, but the moment was horrible! In that short time I saw him exactly as he was – the low straight forehead (that forehead so like my husband's!) under the straw hat; the handsome regular nose and dilated nostrils; the long waxed moustache and short beard; the close-shaved cheeks and sunburnt neck. I hated and feared him; he was utterly repugnant and alien to me. And yet the excitement and passion of this hateful strange man raised a powerful echo in my own heart; I felt an irresistible longing to surrender myself to the kisses of that coarse handsome mouth, and to the pressure of those white hands with their delicate veins and jewelled fingers; I was tempted to throw myself headlong into the abyss of forbidden delights that had suddenly opened up before me.

'I am so unhappy already,' I thought; 'let more and more storms of unhappiness burst over my head!'

He put one arm round me and bent towards my face. 'Better so!' I thought: 'let sin and shame cover me ever deeper and deeper!'

'*Je vous aime!*'[1] he whispered in the voice which was so like my husband's. At once I thought of my husband and child, as creatures once precious to me who had now passed altogether out of my life. At that moment I heard Mme M—'s voice; she called to me from round the corner. I came to myself, tore my hand away without looking at him, and almost ran after her: I only looked at him after she and I were already seated in the carriage. Then I saw him raise his hat and ask some commonplace question with a smile. He little knew the inexpressible aversion I felt for him at that moment.

1 'I love you.'

My life seemed so wretched, the future so hopeless, the past so black! When Mme M— spoke, her words meant nothing to me. I thought that she talked only out of pity, and to hide the contempt I aroused in her. In every word and every look I seemed to detect this contempt and insulting pity. The shame of that kiss burnt my cheek, and the thought of my husband and child was more than I could bear. When I was alone in my own room, I tried to think over my position; but I was afraid to be alone. Without drinking the tea which was brought me, and uncertain of my own motives, I got ready with feverish haste to catch the evening train and join my husband at Heidelberg.

I found seats for myself and my maid in an empty carriage. When the train started and the fresh air blew through the window on my face, I grew more composed and pictured my past and future to myself more clearly. The course of our married life from the time of our first visit to Petersburg now presented itself to me in a new light, and lay like a reproach on my conscience. For the first time I clearly recalled our start at Nikólskoe and our plans for the future; and for the first time I asked myself what happiness had my husband had since then. I felt that I had behaved badly to him. 'But why', I asked myself, 'did he not stop me? Why did he make pretences? Why did he always avoid explanations? Why did he insult me? Why did he not use the power of his love to influence me? Or did he not love me?' But whether he was to blame or not, I still felt the kiss of that strange man upon my cheek. The nearer we got to Heidelberg, the clearer grew my picture of my husband, and the more I dreaded our meeting. 'I shall tell him all,' I thought, 'and wipe out everything with tears of repentance; and he will forgive me.' But I did not know myself what I meant by 'everything'; and I did not believe in my heart that he would forgive me.

As soon as I entered my husband's room and saw his calm though surprised expression, I felt at once that I had nothing to tell him, no confession to make, and nothing to ask forgiveness for. I had to suppress my unspoken grief and penitence.

'What put this into your head?' he asked. 'I meant to go to Baden to-morrow.' Then he looked more closely at me and seemed to take alarm. 'What's the matter with you? What has happened?' he said.

'Nothing at all,' I replied, almost breaking down. 'I am not going back. Let us go home, to-morrow if you like, to Russia.'

For some time he said nothing but looked at me attentively. Then he said, 'But do tell me what has happened to you.'

I blushed involuntarily and looked down. There came into his eyes a flash of anger and displeasure. Afraid of what he might imagine, I said with a power of pretence that surprised myself:

'Nothing at all has happened. It was merely that I grew weary and sad by myself; and I have been thinking a great deal of our way of life and of you. I have long been to blame towards you. Why do you take me abroad, when you can't bear it yourself? I have long been to blame. Let us go back to Nikólskoe and settle there for ever.'

'Spare us these sentimental scenes, my dear,' he said coldly. 'To go back to Nikólskoe is a good idea, for our money is running short; but the notion of stopping there "for ever" is fanciful. I know you would not settle down. Have some tea, and you will feel better,' and he rose to ring for the waiter.

I imagined all he might be thinking about me; and I was offended by the horrible thoughts which I ascribed to him when I encountered the dubious and shame-faced look he directed at me. 'He will not and cannot understand me.' I said I would go and look at the child, and I left the room. I wished to be alone, and to cry and cry and cry...

Chapter IV

THE house at Nikólskoe, so long unheated and uninhabited, came to life again; but much of the past was dead beyond recall. Tatyána Semënovna was no more, and we were now alone together. But far from desiring such close companionship, we even found it irksome. To me that winter was the more trying because I was in bad health, from which I only recovered after the birth of my second son. My husband and I were still on the same terms as during our life in Petersburg: we were coldly friendly to each other; but in the country each room and wall and sofa recalled what he had once been to me, and what I had lost. It was as if some unforgiven grievance held us apart, as if he were punishing me and pretending not to be aware of it. But there was nothing to ask pardon for, no penalty to deprecate; my punishment was merely this, that he did not give his whole heart and mind to me as he used to do; but he did not give it to anyone or to anything; as though he had no longer a heart to give. Sometimes it occurred to me that he was only pretending to be like that, in order to hurt me, and that the old feeling was still alive in his breast; and I tried to call it forth. But I always failed: he always seemed to avoid frankness, evidently suspecting me of insincerity, and dreading the folly of any emotional display. I could read in his face and the tone of his voice, 'What is the good of talking? I know all the facts already, and I know what is on the tip of your tongue, and I know that you will say one thing and do another.' At first I was mortified by his dread of frankness, but I came later to think that it was rather the absence, on his part, of any need of frankness. It would never have occurred to me now, to tell him of a sudden that I loved him, or to ask him to repeat the prayers with me or listen while I played the piano. Our intercourse came to be regulated by a fixed code of good manners. We lived our separate lives: he had his own occupations in which I was not needed, and which I no longer wished to share, while I continued my idle life which no longer vexed or grieved him. The children were still too young to form a bond between us.

But spring came round and brought Kátya and Sónya to spend the summer with us in the country. As the house at Nikólskoe was under repair, we went to live at my old home at Pokróvskoe. The old house was unchanged – the veranda, the folding table and the piano in the sunny drawing-room, and my old bedroom with its white curtains and the dreams of my girlhood which I seemed to have left behind me there. In that room there were two beds: one had been mine, and in it now my plump little Kokósha lay sprawling, when I went at night to sign him with the cross; the other was a crib, in which the little face of my baby, Ványa, peeped out from his swaddling-clothes. Often, when I had made the sign over them and remained standing in the middle of the quiet room, suddenly there rose up from all the corners, from the walls and curtains, old forgotten visions of youth. Old voices began to sing the songs of my girlhood. Where were those visions now? where were those dear old sweet songs? All that I had hardly dared to hope for had come to pass. My vague confused dreams had become a reality, and the reality had become an oppressive, difficult, and joyless life. All remained the same – the garden visible through the window, the grass, the path, the very same bench over there above the dell, the same song of the night-ingale by the pond, the same lilacs in full bloom, the same moon shining above the house; and yet, in everything such a terrible inconceivable change! Such coldness in all that might have been near and dear! Just as in old times, Kátya and I sit quietly alone together in the parlour and talk, and talk of him. But Kátya has grown wrinkled and pale; and her eyes no longer shine with joy and hope, but express only sympathy, sorrow, and regret. We do not go into raptures as we used to, we judge him coolly; we do not wonder what we have done to deserve such happiness, or long to proclaim our thoughts to all the world. No! we whisper together like conspirators and ask each other for the hundredth time why all has changed so sadly. Yet he was still the same man, save for the deeper furrow between his eyebrows and the whiter hair on his temples; but his serious attentive look was constantly veiled from me by a cloud. And I am the same woman, but without love or desire for love, with no longing for work and no content with myself. My religious ecstasies, my love for my husband, the fullness of my former life – all these now seem utterly remote and visionary. Once it seemed so plain and right that to live for others was happiness; but now it has become unintelligible. Why live for others, when life had no attraction even for oneself?

I had given up my music altogether since the time of our first visit to Petersburg; but now the old piano and the old music tempted me to begin again.

One day I was not well and stayed indoors alone. My husband had taken Kátya and Sónya to see the new buildings at Nikólskoe. Tea was laid; I went downstairs and while waiting for them sat down at the piano. I opened the 'Moonlight Sonata' and began to play. There was no one within sight or sound, the windows were open over the garden, and the familiar sounds floated through the room with a solemn sadness. At the end of the first movement I looked round instinctively to the corner where he used once to sit and listen to my playing. He was not there; his chair, long unmoved, was still in its place; through the window I could see a lilac-bush against the light of the setting sun; the freshness of evening streamed in through the open windows. I rested my elbows on the piano and covered my face with both hands; and so I sat for a long time, thinking. I recalled with pain the irrevocable past, and timidly imagined the future. But for me there seemed to be no future, no desires at all and no hopes. 'Can life be over for me?' I thought with horror; then I looked up, and, trying to forget and not to think, I began playing the same movement over again. 'O God!' I prayed, 'forgive me if I have sinned, or restore to me all that once blossomed in my heart, or teach me what to do and how to live now.' There was a sound of wheels on the grass and before the steps of the house; then I heard cautious and familiar footsteps pass along the veranda and cease; but my heart no longer replied to the sound. When I stopped playing the footsteps were behind me and a hand was laid on my shoulder.

'How clever of you to think of playing that!' he said.

I said nothing.

'Have you had tea?' he asked.

I shook my head without looking at him – I was unwilling to let him see the signs of emotion on my face.

'They'll be here immediately,' he said; 'the horse gave trouble, and they got out on the high road to walk home.'

'Let us wait for them,' I said, and went out to the veranda, hoping that he would follow; but he asked about the children and went upstairs to see them. Once more his presence and simple kindly voice made me doubt if I had really lost anything. What more could I wish? 'He is kind and gentle, a good husband, a good father; I don't know myself what more I want.' I sat down under the veranda awning on the very bench on which I had sat when we became engaged. The sun had set, it was growing dark, and a little spring rain-cloud hung over the house and garden, and only behind the trees the horizon was clear, with the fading glow of twilight, in which one star had just begun to twinkle. The landscape, covered by the shadow of the cloud, seemed waiting for the light spring shower. There was not a breath of wind; not a single leaf or blade of grass stirred; the scent of lilac and bird-cherry was so strong in the garden and veranda that it seemed as if all the air was in flower; it came in wafts, now stronger and now weaker, till one longed to shut both eyes and ears and drink in that fragrance only. The dahlias and rose-bushes, not yet in flower, stood motionless on the black mould of the border, looking as if they were growing slowly upwards on their white-shaved props; beyond the dell, the frogs were making the most of their time before the rain drove them to the pond, croaking busily and loudly. Only the high continuous note of water falling at some distance rose above their croaking. From time to time the nightingales called to one another, and I could hear them flitting restlessly from bush to bush. Again this spring a nightingale had tried to build in a bush under the window, and I heard her fly off across the avenue when I went into the veranda. From there she whistled once and then stopped; she, too, was expecting the rain.

I tried in vain to calm my feelings: I had a sense of anticipation and regret.

He came downstairs again and sat down beside me.

'I am afraid they will get wet,' he said.

'Yes,' I answered; and we sat for long without speaking.

The cloud came down lower and lower with no wind. The air grew stiller and more fragrant. Suddenly a drop fell on the canvas awning and seemed to rebound from it; then another broke on the gravel path; soon there was a splash on the burdock leaves, and a fresh shower of big drops came down faster and faster. Nightingales and frogs were both dumb; only the high note of the falling water, though the rain made it seem more distant, still went on; and a bird, which must have sheltered among the dry leaves near the veranda, steadily repeated its two unvarying notes. My husband got up to go in.

'Where are you going?' I asked, trying to keep him; 'it is so pleasant here.'

'We must send them an umbrella and goloshes,' he replied.

'Don't trouble – it will soon be over.'

He thought I was right, and we remained together in the veranda. I rested one hand upon the wet slippery rail and put my head out. The fresh rain wetted my hair and neck in places. The cloud, growing lighter and thinner, was passing overhead; the steady patter of the rain gave place to occasional drops that fell from the sky or dripped from the trees. The frogs began to croak again in the dell; the nightingales woke up and began to call from the dripping bushes from one side and then from another. The whole prospect before us grew clear.

'How delightful!' he said, seating himself on the veranda rail and passing a hand over my wet hair.

This simple caress had on me the effect of a reproach: I felt inclined to cry.

'What more can a man need?' he said; 'I am so content now that I want nothing; I am perfectly happy!'

He told me a different story once, I thought. He had said that, however great his happiness might be, he always wanted more and more. Now he is calm and contented; while my heart is full of unspoken repentance and unshed tears.

'I think it delightful too,' I said; 'but I am sad just because of the beauty of it all. All is so fair and lovely outside me, while my own heart is confused and baffled and full of vague unsatisfied longing. Is it possible that there is no element of pain, no yearning for the past, in your enjoyment of nature?'

He took his hand off my head and was silent for a little.

'I used to feel that too,' he said, as though recalling it, 'especially in spring. I used to sit up all night too, with my hopes and fears for company, and good company they were! But life was all before me then. Now it is all behind me, and I am content with what I have. I find life capital,' he added with such careless confidence, that I believed, whatever pain it gave me to hear it, that it was the truth.

'But is there nothing you wish for?' I asked.

'I don't ask for impossibilities,' he said, guessing my thoughts. 'You go and get your head wet,' he added, stroking my head like a child's and again passing his hand over the wet hair; 'you envy the leaves and the grass their wetting from the rain, and you would like yourself to be the grass and the leaves and the rain. But I am content to enjoy them and everything else that is good and young and happy.'

'And do you regret nothing of the past?' I asked, while my heart grew heavier and heavier.

Again he thought for a time before replying. I saw that he wished to reply with perfect frankness.

'Nothing,' he said shortly.

'Not true! not true!' I said, turning towards him and looking into his eyes. 'Do you really not regret the past?'

'No!' he repeated; 'I am grateful for it, but I don't regret it.'

'But would you not like to have it back?' I asked.

He turned away and looked out over the garden.

'No; I might as well wish to have wings. It is impossible.'

'And would you not alter the past? do you not reproach yourself or me?'

'No, never! It was all for the best.'

'Listen to me!' I said, touching his arm to make him look round. 'Why did you never tell me that you wished me to live as you really wished me to? Why did you give me a freedom for which I was unfit? Why did you stop teaching me? If you had wished it, if you had guided me differently, none of all this would have happened!' said I in a voice that increasingly expressed cold displeasure and reproach, in place of the love of former days.

'What would not have happened?' he asked, turning to me in surprise. 'As it is, there is nothing wrong. Things are all right, quite all right,' he added with a smile.

'Does he really not understand?' I thought; 'or, still worse, does he not wish to understand?'

Then I suddenly broke out. 'Had you acted differently, I should not now be punished, for no fault at all, by your indifference and even contempt, and you would not have taken from me unjustly all that I valued in life!'

'What do you mean, my dear one?' he asked – he seemed not to understand me.

'No! don't interrupt me! You have taken from me your confidence, your love, even your respect; for I cannot believe, when I think of the past, that you still love me. No! don't speak! I must once for all say out what has long been torturing me. Is it my fault that I knew nothing of life, and that you left me to learn experience for myself? Is it my fault that now, when I have gained the knowledge and have been struggling for nearly a year to come back to you, you push me away and pretend not to understand what I want? And you always do it so that it is impossible to reproach you, while I am guilty and unhappy. Yes, you wish to drive me out again to that life which might rob us both of happiness.'

'How did I show that?' he asked in evident alarm and surprise.

'No later than yesterday you said, and you constantly say, that I can never settle down here, and that we must spend this winter too at Petersburg; and I hate Petersburg!' I went on. 'Instead of supporting me, you avoid all plain speaking, you never say a single frank affectionate word to me. And then, when I fall utterly, you will reproach me and rejoice in my fall.'

'Stop!' he said with cold severity. 'You have no right to say that. It only proves that you are ill-disposed towards me, that you don't . . .'

'That I don't love you? Don't hesitate to say it!' I cried, and the tears began to flow. I sat down on the bench and covered my face with my handkerchief.

'So that is how he understood me!' I thought, trying to restrain the sobs which choked me. 'Gone, gone is our former love!' said a voice at my heart. He did not come close or try to comfort me. He was hurt by what I had said. When he spoke, his tone was cool and dry.

'I don't know what you reproach me with,' he began. 'If you mean that I don't love you as I once did...'

'Did love!' I said, with my face buried in the handkerchief, while the bitter tears fell still more abundantly.

'If so, time is to blame for that, and we ourselves. Each time of life has its own kind of love.' He was silent for a moment. 'Shall I tell you the whole truth, if you really wish for frankness? In that summer when I first knew you, I used to lie awake all night, thinking about you, and I made that love myself, and it grew and grew in my heart. So again, in Petersburg and abroad, in the course of horrible sleepless nights, I strove to shatter and destroy that love, which had come to torture me. I did not destroy it, but I destroyed that part of it which gave me pain. Then I grew calm; and I feel love still, but it is a different kind of love.'

'You call it love, but I call it torture!' I said. 'Why did you allow me to go into society, if you thought so badly of it that you ceased to love me on that account?'

'No, it was not society, my dear,' he said.

'Why did you not exercise your authority?' I went on; 'why did you not lock me up or kill me? That would have been better than the loss of all that formed my happiness. I should have been happy, instead of being ashamed.'

I began to sob again and hid my face.

Just then Kátya and Sónya, wet and cheerful, came out to the veranda, laughing and talking loudly. They were silent as soon as they saw us, and went in again immediately.

We remained silent for a long time. I had had my cry out and felt relieved. I glanced at him. He was sitting with his head resting on his hand; he intended to make some reply to my glance, but only sighed deeply and resumed his former position.

I went up to him and removed his hand. His eyes turned thoughtfully to my face.

'Yes,' he began, as if continuing his thoughts aloud, 'all of us, and especially you women, must have personal experience of all the nonsense of life, in order to get back to life itself; the evidence of other people is no good. At that time you had not got near the end of that charming nonsense which I admired in you. So I let you go through it alone, feeling that I had no right to put pressure on you, though my own time for that sort of thing was long past.'

'If you loved me,' I said, 'how could you stand beside me and suffer me to go through it?'

'Because it was impossible for you to take my word for it, though you would have tried to. Personal experience was necessary, and now you have had it.'

'There was much calculation in all that,' I said, 'but little love.'

Again we were silent.

'What you said just now is severe, but it is true,' he began, rising suddenly and beginning to walk about the veranda. 'Yes, it is true. I was to blame,' he added, stopping opposite me; 'I ought either to have kept myself from loving you at all, or to have loved you in a simpler way.'

'Let us forget it all,' I said timidly.

'No,' he said; 'the past can never come back, never'; and his voice softened as he spoke.

'It is restored already,' I said, laying a hand on his shoulder.

He took my hand away and pressed it.

'I was wrong when I said that I did not regret the past. I do regret it; I weep for that past love which can never return. Who is to blame, I do not know. Love remains, but not the old love; its place remains, but it is all wasted away and has lost all strength and substance; recollections are still left, and gratitude; but . . .'

'Do not say that!' I broke in. 'Let all be as it was before! Surely that is possible?' I asked, looking into his eyes; but their gaze was clear and calm, and did not look deeply into mine.

Even while I spoke, I knew that my wishes and my petition were impossible. He smiled calmly and gently; and I thought it the smile of an old man.

'How young you are still!' he said, 'and I am so old. What you seek in me is no longer there. Why deceive ourselves?' he added, still smiling.

I stood silent opposite to him, and my heart grew calmer.

'Don't let us try to repeat life,' he went on. 'Don't let us make pretences to ourselves. Let us be thankful that there is an end of the old emotions and excitements. The excitement of searching is over for us; our quest is done, and happiness enough has fallen to our lot. Now we must stand aside and make room – for him, if you like,' he said, pointing to the nurse who was carrying Ványa out and had stopped at the veranda door. 'That's the truth, my dear one,' he said, drawing down my head and kissing it, not a lover any longer but an old friend.

The fragrant freshness of the night rose ever stronger and sweeter from the garden; the sounds and the silence grew more solemn; star after star began to twinkle overhead. I looked at him, and suddenly my heart grew light; it seemed that the cause of my suffering had been removed like an aching nerve. Suddenly I realized clearly and calmly that the past feeling, like the past time itself, was gone beyond recall, and that it would be not only impossible but painful and uncomfortable to bring it back. And after all, was that time so good which seemed to me so happy? And it was all so long, long ago!

'Time for tea!' he said, and we went together to the parlour. At the door we met the nurse with the baby. I took him in my arms, covered his bare little red legs, pressed him to me, and kissed him with the lightest touch of my lips. Half asleep, he moved the parted fingers of one creased little hand and opened dim little eyes, as if he was looking for something or recalling something. All at once his eyes rested on me, a spark of consciousness shone in them, the little pouting lips, parted before, now met and opened in a smile. 'Mine, mine, mine!' I thought, pressing him to my breast with such an impulse of joy in every limb that I found it hard to restrain myself from hurting him. I fell to kissing the cold little feet, his stomach and hand and head with its thin covering of down. My husband came up to me, and I quickly covered the child's face and uncovered it again.

'Iván Sergéich!' said my husband, tickling him under the chin. But I made haste to cover Iván Sergéich up again. None but I had any business to look long at him. I glanced at my husband. His eyes smiled as he looked at me; and I looked into them with an ease and happiness which I had not felt for a long time.

That day ended the romance of our marriage; the old feeling became a precious irrecoverable remembrance; but a new feeling of love for my children and the father of my children laid the foundation of a new life and a quite different happiness; and that life and happiness have lasted to the present time.

THREE DEATHS

A TALE

I

IT was autumn. Two vehicles were going along the highway
at a quick trot. In the first sat two women: a lady, thin and pale,
and a maidservant, plump and rosy and shining. The maid's
short dry hair escaped from under her faded bonnet and her
red hand in its torn glove kept pushing it back by fits and starts;
her full bosom, covered by a woollen shawl, breathed health,
her quick black eyes now watched the fields as they glided past
the window, now glanced timidly at her mistress, and now
restlessly scanned the corners of the carriage. In front of her
nose dangled her mistress's bonnet, pinned to the luggage
carrier, on her lap lay a puppy, her feet were raised on the
boxes standing on the floor and just audibly tapped against
them to the creaking of the coach-springs and the clatter of the
window-panes.

Having folded her hands on her knees and closed her eyes,
the lady swayed feebly against the pillows placed at her back,
and, frowning slightly, coughed inwardly. On her head
she had a white nightcap, and a blue kerchief was tied round
her delicate white throat. A straight line receding under
the cap parted her light brown, extremely flat, pomaded
hair, and there was something dry and deathly about the
whiteness of the skin of that wide parting. Her features
were delicate and handsome, but her skin was flabby and
rather sallow, though there was a hectic flush on her cheeks.
Her lips were dry and restless, her scanty eyelashes had no
curl in them, and her cloth travelling coat fell in straight folds
over a sunken breast. Though her eyes were closed her
face bore an expression of weariness, irritation, and habitual
suffering.

A footman, leaning on the arms of his seat, was dozing on the box. The mail-coach driver, shouting lustily, urged on his four big sweating horses, occasionally turning to the other driver who called to him from the calèche behind. The broad parallel tracks of the tyres spread themselves evenly and fast on the muddy, chalky surface of the road. The sky was grey and cold and a damp mist was settling on the fields and road. It was stuffy in the coach and there was a smell of Eau-de-Cologne and dust. The invalid drew back her head and slowly opened her beautiful dark eyes, which were large and brilliant.

'Again,' she said, nervously pushing away with her beautiful thin hand an end of her maid's cloak which had lightly touched her foot, and her mouth twitched painfully. Matrësha gathered up her cloak with both hands, rose on her strong legs, and seated herself farther away, while her fresh face grew scarlet. The lady, leaning with both hands on the seat, also tried to raise herself so as to sit up higher, but her strength failed her. Her mouth twisted, and her whole face became distorted by a look of impotent malevolence and irony. 'You might at least help me! . . . No, don't bother! I can do it myself, only don't put your bags or anything behind me, for goodness' sake! . . . No, better not touch me since you don't know how to!' The lady closed her eyes and then, again quickly raising her eyelids, glared at the maid. Matrësha, looking at her, bit her red nether lip. A deep sigh rose from the invalid's chest and turned into a cough before it was completed. She turned away, puckered her face, and clutched her chest with both hands. When the coughing fit was over she once more closed her eyes and continued to sit motionless. The carriage and calèche entered a village. Matrësha stretched out her thick hand from under her shawl and crossed herself.

'What is it?' asked her mistress.

'A post-station, madam.'

'I am asking why you crossed yourself.'

'There's a church, madam.'

The invalid turned to the window and began slowly to cross herself, looking with large wide-open eyes at the big village church her carriage was passing.

The carriage and calèche both stopped at the post-station and the invalid's husband and doctor stepped out of the calèche and went up to the coach.

'How are you feeling?' asked the doctor, taking her pulse.

'Well, my dear, how are you – not tired?' asked the husband in French. 'Wouldn't you like to get out?'

Matrësha, gathering up the bundles, squeezed herself into a corner so as not to interfere with their conversation.

'Nothing much, just the same,' replied the invalid. 'I won't get out.'

Her husband after standing there a while went into the station-house, and Matrësha, too, jumped out of the carriage and ran on tiptoe across the mud and in at the gate.

'If I feel ill, it's no reason for you not to have lunch,' said the sick woman with a slight smile to the doctor, who was standing at her window.

'None of them has any thought for me,' she added to herself as soon as the doctor, having slowly walked away from her, ran quickly up the steps to the station-house. 'They are well, so they don't care. Oh, my God!'

'Well, Edward Ivánovich?' said the husband, rubbing his hands as he met the doctor with a merry smile. 'I have ordered the lunch-basket to be brought in. What do you think about it?'

'A capital idea,' replied the doctor.

'Well, how is she?' asked the husband with a sigh, lowering his voice and lifting his eyebrows.

'As I told you: it is impossible for her to reach Italy – God grant that she gets even as far as Moscow, especially in this weather.'

'But what are we to do? Oh, my God, my God!' and the husband hid his eyes with his hand. 'Bring it here!' he said to the man who had brought in the lunch-basket.

'She ought to have stayed at home,' said the doctor, shrugging his shoulders.

'But what could I do?' rejoined the husband. 'You know I used every possible means to get her to stay. I spoke of the expense, of our children whom we had to leave behind, and of my business affairs, but she would not listen to anything. She is making plans for life abroad as if she were in good health. To tell her of her condition would be to kill her.'

'But she is killed already – you must know that, Vasíli Dmítrich. A person can't live without lungs, and new lungs won't grow. It is sad and hard, but what is to be done? My business and yours is to see that her end is made as peaceful as possible. It's a priest who is needed for that.'

'Oh, my God! Think of my condition, having to remind her about her will. Come what may I can't tell her that, you know how good she is . . .'

'Still, try to persuade her to wait till the roads are fit for sledging,' said the doctor, shaking his head significantly, 'or something bad may happen on the journey.'

'Aksyúsha, hello Aksyúsha!' yelled the station-master's daughter, throwing her jacket over her head and stamping her feet on the muddy back porch. 'Come and let's have a look at the Shírkin lady: they say she is being taken abroad for a chest trouble, and I've never seen what consumptive people look like!'

She jumped onto the threshold, and seizing one another by the hand the two girls ran out of the gate. Checking their pace, they passed by the coach and looked in at the open window. The invalid turned her head towards them but, noticing their curiosity, frowned and turned away.

'De-arie me!' said the station-master's daughter, quickly turning her head away. 'What a wonderful beauty she must have been, and see what she's like now! It's dreadful. Did you see, did you, Aksyúsha?'

'Yes, how thin!' Aksyúsha agreed. 'Let's go and look again, as if we were going to the well. See, she has turned away, and I hadn't seen her yet. What a pity, Másha!'

'Yes, and what mud!' said Másha, and they both ran through the gate.

'Evidently I look frightful,' thought the invalid. 'If only I could get abroad quicker, quicker. I should soon recover there.'

'Well, my dear, how are you?' said her husband, approaching her and still chewing.

'Always the same question,' thought the invalid, 'and he himself is eating.'

'So-so,' she murmured through her closed teeth.

'You know, my dear, I'm afraid you'll get worse travelling in this weather, and Edward Ivánovich says so too. Don't you think we'd better turn back?'

She remained angrily silent.

'The weather will perhaps improve and the roads be fit for sledging; you will get better meanwhile, and we will all go together.'

'Excuse me. If I had not listened to you for so long, I should now at least have reached Berlin, and have been quite well.'

'What could be done, my angel? You know it was impossible. But now if you stayed another month you would get nicely better, I should have finished my business, and we could take the children with us.'

'The children are well, but I am not.'

'But do understand, my dear, that if in this weather you should get worse on the road.... At least you would be at home.'

'What of being at home?... To die at home?' answered the invalid, flaring up. But the word 'die' evidently frightened her, and she looked imploringly and questioningly at her husband. He hung his head and was silent. The invalid's mouth suddenly widened like a child's, and tears rolled down her cheeks. Her husband hid his face in his handkerchief and stepped silently away from the carriage.

'No, I will go on,' said the invalid, and lifting her eyes to the sky she folded her hands and began whispering incoherent words: 'Oh, my God, what is it for?' she said, and her tears flowed faster. She prayed long and fervently, but her chest ached and felt as tight as before; the sky, the fields, and the road were just as grey and gloomy, and the autumnal mist fell, neither thickening nor lifting, and settled on the muddy road, the roofs, the carriage, and the sheepskin coats of the drivers, who talking in their strong merry voices were greasing the wheels and harnessing the horses.

II

THE carriage was ready but the driver still loitered. He had gone into the drivers' room at the station. It was hot, stuffy, and dark there, with an oppressive smell of baking bread, cabbage, sheepskin garments, and humanity. Several drivers were sitting in the room, and a cook was busy at the oven, on the top of which lay a sick man wrapped in sheepskins.

'Uncle Theodore! I say, Uncle Theodore!' said the young driver, entering the room in his sheepskin coat with a whip stuck in his belt, and addressing the sick man.

'What do you want Theodore for, lazybones?' asked one of the drivers. 'There's your carriage waiting for you.'

'I want to ask for his boots; mine are quite worn out,' answered the young fellow, tossing back his hair and straightening the mittens tucked in his belt. 'Is he asleep? I say, Uncle Theodore!' he repeated, walking over to the oven.

'What is it?' answered a weak voice, and a lean face with a red beard looked down from the oven, while a broad, emaciated, pale, and hairy hand pulled up the coat over the dirty shirt covering his angular shoulder.

'Give me a drink, lad. . . . What is it you want?'

The lad handed him up a dipper with water.

'Well, you see, Theodore,' he said, stepping from foot to foot, 'I expect you don't need your new boots now; won't you let me have them? I don't suppose you'll go about any more.'

The sick man, lowering his weary head to the shiny dipper and immersing his sparse drooping moustache in the turbid water, drank feebly but eagerly. His matted beard was dirty, and his sunken clouded eyes had difficulty in looking up at the lad's face. Having finished drinking he tried to lift his hand to wipe his wet lips, but he could not do so, and rubbed them on the sleeve of his coat instead. Silently, and breathing heavily through his nose, he looked straight into the lad's eyes, collecting his strength.

'But perhaps you have promised them to someone else?' asked the lad. 'If so, it's all right. The worst of it is, it's wet outside and I have to go about my work, so I said to myself:

"Suppose I ask Theodore for his boots; I expect he doesn't need them." If you need them yourself – just say so.'

Something began to rumble and gurgle in the sick man's chest; he doubled up and began to choke with an abortive cough in his throat.

'Need them indeed!' the cook snapped out unexpectedly so as to be heard by the whole room. 'He hasn't come down from the oven for more than a month! Hear how he's choking – it makes me ache inside just to hear him. What does he want with boots? They won't bury him in new boots. And it was time long ago – God forgive me the sin! See how he chokes. He ought to be taken into the other room or somewhere. They say there are hospitals in the town. Is it right that he should take up the whole corner? – there's no more to be said. I've no room at all, and yet they expect cleanliness!'

'Hullo, Sergéy! Come along and take your place, the gentle-folk are waiting!' shouted the drivers' overseer, looking in at the door.

Sergéy was about to go without waiting for a reply, but the sick man, while coughing, let him understand by a look that he wanted to give him an answer.

'Take my boots, Sergéy,' he said when he had mastered the cough and rested a moment. 'But listen. . . . Buy a stone for me when I die,' he added hoarsely.

'Thank you, uncle. Then I'll take them, and I'll buy a stone for sure.'

'There, lads, you heard that?' the sick man managed to utter, and then bent double again and began to choke.

'All right, we heard,' said one of the drivers. 'Go and take your seat, Sergéy, there's the overseer running back. The Shírkin lady is ill, you know.'

Sergéy quickly pulled off his unduly big, dilapidated boots and threw them under a bench. Uncle Theodore's new boots just fitted him, and having put them on he went to the carriage with his eyes fixed on his feet.

'What fine boots! Let me grease them,' said a driver, who held some axle-grease in his hand, as Sergéy climbed onto the box and gathered up the reins. 'Did he give them to you for nothing?'

'Why, are you envious?' Sergéy replied, rising and wrapping the skirts of his coat under his legs. 'Off with you! Gee up, my beauties!' he shouted to the horses, flourishing the whip, and the carriage and calèche with their occupants, portmanteaux, and trunks rolled rapidly along the wet road and disappeared in the grey autumnal mist.

The sick driver was left on the top of the oven in the stuffy room and, unable to relieve himself by coughing, turned with an effort onto his other side and became silent.

Till late in the evening people came in and out of the room and dined there. The sick man made no sound. When night came, the cook climbed up onto the oven and stretched over his legs to get down her sheepskin coat.

'Don't be cross with me, Nastásya,' said the sick man. 'I shall soon leave your corner empty.'

'All right, all right, never mind,' muttered Nastásya. 'But what is it that hurts you? Tell me, uncle.'

'My whole inside has wasted away. God knows what it is!'

'I suppose your throat hurts when you cough?'

'Everything hurts. My death has come – that's how it is. Oh, oh, oh!' moaned the sick man.

'Cover up your feet like this,' said Nastásya, drawing his coat over him as she climbed down from the oven.

A night-light burnt dimly in the room. Nastásya and some ten drivers slept on the floor or on the benches, loudly snoring. The sick man groaned feebly, coughed, and turned about on the oven. Towards morning he grew quite quiet.

'I had a queer dream last night,' said Nastásya next morning, stretching herself in the dim light. 'I dreamt that Uncle Theodore got down from the oven and went out to chop wood. "Come, Nastásya," he says, "I'll help you!" and I say, "How can you chop wood now?", but he just seizes the axe and begins chopping quickly, quickly, so that the chips fly all about. "Why," I say, "haven't you been ill?" "No," he says, "I am well," and he swings the axe so that I was quite frightened. I gave a cry and woke up.

I wonder whether he is dead! Uncle Theodore! I say, Uncle Theodore!'

Theodore did not answer.

'True enough he may have died. I'll go and see,' said one of the drivers, waking up.

The lean hand covered with reddish hair that hung down from the oven was pale and cold.

'I'll go and tell the station-master,' said the driver. 'I think he is dead.'

Theodore had no relatives: he was from some distant place. They buried him next day in the new cemetery beyond the wood, and Nastásya went on for days telling everybody of her dream, and of having been the first to discover that Uncle Theodore was dead.

III

SPRING had come. Rivulets of water hurried down the wet streets of the city, gurgling between lumps of frozen manure; the colours of the people's clothes as they moved along the streets looked vivid and their voices sounded shrill. Behind the garden-fences the buds on the trees were swelling and their branches were just audibly swaying in the fresh breeze. Everywhere transparent drops were forming and falling. . . . The sparrows chirped, and fluttered awkwardly with their little wings. On the sunny side of the street, on the fences, houses, and trees, everything was in motion and sparkling. There was joy and youth everywhere in the sky, on the earth, and in the hearts of men.

In one of the chief streets fresh straw had been strewn on the road before a large, important house, where the invalid who had been in a hurry to go abroad lay dying.

At the closed door of her room stood the invalid's husband and an elderly woman. On the sofa a priest sat with bowed head, holding something wrapped in his stole. In a corner of the room the sick woman's old mother lay on an invalid chair weeping bitterly: beside her stood one maidservant holding a clean handkerchief, waiting for her to ask for it; while another was rubbing her temples with something and blowing under the old lady's cap onto her grey head.

'Well, may Christ aid you, dear friend,' the husband said to the elderly woman who stood near him at the door. 'She has such confidence in you and you know so well how to talk to her, so persuade her as well as you can, my dear – go to her.' He was about to open the door, but her cousin stopped him, pressing her handkerchief several times to her eyes and giving her head a shake.

'Well, I don't think I look as if I had been crying now,' said she and, opening the door herself, went in.

The husband was in great agitation and seemed quite distracted. He walked towards the old woman, but while still several steps from her turned back, walked about the room, and went up to the priest. The priest looked at him, raised his eyebrows to heaven, and sighed: his thick, greyish beard also rose as he sighed and then came down again.

'My God, my God!' said the husband.

'What is to be done?' said the priest with a sigh, and again his eyebrows and beard rose and fell.

'And her mother is here!' said the husband almost in despair. 'She won't be able to bear it. You see, loving her as she does . . . I don't know! If you would only try to comfort her, Father, and persuade her to go away.'

The priest got up and went to the old woman.

'It is true, no one can appreciate a mother's heart,' he said – 'but God is merciful.'

The old woman's face suddenly twitched all over, and she began to hiccup hysterically.

'God is merciful,' the priest continued when she grew a little calmer. 'Let me tell you of a patient in my parish who was much worse than Mary Dmítrievna, and a simple tradesman cured her in a short time with various herbs. That tradesman is even now in Moscow. I told Vasíli Dmítrich – we might try him. . . . It would at any rate comfort the invalid. To God all is possible.'

'No, she will not live,' said the old woman. 'God is taking her instead of me,' and the hysterical hiccuping grew so violent that she fainted.

The sick woman's husband hid his face in his hands and ran out of the room.

In the passage the first person he met was his six-year-old son, who was running full speed after his younger sister.

'Won't you order the children to be taken to their mamma?' asked the nurse.

'No, she doesn't want to see them – it would upset her.'

The boy stopped a moment, looked intently into his father's face, then gave a kick and ran on, shouting merrily.

'She pretends to be the black horse, Papa!' he shouted, pointing to his sister.

Meanwhile in the other room the cousin sat down beside the invalid, and tried by skilful conversation to prepare her for the thought of death. The doctor was mixing a draught at another window.

The patient, in a white dressing-gown, sat up in bed supported all round by pillows, and looked at her cousin in silence.

'Ah, my dear friend,' she said, unexpectedly interrupting her, 'don't prepare me! Don't treat me like a child. I am a Christian. I know it all. I know I have not long to live, and know that if my husband had listened to me sooner I should now have been in Italy and perhaps – no, certainly – should have been well. Everybody told him so. But what is to be done? Evidently this is God's wish. We have all sinned heavily. I know that, but I trust in God's mercy everybody will be forgiven, probably all will be forgiven. I try to understand myself. I have many sins to answer for, dear friend, but then how much I have had to suffer! I try to bear my sufferings patiently...'

'Then shall I call the priest, my dear? You will feel still more comfortable after receiving Communion,' said her cousin.

The sick woman bent her head in assent.

'God forgive me, sinner that I am!' she whispered.

The cousin went out and signalled with her eyes to the priest.

'She is an angel!' she said to the husband, with tears in her eyes. The husband burst into tears; the priest went into the next room; the invalid's mother was still unconscious, and all was silent there. Five minutes later he came out again, and after taking off his stole, straightened out his hair.

'Thank God she is calmer now,' she said, 'and wishes to see you.'

The cousin and the husband went into the sick-room. The invalid was silently weeping, gazing at an icon.

'I congratulate you, my dear,'[1] said her husband.

'Thank you! How well I feel now, what inexpressible sweetness I feel!' said the sick woman, and a soft smile played on her thin lips. 'How merciful God is! Is He not? Merciful and all powerful!' and again she looked at the icon with eager entreaty and her eyes full of tears.

Then suddenly, as if she remembered something, she beckoned to her husband to come closer.

'You never want to do what I ask . . .' she said in a feeble and dissatisfied voice.

The husband, craning his neck, listened to her humbly.

'What is it, my dear?'

'How many times have I not said that these doctors don't know anything; there are simple women who can heal, and who do cure. The priest told me . . . there is also a trades-man . . . Send!'

'For whom, my dear?'

'O God, you don't want to understand anything!' . . . And the sick woman's face puckered and she closed her eyes.

The doctor came up and took her hand. Her pulse was beating more and more feebly. He glanced at the husband. The invalid noticed that gesture and looked round in affright. The cousin turned away and began to cry.

'Don't cry, don't torture yourself and me,' said the patient. 'Don't take from me the last of my tranquillity.'

'You are an angel,' said the cousin, kissing her hand.

'No, kiss me here! Only dead people are kissed on the hand. My God, my God!'

---

1 It was customary in Russia to congratulate people who had received Communion.

That same evening the patient was a corpse, and the body lay in a coffin in the music-room of the large house. A deacon sat alone in that big room reading the psalms of David through his nose in a monotonous voice. A bright light from the wax candles in their tall silver candlesticks fell on the pale brow of the dead woman, on her heavy wax-like hands, on the stiff folds of the pall which brought out in awesome relief the knees and the toes. The deacon without understanding the words read on monotonously, and in the quiet room the words sounded strangely and died away. Now and then from a distant room came the sounds of children's voices and the patter of their feet.

'Thou hidest thy face, they are troubled,' said the psalter. 'Thou takest away their breath, they die and return to their dust. Thou sendest forth thy spirit, they are created: and thou renewest the face of the earth. The glory of the Lord shall endure for ever.'

The dead woman's face looked stern and majestic. Neither in the clear cold brow nor in the firmly closed lips was there any movement. She seemed all attention. But had she even now understood those solemn words?

IV

A MONTH later a stone chapel was being erected over the grave of the deceased woman. Over the driver's tomb there was still no stone, and only the light green grass sprouted on the mound which served as the only token of the past existence of a man.

'It will be a sin, Sergéy,' said the cook at the station-house one day, 'if you don't buy a stone for Theodore. You kept saying "It's winter, it's winter!" but why don't you keep your word now? You know I witnessed it. He has already come back once to ask you to do it; if you don't buy him one, he'll come again and choke you.'

'But why? I'm not backing out of it,' replied Sergéy. 'I'll buy a stone as I said I would, and give a ruble and a half for it. I haven't forgotten it, but it has to be fetched. When I happen to be in town I'll buy one.'

'You might at least put up a cross – you ought to – else it's really wrong,' interposed an old driver. 'You know you are wearing his boots.'

'Where can I get a cross? I can't cut one out of a log.'

'What do you mean, can't cut one out of a log? You take an axe and go into the forest early, and you can cut one there. Cut down a young ash or something like that, and you can make a cross of it... you may have to treat the forester to vodka; but one can't afford to treat him for every trifle. There now, I broke my splinter-bar and went and cut a new one, and nobody said a word.'

Early in the morning, as soon as it was daybreak, Sergéy took an axe and went into the wood.

A cold white cover of dew, which was still falling untouched by the sun, lay on everything. The east was imperceptibly growing brighter, reflecting its pale light on the vault of heaven still veiled by a covering of clouds. Not a blade of grass below, nor a leaf on the topmost branches of the trees, stirred. Only occasionally a sound of wings amid the brushwood, or a rustling on the ground, broke the silence of the forest. Suddenly a strange sound, foreign to Nature, resounded and died away at the outskirts of the forest. Again the sound was heard, and was rhythmically repeated at the foot of the trunk of one of the motionless trees. A tree-top began to tremble in an unwonted manner, its juicy leaves whispered something, and the robin who had been sitting in one of its branches fluttered twice from place to place with a whistle, and jerking its tail sat down on another tree.

The axe at the bottom gave off a more and more muffled sound, sappy white chips were scattered on the dewy grass and a slight creaking was heard above the sound of the blows. The tree, shuddering in its whole body, bent down and quickly rose again, vibrating with fear on its roots. For an instant all was still, but the tree bent again, a crashing sound came from its trunk, and with its branches breaking and its boughs hanging down it fell with its crown on the damp earth.

The sounds of the axe and of the footsteps were silenced. The robin whistled and flitted higher. A twig which it brushed with its wings shook a little and then with all its foliage grew still like the rest. The trees flaunted the beauty of their motionless branches still more joyously in the newly cleared space.

The first sunbeams, piercing the translucent cloud, shone out and spread over earth and sky. The mist began to quiver like waves in the hollows, the dew sparkled and played on the verdure, the transparent cloudlets grew whiter, and hurriedly dispersed over the deepening azure vault of the sky. The birds stirred in the thicket and, as though bewildered, twittered joyfully about something; the sappy leaves whispered gladly and peacefully on the tree-tops, and the branches of those that were living began to rustle slowly and majestically over the dead and prostrate tree.

STRIDER: THE STORY OF A HORSE

I

HIGHER and higher receded the sky, wider and wider spread the streak of dawn, whiter grew the pallid silver of the dew, more lifeless the sickle of the moon, and more vocal the forest. People began to get up, and in the owner's stable-yard the sounds of snorting, the rustling of litter, and even the shrill angry neighing of horses crowded together and at variance about something, grew more and more frequent.

'Hold on! Plenty of time! Hungry?' said the old huntsman, quickly opening the creaking gate. 'Where are you going?' he shouted, threateningly raising his arm at a mare that was pushing through the gate.

The keeper, Nester, wore a short Cossack coat with an ornamental leather girdle, had a whip slung over his shoulder, and a hunk of bread wrapped in a cloth stuck in his girdle. He carried a saddle and bridle in his arms.

The horses were not at all frightened or offended at the horseman's sarcastic tone: they pretended that it was all the same to them and moved leisurely away from the gate; only one old brown mare, with a thick mane, laid back an ear and quickly turned her back on him. A small filly standing behind her and not at all concerned in the matter took this opportunity to whinny and kick out at a horse that happened to be near.

'Now then!' shouted the keeper still louder and more sternly, and he went to the opposite corner of the yard.

Of all the horses in the enclosure (there were about a hundred of them) a piebald gelding, standing by himself in a corner under the penthouse and licking an oak post with half-closed eyes, displayed least impatience.

585

It is impossible to say what flavour the piebald gelding found in the post, but his expression was serious and thoughtful while he licked.

'Stop that!' shouted the groom, drawing nearer to him and putting the saddle and a glossy saddle-cloth on the manure heap beside him.

The piebald gelding stopped licking, and without moving gave Nester a long look. The gelding did not laugh, nor grow angry, nor frown, but his whole belly heaved with a profound sigh and he turned away. The horseman put his arm round the gelding's neck and placed the bridle on him.

'What are you sighing for?' said Nester.

The gelding switched his tail as if to say, 'Nothing in particular, Nester!' Nester put the saddle-cloth and saddle on him, and this caused the gelding to lay back his ears, probably to express dissatisfaction, but he was only called a 'good-for-nothing' for it and his saddle-girth was tightened.

At this the gelding blew himself out, but a finger was thrust into his mouth and a knee hit him in the stomach, so that he had to let out his breath. In spite of this, when the saddle-cloth was being buckled on he again laid back his ears and even looked round. Though he knew it would do no good he considered it necessary to show that it was disagreeable to him and that he would always express his dissatisfaction with it. When he was saddled he thrust forward his swollen off foot and began champing his bit, this too for some reason of his own, for he ought to have known by that time that a bit cannot have any flavour at all.

Nester mounted the gelding by the short stirrup, unwound his long whip, straightened his coat out from under his knee, seated himself in the manner peculiar to coachmen, huntsmen, and horsemen, and jerked the reins. The gelding lifted his head to show his readiness to go where ordered, but did not move. He knew that before starting there would be much shouting, and that Nester, from the seat on his back, would give many orders to Váska, the other groom, and to the horses. And Nester did shout: 'Váska! Hullo, Váska. Have you let out the brood mares? Where are you going, you devil? Now then! Are you asleep ... Open the gate! Let the brood mares get out first!' – and so on.

The gate creaked. Váska, cross and sleepy, stood at the gate-post holding his horse by the bridle and letting the other horses pass out. The horses followed one another and stepped care-fully over the straw, smelling at it: fillies, yearling colts with their manes and tails cut, suckling foals, and mares in foal carrying their burden heedfully, passed one by one through the gateway. The fillies sometimes crowded together in twos and threes, throwing their heads across one another's backs and hitting their hoofs against the gate, for which they received a rebuke from the grooms every time. The foals sometimes darted under the legs of the wrong mares and neighed loudly in response to the short whinny of their own mothers.

A playful filly, directly she had got out at the gate, bent her head sideways, kicked up her hind legs, and squealed, but all the same she did not dare to run ahead of old dappled Zhul-dýba who at a slow and heavy pace, swinging her belly from side to side, marched as usual ahead of all the other horses.

In a few minutes the enclosure that had been so animated became deserted, the posts stood gloomily under the empty penthouse, and only trampled straw mixed with manure was to be seen. Used as he was to that desolate sight it probably depressed the piebald gelding. As if making a bow he slowly lowered his head and raised it again, sighed as deeply as the tightly drawn girth would allow, and hobbling along on his stiff and crooked legs shambled after the herd, bearing old Nester on his bony back.

'I know that as soon as we get out on the road he will begin to strike a light and smoke his wooden pipe with its brass mountings and little chain,' thought the gelding. 'I am glad of it because early in the morning when it is dewy I like that smell, it reminds me of much that was pleasant; but it's annoy-ing that when his pipe is between his teeth the old man always begins to swagger and thinks himself somebody and sits side-ways, always sideways – and that side hurts. However, it can't be helped! Suffering for the pleasure of others is nothing new to me. I have even begun to find a certain equine pleasure in it.

Let him swagger, poor fellow! Of course he can only do that when he is alone and no one sees him – let him sit sideways!' thought the gelding, and stepping carefully on his crooked legs he went along the middle of the road.

II

HAVING driven the horses to the riverside where they were to graze, Nester dismounted and unsaddled. Meanwhile the herd had begun gradually to spread over the untrampled meadow, covered with dew and by the mist that rose from it and the encircling river.

When he had taken the bridle off the piebald gelding, Nester scratched him under the neck, in response to which the gelding expressed his gratitude and satisfaction by closing his eyes. 'He likes it, the old dog!' muttered Nester. The gelding however did not really care for the scratching at all, and pretended that it was agreeable merely out of courtesy. He nodded his head in assent to Nester's words; but suddenly Nester quite unexpectedly and without any reason, perhaps imagining that too much familiarity might give the gelding a wrong idea of his importance, pushed the gelding's head away from himself without any warning and, swinging the bridle, struck him painfully with the buckle on his lean leg, and then without saying a word went up the hillock to a tree-stump beside which he generally seated himself.

Though this action grieved the piebald gelding he gave no indication of it, but leisurely switching his scanty tail, sniffed at something and, biting off some wisps of grass merely to divert his mind, walked to the river. He took no notice whatever of the antics of the young mares, colts, and foals around him, who were filled with the joy of the morning; and knowing that, especially at his age, it is healthier to have a good drink on an empty stomach and to eat afterwards, he chose a spot where the bank was widest and least steep, and wetting his hoofs and fetlocks, dipped his muzzle in the water and began to suck it up through his torn lips, to expand his filling sides, and from pleasure to switch his scanty tail with its half bald stump.

An aggressive chestnut filly, who always teased the old fellow and did all kinds of unpleasant things to him, now came up to him in the water as if attending to some business of her own, but in reality merely to foul the water before his nose. But the piebald gelding, who had already had his fill, as though not noticing the filly's intention quietly drew one foot after the other out of the mud in which they had sunk, jerked his head, and stepping aside from the youthful crowd started grazing. Sprawling his feet apart in different ways and not trampling the grass needlessly, he went on eating without unbending himself for exactly three hours. Having eaten till his belly hung down from his steep skinny ribs like a sack, he balanced himself equally on his four sore legs so as to have as little pain as possible, especially in his off foreleg which was the weakest, and fell asleep.

Old age is sometimes majestic, sometimes ugly, and sometimes pathetic. But old age can be both ugly and majestic, and the gelding's old age was just of that kind.

He was tall, rather over fifteen hands high. His spots were black, or rather they had been black, but had now turned a dirty brown. He had three spots, one on his head, starting from a crooked bald patch on the side of his nose and reaching half-way down his neck. His long mane, filled with burrs, was white in some places and brownish in others. Another spot extended down his off side to the middle of his belly, the third, on his croup, touched part of his tail and went half-way down his quarters. The rest of the tail was whitish and speckled. The big bony head, with deep hollows over the eyes and a black hanging lip that had been torn at some time, hung low and heavily on his neck, which was so lean that it looked as though it were carved of wood. The pendant lip revealed a blackish, bitten tongue and the yellow stumps of the worn lower teeth. The ears, one of which was slit, hung low on either side, and only occasionally moved lazily to drive away the pestering flies. Of the forelock, one tuft which was still long hung back behind an ear; the uncovered forehead was dented and rough, and the skin hung down like bags on his broad jaw-bones. The veins of his neck had grown knotty, and twitched and shuddered at every touch of a fly. The expression of his face was one of stern patience, thoughtfulness, and suffering.

His forelegs were crooked to a bow at the knees, there were swellings over both hoofs, and on one leg, on which the piebald spot reached half-way down, there was a swelling at the knee as big as a fist. The hind legs were in better condition, but apparently long ago his haunches had been so rubbed that in places the hair would not grow again. The leanness of his body made all four legs look disproportionately long. The ribs, though straight, were so exposed and the skin so tightly drawn over them, that it seemed to have dried fast to the spaces between. His back and withers were covered with marks of old lashings, and there was a fresh sore behind, still swollen and festering; the black dock of his tail, which showed the vertebrae, hung down long and almost bare. On his dark-brown croup – near the tail – was a scar, as though of a bite, the size of a man's hand and covered with white hair. Another scarred sore was visible on one of his shoulders. His tail and hocks were dirty because of chronic bowel troubles. The hair on the whole body, though short, stood out straight. Yet in spite of the hideous old age of this horse one involuntarily paused to reflect when one saw him, and an expert would have said at once that he had been a remarkably fine horse in his day. The expert would even have said that there was only one breed in Russia that could furnish such breadth of bone, such immense knees, such hoofs, such slender cannons, such a well-shaped neck, and above all such a skull, such eyes – large, black, and clear – and such a thoroughbred network of veins on head and neck, and such delicate skin and hair.

There was really something majestic in that horse's figure and in the terrible union in him of repulsive indications of decrepitude, emphasized by the motley colour of his hair, and his manner which expressed the self-confidence and calm assurance that go with beauty and strength. Like a living ruin he stood alone in the midst of the dewy meadow, while not far from him could be heard the tramping, snorting and youthful neighing and whinnying of the scattered herd.

III

THE sun had risen above the forest and now shone brightly on the grass and the winding river. The dew was drying up and condensing into drops, the last of the morning mist was dispersing like tiny smoke-clouds. The cloudlets were becoming curly but there was as yet no wind. Beyond the river the verdant rye stood bristling, its ears curling into little horns, and there was an odour of fresh verdure and blossom. A cuckoo called rather hoarsely from the forest, and Nester, lying on his back in the grass, was counting the calls to ascertain how many years he still had to live. The larks were rising over the rye and the meadow. A belated hare, finding himself among the horses, leaped into the open, sat down by a bush, and pricked his ears to listen. Váska fell asleep with his head in the grass, the fillies, making a still wider circle about him, scattered over the field below. The old mares went about snorting, and made a shining track across the dewy grass, always choosing a place where no one would disturb them. They no longer grazed, but only nibbled at choice tufts of grass. The whole herd was moving imperceptibly in one direction.

And again it was old Zhuldýba who, stepping sedately in front of the others, showed the possibility of going farther. Black Múshka, a young mare who had foaled for the first time, with uplifted tail kept whinnying and snorting at her bluish foal; the young filly Satin, sleek and brilliant, bending her head till her black silky forelock hid her forehead and eyes, played with the grass, nipping off a little and tossing it and stamping her leg with its shaggy fetlock all wet with dew. One of the older foals, probably imagining he was playing some kind of game, with his curly tail raised like a plume, ran for the twenty-sixth time round his mother, who quietly went on grazing, having grown accustomed to her son's ways, and only occasionally glanced askance at him with one of her large black eyes.

One of the very youngest foals, black, with a big head, a tuft sticking up in astonishment between his ears, and a little tail still twisted to one side as it had been in his mother's womb, stood motionless, his ears pricked and his dull eyes fixed, gazing at the frisking and prancing foal – whether admiring or condemning him it is hard to say. Some of the foals were sucking and butting with their noses, some – heaven knows why – despite their mothers' call were running at an awkward little trot in quite the opposite direction as if searching for something, and then, for no apparent reason, stopping and neighing with desperate shrillness. Some lay on their sides in a row, some were learning to eat grass, some again were scratching themselves behind their ears with their hind legs. Two mares still in foal were walking apart from the rest, and while slowly moving their legs continued to graze. The others evidently respected their condition, and none of the young ones ventured to come near to disturb them. If any saucy youngsters thought of approaching them, the mere movement of an ear or tail sufficed to show them all how improper such behaviour was.

The colts and yearling fillies, pretending to be grown up and sedate, rarely jumped or joined the merry company. They grazed in a dignified manner, curving their close-cropped swan-like necks, and flourished their little broom-like tails as if they also had long ones. Just like the grown-ups they lay down, rolled over, or rubbed one another. The merriest group was composed of the two- and three-year-old fillies and mares not yet in foal. They almost always walked about together like a separate merry virgin crowd. Among them you could hear sounds of tramping, whinnying, neighing, and snorting. They drew close together, put their heads over one another's necks, sniffed at one another, jumped, and sometimes at a semi-trot semi-amble, with tails lifted like an oriflamme, raced proudly and coquettishly past their companions. The most beautiful and spirited of them was the mischievous chestnut filly. What she devised the others did; wherever she went the whole crowd of beauties followed. That morning the naughty one was in a specially playful mood. She was seized with a joyous fit, just as human beings sometimes are. Already at the riverside she had played a trick on the old gelding, and after that she ran

along through the water pretending to be frightened by something, gave a hoarse squeal, and raced full speed into the field
so that Váska had to gallop after her and the others who
followed her. Then after grazing a little she began rolling,
then teasing the old mares by dashing in front of them, then
she drove away a small foal from its dam and chased it as if
meaning to bite it. Its mother was frightened and stopped
grazing, while the little foal cried in a piteous tone, but the
mischievous one did not touch him at all, she only wanted to
frighten him and give a performance for the benefit of her
companions, who watched her escapade approvingly. Then
she set out to turn the head of a little roan horse with which
a peasant was ploughing in a rye-field far beyond the river. She
stopped, proudly lifted her head somewhat to one side, shook
herself, and neighed in a sweet, tender, long-drawn voice.
Mischief, feeling, and a certain sadness, were expressed in
that call. There was in it the desire for and the promise of
love, and a pining for it.

'There in the thick reeds is a corn-crake running backwards
and forwards and calling passionately to his mate; there is the
cuckoo, and the quails are singing of love, and the flowers are
sending their fragrant dust to each other by the wind. And I too
am young and beautiful and strong,' the mischievous one's
voice said, 'but it has not yet been allowed me to know the
sweetness of that feeling, and not only to experience it, but no
lover – not a single one – has ever seen me!'

And this neighing, sad and youthful and fraught with feeling, was borne over the lowland and the field to the roan horse
far away. He pricked up his ears and stopped. The peasant
kicked him with his bast shoe, but the little horse was so
enchanted by the silvery sound of the distant neighing that
he neighed too. The peasant grew angry, pulled at the reins,
and kicked the little roan so painfully in the stomach with his
bast shoes that he could not finish his neigh and walked on.
But the little roan felt a sense of sweetness and sadness, and for
a long time the sounds of unfinished and passionate neighing,
and of the peasant's angry voice, were carried from the distant
rye-field over to the herd.

If the sound of her voice alone so overpowered the little roan that he forgot his duty, what would have happened had he seen the naughty beauty as she stood pricking her ears, breathing in the air with dilated nostrils, ready to run, trembling with her whole beautiful body, and calling to him?

But the mischievous one did not brood long over her impressions. When the neighing of the roan died away she gave another scornful neigh, lowered her head and began pawing the ground, and then she went to wake and to tease the piebald gelding. The piebald gelding was the constant martyr and butt of those happy youngsters. He suffered more from them than at the hands of men. He did no harm to either. People needed him, but why should these young horses torment him?

IV

HE was old, they were young; he was lean, they were sleek; he was miserable, they were gay; and so he was quite alien to them, an outsider, an utterly different creature whom it was impossible for them to pity. Horses only have pity on themselves, and very occasionally on those in whose skins they can easily imagine themselves to be. But was it the old gelding's fault that he was old, poor, and ugly? . . .

One might think not, but in equine ethics it was, and only those were right who were strong, young, and happy – those who had life still before them, whose every muscle quivered with superfluous energy, and whose tails stood erect. Maybe the piebald gelding himself understood this and in his quiet moments was ready to agree that it was his fault that he had already lived his life, and that he had to pay for that life; but after all he was a horse and often could not suppress a sense of resentment, sadness, and indignation, when he looked at those youngsters who tormented him for what would befall them all at the end of their lives. Another cause of the horses' lack of pity was their aristocratic pride. Every one of them traced back its pedigree, through father or mother, to the famous Creamy, while the piebald was of unknown parentage. He was a chance comer, purchased three years before at a fair for eighty assignat rubles.

The chestnut filly, as if taking a stroll, passed close by the piebald gelding's nose and pushed him. He knew at once what it was, and without opening his eyes laid back his ears and showed his teeth. The filly wheeled round as if to kick him. The gelding opened his eyes and stepped aside. He did not want to sleep any more and began to graze. The mischief-maker, followed by her companions, again approached the gelding. A very stupid two-year-old white-spotted filly who always imitated the chestnut in everything, went up with her and, as imitators always do, went to greater lengths than the instigator. The chestnut always went up as if intent on business of her own, and passed by the gelding's nose without looking at him, so that he really did not know whether to be angry or not, and that was really funny.

She did the same now, but the white-spotted one, who followed her and had grown particularly lively, bumped right against the gelding with her chest. He again showed his teeth, whinnied, and with an agility one could not have expected of him, rushed after her and bit her flank. The white-spotted one kicked out with all her strength and dealt the old horse a heavy blow on his thin bare ribs. He snorted heavily and was going to rush at her again, but bethought himself and drawing a deep sigh stepped aside. The whole crowd of young ones must have taken as a personal affront the impertinence the piebald gelding had permitted himself to offer to the white-spotted one, and for the rest of the day did not let him graze in peace for a moment, so that the keeper had to quieten them several times and could not understand what had come over them.

The gelding felt so offended that he went up himself to Nester when the old man was getting ready to drive the horses home, and felt happier and quieter when he was saddled and the old man had mounted him.

God knows what the gelding was thinking as he carried old Nester on his back: whether he thought bitterly of the pertinacious and merciless youngsters, or forgave his tormentors with the contemptuous and silent pride suited to old age. At all events he did not betray his thoughts till he reached home.

That evening, as Nester drove the horses past the huts of the domestic serfs, he noticed a peasant horse and cart tethered to his porch: some friends had come to see him. When driving the horses in he was in such a hurry that he let the gelding in without unsaddling him and, shouting to Váska to do it, shut the gate and went to his friends. Whether because of the affront to the white-spotted filly – Creamy's great-grand-daughter – by that 'mangy trash' bought at the horse fair, who did not know his father or mother, and the consequent outrage to the aristocratic sentiment of the whole herd, or because the gelding with his high saddle and without a rider presented a strangely fantastic spectacle to the horses, at any rate something quite unusual occurred that night in the pad-dock. All the horses, young and old, ran after the gelding, showing their teeth and driving him all round the yard; one heard the sound of hoofs striking against his bare ribs, and his deep groaning. He could no longer endure this, nor could he avoid the blows. He stopped in the middle of the paddock, his face expressing first the repulsive weak malevolence of helpless old age, and then despair: he dropped his ears, and then some-thing happened that caused all the horses to quiet down. The oldest of the mares, Vyazapúrikha, went up to the gelding, sniffed at him and sighed. The gelding sighed too . . .

V

IN the middle of the moonlit paddock stood the tall gaunt figure of the gelding, still wearing the high saddle with its prominent peak at the bow. The horses stood motionless and in deep silence around him as if they were learning something new and unex-pected. And they had learnt something new and unexpected.

This is what they learnt from him . . .

First Night

Yes, I am the son of Affable I and of Bába. My pedigree name is Muzhík, and I was nicknamed Strider by the crowd because of my long and sweeping strides, the like of which was nowhere to be found in all Russia. There is no more thoroughbred horse in the world. I should never have told you this. What good would it have done? You would never have recognized me: even Vyazapúrikha, who was with me in Khrénovo, did not recognize me till now. You would not have believed me if Vyazapúrikha were not here to be my witness, and I should never have told you this. I don't need equine sympathy. But you wished it. Yes, I am that Strider whom connoisseurs are looking for and cannot find — that Strider whom the count himself knew and got rid of from his stud because I outran Swan, his favourite.

When I was born I did not know what *piebald* meant — I thought I was just a horse. I remember that the first remark we heard about my colour struck my mother and me deeply.

I suppose I was born in the night; by the morning, having been licked over by my mother, I already stood on my feet. I remember I kept wanting something and that everything seemed very surprising and yet very simple. Our stalls opened into a long warm passage and had latticed doors through which everything could be seen.

My mother offered me her teats but I was still so innocent that I poked my nose now between her forelegs and now under her udder. Suddenly she glanced at the latticed door and lifting her leg over me stepped aside. The groom on duty was looking into our stall through the lattice.

'Why, Bába has foaled!' he said, and began to draw the bolt. He came in over the fresh bedding and put his arms round me. 'Just look, Tarás!' he shouted, 'what a piebald he is — a regular magpie!'

I darted away from him and fell on my knees.

'Look at him — the little devil!'

My mother became disquieted, but did not take my part, she only stepped a little to one side with a very deep sigh. Other grooms came to look at me, and one of them ran to tell the stud groom.

Everybody laughed when they looked at my spots, and they gave me all kinds of strange names, but neither I nor my mother understood those words. Till then there had been no piebalds among all my relatives. We did not think there was anything bad in it. Everybody even then praised my strength and my form.

'See what a frisky fellow!' said the groom. 'There's no holding him.'

Before long the stud groom came and began to express astonishment at my colour; he even seemed aggrieved.

'And who does the little monster take after?' he said. 'The general won't keep him in the stud. Oh, Bába, you have played me a trick!' he addressed my mother. 'You might at least have dropped one with just a star – but this one is all piebald!'

My mother did not reply, but as usual on such occasions drew a sigh.

'And what devil does he take after – he's just like a peasant-horse!' he continued. 'He can't be left in the stud – he'd shame us. But he's well built – very well!' said he, and so did everyone who saw me.

A few days later the general himself came and looked at me, and again everyone seemed horrified at something, and abused me and my mother for the colour of my hair. 'But he's a fine colt – very fine!' said all who saw me.

Until spring we all lived separately in the brood mares' stable, each with our mother, and only occasionally when the snow on the stable roofs began to melt in the sun were we let out with our mothers into the large paddock strewn with fresh straw. There I first came to know all my near and my distant relations. Here I saw all the famous mares of the day coming out from different doors with their little foals. There was the old mare Dutch, Fly (Creamy's daughter), Ruddy the riding-horse, Wellwisher – all celebrities at that time. They all gathered together with their foals, walking about in the sunshine, rolling on the fresh straw and sniffing at one another like ordinary horses. I have never forgotten the sight of that paddock full of the beauties of that day. It seems strange to you to think, and hard to believe, that I was ever young and frisky, but it was so. This same Vyazapúrikha was then a yearling filly whose mane had just been cut; a dear, merry, lively little thing, but – and I do not say it to offend her – although among you she is now considered a remarkable thoroughbred she was then among the poorest horses in the stud. She will herself confirm this.

My mottled appearance, which men so disliked, was very attractive to all the horses; they all came round me, admired me, and frisked about with me. I began to forget what men said about my mottled appearance, and felt happy. But I soon experienced the first sorrow of my life and the cause of it was my mother. When the thaw had set in, the sparrows twittered under the eaves, spring was felt more strongly in the air, and my mother's treatment of me changed.

Her whole disposition changed: she would frisk about without any reason and run round the yard, which did not at all accord with her dignified age; then she would consider and begin to neigh, and would bite and kick her sister mares, and then begin to sniff at me and snort discontentedly; then on going out into the sun she would lay her head across the shoulder of her cousin, Lady Merchant, dreamily rub her back, and push me away from her teats.

One day the stud groom came and had a halter put on her and she was led out of the stall. She neighed and I answered and rushed after her, but she did not even look back at me. The strapper, Tarás, seized me in his arms while they were closing the door after my mother had been led out.

I bolted and upset the strapper on the straw, but the door was shut and I could only hear the receding sound of my mother's neighing; and that neigh did not sound like a call to me but had another expression. Her voice was answered from afar by a powerful voice – that of Dóbry I, as I learned later, who was being led by two grooms, one on each side, to meet my mother.

I don't remember how Tarás got out of my stall: I felt too sad, for I knew that I had lost my mother's love for ever. 'And it's all because I am piebald!' I thought, remembering what people said about my colour, and such passionate anger overcame me that I began to beat my head and knees against the walls of the stall and continued till I was sweating all over and quite exhausted.

After a while my mother came back to me. I heard her run up the passage at a trot and with an unusual gait. They opened the door for her and I hardly knew her – she had grown so much younger and more beautiful. She sniffed at me, snorted, and began to whinny. Her whole demeanour showed that she no longer loved me.

She told me of Dóbry's beauty and her love of him. Those meetings continued and the relations between my mother and me grew colder and colder.

Soon after that we were let out to pasture. I now discovered new joys which made up to me for the loss of my mother's love. I had friends and companions. Together we learnt to eat grass, to neigh like the grown-ups, and to gallop round our mothers with lifted tails. That was a happy time. Everything was forgiven me, everybody loved me, admired me, and looked indulgently at anything I did. But that did not last long.

Soon afterwards something dreadful happened to me . . .

The gelding heaved a deep sigh and walked away from the other horses.

The dawn had broken long before. The gates creaked. Nester came in, and the horses separated. The keeper straightened the saddle on the gelding's back and drove the horses out.

VI

Second Night

As soon as the horses had been driven in they again gathered round the piebald, who continued:

In August they separated me from my mother and I did not feel particularly grieved. I saw that she was again heavy (with my brother, the famous Usán) and that I could no longer be to her what I had been. I was not jealous, but felt that I had become indifferent to her. Besides I knew that having left my mother I should be put in the general division of foals, where we were kept two or three together and were every day let out in a crowd into the open. I was in the same stall with Darling. Darling was a saddle-horse, who was subsequently ridden by the Emperor and portrayed in pictures and sculpture. At that time he was a mere foal, with soft glossy coat, a swan-like neck, and straight slender legs taut as the strings of an instrument. He was always lively, good-tempered and amiable, always ready to gambol, exchange licks, and play tricks on horse or man. Living together as we did we involuntarily made friends, and our friendship lasted the whole of our youth. He was merry and giddy. Even then he began to make love, courted the fillies, and laughed at my guilelessness. To my misfortune vanity led me to imitate him, and I was soon carried away and fell in love. And this early tendency of mine was the cause of the greatest change in my fate. It happened that I was carried away... Vyazapúrikha was a year older than I, and we were special friends, but towards the autumn I noticed that she began to be shy with me...

But I will not speak of that unfortunate period of my first love; she herself remembers my mad passion, which ended for me in the most important change of my life.

The strappers rushed to drive her away and to beat me. That evening I was shut up in a special stall where I neighed all night as if foreseeing what was to happen next.

In the morning the general, the stud groom, the stablemen, and the strappers came into the passage where my stall was, and there was a terrible hubbub. The general shouted at the stud groom, who tried to justify himself by saying that he had not told them to let me out but that the grooms had done it of their own accord. The general said that he would have everybody flogged, and that it would not do to keep young stallions. The stud groom promised that he would have everything attended to. They grew quiet and went away. I did not understand anything, but could see that they were planning something concerning me.

* * *

The day after that I ceased neighing for ever. I became what I am now. The whole world was changed in my eyes. Nothing mattered any more; I became self-absorbed and began to brood. At first everything seemed repulsive to me. I even ceased to eat, drink, or walk, and there was no idea of playing. Now and then it occurred to me to give a kick, to gallop, or to start neighing, but immediately came the question: Why? What for? and all my energy died away.

One evening I was being exercised just when the horses were driven back from pasture. I saw in the distance a cloud of dust enveloping the indistinct but familiar outlines of all our brood mares. I heard their cheerful snorting and the trampling of their feet. I stopped, though the cord of the halter by which the groom was leading me cut the nape of my neck, and I gazed at the approaching drove as one gazes at a happiness that is lost for ever and cannot return. They approached, and I could distinguish one after another all the familiar, beautiful, stately, healthy, sleek figures. Some of them also turned to look at me. I was unconscious of the pain the groom's jerking at my halter inflicted. I forgot myself and from old habit involuntarily neighed and began to trot, but my neighing sounded sad, ridiculous and meaningless. No one in the drove made sport of me, but I noticed that out of decorum many of them turned away from me. They evidently felt it repugnant, pitiable, indelicate, and above all ridiculous, to look at my thin expressionless neck, my large head (I had grown lean in the meantime), my long, awkward legs, and the silly awkward gait with which by force of habit I trotted round the groom. No one answered my neighing – they all looked away. Suddenly I understood it all, understood how far I was for ever removed from them, and I do not remember how I got home with the groom.

Already before that I had shown a tendency towards gravity and thoughtfulness, but now a decided change came over me. My being piebald, which aroused such curious contempt in men, my terrible and unexpected misfortune, and also my peculiar position in the stud farm which I felt but was unable to explain, made me retire into myself. I pondered over the injustice of men, who blamed me for being piebald; I pondered on the inconstancy of mother-love and feminine love in general and on its dependence on physical conditions; and above all I pondered on the characteristics of that strange race of animals with whom we are so closely connected, and whom we call men – those characteristics which were the source of my own peculiar position in the stud farm, which I felt but could not understand.

The meaning of this peculiarity in people and the characteristic on which it is based was shown me by the following occurrence.

It was in winter at holiday time. I had not been fed or watered all day. As I learnt later this happened because the lad who fed us was drunk. That day the stud groom came in, saw that I had no food, began to use bad language about the missing lad, and then went away.

Next day the lad came into our stable with another groom to give us hay. I noticed that he was particularly pale and sad and that in the expression of his long back especially there was something significant which evoked compassion.

He threw the hay angrily over the grating. I made a move to put my head over his shoulder, but he struck me such a painful blow on the nose with his fist that I started back. Then he kicked me in the belly with his boot.

'If it hadn't been for this scurvy beast,' he said, 'nothing would have happened!'

'How's that?' inquired the other groom.

'You see, he doesn't go to look after the count's horses, but visits his own twice a day.'

'What, have they given him the piebald?' asked the other.

'Given it, or sold it – the devil only knows! The count's horses might all starve – he wouldn't care – but just dare to leave *his* colt without food! "Lie down!" he says, and they begin walloping me! No Christianity in it. He has more pity on a beast than on a man. He must be an infidel – he counted the strokes himself, the barbarian! The general never flogged like that! My whole back is covered with wales. There's no Christian soul in him!'

What they said about flogging and Christianity I understood well enough, but I was quite in the dark as to what they meant by the words '*his* colt', from which I perceived that people considered that there was some connexion between me and the head groom. What that connexion was I could not at all understand then. Only much later when they separated me from the other horses did I learn what it meant. At that time I could not at all understand what they meant by speaking of *me* as being a man's property. The words '*my* horse' applied to me, a live horse, seemed to me as strange as to say 'my land', 'my air', or 'my water'.

But those words had an enormous effect on me. I thought of them constantly and only after long and varied relations with men did I at last understand the meaning they attach to these strange words, which indicate that men are guided in life not by deeds but by words. They like not so much to do or abstain from doing anything, as to be able to apply conventional words to different objects. Such words, considered very important among them, are *my* and *mine*, which they apply to various things, creatures, or objects: even to land, people, and horses. They have agreed that of any given thing only one person may use the word *mine*, and he who in this game of theirs may use that conventional word about the greatest number of things is considered the happiest. Why this is so I do not know, but it is so. For a long time I tried to explain it by some direct advantage they derive from it, but this proved wrong.

For instance many of those who called me their horse did not ride me, quite other people rode me; nor did they feed me – quite other people did that. Again it was not those who called me *their* horse who treated me kindly, but coachmen, veterinaries, and in general quite other people. Later on, having widened my field of observation, I became convinced that not only as applied to us horses, but in regard to other things, the idea of *mine* has no other basis than a low, mercenary instinct in men, which they call the feeling or right of property. A man who never lives in it says 'my house', but only concerns himself with its building and maintenance; and a tradesman talks of 'my cloth business', but has none of his clothes made of the best cloth that is in his shop.

There are people who call land theirs, though they have never seen that land and never walked on it. There are people who call other people theirs, but have never seen those others, and the whole relationship of the owners to the owned is that they do them harm.

There are men who call women their women or their wives; yet these women live with other men. And men strive in life not to do what they think right, but to call as many things as possible *their own*.

I am now convinced that in this lies the essential difference between men and us. Therefore, not to speak of other things in which we are superior to men, on this ground alone we may boldly say that in the scale of living creatures we stand higher than man. The activity of men, at any rate of those I have had to do with, is guided by words, while ours is guided by deeds.

It was this right to speak of me as *my horse* that the stud groom had obtained, and that was why he had the stable lad flogged. This discovery much astonished me and, together with the thoughts and opinions aroused in men by my piebald colour, and the thoughtfulness produced in me by my mother's betrayal, caused me to become the serious and thoughtful gelding that I am.

I was thrice unfortunate: I was piebald, I was a gelding, and people considered that I did not belong to God and to myself, as is natural to all living creatures, but that I belonged to the stud groom.

Their thinking this about me had many consequences. The first was that I was kept apart from the other horses, was better fed, oftener taken out on the line, and was broken in at an earlier age. I was first harnessed in my third year. I remember how the stud groom, who imagined I was his, himself began to harness me with a crowd of other grooms, expecting me to prove unruly or to resist. They put ropes round me to lead me into the shafts; put a cross of broad straps on my back and fastened it to the shafts so that I could not kick, while I was only awaiting an opportunity to show my readiness and love of work.

They were surprised that I started like an old horse. They began to break me and I began to practise trotting. Every day I made greater and greater progress, so that after three months the general himself and many others approved of my pace. But strange to say, just because they considered me not as their own, but as belonging to the head groom, they regarded my paces quite differently.

The stallions who were my brothers were raced, their records were kept, people went to look at them, drove them in gilt sulkies, and expensive horse-cloths were thrown over them. I was driven in a common sulky to Chesménka and other farms on the head groom's business. All this was the result of my being piebald, and especially of my being in their opinion not the count's, but the head groom's property.

To-morrow, if we are alive, I will tell you the chief consequence for me of this right of property the head groom considered himself to have.

All that day the horses treated Strider respectfully, but Nester's treatment of him was as rough as ever. The peasant's little roan horse neighed again on coming up to the herd, and the chestnut filly again coquettishly replied to him.

VII

Third Night

THE new moon had risen and its narrow crescent lit up Strider's figure as he once again stood in the middle of the stable yard. The other horses crowded round him.

The gelding continued:

For me the most surprising consequence of my not being the count's, nor God's, but the head groom's, was that the very thing that constitutes our chief merit – a fast pace – was the cause of my banishment. They were driving Swan round the track, and the head groom, returning from Chesménka, drove me up and stopped there. Swan went past. He went well, but all the same he was showing off and had not the exactitude I had developed in myself – so that directly one foot touched the ground another instantaneously lifted and not the slightest effort was lost but every atom of exertion carried me forward. Swan went by us. I pulled towards the ring and the head groom did not check me. 'Here, shall I try my piebald?' he shouted, and when next Swan came abreast of us he let me go. Swan was already going fast, and so I was left behind during the first round, but in the second I began to gain on him, drew near to his sulky, drew level – and passed him. They tried us again – it was the same thing. I was the faster. And this dismayed everybody. The general asked that I should be sold at once to some distant place, so that nothing more should be heard of me: 'Or else the count will get to know of it and there will be trouble!' So they sold me to a horse-dealer as a shaft-horse. I did not remain with him long. An hussar who came to buy remounts bought me. All this was so unfair, so cruel, that I was glad when they took me away from Khrénovo and parted me for ever from all that had been familiar and dear to me. It was too painful for me among them. They had love, honour, freedom, before them; I had labour, humiliation; humiliation, labour, to the end of my life. And why? Because I was piebald, and because of that had to become somebody's horse. . . .

Strider could not continue that evening. An event occurred in the enclosure that upset all the horses. Kupchíkha, a mare big with foal, who had stood listening to the story, suddenly turned away and walked slowly into the shed, and there began to groan so that it drew the attention of all the horses. Then she lay down, then got up again, and again lay down. The old mares understood what was happening to her, but the young ones became excited and, leaving the gelding, surrounded the invalid. Towards morning there was a new foal standing unsteadily on its little legs. Nester shouted to the groom, and the mare and foal were taken into a stall and the other horses driven to the pasture without them.

VIII

Fourth Night

IN the evening when the gate was closed and all had quieted down, the piebald continued:

I have had opportunity to make many observations both of men and horses during the time I passed from hand to hand.

I stayed longest of all with two masters: a prince (an officer of hussars), and later with an old lady who lived near the church of St Nicholas the Wonder Worker.

The happiest years of my life I spent with the officer of hussars.

Though he was the cause of my ruin, and though he never loved anything or anyone, I loved and still love him for that very reason.

What I liked about him was that he was handsome, happy, rich, and therefore never loved anybody.

You understand that lofty equine feeling of ours. His coldness and my dependence on him gave special strength to my love for him. 'Kill me, drive me till my wind is broken!' I used to think in our good days, 'and I shall be all the happier.'

He bought me from an agent to whom the head groom had sold me for eight hundred rubles, and he did so just because no one else had piebald horses. That was my best time. He had a mistress. I knew this because I took him to her every day and sometimes took them both out.

His mistress was a handsome woman, and he was handsome, and his coachman was handsome, and I loved them all because they were. Life was worth living then. This was how our time was spent: in the morning the groom came to rub me down – not the coachman himself but the groom. The groom was a lad from among the peasants. He would open the door, let out the steam from the horses, throw out the droppings, take off our rugs, and begin to fidget over our bodies with a brush, and lay whitish streaks of dandruff from a curry-comb on the boards of the floor that was dented by our rough horseshoes. I would playfully nip his sleeve and paw the ground. Then we were led out one after another to the trough filled with cold water, and the lad would admire the smoothness of my spotted coat which he had polished, my foot with its broad hoof, my legs straight as an arrow, my glossy quarters, and my back wide enough to sleep on. Hay was piled onto the high racks, and the oak cribs were filled with oats. Then Feofán, the head coachman, would come in.

Master and coachman resembled one another. Neither of them was afraid of anything or cared for anyone but himself, and for that reason everybody liked them. Feofán wore a red shirt, black velveteen knickerbockers, and a sleeveless coat. I liked it on a holiday when he would come into the stable, his hair pomaded, and wearing his sleeveless coat, and would shout:

'Now then, beastie, have you forgotten?' and push me with the handle of the stable fork, never so as to hurt me but just as a joke. I immediately knew that it was a joke, and laid back an ear, making my teeth click.

We had a black stallion, who drove in a pair. At night they used to put me in harness with him. That Polkán, as he was called, did not understand a joke but was simply vicious as the devil. I was in the stall next to his and sometimes we bit one another seriously. Feofán was not afraid of him. He would come up and give a shout: it looked as if Polkán would kill him, but no, he'd miss, and Feofán would put the harness on him.

Once he and I bolted down Smiths Bridge Street. Neither my master nor the coachman was frightened; they laughed, shouted at the people, checked us, and turned so that no one was run over.

In their service I lost my best qualities and half my life. They ruined me by watering me wrongly, and they foundered me. . . . Still for all that it was the best time of my life. At twelve o'clock they would come to harness me, black my hoofs, moisten my forelock and mane, and put me in the shafts.

The sledge was of plaited cane upholstered with velvet; the reins were of silk, the harness had silver buckles, sometimes there was a cover of silken fly-net, and altogether it was such that when all the traces and straps were fastened it was difficult to say where the harness ended and the horse began. We were harnessed at ease in the stable. Feofán would come, broader at his hips than at the shoulders, his red belt up under his arms: he would examine the harness, take his seat, wrap his coat round him, put his foot into the sledge stirrup, let off some joke, and for appearances' sake always hang a whip over his arm though he hardly ever hit me, and would say, 'Let go!', and playfully stepping from foot to foot I would move out of the gate, and the cook who had come out to empty the slops would stop on the threshold and the peasant who had brought wood into the yard would open his eyes wide. We would come out, go a little way, and stop. Footmen would come out and other coachmen, and a chatter would begin. Everybody would wait: sometimes we had to stand for three hours at the entrance, moving a little way, turning back, and standing again.

At last there would be a stir in the hall: old Tíkhon with his paunch would rush out in his dress coat and cry, 'Drive up!' (In those days there was not that stupid way of saying, 'Forward!' as if one did not know that we moved forward and not back.) Feofán would cluck, drive up, and the prince would hurry out carelessly, as though there were nothing remarkable about the sledge, or the horse, or Feofán – who bent his back and stretched out his arms so that it seemed it would be impossible for him to keep them long in that position. The prince would have a shako on his head and wear a fur coat with a grey beaver collar hiding his rosy, black-browed, handsome face, that should never have been concealed. He would come out clattering his sabre, his spurs, and the brass backs of the heels of his overshoes, stepping over the carpet as if in a hurry and taking no notice of me or Feofán whom everybody but he looked at and admired. Feofán would cluck, I would tug at the reins, and respectably, at a foot pace, we would draw up to the entrance and stop. I would turn my eyes on the prince and jerk my thoroughbred head with its delicate forelock. . . . The prince would be in good spirits and would sometimes jest with Feofán. Feofán would reply, half turning his handsome head,

and without lowering his arms would make a scarcely perceptible movement with the reins which I understood: and then
one, two, three... with ever wider and wider strides, every
muscle quivering, and sending the muddy snow against the
front of the sledge, I would go. In those days, too, there was
none of the present-day stupid habit of crying, 'Oh!' as if the
coachman were in pain, instead of the sensible, 'Be off!
Take care!' Feofán would shout 'Be off! Look out there!'
and the people would step aside and stand craning their
necks to see the handsome gelding, the handsome coachman,
and the handsome gentleman...

I was particularly fond of passing a trotter. When Feofán and
I saw at a distance a turn-out worthy of the effort, we would
fly like a whirlwind and gradually gain on it. Now, throwing
the dirt right to the back of the sledge, I would draw level with
the occupant of the vehicle and snort above his head: then
I would reach the horse's harness and the arch of his troyka,
and then would no longer see it but only hear its sounds in the
distance behind. And the prince, Feofán, and I, would all be
silent, and pretend to be merely going on our own business
and not even to notice those with slow horses whom we
happened to meet on our way. I liked to pass another
horse, but also liked to meet a good trotter. An instant,
a sound, a glance, and we had passed each other and were
flying in opposite directions.

The gate creaked and the voices of Nester and Váska were
heard.

Fifth Night

The weather began to break up. It had been dull since morning
and there was no dew, but it was warm and the mosquitoes
were troublesome. As soon as the horses were driven in they
collected round the piebald, and he finished his story as follows:

The happy period of my life was soon over. I lived in that
way only two years. Towards the end of the second winter the

happiest event of my life occurred, and following it came my greatest misfortune. It was during carnival week. I took the prince to the races. Glossy and Bull were running. I don't know what people were doing in the pavilion, but I know the prince came out and ordered Feofán to drive onto the track. I remember how they took me in and placed me beside Glossy. He was harnessed to a racing sulky and I, just as I was, to a town sledge. I outstripped him at the turn. Roars of laughter and howls of delight greeted me.

When I was led in, a crowd followed me and five or six people offered the prince thousands for me. He only laughed, showing his white teeth.

'No,' he said, 'this isn't a horse, but a friend. I wouldn't sell him for mountains of gold. *Au revoir*, gentlemen!'

He unfastened the sledge apron and got in.

'To Ostózhenka Street!'

That was where his mistress lived, and off we flew...

That was our last happy day. We reached her home. He spoke of her as *his*, but she loved someone else and had run away with him. The prince learnt this at her lodgings. It was five o'clock, and without unharnessing me he started in pursuit of her. They did what had never been done to me before, struck me with the whip and made me gallop. For the first time I fell out of step and felt ashamed and wished to correct it, but suddenly I heard the prince shout in an unnatural voice: 'Get on!' The whip whistled through the air and cut me, and I galloped, striking my foot against the iron front of the sledge. We overtook her after going sixteen miles. I got him there, but trembled all night long and could not eat anything. In the morning they gave me water. I drank it and after that was never again the horse that I had been. I was ill, and they tormented me and maimed me – doctoring me, as people call it. My hoofs came off, I had swellings and my legs grew bent; my chest sank in and I became altogether limp and weak. I was sold to a horse-dealer who fed me on carrots and some-thing else and made something of me quite unlike myself, though good enough to deceive one who did not know. My strength and my pace were gone.

When purchasers came the dealer also tormented me by coming into my stall and beating me with a heavy whip to frighten and madden me. Then he would rub down the stripes on my coat and lead me out.

An old woman bought me of him. She always drove to the Church of St Nicholas the Wonder Worker, and she used to have her coachman flogged. He used to weep in my stall and I learnt that tears have a pleasant, salty taste. Then the old woman died. Her steward took me to the country and sold me to a hawker. Then I overate myself with wheat and grew still worse. They sold me to a peasant. There I ploughed, had hardly anything to eat, my foot got cut by a ploughshare and I again became ill. Then a gipsy took me in exchange for something. He tormented me terribly and finally sold me to the steward here. And here I am.

All were silent. A sprinkling of rain began to fall.

IX

The Evening After

As the herd returned home the following evening they encountered their master with a visitor. Zhuldýba when nearing the house looked askance at the two male figures: one was the young master in his straw hat, the other a tall, stout, bloated military man. The old mare gave the man a side-glance and, swerving, went near him; the others, the young ones, were flustered and hesitated, especially when the master and his visitor purposely stepped among them, pointing something out to one another and talking.

'That one, the dapple grey, I bought of Voékov,' said the master.

'And where did you get that young black mare with the white legs? She's a fine one!' said the visitor. They looked over many of the horses, going forward and stopping them. They noticed the chestnut filly too.

'That is one I kept of Khrénov's saddle-horse breed,' said the master.

They could not see all the horses as they walked past, and the master called to Nester, and the old man, tapping the sides of the piebald with his heels, trotted forward. The piebald limped on one leg but moved in a way that showed that as long as his strength lasted he would not murmur on any account, even if they wanted him to run in that way to the end of the world. He was even ready to gallop, and tried to do so with his right leg.

'There, I can say for certain that there is no better horse in Russia than this one,' said the master, pointing to one of the mares. The visitor admired it. The master walked about excitedly, ran forward, and showed his visitor all the horses, mentioning the origin and pedigree of each.

The visitor evidently found the master's talk dull, but devised some questions to show interest.

'Yes, yes,' he said absent-mindedly.

'Just look,' said the master, not answering a question. 'Look at her legs ... She cost me a lot but has a third foal already in harness.'

'And trots well?' asked the guest.

So they went past all the horses till there were no more to show. Then they were silent.

'Well, shall we go now?'

'Yes, let's go.'

They went through the gate. The visitor was glad the exhibition was over and that he could now go to the house where they could eat and drink and smoke, and he grew perceptibly brighter. As he went past Nester, who sat on the piebald waiting for orders, the visitor slapped the piebald's crupper with his big fat hand.

'What an ornamented one!' he said. 'I once had a piebald like him; do you remember my telling you of him?'

The master, finding that it was not his horse that was being spoken about, paid no attention but kept looking round at his own herd.

Suddenly above his ear he heard a dull, weak, senile neigh. It was the piebald that had begun to neigh and had broken off as if ashamed.

Neither the visitor nor the master paid any attention to this neighing, but went into the house.

In the flabby old man Strider had recognized his beloved master, the once brilliant, handsome, and wealthy Serpukhovskóy.

X

It kept on drizzling. In the stable yard it was gloomy, but in the master's house it was very different. The table was laid in a luxurious drawing-room for a luxurious evening tea, and at it sat the host, the hostess, and their guest.

The hostess, her pregnancy made very noticeable by her figure, her strained convex pose, her plumpness, and especially by her large eyes with their mild inward look, sat by the samovar.

The host held in his hand a box of special, ten-year-old cigars, such as he said no one else had, and he was preparing to boast about them to his guest. The host was a handsome man of about twenty-five, fresh-looking, well cared for, and well groomed. In the house he was wearing a new loose thick suit made in London. Large expensive pendants hung from his watch-chain. His gold-mounted turquoise shirt studs were also large and massive. He had a beard à la Napoléon III, and the tips of his moustache stuck out in a way that could only have been learned in Paris.

The hostess wore a dress of silk gauze with a large floral pattern of many colours, and large gold hairpins of a peculiar pattern held up her thick, light-brown hair – beautiful though not all her own. On her arms and hands she wore many bracelets and rings, all of them expensive.

The tea-service was of delicate china and the samovar of silver. A footman, resplendent in dress-coat, white waistcoat and necktie, stood like a statue by the door awaiting orders. The furniture was elegantly carved, and upholstered in bright colours, the wall-paper dark with a large flowered pattern. Beside the table, tinkling the silver bells on its collar, was a particularly fine whippet, whose difficult English name its owners, who neither of them knew English, pronounced badly.

In the corner, surrounded by plants, stood an inlaid piano. Everything gave an impression of newness, luxury, and rarity. Everything was good, but it all bore an imprint of superfluity, wealth, and the absence of intellectual interests.

The host, a lover of trotting races, was sturdy and full-blooded – one of that never-dying race which drives about in sable coats, throws expensive bouquets to actresses, drinks the most expensive wines with the most fashionable labels at the most expensive restaurants, offers prizes engraved with the donor's name, and keeps the most expensive mistresses.

Nikíta Serpukhovskóy, their guest, was a man of over forty, tall, stout, bald-headed, with heavy moustaches and whiskers. He must once have been very handsome, but had now evidently sunk physically, morally, and financially.

He had such debts that he had been obliged to enter the government service to avoid imprisonment for debt, and was now on his way to a provincial town to become the head of a stud farm, a post some important relatives had obtained for him.

He wore a military coat and blue trousers of a kind only a rich man would have had made for himself. His shirt was of similar quality and so was his English watch. His boots had wonderful soles as thick as a man's finger.

Nikíta Serpukhovskóy had during his life run through a fortune of two million rubles, and was now a hundred and twenty thousand in debt. In cases of that kind there always remains a certain momentum of life enabling a man to obtain credit and continue living almost luxuriously for another ten years.

These ten years were however coming to an end, the momentum was exhausted, and life was growing hard for Nikíta. He was already beginning to drink, that is, to get fuddled with wine, a thing that used not to happen, though strictly speaking he had never begun or left off drinking. His decline was most noticeable in the restlessness of his glance (his eyes had grown shifty) and in the uncertainty of his voice and movements. This restlessness struck one the more as it had evidently got hold of him only recently, for one could see that he had all his life been accustomed not to be afraid of anything or anybody, and had only recently, through heavy suffering, reached this state of fear so unnatural to him.

His host and hostess noticed this, and exchanged glances which showed that they understood one another and were only postponing till bedtime a detailed discussion of the subject, putting up meanwhile with poor Nikíta and even showing him attentions.

The sight of his young host's good fortune humiliated Serpukhovskóy, awakening a painful envy in him as he recalled his own irrecoverable past.

'Do you mind my smoking a cigar, Marie?' he asked, addressing the lady in that peculiar tone acquired only by experience – the tone, polite and friendly but not quite respectful, in which men who know the world speak to kept women in contradistinction to wives. Not that he wished to offend her: on the contrary he now wished rather to curry favour with her and with her keeper, though he would on no account have acknowledged the fact to himself. But he was accustomed to speak in that way to such women. He knew she would herself be surprised and even offended were he to treat her as a lady. Besides he had to retain a certain shade of a respectful tone for his friend's real wife. He always treated his friends' mistresses with respect, not because he shared the so-called convictions promulgated in periodicals (he never read trash of that kind) about the respect due to the personality of every man, about the meaninglessness of marriage, and so forth, but because all decent men do so and he was a decent, though fallen, man.

He took a cigar. But his host awkwardly picked up a whole handful and offered them to him.

'Just see how good these are. Take them!'

Serpukhovskóy pushed aside the hand with the cigars, and a gleam of offence and shame showed itself in his eyes.

'Thank you!' he took out his cigar-case. 'Try mine!'

The hostess was sensitive. She noticed his embarrassment and hastened to talk to him.

'I am very fond of cigars. I should smoke myself if everyone about me did not smoke.'

And she smiled her pretty, kindly smile. He smiled in return, but irresolutely. Two of his teeth were missing.

'No, take this!' the tactless host continued. 'The others are weaker. Fritz, *bringen Sie noch einen Kasten*,' he said, '*dort zwei.*'[1]

The German footman brought another box.

'Do you prefer big ones? Strong ones? These are very good. Take them all!' he continued, forcing them on his guest.

He was evidently glad to have someone to boast to of the rare things he possessed, and he noticed nothing amiss. Serpukhovskóy lit his cigar and hastened to resume the conversation they had begun.

'So, how much did you pay for Atlásny?' he asked.

'He cost me a great deal, not less than five thousand, but at any rate I am already safe on him. What colts he gets, I tell you!'

'Do they trot?' asked Serpukhovskóy.

'They trot well! His colt took three prizes this year: in Túla, in Moscow, and in Petersburg; he raced Voékov's Raven. That rascal, the driver, let him make four false steps or he'd have left the other behind the flag.'

'He's a bit green. Too much Dutch blood in him, that's what I say,' remarked Serpukhovskóy.

'Well, but what about the mares? I'll show Goody to you to-morrow. I gave three thousand for her. For Amiable I gave two thousand.'

And the host again began to enumerate his possessions. The hostess saw that this hurt Serpukhovskóy and that he was only pretending to listen.

'Will you have some more tea?' she asked.

'I won't,' replied the host and went on talking. She rose, the host stopped her, embraced her, and kissed her.

---

1 'Bring another box. There are two there.'

As he looked at them Serpukhovskóy for their sakes tried to force a smile, but after the host had got up, embraced her, and led her to the portière, Serpukhovskóy's face suddenly changed. He sighed heavily, and a look of despair showed itself on his flabby face. Even malevolence appeared on it.

The host returned and smilingly sat down opposite him. They were silent awhile.

XI

'YES, you were saying you bought him of Voékov,' remarked Serpukhovskóy with assumed carelessness.

'Oh yes, that was of Atlásny, you know. I always meant to buy some mares of Dubovítzki, but he had nothing but rubbish left.'

'He has failed . . .' said Serpukhovskóy, and suddenly stopped and glanced round. He remembered that he owed that bankrupt twenty thousand rubles, and if it came to talking of being bankrupt it was certainly said that he was one. He laughed.

Both again sat silent for a long time. The host considered what he could brag about to his guest. Serpukhovskóy was thinking what he could say to show that he did not consider himself bankrupt. But the minds of both worked with difficulty, in spite of efforts to brace themselves up with cigars. 'When are we going to have a drink?' thought Serpukhovskóy. 'I must certainly have a drink or I shall die of ennui with this fellow,' thought the host.

'Will you be remaining here long?' Serpukhovskóy asked.

'Another month. Well, shall we have supper, eh? Fritz, is it ready?'

They went into the dining-room. There under a hanging lamp stood a table on which were candles and all sorts of extraordinary things: syphons, and little dolls fastened to corks, rare wine in decanters, unusual hors-d'œuvres and vodka. They had a drink, ate a little, drank again, ate again, and their conversation got into swing. Serpukhovskóy was flushed and began to speak without timidity.

They spoke of women and of who kept this one or that, a gipsy, a ballet-girl, or a Frenchwoman.

'And have you given up Mathieu?' asked the host. (That was the woman who had ruined Serpukhovskóy.)

'No, she left me. Ah, my dear fellow, when I recall what I have got through in my life! Now I am really glad when I have a thousand rubles, and am glad to get away from everybody. I can't stand it in Moscow. But what's the good of talking!'

The host found it tiresome to listen to Serpukhovskóy. He wanted to speak about himself – to brag. But Serpukhovskóy also wished to talk about himself, about his brilliant past. His host filled his glass for him and waited for him to stop, so that he might tell him about himself and how his stud was now arranged as no one had ever had a stud arranged before. And that his Marie loved him with her heart and not merely for his wealth.

'I wanted to tell you that in my stud . . .' he began, but Serpukhovskóy interrupted him.

'I may say that there was a time,' Serpukhovskóy began, 'when I liked to live well and knew how to do it. Now you talk about trotting – tell me which is your fastest horse.'

The host, glad of an opportunity to tell more about his stud, was beginning, when Serpukhovskóy again interrupted him.

'Yes, yes,' he said, 'but you breeders do it just out of vanity and not for pleasure, not for the joy of life. It was different with me. You know I told you I had a driving-horse, a piebald with just the same kind of spots as the one your keeper was riding. Oh, what a horse that was! You can't possibly know: it was in 1842, when I had just come to Moscow; I went to a horse-dealer and there I saw a well-bred piebald gelding. I liked him. The price? One thousand rubles. I liked him, so I took him and began to drive with him. I never had, and you have not and never will have, such a horse. I never knew one like him for speed and for strength. You were a boy then and couldn't have known, but you may have heard of him. All Moscow was talking about him.'

'Yes, I heard of him,' the host unwillingly replied. 'But what I wished to say about mine . . .'

'Ah, then you did hear! I bought him just as he was, without his pedigree and without a certificate; it was only afterwards that I got to know Voékov and found out. He was a colt by Affable I. Strider – because of his long strides. On account of his piebald spots he was removed from the Khrénov stud and given to the head keeper, who had him castrated and sold him to a horse-dealer. There are no such horses now, my dear chap. Ah, those were days! Ah, vanished youth!' – and he sang the words of the gipsy song. He was getting tipsy. – 'Ah, those were good times. I was twenty-five and had eighty thousand rubles a year, not a single grey hair, and all my teeth like pearls.... Whatever I touched succeeded, and now it is all ended ...'

'But there was not the same mettlesomeness then,' said the host, availing himself of the pause. 'Let me tell you that my first horses began to trot without ...'

'Your horses! But they used to be more mettlesome ...'

'How – more mettlesome?'

'Yes, more mettlesome! I remember as if it were to-day how I drove him once to the trotting races in Moscow. No horse of mine was running. I did not care for trotters, mine were thoroughbreds: General Chaulet, Mahomet. I drove up with my piebald. My driver was a fine fellow, I was fond of him, but he also took to drink.... Well, so I got there.

'"Serpukhovskóy," I was asked, "when are you going to keep trotters?" "The devil take your lubbers!" I replied. "I have a piebald hack that can outpace all your trotters!" "Oh no, he won't!" "I'll bet a thousand rubles!" Agreed, and they started. He came in five seconds ahead and I won the thousand rubles. But what of it? I did a hundred versts[1] in three hours with a troyka of thoroughbreds. All Moscow knows it.'

And Serpukhovskóy began to brag so glibly and continuously that his host could not get a single word in and sat opposite him with a dejected countenance, filling up his

---

1 A little over sixty-six miles.

own and his guest's glass every now and then by way of distraction.

The dawn was breaking and still they sat there. It became intolerably dull for the host. He got up.

'If we are to go to bed, let's go!' said Serpukhovskóy rising, and reeling and puffing he went to the room prepared for him.

The host was lying beside his mistress.

'No, he is unendurable,' he said. 'He gets drunk and swaggers incessantly.'

'And makes up to me.'

'I'm afraid he'll be asking for money.'

Serpukhovskóy was lying on the bed in his clothes, breathing heavily.

'I must have been lying a lot,' he thought. 'Well, no matter! The wine was good, but he is an awful swine. There's something cheap about him. And I'm an awful swine,' he said to himself and laughed aloud. 'First I used to keep women, and now I'm kept. Yes, the Winkler girl will support me. I take money of her. Serves him right. Still, I must undress. Can't get my boots off. Hullo! Hullo!' he called out, but the man who had been told off to wait on him had long since gone to bed.

He sat down, took off his coat and waistcoat and somehow managed to kick off his trousers, but for a long time could not get his boots off – his soft stomach being in the way. He got one off at last, and struggled for a long time with the other, panting and becoming exhausted. And so with his foot in the boot-top he rolled over and began to snore, filling the room with a smell of tobacco, wine, and disagreeable old age.

XII

IF Strider recalled anything that night, he was distracted by Váska, who threw a rug over him, galloped off on him, and kept him standing till morning at the door of a tavern, near a peasant horse. They licked one another. In the morning when Strider returned to the herd he kept rubbing himself.

'Something itches dreadfully,' he thought.

Five days passed. They called in a veterinary, who said cheerfully:

'It's the itch, let me sell him to the gipsies.'

'What's the use? Cut his throat, and get it done to-day.'

The morning was calm and clear. The herd went to pasture, but Strider was left behind. A strange man came – thin, dark, and dirty, in a coat splashed with something black. It was the knacker. Without looking at Strider he took him by the halter they had put on him and led him away. Strider went quietly without looking round, dragging along as usual and catching his hind feet in the straw.

When they were out of the gate he strained towards the well, but the knacker jerked his halter, saying: 'Not worth while.'

The knacker and Váska, who followed behind, went to a hollow behind the brick barn and stopped as if there were something peculiar about this very ordinary place. The knacker, handing the halter to Váska, took off his coat, rolled up his sleeves, and produced a knife and a whetstone from his boot-leg. The gelding stretched towards the halter meaning to chew it a little from dullness, but he could not reach it. He sighed and closed his eyes. His nether lip hung down, disclosing his worn yellow teeth, and he began to drowse to the sound of the sharpening of the knife. Only his swollen, aching, outstretched leg kept jerking. Suddenly he felt himself being taken by the lower jaw and his head lifted. He opened his eyes. There were two dogs in front of him; one was sniffing at the knacker, the other was sitting and watching the gelding as if expecting something from him. The gelding looked at them and began to rub his jaw against the arm that was holding him.

'Want to doctor me probably – well, let them!' he thought.

And in fact he felt that something had been done to his throat. It hurt, and he shuddered and gave a kick with one foot, but restrained himself and waited for what would follow. . . . Then he felt something liquid streaming down his neck and chest. He heaved a profound sigh and felt much better.

The whole burden of his life was eased.

He closed his eyes and began to droop his head. No one was holding it. Then his legs quivered and his whole body swayed. He was not so much frightened as surprised.

Everything was so new to him. He was surprised, and started forward and upward, but instead of this, in moving from the spot his legs got entangled, he began to fall sideways, and trying to take a step fell forward and down on his left side.

The knacker waited till the convulsions had ceased; drove away the dogs that had crept nearer, took the gelding by the legs, turned him on his back, told Váska to hold a leg, and began to skin the horse.

'It was a horse, too,' remarked Váska.

'If he had been better fed the skin would have been fine,' said the knacker.

The herd returned down hill in the evening, and those on the left saw down below something red, round which dogs were busy and above which hawks and crows were flying. One of the dogs, pressing its paws against the carcass and swinging his head, with a crackling sound tore off what it had seized hold of. The chestnut filly stopped, stretched out her head and neck, and sniffed the air for a long time. They could hardly drive her away.

At dawn, in a ravine of the old forest, down in an over-grown glade, big-headed wolf cubs were howling joyfully. There were five of them: four almost alike and one little one with a head bigger than his body. A lean old wolf who was shedding her coat, dragging her full belly with its hanging dugs along the ground, came out of the bushes and sat down in front of the cubs. The cubs came and stood round her in a semi-circle. She went up to the smallest, and bending her knee and holding her muzzle down, made some convulsive movements, and opening her large sharp-toothed jaws disgorged a large piece of horseflesh. The bigger cubs rushed towards her, but she moved threateningly at them and let the little one have it all. The little one, growling as if in anger, pulled the horseflesh under him and began to gorge. In the same way the mother wolf coughed up a piece for the second, the third, and all five of them, and then lay down in front of them to rest.

A week later only a large skull and two shoulder-blades lay behind the barn, the rest had all been taken away. In summer a peasant, collecting bones, carried away these shoulder-blades and skull and put them to use.

The dead body of Serpukhovskóy, which had walked about the earth eating and drinking, was put under ground much later. Neither his skin, nor his flesh, nor his bones, were of any use.

Just as for the last twenty years his body that had walked the earth had been a great burden to everybody, so the putting away of that body was again an additional trouble to people. He had not been wanted by anybody for a long time and had only been a burden, yet the dead who bury their dead found it necessary to clothe that swollen body, which at once began to decompose, in a good uniform and good boots and put it into a new and expensive coffin with new tassels at its four corners, and then to place that coffin in another coffin of lead, to take it to Moscow and there dig up some long buried human bones, and to hide in that particular spot this decomposing maggotty body in its new uniform and polished boots, and cover it all up with earth.

THE PORCELAIN DOLL
(A FRAGMENT)

A LETTER written six months after his marriage by Leo Tolstoy to his wife's younger sister, the Natásha of *War and Peace*.

The first few lines are in his wife's handwriting, the rest in his own.

21st March 1863.

Why, Tánya, have you dried up? . . . You don't write to me at all and I so love receiving letters from you, and you have not yet replied to Lëvochka's [Tolstoy's] crazy epistle, of which I did not understand a word.

23rd March.

There, she began to write and suddenly stopped, because she could not continue. And do you know why, Tánya dear? A strange thing has befallen her and a still stranger thing has befallen me. As you know, like the rest of us she has always been made of flesh and blood, with all the advantages and disadvantages of that condition: she breathed, was warm and sometimes hot, blew her nose (and how loud!) and so on, and above all she had control of her limbs, which – both arms and legs – could assume different positions: in a word she was corporeal like all of us. Suddenly on March 21st 1863, at ten o'clock in the evening, this extraordinary thing befell her and me. Tánya! I know you always loved her (I do not know what feeling she will arouse in you now); I know you felt a sympathetic interest in me, and I know your reasonableness, your sane view of the important affairs of life, and your love of your parents (please prepare them and inform them of this event), and so I write to tell you just how it happened.

I got up early that day and walked and rode a great deal. We lunched and dined together and had been reading (she was still able to read) and I felt tranquil and happy. At ten o'clock I said goodnight to Auntie[1] (Sónya was then still as usual and said she would follow me) and I went off to bed. Through my sleep I heard her open the door and heard her breathe as she undressed.... I heard how she came out from behind the screen and approached the bed. I opened my eyes ... and saw − not the Sónya you and I have known − but a porcelain Sónya! Made of that very porcelain about which your parents had a dispute. You know those porcelain dolls with bare cold shoulders, and necks and arms bent forward, but made of the same lump of porcelain as the body. They have black painted hair arranged in large waves, the paint of which gets rubbed off at the top, and protruding porcelain eyes that are too wide and are also painted black at the corners, and the stiff porcelain folds of their skirts are made of the same one piece of porcelain as the rest. And Sónya was like that! I touched her arm − she was smooth, pleasant to feel, and cold porcelain. I thought I was asleep and gave myself a shake, but she remained like that and stood before me immovable. I said: Are you porcelain? And without opening her mouth (which remained as it was, with curved lips painted bright red) she replied: Yes, I am porcelain. A shiver ran down my back. I looked at her legs: they also were porcelain and (you can imagine my horror) fixed on a porcelain stand, made of one piece with herself, representing the ground and painted green to depict grass. By her left leg, a little above and at the back of the knee, there was a porcelain column, coloured brown and probably representing the stump of a tree. This too was in one piece with her. I understood that without this stump she could not remain erect, and I became very sad, as you who loved her can imagine. I still did not believe my senses and began to call her. She could not move without that stump and its base, and only rocked a little − together with the base − to fall in my

1 'Auntie Tatiána' − Tatiána Alexándrovna Érgolski (1795–1874), who brought Tolstoy up.

direction. I heard how the porcelain base knocked against the floor. I touched her again, and she was all smooth, pleasant, and cold porcelain. I tried to lift her hand, but could not. I tried to pass a finger, or even a nail, between her elbow and her side – but it was impossible. The obstacle was the same porcelain mass, such as is made at Auerbach's, and of which sauce-boats are made. She was planned for external appearance only. I began to examine her chemise; it was all of one piece with the body, above and below. I looked more closely, and noticed that at the bottom a bit of the fold of her chemise was broken off and it showed brown. At the top of her head it showed white where the paint had come off a little. The paint had also come off a lip in one place, and a bit was chipped off one shoulder. But it was all so well made and so natural that it was still our same Sónya. And the chemise was one I knew, with lace, and there was a knot of black hair behind, but of porcelain, and the fine slender hands, and large eyes, and the lips – all were the same, but of porcelain. And the dimple in her chin and the small bones in front of her shoulders, were there too, but of porcelain. I was in a terrible state and did not know what to say or do or think. She would have been glad to help me, but what could a porcelain creature do? The half-closed eyes, the eyelashes and eyebrows, were all like her living self when looked at from a distance. She did not look at me, but past me at her bed. She evidently wanted to lie down, and rocked on her pedestal all the time. I quite lost control of myself, seized her, and tried to take her to her bed. My fingers made no impression on her cold porcelain body, and what surprised me yet more was that she had become as light as an empty flask. And suddenly she seemed to shrink, and became quite small, smaller than the palm of my hand, although she still looked just the same. I seized a pillow, put her in a corner of it, pressed down another corner with my fist, and placed her there, then I took her nightcap, folded it in four, and covered her up to the head with it. She lay there still just the same. Then I extinguished the candle and placed her under my beard. Suddenly I heard her voice from the corner of the pillow: 'Lëva, why have I become porcelain?' I did not

know what to reply. She said again: 'Does it make any difference that I am porcelain?' I did not want to grieve her, and
said that it did not matter. I felt her again in the dark – she was
still as before, cold and porcelain. And her stomach was the
same as when she was alive, protruding upwards – rather
unnatural for a porcelain doll. Then I experienced a strange
feeling. I suddenly felt it pleasant that she should be as she was,
and ceased to feel surprised – it all seemed natural. I took her
out, passed her from one hand to the other, and tucked
her under my head. She liked it all. We fell asleep. In the
morning I got up and went out without looking at her. All
that had happened the day before seemed so terrible. When
I returned for lunch she had again become such as she always
was. I did not remind her of what had happened the day
before, fearing to grieve her and Auntie. I have not yet told
anyone but you about it. I thought it had all passed off, but all
these days, every time we are alone together, the same thing
happens. She suddenly becomes small and porcelain. In the
presence of others she is just as she used to be. She is not
oppressed by this, nor am I. Strange as it may seem, I frankly
confess that I am glad of it, and though she is porcelain we are
very happy.

I write to you of all this, dear Tánya, only that you should
prepare her parents for the news, and through papa should find
out from the doctors what this occurrence means, and whether
it will not be bad for our expected child. Now we are alone,
and she is sitting under my necktie and I feel how her sharp
little nose cuts into my neck. Yesterday she had been left in
a room by herself. I went in and saw that Dora (our little dog)
had dragged her into a corner, was playing with her, and nearly
broke her. I whipped Dora, put Sónya in my waistcoat pocket
and took her to my study. To-day however I am expecting
from Túla a small wooden box I have ordered, covered outside
with morocco and lined inside with raspberry-coloured velvet, with a place arranged in it for her so that she can be laid in
it with her elbows, head, and back all supported evenly so that
she cannot break. I shall also cover it completely with chamois
leather.

I had written this letter when suddenly a terrible misfortune occurred. She was standing on the table, when N.P.[1] pushed against her in passing, and she fell and broke off a leg above the knee with the stump. Alexéy[2] says that it can be mended with a cement made of the white of eggs. If such a recipe is known in Moscow please send it me.

1 Natálya Petróvna Okhótnitskaya, an old woman who was living at Yásnaya Polyána.
2 Alexéy Stepánovich Orékhov (who died in 1882), a servant of Tolstoy's who had accompanied him to the Caucasus and to Sevastopol during the Crimean War. He was employed as steward at Yásnaya Polyána.

POLIKÚSHKA

'IT's for you to say, ma'am! Only it would be a pity if it's the Dútlovs. They're all good men and one of them must go if we don't send at least one of the house-serfs,' said the steward. 'As it is, everyone is hinting at them. . . . But it's just as you please, ma'am!'

And he placed his right hand over his left in front of him, inclined his head towards his right shoulder, drew in his thin lips almost with a smack, turned up his eyes, and said no more, evidently intending to keep silent for a long time and to listen without reply to all the nonsense his mistress was sure to utter.

The steward – clean-shaven and dressed in a long coat of a peculiar steward-like cut – who had come to report to his proprietress that autumn evening, was by birth a domestic serf.

The report from the lady's point of view meant listening to a statement of the business done on her estate and giving instructions for further business. From Egór Mikháylovich's (the steward's) point of view, 'reporting' was a ceremony of standing straight on both feet with out-turned toes in a corner facing the sofa, and listening to all sorts of irrelevant chatter, and by various ways and means getting the mistress into a state of mind in which she would quickly and impatiently say, 'All right, all right!' to all that Egór Mikháylovich proposed.

The business under consideration was the conscription. The Pokróvsk estate had to supply three recruits at the Feast of Pokróv.[1] Fate itself seemed to have selected two of them by a coincidence of domestic, moral, and economic circumstances. As far as they were concerned there could be no hesitation or

---

1 The Intercession of the Virgin, the 1st of October old style.

dispute either on the part of the mistress, the Commune, or of public opinion. But who the third was to be was a debatable point. The steward was anxious to save the Dútlovs (in which family there were three men of military age), and to send Polikúshka, a married house-serf with a very bad reputation, who had been caught more than once stealing sacks, harness, and hay; but the mistress, who had often petted Polikúshka's ragged children and improved his morals by exhortations from the Bible, did not wish to give him up. At the same time she did not wish to injure the Dútlovs, whom she did not know and had never even seen. But for some reason she did not seem able to grasp the fact, and the steward could not make up his mind to tell her straight out, that if Polikúshka did not go one of the Dútlovs would have to. 'But I don't wish the Dútlovs any ill!' she said feelingly. 'If you don't – then pay three hundred rubles for a substitute,' should have been the steward's reply; but that would have been bad policy.

So Egór Mikháylovich took up a comfortable position, and even leaned imperceptibly against the door-post, while keeping a servile expression on his face and watching the movements of the lady's lips and the flutter of the frills of her cap and their shadow on the wall beneath a picture. But he did not consider it at all necessary to attend to the meaning of her words. The lady spoke long and said much. A desire to yawn gave him cramp behind his ears, but he adroitly turned the spasm into a cough, and holding his hand to his mouth gave a croak. Not long ago I saw Lord Palmerston sitting with his hat over his face while a member of the Opposition was storming at the Ministry, and then suddenly rise and in a three hours' speech answer his opponent point by point. I saw it without surprise, because I had seen the same kind of thing going on between Egór Mikháylovich and his mistress a thousand times. At last – perhaps he was afraid of falling asleep or thought she was letting herself go too far – he changed the weight of his body from his left to his right foot and began, as he always did, with an unctuous preface:

'Just as you please to order, ma'am. . . . Only there is a gathering of the Commune now being held in front of my office window and we must come to some decision. The order says that the recruits are to be in town before the Feast of Pokróv. Among the peasants the Dútlovs are being suggested, and no one else. The *mir*[1] does not trouble about your interests. What does it care if we ruin the Dútlovs? I know what a hard time they've been having! Ever since I first had the stewardship they have been living in want. The old man's youngest nephew has scarcely had time to grow up to be a help, and now they're to be ruined again! And I, as you well know, am as careful of your property as of my own. . . . It's a pity, ma'am, whatever you're pleased to think! . . . After all they're neither kith nor kin to me, and I've had nothing from them. . . .'

'Why, Egór, as if I ever thought of such a thing!' interrupted the lady, and at once suspected him of having been bribed by the Dútlovs.

' . . . Only theirs is the best-kept homestead in the whole of Pokróvsk. They're God-fearing, hard-working peasants. The old man has been church Elder for thirty years; he doesn't drink or swear, and he goes to church' (the steward well knew with what to bait the hook). ' . . . But the chief thing that I would like to report to you is that he has only two sons – the others are nephews adopted out of charity – and so they ought to cast lots only with the two-men families. Many families have split up because of their own improvidence and their sons have separated from them, and so they are safe now – while these will have to suffer just because they have been charitable.'

Here the lady could not follow at all. She did not understand what he meant by 'two-men families' or 'charitableness'. She only heard sounds and observed the nankeen buttons on the steward's coat. The top one, which he probably did not button up so often, was firmly fixed on, the middle one was hanging loose and ought long ago to have been sewn on again. But it is a well-known fact that in a conversation, especially a business conversation, it is not at all necessary to understand what is being said, but only to remember what you yourself want to say. The lady acted accordingly.

1 The Village Commune.

'How is it you won't understand, Egór Mikháylovich?' she said. 'I have not the least desire that a Dútlov should go as a soldier. One would think that knowing me as you do you might credit me with the wish to do everything in my power to help my serfs, and that I don't want any harm to come to them, and would sacrifice all I possess to escape from this sad necessity and to send neither Dútlov nor Polikúshka.' (I don't know whether it occurred to the steward that to escape the sad necessity there was no need to sacrifice everything – that, in fact, three hundred rubles would suffice; but this thought might well have crossed his mind.)

'I will only tell you this: that I will not give up Polikúshka on any account. When he confessed to me of his own accord after that affair with the clock, and wept, and gave his word to amend, I talked to him for a long time and saw that he was touched and sincerely penitent.' ('There! She's off now!' thought Egór Mikháylovich, and began to scrutinize the syrup she had in a glass of water: 'Is it orange or lemon? Slightly bitter, I expect,' thought he.) 'That is seven months ago now, and he has not once been tipsy, and has behaved splendidly. His wife tells me he is a different man. How can you wish me to punish him now that he has reformed? Besides it would be inhuman to make a soldier of a man who has five children, and only he to keep them. . . . No, you'd better not say any more about it, Egór!'

And the lady took a sip from her glass.

Egór Mikháylovich watched the motion of her throat as the liquid passed down it and then replied shortly and dryly:

'Then Dútlov's decided on?'

The lady clasped her hands together.

'How is it you don't understand? Do I wish Dútlov ill? Have I anything against him? God is my witness I am prepared to do anything for them. . . .' (She glanced at a picture in the corner, but remembered it was not an icon. 'Well, never mind . . . that's not to the point,' she thought. And again, strange to say, the idea of the three hundred rubles did not occur to her. . . .) 'Well, what can I do? What do I know about it? It's impossible for me to know. Well then, I rely on you – you know my wishes. . . . Act so as to satisfy everybody and according to the law. . . . What's to be done? They are not the only ones: everyone has times of trouble. Only Polikúshka can't be sent. You must understand that it would be dreadful of me to do such a thing. . . .'

She was roused and would have continued to speak for a long time had not one of her maidservants entered the room at that moment.

'What is it, Dunyásha?'

'A peasant has come to ask Egór Mikháylovich if the meeting is to wait for him,' said Dunyásha, and glanced angrily at Egór Mikháylovich. ('Oh, that steward!' she thought; 'he's upset the mistress. Now she won't let me get a wink of sleep till two in the morning!')

'Well then, Egór, go and do the best you can.'

'Yes, ma'am.' He did not say anything more about Dútlov. 'And who is to go to the market-gardener to fetch the money?'

'Has not Peter returned from town?'

'No, ma'am.'

'Could not Nicholas go?'

'Father is down with backache,' remarked Dunyásha.

'Shall I go myself to-morrow, ma'am?' asked the steward.

'No, Egór, you are wanted here.' The lady pondered. 'How much is it?'

'Four hundred and sixty-two rubles.'

'Send Polikúshka,' said the lady, with a determined glance at Egór Mikháylovich's face.

Egór Mikháylovich stretched his lips into the semblance of a smile but without parting his teeth, and the expression on his face did not change.

'Yes, ma'am.'

'Send him to me.'

'Yes, ma'am'; and Egór Mikháylovich went to the counting-house.

II

POLIKÉY (or Polikúshka, as he was usually contemptuously called), as a man of little importance, of tarnished reputation, and not a native of the village, had no influence either with the housekeeper, the butler, the steward, or the lady's-maid. His *corner* was the very worst, though there were seven in his family. The late proprietor had had these *corners* built in the following manner: in the middle of a brick building, about twenty-three feet square, there was a large brick baking-oven surrounded by a passage, and the four corners of the building were separated from this 'colidor' (as the domestic serfs called it) by wooden partitions. So there was not much room in these *corners*, especially in Polikéy's, which was nearest to the door. The conjugal couch, with a print quilt and pillow-cases, a cradle with a baby in it, and a small three-legged table (on which the cooking and washing were done and all sorts of domestic articles placed, and at which Polikéy – who was a horse-doctor – worked), tubs, clothing, some chickens, a calf, and the seven members of the family, filled the whole *corner* – and could not have stirred in it had it not been for their quarter of the brick stove (on which both people and things could lie) and for the possibility of going out onto the steps. That, however, was hardly possible, for it is cold in October and the seven of them only possessed one sheepskin cloak between them; but on the other hand the children could keep warm by running about and the grown-ups by working, and both the one and the other could climb on the top of the stove where the temperature rose as high as 120 degrees Fahrenheit. It may seem dreadful to live in such conditions, but they did not mind – it was quite possible to live. Akulína washed and sewed her husband's and her children's clothes, spun, wove, and bleached her linen, cooked and baked in the common oven, and quarrelled and gossiped with her neighbours. The monthly rations sufficed not only for the children, but for an addition to the cow's food. Firewood was free, and so was fodder for the cattle, and a little hay from the stables sometimes came their way. They had a strip of kitchen garden. Their cow had calved, and they had their own fowls. Polikéy was employed in the stables to look after two stallions; he bled horses and cattle, cleaned their hoofs, lanced their sores, administered ointments of his own invention, and for this was paid in money and in kind. Also some of the proprietress's oats used to find their way into his possession, and for two measures of it a peasant in the village gave twenty pounds of mutton regularly every month. Life would have been quite bearable had there been no trouble at heart. But the family had a great trouble. Polikéy in his youth had lived at a stud-farm in another village. The groom into whose hands he happened to fall was the greatest thief in the whole district, and got exiled to Siberia. Under this man Polikéy served his apprenticeship, and in his youth became so used to 'these trifles' that in later life, though he would willingly have left off, he could not rid himself of the habit. He was a young man and weak; he had neither father nor mother nor anyone else to teach him. Polikéy liked drink, and did not like to see anything lying about loose. Whether it was a strap, a piece of harness, a padlock, a bolt, or a thing of greater value, Polikéy found some use for everything. There were people everywhere who would take these things and pay for them in drink or in money, by agreement. Such earnings, so people say, are the easiest to get: no apprenticeship is required, no labour or anything, and he who has once tried that kind of work does not care for any other. It has only one drawback: although you get things cheap and easily and live pleasantly, yet all of a sudden – through somebody's malice – things go all wrong, the trade fails, everything has to be accounted for at once, and you rue the day you were born.

And so it happened to Polikéy. Polikéy had married and God had given him good luck. His wife, the herdsman's daughter, turned out to be a healthy, intelligent, hard-working woman, who bore him one fine baby after another. And though Polikéy still stuck to his trade all went well till one fine day his luck forsook him and he was caught. And it was all about a trifle: he had hidden away some leather reins of a peasant's. They were found, he was beaten, the mistress was told of it, and he was watched. He was caught a second and a third time. People began to taunt him, the steward threatened to have him conscripted, the mistress gave him a scolding, and his wife wept and was broken-hearted. Everything went wrong. He was a good-natured man; not bad, but only weak. He was fond of drink and so in the habit of it that he could not leave it alone. Sometimes his wife would scold him and even beat him when he came home drunk, and he would weep, saying: 'Unfortunate man that I am, what shall I do? Blast my eyes, I'll give it up! Never again!' A month would go by, he would leave home, get drunk, and not be seen for a couple of days. And his neighbours would say: 'He must get the money somewhere to go on the spree with!' His latest trouble had been with the office clock. There was an old wall-clock there that had not been in working order for a long time. He happened to go in at the open door by himself and the clock tempted him. He took it and got rid of it in the town. As ill luck would have it the shopman to whom he sold the clock was related to one of the house-serfs, and coming to see her one holiday he spoke about the clock. People began making inquiries – especially the steward, who disliked Polikéy – just as if it was anybody else's concern! It was all found out and reported to the mistress, and she sent for Polikéy. He fell at her feet at once and pathetically confessed everything, just as his wife had told him to do. He carried out her instructions very well. The mistress began admonishing him; she talked and talked and maundered on about God and virtue and the future life and about wife and children, and at last moved him to tears. Then she said:

'I forgive you; only you must promise me never to do it again!'

'Never in all my life. May I go to perdition! May my bowels gush out!' said Polikéy, and wept touchingly.

Polikéy went home and for the rest of the day lay on the stove blubbering like a calf. Since then nothing more had been traced to him. But his life was no longer pleasant; he was looked on as a thief, and when the time of the conscription drew near everybody hinted at him.

As already mentioned, Polikéy was a horse-doctor. How he had suddenly become one nobody knew, himself least of all. At the stud-farm, when he worked under the head-keeper who got exiled, his only duties were to clean out the dung from the stables, sometimes to groom the horses, and to carry water. He could not have learned it there. Then he became a weaver: after that he worked in a garden, weeding the paths; then he was condemned to break bricks for some offence; then he took a place as yard-porter with a merchant, paying a yearly sum to his mistress for leave to do so. So evidently he could not have had any experience as a veterinary there either; yet somehow during his last stay at home his reputation as a wonderfully and even a rather supernaturally clever horse-doctor began gradually to spread. He bled a horse once or twice, then threw it down and prodded about in its thigh, and then demanded that it should be placed in a trave, where he began cutting its frog till it bled, though the horse struggled and even whined, and he said this meant 'letting off the sub-hoof blood'! Then he explained to a peasant that it was absolutely necessary to let the blood from both veins, 'for greater ease', and began to strike the dull lancet with a mallet; then he bandaged the inn-keeper's horse under its belly with a selvedge torn from his wife's shawl, and finally he began to sprinkle all sorts of sores with vitriol, to drench them with something out of a bottle, and sometimes to give internally whatever came into his head. And the more horses he tormented and did to death, the more he was believed in and the more of them were brought to him.

I feel that for us educated people it is hardly the thing to laugh at Polikéy. The methods he employed to inspire confidence are the same that influenced our fathers, that influence us, and will influence our children. The peasant lying prone on the head of his only mare (which not only constitutes his whole wealth but is almost one of his family) and gazing with faith and horror at Polikéy's frowning look of importance and thin arms with upturned sleeves, as, with the healing rag or a bottle of vitriol between his teeth, he presses upon the very spot that is sore and boldly cuts into the living flesh (with the secret thought, 'The bow-legged brute will be sure to get over it!'), at the same time pretending to know where is blood and where pus, which is a tendon and which a vein – that peasant cannot conceive that Polikéy could lift his hand to cut without knowing where to do it. He himself could not do so. And once the thing is done he will not reproach himself with

LEO TOLSTOY
how you feel about it, but I have gone through the same
experience with a doctor who, at my request, was tormenting
those dear to me. The lancet, the whitish bottle of sublimate,
and the words, 'the staggers – glanders – to let blood, or
matter', and so on, do they not come to the same thing as
'neurosis, rheumatism, organisms', and so forth? *Wage du zu
irren und zu träumen*[1] refers not so much to poets as to doctors
and veterinary surgeons.

III

ON the evening when the village meeting, in the cold darkness of an October night, was choosing the recruits and voci-
ferating in front of the office, Polikéy sat on the edge of his bed
pounding some horse medicine on the table with a bottle – but
what it was he himself did not know. He had there corrosive
sublimate, sulphur, Glauber's salts, and some kind of herb
which he had gathered, having suddenly imagined it to be
good for broken wind and then considered it not amiss for
other disorders. The children were already lying down – two
on the stove, two on the bed, and one in the cradle beside
which Akulína sat spinning. The candle-end – one of
the proprietress's candles which had not been put away carefully enough – was burning in a wooden candlestick on the
window-sill and Akulína every now and then got up to snuff it
with her fingers, so that her husband should not have to break
off his important occupation. There were some free-thinkers
who regarded Polikéy as a worthless veterinary and a worthless
man. Others, the majority, considered him a worthless man
but a great master of his art; but Akulína, though she often
scolded and even beat her husband, thought him undoubtedly
the first of horse-doctors and the best of men. Polikéy
sprinkled some kind of simple on the palm of his hand (he
never used scales, and spoke ironically of the Germans who use
them: 'This,' he used to say, 'is not an apothecary's!'). Polikéy

1 'Dare to err and dream.'

weighed the simple on his hand and tossed it up, but there did not seem enough of it and he poured in ten times more. 'I'll put in the lot,' he said to himself. 'It will pick 'em up better.' Akulína quickly turned round at the sound of her lord and master's voice, expecting some command; but seeing that the business did not concern her she shrugged her shoulders. 'What knowledge!... Where does he get it?' she thought, and went on spinning. The paper which had held the simple fell to the floor. Akulína did not overlook this.

'Annie,' she cried, 'look! Father has dropped something. Pick it up!'

Annie put out her thin little bare legs from under the cloak with which she was covered, slid down under the table like a kitten, and got the paper.

'Here, daddy,' she said, and darted back into bed with her chilled little feet.

'Don't puth!' squeaked her lisping younger sister sleepily.

'I'll give it you!' muttered Akulína, and both heads disappeared again under the cloak.

'He'll give me three rubles,' said Polikéy, corking up the bottle. 'I'll cure the horse. It's even too cheap,' he added, 'brain-splitting work!... Akulína, go and ask Nikíta for a little 'baccy. I'll pay him back to-morrow.'

Polikéy took out of his trouser-pocket a lime-wood pipe-stem, which had once been painted, with a sealing-wax mouthpiece, and began fixing it onto the bowl.

Akulína left her spindle and went out, managing to steer clear of everything – though this was not easy. Polikéy opened the cupboard and put away the medicine, then tilted a vodka bottle into his mouth, but it was empty and he made a grimace. But when his wife brought the tobacco he sat down on the edge of the bed, after filling and lighting his pipe, and his face beamed with the content and pride of a man who has completed his day's task. Whether he was thinking how on the morrow he would catch hold of the horse's tongue and pour his wonderful mixture down its throat, or reflecting that a useful person never gets a refusal – 'There, now! Hadn't Nikíta sent him the tobacco?' – anyhow he felt happy.

Suddenly the door, which hung on one hinge, was thrown open and a maidservant from *up there* – not the second maid but the third, the little one that was kept to run errands – entered their *corner*. (*Up there*, as everyone knows, means the master's house, even if it stands on lower ground.) Aksyútka – that was the girl's name – always flew like a bullet, and did it without bending her arms, which keeping time with the speed of her flight swung like pendulums, not at her sides but in front of her. Her cheeks were always redder than her pink dress, and her tongue moved as fast as her legs. She flew into the room, and for some reason catching hold of the stove, began to sway to and fro; then as if intent on not emitting more than two or three words at once, she suddenly addressed Akulína breathlessly as follows:

'The mistress . . . has given orders . . . that Polikéy should come this minute . . . orders to come up. . . .'

She stopped, drawing breath with difficulty.

'Egór Mikháylovich has been with the mistress . . . they talked about *rickruits* . . . they mentioned Polikéy . . . Avdótya Nikoláevna . . . has ordered him to come this minute . . . Avdótya Nikoláevna has ordered . . .' again a sigh, 'to come this minute. . . .'

For half a minute Aksyútka looked round at Polikéy and at Akulína and the children – who had put out their heads from under their coverlets – picked up a nutshell that lay on the stove and threw it at little Annie. Then she repeated: 'To come this minute! . . .' and rushed out of the room like a whirlwind, the pendulums swinging as usual across her line of flight.

Akulína again rose and got her husband his boots – abominable soldier's boots with holes in them – and took down his coat from the stove and handed it to him without looking at him.

'Won't you change your shirt, Polikéy?'

'No,' he answered.

Akulína never once looked at his face while he put on his boots and coat, and she did well not to look. Polikéy's face was pale, his nether jaw twitched, and in his eyes there was that tearful, meek, and deeply mournful look one only sees in the eyes of kindly, weak, and guilty people. – He combed his hair and was going out; but his wife stopped him, tucked in the string of his shirt that hung down from under his coat, and put his cap on for him.

'What's that, Polikéy? Has the mistress sent for you?' came the voice of the carpenter's wife from behind the partition.

Only that very morning the carpenter's wife had had high words with Akulína about her pot of lye[1] that Polikéy's children had upset in her *corner*, and at first she was pleased to hear Polikéy being summoned to the mistress – most likely for no good. She was a subtle, diplomatic lady, with a biting tongue. Nobody knew better than she how to cut one with a word: so at least she imagined.

'I expect you'll be sent to town to buy things,' she continued. 'I suppose a trusty person is wanted for that job so she is sending you! You might buy me a quarter of a pound of tea there, Polikéy.'

Akulína forced back her tears, and an angry expression distorted her lips. She felt as if she could have clutched 'that vixen, the joiner's wife, by her mangy hair'. But as she looked at her children and thought that they would be left fatherless and she herself be a soldier's wife and as good as widowed, she forgot the sharp-tongued carpenter's wife, hid her face in her hands, sat down on the bed, and let her head sink in the pillows.

'Mammy, you're cwushing me!' lisped the little girl, pulling the cloak with which she was covered from under her mother's elbow.

'If only you'd die, all of you! I've brought you into the world for nothing but sorrow!' cried Akulína, and sobbed aloud, to the delight of the carpenter's wife who had not yet forgotten the lye spilt that morning.

IV

H A L F an hour passed. The baby began to cry. Akulína got up and gave it the breast. Weeping no longer, but resting her thin

---

1 Made by scalding wood-ash taken from the stove, and used for washing clothes.

though still handsome face on her hand and fixing her eyes on the last flickerings of the candle, she sat thinking why she had married, wondering why so many soldiers were needed, and also how she could pay out the carpenter's wife.

She heard her husband's footsteps and, wiping her tears, got up to let him pass. Polikéy entered like a conqueror, threw his cap on the bed, puffed, and undid his girdle.

'Well, what did she want you for?'

'H'm! Of course! Polikúshka is the least of men...but when there's business to be done, who's wanted? Why, Polikúshka....'

'What business?'

Polikéy was in no hurry to reply. He lit his pipe and spat.

'To go and fetch money from a merchant.'

'To fetch money?' Akulína asked.

Polikéy chuckled and wagged his head.

'Ah! Ain't she clever at words?... "You have been regarded," she says, "as an untrustworthy man, but I trust you more than another"' (Polikéy spoke loud that the neighbours might hear). '"You promised me you'd reform; here", she says, "is the first proof that I believe you. Go", she says, "to the merchant, fetch the money he owes, and bring it back to me." And I say: "We are all your serfs, ma'am," I say, "and must serve you as we serve God; so I feel that I can do anything for your honour and cannot refuse any kind of work; whatever you order I will do, because I am your slave."' (He again smiled that peculiar, weak, kindly, guilty smile.) '"Well, then," she says, "you will do it faithfully?... You understand," she says, "that your fate depends on it?" – "How could I fail to understand that I can do it all? If they have told tales about me – well, anyone can tell tales about another...but I never in any way, I believe, have even had a thought against your honour..." In a word, I buttered her up till my lady was quite softened.... "I shall think highly of you," she says.' (He kept silent a minute, then the smile again appeared on his face.) 'I know very well how to talk to the likes of them! Formerly, when I used to go out to work on my own, at times someone would come down hard on me; but only let me get in a word or two and I'd butter him up till he'd be as smooth as silk!'

'Is it much money?'

'Fifteen hundred rubles,' carelessly replied Polikéy.

She shook her head.

'When are you to go?'

'"To-morrow," she says. "Take any horse you like," she says, "call at the office, and then start and God be with you!"'

'The Lord be praised!' said Akulína, rising and crossing herself. 'May God help you, Polikéy,' she added in a whisper, so that she might not be heard beyond the partition and holding him by his shirt-sleeve. 'Polikéy, listen to me! I beseech you in the name of Christ our God: kiss the cross when you start, and promise that not a drop shall pass your lips.'

'A likely thing!' he ejaculated; 'drink when carrying all that money! . . . Ah! how somebody was playing the piano up there! Fine! . . .' he said, after a pause, and smiled. 'I suppose it was the young lady. I was standing like this in front of the mistress, beside the whatnot, and the young lady was rattling away behind the door. She rattled and rattled on, fitting it together so pat! O my! Wouldn't I like to play a tune! I'd soon master it, I would. I'm awfully good at that sort of thing. . . . Let me have a clean shirt to-morrow!'

And they went to bed happy.

V

MEANWHILE the meeting in front of the office had been noisy. The business before them was no trifle. Almost all the peasants were present. While the steward was with the mistress they kept their caps on, more voices were heard, and they talked more loudly. The hum of deep voices, interrupted at rare intervals by breathless, husky, and shrill tones, filled the air and, entering through the windows of the mistress's house, sounded like the noise of a distant sea, making her feel a nervous agitation like that produced by a heavy thunderstorm – a sensation between fear and discomfort. She felt as if the voices might at any moment grow yet louder and faster and then something would happen. 'As if it could not all be done quietly, peaceably, without disputing and shouting,' she thought, 'according to the Christian law of brotherly love and meekness!'

Many voices were speaking at once, but Theodore Rezún, the carpenter, shouted loudest. There were two grown-up young men in his family and he was attacking the Dútlovs. Old Dútlov was defending himself: he stepped forward from the crowd behind which he had at first been standing. Now spreading out his arms, now clutching his little beard, he sputtered and snuffled in such a way that it would have been hard for him to understand what he himself was saying. His sons and nephews — splendid fellows all of them — stood huddled behind him, and the old man resembled the mother-hen in the game of Hawk and Chickens. The hawk was Rezún; and not only Rezún, but all the men who had two grown lads in family, and the fathers of only sons, and almost the whole meeting, were attacking Dútlov. The point was that Dútlov's brother had been recruited thirty years before, and that Dútlov wished therefore to be excused from taking his turn with the families in which there were three eligible young men, and wanted his brother's service in the army to be reckoned to the credit of his family, so that it should be given the same chance as those in which there were only two young men; and that these families should all draw lots equally and the third recruit be chosen from among all of them. Besides Dútlov's family there were four others in which there were three young men, but one was the village Elder's family and the mistress had exempted him. From the second a recruit had been taken the year before, and from each of the remaining families a recruit was now being taken. One of them had not even come to this meeting, but his wife stood sorrowfully behind all the others, vaguely hoping that the wheel of fortune might somehow turn her way. The red-haired Román, the father of the other recruit, in a tattered coat — though he was not poor — hung his head and silently leaned against the porch, only now and then looking up attentively at anyone who raised his voice, and then hanging his head again. Misery seemed to breathe from his whole figure. Old Semën Dútlov was a man to whose keeping anyone who knew anything of him would have trusted hundreds and thousands of rubles. He was a steady, God-fearing, reliable man, and was the church Elder. Therefore the excitement he was now in was all the more striking.

Rezún the carpenter, a tall dark man, was, on the contrary, a riotous drunkard, very smart in a dispute and in arguing with workmen, tradespeople, peasants, or gentlefolk, at meetings and fairs. Now he was self-possessed and sarcastic, and from his superior height was crushing down the spluttering church Elder with the whole strength of his ringing voice and oratorical talent. The church Elder was exasperated out of his usual sober groove. Besides these, the youngish, round-faced, square-headed, curly-bearded, thick-set Garáska Kopýlov, one of the speakers of the younger generation, followed Rezún and took part in the dispute. He had already gained some weight at village meetings, having distinguished himself by his trenchant speeches. Then there was Theodore Mélnichny, a tall, thin, yellow-faced, round-shouldered man, also young, with a scanty beard and small eyes, always embittered and gloomy, seeing the dark side of everything and often bewildering the meeting by unexpected and abrupt questions and remarks. Both these speakers sided with Rezún. Besides these there were two babblers who now and then joined in: one, called Khrapkóv, with a most good-humoured face and flowing brown beard, who kept repeating the words, 'Oh, my dearest friend!' the other, Zhidkóv, a little fellow with a bird-like face who also kept remarking at every opportunity, 'That's how it is, brothers mine!' addressing himself to everybody and speaking fluently but never to the point. Both of these sided first with one and then with the other party, but no one listened to them. There were others like them, but these two, who kept moving through the crowd and shouting louder than anybody and frightening the mistress, were listened to less than anyone else. Intoxicated by the noise and shouting, they gave themselves up entirely to the pleasure of letting their tongues wag. There were many other characters among the members of the commune, stern, respectable, indifferent, or depressed; and there were women standing behind the men with sticks in their hands, but, God willing, I'll speak of them some other time. The greater part of the crowd, however, consisted of peasants who stood as if they were in church, whispering behind each other's backs about home affairs, or of when to cut faggots in the wood, or silently awaiting the end of the jabber. There were also rich peasants whose well-being the meeting could not add to nor diminish. Such was Ermíl, with his broad shiny face, whom the peasants called the 'big-bellied', because he was rich. Such too was Stárostin, whose face showed a self-satisfied expression of power that seemed to say, 'You may talk away, but no one will touch me! I have four sons, but not one of them will have to go.' Now and then these two were attacked by some independent thinker such as Kopýlov and Rezún, but they replied quietly and firmly and with a consciousness of their own inviolability. If Dútlov was like the mother-hen in the game of Hawk and Chickens, his lads did not much resemble the chickens. They did not flutter about and squeak, but stood quietly behind him. His eldest son, Ignát, was already thirty; the second, Vasíli, also was already a married man and moreover not fit for a recruit; the third, his nephew Elijah, who had just got married – a fair, rosy young man in a smart sheepskin coat (he was a post-chaise driver) – stood looking at the crowd, sometimes scratching his head under his hat, as if the whole matter was no concern of his, though it was just on him that the hawks wished to swoop down.

'If it comes to that, my grandfather was a soldier,' said one, 'and so I might refuse to draw lots in just the same way! ... There's no such law, friend. Last recruiting, Mikhéchev was taken though his uncle had not even returned from service then.'

'Neither your father nor your uncle ever served the Tsar,' Dútlov was saying at the same time. 'Why, you don't even serve the mistress or the commune, but spend all your time in the pub. Your sons have separated from you because it's impossible to live with you, so you go suggesting other people's sons for recruits! But I have done police duty for ten years, and served as Elder. Twice I have been burnt out, and no one helped me over it; and now, because things are peaceable and decent in my home, am I to be ruined? . . . Give me back my brother, then! He has died in service for sure. . . . Judge honestly according to God's law, Christian commune, and don't listen to a drunkard's drivel.'

And at the same time Geráska was saying to Dútlov:

'You are making your brother an excuse; but he was not sent by the commune. He was sent by the master because of his evil ways, so he's no excuse for you.'

Geráska had not finished when the lank yellow-faced Theodore Mélnichny stepped forward and began dismally:

'Yes, that's the way! The masters send whom they please, and then the commune has to get the muddle straight. The commune has fixed on your lad, and if you don't like it, go and ask the lady. Perhaps she will order me, the one man of our family, to leave my children and go! . . . There's law for you!' he said bitterly, and waving his hand he went back to his former place.

Red-haired Román, whose son had been chosen as a recruit, raised his head and muttered: 'That's it, that's it!' and even sat down on the step in vexation.

But these were not the only ones who were speaking at once. Besides those at the back who were talking about their own affairs, the babblers did not forget to do their part.

'And so it is, faithful commune,' said little Zhidkóv, supporting Dútlov. 'One must judge in a Christian way. . . . Like Christians I mean, brothers, we must judge.'

'One must judge according to one's conscience, my dear friend,' spoke the good-humoured Khrapkóv, repeating Garáska Kopýlov's words and pulling Dútlov by his sheepskin coat. 'It was the master's will and not the commune's decision.'

'That's right! So it was!' said others.

'What drunkard is drivelling there?' Rezún retorted to Dútlov. 'Did you stand me any drinks? Or is your son, whom they pick up by the roadside, going to reproach me for drinking? . . . Friends, we must decide! If you want to spare the Dútlovs, choose not only out of families with two men, but even an only son, and he will have the laugh of us!'

'A Dútlov will have to go! What's the good of talking?'

'Of course the three-men families must be the first to draw lots,' began different voices.

'We must first see what the mistress will say. Egór Mikháy-lovich was saying that they wished to send a house-serf,' put in a voice.

This remark checked the dispute for a while, but soon it flared up anew and again came to personalities.

Ignát, whom Rezún had accused of being picked up drunk by the roadside, began to make out that Rezún had stolen a saw from some travelling carpenters, and that he had almost beaten his wife to death when he was drunk.

Rezún replied that he beat his wife drunk or sober, and still it was not enough, and this set everybody laughing. But about the saw he became suddenly indignant, stepped closer to Ignát and asked:

'Who stole? . . .'

'You did,' replied the sturdy Ignát, drawing still closer.

'Who stole? . . . Wasn't it you?' shouted Rezún.

'No, it was you,' said Ignát.

From the saw they went on to the theft of a horse, a sack of oats, some strip of communal kitchen-garden, and to a certain dead body; and the two peasants said such terrible things of one another that if a hundredth part of them had been true they would by law at the very least have deserved exile to Siberia.

In the meantime old Dútlov had chosen another way of defending himself. He did not like his son's shouting, and tried to stop him, saying: 'It's a sin. . . . Leave off, I tell you!' At the same time he argued that not only those who had three young men at home were three-men families, but also those whose sons had separated from them, and he also pointed to Stárostin.

Stárostin smiled slightly, cleared his throat, and stroking his beard with the air of a well-to-do peasant, answered that it all depended on the mistress, and that evidently his sons had deserved well, since the order was for them to be exempt.

Garáska smashed Dútlov's arguments about the families that had broken up, by the remark that they ought not to have been allowed to break up, as was the rule during the lifetime of the late master; but that no one went raspberry-picking when summer was over, and that one could not now conscript the only man left in a household.

'Did they break up their households for fun? Why should they now be quite ruined?' came the voices of the men whose families had separated; and the babblers joined in too.

'You'd better buy a substitute if you're not satisfied. You can afford it!' said Rezún to Dútlov.

Dútlov wrapped his coat round him with a despairing gesture and stepped back behind the others.

'It seems you've counted my money!' he muttered angrily. 'We shall see what Egór Mikháylovich will say when he comes from the mistress.'

VI

At that very moment Egór Mikháylovich came out of the house. One cap after another was lifted, and as the steward approached all the heads – grey, grizzled, red, brown, fair, or bald in front or on top – were uncovered, and the voices were gradually silenced till at last all was quiet. Egór Mikháylovich stepped onto the porch, evidently intending to speak. In his long coat, his hands awkwardly thrust into the front pockets, his town-made cap pulled over his forehead, he stood firmly, with feet apart, in this elevated position, towering above all these heads – mostly old, bearded, and handsome – that were turned towards him. He was now a different man from what he had been when he stood before his mistress. He was majestic.

'This is the mistress's decision, men! It is not her pleasure to give up any of the house-serfs, but from among you – whom you yourselves decide on shall go. Three are wanted this time. By rights only two and a half are wanted, but the half will be taken into account next time. It comes to the same thing: if not to-day it would have to be to-morrow.'

'Of course, that's quite right!' some voices said.

'In my opinion,' continued Egór Mikháylovich, 'Kharyúshkin and Váska Mityúkhin must go, that is evidently God's will.'

'Yes, that's quite right!' said the voices.

' . . . The third will have to be one of the Dútlovs, or one out of a two-men family. . . . What do you say?'

'Dútlov!' cried the voices. 'There are three of them of the right age!'

And again, little by little, the shouting increased, and somehow the question of the strip of kitchen-garden and certain sacks stolen from the mistress's yard came up again. Egór Mikháylovich had been managing the estate for the last twenty years and was a shrewd and experienced man. He stood and listened for about a quarter of an hour, then he ordered all to be silent, and the three younger Dútlovs to draw lots to see which of them was to go. The lots were prepared, shaken up in a hat, and Khrapkóv drew one out. It was Elijah's. All became silent.

'Is it mine? Let me see it!' said Elijah in a faltering voice.

All remained silent. Egór Mikháylovich ordered that everybody should bring the recruit money – seven kopéks from each household – next day, and saying that all was over, dismissed the meeting. The crowd moved off, the men covered their heads as they turned the corner, and their voices and the sound of their footsteps mingled into a hum. The steward stood on the porch watching the departing crowd, and when the young Dútlovs were round the corner he beckoned old Dútlov, who had stopped of his own accord, and they went into the office.

'I am sorry for you, old man,' said Egór Mikháylovich, sitting down in an arm-chair before the table. 'It was your turn though. Will you buy a recruit to take your nephew's place, or not?'

The old man, without speaking, gave Egór Mikháylovich a significant look.

'There's no getting out of it,' said Egór Mikháylovich in answer to that look.

'We'd be glad enough to buy a substitute, Egór Mikháylovich, but we haven't the means. Two horses went to the knacker's this summer, and there was my nephew's wedding. . . . Evidently it's our fate . . . for living honestly. It's very well for him to talk!' (He was thinking of Rezún.)

Egór Mikháylovich rubbed his face with his hand and yawned. He was evidently tired of the business and was ready for his tea.

'Eh, old fellow, don't be mean!' said he. 'Have a hunt under your floor, I dare say you'll turn up some four hundred old ruble notes, and I'll get you a substitute – a regular wonder! . . . The other day a fellow came offering himself.'

'In the *government*?' asked Dútlov, meaning the town.

'Well, will you buy him?'

'I'd be glad enough, God is my witness! . . . but . . . '

Egór Mikháylovich interrupted him sternly.

'Well then, listen to me, old man! See that Elijah does himself no mischief,[1] and as soon as I send word – whether to-day or to-morrow – he is to be taken to town at once. You will take him and you will be answerable for him, but if anything should happen to him – which God forbid! – I'll send your eldest son instead! Do you hear?'

'But could not one be sent from a two-man family? . . . Egór Mikháylovich, this is not fair!' he said. Then after a pause he went on, almost with tears: 'When my brother has died a soldier, now they are taking my son! How have I deserved such a blow?' and he was ready to fall on his knees.

'Well, well, go away!' said Egór Mikháylovich. 'Nothing can be done. It's the law. Keep an eye on Elijah: you'll have to answer for him!'

Dútlov went home, thoughtfully tapping the ruts with his linden stick as he walked.

---

1 It sometimes happened that to escape service men mutilated themselves, for instance by cutting off the finger needed to pull the trigger.

VII

EARLY next morning a big-boned bay gelding (for some reason called Drum) harnessed to a small cart (the steward himself used to drive in that cart), stood at the porch of the house-serfs' quarters. Annie, Polikéy's eldest daughter, barefoot in spite of the falling sleet and the cold wind, and evidently frightened, stood at the horse's head holding the bridle at arm's length, and with her other hand held a faded yellowy-green jacket that was thrown over her head, and which served the family as blanket, cloak, hood, carpet, overcoat for Polikéy, and many other things besides. Polikéy's *corner* was all in a bustle. The dim light of a rainy morning was just glimmering in at the window, which was broken here and there and mended with paper. Akulína had left her cooking in the oven, and left her children – of whom the younger were still in bed – shivering, because the jacket that served them as blanket had been taken away to serve as a garment and only replaced by the shawl off their mother's head. Akulína was busy getting her husband ready for his journey. His shirt was clean, but his boots, which as the saying is were 'begging for porridge', gave her much trouble. She had taken off her thick worsted stockings (her only pair) and given them to her husband, and had managed to cut out a pair of inner soles from a saddle-cloth (which had been carelessly left about in the stable and had been brought home by Polikéy two days before) in such a way as to stop up the holes in his boots and keep his feet dry. Polikéy sat, feet and all, on the bed, untwisting his girdle so that it should not look like a dirty cord. The cross, lisping little girl, wrapped in the sheepskin (which though it covered her head was trailing round her feet), had been dispatched to ask Nikíta to lend them a cap. The bustle was increased by house-serfs coming in to ask Polikéy to get different things for them in town. One wanted needles, another tea, a third some tobacco, and another some olive oil. The carpenter's wife – who to conciliate Polikéy had already found time to make her samovar boil and bring him a mug full of liquid which she called tea – wanted some sugar. Though Nikíta refused to lend a cap and they had to mend his own — that is, to push in the protruding bits of wadding and sew them up with a veterinary needle; though at first the boots with the saddle-cloth soles would not go on his feet; though Annie, chilled through, nearly let Drum get out of hand, and Mary in the long sheep-skin had to take her place, and then Mary had to take off the sheepskin and Akulína had to hold the horse herself — it all ended by Polikéy successfully getting all the warm family garments on himself, leaving only the jacket and a pair of slippers behind. When ready, he got into the little cart, wrapped the sheepskin round him, shook up the bag of hay at the bottom of the cart, again wrapped himself up, took the reins, wrapped the coat still closer round him as very important people do, and started.

His little boy Míshka, running out onto the steps, begged to have a ride; the lisping Mary also begged that she might 'have a lide', and was 'not cold even without the theepthkin'; so Polikéy stopped Drum and smiled his weak smile while Aku-lína put the children into the cart and, bending towards him, begged him in a whisper to remember his oath and not drink anything on the way. Polikéy took the children through the village as far as the smithy, put them down, wrapped himself up and put his cap straight again, and drove off at a slow, sedate trot, his cheeks quivering at every jolt and his feet knocking against the bark sides of the cart. Mary and Míshka, barefoot, rushed down the slippery hill to the house at such a rate and yelling so loudly that a stray dog from the village looked up at them and scurried home with its tail between its legs, which made Polikéy's heirs yell ten times louder.

It was abominable weather: the wind was cutting, and something between rain and snow, and now and then fine hail, beat on Polikéy's face and on his bare hands which held the reins — and over which he kept drawing the sleeves of his coat — and on the leather of the horse-collar, and on the head of old Drum, who set back his ears and half closed his eyes.

Then suddenly the rain stopped and it brightened up in a moment. The bluish snow clouds stood out clear and the sun began to come out, but uncertainly and cheerlessly like

Polikéy's own smile. Notwithstanding all this, Polikéy was
deep in pleasant thoughts. He whom they threatened to exile
and conscript, whom only those who were too lazy did not
scold and beat, who was always shoved into the worst places,
he was driving now to fetch *a sum of money*, and a large sum too,
and his mistress trusted him, and he was driving in the steward's cart behind Drum – with whom the lady herself sometimes drove out – just as if he were some proprietor with
leather collar-strap and reins instead of ropes. And Polikéy
sat up straighter, pushed in the bits of wadding hanging out
of his cap, and again wrapped his coat closer.

If Polikéy, however, imagined that he looked just like
a wealthy peasant proprietor he deluded himself. It is true, as
everyone knows, that tradesmen worth ten thousand rubles
drive in carts with leather harness, only this was not quite the
same thing. A bearded man in a blue or black coat drives past
sitting alone in a cart, driving a well-fed horse, and you just
glance to see if the horse is sleek and he himself well fed, and at
the way he sits, at the horse's harness, and the tyres on the
cartwheels, and at his girdle, and you know at once whether
the man does business in hundreds or in thousands of rubles.
Every experienced person looking closer at Polikéy, at his
hands, his face, his newly-grown beard, his girdle, at the hay
carelessly thrown into the cart, at lean Drum, at the worn
tyres, would know at once that it was only a serf driving past,
and not a merchant or a cattle-dealer or even a peasant proprietor, and that he did not deal in thousands or hundreds, or
even tens of rubles. But Polikéy did not think so: he deceived
himself, and deceived himself agreeably. He is going to carry
home fifteen hundred rubles in the bosom of his coat. If he
liked, he might turn Drum's head towards Odessa instead of
homewards, and drive off where Fate might take him. But he
will not do such a thing; he will bring the lady her money all in
order, and will talk about having had larger sums than that on
him. When they came to an inn Drum began pulling at the left
rein, turning towards the inn and stopping; but Polikéy,
though he had the money given him to do the shopping
with, gave Drum the whip and drove on. The same thing

happened at the next inn, and about noon he got out of the cart, and opening the gate of the inn-keeper's house where all his mistress's people put up, he led the horse and cart into the yard. There he unharnessed, gave the horse some hay, dined with the inn-keeper's men, not omitting to mention what important business he had come on, and then went out with the market-gardener's bill in the crown of his cap.

The market-gardener (who knew and evidently mistrusted Polikéy) having read the letter questioned him as to whether he had really been sent for the money. Polikéy tried to seem offended, but could not manage it, and only smiled his peculiar smile. The market-gardener read the letter over once more and handed him the money. Having received the money, Polikéy put it into his bosom and went back to the inn. Neither the beer-shop nor the tavern nor anything tempted him. He felt a pleasant agitation through his whole being, and stopped more than once in front of shops that showed tempting wares: boots, coats, caps, chintz, and foodstuffs, and went on with the pleasant feeling: 'I could buy it all, but there now, I won't do it!' He went to the bazaar for the things he had been asked to buy, got them all, and started bargaining for a lined sheepskin coat, for which he was asked twenty-five rubles. For some reason the dealer, after looking at Polikéy, seemed to doubt his ability to buy it. But Polikéy pointed to his bosom, saying that he could buy the whole shop if he liked, and insisted on trying the coat on; felt it, patted it, blew into the wool till he became permeated with the smell of it, and then took it off with a sigh. 'The price does not suit me. If you'll let it go for fifteen rubles, now!' he said. The dealer angrily threw the coat across the table, and Polikéy went out and cheerfully returned to his inn. After supper, having watered Drum and given him some oats, he climbed up on the stove, took out the envelope with the money and examined it for a long time, and then asked a porter who knew how to read to read him the address and the inscription: 'With enclosure of one thousand six hundred and seventeen assignation rubles.'[1] The envelope

1 Equal to 462 'silver rubles', at $3\frac{1}{2}$ assignations for one silver ruble.

was made of common paper and sealed with brown sealing-wax with the impression of an anchor. There was one large seal in the middle, four at the corners, and there were some drops of sealing-wax near the edge. Polikéy examined all this, and studied it. He even felt the sharp edges of the notes. It gave him a kind of childish pleasure to know that he had such a sum in his hands. He thrust the envelope into a hole in the lining of his cap, and lay down with the cap under his head; but even in the night he kept waking and feeling the envelope. And each time he found it in its place he experienced the pleasant feeling that here was he, the disgraced, the down-trodden Polikéy, carrying such a sum and delivering it up more accurately than even the steward could have done.

VIII

About midnight the inn-keeper's men and Polikéy were awakened by a knocking at the gate and the shouting of peasants. It was the party of recruits from Pokróvsk. There were about ten people: Khoryúshkin, Mityúkin, and Elijah (Dútlov's nephew), two substitutes in case of need, the village Elder, old Dútlov, and the men who had driven them. A night-light was burning in the room, and the cook was sleeping on a bench under the icons. She jumped up and began lighting a candle. Polikéy also awoke, and leaning over from the top of the stove looked at the peasants as they came in. They came in crossing themselves, and sat down on the benches round the room. They all seemed perfectly calm, so that one could not tell which of them were the conscripts and which their escorts. They were greeting the people of the inn, talking loudly, and asking for food. It is true that some were silent and sad; but on the other hand others were unusually merry, evidently drunk. Among these was Elijah, who had never had too much to drink before.

'Well, lads, shall we go to sleep or have some supper?' asked the Elder.

'Supper!' said Elijah, throwing open his coat and setting himself on a bench. 'Send for some vodka.'

'Enough of your vodka!' answered the Elder shortly, and turning to the others he said: 'You just cut yourselves a bit of bread, lads! Why wake people up?'

'Give me vodka!' Elijah repeated, without looking at anybody, and in a voice that showed that he would not soon stop.

The peasants took the Elder's advice, fetched some bread out of their carts, ate it, asked for a little kvas, and lay down, some on the floor and some on the stove.

Elijah kept repeating at intervals: 'Let me have some vodka, I say, let me have some.' Then, noticing Polikéy: 'Polikéy! Hi, Polikéy! You here, dear friend? Why, I am going for a soldier.... Have said good-bye to my mother and my missus. ... How she howled! They've bundled me off for a soldier. ... Stand me some vodka!'

'I haven't got any money,' answered Polikéy, and to comfort him added: 'Who knows? By God's aid you may be rejected!...'

'No, friend. I'm as sound as a young birch. I've never had an illness. There's no rejecting for me! What better soldier can the Tsar want?'

Polikéy began telling him how a peasant gave a doctor a five-ruble note and got rejected.

Elijah drew nearer the oven, and they talked more freely.

'No, Polikéy, it's all up now! I don't want to stay now myself. Uncle has done for me. As if he couldn't have bought a substitute!... No, he grudged his son, and grudges the money, so they send me. No! I don't myself want to stay.' (He spoke gently, confidingly, under the influence of quiet sorrow.) 'One thing only – I am sorry for mother, dear heart!... How she grieved! And the wife, too!... They've ruined the woman just for nothing; now she'll perish – in a word, she'll be a soldier's wife! Better not to have married. What did they marry me for?... They're coming here to-morrow.'

'But why have they brought you so soon?' asked Polikéy; 'nothing was heard about it, and then, all of a sudden...'

'Why, they're afraid I shall do myself some mischief,' answered Elijah, smiling. 'No fear! I'll do nothing of the kind.

I shall not be lost even as a soldier; only I'm sorry for mother. . . . Why did they get me married?' he said gently and sadly.

The door opened and shut with a loud slam as old Dútlov came in, shaking the wet off his cap, and as usual in bast shoes so big that they looked like boats.

'Afanásy,' he said to the porter, when he had crossed himself, 'isn't there a lantern to get some oats by?'

And without looking at Elijah he began slowly lighting a bit of candle. His mittens and whip were stuck into the girdle tied neatly round his coat, and his toil-worn face appeared as usual, simple, quiet, and full of business cares, as if he had just arrived with a train of loaded carts.

Elijah became silent when he saw his uncle, and looked dismally down at the bench again. Then, addressing the Elder, he muttered:

'Vodka, Ermíl! I want some drink!' His voice sounded wrathful and dejected.

'Drink, at this time?' answered the Elder, who was eating something out of a bowl. 'Don't you see the others have had a bite and lain down? Why are you making a row?'

The word 'row' evidently suggested to Elijah the idea of violence.

'Elder, I'll do some mischief if you don't give me vodka!'

'Couldn't you bring him to reason?' the Elder said, turning to Dútlov, who had lit the lantern, but had stopped, evidently to see what would happen, and was looking pityingly at his nephew out of the corner of his eyes, as if surprised at his childishness.

Elijah, looking down, again muttered:

'Vodka! Give . . . do mischief!'

'Leave off, Elijah!' said the Elder mildly. 'Really, now, leave off! You'd better!'

But before the words were out Elijah had jumped up and hit a window-pane with his fist, and shouting at the top of his voice: 'You would not listen to me, so there you have it!' rushed to the other window to break that too.

Políkey in the twinkling of an eye rolled over twice and hid in the farthest corner of the top of the stove, so quickly that he

scared all the cockroaches there. The Elder threw down his
spoon and rushed towards Elijah. Dútlov slowly put down his
lantern, untied his girdle, and shaking his head and making
a clicking noise with his tongue, went up to Elijah, who was
already struggling with the Elder and the inn-keeper's man,
who were keeping him away from the window. They had
caught his arms and seemed to be holding him fast; but the
moment he saw his uncle with the girdle his strength increased
tenfold and he tore himself away, and with rolling eyes and
clenched fists stepped up to Dútlov.

'I'll kill you! Keep away, you brute! . . . You have ruined me,
you and your brigands of sons, you've ruined me! . . . Why did
they get me married? . . . Keep away! I'll kill you! . . .'

Elijah was terrible. His face was purple, his eyes rolled, the
whole of his healthy young body trembled as in a fever. He
seemed to wish and to be able to kill all the three men who
were facing him.

'You're drinking your brother's blood, you blood-sucker!'

Something flashed across Dútlov's ever-serene face. He
took a step forward.

'You won't take it peaceably!' said he suddenly. The wonder was where he got the energy; for with a quick motion he
caught hold of his nephew, rolled to the ground with him, and
with the aid of the Elder began binding his hands with the
girdle. They struggled for about five minutes. At last with the
help of the peasants Dútlov rose, pulling his coat out of Elijah's
clutch. Then he raised Elijah, whose hands were tied behind
his back, and made him sit down on a bench in a corner.

'I told you it would be the worse for you,' he said, still out of
breath with the struggle, and pulling straight the narrow girdle
tied over his shirt. 'Why sin? We shall all have to die! . . . Fold
a coat for a pillow for him,' he said, turning to the inn-keeper's
men, 'or the blood will go to his head.' And he tied the cord
round his waist over his sheepskin and, taking up the lantern,
went to see after the horses.

Elijah, pale, dishevelled, his shirt pulled out of place, was
gazing round the room as though trying to remember where
he was. The inn-keeper's men picked up the broken bits of

glass and stuffed a coat into the hole in the window to keep the draught out. The Elder sat down again to his bowl.

'Ah, Elijah, Elijah! I'm sorry for you, really! What's to be done? There's Khoryúshkin . . . he, too, is married. Seems it can't be helped!'

'It's all on account of that fiend, my uncle, that I'm being ruined!' Elijah repeated, dryly and bitterly. 'He was chary of his own son! . . . Mother says the steward told him to buy me off. He won't: he says he can't afford it. As if what my brother and I have brought into his house were a trifle! . . . He is a fiend!'

Dútlov returned to the room, said a prayer in front of the icons, took off his outdoor things, and sat down beside the Elder. The cook brought more kvas and another spoon. Elijah grew silent, and closing his eyes lay down on the folded coat. The Elder pointed to him and shook his head silently. Dútlov waved his hand.

'As if one was not sorry! . . . My own brother's son! . . . And as if things were not bad enough it seems they also made me out a villain to him. . . . Whether it's his wife – she's a cunning little woman for all she's so young – that has put it into his head that we could afford to buy a substitute! . . . Anyhow, he's reproaching me. But one does pity the lad! . . .'

'Ah! he's a fine lad,' said the Elder.

'But I'm at the end of my tether with him! To-morrow I shall let Ignát come, and his wife wanted to come too.'

'All right – let them come,' said the Elder, rising and climbing onto the stove. 'What is money? Money is dross!'

'If one had the money, who would grudge it?' muttered one of the inn-keeper's men, lifting his head.

'Ah, money, money! It causes much sin,' replied Dútlov. 'Nothing in the world causes so much sin, and the Scriptures say so too.'

'Everything is said there,' the workman agreed. 'There was a man told me how a merchant had stored up a heap of money and did not want to leave any behind; he loved it so that he took it with him to the grave. As he was dying he asked to have a small pillow buried with him. No one suspected anything, and so it was done. Then his sons began looking for his money and nothing was to be found. At last one of them guessed that probably the notes were all in the pillow. The matter went to the Tsar, and he allowed the grave to be opened. And what do you think? They opened the coffin. There was nothing in the pillow, but the coffin was full of small snakes, and so it was buried again. . . . You see what money does!'

'It's a fact, it brings much sin,' said Dútlov, and he got up and began saying his prayers.

When he had finished he looked at his nephew. The lad was asleep. Dútlov came up to him, untied the girdle with which he was bound, and then lay down. Another peasant went out to sleep with the horses.

IX

As soon as all was quiet Polikéy climbed down softly, like a guilty man, and began to get ready. For some reason he felt uneasy at the thought of spending the night there among the recruits. The cocks were already crowing to one another more often. Drum had eaten all his oats and was straining towards the drinking-trough. Polikéy harnessed him and led him out past the peasants' carts. His cap with its contents was safe, and the wheels of the cart were soon rattling along the frosty road to Pokróvsk. Polikéy felt more at ease only when he had left the town behind. Till then he kept imagining that at any moment he might hear himself being pursued, that he would be stopped, and they would tie up his arms instead of Elijah's, and he would be taken to the recruiting station next morning. It might have been the frost, or it might have been fear, but something made cold shivers run down his back, and again and again he touched Drum up. The first person he met was a priest in a tall fur cap, accompanied by a one-eyed labourer. Taking this for an evil omen Polikéy grew still more alarmed, but outside the town this fear gradually passed. Drum went on at a walking pace and the road in front became more visible. Polikéy took off his cap and felt the notes. 'Shall I hide it in my bosom?' he thought. 'No; I should have to undo my girdle. . . . Wait a bit! When I get to the foot of the hill I'll get down and put myself to rights. . . . The cap is sewn up tight at the top, and it can't fall through the lining. After all, I'd better not take the cap off till I get home.' When he had reached the foot of the incline Drum of his own accord galloped up the next hill and Polikéy, who was as eager as Drum to get home, did not check him. All was well – at any rate so Polikéy imagined, and he gave himself up to dreams of his mistress's gratitude, of the five rubles she would give him, and of the joy of his family. He took off his cap, felt for the envelope, and, smiling, put the cap tighter on his head. The velveteen crown of the cap was very rotten, and just because Akulína had carefully sewn up the rents in one place, it burst open in another; and the very movement by which Polikéy in the dusk had thought to push the envelope with the money deeper under the wadding, tore the cap farther and pushed out a corner of the envelope through the velveteen crown.

The dawn was appearing, and Polikéy, who had not slept all night, began to drowse. Pulling his cap lower down and thereby pushing the envelope still farther out, Polikéy in his drowsiness let his head knock against the front of the cart. He woke up near home and was about to catch hold of his cap, but feeling that it sat firmly on his head he did not take it off, convinced that the envelope was inside. He gave Drum a touch, arranged the hay in the cart again, assumed once more the appearance of a well-to-do peasant, and proudly looking about him rattled homewards.

There was the kitchen, there the house-serfs' quarters. There was the carpenter's wife carrying some linen; there was the office, and there the mistress's house where in a few moments Polikéy would show that he was a trustworthy and honest man. 'One can say anything about anybody,' he would say; and the lady would reply, 'Well, thank you, Polikéy! Here are three (or perhaps five, perhaps even ten) rubles,' and she would tell them to give him some tea, or even some vodka. It would not be amiss, after being out in the cold! 'With ten rubles we would have a treat for the holiday, and buy boots, and return Nikíta his four and a half rubles (it can't be

helped!... He has begun bothering)....' When he was about
a hundred paces from the house, Polikéy wrapped his coat
round him, pulled his girdle straight and his collar, took off his
cap, smoothed his hair, and without haste thrust his hand
under the lining. The hand began to fumble faster and faster
inside the lining, then the other hand went in too, while his
face grew paler and paler. One of the hands went right through
the cap. Polikéy fell on his knees, stopped the horse, and began
searching in the cart among the hay and the things he had
bought, feeling inside his coat and in his trousers. The money
was nowhere to be found.

'Heavens! What does it mean?... What will happen?...'
He began to roar, clutching at his hair.

But recollecting that he might be seen, he turned the horse
round, pulled the cap on, and drove the surprised and disgusted Drum back along the road.

'I can't bear going out with Polikéy,' Drum must have
thought. 'For once in his life he has fed and watered me
properly, and then only to deceive me so unpleasantly! How
hard I tried, running home! I am tired, and hardly have we got
within smell of our hay than he starts driving me back!'

'Now then, you devil's jade!' shouted Polikéy through his
tears, standing up in the cart, pulling at Drum's mouth, and
beating him with the whip.

X

ALL that day no one saw Polikéy in Pokróvsk. The mistress
asked for him several times after dinner, and Aksyútka flew
down to Akulína; but Akulína said he had not yet returned,
and that evidently the market-gardener had detained him or
something had happened to the horse. 'If only it has not gone
lame!' she said. 'Last time, when Maxím went, he was on the
road a whole day – had to walk back all the way.'

And Aksyútka turned her pendulums back to the house
again, while Akulína, trying to calm her own fears, invented
reasons to account for her husband's absence, but in vain! Her
heart was heavy and she could not work with a will at any of

the preparations for the morrow's holiday. She suffered all the more because the carpenter's wife assured her that she herself had seen 'a man just like Polikéy drive up to the avenue and then turn back again'. The children, too, were anxiously and impatiently expecting 'Daddy', but for another reason. Annie and Mary, being left without the sheepskin and the coat which made it possible to take turns out of doors, could only run out in their indoor dresses with increasing rapidity in a small circle round the house. This was not a little inconvenient to all the dwellers in the serfs' quarters who wanted to go in or out. Once Mary ran against the legs of the carpenter's wife who was carrying water, and though she began to howl in anticipation as soon as she knocked against the woman's knees, she got her curls cuffed all the same, and cried still louder. When she did not knock against anyone, she flew in at the door, and immediately climbing up by means of a tub, got onto the top of the oven. Only the mistress and Akulína were really anxious about Polikéy; the children were concerned only about what he had on.

Egór Mikháylovich reporting to his mistress, in answer to her questions, 'Hasn't Polikéy come back yet?' and 'Where can he be?' answered: 'I can't say,' and seemed pleased that his expectations were being fulfilled. 'He ought to have been back by noon,' he added significantly.

All that day no one heard anything of Polikéy; only later on it was known that some neighbouring peasants had seen him running about on the road bareheaded, and asking everyone whether they hadn't found a letter. Another man had seen him asleep by the roadside beside a tied-up horse and cart. 'I thought he was tipsy,' the man said, 'and the horse looked as if it had not been watered or fed for two days, its sides were so fallen in.' Akulína did not sleep all night and kept listening, but Polikéy did not return. Had she been alone, or had she kept a cook or a maid, she would have felt still more unhappy; but as soon as the cocks crowed and the carpenter's wife got up, Akulína was obliged to rise and light the fire. It was a holiday. The bread had to come out of the oven before daybreak, kvas had to be made, cakes baked, the cow milked, frocks and shirts ironed, the children washed, water fetched, and her neighbour prevented from taking up the whole oven. So Akulína, still listening, set to work. It had grown light and the church bells were ringing, the children were up, but still Polikéy had not returned. There had been a first frost the day before, a little snow had fallen and lay in patches on the fields, on the road, and on the roofs; and now, as if in honour of the holiday, the day was fine, sunny, and frosty, so that one could see and hear a long way. But Akulína, standing by the brick oven, her head thrust into the opening, was so busy with her cakes that she did not hear Polikéy drive up, and only knew from the children's cries that her husband had returned.

Annie, as the eldest, had greased her hair and dressed herself without help. She wore a new but crumpled print dress – a present from the mistress. It stuck out as stiff as if it were made of bast, and was an object of envy to the neighbours; her hair glistened; she had smeared half an inch of tallow candle onto it. Her shoes, though not new, were thin ones. Mary was still wrapped in the old jacket and was covered with mud, and Annie would not let her come near her for fear of getting soiled. Mary was outside. She saw her father drive up with a sack. 'Daddy has come!' she shrieked, and rushed headlong through the door past Annie, dirtying her. Annie, no longer fearing to be soiled, went for her at once and hit her. Akulína could not leave her work, and only shouted at the children: 'Now, then...I'll whip you all!' and looked round at the door. Polikéy came in with a sack, and at once made his way to his own corner. It seemed to Akulína that he was pale, and his face looked as if he were either smiling or crying, but she had no time to find out which it was.

'Well, Polikéy, is it all right?' she called to him from the oven.

Polikéy muttered something that she did not understand.

'Eh?' she cried. 'Have you been to the mistress?'

Polikéy sat down on the bed in his corner looking wildly round him and smiling his guilty, intensely miserable smile. He did not answer for a long time.

'Eh, Polikéy? Why have you been so long?' came Akulína's voice.

'Yes, Akulína, I have handed the lady her money. How she thanked me!' he said suddenly, and began looking round and smiling still more uneasily. Two things attracted his feverishly staring eyes: the baby, and the cords attached to the hanging cradle. He went up to where the cradle hung, and began hastily undoing the knot of the rope with his thin fingers. Then his eyes fixed themselves on the baby; but just then Akulína entered, carrying a board of cakes, and Polikéy quickly hid the rope in his bosom and sat down on the bed.

'What is it, Polikéy? You are not like yourself,' said Akulína.

'Haven't slept,' he answered.

Suddenly something flitted past the window, and in a moment Aksyútka, the maid from 'up there', darted in like an arrow.

'The mistress orders Polikéy to come this minute,' she said – 'this minute, Avdótya Nikoláevna's orders are . . . this minute!'

Polikéy looked at Akulína, then at the girl.

'I'm coming. What can she want?' he said, so simply that Akulína grew quieter. 'Perhaps she wants to reward me. Tell her I'm coming.'

He rose and went out. Akulína took the washing-trough, put it on a bench, filled it with water from the pails which stood by the door and from the cauldron in the oven, rolled up her sleeves, and tried the water.

'Come, Mary, I'll wash you.'

The cross, lisping little girl began howling.

'Come, you brat! I'll give you a clean smock. Now then, don't make a fuss. Come along. . . . I've still got your brother to wash.'

Meanwhile Polikéy had not followed the maid from 'up there', but had gone to quite a different place. In the passage by the wall was a ladder leading to the loft. Polikéy, when he came out, looked round, and seeing no one, bent down and climbed that ladder almost at a run, nimbly and hurriedly.

'Why ever doesn't Polikéy come?' asked the mistress impatiently of Dunyásha, who was dressing her hair. 'Where is Polikéy? Why hasn't he come?'

Aksyútka again flew to the serfs' quarters, and again rushed into the entry, calling Polikéy to her mistress.

'Why, he went long ago,' answered Akulína, who, having washed Mary, had just put her suckling baby-boy into the wash-trough and was moistening his thin short hair, regardless of his cries. The boy screamed, puckered his face, and tried to clutch something with his helpless little hands. Akulína supported his soft, plump, dimpled little back with one large hand, while she washed him with the other.

'See if he has not fallen asleep somewhere,' said she, looking round anxiously.

Just then the carpenter's wife, unkempt and with her dress unfastened and holding up her skirts, went up into the loft to get some things she had hung there to dry. Suddenly a shriek of horror filled the loft, and the carpenter's wife, like one demented, with her eyes closed, came down the steps on all fours, backwards, sliding rather than running.

'Polikéy!' she screamed.

Akulína let go the baby.

'Has hung himself!' roared the carpenter's wife.

Akulína rushed out into the passage, paying no heed to the baby, who rolled over like a ball and fell backwards with his little legs in the air and his head under water.

'On a rafter . . . hanging!' the carpenter's wife ejaculated, but stopped when she saw Akulína.

Akulína darted up the ladder, and before anyone could stop her she was at the top, but from there with a terrible scream she fell back like a corpse, and would have been killed if the people who had come running from every corner had not been in time to catch her.

XI

FOR several minutes nothing could be made out amidst the general uproar. A crowd of people had collected, everyone was shouting and talking, and the children and old women were crying. Akulína lay unconscious. At last the men, the carpenter and the steward who had run to the place, went up the ladder, and the carpenter's wife began telling for the twentieth time how she, 'suspecting nothing, went to fetch a dress, and just looked round like this – and saw . . . a man; and I looked again, and a cap is lying inside out, close by. I look . . . his legs are dangling. I went cold all over! Is it pleasant? . . . To think of a man hanging himself, and that I should be the one to see him! . . . How I came clattering down I myself don't remember . . . it's a miracle how God preserved me! Truly, the Lord has had mercy on me! . . . Is it a trifle? . . . so steep and from such a height. Why, I might have been killed!'

The men who had gone up had the same tale to tell. Políkey, in his shirt and trousers, was hanging from a rafter by the cord he had taken from the cradle. His cap, turned inside out, lay beside him, his coat and sheepskin were neatly folded and lay close by. His feet touched the ground, but he no longer showed signs of life. Akulína regained consciousness, and again made for the ladder, but was held back.

'Mamma, Sëmka is dwownded!' the lisping little girl suddenly cried from their *corner*. Akulína tore herself away and ran to the *corner*. The baby lay on his back in the trough and did not stir, and his little legs were not moving. Akulína snatched him out, but he did not breathe or move. She threw him on the bed, and with arms akimbo burst into such loud, piercing, terrible laughter that Mary, who at first laughed too, covered her ears with her hands, and ran out into the passage crying. The neighbours thronged into the *corner*, wailing and weeping. They carried out the little body and began rubbing it, but in vain. Akulína tossed about on the bed and laughed – laughed so that all who heard her were horror-stricken. Only now, seeing this motley crowd of men and women, old people and children, did one realize what a number of people and what sort of people lived in the serfs' quarters. All were bustling and talking, many wept, but nobody did anything. The carpenter's wife still found people who had not heard her tale of how her sensitive feelings were shocked by the unexpected sight, and how God had preserved her from falling down the ladder. An old man who had been a footman, with a woman's jacket thrown over his shoulders, was telling how in the days of the old master a woman had drowned herself in the pond. The steward sent messengers to the priest and to the constable, and appointed men to keep guard. Aksyútka, the maid from 'up there', kept gazing with staring eyes at the opening that led to the loft, and though she could not see anything was unable to tear herself away and go back to her mistress. Agatha Mikháylovna, who had been lady's-maid to the former proprietress, was weeping and asking for some tea to soothe her nerves. Anna the midwife was laying out the little body on the table, with her plump practised hands moistened with olive oil. Other women stood round Akulína, silently looking at her. The children, huddled together in the corner, peeped at their mother and burst into howls; and then subsiding for a moment, peeped again, and huddled still closer. Boys and men thronged round the porch, looking in at the door and the windows with frightened faces unable to see or understand anything, and asking one another what was the matter. One said the carpenter had chopped off his wife's foot with an axe. Another said that the laundress had been brought to bed of triplets; a third that the cook's cat had gone mad and bitten several people. But the truth gradually spread, and at last it reached the mistress; and it seems no one understood how to break it to her. That rough Egór blurted the facts straight out to her, and so upset the lady's nerves that it was a long time before she could recover. The crowd had already begun to quiet down, the carpenter's wife set the samovar to boil and made tea, and the outsiders, not being invited, thought it improper to stay longer. Boys had begun fighting outside the porch. Everybody now knew what had happened, and crossing themselves they began to disperse, when suddenly the cry was raised: 'The mistress! The mistress!' and everybody crowded and pressed together to make way for her, but at the same time everybody wanted to see what she was going to do. The lady, with pale and tear-stained face, entered the passage, crossed the threshold, and went into Akulína's *corner*. Dozens of heads squeezed together and gazed in at the door. One pregnant woman was squeezed so that she gave a squeal, but took advantage of that very circumstance to secure a front place for herself. And how could one help wishing to see the lady in Akulína's *corner*? For the house-serfs it was just what the

coloured lights are at the end of a show. It's sure to be great
when they burn the coloured fires; and it must be an important
occasion when the lady in her silks and lace enters Akulína's
corner. The lady went up and took Akulína's hand, but Akulína
snatched it away. The old house-serfs shook their heads
reprovingly.

'Akulína!' said the lady. 'You have your children – so take
care of yourself!'

Akulína burst out laughing and got up.

'My children are all silver, all silver! I don't keep
paper money,' she muttered very rapidly. 'I told Polikéy,
"Take no notes," and there now, they've smeared him,
smeared him with tar – tar and soap, madam! Any scabbiness
you may have it will get rid of at once . . .' and she laughed still
louder.

The mistress turned away, and gave orders that the
doctor's assistant should come with mustard poultices. 'Bring
some cold water!' she said, and began looking for it herself;
but seeing the dead baby with Granny Anna the midwife
beside it, the lady turned away, and everybody saw how she
hid her face in her handkerchief and burst into tears; while
Granny Anna (it was a pity the lady did not see it – she would
have appreciated it, and it was all done for her benefit) covered
the baby with a piece of linen, straightened his arms with
her plump, deft hands, shook her head, pouted, drooped
her eyelids, and sighed with so much feeling that everybody
could see how excellent a heart she had. But the lady did
not see it, she could not see anything. She burst out sobbing
and went into hysterics. Holding her up under the arms they
led her out into the porch and took her home. 'That's all there
was to be seen of her!' thought many, and again began to
disperse. Akulína went on laughing and talking nonsense.
She was taken into another room and bled, and plastered
over with mustard poultices, and ice was put on her head.
Yet she did not come to her senses, and did not weep, but
laughed, and kept doing and saying such things that the kind
people who were looking after her could not help laughing
themselves.

XII

THE holiday was not a cheerful one at Pokróvsk. Though the day was beautiful the people did not go out to amuse themselves: no girls sang songs in the street, the factory hands who had come home from town for the day did not play on their concertinas and balaláykas and did not play with the girls. Everybody sat about in corners, and if they spoke did so as softly as if an evil one were there who could hear them. It was not quite so bad in the daytime, but when the twilight fell and the dogs began to howl, and when, to make matters worse, a wind sprang up and whistled down the chimneys, such fear seized all the people of the place that those who had tapers lit them before their icons. Anyone who happened to be alone in his *corner* went to ask the neighbours' permission to stay the night with them, to be less lonely, and anyone whose business should have taken him into one of the out-houses did not go, but pitilessly left the cattle without fodder that night. And the holy water, of which everyone kept a little bottle to charm away anything evil, was all used up during the night. Many even heard something walking about with heavy steps up in the loft, and the blacksmith saw a serpent fly straight towards it. In Polikéy's *corner* there was no one; the children and the mad woman had been taken elsewhere. Only the little dead body lay there, and two old women sat and watched it, while a third, a pilgrim woman, was reading the psalms, actuated by her own zeal, not for the sake of the baby but in a vague way because of the whole calamity. The mistress had willed it so. The pilgrim woman and these old women themselves heard how, as soon as they finished reading a passage of the Psalter, the rafters above would tremble and someone would groan. Then they would say, 'Let God arise,' and all would be quiet again. The carpenter's wife invited a friend and, not sleeping all night, with her aid drank up all the tea she had laid in for the whole week. They, too, heard how the rafters creaked overhead, and a noise as if sacks were tumbling down. The presence of the peasant watchmen kept up the courage of the house-serfs somewhat, or they would have died of fear that night. The peasants lay on some hay in the passage, and

afterwards declared that they too had heard wonderful things up
in the loft, though at the time they were conversing very calmly
together about the conscription, munching crusts of bread,
scratching themselves, and above all so filling the passage with
the peculiar odour characteristic of peasants that the carpenter's
wife, happening to pass by, spat and called them 'peasant-
brood'. However that might be, the dead man was still dangling
in the loft, and it seemed as if the evil one himself had over-
shadowed the serfs' quarters with his huge wings that night,
showing his power and coming closer to these people than he
had ever done before. So at least they all felt. I do not know if
they were right; I even think they were quite mistaken. I think
that if some bold fellow had taken a candle or lantern that
terrible night, and crossing himself, or even without crossing
himself, had gone up into the loft – slowly dispelling before him
the horror of the night with the candle, lighting up the rafters,
the sand, the cobweb-covered flue-pipe, and the tippets left
behind by the carpenter's wife – till he came to Polikéy, and,
conquering his fears, had raised the lantern to the level of the
face, he would have beheld the familiar spare figure: the feet
touching the ground (the cord had stretched), the body bending
lifelessly to one side, no cross visible under the open shirt, the
head drooping on the breast, the good-natured face with open
sightless eyes, and the meek, guilty smile, and a solemn calmness
and silence over all. Really the carpenter's wife, crouching in a
corner of her bed with dishevelled hair and frightened eyes and
telling how she heard the sacks falling, was far more terrible and
frightful than Polikéy, though his cross was off and lay on a
rafter.

'Up there', that is, in the mistress's house, reigned the same
horror as in the serfs' quarters. Her bedroom smelt of eau-de-
cologne and medicine. Dunyásha was melting yellow wax and
making a plaster. What the plaster was for I don't know, but it
was always made when the lady was unwell. And now she was
so upset that she was quite ill. To keep Dunyásha's courage up
her aunt had come to stay the night, so there were four of
them, including the girl, sitting in the maid's room, and talking
in low voices.

'Who will go to get some oil?' asked Dunyásha.

'Nothing will induce me to go, Avdótya Pávlovna!' the second maid said decidedly.

'Nonsense! You and Aksyútka go together.'

'I'll run across alone. I'm not afraid of anything!' said Aksyútka, and at once became frightened.

'Well then, go, dear; ask Granny Anna to give you some in a tumbler and bring it here; don't spill any,' said Dunyásha.

Aksyútka lifted her skirt with one hand, and being thereby prevented from swinging both arms, swung one of them twice as violently across the line of her progression, and darted away. She was afraid, and felt that if she should see or hear anything, even her own living mother, she would perish with fright. She flew, with her eyes shut, along the familiar pathway.

XIII

'Is the mistress asleep or not?' suddenly asked a deep peasant-voice close to Aksyútka. She opened her eyes, which she had kept shut, and saw a figure that seemed to her taller than the house. She screeched, and flew back so fast that her skirts floated behind her. With one bound she was on the porch and with another in the maid's room, where she threw herself on her bed with a wild yell. Dunyásha, her aunt, and the second maid almost died of terror, and before they had time to recover they heard heavy, slow, hesitating steps in the passage and at their door. Dunyásha rushed to her mistress, spilling the melted wax. The second maid hid herself behind the skirts that hung on the wall; the aunt, a more determined character, was about to hold the door to the passage closed, but it opened and a peasant entered the room. It was Dútlov, with his boat-like shoes. Paying no heed to the maids' fears, he looked round for an icon, and not seeing the tiny one in the left-hand corner of the room, he crossed himself in front of a cupboard in which teacups were kept, laid his cap on the window-sill, and thrusting his arm deep into the bosom of his coat as if he were going to scratch himself under his other arm, he pulled out the letter with the five brown seals stamped with an anchor. Dunyásha's aunt held her hands to her heart and with difficulty brought out the words:

'Well, you did give me a fright, Naúmych! I can't utter a wo . . . ord! I thought my last moment had come!'

'Is that the way to behave?' said the second maid, appearing from under the skirts.

'The mistress herself is upset,' said Dunyásha, coming out of her mistress's door. 'What do you mean, shoving yourself in through the maids' entrance without leave? . . . Just like a peasant lout!'

Dútlov, without excusing himself, explained that he wanted to see the lady.

'She is not well,' said Dunyásha.

At this moment Aksyútka burst into such loud and unseemly laughter that she was obliged to hide her face in the pillow on the bed, from which for a whole hour, in spite of Dunyásha's and the aunt's threats, she could not for long lift it without going off again as if something were bursting in her pink print bosom and rosy cheeks. It seemed to her so funny that everybody should have been so scared, that she again hid her head in the pillows and scraped the floor with her shoe and jerked her whole body as if in convulsions.

Dútlov stopped and looked at her attentively, as if to ascertain what was happening to her, but turned away again without having discovered what it was all about, and continued:

'You see, it's just this – it's a very important matter,' he said. 'You just go and say that a peasant has found the letter with the money.'

'What money?'

Dunyásha, before going to report, read the address and questioned Dútlov as to when and how he had found this money which Polikéy was to have brought back from town. Having heard all the details and pushed the little errand-girl, who was still convulsed with laughter, out into the vestibule, Dunyásha went to her mistress; but to Dútlov's surprise the mistress would not see him and did not say anything intelligible to Dunyásha.

'I know nothing about it and don't want to know anything!'

the lady said. 'What peasant? What money?... I can't and won't see anyone! He must leave me in peace.'

'What am I to do?' said Dútlov, turning the envelope over; 'it's not a small sum. What is written on it?' he asked Dunyásha, who again read the address to him.

Dútlov seemed in doubt. He was still hoping that perhaps the money was not the mistress's and that the address had not been read to him right, but Dunyásha confirmed it, and he put the envelope back into his bosom with a sigh, and was about to go.

'I suppose I shall have to hand it over to the police-constable,' he said.

'Wait a bit! I'll try again,' said Dunyásha, stopping him, after attentively following the disappearance of the envelope into the bosom of the peasant's coat. 'Let me have the letter.'

Dútlov took it out again, but did not at once put it into Dunyásha's outstretched hand.

'Say that Semën Dútlov found it on the road....'

'Well, let me have it!'

'I did think it was just nothing – only a letter; but a soldier read out to me that there was money inside....'

'Well then, let me have it.'

'I dared not even go home first to...' Dútlov continued, still not parting with the precious envelope. 'Tell the lady so.'

Dunyásha took it from him and went again to her mistress.

'O my God, Dunyásha, don't speak to me of that money!' said the lady in a reproachful tone. 'Only to think of that little baby...'

'The peasant does not know to whom you wish it to be given, madam,' Dunyásha again said.

The lady opened the envelope, shuddering at the sight of the money, and pondered.

'Dreadful money! How much evil it does!' she said.

'It is Dútlov, madam. Do you order him to go, or will you please come out and see him – and is the money all safe?' asked Dunyásha.

'I don't want this money. It is terrible money! What it has done! Tell him to take it himself if he likes,' said the lady suddenly, feeling for Dunyásha's hand. 'Yes, yes, yes!' she repeated to the astonished Dunyásha; 'let him take it altogether and do what he likes with it.'

'Fifteen hundred rubles,' remarked Dunyásha, smiling as if at a child.

'Let him take it all!' the lady repeated impatiently. 'How is it you don't understand me? It is unlucky money. Never speak of it to me again! Let the peasant who found it take it. Go, go along!'

Dunyásha went out into the maids' room.

'Is it all there?' asked Dútlov.

'You'd better count it yourself,' said Dunyásha, handing him the envelope. 'My orders are to give it to you.'

Dútlov put his cap under his arm, and, bending forward, began to count the money.

'Have you got a counting-frame?'[1]

Dútlov had an idea that the lady was stupid and could not count, and that that was why she ordered him to do so.

'You can count it at home – the money is yours...!' Dunyásha said crossly. '"I don't want to see it," she says; "give it to the man who brought it."'

Dútlov, without unbending his back, stared at Dunyásha.

Dunyásha's aunt flung up her hands.

'O holy Mother! What luck the Lord has sent him! O holy Mother!'

The second maid would not believe it.

'You don't mean it, Avdótya Pávlovna; you're joking!'

'Joking, indeed! She told me to give it to the peasant.... There, take your money and go!' said Dunyásha, without hiding her vexation. 'One man's sorrow is another man's luck!'

'It's not a joke ... fifteen hundred rubles!' said the aunt.

'It's even more,' stated Dunyásha. 'Well, you'll have to give a ten-kopek candle to St Nicholas,' she added sarcastically. 'Why don't you come to your senses? If it had come to a poor man, now!... But this man has plenty of his own.'

Dútlov at last grasped that it was not a joke, and began gathering together the notes he had spread out to count and putting them back into the envelope. But his hands trembled,

___

1 The abacus, with wires and beads to count on, was much used in Russia.

and he kept glancing at the maids to assure himself that it was not a joke.

'See! He can't come to his senses he's so pleased,' said Dunyásha, implying that she despised both the peasant and the money. 'Come, I'll put it up for you.'

She was going to take the notes, but Dútlov would not let her. He crumpled them together, pushed them in deeper, and took his cap.

'Are you glad?'

'I hardly know what to say! It's really...'

He did not finish, but waved his hand, smiled, and went out almost crying.

The mistress rang.

'Well, have you given it to him?'

'I have.'

'Well, was he very glad?'

'He was just like a madman.'

'Ah! call him back. I want to ask him how he found it. Call him in here; I can't come out.'

Dunyásha ran out and found the peasant in the entry. He was still bareheaded, but had drawn out his purse and was stooping, untying its strings, while he held the money between his teeth. Perhaps he imagined that as long as the money was not in his purse it was not his. When Dunyásha called him he grew frightened.

'What is it, Avdótya... Avdótya Pávlovna? Does she want to take it back? Couldn't you say a word for me?... Now really, and I'd bring you some nice honey.'

'Indeed! Much you ever brought!'

Again the door was opened, and the peasant was brought in to the lady. He felt anything but cheerful. 'Oh dear, she'll want it back!' he thought on his way through the rooms, lifting his feet for some reason as if he were walking through high grass, and trying not to stamp with his bast shoes. He could make nothing of his surroundings. Passing by a mirror he saw flowers of some sort and a peasant in bast shoes lifting his feet high, a gentleman with an eyeglass painted on the wall, some kind of green tub, and something white.... There, now!

The something white began to speak. It was his mistress. He did not understand anything but only stared. He did not know where he was, and everything appeared as in a fog.

'Is that you, Dútlov?'

'Yes, lady.... Just as it was, so I left it...' he said. 'I was not glad so help me God! How I've tired out my horse!...'

'Well, it's your luck!' she remarked contemptuously, though with a kindly smile. 'Take it, take it for yourself.'

He only rolled his eyes.

'I am glad that you got it. God grant that it may be of use. Well, are you glad?'

'How could I help being glad? I'm so glad, ma'am, so glad! I will pray for you always!... So glad that, thank Heaven, our lady is alive! It was not my fault.'

'How did you find it?'

'Well, I mean, we can always do our best for our lady, quite honourably, and not anyhow...'

'He is in a regular muddle, madam,' said Dunyásha.

'I had taken my nephew, the conscript, and as I was driving back along the road I found it. Polikéy must have dropped it.'

'Well, then, go – go, my good man! I am glad you found it!'

'I am so glad, lady!' said the peasant.

Then he remembered that he had not thanked her properly, and did not know how to behave. The lady and Dunyásha smiled, and then he again began stepping as if he were walking in very high grass, and could hardly refrain from running so afraid was he that he might be stopped and the money taken from him.

XIV

WHEN he got out into the fresh air Dútlov stepped aside from the road to the lindens, even undoing his belt to get at his purse more easily, and began putting away the money. His lips were twitching, stretching and drawing together again, though he uttered no sound. Having put away his money and fastened his belt, he crossed himself and went staggering along the road as though he were drunk, so full was he of the thoughts that came rushing to his mind. Suddenly he saw the figure of a man coming towards him. He called out; it was Efím, with a cudgel in his hand, on watch at the serfs' quarters.

'Ah, Daddy Semën!' said Efím cheerfully, drawing nearer (Efím felt it uncanny to be alone). 'Have you got the conscripts off, daddy?'

'We have. What are you after?'

'Why, I've been put here to watch over Polikéy who's hanged himself.'

'And where is he?'

'Up there, hanging in the loft, so they say,' answered Efím, pointing with his cudgel through the darkness to the roof of the serfs' quarters.

Dútlov looked in the direction of the arm, and though he could see nothing he puckered his brows, screwed up his eyes, and shook his head.

'The police-constable has come,' said Efím, 'so the coachman said. He'll be taken down at once. Isn't it horrible at night, daddy? Nothing would make me go up at night even if they ordered me to. If Egór Mikháylovich were to kill me outright I wouldn't go . . .'

'What a sin, oh, what a sin!' Dútlov kept repeating, evidently for propriety's sake and not even thinking what he was saying. He was about to go on his way, but the voice of Egór Mikháylovich stopped him.

'Hi! watchman! Come here!' shouted Egór Mikháylovich from the porch of the office.

Efím replied to him.

'Who was that other peasant standing with you?'

'Dútlov.'

'Ah! and you too, Semën! Come here!'

Having drawn near, Dútlov, by the light of a lantern the coachman was carrying, recognized Egór Mikháylovich and a short man with a cockade on his cap, dressed in a long uniform overcoat. This was the police-constable.

'Here, this old man will come with us too,' said Egór Mikháylovich on seeing him.

The old man felt a bit uncomfortable, but there was no getting out of it.

'And you, Efím – you're a bold lad! Run up into the loft where he's hanged himself, and set the ladder straight for his honour to mount.'

Efím, who had declared that he would not go near the loft for anything in the world, now ran towards it, clattering with his bast shoes as if they were logs.

The police-officer struck a light and lit a pipe. He lived about a mile and a half off, and having just been severely reprimanded for drunkenness by his superior, was in a zealous mood. Having arrived at ten o'clock at night, he wished to view the corpse at once. Egór Mikháylovich asked Dútlov how he came to be there. On the way Dútlov told the steward about the money he had found and what the lady had done, and said he was coming to ask Egór Mikháylovich's sanction. To Dútlov's horror the steward asked for the envelope and examined it. The police-constable even took the envelope in his hand and briefly and dryly asked the details.

'Oh dear, the money is gone!' thought Dútlov, and began justifying himself. But the police-constable handed him back the money.

'What a piece of luck for the clodhopper!' he said.

'It comes handy for him,' said Egór Mikháylovich. 'He's just been taking his nephew to be conscripted, and now he'll buy him out.'

'Ah!' said the policeman, and went on in front.

'Will you buy him off – Elijah, I mean?' asked Egór Mikháylovich.

'How am I to buy him off? Will there be money enough? And perhaps it's too late ...'

'Well, you know best,' said the steward, and they both followed the police-constable.

They approached the serfs' house, where the ill-smelling watchmen stood waiting in the passage with a lantern. Dútlov followed them. The watchmen looked guilty, perhaps because of the smell they were spreading, for they had done nothing wrong. All were silent.

'Where is he?' asked the police-constable.

'Here,' said Egór Mikháylovich in a whisper. 'Efím,' he added, 'you're a bold lad, go on in front with the lantern.'

Efím had already put a plank straight at the top of the ladder, and seemed to have lost all fear. Taking two or three steps at a time, he clambered up with a cheerful look, only turning round to light the way for the police-constable. The constable was followed by Egór Mikháylovich. When they had disappeared above, Dútlov, with one foot on the bottom step, sighed and stopped. Two or three minutes passed. The footsteps in the loft were no longer heard; they had no doubt reached the body.

'Daddy, they want you,' Efím called down through the opening.

Dútlov began going up. The light of the lantern showed only the upper part of the bodies of the police-constable and of Egór Mikháylovich beyond the rafters. Beyond them again someone else was standing with his back turned. It was Polikéy. Dútlov climbed over a rafter and stopped, crossing himself.

'Turn him round, lads!' said the police-constable.

No one stirred.

'Efím, you're a bold lad,' said Egór Mikháylovich.

The 'bold lad' stepped across a rafter, turned Polikéy round, and stood beside him, looking with a most cheerful face now at Polikéy now at the constable, as a showman exhibiting an albino or Julia Pastrana[1] looks now at the public and now at what he is exhibiting, ready to do anything the spectators may wish.

'Turn him round again.'

Polikéy was turned round, his arms slightly swaying and his feet dragging in the sand on the floor.

'Catch hold, and take him down.'

'Shall we cut the rope through, your honour?' asked Egór Mikháylovich. 'Hand us an axe, lads!'

---

1 Julia Pastrana was exhibited as being half-woman half-monkey, and created a considerable sensation.

The watchmen and Dútlov had to be told twice before they set to, but the 'bold lad' handled Polikéy as he would have handled a sheep's carcass. At last the rope was cut through and the body taken down and covered up. The police-constable said that the doctor would come next day, and dismissed them all.

XV

DÚTLOV went homeward, still moving his lips. At first he had an uncanny feeling, but it passed as he drew nearer home, and a feeling of gladness gradually penetrated his heart. In the village he heard songs and drunken voices. Dútlov never drank, and this time too he went straight home. It was late when he entered his hut. His old wife was asleep. His eldest son and grandsons were asleep on the stove, and his second son in the store-room. Elijah's wife alone was awake, and sat on the bench bare-headed, in a dirty, working-day smock, wailing. She did not come out to meet her uncle, but only sobbed louder, lamenting her fate, when he entered. According to the old woman, she 'lamented' very fluently and well, taking into consideration the fact that at her age she could not have had much practice.

The old woman rose and got supper for her husband. Dútlov turned Elijah's wife away from the table, saying: 'That's enough, that's enough!' Aksínya went away, and lying down on a bench continued to lament. The old woman put the supper on the table and afterwards silently cleared it away again. The old man did not speak either. When he had said grace he hiccuped, washed his hands, took the counting-frame from a nail in the wall, and went into the store-room. There he and the old woman spoke in whispers for a little while, and then, after she had gone away, he began counting on the frame, making the beads click. Finally he banged the lid of the chest standing there, and clambered into the space under the floor. For a long time he went on bustling about in the room and in the space below. When he came back to the living-room it was dark in the hut. The

wooden splint that served for a candle had gone out. His old
woman, quiet and silent in the daytime, had rolled herself up
on the sleeping-bunk and filled the hut with her snoring.
Elijah's noisy young wife was also asleep, breathing quietly.
She lay on the bench dressed just as she had been, and with
nothing under her head for a pillow. Dútlov began to pray,
then looked at Elijah's wife, shook his head, put out the light,
hiccuped again, and climbed up on the stove, where he lay
down beside his little grandson. He threw down his plaited
bast shoes from the stove in the dark, and lay on his back
looking up at the rafter which was hardly discernible just over
his head above the stove, and listening to the sounds of the
cockroaches swarming along the walls, and to the sighs, the
snoring, the rubbing of one foot against another, and the noise
made by the cattle outside. It was a long time before he could
sleep. The moon rose. It grew lighter in the hut. He could see
Aksínya in her corner and something he could not make out:
was it a coat his son had forgotten, or a tub the women had put
there, or a man standing there? Perhaps he was drowsing,
perhaps not: anyhow he began to peer into the darkness.
Evidently that evil spirit who had led Polikéy to commit his
awful deed and whose presence was felt that night by all the
house-serfs, had stretched out his wing and reached across the
village to the house in which lay the money that *he* had used to
ruin Polikéy. At least, Dútlov felt *his* presence and was ill at
ease. He could neither sleep nor get up. After noticing the
something he could not make out, he remembered Elijah with
his arms bound, and Aksínya's face and her eloquent lamentations; and he recalled Polikéy with his swaying hands. Suddenly it seemed to the old man that someone passed by the
window. 'Who was that? Could it be the village elder coming
so early with a notice?' thought he. 'How did he open the
door?' thought the old man, hearing a step in the passage. 'Had
the old woman not put up the bar when she went out into the
passage?' The dog began to howl in the yard and *he* came
stepping along the passage, so the old man related afterwards,
as though he were trying to find the door, then passed on and
began groping along the wall, stumbled over a tub and made it

clatter, and again began groping as if feeling for the latch. Now *he* had hold of the latch. A shiver ran down the old man's body. Now *he* pulled the latch and entered in the shape of a man. Dútlov knew it was *he*. He wished to cross himself, but could not. *He* went up to the table which was covered with a cloth, and, pulling it off, threw it on the floor and began climbing onto the stove. The old man knew that *he* had taken the shape of Polikéy. *He* was showing his teeth and his hands were swinging about. *He* climbed up, fell on the old man's chest, and began to strangle him.

'The money's mine!' muttered Polikéy.

'Let me go! I won't do it!' Semën tried to say, but could not.

Polikéy was pressing down on him with the weight of a mountain of stone. Dútlov knew that if he said a prayer *he* would let him go, and he knew which prayer he ought to recite, but could not utter it. His grandson sleeping beside him uttered a shrill scream and began to cry. His grandfather had pressed him against the wall. The child's cry loosened the old man's lips. 'Let God arise! . . .' he said. *He* pressed less hard. 'And let his enemies be scattered . . .' spluttered Dútlov. *He* got off the stove. Dútlov heard his two feet strike the floor. Dútlov went on repeating in turn all the prayers he knew. *He* went towards the door, passed the table, and slammed the door so that the whole hut shook. Everybody but the grandfather and grandson continued to sleep however. The grandfather, trembling all over, muttered prayers, while the grandson was crying himself to sleep and pressing close to his grandfather. All became quiet once more. The old man lay still. A cock crowed behind the wall close to Dútlov's ear. He heard the hens stirring, and a cockerel unsuccessfully trying to crow in answer to the old cock. Something moved over the old man's legs. It was the cat; she jumped on her soft pads from the stove to the floor, and stood mewing by the door. The old man got up and opened the window. It was dark and muddy in the street. The front of the cart was standing there close to the window. Crossing himself he went out barefoot into the yard to the horses. One could see that *he* had been there too. The mare, standing under the lean-to beside a tub of chaff, had got her foot into the cord of her halter and had spilt the chaff, and now, lifting her foot, turned her head and waited for her master. Her foal had tumbled over a heap of manure. The old man raised him to his feet, disentangled the mare's foot and fed her, and went back to the hut. The old woman got up and lit the splint. 'Wake the lads, I'm going to the town!' And taking a wax taper from before the icon Dútlov lit it and went down with it into the opening under the floor. When he came up again lights were burning not only in his hut but in all the neighbouring houses. The young fellows were up and preparing to start. The women were coming in and out with pails of milk. Ignát was harnessing the horse to one cart and the second son was greasing the wheels of another. The young wife was no longer wailing. She had made herself neat and had bound a shawl over her head, and now sat waiting till it would be time to go to town to say good-bye to her husband.

The old man seemed particularly stern. He did not say a word to anyone, put on his best coat, tied his belt round him, and with all Polikéy's money in the bosom of his coat, went to Egór Mikháylovich.

'Don't dawdle,' he called to his son, who was turning the wheels round on the raised and newly greased axle. 'I'll be back in a minute; see that everything is ready.'

The steward had only just got up and was drinking tea. He himself was preparing to go to town to deliver up the recruits.

'What is it?' he asked.

'Egór Mikháylovich, I want to buy the lad off. Do be so good! You said t'other day that you knew one in the town that was willing. . . . Explain to me how to do it; we are ignorant people.'

'Why, have you reconsidered it?'

'I have, Egór Mikháylovich. I'm sorry for him. My brother's child after all, whatever he may be. I'm sorry for him! It's the cause of much sin, money is. Do be good enough to explain it to me!' he said, bowing to his waist.

Egór Mikháylovich, as was his wont on such occasions, stood for a long time thoughtfully smacking his lips. Then, having considered the matter, he wrote two notes and told him what to do in town and how to do it.

When Dútlov got home, the young wife had already set off with Ignát. The fat roan mare stood ready harnessed at the gate. Dútlov broke a stick out of the hedge and, lapping his coat over, got into the cart and whipped up the horse. He made the mare run so fast that her fat sides quickly shrank, and Dútlov did not look at her so as not to feel sorry for her. He was tormented by the thought that he might come too late for the recruiting, that Elijah would go as a soldier and the devil's money would be left on his hands.

I will not describe all Dútlov's proceedings that morning. I will only say that he was specially lucky. The man to whom Egór Mikháylovich had given him a note had a volunteer quite ready who was already twenty-three silver rubles in debt and had been passed by the recruiting-board. His master wanted four hundred silver rubles for him and a buyer in the town had for the last three weeks been offering him three hundred. Dútlov settled the matter in a couple of words. 'Will you take three twenty-five?' he said, holding out his hand, but with a look that showed that he was prepared to give more. The master held back his hand and went on asking four hundred. 'You won't take three and a quarter?' Dútlov said, catching hold with his left hand of the man's right and preparing to slap his own right hand down on it. 'You won't take it? Well, God be with you!' he said suddenly, smacking the master's hand with the full swing of his other hand and turning away with his whole body. 'It seems it has to be so ... take three and a half hundred! Get out the discharge and bring the fellow along. And now here are two ten-ruble notes on account. Is it enough?'

And Dútlov unfastened his girdle and got out the money.

The man, though he did not withdraw his hand, yet did not seem quite to agree and, not accepting the deposit money, went on stipulating that Dútlov should wet the bargain and stand treat to the volunteer.

'Don't commit a sin,' Dútlov kept repeating as he held out the money. 'We shall all have to die some day,' he went on, in such a mild, persuasive and assured tone that the master said:

'So be it, then!' and again clapped Dútlov's hand and began praying for God's blessing. 'God grant you luck,' he said.

They woke the volunteer, who was still sleeping after yesterday's carouse, examined him for some reason, and went with him to the offices of the Administration. The recruit was merry. He demanded rum as a refresher, for which Dútlov gave him some money, and only when they came into the vestibule of the recruiting-board did his courage fail him. For a long time they stood in the entrance-hall, the old master in his full blue cloak and the recruit in a short sheepskin, his eyebrows raised and his eyes staring. For a long time they whispered, tried to get somewhere, looked for somebody, and for some reason took off their caps and bowed to every copying-clerk they met, and meditatively listened to the decision which a scribe whom the master knew brought out to them. All hope of getting the business done that day began to vanish, and the recruit was growing more cheerful and unconstrained again, when Dútlov saw Egór Mikháylovich, seized on him at once, and began to beg and bow to him. Egór Mikháylovich helped him so efficiently that by about three o'clock the recruit, to his great dissatisfaction and surprise, was taken into the hall and placed for examination, and amid general merriment (in which for some reason everybody joined, from the watchmen to the President), he was undressed, dressed again, shaved, and led out at the door; and five minutes later Dútlov counted out the money, received the discharge and, having taken leave of the volunteer and his master, went to the lodging-house where the Pokróvsk recruits were staying. Elijah and his young wife were sitting in a corner of the kitchen, and as soon as the old man came in they stopped talking and looked at him with a resigned expression, but not with goodwill. As was his wont the old man said a prayer, and he then unfastened his belt, got out a paper, and called into the room his eldest son Ignát and Elijah's mother, who were in the yard.

'Don't sin, Elijah,' he said, coming up to his nephew. 'Last night you said a word to me. . . . Don't I pity you? I remember how my brother left you to me. If it had been in my power would I have let you go? God has sent me luck, and I am not grudging it you. Here it is, the paper'; and he put the discharge on the table and carefully smoothed it out with his stiff, unbending fingers.

All the Pokróvsk peasants, the inn-keeper's men, and even some outsiders, came in from the yard. All guessed what was happening, but no one interrupted the old man's solemn discourse.

'Here it is, the paper! Four hundred silver rubles I've given for it. Don't reproach your uncle.'

Elijah rose, but remained silent not knowing what to say. His lips quivered with emotion. His old mother came up and would have thrown herself sobbing on his neck; but the old man motioned her away slowly and authoritatively and continued speaking.

'You said a word to me yesterday,' the old man again repeated. 'You stabbed me to the heart with that word as with a knife! Your dying father left you to me and you have been as my own son to me, and if I have wronged you in any way, well, we all live in sin! Is it not so, good Christian folk?' he said, turning to the peasants who stood round. 'Here is your own mother and your young wife, and here is the discharge for you. I don't regret the money, but forgive me for Christ's sake!'

And, turning up the skirts of his coat, he deliberately sank to his knees and bowed down to the ground before Elijah and his wife. The young people tried in vain to restrain him, but not till his forehead had touched the floor did he get up. Then, after giving his skirts a shake, he sat down on a bench. Elijah's mother and wife howled with joy, and words of approval were heard among the crowd. 'That is just, that's the godly way,' said one. 'What's money? You can't buy a fellow for money,' said another. 'What happiness!' said a third; 'no two ways about it, he's a just man!' Only the peasants who were to go as recruits said nothing, and went quietly out into the yard.

Two hours later Dútlov's two carts were driving through the outskirts of the town. In the first, to which was harnessed the roan mare, her sides fallen in and her neck moist with sweat, sat the old man and Ignát. Behind them jerked strings of ring-shaped fancy-bread. In the second cart, in which nobody held the reins, the young wife and her mother-in-law, with shawls over their heads, were sitting, sedate and happy. The former held a bottle of vodka under her apron. Elijah, very red in the face, sat all in a heap with his back to the horse, jolting against the front of the cart, biting into a roll and talking incessantly. The voices, the rumbling of the cart-wheels on the stony road, and the snorting of the horses, blent into one note of merriment. The horses, swishing their tails, increased their speed more and more, feeling themselves on the home-ward road. The passers-by, whether driving or on foot, in-voluntarily turned round to look at the happy family party.

Just as they left the town the Dútlovs overtook a party of recruits. A group of them were standing in a ring outside a tavern. One of the recruits, with that unnatural expression on his face which comes of having the front of the head shaved,[1] his grey cap pushed back, was vigorously strumming a balaláyka; another, bareheaded and with a bottle of vodka in his hand, was dancing in the middle of the ring. Ignát stopped his horse and got down to tighten the traces. All the Dútlovs looked with curiosity, approval, and amusement at the dancer. The recruit seemed not to see anyone, but felt that the public admiring him had grown larger, and this added to his strength and agility. He danced briskly. His brows were knitted, his flushed face was set, and his lips were fixed in a grin that had long since lost all meaning. It seemed as if all the strength of his soul was concentrated on placing one foot as quickly as poss-ible after the other, now on the heel and now on the toe. Sometimes he stopped suddenly and winked to the balaláyka-player, who began playing still more briskly, strumming on all the strings and even striking the case with his knuckles. The recruit would stop, but even when he stood still he still seemed to be dancing all over. Then he began slowly jerking his

---

1 On being conscripted a man's head was partially shaved to make desertion more difficult.

shoulders, and suddenly twirling round, leaped in the air with a wild cry, and descending, crouched down, throwing out first one leg and then the other. The little boys laughed, the women shook their heads, the men smiled approvingly. An old sergeant stood quietly by, with a look that seemed to say: 'You think it wonderful, but we have long been familiar with it.' The balaláyka–player seemed tired; he looked lazily round, struck a false chord, and suddenly knocked on the case with his knuckles, and the dance came to an end.

'Eh, Alëkha,' he said to the dancer, pointing at Dútlov, 'there's your sponsor!'

'Where? You, my dearest friend!' shouted Alëkha, the very recruit whom Dútlov had bought; and staggering forward on his weary legs and holding the bottle of vodka above his head he moved towards the cart. 'Míshka, a glass!' he cried to the player. 'Master! My dearest friend! What a pleasure, really!' he shouted, drooping his tipsy head over the cart, and he began to treat the men and women to vodka. The men drank, but the women refused. 'My dear friends, what can I offer you?' exclaimed Alëkha, embracing the old women.

A woman selling eatables was standing among the crowd. Alëkha noticed her, seized her tray, and poured its contents into the cart.

'I'll pay, no fear, you devil!' he howled tearfully, pulling a purse from his pocket and throwing it to Míshka.

He stood leaning with his elbows on the cart and looking with moist eyes at those who sat in it.

'Which is the mother . . . you?' he asked. 'I must treat you too.'

He stood thinking for a moment, then he put his hand in his pocket and drew out a new folded handkerchief, hurriedly took off a sash which was tied round his waist under his coat, and also a red scarf he was wearing round his neck, and, crumpling them all together, thrust them into the old woman's lap.

'There! I'm sacrificing them for you,' he said in a voice that was growing more and more subdued.

'What for? Thank you, sonny! Just see what a simple lad it is!' said the old woman, addressing Dútlov, who had come up to their cart.

Alëkha was now quite quiet, quite stupefied, and looked as if he were falling asleep. He drooped his head lower and lower.

'It's for you I am going, for you I am perishing!' he muttered; 'that's why I am giving you gifts.'

'I dare say he, too, has a mother,' said someone in the crowd. 'What a simple fellow! What a pity!'

Alëkha lifted his head.

'I have a mother,' said he; 'I have a father too. All have given me up. Listen to me, old woman,' he went on, taking Elijah's mother by the hand. 'I have given you presents. Listen to me for Christ's sake! Go to Vódnoe village, ask for the old woman Nikónovna – she's my own mother, see? Say to this same old woman, Nikónovna, the third hut from the end, by the new well. Tell her that Alëkha – her son, you see. . . . Eh! musician! strike up!' he shouted.

And muttering something he immediately began dancing again, and hurled the bottle with the remaining vodka to the ground.

Ignát got into the cart and was about to start.

'Good-bye! May God bless you!' said the old woman, wrapping her cloak closer round her.

Alëkha suddenly stopped.

'Go to the devil!' he shouted, clenching his fists threateningly. 'May your mother be . . . '

'O Lord!' exclaimed Elijah's mother, crossing herself.

Ignát touched the reins, and the carts rattled on again. Alëkha, the recruit, stood in the middle of the road with clenched fists and with a look of fury on his face, and abused the peasants with all his might.

'What are you stopping for? Go on, devils! cannibals!' he cried. 'You won't escape me! . . . Devil's clodhoppers!'

At these words his voice broke, and he fell full length to the ground just where he stood.

Soon the Dútlovs reached the open fields, and looking back could no longer see the crowd of recruits. Having gone some four miles at a walking pace Ignát got down from his father's cart, in which the old man lay asleep, and walked beside Elijah's cart.

Between them they emptied the bottle they had brought from town. After a while Elijah began a song, the women joined in, and Ignát shouted merrily in time with the song. A post-chaise drove merrily towards them. The driver called lustily to his horses as he passed the two festive carts, and the post-boy turned round and winked at the men and women who with flushed faces sat jolting inside singing their jovial song.

Three Tales for Children

(1) GOD SEES THE TRUTH, BUT WAITS

IN the town of Vladímir lived a young merchant named Iván Dmítritch Aksyónof. He had two shops and a house of his own.

Aksyónof was a handsome, fair-haired, curly-headed fellow, full of fun, and very fond of singing. When quite a young man he had been given to drink, and was riotous when he had had too much; but after he married he gave up drinking, except now and then.

One summer Aksyónof was going to the Nízhny Fair, and as he bade good-bye to his family his wife said to him, 'Iván Dmítritch, do not start to-day; I have had a bad dream about you.'

Aksyónof laughed, and said, 'You are afraid that when I get to the fair I shall go on the spree.'

His wife replied: 'I do not know what I am afraid of; all I know is that I had a bad dream. I dreamt you returned from the town, and when you took off your cap I saw that your hair was quite grey.'

Aksyónof laughed. 'That's a lucky sign,' said he. 'See if I don't sell out all my goods, and bring you some presents from the fair.'

So he said good-bye to his family, and drove away.

When he had travelled half-way, he met a merchant whom he knew, and they put up at the same inn for the night. They had some tea together, and then went to bed in adjoining rooms.

It was not Aksyónof's habit to sleep late, and, wishing to travel while it was still cool, he aroused his driver before dawn, and told him to put in the horses.

Then he made his way across to the landlord of the inn (who lived in a cottage at the back), paid his bill, and continued his journey.

When he had gone about twenty-five miles, he stopped for the horses to be fed. Aksyónof rested a while in the passage of the inn, then he stepped out into the porch, and, ordering a samovar to be heated, got out his guitar and began to play.

Suddenly a tróyka drove up with tinkling bells, and an official alighted, followed by two soldiers. He came to Aksyónof and began to question him, asking him who he was and whence he came. Aksyónof answered him fully, and said, 'Won't you have some tea with me?' But the official went on cross-questioning him and asking him, 'Where did you spend last night? Were you alone, or with a fellow-merchant? Did you see the other merchant this morning? Why did you leave the inn before dawn?'

Aksyónof wondered why he was asked all these questions, but he described all that had happened, and then added, 'Why do you cross-question me as if I were a thief or a robber? I am travelling on business of my own, and there is no need to question me.'

Then the official, calling the soldiers, said, 'I am the police-officer of this district, and I question you because the merchant with whom you spent last night has been found with his throat cut. We must search your things.'

They entered the house. The soldiers and the police-officer unstrapped Aksyónof's luggage and searched it. Suddenly the officer drew a knife out of a bag, crying, 'Whose knife is this?'

Aksyónof looked, and seeing a blood-stained knife taken from his bag, he was frightened.

'How is it there is blood on this knife?'

Aksyónof tried to answer, but could hardly utter a word, and only stammered: 'I – I don't know – not mine.'

Then the police-officer said, 'This morning the merchant was found in bed with his throat cut. You are the only person who could have done it. The house was locked from inside, and no one else was there. Here is this blood-stained knife in your bag, and your face and manner betray you! Tell me how you killed him, and how much money you stole?'

Aksyónof swore he had not done it; that he had not seen the merchant after they had had tea together; that he had no money except eight thousand rubles of his own, and that the knife was not his. But his voice was broken, his face pale, and he trembled with fear as though he were guilty.

The police-officer ordered the soldiers to bind Aksyónof and to put him in the cart. As they tied his feet together and flung him into the cart, Aksyónof crossed himself and wept. His money and goods were taken from him, and he was sent to the nearest town and imprisoned there. Enquiries as to his character were made in Vladímir. The merchants and other inhabitants of that town said that in former days he used to drink and waste his time, but that he was a good man. Then the trial came on: he was charged with murdering a merchant from Ryazán, and robbing him of twenty thousand rubles.

His wife was in despair, and did not know what to believe. Her children were all quite small; one was a baby at her breast. Taking them all with her, she went to the town where her husband was in gaol. At first she was not allowed to see him; but, after much begging, she obtained permission from the officials, and was taken to him. When she saw her husband in prison-dress and in chains, shut up with thieves and criminals, she fell down, and did not come to her senses for a long time. Then she drew her children to her, and sat down near him. She told him of things at home, and asked about what had happened to him. He told her all, and she asked, 'What can we do now?'

'We must petition the Tsar not to let an innocent man perish.'

His wife told him that she had sent a petition to the Tsar, but that it had not been accepted.

Aksyónof did not reply, but only looked downcast.

Then his wife said, 'It was not for nothing I dreamt your hair had turned grey. You remember? You should not have started that day.' And passing her fingers through his hair, she said: 'Ványa dearest, tell your wife the truth; was it not you who did it?'

'So you, too, suspect me!' said Aksyónof, and, hiding his face in his hands, he began to weep. Then a soldier came to say that the wife and children must go away; and Aksyónof said good-bye to his family for the last time.

When they were gone, Aksyónof recalled what had been said, and when he remembered that his wife also had suspected him, he said to himself, 'It seems that only God can know the truth; it is to Him alone we must appeal, and from Him alone expect mercy.'

And Aksyónof wrote no more petitions; gave up all hope, and only prayed to God.

Aksyónof was condemned to be flogged and sent to the mines. So he was flogged with a knout, and when the wounds made by the knout were healed, he was driven to Siberia with other convicts.

For twenty-six years Aksyónof lived as a convict in Siberia. His hair turned white as snow, and his beard grew long, thin, and grey. All his mirth went; he stooped; he walked slowly, spoke little, and never laughed, but he often prayed.

In prison Aksyónof learnt to make boots, and earned a little money, with which he bought *The Lives of the Saints*. He read this book when there was light enough in the prison; and on Sundays in the prison-church he read the lessons and sang in the choir; for his voice was still good.

The prison authorities liked Aksyónof for his meekness, and his fellow-prisoners respected him: they called him 'Grandfather', and 'The Saint'. When they wanted to petition the prison authorities about anything, they always made Aksyónof their spokesman, and when there were quarrels among the prisoners they came to him to put things right, and to judge the matter.

No news reached Aksyónof from his home, and he did not even know if his wife and children were still alive.

One day a fresh gang of convicts came to the prison. In the evening the old prisoners collected round the new ones and asked them what towns or villages they came from, and what they were sentenced for. Among the rest Aksyónof sat down

near the new-comers, and listened with downcast air to what
was said.

One of the new convicts, a tall, strong man of sixty, with
a closely-cropped grey beard, was telling the others what he
had been arrested for.

'Well, friends,' he said, 'I only took a horse that was tied to a
sledge, and I was arrested and accused of stealing. I said I had
only taken it to get home quicker, and had then let it go;
besides, the driver was a personal friend of mine. So I said, "It's
all right." "No," said they, "you stole it." But how or where
I stole it they could not say. I once really did something wrong,
and ought by rights to have come here long ago, but that time
I was not found out. Now I have been sent here for nothing at
all. . . . Eh, but it's lies I'm telling you; I've been to Siberia
before, but I did not stay long.'

'Where are you from?' asked someone.

'From Vladímir. My family are of that town. My name is
Makár, and they also call me Semyónitch.'

Aksyónof raised his head and said: 'Tell me, Semyónitch, do
you know anything of the merchants Aksyónof, of Vladímir?
Are they still alive?'

'Know them? Of course I do. The Aksyónofs are rich,
though their father is in Siberia: a sinner like ourselves, it
seems! As for you, Gran'dad, how did you come here?'

Aksyónof did not like to speak of his misfortune. He only
sighed, and said, 'For my sins I have been in prison these
twenty-six years.'

'What sins?' asked Makár Semyónitch.

But Aksyónof only said, 'Well, well – I must have deserved
it!' He would have said no more, but his companions told
the new-comer how Aksyónof came to be in Siberia:
how someone had killed a merchant, and had put a knife
among Aksyónof's things, and Aksyónof had been unjustly
condemned.

When Makár Semyónitch heard this, he looked at Aksyónof, slapped his own knee, and exclaimed, 'Well, this is
wonderful! Really wonderful! But how old you've grown,
Gran'dad!'

The others asked him why he was so surprised, and where he had seen Aksyónof before; but Makár Semyónitch did not reply. He only said: 'It's wonderful that we should meet here, lads!'

These words made Aksyónof wonder whether this man knew who had killed the merchant; so he said, 'Perhaps, Semyónitch, you have heard of that affair, or maybe you've seen me before?'

'How could I help hearing? The world's full of rumours. But it's long ago, and I've forgotten what I heard.'

'Perhaps you heard who killed the merchant?' asked Aksyónof.

Makár Semyónitch laughed, and replied, 'It must have been him in whose bag the knife was found! If someone else hid the knife there, "He's not a thief till he's caught," as the saying is. How could anyone put a knife into your bag while it was under your head? It would surely have woke you up?'

When Aksyónof heard these words, he felt sure this was the man who had killed the merchant. He rose and went away. All that night Aksyónof lay awake. He felt terribly unhappy, and all sorts of images rose in his mind. There was the image of his wife as she was when he parted from her to go to the fair. He saw her as if she were present; her face and her eyes rose before him; he heard her speak and laugh. Then he saw his children, quite little, as they were at that time: one with a little cloak on, another at his mother's breast. And then he remembered himself as he used to be – young and merry. He remembered how he sat playing the guitar in the porch of the inn where he was arrested, and how free from care he had been. He saw, in his mind, the place where he was flogged, the executioner, and the people standing around; the chains, the convicts, all the twenty-six years of his prison life, and his premature old age. The thought of it all made him so wretched that he was ready to kill himself.

'And it's all that villain's doing!' thought Aksyónof. And his anger was so great against Makár Semyónitch that he longed for vengeance, even if he himself should perish for it. He kept repeating prayers all night, but could get no peace. During the day he did not go near Makár Semyónitch, nor even look at him.

A fortnight passed in this way. Aksyónof could not sleep at nights, and was so miserable that he did not know what to do.

One night as he was walking about the prison he noticed some earth that came rolling out from under one of the shelves on which the prisoners slept. He stopped to see what it was. Suddenly Makár Semyónitch crept out from under the shelf, and looked up at Aksyónof with frightened face. Aksyónof tried to pass without looking at him, but Makár seized his hand and told him that he had dug a hole under the wall, getting rid of the earth by putting it into his high-boots, and emptying it out every day on the road when the prisoners were driven to their work.

'Just you keep quiet, old man, and you shall get out too. If you blab they'll flog the life out of me, but I will kill you first.'

Aksyónof trembled with anger as he looked at his enemy. He drew his hand away, saying, 'I have no wish to escape, and you have no need to kill me; you killed me long ago! As to telling of you – I may do so or not, as God shall direct.'

Next day, when the convicts were led out to work, the convoy soldiers noticed that one or other of the prisoners emptied some earth out of his boots. The prison was searched, and the tunnel found. The Governor came and questioned all the prisoners to find out who had dug the hole. They all denied any knowledge of it. Those who knew, would not betray Makár Semyónitch, knowing he would be flogged almost to death. At last the Governor turned to Aksyónof, whom he knew to be a just man, and said:

'You are a truthful old man; tell me, before God, who dug the hole?'

Makár Semyónitch stood as if he were quite unconcerned, looking at the Governor and not so much as glancing at Aksyónof. Aksyónof's lips and hands trembled, and for a long time he could not utter a word. He thought, 'Why should I screen him who ruined my life? Let him pay for what I have suffered. But if I tell, they will probably flog the life out of him, and maybe I suspect him wrongly. And, after all, what good would it be to me?'

'Well, old man,' repeated the Governor, 'tell us the truth: who has been digging under the wall?'

Aksyónof glanced at Makár Semyónitch, and said, 'I cannot say, your honour. It is not God's will that I should tell! Do what you like with me; I am in your hands.'

However much the Governor tried, Aksyónof would say no more, and so the matter had to be left.

That night, when Aksyónof was lying on his bed and just beginning to doze, someone came quietly and sat down on his bed. He peered through the darkness and recognized Makár.

'What more do you want of me?' asked Aksyónof. 'Why have you come here?'

Makár Semyónitch was silent. So Aksyónof sat up and said, 'What do you want? Go away, or I will call the guard!'

Makár Semyónitch bent close over Aksyónof, and whispered, 'Iván Dmítritch, forgive me!'

'What for?' asked Aksyónof.

'It was I who killed the merchant and hid the knife among your things. I meant to kill you too, but I heard a noise outside; so I hid the knife in your bag and escaped out of the window.'

Aksyónof was silent, and did not know what to say. Makár Semyónitch slid off the bed-shelf and knelt upon the ground. 'Iván Dmítritch,' said he, 'forgive me! For the love of God, forgive me! I will confess that it was I who killed the merchant, and you will be released and can go to your home.'

'It is easy for you to talk,' said Aksyónof, 'but I have suffered for you these twenty-six years. Where could I go to now? . . . My wife is dead, and my children have forgotten me. I have nowhere to go. . . .'

Makár Semyónitch did not rise, but beat his head on the floor. 'Iván Dmítritch, forgive me!' he cried. 'When they flogged me with the knout it was not so hard to bear as it is to see you now . . . yet you had pity on me, and did not tell. For Christ's sake forgive me, wretch that I am!' And he began to sob.

When Aksyónof heard him sobbing he, too, began to weep. 'God will forgive you!' said he. 'Maybe I am a hundred times worse than you.' And at these words his heart grew light, and the longing for home left him. He no longer had any desire to leave the prison, but only hoped for his last hour to come.

In spite of what Aksyónof had said, Makár Semyónitch confessed his guilt. But when the order for his release came, Aksyónof was already dead.

(2) A PRISONER IN THE CAUCASUS

I

An officer named Zhílin was serving in the army in the Caucasus.

One day he received a letter from home. It was from his mother, who wrote: 'I am getting old, and should like to see my dear son once more before I die. Come and say good-bye to me and bury me, and then, if God pleases, return to service again with my blessing. But I have found a girl for you, who is sensible and good and has some property. If you can love her, you might marry her and remain at home.'

Zhílin thought it over. It was quite true, the old lady was failing fast and he might not have another chance to see her alive. He had better go, and, if the girl was nice, why not marry her?

So he went to his colonel, obtained leave of absence, said good-bye to his comrades, stood the soldiers four pailfuls of vodka as a farewell treat, and got ready to go.

It was a time of war in the Caucasus. The roads were not safe by night or day. If ever a Russian ventured to ride or walk any distance away from his fort, the Tartars killed him or carried him off to the hills. So it had been arranged that twice every week a body of soldiers should march from one fortress to the next to convey travellers from point to point.

It was summer. At daybreak the baggage-train got ready under shelter of the fortress; the soldiers marched out; and all started along the road. Zhílin was on horseback, and a cart with his things went with the baggage-train. They had sixteen miles to go. The baggage-train moved slowly; sometimes the soldiers stopped, or perhaps a wheel would come off one of the carts, or a horse refuse to go on, and then everybody had to wait.

When by the sun it was already past noon, they had not gone half the way. It was dusty and hot, the sun was scorching, and there was no shelter anywhere: a bare plain all round – not a tree, not a bush, by the road.

Zhílin rode on in front, and stopped, waiting for the baggage to overtake him. Then he heard the signal-horn sounded behind him: the company had again stopped. So he began to think: 'Hadn't I better ride on by myself? My horse is a good one: if the Tartars do attack me, I can gallop away. Perhaps, however, it would be wiser to wait.'

As he sat considering, Kostílin, an officer carrying a gun, rode up to him and said:

'Come along, Zhílin, let's go on by ourselves. It's dreadful; I am famished, and the heat is terrible. My shirt is wringing wet.'

Kostílin was a stout, heavy man, and the perspiration was running down his red face. Zhílin thought awhile, and then asked: 'Is your gun loaded?'

'Yes, it is.'

'Well, then, let's go, but on condition that we keep together.'

So they rode forward along the road across the plain, talking, but keeping a look-out on both sides. They could see afar all round. But after crossing the plain the road ran through a valley between two hills, and Zhílin said: 'We had better climb that hill and have a look round, or the Tartars may be on us before we know it.'

But Kostílin answered: 'What's the use? Let us go on.'

Zhílin, however, would not agree.

'No,' he said; 'you can wait here if you like, but I'll go and look round.' And he turned his horse to the left, up the hill. Zhílin's horse was a hunter, and carried him up the hillside as if it had wings. (He had bought it for a hundred rubles as a colt out of a herd, and had broken it in himself.) Hardly had he reached the top of the hill, when he saw some thirty Tartars not much more than a hundred yards ahead of him. As soon as he caught sight of them he turned round, but the Tartars had also seen him, and rushed after him at full gallop, getting their guns out as they went. Down galloped Zhílin as fast as the horse's legs could go, shouting to Kostílin: 'Get your gun ready!'

And, in thought, he said to his horse: 'Get me well out of this, my pet; don't stumble, for if you do it's all up. Once I reach the gun, they shan't take me prisoner.'

But, instead of waiting, Kostílin, as soon as he caught sight of the Tartars, turned back towards the fortress at full speed, whipping his horse now on one side now on the other, and its switching tail was all that could be seen of him in the dust.

Zhílin saw it was a bad look-out; the gun was gone, and what could he do with nothing but his sword? He turned his horse towards the escort, thinking to escape, but there were six Tartars rushing to cut him off. His horse was a good one, but theirs were still better; and besides, they were across his path. He tried to rein in his horse and to turn another way, but it was going so fast it could not stop, and dashed on straight towards the Tartars. He saw a red-bearded Tartar on a grey horse, with his gun raised, come at him, yelling and showing his teeth.

'Ah,' thought Zhílin, 'I know you, devils that you are. If you take me alive, you'll put me in a pit and flog me. I will not be taken alive!'

Zhílin, though not a big fellow, was brave. He drew his sword and dashed at the red-bearded Tartar, thinking: 'Either I'll ride him down, or disable him with my sword.'

He was still a horse's length away from him, when he was fired at from behind, and his horse was hit. It fell to the ground with all its weight, pinning Zhílin to the earth.

He tried to rise, but two ill-savoured Tartars were already sitting on him and binding his hands behind his back. He made an effort and flung them off, but three others jumped from their horses and began beating his head with the butts of their guns. His eyes grew dim, and he fell back. The Tartars seized him, and, taking spare girths from their saddles, twisted his hands behind him and tied them with a Tartar knot. They knocked his cap off, pulled off his boots, searched him all over, tore his clothes, and took his money and his watch.

Zhílin looked round at his horse. There it lay on its side, poor thing, just as it had fallen; struggling, its legs in the air, unable to touch the ground. There was a hole in its head, and black blood was pouring out, turning the dust to mud for a couple of feet around.

One of the Tartars went up to the horse and began taking the saddle off; it still kicked, so he drew a dagger and cut its windpipe. A whistling sound came from its throat, the horse gave one plunge, and all was over.

The Tartars took the saddle and trappings. The red-bearded Tartar mounted his horse, and the others lifted Zhílin into the saddle behind him. To prevent his falling off, they strapped him to the Tartar's girdle; and then they all rode away to the hills.

So there sat Zhílin, swaying from side to side, his head striking against the Tartar's stinking back. He could see nothing but that muscular back and sinewy neck, with its closely shaven, bluish nape. Zhílin's head was wounded: the blood had dried over his eyes, and he could neither shift his position on the saddle nor wipe the blood off. His arms were bound so tightly that his collar-bones ached.

They rode up and down hills for a long way. Then they reached a river which they forded, and came to a hard road leading across a valley.

Zhílin tried to see where they were going, but his eyelids were stuck together with blood, and he could not turn.

Twilight began to fall; they crossed another river, and rode up a stony hillside. There was a smell of smoke here, and dogs were barking. They had reached an Aoul (a Tartar village). The Tartars got off their horses; Tartar children came and stood round Zhílin, shrieking with pleasure and throwing stones at him.

The Tartar drove the children away, took Zhílin off the horse, and called his man. A Nogáy[1] with high cheek-bones, and nothing on but a shirt (and that so torn that his breast was all bare), answered the call. The Tartar gave him an order. He went and fetched shackles: two blocks of oak with iron rings attached, and a clasp and lock fixed to one of the rings.

---

1 One of a certain Tartar tribe.

They untied Zhílin's arms, fastened the shackles on his leg, and dragged him to a barn, where they pushed him in and locked the door.

Zhílin fell on a heap of manure. He lay still awhile, then groped about to find a soft place, and settled down.

II

THAT night Zhílin hardly slept at all. It was the time of year when the nights are short, and daylight soon showed itself through a chink in the wall. He rose, scratched to make the chink bigger, and peeped out.

Through the hole he saw a road leading down-hill; to the right was a Tartar hut with two trees near it, a black dog lay on the threshold, and a goat and kids were moving about wagging their tails. Then he saw a young Tartar woman in a long, loose, bright-coloured gown, with trousers and high boots showing from under it. She had a coat thrown over her head, on which she carried a large metal jug filled with water. She was leading by the hand a small, closely-shaven Tartar boy, who wore nothing but a shirt; and as she went along balancing herself, the muscles of her back quivered. This woman carried the water into the hut, and, soon after, the red-bearded Tartar of yesterday came out dressed in a silk tunic, with a silver-hilted dagger hanging by his side, shoes on his bare feet, and a tall black sheepskin cap set far back on his head. He came out, stretched himself, and stroked his red beard. He stood awhile, gave an order to his servant, and went away.

Then two lads rode past from watering their horses. The horses' noses were wet. Some other closely-shaven boys ran out, without any trousers, and wearing nothing but their shirts. They crowded together, came to the barn, picked up a twig, and began pushing it in at the chink. Zhílin gave a shout, and the boys shrieked and scampered off, their little bare knees gleaming as they ran.

Zhílin was very thirsty: his throat was parched, and he thought: 'If only they would come and so much as look at me!'

Then he heard someone unlocking the barn. The red-bearded Tartar entered, and with him was another, a smaller man, dark, with bright black eyes, red cheeks, and a short beard. He had a merry face, and was always laughing. This man was even more richly dressed than the other. He wore a blue silk tunic trimmed with gold, a large silver dagger in his belt, red morocco slippers worked with silver, and over these a pair of thick shoes, and he had a white sheepskin cap on his head.

The red-bearded Tartar entered, muttered something as if he were annoyed, and stood leaning against the doorpost, playing with his dagger, and glaring askance at Zhílin, like a wolf. The dark one, quick and lively, and moving as if on springs, came straight up to Zhílin, squatted down in front of him, slapped him on the shoulder, and began to talk very fast in his own language. His teeth showed, and he kept winking, clicking his tongue, and repeating, 'Good Russ, good Russ.'

Zhílin could not understand a word, but said, 'Drink! give me water to drink!'

The dark man only laughed. 'Good Russ,' he said, and went on talking in his own tongue.

Zhílin made signs with lips and hands that he wanted something to drink.

The dark man understood, and laughed. Then he looked out of the door, and called to someone: 'Dina!'

A little girl came running in: she was about thirteen, slight, thin, and like the dark Tartar in face. Evidently she was his daughter. She, too, had clear black eyes, and her face was good-looking. She had on a long blue gown with wide sleeves, and no girdle. The hem of her gown, the front, and the sleeves, were trimmed with red. She wore trousers and slippers, and over the slippers stouter shoes with high heels. Round her neck she had a necklace made of Russian silver coins. She was bareheaded, and her black hair was plaited with a ribbon and ornamented with gilt braid and silver coins.

Her father gave an order, and she ran away and returned with a metal jug. She handed the water to Zhílin and sat down, crouching so that her knees were as high as her head; and there she sat with wide open eyes watching Zhílin drink, as though he were a wild animal.

When Zhílin handed the empty jug back to her, she gave such a sudden jump back, like a wild goat, that it made her father laugh. He sent her away for something else. She took the jug, ran out, and brought back some unleavened bread on a round board, and once more sat down, crouching, and looking on with staring eyes.

Then the Tartars went away and again locked the door.

After a while the Nogáy came and said: '*Ayda*, the master, *Ayda!*'

He, too, knew no Russian. All Zhílin could make out was that he was told to go somewhere.

Zhílin followed the Nogáy, but limped, for the shackles dragged his feet so that he could hardly step at all. On getting out of the barn he saw a Tartar village of about ten houses, and a Tartar church with a small tower. Three horses stood saddled before one of the houses; little boys were holding them by the reins. The dark Tartar came out of this house, beckoning with his hand for Zhílin to follow him. Then he laughed, said something in his own language, and returned into the house.

Zhílin entered. The room was a good one: the walls smoothly plastered with clay. Near the front wall lay a pile of bright-coloured feather beds; the side walls were covered with rich carpets used as hangings, and on these were fastened guns, pistols and swords, all inlaid with silver. Close to one of the walls was a small stove on a level with the earthen floor. The floor itself was as clean as a threshing-ground. A large space in one corner was spread over with felt, on which were rugs, and on these rugs were cushions stuffed with down. And on these cushions sat five Tartars, the dark one, the red-haired one, and three guests. They were wearing their indoor slippers, and each had a cushion behind his back. Before them were standing millet cakes on a round board, melted butter in a bowl, and a jug of *buza*, or Tartar beer. They ate both cakes and butter with their hands.

The dark man jumped up and ordered Zhílin to be placed on one side, not on the carpet but on the bare ground, then he sat down on the carpet again, and offered millet cakes and *buza* to his guests. The servant made Zhílin sit down, after which he took off his own overshoes, put them by the door where the other shoes were standing, and sat down nearer to his masters on the felt, watching them as they ate, and licking his lips.

The Tartars ate as much as they wanted, and a woman dressed in the same way as the girl – in a long gown and trousers, with a kerchief on her head – came and took away what was left, and brought a handsome basin, and an ewer with a narrow spout. The Tartars washed their hands, folded them, went down on their knees, blew to the four quarters, and said their prayers. After they had talked for a while, one of the guests turned to Zhílin and began to speak in Russian.

'You were captured by Kazi-Mohammed,' he said, and pointed at the red-bearded Tartar. 'And Kazi-Mohammed has given you to Abdul Murat,' pointing at the dark one. 'Abdul Murat is now your master.'

Zhílin was silent. Then Abdul Murat began to talk, laughing, pointing to Zhílin, and repeating, 'Soldier Russ, good Russ.'

The interpreter said, 'He orders you to write home and tell them to send a ransom, and as soon as the money comes he will set you free.'

Zhílin thought for a moment, and said, 'How much ransom does he want?'

The Tartars talked awhile, and then the interpreter said, 'Three thousand rubles.'

'No,' said Zhílin, 'I can't pay so much.'

Abdul jumped up and, waving his arms, talked to Zhílin, thinking, as before, that he would understand. The interpreter translated: 'How much will you give?'

Zhílin considered, and said, 'Five hundred rubles.' At this the Tartars began speaking very quickly, all together. Abdul began to shout at the red-bearded one, and jabbered so fast that the spittle spurted out of his mouth. The red-bearded one only screwed up his eyes and clicked his tongue.

They quietened down after a while, and the interpreter said, 'Five hundred rubles is not enough for the master. He paid two hundred for you himself. Kazi-Mohammed was in debt to him, and he took you in payment. Three thousand rubles! Less than that won't do. If you refuse to write, you will be put into a pit and flogged with a whip!'

'Eh!' thought Zhílin, 'the more one fears them the worse it will be.'

So he sprang to his feet, and said, 'You tell that dog that if he tries to frighten me I will not write at all, and he will get nothing. I never was afraid of you dogs, and never will be!'

The interpreter translated, and again they all began to talk at once.

They jabbered for a long time, and then the dark man jumped up, came to Zhílin, and said: '*Dzhigit Russ, dzhigit Russ!*' (*Dzhigit* in their language means 'brave'.) And he laughed, and said something to the interpreter, who translated: 'One thousand rubles will satisfy him.'

Zhílin stuck to it: 'I will not give more than five hundred. And if you kill me you'll get nothing at all.'

The Tartars talked awhile, then sent the servant out to fetch something, and kept looking, now at Zhílin, now at the door. The servant returned, followed by a stout, bare-footed, tattered man, who also had his leg shackled.

Zhílin gasped with surprise: it was Kostílin. He, too, had been taken. They were put side by side, and began to tell each other what had occurred. While they talked, the Tartars looked on in silence. Zhílin related what had happened to him; and Kostílin told how his horse had stopped, his gun missed fire, and this same Abdul had overtaken and captured him.

Abdul jumped up, pointed to Kostílin, and said something. The interpreter translated that they both now belonged to one master, and the one who first paid the ransom would be set free first.

'There now,' he said to Zhílin, 'you get angry, but your comrade here is gentle; he has written home, and they will send five thousand rubles. So he will be well fed and well treated.'

Zhílin replied: 'My comrade can do as he likes; maybe he is rich, I am not. It must be as I said. Kill me, if you like – you will gain nothing by it; but I will not write for more than five hundred rubles.'

They were silent. Suddenly up sprang Abdul, brought a little box, took out a pen, ink, and a bit of paper, gave them to Zhílin, slapped him on the shoulder, and made a sign that he should write. He had agreed to take five hundred rubles.

'Wait a bit!' said Zhílin to the interpreter; 'tell him that he must feed us properly, give us proper clothes and boots, and let us be together. It will be more cheerful for us. And he must have these shackles taken off our feet,' and Zhílin looked at his master and laughed.

The master also laughed, heard the interpreter, and said: 'I will give them the best of clothes: a cloak and boots fit to be married in. I will feed them like princes; and if they like they can live together in the barn. But I can't take off the shackles, or they will run away. They shall be taken off, however, at night.' And he jumped up and slapped Zhílin on the shoulder, exclaiming: 'You good, I good!'

Zhílin wrote the letter, but addressed it wrongly, so that it should not reach its destination, thinking to himself: 'I'll run away!'

Zhílin and Kostílin were taken back to the barn and given some maize straw, a jug of water, some bread, two old cloaks, and some worn-out military boots – evidently taken from the corpses of Russian soldiers. At night their shackles were taken off their feet, and they were locked up in the barn.

III

ZHÍLIN and his friend lived in this way for a whole month. The master always laughed and said: 'You, Iván, good! I, Abdul, good!' But he fed them badly, giving them nothing but unleavened bread of millet-flour baked into flat cakes, or sometimes only unbaked dough.

Kostílin wrote home a second time, and did nothing but mope and wait for the money to arrive. He would sit for days together in the barn sleeping, or counting the days till a letter could come.

Zhílin knew his letter would reach no one, and he did not write another. He thought: 'Where could my mother get enough money to ransom me? As it is she lived chiefly on what I sent her. If she had to raise five hundred rubles, she would be quite ruined. With God's help I'll manage to escape!'

So he kept on the look-out, planning how to run away.

He would walk about the Aoul whistling; or would sit working, modelling dolls of clay, or weaving baskets out of twigs: for Zhílin was clever with his hands.

Once he modelled a doll with a nose and hands and feet and with a Tartar gown on, and put it up on the roof. When the Tartar women came out to fetch water, the master's daughter, Dina, saw the doll and called the women, who put down their jugs and stood looking and laughing. Zhílin took down the doll and held it out to them. They laughed, but dared not take it. He put down the doll and went into the barn, waiting to see what would happen.

Dina ran up to the doll, looked round, seized it, and ran away.

In the morning, at daybreak, he looked out. Dina came out of the house and sat down on the threshold with the doll, which she had dressed up in bits of red stuff, and she rocked it like a baby, singing a Tartar lullaby. An old woman came out and scolded her, and snatching the doll away she broke it to bits, and sent Dina about her business.

But Zhílin made another doll, better than the first, and gave it to Dina. Once Dina brought a little jug, put it on the ground, sat down gazing at him, and laughed, pointing to the jug.

'What pleases her so?' wondered Zhílin. He took the jug thinking it was water, but it turned out to be milk. He drank the milk and said: 'That's good!'

How pleased Dina was! 'Good, Iván, good!' said she, and she jumped up and clapped her hands. Then, seizing the jug, she ran away. After that, she stealthily brought him some milk every day.

The Tartars make a kind of cheese out of goat's milk, which they dry on the roofs of their houses; and sometimes, on the sly, she brought him some of this cheese. And once, when Abdul had killed a sheep, she brought Zhílin a bit of mutton in her sleeve. She would just throw the things down and run away.

One day there was a heavy storm, and the rain fell in torrents for a whole hour. All the streams became turbid. At the ford, the water rose till it was seven feet high, and the current was so strong that it rolled the stones about. Rivulets flowed everywhere, and the rumbling in the hills never ceased. When the storm was over, the water ran in streams down the village street. Zhílin got his master to lend him a knife, and with it he shaped a small cylinder, and cutting some little boards, he made a wheel to which he fixed two dolls, one on each side. The little girls brought him some bits of stuff, and he dressed the dolls, one as a peasant, the other as a peasant woman. Then he fastened them in their places, and set the wheel so that the stream should work it. The wheel began to turn and the dolls danced.

The whole village collected round. Little boys and girls, Tartar men and women, all came and clicked their tongues.

'Ah, Russ! Ah, Iván!'

Abdul had a Russian clock, which was broken. He called Zhílin and showed it to him, clicking his tongue.

'Give it me; I'll mend it for you,' said Zhílin.

He took it to pieces with the knife, sorted the pieces, and put them together again, so that the clock went all right.

The master was delighted, and made him a present of one of his old tunics which was all in holes. Zhílin had to accept it. He could, at any rate, use it as a coverlet at night.

After that Zhílin's fame spread; and Tartars came from distant villages, bringing him now the lock of a gun or of a pistol, now a watch, to mend. His master gave him some tools – pincers, gimlets, and a file.

One day a Tartar fell ill, and they came to Zhílin, saying, 'Come and heal him!' Zhílin knew nothing about doctoring, but he went to look, and thought to himself, 'Perhaps he will get well anyway.'

He returned to the barn, mixed some water with sand, and then in the presence of the Tartars whispered some words over it and gave it to the sick man to drink. Luckily for him, the Tartar recovered.

Zhílin began to pick up their language a little, and some of the Tartars grew familiar with him. When they wanted him, they would call: 'Iván! Iván!' Others, however, still looked at him askance, as at a wild beast.

The red-bearded Tartar disliked Zhílin. Whenever he saw him he frowned and turned away, or swore at him. There was also an old man there who did not live in the Aoul, but used to come up from the foot of the hill. Zhílin only saw him when he passed on his way to the mosque. He was short, and had a white cloth wound round his hat. His beard and moustaches were clipped, and white as snow; and his face was wrinkled and brick-red. His nose was hooked like a hawk's, his grey eyes looked cruel, and he had no teeth except two tusks. He would pass, with his turban on his head, leaning on his staff, and glaring round him like a wolf. If he saw Zhílin he would snort with anger and turn away.

Once Zhílin descended the hill to see where the old man lived. He went down along the pathway and came to a little garden surrounded by a stone wall; and behind the wall he saw cherry and apricot trees, and a hut with a flat roof. He came closer, and saw hives made of plaited straw, and bees flying about and humming. The old man was kneeling, busy doing something with a hive. Zhílin stretched to look, and his shackles rattled. The old man turned round, and, giving a yell, snatched a pistol from his belt and shot at Zhílin, who just managed to shelter himself behind the stone wall.

The old man went to Zhílin's master to complain. The master called Zhílin, and said with a laugh, 'Why did you go to the old man's house?'

'I did him no harm,' replied Zhílin. 'I only wanted to see how he lived.'

The master repeated what Zhílin said.

But the old man was in a rage; he hissed and jabbered, showing his tusks, and shaking his fists at Zhílin.

Zhílin could not understand all, but he gathered that the old man was telling Abdul he ought not to keep Russians in the Aoul, but ought to kill them. At last the old man went away.

Zhílin asked the master who the old man was.

'He is a great man!' said the master. 'He was the bravest of our fellows; he killed many Russians, and was at one time very rich. He had three wives and eight sons, and they all lived in one village. Then the Russians came and destroyed the village, and killed seven of his sons. Only one son was left, and he gave himself up to the Russians. The old man also went and gave himself up, and lived among the Russians for three months. At the end of that time he found his son, killed him with his own hands, and then escaped. After that he left off fighting, and went to Mecca to pray to God; that is why he wears a turban. One who has been to Mecca is called "Hadji", and wears a turban. He does not like you fellows. He tells me to kill you. But I can't kill you. I have paid money for you and, besides, I have grown fond of you, Iván. Far from killing you, I would not even let you go if I had not promised.' And he laughed, saying in Russian, 'You, Iván, good; I, Abdul, good!'

IV

ZHÍLIN lived in this way for a month. During the day he sauntered about the Aoul or busied himself with some handicraft, but at night, when all was silent in the Aoul, he dug at the floor of the barn. It was no easy task digging, because of the stones; but he worked away at them with his file, and at last had made a hole under the wall large enough to get through.

'If only I could get to know the lay of the land,' thought he, 'and which way to go! But none of the Tartars will tell me.'

So he chose a day when the master was away from home, and set off after dinner to climb the hill beyond the village, and to look around. But before leaving home the master always gave orders to his son to watch Zhílin, and not to lose sight of him. So the lad ran after Zhílin, shouting: 'Don't go! Father does not allow it. I'll call the neighbours if you won't come back.'

Zhílin tried to persuade him, and said: 'I'm not going far; I only want to climb that hill. I want to find a herb – to cure sick people with. You come with me if you like. How can I run away with these shackles on? To-morrow I'll make a bow and arrows for you.'

So he persuaded the lad, and they went. To look at the hill, it did not seem far to the top; but it was hard walking with shackles on his leg. Zhílin went on and on, but it was all he could do to reach the top. There he sat down and noted how the land lay. To the south, beyond the barn, was a valley in which a herd of horses was pasturing and at the bottom of the valley one could see another Aoul. Beyond that was a still steeper hill, and another hill beyond that. Between the hills, in the blue distance, were forests, and still further off were mountains, rising higher and higher. The highest of them were covered with snow, white as sugar; and one snowy peak towered above all the rest. To the east and to the west were other such hills, and here and there smoke rose from Aouls in the ravines. 'Ah,' thought he, 'all that is Tartar country.' And he turned towards the Russian side. At his feet he saw a river, and the Aoul he lived in, surrounded by little gardens. He could see women, like tiny dolls, sitting by the river rinsing clothes. Beyond the Aoul was a hill, lower than the one to the south, and beyond it two other hills well wooded; and between these, a smooth bluish plain, and far, far across the plain something that looked like a cloud of smoke. Zhílin tried to remember where the sun used to rise and set when he was living in the fort, and he saw that there was no mistake: the Russian fort must be in that plain. Between those two hills he would have to make his way when he escaped.

The sun was beginning to set. The white, snowy mountains turned red, and the dark hills turned darker; mists rose from the ravine, and the valley, where he supposed the Russian fort to be, seemed on fire with the sunset glow. Zhílin looked carefully. Something seemed to be quivering in the valley like smoke from a chimney, and he felt sure the Russian fortress was there.

It had grown late. The Mullah's cry was heard. The herds were being driven home, the cows were lowing, and the lad kept saying, 'Come home!' But Zhílin did not feel inclined to go away.

At last, however, they went back. 'Well,' thought Zhílin, 'now that I know the way, it is time to escape.' He thought of running away that night. The nights were dark – the moon had waned. But as ill-luck would have it, the Tartars returned home that evening. They generally came back driving cattle before them and in good spirits. But this time they had no cattle. All they brought home was the dead body of a Tartar – the red one's brother – who had been killed. They came back looking sullen, and they all gathered together for the burial. Zhílin also came out to see it.

They wrapped the body in a piece of linen, without any coffin, and carried it out of the village, and laid it on the grass under some plane-trees. The Mullah and the old men came. They wound clothes round their caps, took off their shoes, and squatted on their heels, side by side, near the corpse.

The Mullah was in front: behind him in a row were three old men in turbans, and behind them again the other Tartars. All cast down their eyes and sat in silence. This continued a long time, until the Mullah raised his head and said: 'Allah!' (which means God). He said that one word, and they all cast down their eyes again, and were again silent for a long time. They sat quite still, not moving or making any sound.

Again the Mullah lifted his head and said, 'Allah!' and they all repeated: 'Allah! Allah!' and were again silent.

The dead body lay immovable on the grass, and they sat as still as if they too were dead. Not one of them moved. There was no sound but that of the leaves of the plane-trees stirring in the breeze. Then the Mullah repeated a prayer, and they all rose. They lifted the body and carried it in their arms to a hole in the ground. It was not an ordinary hole, but was hollowed out under the ground like a vault. They took the body under the arms and by the legs, bent it, and let it gently down, pushing it under the earth in a sitting posture, with the hands folded in front.

The Nogáy brought some green rushes, which they stuffed into the hole, and, quickly covering it with earth, they smoothed the ground, and set an upright stone at the head of the grave. Then they trod the earth down, and again sat in a row before the grave, keeping silence for a long time.

At last they rose, said 'Allah! Allah! Allah!' and sighed.

The red-bearded Tartar gave money to the old men; then he too rose, took a whip, struck himself with it three times on the forehead, and went home.

The next morning Zhílin saw the red Tartar, followed by three others, leading a mare out of the village. When they were beyond the village, the red-bearded Tartar took off his tunic and turned up his sleeves, showing his stout arms. Then he drew a dagger and sharpened it on a whetstone. The other Tartars raised the mare's head, and he cut her throat, threw her down, and began skinning her, loosening the hide with his big hands. Women and girls came and began to wash the entrails and the innards. The mare was cut up, the pieces taken into the hut, and the whole village collected at the red Tartar's hut for a funeral feast.

For three days they went on eating the flesh of the mare, drinking *buza*, and praying for the dead man. All the Tartars were at home. On the fourth day at dinner-time Zhílin saw them preparing to go away. Horses were brought out, they got ready, and some ten of them (the red one among them) rode away; but Abdul stayed at home. It was new moon, and the nights were still dark.

'Ah!' thought Zhílin, 'to-night is the time to escape.' And he told Kostílin; but Kostílin's heart failed him.

'How can we escape?' he said. 'We don't even know the way.'

'I know the way,' said Zhílin.

'Even if you do,' said Kostílin, 'we can't reach the fort in one night.'

'If we can't,' said Zhílin, 'we'll sleep in the forest. See here, I have saved some cheeses. What's the good of sitting and moping here? If they send your ransom – well and good; but suppose they don't manage to collect it? The Tartars are angry now, because the Russians have killed one of their men. They are talking of killing us.'

Kostílin thought it over.

'Well, let's go,' said he.

V

ZHÍLIN crept into the hole, widened it so that Kostílin might also get through, and then they both sat waiting till all should be quiet in the Aoul.

As soon as all was quiet, Zhílin crept under the wall, got out, and whispered to Kostílin, 'Come!' Kostílin crept out, but in so doing he caught a stone with his foot and made a noise. The master had a very vicious watch-dog, a spotted one called Oulyashin. Zhílin had been careful to feed him for some time before. Oulyashin heard the noise and began to bark and jump, and the other dogs did the same. Zhílin gave a slight whistle, and threw him a bit of cheese. Oulyashin knew Zhílin, wagged his tail, and stopped barking.

But the master had heard the dog, and shouted to him from his hut, 'Hayt, hayt, Oulyashin!'

Zhílin, however, scratched Oulyashin behind the ears, and the dog was quiet, and rubbed against his legs, wagging his tail.

They sat hidden behind a corner for awhile. All became silent again, only a sheep coughed inside a shed, and the water rippled over the stones in the hollow. It was dark, the stars were high overhead, and the new moon showed red as it set, horns upward, behind the hill. In the valleys the fog was white as milk.

Zhílin rose and said to his companion, 'Well, friend, come along!'

They started; but they had only gone a few steps when they heard the Mullah crying from the roof, 'Allah, Beshmillah! Ilrahman!' That meant that the people would be going to the mosque. So they sat down again, hiding behind a wall, and waited a long time till the people had passed. At last all was quiet again.

'Now then! May God be with us!' They crossed themselves, and started once more. They passed through a yard and went down the hillside to the river, crossed the river, and went along the valley.

The mist was thick, but only near the ground; overhead the stars shone quite brightly. Zhílin directed their course by the stars. It was cool in the mist, and easy walking; only their boots were uncomfortable, being worn out and trodden down. Zhílin took his off, threw them away, and went barefoot, jumping from stone to stone, and guiding his course by the stars. Kostílin began to lag behind.

'Walk slower,' he said, 'these confounded boots have quite blistered my feet.'

'Take them off!' said Zhílin. 'It will be easier walking without them.'

Kostílin went barefoot, but got on still worse. The stones cut his feet, and he kept lagging behind. Zhílin said: 'If your feet get cut, they'll heal again; but if the Tartars catch us and kill us, it will be worse!'

Kostílin did not reply, but went on, groaning all the time.

Their way lay through the valley for a long time. Then, to the right, they heard dogs barking. Zhílin stopped, looked about, and began climbing the hill, feeling with his hands.

'Ah!' said he, 'we have gone wrong, and have come too far to the right. Here is another Aoul, one I saw from the hill. We must turn back and go up that hill to the left. There must be a wood there.'

But Kostílin said: 'Wait a minute! Let me get breath. My feet are all cut and bleeding.'

'Never mind, friend! They'll heal again. You should spring more lightly. Like this!'

And Zhílin ran back and turned to the left up the hill towards the wood.

Kostílin still lagged behind, and groaned. Zhílin only said 'Hush!' and went on and on.

They went up the hill and found a wood as Zhílin had said. They entered the wood and forced their way through the brambles, which tore their clothes. At last they came to a path and followed it.

'Stop!' They heard the tramp of hoofs on the path, and waited, listening. It sounded like the tramping of a horse's feet, but then ceased. They moved on, and again they heard the tramping. When they paused, it also stopped. Zhílin crept nearer to it, and saw something standing on the path where it was not quite so dark. It looked like a horse, and yet not quite like one, and on it was something queer, not like a man. He heard it snorting. 'What can it be?' Zhílin gave a low whistle, and off it dashed from the path into the thicket, and the woods were filled with the noise of crackling, as if a hurricane were sweeping through, breaking the branches.

Kostílin was so frightened that he sank to the ground. But Zhílin laughed and said: 'It's a stag. Don't you hear him breaking the branches with his antlers? We were afraid of him, and he is afraid of us.'

They went on. The Great Bear was already setting. It was near morning, and they did not know whether they were going the right way or not. Zhílin thought it was the way he had been brought by the Tartars, and that they were still some seven miles from the Russian fort; but he had nothing certain to go by, and at night one easily mistakes the way. After a time they came to a clearing. Kostílin sat down and said: 'Do as you like, I can go no farther! My feet won't carry me.'

Zhílin tried to persuade him.

'No, I shall never get there; I can't!'

Zhílin grew angry, and spoke roughly to him.

'Well, then, I shall go on alone. Good-bye!'

Kostílin jumped up and followed. They went another three miles. The mist in the wood had settled down still more densely; they could not see a yard before them, and the stars had grown dim.

Suddenly they heard the sound of a horse's hoofs in front of them. They heard its shoes strike the stones. Zhílin lay down flat, and listened with his ear to the ground.

'Yes, so it is! A horseman is coming towards us.'

They ran off the path, crouched among the bushes, and waited. Zhílin crept to the road, looked, and saw a Tartar on horseback driving a cow and humming to himself. The Tartar rode past. Zhílin returned to Kostílin.

'God has led him past us; get up and let's go on!'

Kostílin tried to rise, but fell back again.

'I can't; on my word I can't! I have no strength left.'

He was heavy and stout, and had been perspiring freely. Chilled by the mist, and with his feet all bleeding, he had grown quite limp.

Zhílin tried to lift him, when suddenly Kostílin screamed out: 'Oh, how it hurts!'

Zhílin's heart sank.

'What are you shouting for? The Tartar is still near; he'll have heard you!' And he thought to himself, 'He is really quite done up. What am I to do with him? It won't do to desert a comrade.'

'Well, then, get up, and climb up on my back. I'll carry you if you really can't walk.'

He helped Kostílin up, and put his arms under his thighs. Then he went out on to the path, carrying him.

'Only, for the love of heaven,' said Zhílin, 'don't throttle me with your hands! Hold on to my shoulders.'

Zhílin found his load heavy; his feet, too, were bleeding, and he was tired out. Now and then he stooped to balance Kostílin better, jerking him up so that he should sit higher, and then went on again.

The Tartar must, however, really have heard Kostílin scream. Zhílin suddenly heard someone galloping behind and shouting in the Tartar tongue. He darted in among the bushes. The Tartar seized his gun and fired, but did not hit them, shouted in his own language, and galloped off along the road.

'Well, now we are lost, friend!' said Zhílin. 'That dog will gather the Tartars together to hunt us down. Unless we can get a couple of miles away from here we are lost!' And he thought to himself, 'Why the devil did I saddle myself with this block? I should have got away long ago had I been alone.'

'Go on alone,' said Kostílin. 'Why should you perish because of me?'

'No, I won't go. It won't do to desert a comrade.'

Again he took Kostílin on his shoulders and staggered on. They went on in that way for another half-mile or more. They were still in the forest, and could not see the end of it. But the mist was already dispersing, and clouds seemed to be gathering; the stars were no longer to be seen. Zhílin was quite done up. They came to a spring walled in with stones by the side of the path. Zhílin stopped and set Kostílin down.

'Let me have a rest and a drink,' said he, 'and let us eat some of the cheese. It can't be much farther now.'

But hardly had he lain down to get a drink, when he heard the sound of horses' feet behind him. Again they darted to the right among the bushes, and lay down under a steep slope.

They heard Tartar voices. The Tartars stopped at the very spot where they had turned off the path. The Tartars talked a bit, and then seemed to be setting a dog on the scent. There was a sound of crackling twigs, and a strange dog appeared from behind the bushes. It stopped, and began to bark.

Then the Tartars, also strangers, came climbing down, seized Zhílin and Kostílin, bound them, put them on horses, and rode away with them.

When they had ridden about two miles, they met Abdul, their owner, with two other Tartars following him. After talking with the strangers, he put Zhílin and Kostílin on two of his own horses and took them back to the Aoul.

Abdul did not laugh now, and did not say a word to them.

They were back at the Aoul by daybreak, and were set down in the street. The children came crowding round, throwing stones, shrieking, and beating them with whips.

The Tartars gathered together in a circle, and the old man from the foot of the hill was also there. They began discussing; and Zhílin heard them considering what should be done with him and Kostílin. Some said they ought to be sent farther into the mountains; but the old man said: 'They must be killed!'

Abdul disputed with him, saying: 'I gave money for them, and I must get ransom for them.' But the old man said: 'They will pay you nothing, but will only bring misfortune. It is a sin to feed Russians. Kill them, and have done with it!'

They dispersed. When they had gone, the master came up to Zhílin and said: 'If the money for your ransom is not sent within a fortnight, I will flog you; and if you try to run away again, I'll kill you like a dog! Write a letter, and write properly!'

Paper was brought to them, and they wrote the letters. Shackles were put on their feet, and they were taken behind the mosque to a deep pit about twelve feet square, into which they were let down.

VI

LIFE was now very hard for them. Their shackles were never taken off, and they were not let out into the fresh air. Unbaked dough was thrown to them as if they were dogs, and water was let down in a can.

It was wet and close in the pit, and there was a horrible stench. Kostílin grew quite ill, his body became swollen and he ached all over, and moaned or slept all the time. Zhílin, too, grew downcast; he saw it was a bad look-out, and could think of no way of escape.

He tried to make a tunnel, but there was nowhere to put the earth. His master noticed it, and threatened to kill him.

He was sitting on the floor of the pit one day, thinking of freedom and feeling very downhearted, when suddenly a cake fell into his lap, then another, and then a shower of cherries. He looked up, and there was Dina. She looked at him, laughed, and ran away. And Zhílin thought: 'Might not Dina help me?'

He cleared out a little place in the pit, scraped up some clay, and began modelling toys. He made men, horses, and dogs, thinking, 'When Dina comes I'll throw them up to her.'

But Dina did not come next day. Zhílin heard the tramp of horses; some men rode past, and the Tartars gathered in council near the mosque. They shouted and argued; the word 'Russians' was repeated several times. He could hear the voice of the old man. Though he could not distinguish what was said, he guessed that Russian troops were somewhere near, and that the Tartars, afraid they might come into the Aoul, did not know what to do with their prisoners.

After talking awhile, they went away. Suddenly he heard a rustling overhead, and saw Dina crouching at the edge of the pit, her knees higher than her head, and bending over so that the coins of her plait dangled above the pit. Her eyes gleamed like stars. She drew two cheeses out of her sleeve and threw them to him. Zhílin took them and said, 'Why did you not come before? I have made some toys for you. Here, catch!' And he began throwing the toys up, one by one.

But she shook her head and would not look at them.

'I don't want any,' she said. She sat silent for awhile, and then went on, 'Iván, they want to kill you!' And she pointed to her own throat.

'Who wants to kill me?'

'Father; the old men say he must. But I am sorry for you!'

Zhílin answered: 'Well, if you are sorry for me, bring me a long pole.'

She shook her head, as much as to say, 'I can't!'

He clasped his hands and prayed her: 'Dina, please do! Dear Dina, I beg of you!'

'I can't!' she said, 'they would see me bringing it. They're all at home.' And she went away.

So when evening came Zhílin still sat looking up now and then, and wondering what would happen. The stars were there, but the moon had not yet risen. The Mullah's voice was heard; then all was silent. Zhílin was beginning to doze, thinking: 'The girl will be afraid to do it!'

Suddenly he felt clay falling on his head. He looked up, and saw a long pole poking into the opposite wall of the pit. It kept poking about for a time, and then it came down, sliding into the pit. Zhílin was glad indeed. He took hold of it and lowered it. It was a strong pole, one that he had seen before on the roof of his master's hut.

He looked up. The stars were shining high in the sky, and just above the pit Dina's eyes gleamed in the dark like a cat's.

She stooped with her face close to the edge of the pit, and whispered, 'Iván! Iván!' waving her hand in front of her face to show that he should speak low.

'What?' said Zhílin.

'All but two have gone away.'

Then Zhílin said, 'Well, Kostílin, come; let us have one last try; I'll help you up.'

But Kostílin would not hear of it.

'No,' said he, 'it's clear I can't get away from here. How can I go, when I have hardly strength to turn round?'

'Well, good-bye, then! Don't think ill of me!' and they kissed each other. Zhílin seized the pole, told Dina to hold on, and began to climb. He slipped once or twice; the shackles hindered him. Kostílin helped him, and he managed to get to the top. Dina, with her little hands, pulled with all her might at his shirt, laughing.

Zhílin drew out the pole, and said, 'Put it back in its place, Dina, or they'll notice, and you will be beaten.'

She dragged the pole away, and Zhílin went down the hill. When he had gone down the steep incline, he took a sharp stone and tried to wrench the lock off the shackles. But it was a strong lock and he could not manage to break it, and besides, it was difficult to get at. Then he heard someone running down the hill, springing lightly. He thought: 'Surely, that's Dina again.'

Dina came, took a stone, and said, 'Let me try.'

She knelt down and tried to wrench the lock off, but her little hands were as slender as little twigs, and she had not the strength. She threw the stone away and began to cry. Then Zhílin set to work again at the lock, and Dina squatted beside him with her hand on his shoulder.

Zhílin looked round and saw a red light to the left behind the hill. The moon was just rising. 'Ah!' he thought, 'before the moon has risen I must have passed the valley and be in the forest.' So he rose and threw away the stone. Shackles or no, he must go on.

'Good-bye, Dina dear!' he said. 'I shall never forget you!'

Dina seized hold of him and felt about with her hands for a place to put some cheeses she had brought. He took them from her.

'Thank you, my little one. Who will make dolls for you when I am gone?' And he stroked her head.

Dina burst into tears, hiding her face in her hands. Then she ran up the hill like a young goat, the coins in her plait clinking against her back.

Zhílin crossed himself, took the lock of his shackles in his hand to prevent its clattering, and went along the road, dragging his shackled leg, and looking towards the place where the moon was about to rise. He now knew the way. If he went straight he would have to walk nearly six miles. If only he could reach the wood before the moon had quite risen! He crossed the river; the light behind the hill was growing whiter. Still looking at it, he went along the valley. The moon was not yet visible. The light became brighter, and one side of the valley was growing lighter and lighter, and shadows were drawing in towards the foot of the hill, creeping nearer and nearer to him.

Zhílin went on, keeping in the shade. He was hurrying, but the moon was moving still faster; the tops of the hills on the right were already lit up. As he got near the wood the white moon appeared from behind the hills, and it became light as day. One could see all the leaves on the trees. It was light on the hill, but silent, as if nothing were alive; no sound could be heard but the gurgling of the river below.

Zhílin reached the wood without meeting anyone, chose a dark spot, and sat down to rest.

He rested, and ate one of the cheeses. Then he found a stone and set to work again to knock off the shackles. He knocked his hands sore, but could not break the lock. He rose and went along the road. After walking the greater part of a mile he was quite done up, and his feet were aching. He had to stop every ten steps. 'There is nothing else for it,' thought he. 'I must drag on as long as I have any strength left. If I sit down, I shan't be able to rise again. I can't reach the fortress; but when day breaks I'll lie down in the forest, remain there all day, and go on again at night.'

He went on all night. Two Tartars on horseback passed him; but he heard them a long way off, and hid behind a tree.

The moon began to grow paler, the dew to fall. It was getting near dawn, and Zhílin had not reached the end of the forest. 'Well,' thought he, 'I'll walk another thirty steps, and then turn in among the trees and sit down.'

He walked another thirty steps, and saw that he was at the end of the forest. He went to the edge; it was now quite light, and straight before him was the plain and the fortress. To the left, quite close at the foot of the slope, a fire was dying out, and the smoke from it spread round. There were men gathered about the fire.

He looked intently, and saw guns glistening. They were soldiers – Cossacks!

Zhílin was filled with joy. He collected his remaining strength and set off down the hill, saying to himself: 'God forbid that any mounted Tartar should see me now, in the open field! Near as I am, I could not get there in time.'

Hardly had he said this when, a couple of hundred yards off, on a hillock to the left, he saw three Tartars.

They saw him also and made a rush. His heart sank. He waved his hands, and shouted with all his might, 'Brothers, brothers! Help!'

The Cossacks heard him, and a party of them on horseback darted to cut across the Tartars' path. The Cossacks were far and the Tartars were near; but Zhílin, too, made a last effort. Lifting the shackles with his hand, he ran towards the Cossacks, hardly knowing what he was doing, crossing himself and shouting, 'Brothers! Brothers! Brothers!'

There were some fifteen Cossacks. The Tartars were frightened, and stopped before reaching him. Zhílin staggered up to the Cossacks.

They surrounded him and began questioning him. 'Who are you? What are you? Where from?'

But Zhílin was quite beside himself, and could only weep and repeat, 'Brothers! Brothers!'

Then the soldiers came running up and crowded round Zhílin – one giving him bread, another buckwheat, a third vodka: one wrapping a cloak round him, another breaking his shackles.

The officers recognized him, and rode with him to the fortress. The soldiers were glad to see him back, and his comrades all gathered round him.

Zhílin told them all that had happened to him.

'That's the way I went home and got married!' said he. 'No. It seems plain that fate was against it!'

So he went on serving in the Caucasus. A month passed before Kostílin was released, after paying five thousand rubles ransom. He was almost dead when they brought him back.

(3) THE BEAR-HUNT

[The adventure here narrated is one that happened to Tolstoy himself in 1858. More than twenty years later he gave up hunting, on humanitarian grounds.]

WE were out on a bear-hunting expedition. My comrade had shot at a bear, but only gave him a flesh-wound. There were traces of blood on the snow, but the bear had got away.

We all collected in a group in the forest, to decide whether we ought to go after the bear at once, or wait two or three days till he should settle down again. We asked the peasant bear-drivers whether it would be possible to get round the bear that day.

'No. It's impossible,' said an old bear-driver. 'You must let the bear quiet down. In five days' time it will be possible to surround him; but if you followed him now, you would only frighten him away, and he would not settle down.'

But a young bear-driver began disputing with the old man, saying that it was quite possible to get round the bear now.

'On such snow as this,' said he, 'he won't go far, for he is a fat bear. He will settle down before evening; or, if not, I can overtake him on snow-shoes.'

The comrade I was with was against following up the bear, and advised waiting. But I said:

'We need not argue. You do as you like, but I will follow up the track with Damian. If we get round the bear, all right. If not, we lose nothing. It is still early, and there is nothing else for us to do to-day.'

So it was arranged.

The others went back to the sledges, and returned to the village. Damian and I took some bread, and remained behind in the forest.

When they had all left us, Damian and I examined our guns, and after tucking the skirts of our warm coats into our belts, we started off, following the bear's tracks.

The weather was fine, frosty and calm; but it was hard work snow-shoeing. The snow was deep and soft: it had not caked together at all in the forest, and fresh snow had fallen the day before, so that our snow-shoes sank six inches deep in the snow, and sometimes more.

The bear's tracks were visible from a distance, and we could see how he had been going; sometimes sinking in up to his belly and ploughing up the snow as he went. At first, while under large trees, we kept in sight of his track; but when it turned into a thicket of small firs, Damian stopped.

'We must leave the trail now,' said he. 'He has probably settled somewhere here. You can see by the snow that he has been squatting down. Let us leave the track and go round; but we must go quietly. Don't shout or cough, or we shall frighten him away.'

Leaving the track, therefore, we turned off to the left. But when we had gone about five hundred yards, there were the bear's traces again right before us. We followed them, and they brought us out on to the road. There we stopped, examining the road to see which way the bear had gone. Here and there in the snow were prints of the bear's paw, claws and all, and here and there the marks of a peasant's bark shoes. The bear had evidently gone towards the village.

As we followed the road, Damian said:

'It's no use watching the road now. We shall see where he has turned off, to right or left, by the marks in the soft snow at the side. He must have turned off somewhere; for he won't have gone on to the village.'

We went along the road for nearly a mile, and then saw, ahead of us, the bear's track turning off the road. We examined it. How strange! It was a bear's track right enough, only not going from the road into the forest, but from the forest on to the road! The toes were pointing towards the road.

'This must be another bear,' I said.

Damian looked at it, and considered a while.

'No,' said he. 'It's the same one. He's been playing tricks, and walked backwards when he left the road.'

We followed the track, and found it really was so! The bear had gone some ten steps backwards, and then, behind a fir tree, had turned round and gone straight ahead. Damian stopped and said:

'Now, we are sure to get round him. There is a marsh ahead of us, and he must have settled down there. Let us go round it.'

We began to make our way round, through a fir thicket. I was tired out by this time, and it had become still more difficult to get along. Now I glided on to juniper bushes and caught my snow-shoes in them, now a tiny fir tree appeared between my feet, or, from want of practice, my snow-shoes slipped off; and now I came upon a stump or a log hidden by the snow. I was getting very tired, and was drenched with perspiration; and I took off my fur cloak. And there was Damian all the time, gliding along as if in a boat, his snow-shoes moving as if of their own accord, never catching against anything, nor slipping off. He even took my fur and slung it over his shoulder, and still kept urging me on.

We went on for two more miles, and came out on the other side of the marsh. I was lagging behind. My snow-shoes kept slipping off, and my feet stumbled. Suddenly Damian, who was ahead of me, stopped and waved his arm. When I came up to him, he bent down, pointing with his hand, and whispered:

'Do you see the magpie chattering above that undergrowth? It scents the bear from afar. That is where he must be.'

We turned off and went on for more than another half-mile, and presently we came on to the old track again. We had, therefore, been right round the bear, who was now within the track we had left. We stopped, and I took off my cap and loosened all my clothes. I was as hot as in a steam bath, and as wet as a drowned rat. Damian too was flushed, and wiped his face with his sleeve.

'Well, sir,' he said, 'we have done our job, and now we must have a rest.'

The evening glow already showed red through the forest. We took off our snow-shoes and sat down on them, and got some bread and salt out of our bags. First I ate some snow, and then some bread; and the bread tasted so good, that I thought I had never in my life had any like it before. We sat there resting until it began to grow dusk, and then I asked Damian if it was far to the village.

'Yes,' he said. 'It must be about eight miles. We will go on there to-night, but now we must rest. Put on your fur coat, sir, or you'll be catching cold.'

Damian flattened down the snow, and breaking off some fir branches made a bed of them. We lay down side by side, resting our heads on our arms. I do not remember how I fell asleep. Two hours later I woke up, hearing something crack.

I had slept so soundly that I did not know where I was. I looked around me. How wonderful! I was in some sort of a hall, all glittering and white with gleaming pillars, and when I looked up I saw, through delicate white tracery, a vault, raven black and studded with coloured lights. After a good look, I remembered that we were in the forest, and that what I took for a hall and pillars, were trees covered with snow and hoar-frost, and the coloured lights were stars twinkling between the branches.

Hoar-frost had settled in the night; all the twigs were thick with it, Damian was covered with it, it was on my fur coat, and it dropped down from the trees. I woke Damian; and we put on our snow-shoes and started. It was very quiet in the forest. No sound was heard but that of our snow-shoes pushing through the soft snow; except when now and then a tree, cracked by the frost, made the forest resound. Only once we heard the sound of a living creature. Something rustled close to us, and then rushed away. I felt sure it was the bear, but when we went to the spot whence the sound had come, we found the footmarks of hares, and saw several young aspen trees with their bark gnawed. We had startled some hares while they were feeding.

We came out on the road, and followed it, dragging our snow-shoes behind us. It was easy walking now. Our snow-shoes clattered as they slid behind us from side to side of the hard-trodden road. The snow creaked under our boots, and the cold hoar-frost settled on our faces like down. Seen through the branches, the stars seemed to be running to meet us, now twinkling, now vanishing, as if the whole sky were on the move.

I found my comrade sleeping, but woke him up, and related how we had got round the bear. After telling our peasant host to collect beaters for the morning, we had supper and lay down to sleep.

I was so tired that I could have slept on till midday, if my comrade had not roused me. I jumped up, and saw that he was already dressed, and busy doing something to his gun.

'Where is Damian?' said I.

'In the forest, long ago. He has already been over the tracks you made, and been back here, and now he has gone to look after the beaters.'

I washed and dressed, and loaded my guns; and then we got into a sledge, and started.

The sharp frost still continued. It was quiet, and the sun could not be seen. There was a thick mist above us, and hoar-frost still covered everything.

After driving about two miles along the road, as we came near the forest, we saw a cloud of smoke rising from a hollow, and presently reached a group of peasants, both men and women, armed with cudgels.

We got out and went up to them. The men sat roasting potatoes, and laughing and talking with the women.

Damian was there too; and when we arrived the people got up, and Damian led them away to place them in the circle we had made the day before. They went along in single file, men and women, thirty in all. The snow was so deep that we could only see them from their waists upwards. They turned into the forest, and my friend and I followed in their track.

Though they had trodden a path, walking was difficult; but, on the other hand, it was impossible to fall: it was like walking between two walls of snow.

We went on in this way for nearly half a mile, when all at once we saw Damian coming from another direction –

running towards us on his snow-shoes, and beckoning us to join him. We went towards him, and he showed us where to stand. I took my place, and looked round me.

To my left were tall fir trees, between the trunks of which I could see a good way, and, like a black patch just visible behind the trees, I could see a beater. In front of me was a thicket of young firs, about as high as a man, their branches weighed down, and stuck together with snow. Through this copse ran a path thickly covered with snow, and leading straight up to where I stood. The thicket stretched away to the right of me, and ended in a small glade, where I could see Damian placing my comrade.

I examined both my guns, and considered where I had better stand. Three steps behind me was a tall fir.

'That's where I'll stand,' thought I, 'and then I can lean my second gun against the tree'; and I moved towards the tree, sinking up to my knees in the snow at each step. I trod the snow down, and made a clearance about a yard square, to stand on. One gun I kept in my hand; the other, ready cocked, I placed leaning up against the tree. Then I unsheathed and replaced my dagger, to make sure that I could draw it easily in case of need.

Just as I had finished these preparations, I heard Damian shouting in the forest:

'He's up! He's up!'

And as soon as Damian shouted, the peasants round the circle all replied in their different voices.

'Up, up, up! Ou! Ou! Ou!' shouted the men.

'Ay! Ay! Ay!' screamed the women in high-pitched tones.

The bear was inside the circle, and as Damian drove him on, the people all round kept shouting. Only my friend and I stood silent and motionless, waiting for the bear to come towards us. As I stood gazing and listening, my heart beat violently. I trembled, holding my gun fast.

'Now, now,' I thought. 'He will come suddenly. I shall aim, fire, and he will drop —'

Suddenly, to my left, but at a distance, I heard something falling on the snow. I looked between the tall fir trees, and, some fifty paces off, behind the trunks, saw something big and black. I took aim and waited, thinking:

'Won't he come any nearer?'

As I waited I saw him move his ears, turn, and go back; and then I caught a glimpse of the whole of him in profile. He was an immense brute. In my excitement, I fired, and heard my bullet go 'flop' against a tree. Peering through the smoke, I saw my bear scampering back into the circle, and disappearing among the trees.

'Well,' thought I. 'My chance is lost. He won't come back to me. Either my comrade will shoot him, or he will escape through the line of beaters. In any case he won't give me another chance.'

I reloaded my gun, however, and again stood listening. The peasants were shouting all round, but to the right, not far from where my comrade stood, I heard a woman screaming in a frenzied voice:

'Here he is! Here he is! Come here, come here! Oh! Oh! Ay! Ay!'

Evidently she could see the bear. I had given up expecting him, and was looking to the right at my comrade. All at once I saw Damian with a stick in his hand, and without his snow-shoes, running along a footpath towards my friend. He crouched down beside him, pointing his stick as if aiming at something, and then I saw my friend raise his gun and aim in the same direction. Crack! He fired.

'There,' thought I. 'He has killed him.'

But I saw that my comrade did not run towards the bear. Evidently he had missed him, or the shot had not taken full effect.

'The bear will get away,' I thought. 'He will go back, but he won't come a second time towards me. — But what is that?'

Something was coming towards me like a whirlwind, snorting as it came; and I saw the snow flying up quite near me. I glanced straight before me, and there was the bear, rushing along the path through the thicket right at me, evidently beside himself with fear. He was hardly half a dozen paces off, and I could see the whole of him — his black chest and enormous head with a reddish patch. There he was, blundering straight at me, and scattering the snow about as he came. I could see by his eyes that he did not see me, but, mad with fear, was rushing blindly along; and his path led him straight at the tree under which I was standing. I raised my gun and fired. He was almost upon me now, and I saw that I had missed. My bullet had gone past him, and he did not even hear me fire, but still came headlong towards me. I lowered my gun, and fired again, almost touching his head. Crack! I had hit, but not killed him!

He raised his head, and laying his ears back, came at me, showing his teeth.

I snatched at my other gun, but almost before I had touched it, he had flown at me and, knocking me over into the snow, had passed right over me.

'Thank goodness, he has left me,' thought I.

I tried to rise, but something pressed me down, and prevented my getting up. The bear's rush had carried him past me, but he had turned back, and had fallen on me with the whole weight of his body. I felt something heavy weighing me down, and something warm above my face, and I realized that he was drawing my whole face into his mouth. My nose was already in it, and I felt the heat of it, and smelt his blood. He was pressing my shoulders down with his paws so that I could not move: all I could do was to draw my head down towards my chest away from his mouth, trying to free my nose and eyes, while he tried to get his teeth into them. Then I felt that he had seized my forehead just under the hair with the teeth of his lower jaw, and the flesh below my eyes with his upper jaw, and was closing his teeth. It was as if my face were being cut with knives. I struggled to get away, while he made haste to close his jaws like a dog gnawing. I managed to twist my face away, but he began drawing it again into his mouth.

'Now,' thought I, 'my end has come!'

Then I felt the weight lifted, and looking up, I saw that he was no longer there. He had jumped off me and run away.

When my comrade and Damian had seen the bear knock me down and begin worrying me, they rushed to the rescue.

My comrade, in his haste, blundered, and instead of following the trodden path, ran into the deep snow and fell down. While he was struggling out of the snow, the bear was gnawing at me. But Damian just as he was, without a gun, and with only a stick in his hand, rushed along the path shouting:

'He's eating the master! He's eating the master!'

And, as he ran, he called to the bear:

'Oh, you idiot! What are you doing? Leave off! Leave off!'

The bear obeyed him, and leaving me ran away. When I rose, there was as much blood on the snow as if a sheep had been killed, and the flesh hung in rags above my eyes, though in my excitement I felt no pain.

My comrade had come up by this time, and the other people collected round: they looked at my wound, and put snow on it. But I, forgetting about my wounds, only asked:

'Where's the bear? Which way has he gone?'

Suddenly I heard:

'Here he is! Here he is!'

And we saw the bear again running at us. We seized our guns, but before anyone had time to fire, he had run past. He had grown ferocious, and wanted to gnaw me again, but seeing so many people he took fright. We saw by his track that his head was bleeding, and we wanted to follow him up; but, as my wounds had become very painful, we went, instead, to the town to find a doctor.

The doctor stitched up my wounds with silk, and they soon began to heal.

A month later we went to hunt that bear again, but I did not get a chance of finishing him. He would not come out of the circle, but went round and round, growling in a terrible voice.

Damian killed him. The bear's lower jaw had been broken, and one of his teeth knocked out by my bullet.

He was a huge creature, and had splendid black fur.

I had him stuffed, and he now lies in my room. The wounds on my forehead healed up so that the scars can scarcely be seen.

WHAT MEN LIVE BY

'We know that we have passed out of death into life, because we love the brethren. He that loveth not abideth in death.' – I Epistle St John iii. 14.

'Whoso hath the world's goods, and beholdeth his brother in need, and shutteth up his compassion from him, how doth the love of God abide in him? My little children, let us not love in word, neither with the tongue; but in deed and truth.' – iii. 17–18.

'Love is of God; and every one that loveth is begotten of God, and knoweth God. He that loveth not knoweth not God; for God is love.' – iv. 7–8.

'No man hath beheld God at any time; if we love one another, God abideth in us.' – iv. 12.

'God is love; and he that abideth in love abideth in God, and God abideth in him.' – iv. 16.

'If a man say, I love God, and hateth his brother, he is a liar; for he that loveth not his brother whom he hath seen, how can he love God whom he hath not seen?' – iv. 20.

I

A SHOEMAKER named Simon, who had neither house nor land of his own, lived with his wife and children in a peasant's hut, and earned his living by his work. Work was cheap but bread was dear, and what he earned he spent for food. The man and his wife had but one sheepskin coat between them for winter wear, and even that was worn to tatters, and this was the second year he had been wanting to buy sheep-skins for a new coat. Before winter Simon saved up a little money: a three-ruble note lay hidden in his wife's box, and five rubles and twenty kopeks were owed him by customers in the village.

So one morning he prepared to go to the village to buy the sheep-skins. He put on over his shirt his wife's wadded nankeen jacket, and over that he put his own cloth coat. He took the three-ruble note in his pocket, cut himself a stick to serve as a staff, and started off after breakfast. 'I'll collect the five rubles that are due to me,' thought he, 'add the three I have got, and that will be enough to buy sheep-skins for the winter coat.'

He came to the village and called at a peasant's hut, but the man was not at home. The peasant's wife promised that the money should be paid next week, but she would not pay it herself. Then Simon called on another peasant, but this one swore he had no money, and would only pay twenty kopeks which he owed for a pair of boots Simon had mended. Simon then tried to buy the sheep-skins on credit, but the dealer would not trust him.

'Bring your money,' said he, 'then you may have your pick of the skins. We know what debt-collecting is like.'

So all the business the shoemaker did was to get the twenty kopeks for boots he had mended, and to take a pair of felt boots a peasant gave him to sole with leather.

Simon felt downhearted. He spent the twenty kopeks on vodka, and started homewards without having bought any skins. In the morning he had felt the frost; but now, after drinking the vodka, he felt warm even without a sheepskin coat. He trudged along, striking his stick on the frozen earth with one hand, swinging the felt boots with the other, and talking to himself.

'I'm quite warm,' said he, 'though I have no sheepskin coat. I've had a drop, and it runs through all my veins. I need no sheep-skins. I go along and don't worry about anything. That's the sort of man I am! What do I care? I can live without sheep-skins. I don't need them. My wife will fret, to be sure. And, true enough, it *is* a shame; one works all day long, and then does not get paid. Stop a bit! If you don't bring that money along, sure enough I'll skin you, blessed if I don't. How's that? He pays twenty kopeks at a time! What can I do with twenty kopeks? Drink it – that's all one can do! Hard up, he says he is! So he may be – but what about me? You have house, and cattle, and everything; I've only what I stand up in! You have corn of your own growing; I have to buy every grain. Do what I will, I must spend three rubles every week for bread alone. I come home and find the bread all used up, and I have to fork out another ruble and a half. So just you pay up what you owe, and no nonsense about it!'

By this time he had nearly reached the shrine at the bend of the road. Looking up, he saw something whitish behind the shrine. The daylight was fading, and the shoemaker peered at the thing without being able to make out what it was. 'There was no white stone here before. Can it be an ox? It's not like an ox. It has a head like a man, but it's too white; and what could a man be doing there?'

He came closer, so that it was clearly visible. To his surprise it really was a man, alive or dead, sitting naked, leaning motionless against the shrine. Terror seized the shoe-maker, and he thought, 'Someone has killed him, stripped him, and left him here. If I meddle I shall surely get into trouble.'

So the shoemaker went on. He passed in front of the shrine so that he could not see the man. When he had gone some way, he looked back, and saw that the man was no longer leaning against the shrine, but was moving as if looking towards him. The shoemaker felt more frightened than before, and thought, 'Shall I go back to him, or shall I go on? If I go near him something dreadful may happen. Who knows who the fellow is? He has not come here for any good. If I go near him he may jump up and throttle me, and there will be no getting away. Or if not, he'd still be a burden on one's hands. What could I do with a naked man? I couldn't give him my last clothes. Heaven only help me to get away!'

So the shoemaker hurried on, leaving the shrine behind him – when suddenly his conscience smote him, and he stopped in the road.

'What are you doing, Simon?' said he to himself. 'The man may be dying of want, and you slip past afraid. Have you grown so rich as to be afraid of robbers? Ah, Simon, shame on you!'

So he turned back and went up to the man.

II

SIMON approached the stranger, looked at him, and saw that he was a young man, fit, with no bruises on his body, only evidently freezing and frightened, and he sat there leaning back without looking up at Simon, as if too faint to lift his eyes. Simon went close to him, and then the man seemed to wake up. Turning his head, he opened his eyes and looked into Simon's face. That one look was enough to make Simon fond of the man. He threw the felt boots on the ground, undid his sash, laid it on the boots, and took off his cloth coat.

'It's not a time for talking,' said he. 'Come, put this coat on at once!' And Simon took the man by the elbows and helped him to rise. As he stood there, Simon saw that his body was clean and in good condition, his hands and feet shapely, and his face good and kind. He threw his coat over the man's shoulders, but the latter could not find the sleeves. Simon guided his arms into them, and drawing the coat well on, wrapped it closely about him, tying the sash round the man's waist.

Simon even took off his torn cap to put it on the man's head, but then his own head felt cold, and he thought: 'I'm quite bald, while he has long curly hair.' So he put his cap on his own head again. 'It will be better to give him something for his feet,' thought he; and he made the man sit down, and helped him to put on the felt boots, saying, 'There, friend, now move about and warm yourself. Other matters can be settled later on. Can you walk?'

The man stood up and looked kindly at Simon, but could not say a word.

'Why don't you speak?' said Simon. 'It's too cold to stay here, we must be getting home. There now, take my stick, and if you're feeling weak, lean on that. Now step out!'

The man started walking, and moved easily, not lagging behind.

As they went along, Simon asked him, 'And where do you belong to?'

'I'm not from these parts.'

'I thought as much. I know the folks hereabouts. But how did you come to be there by the shrine?'

'I cannot tell.'

'Has someone been ill-treating you?'

'No one has ill-treated me. God has punished me.'

'Of course God rules all. Still, you'll have to find food and shelter somewhere. Where do you want to go to?'

'It is all the same to me.'

Simon was amazed. The man did not look like a rogue, and he spoke gently, but yet he gave no account of himself. Still Simon thought, 'Who knows what may have happened?' And he said to the stranger: 'Well then, come home with me, and at least warm yourself awhile.'

So Simon walked towards his home, and the stranger kept up with him, walking at his side. The wind had risen and Simon felt it cold under his shirt. He was getting over his tipsiness by now, and began to feel the frost. He went along sniffling and wrapping his wife's coat round him, and he thought to himself: 'There now – talk about sheep-skins! I went out for sheep-skins and come home without even a coat to my back, and what is more, I'm bringing a naked man along with me. Matryóna won't be pleased!' And when he thought of his wife he felt sad; but when he looked at the stranger and remembered how he had looked up at him at the shrine, his heart was glad.

III

SIMON'S wife had everything ready early that day. She had cut wood, brought water, fed the children, eaten her own meal, and now she sat thinking. She wondered when she ought to make bread: now or to-morrow? There was still a large piece left.

'If Simon has had some dinner in town,' thought she, 'and does not eat much for supper, the bread will last out another day.'

She weighed the piece of bread in her hand again and again, and thought: 'I won't make any more to-day. We have only enough flour left to bake one batch. We can manage to make this last out till Friday.'

So Matryóna put away the bread, and sat down at the table to patch her husband's shirt. While she worked she thought how her husband was buying skins for a winter coat.

'If only the dealer does not cheat him. My good man is much too simple; he cheats nobody, but any child can take him in. Eight rubles is a lot of money – he should get a good coat at that price. Not tanned skins, but still a proper winter coat. How difficult it was last winter to get on without a warm coat. I could neither get down to the river, nor go out anywhere. When he went out he put on all we had, and there was nothing left for me. He did not start very early to-day, but still it's time he was back. I only hope he has not gone on the spree!'

Hardly had Matryóna thought this, when steps were heard on the threshold, and someone entered. Matryóna stuck her needle into her work and went out into the passage. There she saw two men: Simon, and with him a man without a hat, and wearing felt boots.

Matryóna noticed at once that her husband smelt of spirits. 'There now, he has been drinking,' thought she. And when she saw that he was coatless, had only her jacket on, brought no parcel, stood there silent, and seemed ashamed, her heart was ready to break with disappointment. 'He has drunk the money,' thought she, 'and has been on the spree with some good-for-nothing fellow whom he has brought home with him.'

Matryóna let them pass into the hut, followed them in, and saw that the stranger was a young, slight man, wearing her husband's coat. There was no shirt to be seen under it, and he had no hat. Having entered, he stood neither moving, nor raising his eyes, and Matryóna thought: 'He must be a bad man – he's afraid.'

Matryóna frowned, and stood beside the oven looking to see what they would do.

Simon took off his cap and sat down on the bench as if things were all right.

'Come, Matryóna; if supper is ready, let us have some.'

Matryóna muttered something to herself and did not move, but stayed where she was, by the oven. She looked first at the one and then at the other of them, and only shook her head. Simon saw that his wife was annoyed, but tried to pass it off. Pretending not to notice anything, he took the stranger by the arm.

'Sit down, friend,' said he, 'and let us have some supper.'

The stranger sat down on the bench.

'Haven't you cooked anything for us?' said Simon.

Matryóna's anger boiled over. 'I've cooked, but not for you. It seems to me you have drunk your wits away. You went to buy a sheepskin coat, but come home without so much as the coat you had on, and bring a naked vagabond home with you. I have no supper for drunkards like you.'

'That's enough, Matryóna. Don't wag your tongue without reason! You had better ask what sort of man —'

'And you tell me what you've done with the money?'

Simon found the pocket of the jacket, drew out the three-ruble note, and unfolded it.

'Here is the money. Trífonof did not pay, but promises to pay soon.'

Matryóna got still more angry; he had bought no sheep-skins, but had put his only coat on some naked fellow and had even brought him to their house.

She snatched up the note from the table, took it to put away in safety, and said: 'I have no supper for you. We can't feed all the naked drunkards in the world.'

'There now, Matryóna, hold your tongue a bit. First hear what a man has to say —!'

'Much wisdom I shall hear from a drunken fool. I was right in not wanting to marry you – a drunkard. The linen my mother gave me you drank; and now you've been to buy a coat – and have drunk it too!'

Simon tried to explain to his wife that he had only spent twenty kopeks; tried to tell how he had found the man – but Matryóna would not let him get a word in. She talked nine-teen to the dozen, and dragged in things that had happened ten years before.

Matryóna talked and talked, and at last she flew at Simon and seized him by the sleeve.

'Give me my jacket. It is the only one I have, and you must needs take it from me and wear it yourself. Give it here, you mangy dog, and may the devil take you.'

Simon began to pull off the jacket, and turned a sleeve of it inside out; Matryóna seized the jacket and it burst its seams. She snatched it up, threw it over her head and went to the door. She meant to go out, but stopped undecided – she wanted to work off her anger, but she also wanted to learn what sort of a man the stranger was.

IV

MATRYÓNA stopped and said: 'If he were a good man he would not be naked. Why, he hasn't even a shirt on him. If he were all right, you would say where you came across the fellow.'

'That's just what I am trying to tell you,' said Simon. 'As I came to the shrine I saw him sitting all naked and frozen. It isn't quite the weather to sit about naked! God sent me to him, or he would have perished. What was I to do? How do we know what may have happened to him? So I took him, clothed him, and brought him along. Don't be so angry, Matryóna. It is a sin. Remember, we all must die one day.'

Angry words rose to Matryóna's lips, but she looked at the stranger and was silent. He sat on the edge of the bench, motionless, his hands folded on his knees, his head drooping on his breast, his eyes closed, and his brows knit as if in pain. Matryóna was silent, and Simon said: 'Matryóna, have you no love of God?'

Matryóna heard these words, and as she looked at the stranger, suddenly her heart softened towards him. She came back from the door, and going to the oven she got out the supper. Setting a cup on the table, she poured out some kvas. Then she brought out the last piece of bread, and set out a knife and spoons.

'Eat, if you want to,' said she.

Simon drew the stranger to the table.

'Take your place, young man,' said he.

Simon cut the bread, crumbled it into the broth, and they began to eat. Matryóna sat at the corner of the table, resting her head on her hand and looking at the stranger.

And Matryóna was touched with pity for the stranger, and began to feel fond of him. And at once the stranger's face lit up; his brows were no longer bent, he raised his eyes and smiled at Matryóna.

When they had finished supper, the woman cleared away the things and began questioning the stranger. 'Where are you from?' said she.

'I am not from these parts.'

'But how did you come to be on the road?'

'I may not tell.'

'Did someone rob you?'

'God punished me.'

'And you were lying there naked?'

'Yes, naked and freezing. Simon saw me and had pity on me. He took off his coat, put it on me and brought me here. And you have fed me, given me drink, and shown pity on me. God will reward you!'

Matryóna rose, took from the window Simon's old shirt she had been patching, and gave it to the stranger. She also brought out a pair of trousers for him.

'There,' said she, 'I see you have no shirt. Put this on, and lie down where you please, in the loft or on the oven.'

The stranger took off the coat, put on the shirt, and lay down in the loft. Matryóna put out the candle, took the coat, and climbed to where her husband lay.

Matryóna drew the skirts of the coat over her and lay down, but could not sleep; she could not get the stranger out of her mind.

When she remembered that he had eaten their last piece of bread and that there was none for to-morrow, and thought of the shirt and trousers she had given away, she felt grieved; but when she remembered how he had smiled, her heart was glad.

Long did Matryóna lie awake, and she noticed that Simon also was awake – he drew the coat towards him.

'Simon!'

'Well?'

'You have had the last of the bread, and I have not put any to rise. I don't know what we shall do to-morrow. Perhaps I can borrow some off neighbour Martha.'

'If we're alive we shall find something to eat.'

The woman lay still awhile, and then said, 'He seems a good man, but why does he not tell us who he is?'

'I suppose he has his reasons.'

'Simon!'

'Well?'

'We give; but why does nobody give us anything?'

Simon did not know what to say; so he only said, 'Let us stop talking,' and turned over and went to sleep.

V

IN the morning Simon awoke. The children were still asleep; his wife had gone to the neighbour's to borrow some bread. The stranger alone was sitting on the bench, dressed in the old shirt and trousers, and looking upwards. His face was brighter than it had been the day before.

Simon said to him, 'Well, friend; the belly wants bread, and the naked body clothes. One has to work for a living. What work do you know?'

'I do not know any.'

This surprised Simon, but he said, 'Men who want to learn can learn anything.'

'Men work, and I will work also.'

'What is your name?'

'Michael.'

'Well, Michael, if you don't wish to talk about yourself, that is your own affair; but you'll have to earn a living for yourself. If you will work as I tell you, I will give you food and shelter.'

'May God reward you! I will learn. Show me what to do.'

Simon took yarn, put it round his thumb and began to twist it.

'It is easy enough – see!'

Michael watched him, put some yarn round his own thumb in the same way, caught the knack, and twisted the yarn also.

Then Simon showed him how to wax the thread. This also Michael mastered. Next Simon showed him how to twist the bristle in, and how to sew, and this, too, Michael learned at once.

Whatever Simon showed him he understood at once, and after three days he worked as if he had sewn boots all his life. He worked without stopping, and ate little. When work was over he sat silently, looking upwards. He hardly went into the street, spoke only when necessary, and neither joked nor laughed. They never saw him smile, except that first evening when Matryóna gave them supper.

VI

DAY by day and week by week the year went round. Michael lived and worked with Simon. His fame spread till people said that no one sewed boots so neatly and strongly as Simon's workman, Michael; and from all the district round people came to Simon for their boots, and he began to be well off.

One winter day, as Simon and Michael sat working, a carriage on sledge-runners, with three horses and with bells, drove up to the hut. They looked out of the window; the carriage stopped at their door, a fine servant jumped down from the box and opened the door. A gentleman in a fur coat got out and walked up to Simon's hut. Up jumped Matryóna and opened the door wide. The gentleman stooped to enter the hut, and when he drew himself up again his head nearly reached the ceiling, and he seemed quite to fill his end of the room.

Simon rose, bowed, and looked at the gentleman with astonishment. He had never seen anyone like him. Simon himself was lean, Michael was thin, and Matryóna was dry as a bone, but this man was like someone from another world: red-faced, burly, with a neck like a bull's, and looking altogether as if he were cast in iron.

The gentleman puffed, threw off his fur coat, sat down on the bench, and said, 'Which of you is the master bootmaker?'

'I am, your Excellency,' said Simon, coming forward.

Then the gentleman shouted to his lad, 'Hey, Fédka, bring the leather!'

The servant ran in, bringing a parcel. The gentleman took the parcel and put it on the table.

'Untie it,' said he. The lad untied it.

The gentleman pointed to the leather.

'Look here, shoemaker,' said he, 'do you see this leather?'

'Yes, your honour.'

'But do you know what sort of leather it is?'

Simon felt the leather and said, 'It is good leather.'

'Good, indeed! Why, you fool, you never saw such leather before in your life. It's German, and cost twenty rubles.'

Simon was frightened, and said, 'Where should I ever see leather like that?'

'Just so! Now, can you make it into boots for me?'

'Yes, your Excellency, I can.'

Then the gentleman shouted at him: 'You *can*, can you? Well, remember whom you are to make them for, and what the leather is. You must make me boots that will wear for a year, neither losing shape nor coming unsewn. If you can do it, take the leather and cut it up; but if you can't, say so. I warn you now, if your boots come unsewn or lose shape within a year, I will have you put in prison. If they don't burst or lose shape for a year, I will pay you ten rubles for your work.'

Simon was frightened, and did not know what to say. He glanced at Michael and nudging him with his elbow, whispered: 'Shall I take the work?'

Michael nodded his head as if to say, 'Yes, take it.'

Simon did as Michael advised, and undertook to make boots that would not lose shape or split for a whole year.

Calling his servant, the gentleman told him to pull the boot off his left leg, which he stretched out.

'Take my measure!' said he.

Simon stitched a paper measure seventeen inches long, smoothed it out, knelt down, wiped his hands well on his apron so as not to soil the gentleman's sock, and began to measure. He measured the sole, and round the instep, and began to measure the calf of the leg, but the paper was too short. The calf of the leg was as thick as a beam.

'Mind you don't make it too tight in the leg.'

Simon stitched on another strip of paper. The gentleman twitched his toes about in his sock, looking round at those in the hut, and as he did so he noticed Michael.

'Whom have you there?' asked he.

'That is my workman. He will sew the boots.'

'Mind,' said the gentleman to Michael, 'remember to make them so that they will last me a year.'

Simon also looked at Michael, and saw that Michael was not looking at the gentleman, but was gazing into the corner behind the gentleman, as if he saw someone there. Michael looked and looked, and suddenly he smiled, and his face became brighter.

'What are you grinning at, you fool?' thundered the gentleman. 'You had better look to it that the boots are ready in time.'

'They shall be ready in good time,' said Michael.

'Mind it is so,' said the gentleman, and he put on his boots and his fur coat, wrapped the latter round him, and went to the door. But he forgot to stoop, and struck his head against the lintel.

He swore and rubbed his head. Then he took his seat in the carriage and drove away.

When he had gone, Simon said: 'There's a figure of a man for you! You could not kill him with a mallet. He almost knocked out the lintel, but little harm it did him.'

And Matryóna said: 'Living as he does, how should he not grow strong? Death itself can't touch such a rock as that.'

VII

THEN Simon said to Michael: 'Well, we have taken the work, but we must see we don't get into trouble over it. The leather is dear, and the gentleman hot-tempered. We must make no mistakes. Come, your eye is truer and your hands have become nimbler than mine, so you take this measure and cut out the boots. I will finish off the sewing of the vamps.'

Michael did as he was told. He took the leather, spread it out on the table, folded it in two, took a knife and began to cut out.

Matryóna came and watched him cutting, and was surprised to see how he was doing it. Matryóna was accustomed to seeing boots made, and she looked and saw that Michael was not cutting the leather for boots, but was cutting it round.

She wished to say something, but she thought to herself: 'Perhaps I do not understand how gentlemen's boots should be made. I suppose Michael knows more about it – and I won't interfere.'

When Michael had cut up the leather, he took a thread

and began to sew not with two ends, as boots are sewn, but with a single end, as for soft slippers.

Again Matryóna wondered, but again she did not interfere. Michael sewed on steadily till noon. Then Simon rose for dinner, looked around, and saw that Michael had made slippers out of the gentleman's leather.

'Ah!' groaned Simon, and he thought, 'How is it that Michael, who has been with me a whole year and never made a mistake before, should do such a dreadful thing? The gentleman ordered high boots, welted, with whole fronts, and Michael has made soft slippers with single soles, and has wasted the leather. What am I to say to the gentleman? I can never replace leather such as this.'

And he said to Michael, 'What are you doing, friend? You have ruined me! You know the gentleman ordered high boots, but see what you have made!'

Hardly had he begun to rebuke Michael, when 'rat-tat' went the iron ring that hung at the door. Someone was knocking. They looked out of the window; a man had come on horseback, and was fastening his horse. They opened the door, and the servant who had been with the gentleman came in.

'Good day,' said he.

'Good day,' replied Simon. 'What can we do for you?'

'My mistress has sent me about the boots.'

'What about the boots?'

'Why, my master no longer needs them. He is dead.'

'Is it possible?'

'He did not live to get home after leaving you, but died in the carriage. When we reached home and the servants came to help him alight, he rolled over like a sack. He was dead already, and so stiff that he could hardly be got out of the carriage. My mistress sent me here, saying: "Tell the bootmaker that the gentleman who ordered boots of him and left the leather for them no longer needs the boots, but that he must quickly make soft slippers for the corpse. Wait till they are ready, and bring them back with you." That is why I have come.'

Michael gathered up the remnants of the leather; rolled them up, took the soft slippers he had made, slapped them together, wiped them down with his apron, and handed them and the roll of leather to the servant, who took them and said: 'Good-bye, masters, and good day to you!'

VIII

ANOTHER year passed, and another, and Michael was now living his sixth year with Simon. He lived as before. He went nowhere, only spoke when necessary, and had only smiled twice in all those years – once when Matryóna gave him food, and a second time when the gentleman was in their hut. Simon was more than pleased with his workman. He never now asked him where he came from, and only feared lest Michael should go away.

They were all at home one day. Matryóna was putting iron pots in the oven; the children were running along the benches and looking out of the window; Simon was sewing at one window, and Michael was fastening on a heel at the other.

One of the boys ran along the bench to Michael, leant on his shoulder, and looked out of the window.

'Look, Uncle Michael! There is a lady with little girls! She seems to be coming here. And one of the girls is lame.'

When the boy said that, Michael dropped his work, turned to the window, and looked out into the street.

Simon was surprised. Michael never used to look out into the street, but now he pressed against the window, staring at something. Simon also looked out, and saw that a well-dressed woman was really coming to his hut, leading by the hand two little girls in fur coats and woollen shawls. The girls could hardly be told one from the other, except that one of them was crippled in her left leg and walked with a limp.

The woman stepped into the porch and entered the passage. Feeling about for the entrance she found the latch, which she lifted, and opened the door. She let the two girls go in first, and followed them into the hut.

'Good day, good folk!'

'Pray come in,' said Simon. 'What can we do for you?'

The woman sat down by the table. The two little

girls pressed close to her knees, afraid of the people in the hut.

'I want leather shoes made for these two little girls, for spring.'

'We can do that. We never have made such small shoes, but we can make them; either welted or turnover shoes, linen lined. My man, Michael, is a master at the work.'

Simon glanced at Michael and saw that he had left his work and was sitting with his eyes fixed on the little girls. Simon was surprised. It was true the girls were pretty, with black eyes, plump, and rosy-cheeked, and they wore nice kerchiefs and fur coats, but still Simon could not understand why Michael should look at them like that – just as if he had known them before. He was puzzled, but went on talking with the woman, and arranging the price. Having fixed it, he prepared the measure. The woman lifted the lame girl on to her lap and said: 'Take two measures from this little girl. Make one shoe for the lame foot and three for the sound one. They both have the same sized feet. They are twins.'

Simon took the measure and, speaking of the lame girl, said: 'How did it happen to her? She is such a pretty girl. Was she born so?'

'No, her mother crushed her leg.'

Then Matryóna joined in. She wondered who this woman was, and whose the children were, so she said: 'Are not you their mother, then?'

'No, my good woman; I am neither their mother nor any relation to them. They were quite strangers to me, but I adopted them.'

'They are not your children and yet you are so fond of them?'

'How can I help being fond of them? I fed them both at my own breasts. I had a child of my own, but God took him. I was not so fond of him as I now am of them.'

'Then whose children are they?'

IX

THE woman, having begun talking, told them the whole story.

'It is about six years since their parents died, both in one week: their father was buried on the Tuesday, and their mother died on the Friday. These orphans were born three days after their father's death, and their mother did not live another day. My husband and I were then living as peasants in the village. We were neighbours of theirs, our yard being next to theirs. Their father was a lonely man; a wood-cutter in the forest. When felling trees one day, they let one fall on him. It fell across his body and crushed his bowels out. They hardly got him home before his soul went to God; and that same week his wife gave birth to twins – these little girls. She was poor and alone; she had no one, young or old, with her. Alone she gave them birth, and alone she met her death.

'The next morning I went to see her, but when I entered the hut, she, poor thing, was already stark and cold. In dying she had rolled on to this child and crushed her leg. The village folk came to the hut, washed the body, laid her out, made a coffin, and buried her. They were good folk. The babies were left alone. What was to be done with them? I was the only woman there who had a baby at the time. I was nursing my first-born – eight weeks old. So I took them for a time. The peasants came together, and thought and thought what to do with them; and at last they said to me: "For the present, Mary, you had better keep the girls, and later on we will arrange what to do for them." So I nursed the sound one at my breast, but at first I did not feed this crippled one. I did not suppose she would live. But then I thought to myself, why should the poor innocent suffer? I pitied her, and began to feed her. And so I fed my own boy and these two – the three of them – at my own breast. I was young and strong, and had good food, and God gave me so much milk that at times it even overflowed. I used sometimes to feed two at a time, while the third was waiting. When one had had enough I nursed the third. And God so ordered it that these grew up, while my own was buried before he was two years old. And I had no more children, though we prospered. Now my husband is working for the corn merchant at the mill. The pay is good, and we are well off. But I have no children of my own, and how lonely I should be without these little girls! How can I help loving them! They are the joy of my life!'

She pressed the lame little girl to her with one hand, while with the other she wiped the tears from her cheeks.

And Matryóna sighed, and said: 'The proverb is true that says, "One may live without father or mother, but one cannot live without God."'

So they talked together, when suddenly the whole hut was lighted up as though by summer lightning from the corner where Michael sat. They all looked towards him and saw him sitting, his hands folded on his knees, gazing upwards and smiling.

X

THE woman went away with the girls. Michael rose from the bench, put down his work, and took off his apron. Then, bowing low to Simon and his wife, he said: 'Farewell, masters. God has forgiven me. I ask your forgiveness, too, for anything done amiss.'

And they saw that a light shone from Michael. And Simon rose, bowed down to Michael, and said: 'I see, Michael, that you are no common man, and I can neither keep you nor question you. Only tell me this: how is it that when I found you and brought you home, you were gloomy, and when my wife gave you food you smiled at her and became brighter? Then when the gentleman came to order the boots, you smiled again and became brighter still? And now, when this woman brought the little girls, you smiled a third time, and have become as bright as day? Tell me, Michael, why does your face shine so, and why did you smile those three times?'

And Michael answered: 'Light shines from me because I have been punished, but now God has pardoned me. And I smiled three times, because God sent me to learn three truths, and I have learnt them. One I learnt when your wife pitied me, and that is why I smiled the first time. The second I learnt when the rich man ordered the boots, and then I smiled again.

And now, when I saw those little girls, I learnt the third and last truth, and I smiled the third time.'

And Simon said, 'Tell me, Michael, what did God punish you for? and what were the three truths? that I, too, may know them.'

And Michael answered: 'God punished me for disobeying Him. I was an angel in heaven and disobeyed God. God sent me to fetch a woman's soul. I flew to earth, and saw a sick woman lying alone, who had just given birth to twin girls. They moved feebly at their mother's side, but she could not lift them to her breast. When she saw me, she understood that God had sent me for her soul, and she wept and said: "Angel of God! My husband has just been buried, killed by a falling tree. I have neither sister, nor aunt, nor mother: no one to care for my orphans. Do not take my soul! Let me nurse my babes, feed them, and set them on their feet before I die. Children cannot live without father or mother." And I hearkened to her. I placed one child at her breast and gave the other into her arms, and returned to the Lord in heaven. I flew to the Lord, and said: "I could not take the soul of the mother. Her husband was killed by a tree; the woman has twins, and prays that her soul may not be taken. She says: 'Let me nurse and feed my children, and set them on their feet. Children cannot live without father or mother.' I have not taken her soul." And God said: "Go – take the mother's soul, and learn three truths: Learn *What dwells in man*, *What is not given to man*, and *What men live by*. When thou hast learnt these things, thou shalt return to heaven." So I flew again to earth and took the mother's soul. The babes dropped from her breasts. Her body rolled over on the bed and crushed one babe, twisting its leg. I rose above the village, wishing to take her soul to God; but a wind seized me, and my wings drooped and dropped off. Her soul rose alone to God, while I fell to earth by the roadside.'

XI

AND Simon and Matryóna understood who it was that had lived with them, and whom they had clothed and fed. And they wept with awe and with joy. And the angel said: 'I was alone in the field, naked. I had never known human needs, cold and hunger, till I became a man. I was famished, frozen, and did not know what to do. I saw, near the field I was in, a shrine built for God, and I went to it hoping to find shelter. But the shrine was locked, and I could not enter. So I sat down behind the shrine to shelter myself at least from the wind. Evening drew on. I was hungry, frozen, and in pain. Suddenly I heard a man coming along the road. He carried a pair of boots, and was talking to himself. For the first time since I became a man I saw the mortal face of a man, and his face seemed terrible to me and I turned from it. And I heard the man talking to himself of how to cover his body from the cold in winter, and how to feed wife and children. And I thought: "I am perishing of cold and hunger, and here is a man thinking only of how to clothe himself and his wife, and how to get bread for themselves. He cannot help me." When the man saw me he frowned and became still more terrible, and passed me by on the other side. I despaired; but suddenly I heard him coming back. I looked up, and did not recognize the same man: before, I had seen death in his face; but now he was alive, and I recognized in him the presence of God. He came up to me, clothed me, took me with him, and brought me to his home. I entered the house; a woman came to meet us and began to speak. The woman was still more terrible than the man had been; the spirit of death came from her mouth; I could not breathe for the stench of death that spread around her. She wished to drive me out into the cold, and I knew that if she did so she would die. Suddenly her husband spoke to her of God, and the woman changed at once. And when she brought me food and looked at me, I glanced at her and saw that death no longer dwelt in her; she had become alive, and in her too I saw God.

'Then I remembered the first lesson God had set me: "*Learn what dwells in man*." And I understood that in man dwells Love! I was glad that God had already begun to show me what He had promised, and I smiled for the first time. But I had not yet learnt all. I did not yet know *What is not given to man*, and *What men live by*.

'I lived with you, and a year passed. A man came to order boots that should wear for a year without losing shape or cracking. I looked at him, and suddenly, behind his shoulder, I saw my comrade – the angel of death. None but me saw that angel; but I knew him, and knew that before the sun set he would take that rich man's soul. And I thought to myself, "The man is making preparations for a year, and does not know that he will die before evening." And I remembered God's second saying, "*Learn what is not given to man.*"

'What dwells in man I already knew. Now I learnt what is not given him. It is not given to man to know his own needs. And I smiled for the second time. I was glad to have seen my comrade angel – glad also that God had revealed to me the second saying.

'But I still did not know all. I did not know *What men live by.* And I lived on, waiting till God should reveal to me the last lesson. In the sixth year came the girl-twins with the woman; and I recognized the girls, and heard how they had been kept alive. Having heard the story, I thought, "Their mother besought me for the children's sake, and I believed her when she said that children cannot live without father or mother; but a stranger has nursed them, and has brought them up." And when the woman showed her love for the children that were not her own, and wept over them, I saw in her the living God, and understood *What men live by.* And I knew that God had revealed to me the last lesson, and had forgiven my sin. And then I smiled for the third time.'

XII

AND the angel's body was bared, and he was clothed in light so that eye could not look on him; and his voice grew louder, as though it came not from him but from heaven above. And the angel said:

'I have learnt that all men live not by care for themselves, but by love.

'It was not given to the mother to know what her children needed for their life. Nor was it given to the rich man to know what he himself needed. Nor is it given to any man to know whether, when evening comes, he will need boots for his body or slippers for his corpse.

'I remained alive when I was a man, not by care of myself, but because love was present in a passer-by, and because he and his wife pitied and loved me. The orphans remained alive, not because of their mother's care, but because there was love in the heart of a woman a stranger to them, who pitied and loved them. And all men live not by the thought they spend on their own welfare, but because love exists in man.

'I knew before that God gave life to men and desires that they should live; now I understood more than that.

'I understood that God does not wish men to live apart, and therefore he does not reveal to them what each one needs for himself; but he wishes them to live united, and therefore reveals to each of them what is necessary for all.

'I have now understood that though it seems to men that they live by care for themselves, in truth it is love alone by which they live. He who has love, is in God, and God is in him, for God is love.'

And the angel sang praise to God, so that the hut trembled at his voice. The roof opened, and a column of fire rose from earth to heaven. Simon and his wife and children fell to the ground. Wings appeared upon the angel's shoulders, and he rose into the heavens.

And when Simon came to himself the hut stood as before, and there was no one in it but his own family.

MEMOIRS OF A
MADMAN

TO-DAY I was taken to the Provincial Government Board to be certified. Opinions differed. They disputed, and finally decided that I was not insane – but they arrived at this decision only because during the examination I did my utmost to restrain myself and not give myself away. I did not speak out, because I am afraid of the madhouse, where they would prevent me from doing my mad work. So they came to the conclusion that I am subject to hallucinations and something else, but am of sound mind.

They came to that conclusion, but I myself know that I am mad. A doctor prescribed a treatment for me, and assured me that if I would follow his instructions exactly all would be right – all that troubled me would pass. Ah, what would I not give that it might pass! The torment is too great. I will tell in due order how and from what this medical certification came about – how I went mad and how I betrayed myself.

Up to the age of thirty-five I lived just as everybody else does and nothing strange was noticed about me. Perhaps in early childhood, before the age of ten, there was at times something resembling my present condition, but only by fits, and not continually as now. Moreover in childhood it used to affect me rather differently. For instance I remember that once when going to bed, at the age of five or six, my nurse Eupraxia, a tall thin woman who wore a brown dress and a cap and had flabby skin under her chin, was undressing me and lifting me up to put me into my cot. 'I will get into bed by myself – myself!' I said, and stepped over the side of the cot.

'Well, lie down then. Lie down, Fédya! Look at Mítya. He's a good boy and is lying down already,' she said, indicating my brother with a jerk of her head.

I jumped into the bed still holding her hand, and then let it go, kicked about under my bed-clothes, and wrapped myself up. And I had such a pleasant feeling. I grew quiet and thought: 'I love Nurse; Nurse loves me and Mítya; and I love Mítya, and Mítya loves me and Nurse. Nurse loves Tarás, and I love Tarás, and Mítya loves him. And Tarás loves me and Nurse. And Mamma loves me and Nurse, and Nurse loves Mamma and me and Papa – and everybody loves everybody and everybody is happy!'

Then suddenly I heard the housekeeper run in and angrily shout something about a sugar-basin, and nurse answering indignantly that she had not taken it. And I felt pained, frightened, and bewildered, and horror, cold horror, seized me, and I hid my head under the bed-clothes but felt no better in the dark.

I also remembered how a serf-boy was once beaten in my presence, how he screamed, and how dreadful Fóka's face looked when he was beating the boy. 'Then you won't do it any more, you won't?' he kept repeating as he went on beating. The boy cried, 'I won't!' but Fóka still repeated, 'You won't!' and went on beating him.

And then it came upon me! I began to sob, and went on so that they could not quiet me for a long time. That sobbing and despair were the first attacks of my present madness.

I remember another attack when my aunt told us about Christ. She told the story and was about to go away, but we said: 'Tell us some more about Jesus Christ!'

'No, I have no time now,' she said.

'Yes, do tell us!'

Mítya also asked her to, and my aunt began to repeat what she had told us. She told us how they crucified, beat, and tortured him, and how he went on praying and did not reproach them.

'Why did they torment him, Auntie?'

'They were cruel people.'

'But why, when he was good?'

'There, that's enough. It's past eight! Do you hear?'

'Why did they beat him? He forgave them, then why did they hit him? Did it hurt him, Auntie? Did it hurt?'

'That will do! I'm going to have tea now.'

'But perhaps it isn't true and they didn't beat him?'

'Now, now, that will do!'

'No, no! Don't go away!'

And again I was overcome by it. I sobbed and sobbed, and began knocking my head against the wall.

That was how it befell me in my childhood. But by the time I was fourteen, and from the time the instincts of sex were aroused and I yielded to vice, all that passed away and I became a boy like other boys, like all the rest of us reared on rich, over-abundant food, effeminate, doing no physical work, surrounded by all possible temptations that inflamed sensuality, and among other equally spoilt children. Boys of my own age taught me vice, and I indulged in it. Later on that vice was replaced by another, and I began to know women. And so, seeking enjoyments and finding them, I lived till the age of thirty-five. I was perfectly well and there were no signs of my madness.

Those twenty years of my healthy life passed for me so that I can hardly remember anything of them, and now recall them with difficulty and disgust. Like all mentally healthy boys of our circle I entered the high school and afterwards the university, where I completed the course of law-studies. Then I was in the Civil Service for a short time, and then I met my present wife, married, had a post in the country and, as it is called, 'brought up' our children, managed the estates, and was Justice of the Peace.

In the tenth year of my married life I again had an attack – the first since my childhood.

My wife and I had saved money – some inherited by her and some from the bonds I, like other landowners, received from the Government at the time of the emancipation of the serfs – and we decided to buy an estate. I was much interested, as was proper, in the growth of our property and in increasing it in the shrewdest way – better than other people. At that time I inquired everywhere where there were estates for sale, and read all the advertisements in the papers. I wanted to buy an estate so that the income from it, or the timber on it, should cover the whole purchase price and I should get it for nothing. I looked out for some fool who did not understand business, and thought I had found such a man.

An estate with large forests was being sold in Pénza province. From all I could learn about it, it seemed that its owner was just such a fool as I wanted and the timber would cover the whole cost of the estate. So I got ready and set out.

We (my servant and I) travelled at first by rail and then by road in a post-chaise. The journey was a very pleasant one for me. My servant, a young good-natured fellow, was in just as good spirits as I. We saw new places and met new people and enjoyed ourselves. To reach our destination we had to go about a hundred and forty miles, and decided to go without stopping except to change horses. Night came and we still went on. We grew drowsy. I fell asleep, but suddenly awoke feeling that there was something terrifying. As often happens, I woke up thoroughly alert and feeling as if sleep had gone for ever. 'Why am I going? Where am I going to?' I suddenly asked myself. It was not that I did not like the idea of buying an estate cheaply, but it suddenly occurred to me that there was no need for me to travel all that distance, that I should die here in this strange place, and I was filled with dread. Sergéy, my servant, woke up, and I availed myself of the opportunity to talk to him. I spoke about that part of the country, he replied and joked, but I felt depressed. I spoke about our folks at home, and of the business before us, and I was surprised that his answers were so cheerful. Everything seemed pleasant and amusing to him while it nauseated me. But for all that while we were talking I felt easier. But besides everything seeming wearisome and uncanny, I began to feel tired and wished to stop. It seemed to me that I should feel better if I could enter a house, see people, drink tea, and above all have some sleep.

We were nearing the town of Arzamás.

'Shall we put up here and rest a bit?'

'Why not? Splendid!'

'Are we still far from the town?'

'About five miles from the last mile-post.'

The driver was a respectable man, careful and taciturn, and he drove rather slowly and wearily.

We drove on. I remained silent and felt better because I was looking forward to a rest and hoped that the discomfort would pass. We went on and on in the darkness for a terribly long time as it seemed to me. We reached the town. Everybody was already in bed. Mean little houses showed up through the darkness, and the sound of our jingling bells and the clatter of the horses' feet re-echoed, especially near the houses, and all this was far from cheerful. We passed large white houses here and there. I was impatient to get to the post-station and a samovar, and to lie down and rest.

At last we came up to a small house with a post beside it. The house was white, but appeared terribly melancholy to me, so much so that it seemed uncanny and I got out of the carriage slowly.

Sergéy briskly took out all that would be wanted, running clattering up the porch, and the sound of his steps depressed me. I entered a little corridor. A sleepy man with a spot on his cheek (which seemed to me terrifying) showed us into a room. It was gloomy. I entered, and the uncanny feeling grew worse.

'Haven't you got a bedroom? I should like to rest.'

'Yes, we have. This is it.'

It was a small square room, with whitewashed walls. I remember that it tormented me that it should be square. It had one window with a red curtain, a birchwood table, and a sofa with bent-wood arms. We went in. Sergéy prepared the samovar and made tea, while I took a pillow and lay down on the sofa. I was not asleep and heard how Sergéy was busy with the tea and called me to have some. But I was afraid of getting up and arousing myself completely, and I thought how frightful it would be to sit up in that room. I did not get up but began to doze. I must have fallen asleep, for when I awoke I found myself alone in the room and it was dark. I was again as wide awake as I had been in the chaise. I felt that to sleep would be quite impossible. 'Why have I come here? Where am I betaking myself? Why and whither am I escaping? I am running away from something dreadful and cannot escape it. I am always with myself, and it is I who am my tormentor. Here I am, the whole of me. Neither the Pénza nor any other property will add anything to or take anything from me. And it is myself I am weary of and find intolerable and a torment. I want to fall asleep and forget myself and cannot. I cannot get away from myself!'

I went out into the passage. Sergéy was sleeping on a narrow bench with one arm hanging down, but he was sleeping peacefully and the man with the spot was also asleep. I had gone out into the corridor thinking to escape from what tormented me. But *it* had come out with me and cast a gloom over everything. I felt just as filled with horror or even more so.

'But what folly this is!' I said to myself. 'Why am I depressed? What am I afraid of?'

'Me!' answered the voice of Death, inaudibly. 'I am here!'

A cold shudder ran down my back. Yes! Death! It will come – here it is – and it ought not to be. Had I been actually facing death I could not have suffered as much as I did then. Then I should have been frightened. But now I was not frightened. I saw and felt the approach of death, and at the same time I felt that such a thing ought not to exist.

My whole being was conscious of the necessity and the right to live, and yet I felt that Death was being accomplished. And this inward conflict was terrible. I tried to throw off the horror. I found a brass candlestick, the candle in which had a long wick, and lighted it. The red glow of the candle and its size – little less than the candlestick itself – told me the same thing. Everything told me the same: 'There is nothing in life. Death is the only real thing, and death ought not to exist.'

I tried to turn my thoughts to things that had interested me – to the estate I was to buy, and to my wife – but found nothing to cheer me. It had all become nothing. Everything was hidden by the terrible consciousness that my life was ebbing away. I needed sleep. I lay down, but the next instant

I jumped up again in terror. A fit of the spleen seized me – spleen such as the feeling before one is sick, but spiritual spleen. It was uncanny and dreadful. It seems that death is terrible, but when remembering and thinking of life it is one's dying life that is terrible. Life and death somehow merged into one another. Something was tearing my soul apart and could not complete the severance. Again I went to look at the sleepers, and again I tried to go to sleep. Always the same horror: red, white, and square. Something tearing within that yet could not be torn apart. A painful, painfully dry and spiteful feeling, no atom of kindliness, but just a dull and steady spitefulness towards myself and towards that which had made me.

What created me? God, they say. God... what about prayer? I remembered. For some twenty years I had not prayed, and I did not believe in anything, though as a matter of propriety I fasted and went to Communion every year. Now I began to pray. 'Lord have mercy!' 'Our Father'. 'Holy Virgin'. I began to compose new prayers, crossing myself, bowing down to the ground and glancing around me for fear that I might be seen. This seemed to divert me – the fear of being seen distracted my terror – and I lay down. But I had only to lie down and close my eyes for the same feeling of terror to knock and rouse me. I could bear it no longer. I woke the hotel servant and Sergéy, gave orders to harness, and we drove off again.

The fresh air and the drive made me feel better. But I realized that something new had come into my soul and poisoned my former life.

* * *

By nightfall we reached our destination. The whole day I had been fighting my depression and had mastered it, but it had left its terrible dregs in my soul as if some misfortune had befallen me, and I could forget it only for a time. There it remained at the bottom of my soul and had me in its power.

The old steward of the estate received me well, though without any pleasure. He was sorry the estate was to be sold.

The furniture in the little rooms was upholstered. There was a new, brightly polished samovar, a large-sized tea-service, and honey for tea. Everything was good. But I questioned him about the estate unwillingly, as if it were some old forgotten lesson. However, I fell asleep without any depression, and this I attributed to my having prayed again before going to bed.

After that I went on living as before, but the fear of that spleen always hung over me. I had to live without stopping to think, and above all to live in my accustomed surroundings. As a schoolboy repeats a lesson learnt by heart without thinking, so I had to live to avoid falling a prey to that awful depression I had first experienced at Arzamás.

I returned home safely. I did not buy the estate – I had not enough money – and I continued to live as before, only with this difference, that I began to pray and went to church. As before – it seemed to me, but I now remember that it was not as before – I lived on what had been previously begun. I continued to go along the rails already laid by my former strength, but I did not undertake anything new. And I took less part in those things I had previously begun. Everything seemed dull to me and I became pious. My wife noticed this, and scolded and nagged me on account of it. But my spleen did not recur at home.

But once I had unexpectedly to go to Moscow. I got ready in the afternoon and left in the evening. It was in connexion with a lawsuit. I arrived in Moscow cheerful. On the way I had talked with a landowner from Khárkov about estate-management and banks, and about where to put up, and about the theatre. We both decided to stop at the Moscow Hotel on the Myasnítsky Street, and to go to see *Faust* that same evening.

When we arrived I was shown into a small room. The oppressive air of the corridor filled my nostrils. A porter brought in my portmanteau and a chambermaid lighted a candle. The wick was lighted and then as usual the flame went down. In the next room someone coughed, probably an old man. The maid went out, but the porter remained and asked if he should uncord my luggage. The flame of the candle burnt up, revealing the blue wall-paper with yellow stripes on the partition, a shabby table, a small sofa, a looking-glass, a window, and the narrow dimensions of the room. And suddenly I was seized with an attack of the same horror as in Arzamás. 'My God! How can I stay here all night?' I thought.

'Yes, uncord, my good fellow,' I told the porter to keep him longer in the room. 'I'll dress quickly and go to the theatre.' When the porter had uncorded, I said: 'Please go to Number Eight and tell the gentleman who came here with me that I shall be ready immediately and will come to him.'

The porter went out and I dressed hurriedly, afraid to look at the walls. 'What nonsense!' I thought. 'What am I afraid of? Just like a child! I am not afraid of ghosts. Ghosts! Ghosts would be better than what I am afraid of. Why, what is it? Nothing. Myself. . . . Oh, nonsense!'

However, I put on a hard, cold, starched shirt, inserted the studs, donned my evening coat and new boots, and went to find the Khárkov landowner, who was ready. We started for the opera. He stopped on the way at a hairdresser's to have his hair curled, and I had mine cut by a French assistant and had a chat with him, and bought a pair of gloves. All was well, and I quite forgot my oblong room with its partition. In the theatre, too, it was pleasant. After the opera the Khárkov landowner suggested that we should have supper. That was contrary to my habit, but just then I again remembered the partition in my room and accepted his suggestion.

We got back after one. I had had two glasses of wine, to which I was unaccustomed, but in spite of that I felt cheerful. But no sooner had we entered the corridor in which the lamp was turned low and I was surrounded by the hotel smell, than a shiver of horror ran down my spine. There was nothing to be done however, and I pressed my companion's hand and went into my room.

I spent a terrible night – worse than at Arzamás. Not till dawn, when the old man at the other side of the door was coughing again, did I fall asleep, and then not in the bed, in which I had lain down several times during the night, but on the sofa. I had suffered all night unbearably. Again my soul and body were being painfully torn asunder. 'I am living, have lived, and ought to live, and suddenly – here is death to destroy everything. Then what is life for? To die? To kill myself at once? No, I am afraid. To wait for death till it comes? I fear that even more. Then I must live. But what for? In order to die?' And I could not escape from that circle. I took up a book, read, and forgot myself for a moment, but then again the same question and the same horror. I lay down in bed and closed my eyes. It was worse still!

God has so arranged it. Why? They say: 'Don't ask, but pray!' Very well. I prayed, and prayed as I had done at Arzamás. Then and afterwards I prayed simply, like a child. But now my prayers had a meaning. 'If Thou dost exist, reveal to me why and what I am!' I bowed down, repeated all the prayers I knew, composed my own, and added: 'Then reveal it!' and became silent, awaiting an answer. But no answer came. It was just as if there were no one who could give an answer. And I remained alone with myself. And in place of Him who would not reply I answered my own questions. 'Why? In order to live in a future life,' I said to myself. 'Then why this obscurity, this torment? I cannot believe in a future life. I believed when I did not ask with my whole soul, but now I cannot, I cannot. If Thou didst exist Thou wouldst speak to me and to all men. And if Thou dost not exist there is nothing but despair. And I do not want that. I do not want that!'

I became indignant. I asked Him to reveal the truth to me, to reveal Himself to me. I did all that everybody does, but He did not reveal Himself. 'Ask and it shall be given you' I remembered, and I had asked and in that asking had found not consolation but relaxation. Perhaps I did not pray to Him but repudiated Him. 'You recede a span and He recedes a mile' as the proverb has it. I did not believe in Him but I asked, and He did not reveal anything to me. I was balancing accounts with Him and blaming Him. I simply did not believe.

* * *

The next day I did all in my power to get through my ordinary affairs so as to avoid another night in the hotel. Although I did not finish everything, I left for home that evening. I did not feel any spleen. That night in Moscow still further changed my life which had begun to change from the time I was at Arzamás. I now attended still less to my affairs and became apathetic. I also grew weaker in health. My wife insisted that I should undergo a treatment. She said that my talks about faith and God arose from ill health. But I knew that my weakness and ill health were the effect of the unsolved question within me. I tried not to let that question dominate me, and tried to fill my life amid my customary surroundings. I went to church on Sundays and feast days, prepared to receive Communion, and even fasted, as I had begun to do since my visit to Pénza, and I prayed, though more as a custom. I did not expect any result from this, but as it were kept the demand-note and presented it at the due date, though I knew it was impossible to secure payment. I only did it on the chance. I did not fill my life by estate management − it repelled me by the struggle it involved (I had no energy) − but by reading magazines, news-papers, and novels, and playing cards for small stakes. I only showed energy by hunting, which I did from habit. I had been fond of hunting all my life.

One winter day a neighbouring huntsman came with his wolf-hounds. I rode out with him. When we reached the place we put on snow-shoes and went to the spot where the wolf might be found. The hunt was unsuccessful, the wolves broke through the ring of beaters. I became aware of this from a distance and went through the forest following the fresh tracks of a hare. These led me far into a glade, where I spied the hare, but it jumped out so that I lost it. I went back through the thick forest. The snow was deep, my snow-shoes sank in, and branches of the trees entangled me. The trees grew ever more and more dense. I began to ask myself: 'Where am I?' The snow had altered the look of everything.

Suddenly I realized that I had lost my way. I was far from the house and from the hunters too, and could hear nothing. I was tired and bathed in perspiration. If I stopped I should freeze. If I went on my strength would fail me. I shouted. All was still. No one answered. I turned back, but it was the same again.

I looked around – nothing but trees, impossible to tell which was east or west. Again I turned back. My legs were tired. I grew frightened, stopped, and was seized with the same horror as in Arzamás and Moscow, but a hundred times worse. My heart palpitated, my arms and legs trembled. 'Is this death? I won't have it! Why death? What is death?' Once again I wanted to question and reproach God, but here I suddenly felt that I dare not and must not do so, that it is impossible to present one's account to God, that He had said what is needful and I alone was to blame. I began to implore His forgiveness, and felt disgusted with myself.

The horror did not last long. I stood there for awhile, came to myself, went on in one direction and soon emerged from the forest. I had not been far from its edge, and came out on to the road. My arms and legs still trembled and my heart was beating, but I felt happy. I found the hunting party and we returned home. I was cheerful, but I knew there was something joyful which I would make out when alone. And so it was. I remained by myself in my study and began to pray, asking forgiveness and remembering my sins. There seemed to me to be but few, but when I recalled them they became hateful to me.

* * *

After that I began to read the scriptures. The Old Testament I found unintelligible though enchanting, but the Gospels moved me profoundly. But most of all I read the Lives of the Saints, and that reading consoled me, presenting examples that it seemed more and more possible to follow. From that time forth farming and family matters occupied me less and less. They even repelled me. They all seemed to me wrong. What it was that was 'right' I did not know, but what had formerly constituted my life had now ceased to do so. This became plain to me when I was going to buy another estate.

Not far from us an estate was for sale on very advantageous terms. I went to see it. Everything was excellent and advantageous; especially so was the fact that the peasants there had no land of their own except their kitchen-gardens. I saw that they would have to work on the landlord's land merely for permission to use his pastures. And so it was. I grasped all this, and by old habit felt pleased about it. But on my way home I met an old woman who asked her way. I had a talk with her, during which she told me about her poverty. I got home, and when telling my wife of the advantages that estate offered, I suddenly felt ashamed and disgusted. I told her I could not buy it because the advantages we should get would be based on the peasants' destitution and sorrow. As I said this I suddenly realized the truth of what I was saying – the chief truth, that the peasants, like ourselves, want to live, that they are human beings, our brothers, and sons of the Father as the Gospels say. Suddenly something that had long troubled me seemed to have broken away, as though it had come to birth. My wife was vexed and scolded me, but I felt glad.

That was the beginning of my madness. But my utter madness began later – about a month after that.

It began by my going to church. I stood there through the liturgy and prayed well, and listened and was touched. Then suddenly they brought me some consecrated bread: after that we went up to the Cross, and people began pushing one another. Then at the exit there were beggars. And it suddenly became clear to me that this ought not to be, and not only ought not to be but in reality was not. And if this was not, then neither was there either death or fear, and there was no longer the former tearing asunder within me and I no longer feared anything.

Then the light fully illumined me and I became what I now am. If there is nothing of all that – then it certainly does not exist within me. And there at the church door I gave away to the beggars all I had with me – some thirty-five rubles – and went home on foot talking with the peasants.

ABOUT THE TRANSLATORS

LOUISE and AYLMER MAUDE spent much of their lives in Russia. Their Quaker background led them to share many of Tolstoy's views on spiritual life, moral obligation and passive resistance to violence, and they helped him to organize the Doukhobor migration to Canada in 1893. Aylmer Maude, whose business activities left him time to write a biography of his friend, also translated most of Tolstoy's major works in partnership with his wife. These translations, which were commended by the author himself, are still widely regarded as the best.

NIGEL J. COOPER read French and Russian at Christ Church, Oxford. He has recently retired from Middlesex University where he was a Principal Lecturer in Modern Languages.

ABOUT THE INTRODUCER

JOHN BAYLEY is former Thomas Warton Professor of English Literature at the University of Oxford. His many books include *Tolstoy and the Novel*; *Pushkin: A Comparative Commentary*; *The Short Story: Henry James to Elizabeth Bowen*; *An Essay on Hardy*, *Shakespeare and Tragedy* and a detailed study of A. E. Housman's poems. He has also written several novels.